STÉPHANIE-FÉLICITÉ DE GENLIS, ADELAIDE AND THEODORE, OR LETTERS ON EDUCATION (1783)

CHAWTON HOUSE LIBRARY SERIES:
WOMEN'S NOVELS

Series Editors: Stephen Bending
                       Stephen Bygrave

TITLES IN THIS SERIES

The Histories of Some of the Penitents in the Magdalen-House
edited by Jennie Batchelor and Megan Hiatt

FORTHCOMING TITLES

Sarah Harriet Burney, *The Romance of Private Life*
edited by Lorna J. Clark

E. M. Foster, *The Corinna of England*
edited by Sylvia Bordoni

Stéphanie-Félicité de Genlis,
Adelaide and Theodore, or Letters on Education (1783)

EDITED BY

Gillian Dow

Routledge
Taylor & Francis Group
LONDON AND NEW YORK

First published 2007 by Pickering & Chatto (Publishers) Limited

Published 2016 by Routledge
2 Park Square, Milton Park, Abingdon, Oxfordshire OX14 4RN
711 Third Avenue, New York, NY 10017, USA

First issued in paperback 2016

Routledge is an imprint of the Taylor & Francis Group, an informa business

BRITISH LIBRARY CATALOGUING IN PUBLICATION DATA

Genlis, Stephanie Felicite, comtesse de, 1746–1830
Adelaide and Theodore
  1. Education – Fiction 2. Girls – Education – Fiction
  I. Title II. Dow, Gillian, 1975–
843.5[F]

ISBN 13: 978-1-138-23594-6 (pbk)
ISBN 13: 978-1-8519-6872-5 (hbk)

Typeset by Pickering & Chatto (Publishers) Limited

CONTENTS

Acknowledgments	vii
Introduction	ix
Select Bibliography	xxi
Note on the Text	xxv
Adelaide and Theodore, or Letters on Education	1
Endnotes	479

ACKNOWLEDGEMENTS

The publication of this edition is the result of doctoral and post-doctoral research on the reception of Stéphanie-Félicité de Genlis in Britain. I am naturally indebted to many colleagues, friends, Genlis scholars and those who work on women's writing more generally. Alison Finch was a constant source of encouragement in the early stages of my research, and has long been convinced of the importance of re-editing Genlis in translation. The organizers of the Twelfth Annual Eighteenth- and Nineteenth-Century British Women Writers Conference in Athens, Georgia, 2004 were the first to hear my thoughts on British women writers' responses to *Adelaide and Theodore*. In France, comments and encouragement from Marie-Emmanuelle Plagnol-Diéval were particularly valuable. Isabelle Brouard-Arends and I were contracted to work on new editions of *Adèle et Théodore* and *Adelaide and Theodore* unknown to each other, and only met when the original French text had already been published late in 2006. I have benefited enormously from Brouard-Arends's scholarship in the final months of this project.

My colleagues at Southampton have been very supportive, and particular thanks must of course go to Stephen Bending and Stephen Bygrave, series editors. I have been fortunate to spend time on the edition whilst undertaking a post-doctoral research fellowship at Chawton House Library, home to many editions of Genlis's writings, in both French and English, and many female-authored *Letters on Education* inspired by or reacting to her work. I would like to thank all my colleagues at Chawton House, and in particular the librarian Helen Scott.

INTRODUCTION

i

When Stéphanie-Félicité de Genlis's[1] 1782 *Adèle et Théodore ou lettres sur l'éducation* was translated into English and published as *Adelaide and Theodore, or Letters on Education* in 1783, it was heralded by the *English Review* as 'by much the best system of education ever published in France'.[2] High praise indeed for a work which appeared just twenty years after Rousseau's *Émile, or On Education*.[3] *Adelaide and Theodore* clearly captured the imaginations of both British readers and publishers in the 1780s and 1790s: a new edition of the translation was published in 1784, and this was reprinted in 1788 and 1796. It could even been argued that the work was a late eighteenth-century pan-European phenomenon, since Spanish, Italian, Dutch, Polish and Russian translations appeared at various points throughout this period.[4]

Part of the attraction of the publication was due to the celebrity of the author herself. Stéphanie-Félicité Ducrest de Saint-Aubin was born at Champcery near Autun in Burgundy in 1746, the oldest child of Pierre-César Ducrest and Marie-Françoise-Félicité Mauget de Mézières.[5] The chateau of St. Aubin, Genlis tells

---

1 The problem of names plagues those who work on Genlis. She seems to have been christened Caroline-Stéphanie-Félicité Ducrest de St Aubin, but the Caroline was only rarely used. It was standard for aristocratic women to use the third first name (Germaine de Staël was actually Anne-Louise-Germaine) and most biographers refer to her as Félicité. In French scholarship, she is always Madame de Genlis. I have chosen to refer to her simply as Genlis, omitting the 'de', as is always the case with canonical male French Enlightenment figures such as Montesquieu (Charles de Secondat, Baron de Montesquieu) and Buffon (George-Louis Leclerc, Comte de Buffon).

2 *English Review*, 2 (August 1783), pp. 106–9.

3 First published in French in 1762, and translated almost immediately into English by William Kendrick in 1763, and by William Nugent in 1765, Rousseau's *Émile, or On Education* has been and continues to be hugely influential in debates on education.

4 For details of these translations, see Marie-Emmanuelle Plagnol-Diéval's bibliography *Madame de Genlis* (Paris, Rome: Memini, 1996).

5 These brief biographical details have been compiled from Genlis's own *Mémoires* (1825) of which an English translation appeared in the same year, and several published biographies. The most recent biography, in French, is by Gabriel de Broglie, *Madame de Genlis* (Paris: Librarie Académique Perrin, 2001). Two English biographies are also available. The first is a translation of Jean Harmand's 1912 *Madame de Genlis, sa vie intime et politique* (1912), which appeared as *A Keeper*

the readers of her 1825 *Memoirs* 'resembled those which Mrs. Radcliffe has since described. It was ancient and ruinous, and had old towers, and immense courtyards'.[6] In this state of genteel poverty, Genlis's early education was largely neglected: she was cared for by the staff in her parents' house and taught a little catechism. Genlis's parents' involvement in her education seems to have been minimal as she recounts in her *Memoirs*:

> My father had the utmost affection for me; but he did not interfere with my educa-
> tion in any point but one: he wished to make me a woman of firm mind, and I was
> born with numberless little antipathies: I had a horror of all insects, particularly of
> spiders and frogs; I was also afraid of mice, and he made me feed and bring up one.[7]

The parental disinterest was only marginally rectified when the young Félicité turned seven. The Ducrests decided she should have a governess, and went on to appoint a Breton girl, Mademoiselle de Mars, who had little formal education herself apart from some knowledge of the harpsichord. The two girls were left to their own devices in devising their educational programme, and had access to the family library, where they read many romances and novels. Although the above quoted passage is reminiscent of the account the Baron d'Almane gives of his daughter Adelaide crying over a pet frog (see p. 47), in all other respects, Genlis's lack of formal education is striking for one who was to write a work containing not only 'Letters on Education', but 'All the principles relative to three different Plans of Education; to that of Princes, and to those of young persons of both Sexes'.

A financial disaster in Genlis's early teenage years meant that the family could no longer pay Mademoiselle de Mars's wages. Genlis and her mother travelled to Paris, where they depended on the benevolence of various family acquaintances to establish themselves, and to continue Genlis's training on the harp, an instrument for which she showed considerable aptitude. In 1763, Genlis's fortunes were reversed when she married Count Charles-Alexis de Genlis (later the Marquis of Sillery). The marriage was seen as a disappointing one by Charles-Alexis de Genlis's family, and Genlis herself only managed to bring them round to the idea of a daughter-in-law from impoverished circumstances in the months and years following the union.

The most important rise in fortune and influence came in 1772 owing to the position of Genlis's aunt, Madame de Montesson (1738–1806), who had long been the mistress of the Duke of Orléans, Louis-Philippe (1725–85), and indeed was to marry him in 1773. This connection with the Orléans family

---

of Royal Secrets, the Private and Political Life of Madame de Genlis (London: Nash, 1913). The second is Violet Wyndham's *Madame de Genlis: A Biography* (London: Andre Deutsch, 1958).
6   See *Memoirs of the Countess de Genlis, Illustrative of the History of the Eighteenth and Nineteenth Centuries, Written by Herself*, 8 vols (London: Henry Colburn, 1825), vol. 1, p. 8.
7   Ibid., vol. 1, p. 23.

gave Genlis the position of lady-in-waiting to Orléans's daughter-in-law, Louise Marie Adélaïde de Bourbon-Penthièvre, Duchess of Chartres (1753–1821) and the richest heiress of her day. Shortly after Genlis's arrival at the Palais-Royal, the central Paris seat of the Orléans family, she became the mistress of Louis-Philippe-Joseph Duke of Chartres (1749–93), Orléans's son. This liaison was the subject of much speculation and gossip. After five years in the Chartres household in 1777, Genlis was made governess to the family's newborn twin daughters, and moved to an estate at Belle Chasse in the outskirts of Paris. She was the first woman to be appointed as 'gouverneur' to Royal children when on 6 January 1782 the care of the sons, the Duke of Valois (future head of the Orléans household, King Louis-Philippe, king of the French, in the July Monarchy of 1830–48), the Duke of Montpensier and the Count Beaujolais, was also entrusted to her. Genlis gave a matter-of-fact account of the appointment in her *Memoirs*:

> One evening the Duke of Chartres came, as he generally did to Belle Chasse between eight and nine o'clock, finding me alone, he told me that there was no time to lose in procuring a tutor for his son, for that otherwise his children would have the manners of *shopmen* [...] He consulted me on the selection of one: I proposed M. de Schomberg, whom he refused to accept, alleging, that he would render the children pedantic. I then named the Chevalier de Durfort, who he said would give them a tone of bombast. I next spoke of M. de Thiars, but the Duke of Chartres objected to him as being too careless; and said that he would pay no attention at all to the children. I then began to laugh, and said, 'Well then, what do you think of me?' 'Why not,' replied he seriously.[8]

Genlis, then, was an important member of one of the most notorious French households in the 1770s and 1780s.[9] After 1789, Chartres himself (he became Duke of Orléans on his father's death in 1785, and was known as Philippe Égalité during the revolutionary years) voted for the execution of Louis XVI, and was guillotined in 1793. For reasons of self-preservation in the 1790s, Genlis was to deny that she had had any relationship with Chartres other than as governor to his children, a concealment she maintained in her *Memoirs*.[10]

It was against the background of her controversial appointment as 'gouverneur' to the Orléans heirs that Genlis's educational treaty *Adelaide and Theodore* was published. Contemporary French commentators did not hesitate

---

8   Ibid, vol. 3, pp. 112–13.
9   The Palais-Royal was the centre of Jacobin activity and political pamphleteering in the years leading up to the Revolution. See Chantal Thomas, *La Reine scélérate: Marie-Antoinette dans les pamphlets* (Paris: Le Seuil, 1989) and Robert Darnton, *The Corpus of Clandestine Literature in France, 1769–1789* (London: W. W. Norton, 1995).
10   The *Memoirs* are a valuable source of information about the composition and publication of Genlis's works, but are of less value concerning her involvement in events leading up to the Revolution and her years in exile, when, for obvious reasons, she wanted to deny close involvement in the Orléaniste faction's affairs.

to draw attention to her relationship with Chartres in an abusive and mocking campaign which also attacked Genlis's perceived 'gender-bending', noting her insistence on the male form of the title, 'governeur', rather than 'governante'. One verse ended with the lines 'Je suis monsieur dans le lycée / Et madame dans le boudoir'.[11] As Ellen Moers pointed out, 'the official change in title from *la Gouvernante* to *le Gouverneur* [...] is a change as momentous in French as it is in English, for *Governess* is in the nursery, and *Governor* rules the world.'[12] Through the appointment and through the publication of her 'treaty' in 1782, Genlis positioned herself as the authority on the education of princes and children of both sexes. It was a bold statement for a thirty-six-year-old woman to make.

ii

The schema of *Adelaide and Theodore* is relatively straightforward. The Baron and Baroness d'Almane have retreated to an estate in the south of France, and the Baroness is educating Adelaide and Theodore herself, with the assistance of various tutors, away from the damaging influence of the city. She focuses on the eighteenth-century preoccupation that education should move away from rote-learning from books, and that children should learn by absorbing material from their everyday lives. She places a great importance on the study of modern languages, as opposed to Latin and Greek, and these are learnt in conversation with the gardener, the English governess Miss Bridget and the Italian art tutor Dainville, as well as various other foreign employees. History lessons are taught by looking at a series of magic lantern images, and by examining the décor of their apartments. The regime both children follow is not fundamentally different, and their gender does not affect their education. Both Adelaide and Theodore have a similar daily routine which is carefully thought out, and involves much washing in cold water, and bracing walks. They sleep on hard beds, wear no restrictive clothing, eat plenty of fruit and vegetables but few sweetmeats and follow a programme of gymnastics. They are encouraged to act charitably towards those who are less well-off. The emphasis, as is appropriate for the time, is on instruction alongside delight. Indeed, when another character gives an account of a stay at the Almane estate in Letter XIII of Volume II, she claims 'I am here as much instructed as entertained' (p. 214). Later, the programme of reading for the two children is carefully supervised, and Adelaide's 'Course of Reading' is annexed to

---

11 An approximate translation would be 'I am Mr in the high-school / and Mrs in the bedroom'. Quoted in Louis Petit de Bachaumont, *Mémoires secrets pour servir à l'histoire de la République des Lettres en France, depuis MDCCLXII jusqu'à nos jours, ou journal d'un observateur, contenant les analyses des Pièces de Théâtre qui ont paru dans cet intervalle &c.* (Paris: 1782), vol. 20, p. 53, entry dated 15 February 1782.

12 Ellen Moers, *Literary Women* (London: W. H. Allen, 1977), p. 214.

the main text (pp. 473–7). It is an ambitious programme that takes in the French classics, naturally, but also many works of European literature and philosophy.

All the experiments in education are related back to friends in Paris in letters from both the Baron and the Baroness. The Baroness's main correspondents are the Viscountess de Limours, a mother of two children, Flora and Constantia, and Madame d'Ostalis, a younger woman who the Baroness had 'adopted' in the early years of her marriage, when she was still childless herself. Madame d'Ostalis has been brought up to be a perfect society lady; the Viscountess is a flawed character who is often in need of the Baroness's guidance and advice. The Baron corresponds with the Viscount de Limours, and the Count de Roseville, the Viscountess de Limours's brother, who is the preceptor of 'a Prince, born to be a sovereign' (p. 61).

The novel is primarily a work of parallel educations, in which every character to be educated has their counterpart, and we watch the characters develop over a period of around twelve years. Despite the title suggesting an equal focus on the male and female child, it is Adelaide's story. She is the child whose education is described in great detail, and she is the child to whom those with flawed educations are compared. She has an older example of a solid education in Madame d'Ostalis, her mother's first 'experiment', and indeed she herself is encouraged to take on the duty of educating a young Italian orphan, Hermine, as a way of learning skills that will later serve her in the education of her own children. 'Oh, the charming little creature! I will be her Governess!' Adelaide exclaims (p. 321) but as Olwen Hufton points out, 'Madame de Genlis does not permit the borrowed child to pass judgment on the success or failure of the care given – she is presumably one of the lower orders'.[13] No matter how sceptical a modern reader may be of the benefits of letting children practise educating on other children, according to the novel, the experiment is an astonishing success. The picture of Adelaide's perfections is given to her future husband in the following terms:

> Mademoiselle Almane was the handsomest person living; the most amiable, the most natural; [...] she possessed all the candour and simplicity of infancy, and all the graces of youth; [...] she sings in Italian, and plays on the harp like an Angel; that she draws in a superior style; [...] she educates a little orphan; [...] she is the best as well as the most charming of mothers. (p. 360)

Here, the emphasis is on female accomplishments, and the attractions of Adelaide as a future wife. But it is Flora, the largely neglected daughter of the Viscountess de Limours and counterpart both to Madame d'Ostalis and Adelaide herself, who recognizes that the benefits of the Almane method of education run deeper

---

13 See Olwen Hufton, *The Prospect Before Her: A History of Women in Western Europe: Volume One, 1500–1800* (London: HarperCollins, 1995), p. 454.

than singing and dancing. Complaining of her mother and the Baroness's constant praise of Madame d'Ostalis, the girl who becomes Madame de Valcy says:

> If they look on her as so perfect a pattern, why did they not educate me as they did her? We are both 'just as they made us.' She is very prudent, very reasonable; I am very giddy, very trifling; she knows how to employ herself, to paint, and play on the harp; I know how to dance. We have profited alike, each of us, of the examples, attentions, and education we have received. (p. 245)

It is the responsibility, then, of individual families to educate their daughters. A well-educated daughter will, like Adelaide, live a happy and contented life as a devoted wife and mother, a woman who is also the intellectual companion of her husband. A badly educated daughter can only come to ruin and despair, as the Baroness tells the Madame d'Ostalis with perhaps too much relish:

> Madame de Valcy has consumed all her fortune, for her debts far exceed the portion she received. Her husband went away last night; it is said she means to travel for two or three years. Madame de Valcy remains here without assistance, without advice, without resource, abandoned by all her friends, and even by Mons. de Remicourt [her lover]. She is very ill and keeps her bed; at this moment the Viscountess sees only her misfortunes; she forgets the causes of them. (p. 448)

The Viscountess herself is punished for the lack of attention that she has given her eldest daughter. Her younger daughter, Constantia, was educated with the Baroness's guidance, and she is rewarded by becoming Theodore's wife.

When the Baroness herself presents both her children with a book on their wedding day, entitled 'Letters on Education', she tells them that 'the work reveals all the secrets of education' (p. 472), and moreover that if they find it successful in the education of their own children 'my plan is a good one; my system is not chimerical; and my work is no romance.'[14] (p. 472) The question of whether *Adelaide and Theodore* is a novel or treaty on education is not an idle one, since it is one with which the characters themselves engage. It is certainly a work that reacts and responds to previously published works on education. From Locke's *Some Thoughts Concerning* (1693) to Fénelon's *Les Aventures de Télémaque* (1699), to Rousseau's *Émile, or On Education* (1762), Genlis has read all the major (and many of the minor) writers on education, and engages with their writing both in the letters themselves, and in extensive authorial footnotes. From the opening pages, opposition to Rousseau is set up, as in Letter V, from the Baroness d'Almane to the Viscountess de Limours:

> J. J. Rousseau say, 'Most people chuse Governors for their children who have been accustomed to that employment. But this is too much to expect; the same man can never compleat more than the education of one'. Experience has proved to me that

14 The French word is 'roman', which would be more likely to be translated as 'novel' today, although both romance and novel were common translations in the eighteenth century.

Rousseau opposes an opinion well founded: the deepest study of the human heart, with every talent united, which is so essentially necessary in a Tutor, will avail nothing, without that experience which alone can be acquired by long practice. (p. 7)

By suggesting that Rousseau knew nothing of the practicalities of educating children, the Baroness – a mother who has chosen to keep her children with her and indeed to devote her life to their education – gives herself authority to speak on this most important of topics, setting out in Letter XI of Volume I, her 'principles of education' (p. 25). With regard to strengthening children, and encouraging good health, she tells us that Rousseau 'exactly follows the system of Mr. Locke; for though he doesn't quote him, he copies him literally' (p. 29) – a dependence on other educationalists also stressed, for example, by the Count de Roseville in Letter XXIV of volume I, who writes that 'Rousseau is indebted to Senecca, to Montaigne, to Locke, and to Monsieur de Fénelon for every thing that is truly useful in his book' (p. 61). The Baroness similarly challenges another of Rousseau's statements – that women should breastfeed their children – in Letter XXI, addressed to her adopted daughter Madame d'Ostalis, who admires his views on the issue. The 'interested and mercenary' (p. 50) wet nurses that Rousseau scorns, are, the Baroness shows, acting out of desire to benefit their own children: 'far from being a "bad mother"', the wet nurse 'has on the contrary shewed herself to be possessed of real tenderness' (p. 50). The letter concludes that the situation is more complex than Rousseau depicts it when he claims that women who do not breastfeed their children are selfish and unnatural: 'reflect on the numerous obligations you bring on yourself by determining to suckle your child; and remember, it is better not to impose on yourself such a duty, than to fulfil it imperfectly' (p. 51). While modern debates on this issue tend to side with Rousseau on the benefits for both the mother and child, Genlis's argument for the rational individual woman's right to choose when presented with the evidence must appeal to the feminist reader.

Genlis suffered for her attacks on Rousseau as she admitted in later works, including one written in 1811 in which she addresses her critics:

After the publication of *Adelaide and Theodore*, it was said [...] that I had disproportional pride. To speak on education after Jean-Jacques, to say that his methods were not practical (whilst acknowledging his talents fully) what presumption![15]

It was, however, a matter of fact that Genlis had experience in educating children where Rousseau did not. As a mother of three children herself, the governor of

15 My translation. The original French reads 'Après la publication d'*Adèle et Théodore*, on dit alors, [...] que j'avois un *orgueil démésuré*. Parler sur l'éducation après Jean-Jacques, dire que les systèmes de J. J. sont impracticables (en rendant justice entière à ses éminens talens), quelle présomption!' See *Observations critiques pour servir à l'histoire de la littérature française du XIXième siècle ou réponse de Mme de Genlis à Messieurs M. T. et N. L. etc sur les critiques de son dernier ouvrage intitulé: de l'influence des femmes* (Paris: Maradan, 1811), p. 94.

the Orléans children, and the adoptive mother of two English girls, Pamela and Hermine, adopted to speak English to her young pupils,[16] Genlis could claim first-hand experience of educating, just as Maria Edgeworth was to do in her *Practical Education* (1798).[17] Her account of the Belle Chasse estate in volume 3 of her memoirs is so close to the Languedoc estate in Letter IX of *Adelaide and Theodore* as to be almost indistinguishable:

> I tried to render everything useful to my plan of education, even to the furniture of Belle Chasse. The tapestry of the princesses' room was painted in oil, and on a blue ground were represented in rough sketches, from medals, busts of the seven kings of Rome and the emperors and empresses down to Constantine the Great. Over the doors were painted particular scenes from the same history, and over the medallions were the dates and the names of the personages represented. Two large fire-screens represented the kings of France; the hand-screens, &c. and the tops of the dining-room doors were all covered with mythological pictures. The staircase was entirely covered with maps, which could be taken down for the lessons; the maps of the south were at the foot of the stair, and those of the north at the top. I have detailed all these things in *Adèle et Théodore*.[18]

Naturally, French contemporaries believed that the characters represented were friends and acquaintances of Genlis's, and as Genlis wrote in her *Memoirs*, there were many who thought they could furnish a key to the work. Genlis defended herself: 'I have painted pictures, and not portraits; I have collected several features to be found in nature, but I always interdicted myself all personality that could offend; and when I have recalled the remembrance of persons either ridiculous or vicious, I have so disguised the likeness as to conceal the person, or in general I have given the likeness a different sex from the original'.[19]

Genlis left herself somewhat open to these accusations when she insisted that the inset stories such as the Gothic Duchess of C*** (pp. 267–96) were true, that she had met the Lagarayes personally (p. 164 and note 138 to Volume I, p. 497) and that she knew a mother exactly like the Baroness d'Almane, that is to say,

16 The story of the adoption of Pamela and Hermine into the Orléans household is a complex one. Contemporary observers, in Britain in particular, believed Pamela to be the illegitimate child of Genlis and Chartres, sent to England to avoid scandal, and then brought back under cover as an 'educational tool'. Today, generally speaking, French scholars believe that Pamela was, as Genlis always argued, Nancy Sims, born in Newfoundland, whereas British scholars believe that she was an illegitimate child. Pamela became the celebrated Pamela Fitzgerald, wife of United Irishman Lord Edward Fitzgerald (1763–98). For different views of her parentage, see *La Belle Pamela (Lady Edward Fitzgerald)* (London: Herbert Jenkins, 1924), a biography of Pamela by her great-grand-daughter Lucy Ellis and Joseph Turquan, and Jacques Bertaud's unpublished thesis, 'Madame de Genlis et l'Angleterre: La femme et l'œuvre de 1779 à 1792' (University of Paris III: Sorbonne Nouvelle, 1974).

17 See *The Novels and Selected Works of Maria Edgeworth*, 12 vols (London: Pickering and Chatto, 2003), vol. 11, ed. Susan Manly.

18 See *Memoirs of the Countess de Genlis*, vol. 3, pp. 76–9.

19 Ibid., vol. 3, p. 147.

herself (p. 394 and note 45 to Volume III, p. 510). Even the tragic tale of Cécile, the beautiful nun had its roots in a true story. Cécile 'was Madame de Rochefort, daughter of the Marquis of St. Pouen, and sister of Madame de Balicour. Her father has forced her to take the vows, at the age of seventeen.'[20] The blending of fact with fiction is characteristic of Genlis's later works, including her *Memoirs*, and was a technique that she used to great effect in her historical romances when she was to frustrate British critics with hybrid compositions that blended 'truth with fiction in such a manner as to confound our knowledge of past events'.[21]

In many ways, *Adelaide and Theodore* can be seen as Genlis's doctoral dissertation, a thesis from which she was to draw articles and expand comments for future publications over the remaining fifty years of her writing career in further works on religion, education and what could be called anti-*philosophe* writings and fiction.

iii

In France, the reception of *Adèle et Théodore* was inextricably linked to Genlis's public position, but the work was still extremely popular: the first edition sold out before any announcements had appeared in the press, and a total of twenty-nine editions appeared between 1782 and 1810. Malcolm Cook has compared the French re-editions of Genlis's novel with the late eighteenth-century classic of the epistolary genre, Laclos's *Les Liaisons Dangereuses*, also published in 1782, in this case anonymously.[22] *Adèle et Théodore* far outsold Laclos's work in the 1780s and 1790s, and even in 1810 the editions of *Les Liaisons Dangereuses* numbered only one more, thirty. As portraits of decaying and corrupt Ancien-Régime high society, the two novels are remarkably similar, although, whereas Genlis suggests that the 'solution' to the problem is individualism, religion and education, Laclos's novel offers no 'solutions' as such – simply punishing the evil Merteuil and Valmont, in much the same way as Monsieur and Madame de Valcy are punished, and sacrificing the young Cécile de Volanges and the Présidente de Tourvel in much the same way as Cecilia is sacrificed in *Adelaide and Theodore*. Of course if Genlis had shocked her French contemporaries by daring to write on female education, they would naturally been more shocked had she been the author of *Les Liaisons Dangereuses*. She gives an account of the confusion that arose when one friend mixed up the two novels, sending *Adèle et Théodore* without a note to a friend in Italy, swiftly followed by *Les Liaisons Dangereuses*, with a letter saying the author was Genlis:

---

20 Ibid., vol. 3, p. 140.
21 See the review of Genlis's *The Duke de Lauzun, in Continuation of the History of the Duchess de la Vallière* (1808) in the *Critical Review*, appendix to third series (1808), pp. 449–57.
22 See Malcolm Cook, 'Adèle et Théodore ou les liaisons dangereuses', *Studies on Voltaire & the Eighteenth Century*, 284 (1991), 371–83.

M. d'Hericourt thought for about a fortnight that I was the author of the *Liaisons Dangereuses*. He thereupon wrote to M. de Rulhières to express how great was his surprise, to find that a woman who was still young, and the instructress of the princes of the blood, had the inconceivable effrontery to publish such a work. M. de Rulhières showed me this letter, which affected me deeply; I could not support the thought that a person of understanding should have entertained such an opinion of me, and I was not restored to a state of self-satisfaction until M. de Rulhières brought me a second letter from M. d'Hericourt, which proved that he was undeceived, and that he had read *Adèle et Théodore*.[23]

The reception of *Adelaide and Theodore* in the British periodicals and reviews was less connected to the scandalous reputation Genlis was gaining in her native country, and was almost uniformly enthusiastic, as the quotation from the *English Review* at the beginning of this introduction made clear. There was much in the novel for British reviewers to admire: the citing of Richardson's works as the only novels 'which have any morality in them' (p. 114), the inclusion of many British works in Adelaide's course of reading and the placing of Locke above Rousseau. There were, however, some reservations. In the *European Magazine*, although the reviewer admired the novel, finding the characters 'various and well-supported', the sentiments 'virtuous' and the strategies adopted 'ingenious', the work on the whole, he judged, 'suits France rather than England'.[24] The *Critical Review* went further, seeing a clear danger from French morals:

> to hear of a married woman's lover, without it being followed with marks of infamy and disgust, might blunt that acute sensibility, which makes every approach to vice, and every hint of impropriety, so painful to a female of delicacy and virtue.[25]

Concerns about depictions of French morals and manners did not prevent the novel from being widely serialized in the British Magazines, or represented in the form of the interpolated stories, such as that of Cecilia, the beautiful nun (pp. 52–9), the Dutchess of C*** (pp. 267–96) and St André (pp. 174–86). As Robert Mayo's research has demonstrated, Genlis was one of the most widely translated French authors in British magazines, second only to Marmontel.[26] *Adèle et Théodore* was the most popular single work in the magazines, with two rival translations. The first was published in the *Universal*, which serialized the novel rapidly after the French publication, between June 1782 and December

23 See *Memoirs of the Countess of Genlis*, vol. 3, pp. 145–7.

24 *European Magazine*, 4 (August 1783), pp. 117–18.

25 *Critical Review*, 56 (1783), pp. 300–3. There are several occasions when there is a reference to a married woman's lover in the novel. On the whole, however, Genlis prizes virtue and condemns licentiousness, as the comparison between Madame de Valcy and Adelaide, quoted above, makes clear.

26 See Robert Mayo, *The English Novel in the Magazines 1740–1815* (Evanston, IL: Northwestern University Press, 1962), in particular his catalogue of serialized fiction, entries 9 and 12, which give full bibliographic references to the translations in the *Universal* and *Lady's* Magazines.

1786. This serialization, running to twenty-seven parts, was the longest novel this magazine offered. The second was published some years later, in the *Lady's Magazine*. It ran between May 1785 and April 1789, in forty-nine instalments. British women readers were clearly considered able to judge for themselves whether the work was worthy of their attention. Notable women writers of the 1780s and 1790s such as Mary Wollstonecraft, Catherine Macaulay, Hannah More, Clara Reeve, Anna Seward and Frances Burney all read and responded to Genlis. Nor did later Romantics neglect her: Mary Shelley and Susan Ferrier's journals both give accounts of reading *Adelaide and Theodore*.[27] When Jane Austen published *Emma* in 1814, she included a telling reference to the work which she clearly expected her readers to be familiar with. Speaking of the birth of a daughter to her former governess, Emma rejoices that Mrs Weston has already had experience of educating:

> 'She has had the advantage, you know, of practising on me,' she continued – 'like La Baronne d'Almane on La Comtesse d'Ostalis, in Madame de Genlis's *Adelaide and Theodore*, and we shall now see her own little Adelaide educated on a more perfect plan'.[28]

Austen's comments are clearly light-hearted: Emma herself is hardly the model of a good female education that Madame d'Ostalis, at only fifteen, represented: 'the most distinguished young person of her age, for her talents, knowledge, and disposition' (p. 7). Nor does Austen suggest that such a character is desirable in a novel, or in life: 'pictures of perfection', she famously wrote in a letter from Chawton 'make me sick and wicked'.[29]

Despite Austen's and the English critics' reservations about *Adelaide et Theodore*'s suitability as an educational manual for the mothers and daughters of England, one mother used the work in exactly that way, and the experiment was much more successful than Richard Lovell Edgeworth's attempt to bring up his eldest son 'à la Jean-Jacques'. Margaret Chinnery adopted Genlis's ideas for the learning of modern languages, history, gymnastics – indeed, her entire programme was taken from Genlis, and applied enthusiastically. The two women became friends, corresponded for several years, and Genlis was to dedicate her 1806 historical novel *Madame de Maintenon* to Chinnery.[30]

27 For an account of these responses, see my doctoral dissertation 'Reviewing Madame de Genlis: 'Gouverneur', 'Mère de l'Église', 'Hypocrite'' (University of Oxford, 2004).

28 *The Cambridge Edition of the Works of Austen: Emma*, ed. Richard Cronin and Dorothy Macmillan, (Cambridge: Cambridge University Press, 2005), p. 375.

29 Letter to Fanny Knight, 23 March 1817, in *Jane Austen's Letters*, ed. Deirdre Le Faye (Oxford: Oxford University Press, 1997), p. 335.

30 For more details about this friendship, and its eventual rupture, see both Denise Yim, 'The Chinnery Family Papers (1793–1843)' (Doctoral Dissertation, University of Sydney, 2000) and

Many British women took advantage of the Peace of Amiens to visit Genlis in her apartments in the Arsenal. In a published portrait of Genlis, appearing just after her death in 1831, Joseph Fiévée wrote of a 'hoard of foreigners', for whom Genlis held a saint-like position, especially 'English women who came to have their children blessed'.[31] One of these women, Maria Edgeworth, came without children, but with a background of distinguished contributions to the debate on education herself: *Letters from Literary Ladies* (1795), *Practical Education* (1798) and even a much earlier, unpublished, translation of *Adèle et Théodore* of her own.[32] Her letter to her aunt Mary Sneyd dated 19 March 1803 gives an account of the visit. It paints a picture of Genlis as an embittered old woman, tied up in political scandal and intrigue. Edgeworth says she 'could not like her', although she confesses that 'I might be prejudiced or mortified by Mme de Genlis' assuring me that she had never seen any thing I had written except *Belinda* – that she had heard of *Practical Education* – had seen it mentioned in Miss Hamilton which she was just reading – heard it much praised but had never seen it'.[33] Despite this blow to her pride, Edgeworth remains admiring of Genlis's talents as an educator. She comments in the letter on the excellence of a translation that one of Genlis's pupils is working on, and tells the anecdote of Louis-Philippe being turned into such an accomplished Mathematician by Genlis that he had been able to find work as a university professor in exile in Germany.

Edgeworth concludes:

> If we could see and converse with one of her pupils we should be able to form a better judgment than from all that her books and her enemies say for and against her. I say her books and enemies, not her friends and enemies for I fear she has no friends to plead for her except her books.'[34]

If any work can indeed 'plead for' Genlis's importance as a writer, it is the ambitious *Adelaide and Theodore*. Often controversial, always impressive in both scope and aims, it deserves to be resituated within the context of the late eighteenth- and early nineteenth-century debate on female education, as a key work of instruction and delight.

Denise Yim, *The Unpublished Correspondence of Mme de Genlis and Margaret Chinnery and related documents in the Chinnery family papers* (Oxford: Voltaire Foundation, 2003).
31 My translation: original French read 'foule des étrangers [...] Les Anglaises qui venait faire bénir leurs enfants'. See Joseph Fiévée, 'Madame de Genlis', *L'Artiste*, 1 (1831), pp. 5–9. Also quoted in Yim, *Correspondence of Genlis and Chinnery*, p. 30.
32 For details of Edgeworth's work on *Adèle et Théodore*, see Marilyn Butler, *Maria Edgeworth: A Literary Biography* (Oxford: Clarendon Press, 1972) pp. 147–9.
33 Christina Colvin (ed.), *Maria Edgeworth in France and Switzerland* (Oxford: Clarendon Press, 1979), p. 101. Elizabeth Hamilton's *Letters on Education* were published in 1801–2.
34 Colvin (ed.), *Maria Edgeworth in France and Switzerland*, p. 102.

SELECT BIBLIOGRAPHY

Primary Material

Reviews

[Anon.], *European Magazine* (July 1783), pp. 54–5; (August 1783), pp. 117–18.

[Anon.], *English Review*, 2 (August 1783), pp. 106–9.

[Anon.], *New Annual Register* (September 1783), p. 281.

[Anon.], *British Magazine and Review* (October 1783), pp. 293–5.

[Anon.], *Town and Country Magazine* (November 1783), p. 599.

[Anon.], *Gentleman's Magazine*, 53 (1783), pp. 860–2, 946–7.

[Anon.], *Critical Review*, 56 (1783), pp. 300–3.

[Anon.], *Monthly Review*, 70 (1784), pp. 338–45.

Works by Genlis

Only a small number of Genlis's most relevant publications have been included here. For details of others, see the following bibliography: Marie-Emmanuelle Plagnol-Diéval, *Madame de Genlis* (Paris; Rome: Memini, 1996).

In French

Théâtre à l'usage des jeunes personnes (Paris: M. Lambert et F. J. Baudoin, 1779–80).

Annales de la vertu ou cours d'histoire à l'usage des jeunes personnes par l'auteur du théâtre d'éducation (Paris: M. Lambert et F. J. Baudoin, 1781).

Adèle et Théodore ou Lettres sur l'éducation contenant tous les principes relatifs aux trois plans d'éducation des princes, des jeunes personnes et des hommes (Paris: M. Baudoin et F. J. Lambert, 1782).

Les Veillées du château, ou Cours de morale à l'usage des enfants, par l'auteur d'Adèle et Théodore (Paris: M. Lambert et F. J. Baudoin, 1782).

La Religion considérée comme l'unique base du bonheur et de la véritable philosophie (Paris: Imprimerie polytype, 1787).

Discours sur l'Education de M. le Dauphin et sur l'adoption (Paris: Onfroy, 1790).

Discours sur la suppression des couvens de religieuses et l'éducation publique des femmes (Paris, 1791).

Discours sur l'Education publique du peuple (Paris, 1791).

Leçons d'une Gouvernante à ses Elèves, ou fragment d'un journal qui a été fait pour l'éducation des enfants de M. d'Orleans (Paris: Onfroy, 1791).

Nouvelles heures à l'usage des enfants (Paris: Maradan, 1801).

Nouvelle méthode d'Enseignement pour la première enfance (Paris: Maradan, 1801).

Projet d'une école rurale pour l'éducation des filles (Paris, 1801).

De l'influence des femmes sur la littérature française comme protectrices des Lettres ou comme auteurs. Précis de l'histoire des femmes françaises les plus célèbres (Paris: Maradan, 1811).

Émile, avec des retranchements, une note et une préface (Paris: Maradan, 1820).

Mémoires inédits sur le XVIIIième siècle et la Révolution française, 10 vols (Paris: Ladvocat, 1825–8).

In English

Theatre of education, Translated from the French of the Countess of Genlis, 4 vols (London: T. Cadell and P. Elmsly, 1781).

Tales of the Castle, or Stories of instruction and delight, being les Veillées du château Written in French by the Comtesse de Genlis (London: G. Robinson, 1785).

The Beauties of Genlis; Being a Collection of the Most Beautiful Tales and other Striking Extracts from Adela and Theodore; the Tales of the Castle; The Theatre of Education and Sacred Dramas (Perth: R. Morrison and Sons, 1787).

Religion Considered as the Only Basis of Happiness and True Philosophy (London: T. Payne and Son, 1787).

Selections from the Works of Madame de Genlis; Consisting Principally of Precepts, Maxims, and Reflections to which are Prefixed a Portrait and Life of the Author (London: James Cundee, 1806).

Memoirs of the Countess of Genlis, Illustrative of the Eighteenth and Nineteenth centuries. Written by Herself (London: Henry Colburn, 1825).

Secondary Material

Allen Ford, Susan, 'Romance, Pedagogy and Power: Jane Austen Re-writes Madame de Genlis', *Persuasions*, 21 (2001), pp. 172–187.

Bertaud, Jacques, 'Madame de Genlis et l'Angleterre: La femme et l'œuvre de 1779 à 1792' (unpublished doctoral thesis, University of Paris III: Sorbonne Nouvelle, 1974).

—, 'Madame de Genlis et ses deux voyages en Angleterre', in *Studies in Eighteenth Century Literature*, ed. Miklos J. Szenczi and Laslo Ferenczi (Budapest: Akadémiai Kiadó, 1974), pp. 275–300.

—, 'Madame de Genlis, John Wilson Croker et la Révolution Française', *Revue de Littérature Comparée*, 3 (1977), pp. 356–65.

Brown, Penny, '"Candidates for my friendship" or How Madame de Genlis and Mary Wollstonecraft Sought to Regulate the Affections and Form the Mind to Truth and Goodness', *New Comparison*, 20 (1995), pp. 46–60.

Clancy, P., 'Madame de Genlis, Elizabeth Inchbald, and the Child of Nature', *Australian Journal of French Studies*, 30 (1993), pp. 324–40.

Colvin, Christina (ed.), *Maria Edgeworth in France and Switzerland* (Oxford: Clarendon Press, 1979).

Cook, Malcolm, '*Adèle et Théodore* ou les liaisons dangereuses', *Studies on Voltaire & the Eighteenth Century*, 284 (1991), pp. 371–83.

Dow, Gillian, 'The good sense of British readers has encouraged the translation of the whole: les traductions anglaises des œuvres de Mme de Genlis dans les années 1780', in *La Traduction des genres non-romanesques au XVIIIième siècle*, ed. Annie Cointre and Annie Rivara (Metz: Centre d'études de la traduction, 2003), pp. 285–97.

—, 'The British Reception of Madame de Genlis's Writings for Children: Tales and Plays of Instruction and Delight', *British Journal for Eighteenth-Century Studies*, 29 (2006), pp. 367–81.

France, Peter (ed.), *The New Oxford Companion to Literature in French* (Oxford: Clarendon Press, 1995).

—, *The Oxford Guide to Literature in English Translation* (Oxford: Oxford University Press, 2000).

Gillespie, Stuart and David Hopkins (eds), *The Oxford History of Literary Translation in English: Vol. 3 1660–1790* (Oxford: Oxford University Press, 2005).

Kavanagh, Julia, *French Women of Letters: Biographical Sketches* (London: Hurst and Blackett, 1862).

Kerby, William Mosely, *The Educational Ideas and Activities of Madame la Comtesse de Genlis, with Special Reference to her Work Adèle et Théodore* (Paris: Presses Universitaires de France, 1926).

Krakeur, Lester Gilbert, 'A Forgotten Participant in the Attack on the Convent: Madame de Genlis', *Modern Language Notes*, 52 (1937), pp. 89–95.

Maza, Sarah, 'The Rose-Girl of Salency: Representations of Virtue in Prerevolutionary France', *Eighteenth-Century Studies*, 22 (1989), pp. 395–412.

Moers, Ellen, *Literary Women* (London: W. H. Allen, 1977).

Ó Gallchoir, Clíona, 'Gender, Nation and Revolution: Maria Edgeworth and Stéphanie-Félicité de Genlis', in *Women, Writing and the Public Sphere 1700–1830*, ed. Elizabeth

Eger, Charlotte Grant, Clíona Ó Gallchoir and Penny Warburton (Cambridge: Cambridge University Press, 2001), pp. 200–16.

Plagnol-Diéval, Marie-Emmanuelle, *Madame de Genlis* (Paris; Rome: Memini, 1996).

—, *Madame de Genlis et le théatre d'éducation au XVIIIe siècle* (Oxford: Voltaire Foundation, 1997).

Schaneman, J. C., 'Rewriting *Adèle et Théodore*: Intertextual Connections Between Madame de Genlis and Ann Radcliffe', *Comparative Literature Studies*, 38 (2001), pp. 31–45.

van Dijk, Suzan, 'Gender et traduction: Madame de Genlis traduite par une romancière hollandaise, Elisabeth Bekker (Betje Wolff)', in *La traduction des genres non romanesques au XVIIIième siècle*, ed. Annie Cointre and Annie Rivara (Metz: Centre d'études de la traduction, 2003), pp. 299–311.

Wahba, Magdi, 'Madame de Genlis in England', *Comparative Literature*, 13 (1961), pp. 221–38.

NOTE ON THE TEXT

The original French text of *Adèle et Théodore ou Lettres sur l'éducation contenant tous les principes relatifs aux trois différerents plans d'éducation des Princes et des jeunes personnes de l'un et l'autre sexe* published in January 1782 (Paris: Lambert et J. F. Baudouin, 1782) was followed a few months later by a second edition, also published by Lambert et J. F. Baudoin. Although the text of the second edition is almost identical, it contains a lengthy preface by Genlis where she reacts to the criticism of her work, explains the background to its composition, and comments in particular on criticisms that she did not acknowledge the importance of Rousseau's *Émile*. She also carefully points out where a very few changes have been made in the text. For those who are interested in Genlis's preface to the second French edition, and to the textual history of *Adèle et Théodore* in France more generally, I refer you to *Adèle et Théodore ou Lettres sur l'éducation contenant tous les principes relatifs aux trois différerents plans d'éducation des Princes et des jeunes personnes de l'un et l'autre sexe* (Rennes: Presses universitaires de Rennes, 2006), ed. Isabelle Brouard-Arends, and in particular pp. 38–55, where Brouard-Arends's note on the text and Genlis's preface can be read in French.

I have chosen for this edition to use the text that would have been familiar to the first English-speaking readers, the 1783 English translation of the initial 1782 edition, the copy taken from the Chawton House Library. When compared to the first edition of the French text, some differences are immediately apparent. The original 'Avertissement' (Advertisement to the Reader) is not translated. Nor does the English translator include Genlis's notes to the main body of the text. These notes are numerous and frequently lengthy and to omit them gives quite a different impression of the work, which in English becomes more of a novel and less of an educational treaty. I have included in the Endnotes all examples of where Genlis's original notes have been omitted or incorporated into the main body of the text.

As far as the translation is concerned, British reviewers saw it as their duty to comment on the 'purity and elegance' of expression in late eighteenth-century translations. The *English Review* writes approvingly of this translation that 'the stile [*sic*] is almost uniformly elegant – we mean in the original – but we must so far do justice to the translator as to allow that he has seldom failed in transplanting the beauties of the original, unless where these beauties could not be moved'. The reviewer in the *Gentleman's Magazine*, on the other hand, grumbles about 'solecisms in the translation, such as that of *lay* for *lie*, &c. [and] constantly using *you was* for *you were*, a singular and a plural, as absurd, though not so obvious, as that of *you is* for *you are*.' The *British Magazine and Review* goes even further, and suggests that 'a lady of the first literary talents', probably Maria Edgeworth, should complete and publish her own translation:

> Should *that lady* renew her intention, the present performance, we apprehend, would be but little read. To say the truth, this translation is so indifferently executed, being in many places egregiously ungrammatical, and generally very inelegant, that if even the lady in question should not be induced to take up her pen, we hope, at least, some person of respectable talents may be prevailed on to render the excellent Letters of Madame la Comtesse de Genlis worthy of the attention of the English nation.

Perhaps partly in response to these criticisms, a second edition of the translation was published in 1784: *Adelaide and Theodore; or Letters on Education: Containing all the Principles Relative to three Different Plans of Education; to that of Princes, and to those of Young Persons of both Sexes. Translated from the French of Madame la Comtesse de Genlis. The Second Edition, Carefully Corrected and Amended*, 3 vols (London: C. Bathurst and T. Cadell, 1784). In many English translations of Genlis's works the names of the translators were published (Thomas Holcroft, for example, who translated *Les Veillées du chateau*); in other cases, formerly unknown translators have since been identified (for instance, the translators of the 1788 version of the *Theatre of Education*, Mariana Starke and Millecent Thomas).[1] In the second English edition, the translators include a preface, which identifies them only as:

> some Ladies, who through misfortunes, too common at this time, are reduced from ease and opulence, to the necessity of applying, to the support of life, those accomplishments which were given them in their youth, for the amusement and embellishment of it.
>
> They are sensible that the favourable reception of the Work, and the quick sale of the former Edition, are owing more to the great merit of the Original, than to the accuracy of the Translation: In gratitude therefore to the Public, and in justice to the celebrated Author, Madame de Genlis, they have endeavoured at a thorough revisal of it, and they hope that, by the obliging criticisms of their friends, and by the experience they have gained in practice, they have made it more worthy of her, and of the Reader.

1 See Edward W. Pitcher, 'Mariana Starke and Millecent Thomas: Early Translators of Genlis's 'Le théâtre à l'usage des jeunes personnes (1779–1780)', *Notes and Queries*, 45:243 (March 1998), pp. 81–2.

In the 1784 edition, the translators also include Genlis's Advertisement to the Reader:

> These Letters contain a period of twelve years: and it is necessary to say, that these are not the whole of what passed between the different parties during that time, but that those least interesting have been suppressed, which frequently occasions chasms of several months, but is no interruption to the history contained in them.

Another valuable inclusion is a page which gives 'Names of the principal Persons'. There are many more notes from the translators, and more of Genlis's own notes have been included. The second edition does not always differentiate between Genlis's notes and notes included by the translators, but I have highlighted all these textual differences in the Endnotes. The editions that followed in 1788 and 1796 used the text of the second edition, and I have therefore only compared the first two editions, both against each other and against the first and second editions of the French text.

Finally, I have made very few changes to the substance of the first English edition text, keeping, for example, the 'solecisms in the translation' that the *Gentleman's Magazine* objected to (such as 'you was') even though the second edition removes these. The following changes have been made in order to make the text more accessible to the modern reader and remove some of the obstacles which naturally arise when different translators translate different sections of the same novel. I have made the spelling of names of characters consistent throughout the text, choosing the name that is closest to the French original, and making titles consistently French throughout: Madame and Mons., for example, rather than the Mr. that the translator of the second volume preferred. I have removed the italics of proper nouns, whilst italicising the titles of publications. I have also silently corrected typographical errors, changed the long *s* to the roman *s* and eliminated running quotation marks. Finally, I have only commented on the accuracy of the translation when the English version renders it incomprehensible, misses an important allusion, or leaves words in the original French, an occurrence which, in fact, is remarkably rare. The text, then, a flawed but nonetheless popular translation, is almost exactly as the first English readers of *Adelaide and Theodore* would have encountered it.

ADELAIDE AND THEODORE;

OR

LETTERS ON EDUCATION:

CONTAINING

All the Principles relative to three different
Plans of Education; to that of Princes, and
to those of young Persons of both Sexes.

*Translated from the French of Madame la Comtesse
de Genlis.*

VOL. I

LONDON

Printed for C. BATHURST, in Fleet-street; and
T. CADELL, in the Strand.
MDCCLXXXIII.

ADELAIDE

AND

THEODORE.

LETTER I.

From the Baron d' Almane to the Viscount de Limours.

Feb. 2, Three o'Clock in the Morning.

B Y the time you receive this letter, my dear Viscount, I shall be twenty leagues from Paris.[1] I am setting off immediately with my wife and two children for four years. I have neither been able to give you an account of my intentions, nor to bid you adieu, and fearing the remonstrances and solicitations of your friendship, I have carefully concealed from you my intentions. The manner in which I now proceed, after long and deliberate reflection, is only the result of that lively tenderness, which you well know I feel for my children. It is from them I expect the happiness of my future life, and I dedicate myself entirely to their education. I shall perhaps appear to the world to make a great and painful sacrifice: I shall also be accused of singularity and caprice, and indeed with reason. I cannot in this letter lay open to you all my ideas. They are too numerous and extensive. When I arrive at B—,[2] I shall write you all the particulars, which you have a right to expect from my confidence and friendship. Be assured, my dear Viscount, that I shall not lose sight of the delightful project we have formed, and which ought to draw still closer the bonds which unite us. Removing my son in his infancy from the examples of vice, in becoming his governor and his friend, am I not working for you as well as for myself? Since it is virtue alone can render him worthy the happiness you design for him. Farewell, dear Viscount: let me hear from you; be not too hasty in judging me, and above all do not condemn me, before you know all the motives which may influence my conduct. My wife is writing to yours a long letter: but knowing so well the Viscountess, she fears her vivacity, and entreats you to moderate its effects as much as possible. We are only in fear of her first letter, as we are sure time and reflection will not fail to justify us.

LETTER II.

Baroness d'Almane to the Viscountess de Limours.

Feb. 2.

WE arrived at B—, my dear friend, all in good health. My boy and girl, at six and seven years old, bore their journey perfectly well; and as they slept as easy in the carriage, as in their beds, are infinitely less fatigued than I was myself. This country is charming, though I am not yet acquainted with its environs; yet the delightful views which may be seen from the castle, are sufficient to give me an idea of them. Every thing here puts on a plain and humble appearance; I have left pomp and magnificence behind me at Paris, in that large and disagreeable house we lived, and which was always so displeasing to me. I at length find myself lodged according to my taste and my wishes. My little Adelaide too is charmed with this country, and our habitation. She says she likes instructive pictures much better than damask hangings, and that 'the Sun of Languedoc is brighter than that of Paris.' As I conclude my dear friend is at this time a little displeased with me, I shall reserve my more particular accounts and descriptions for the happy moment of reconciliation. When you have read my heart, I dare believe, far from condemning me, you will approve every step I have taken. Consider, though you may be permitted to quarrel with your friend, when in the space of five minutes you can ask her pardon, you have no longer that privilege when she is at the distance of two hundred leagues. Besides, what crime have I been guilty of more than concealing a secret from you, which was not my own to divulge? Mons. d'Almane positively forbid my trusting you with it. But do you not remember the last time we supped together? In truth, you might have guessed from my melancholy, from my tenderness, what it was impossible to acquaint you with! Adieu, my dear friend! I shall expect your answer with the utmost impatience, for I cannot be happy, whilst I think you are displeased with me. I embrace Flora, and the sweet little Constantia with all my heart; and I entreat the former will sometimes talk to you about the best friend you have in the world.

LETTER III.

The Countess d' Ostalis, to the Baroness d' Almane.

THE day of your departure, my dear aunt, I went as you desired to Madame de Limours. In the morning she was denied to me; but in the evening she gave me admittance. I found her a little angry, but more grieved. She wept on seeing me, and then gave a loose to complaints against you; and treated me with a coolness, the cause of which I easily penetrated, and which was nothing more than an impulse of jealousy, occasioned by the idea of my having been entrusted with the secret, you had so carefully concealed from her. I could have said to her, 'How, my dear Madam, was it possible that my aunt, my benefactress, my mother, that she, to whom I owe my education, my establishment, almost my existence, could have any reserves with her child, or could fear from me, either the objections or the oppositions she dreaded from you?' But I happily recalled to my mind one of your maxims, which forbids our making use of reason to oppose ill humour, and I remained silent. I dined yesterday at her house, and found her nearly in the same temper. She had many people with her; and I perceived several of her visitors endeavoured to irritate her against you, my dear aunt, by repeating with ill nature, how 'incredible and inconceivable it was, that you should not have imparted your secret to her:' this has given such a wound to her self-love, that at this moment you must not expect your letters will have that effect on her which you hope for. But her heart is so good, she loves you so tenderly, and has so much frankness and vivacity in her disposition, that it is impossible she should long retain these disagreeable impressions.

Mons. d' Ostalis does not go to his regiment till the first of June: and I shall set out the same day for Languedoc. How happy, my dear aunt, shall I be to find myself in your arms, after an absence of upwards of four months! To see my uncle again; the amiable Theodore, and the charming little Adelaide! And, ah, how cruel will it be to be separated again from these objects so dear to my heart! Adieu, my dear aunt; do not forget your eldest, your adopted child, who every moment of her life thinks of you, and loves you as much as she admires and respects you.

My little twins are perfectly well; they begin to pronounce some words both of French and English: and they already afford me the greatest pleasure I am able to enjoy in your absence.

LETTER IV.

Viscountess de Limours, to the Baroness d' Almane.

YOU say one must not find fault with a friend, when she is two hundred leagues off. But is it also necessary one must pardon her, if she fails in all the duties of friendship? If you know any maxim which enforces this doctrine, you will do well to quote it, for that alone can support your argument. You say I pout, and am in the sullens, but it is no such thing. I do not pout, but I am wounded and vexed to the very bottom of my soul! You have no nearer relation, not even Madame d' Ostalis, since I am your first cousin, and she is only your niece in the thousandth degree. You had not a more tender friend, nor one who had known you longer; and yet in the only occasion of your life, when you could have given me the strongest proof of your confidence, you treat me as a stranger! Surely this is enough to make me angry! *It was not entirely your own secret, it was another's*! You go away for four years! My God, what a slave you are become! 'Mons. d' Almane prevented you from telling it,' in other words 'he forbid you.' You are to be sure a most submissive wife, and he is an imperious tyrant. Now indeed I can hear Mons. de Limours' secrets without even being tempted to disclose them to you. But whilst I was persuaded you loved me, I should have betrayed all the husbands in the world for you: you have convinced me I was wrong, and I will correct myself. You pretend to say I might have divined what you dared not to tell me, because you was 'melancholy' at supper; now as I never saw you remarkably gay, and as your avocations often made you serious, I confess I was not struck with this pretended sadness. Besides, as it was only the eve of your departure; supposing I had discovered this project, which had been for two years determined on, I should not have been more satisfied with you. I know you set little value on the opinion of the world, when your honour is not concerned; and it is happy for you that it is so in this particular instance, for at present you are universally blamed. It is thought strange you should go and educate your children in the farthest part of Languedoc, when you had a delightful estate only six leagues from Paris, where you might have lived retired without abandoning your friends, and without being deprived of the assistance of those masters you will stand in need of, where you are: some people say you have fixed on this plan from motives of vanity, that you may appear to make a greater sacrifice: others, and the greater part, say that you are ruined; and that the disrangement of your affairs is the sole cause of your quitting Paris. There are many other conjectures formed, but they are so absurd they are not worth relating. What reply can I make to all these opinions? Only that *the Sun is brighter in Languedoc than it is in Paris, or its environs.* This is the only reason you have as yet given me; doubtless, you have many others, therefore I intreat you will acquaint me with them. It will be cruel for me to be always silent, when I hear you accused of caprice and inconsistency. Adieu! ... It is not an adieu for a few hours, it is for four years, perhaps for ever! What a pleasant thought this is. How does one melancholy idea soften the heart? My eyes are filled with tears! I am now scarcely angry with you, but I am afflicted, I am melancholy to the greatest degree! Write to me, write to me immediately, and be very particular in your accounts. You see what malice I have been capable of, and at the same time how weak I am! After this acknowledgment, I may still confess I shall ever love you, and that it is impossible for me to live without telling you so, and without knowing that you are perfectly convinced of it.

LETTER V.

Baroness d' Almane to the Viscountess de Limours.

How much do I owe to that 'melancholy idea,' which presented me four such tender and sweet lines! Although you have at present forgiven me, with so much kindness and generosity, I am still apprehensive we may have more disputes; but, however, attend to all that may serve to justify me. I never was fond of the bustle and amusements of the gay world, and you know with what ardour and anxiety I wished for children, and how much of my time has been employed during my whole life, in whatever concerned their education. Married at seventeen years of age, and not being a mother till I was twenty-one, I was apprehensive I should never enjoy that happiness for which I had so ardently wished, and to make myself as much amends as I possibly could for this disappointment, I adopted Madame d' Ostalis; she was at that time ten years old, and was of an excellent disposition. I educated her with all the care of which I was then capable; and every body was pleased with the method I had pursued. My scholar at fifteen, was the most distinguished young person of her age, for her talents, knowledge, and disposition. I alone was sensible by the experience I had acquired, that I could do much better in future. J. J. Rousseau says, 'Most people chuse Governors for their children who have been accustomed to that employment. But this is too much to expect; the same man can never complete more than the education of one.'[3] Experience has proved to me that Rousseau opposes an opinion well founded: the deepest study of the human heart, with every talent united, which is so essentially necessary in a Tutor, will avail nothing, without that experience which alone can be acquired by long practice. It was with great concern I made this discovery, yet it increased the extreme desire

I always had for children; certain, that the greatest pleasure of my life would be to dedicate my time to their improvement. I cannot express what I felt at being disappointed of such happiness. Heaven at length heard my prayer: the birth of Theodore, and that of Adelaide a twelve-month after, made me the happiest creature in the world. I had already finished some Works on Education.[4] I laboured at it again with such earnestness, that it affected my health; I then found I could not follow my plan in the extent I wished, without breaking those bonds of society to which custom subjects us: in short, I saw it was necessary either to quit the world, or to renounce for ever the project I had formed, and which was so dear to my heart. Mons. d' Almane was entirely of my opinion, and he declared himself determined to leave Paris, as soon as Theodore had reached his seventh year. The difficulty was, what retreat to fix upon? We were desirous of inspiring our children with a taste for humble pleasures, and of removing them far from the pomp and magnificence of the metropolis. Could we therefore have been contented to go to a villa we had at only six leagues from Paris? Would it have been possible to prevent our acquaintance from following us thither? Would not Adelaide and Theodore have heard every day of Operas, Comedies, &c. And how could we have prevented their regretting these amusements, which they would have heard mentioned with so much pleasure? The result of these reflections, and many others, determined our preference of an estate of Mons. d' Almane's, in the province of Languedoc; where we should meet with freedom and retirement. From that moment Mons. d' Almane began to arrange every thing at the castle for our reception. If you wish to know in what manner we have furnished our apartments, I will give you an exact description of it in my next letter. And now, my dear friend, I must intreat you for one moment to put yourself in my place; do not judge me by yourself, formed as you are for society, and to give and receive pleasure in the high stile of life which you have been used to; but represent me in the way you have always found me, fond of study and attention to my domestic duties, unable to bear restraint, where no rational aim was in view; and indifferent to the last degree to those trifling matters, which employ so many people in the world; I find myself interested in things only which are useful; not conceiving it possible to have any desire to please those we do not love, and detesting grand entertainments, dress, and cards; in short, expecting and looking for happiness only in my children, have I not followed the course most suitable to my disposition? And can you after this accuse me of 'caprice?' It is very true, as you observe, my children can have no masters in Languedoc; but Mons. d' Almane and I shall be able to supply their places, at least during their infancy. Besides, I have with me two persons well qualified to instruct children, who will remain here till their education is compleated. When four years are elapsed, I mean to spend all my winters at Paris, and then I shall procure all the masters we shall think necessary to finish their improvements. Now confess, my dear friend; had I communicated this scheme to you two years ago, would you have thought yourself much obliged to me? No persons love to have secrets entrusted to them, but when you communicate them by way of asking advice. Our resolution was not to be shaken; so that in trusting the secret to you, we should have only exposed ourselves to oppositions and to arguments which could only have vexed both parties, and perhaps have produced a mutual coolness. Here, my dear friend, is a part of my justification. When you know the plan of education we have formed, you will be more convinced how indispensably necessary it was for us to leave Paris. Let the world censure me as it pleases, the testimony of my own conscience will easily console me for their injustice, provided I can but attain the approbation of my friend. Those who make a sacrifice of their pleasures to their duty, may be sure the publick will turn to ridicule actions which are influenced by such laudable motives; and will find out imaginary causes to take away all their merit. This unjust way of judging is not always the effect of envy, but frequently takes place without any ill intention; for in effect the greater part of mankind are unable well to believe motives of which they themselves do not see the propriety, in which case their incredulity is more flattering than their approbation. In short, my dear friend, if you approve my conduct, and will always love me, I shall be satisfied, and perfectly happy.

LETTER VI.

Viscountess de Limours to the Baroness.

OUR disputes always end in the same manner. I find you in the right, and I am obliged to confess my faults; and I perceive this will ever be the case between us. Yes, my dear friend, you are still right, when the motives of your conduct are explained, however I may find fault with you on the first appearance, in which I constantly see irregularity. Your plans always succeed well in the end. This is at present as much as I can allow you. But I cannot answer for its being my last word upon this subject. You have acted in every respect according to your disposition and sentiments. And though your scheme should not succeed so well as I suppose, you are setting an example, which in these days must have great merit; therefore it is impossible for me to disapprove your conduct any longer. Nothing can be more like than the picture you draw of yourself. At each word I read, I cried out, 'how true that is!' And I then said to myself, but how can I love a person so tenderly, who bears so little resemblance to myself! You, who have so much knowledge, must explain this to me. Friendship has its caprices as well as love. All you have told me concerning the education of Madame d' Ostalis, has struck me in the most lively manner. I sincerely think, there can be no mother who would not be proud of such a daughter; yet from your sentiments I apprehend, if Adelaide has as good a disposition, she will infinitely surpass her. This, however, is a melancholy consideration for eldest daughters, since it is the youngest only who can be compleatly educated. How then is this inconvenience to be remedied? There must be some method, and you ought to employ yourself in finding it out. Think about it, I intreat you. I am this day thirty-one years old. I have a daughter in her fifteenth year. It is time I should renounce some of the follies of the world, which I have hitherto been engaged in; and, perhaps, it may be even now too late for me to repair the faults I have committed in Flora's education. Her sister, you know, is only five years old. Inform me of the plan you have laid out for Adelaide, and I will pursue it with as much steadiness as I possibly can in my situation. I have the greatest desire to render her worthy of being one day your daughter-in-law. Instruct me, guide me, my dear friend! How delightful will it be for me to be indebted to you for new virtues, and consequently for new sources of happiness! You have known me very gay and dissipated; but indeed my faults are more to be attributed to the neglected education I received, than to my natural disposition. When I first entered into the world, having just left the convent, one single idea had possession of my mind, which was that of making myself amends for a long and painful slavery, by entering into all the pleasures and amusements of life. All the instructions I received at that time was how to dress myself to advantage, and to dance well. I never missed an assembly; and the consequence was, that towards the end of the winter, I had an inflammation in my lungs, which I thought would have been fatal, and I was in debt to my mantua maker, fifteen thousand livres! You see how tractable I was, and how strictly I followed the advice you gave me. Nevertheless, I can assure you with the greatest truth, that dissipation never charmed me but in idea, and I always returned from those noisy and tumultuous scenes, with a weariness and disgust, which ought to have convinced me, that they were not designed for me, at least not in the degree I had imagined. Yet I suffered myself to be led to them again by custom and complaisance. And thus it is I have passed my life; giving myself up to the pleasures of the world without loving them, and committing follies which my reflection condemned. And what is the consequence of all this? I enjoy not one agreeable recollection; my health is impaired; and now, when it is too late, I regret the time past. My vivacity is much talked of. I myself do not think it is natural to me; though I am praised for the appearance of it, you, who seem so serious in your manner, are in reality much more chearful than I am. I never saw you entertain 'gloomy ideas,' you know not what they mean. But as to myself, I am sometimes seized on a sudden with the most melancholy thoughts, and they present themselves to my imagination at the most unseasonable times, and even when I have been in the gayest humour. For instance, I find myself at this moment so sad and so peevish, that I will not lengthen my letter. Adieu, my dear friend! send me the description of your castle, and all the other accounts you have promised me. I received a letter yesterday from my brother; he appears charmed with his young Prince, and every day congratulates himself on having undertaken his education. There is certainly much honour to be acquired, in well educating a Prince born to sovereignty. But it will cost my brother dear; for is it not a cruel sacrifice to be banished from one's own country for twelve years? He desires me to tell you, that the plan you have formed adds still more to the high esteem and attachment with which you have always inspired him, and that he will himself write to the Baron, to express to him the admiration he has conceived for you both. You most certainly set excellent examples, but such are not always the most useful; for if it be difficult to avoid praising you, it is still more difficult to imitate you.

LETTER VII.

The Baroness to the Viscountess.

YOU ask me so many questions, it is impossible one letter should contain all you desire to know. But since you are fond of particulars, be assured I shall not be sparing of them, as nothing can give me more pleasure than to inform you of my employments, and to receive an account of whatever interests you. Is it then so necessary for us to see each other, in order to give and receive proofs of our mutual regard? Friendship, that pure and disinterested sentiment, is nourished and strengthened by absence. Absence also serves to prove to us the constancy and sincerity of the attachment. The pleasure of writing to each other, the delightful intercourse between two hearts united by esteem and confidence is perhaps one of our greatest delights; and in this case there does not exist that cold conformity of sentiment which you meet with amongst persons who are drawn together by mere chance, without any other ties: for you are never enslaved but by choice and inclination. This intimate correspondence of thoughts is an enjoyment as new as it is interesting. Besides, one finds in absence many other advantages. All defects in the temper and disposition disappear; you only see in your friend's letter, her tenderness, her understanding, and her amiable qualities. No disputes can arise, no opposition can occasion a coolness! but it is not an account of my sentiments you ask for, it is my plan of education. It will not be in one letter, nor in a correspondence of three months, that I can explain it to you in its utmost extent; for it is only by giving you examples, that it will be possible for me to communicate to you my ideas, and nothing but the history of Adelaide, can sufficiently inform you of my system and opinions. You must therefore consider, my dear friend, whether you will have courage to support the fatigue of those minute recitals, which will only describe to you the actions of a child of six years of age; her employments, faults, and improvements, the questions she puts to us, and our answers. I should first acquaint you with the persons we brought here to assist us, and I begin with Miss Bridget, with whom you are already acquainted, and on whose account you, and many others, ridiculed my idea of sending to England for a person to teach Adelaide the language of that country,[5] when she was only six months old. I have not forgot your raillery upon that subject, and the stupidity you attributed to my plan of giving a governess to a baby in swaddling clothes. And though I told you that manner of teaching children the living languages, was universally established all over Europe, except in France, nothing could stop the unmerciful career of your wit. It is very true I ought not to reproach you with it, as you have certainly made ample amends by the surprize and admiration you expressed at the first English words spoken by Theodore and Adelaide, who at this time, to your great astonishment, speak English as well as they speak French. Miss Bridget will remain with us till their education is perfected; and though you could not bear to see her with her long waist, and her stiff stays, to which she has used herself these five and forty years, yet she will be very useful to me, for she has great good sense, an even temper, and a perfect knowledge of English literature. A young man named Dainville, some of whose little drawings I believe you have seen, is also with us; he is by birth an Italian, paints delightfully, and you would find him more agreeable than Miss Bridget, for he has cheerfulness, wit, and genius. With regard to our servants, (as the number we had at Paris would be very troublesome here) we have only retained those on whom we could depend. You are quite right in supposing Mademoiselle Blondin would follow me, but Lucile was too proud to think of it; therefore I have taken in her place a young woman who understands embroidery, and all other works of ingenuity; for I would have Adelaide instructed in all these feminine amusements, and not despise them because she has been taught other branches of knowledge. At Paris you know Miss Bridget used to dine in her own chamber; but as we live here quite in a family way, she and Dainville both eat with us:[6] and as you know her pride, you may easily guess how much on this account she prefers Languedoc to Paris. She is also continually praising the pleasures of a country life, and the happiness which is to be found in solitude. And now, my dear friend, that I have given you an account of our household, I will proceed to inform you of my daily employment. I rise at seven o'clock; from that hour till nine, my time is taken up with my toilet, breakfast, and other family affairs. I go then to chapel, and if there is time afterwards, walk till eleven. I then take Adelaide into my apartment, where I make her read to me, and repeat some little stories made on purpose for her to get by heart. And we talk together till twelve, when we all assemble to dinner. As soon as dinner is over, we either walk in the garden for an hour, or amuse ourselves in the saloon, with maps, drawings, or conversation. At two, we return to our respective apartments, Adelaide always with me, whom she never quits but to take a walk for exercise. I write till four, without interruption, whilst Adelaide amuses herself with running and playing about the room. At five, Dainville brings Theodore to take a lesson of drawing with his sister for an hour, during which I continue my writing. When they have finished, they bring me what they have done, which I blame or approve according to its merit. Theodore then returns to his father, and I again employ myself with Adelaide, either teaching her arithmetic with counters, or talking on different subjects till seven o'clock. I afterwards play on the harp or harpsichord till half past eight, when we go to supper. At nine the children go to bed, and we stay and converse about them for an hour longer. I then go to my chamber, and read for another hour, when I retire to my bed, perfectly satisfied with the manner in which I have been employed, and can say to myself, here is a day gone, but it is not lost. I go to sleep thinking of my children. I see them in my dreams, and I awake again with the desire of continuing these pleasing cares. In my next I will give you the rest of the particulars you have desired, but it is time to end this letter. I will now talk to you about your daughters. Are you better satisfied with Flora? Is my sweet little Constantia as gentle, and as sensible as ever? Ah! improve that amiable disposition of hers, you have understanding enough, and you love her with sufficient tenderness, to make it very easy to you to educate her as perfectly as I wish. If it be true, as I make no doubt it is, that you have resolved to stay more at home, to go seldomer to public places, to give up balls and operas, and to keep early hours, you will be one of the best, as well as the tenderest of mothers!

LETTER VIII.

Answer from the Viscountess.

IT is very easy for you to say, go no more to public places, renounce balls, operas, &c. But what am I to put in their places? I no longer delight in them, yet how otherwise can I fill up my time? Flora is fourteen; she knows nothing, has no taste for any accomplishment but dancing, and this misfortune is now without remedy. Her sister is only four years old, consequently she cannot take up the whole day. One is too old for my cares to be of any use, the other too young to want them at present. What then must I do with all the time you would give me? I see your indignation at this distance. I hear you say, 'Why not read and reflect, and wait till you can act?' All this is mighty well, but reading hurts my eyes, and reflection is death to me. Besides, you have read and reflected enough for us both. I still entirely rely on your advice; you shall dictate what I must say and do, I shall punctually execute it. Only do not require study or meditation of me, I am incapable of it. But I promise you to keep the secret, and to be very tractable. To be serious; I cannot take a better method; I distrust my own understanding, and depend on yours. It is better to take a person for our guide, whose sense we are convinced of, than to employ our own, when we are in doubt that we shall not be able to succeed.

I wait with impatience for the rest of the particulars you have promised me, certain they will be interesting, and that I shall be able to draw from them the most useful and instructive lessons. I have been too little accustomed to study to make it possible for you to fix my attention to precepts and maxims. I must have pictures and examples of real life. However, I desire you will give me a general idea of the principles in which you mean to instruct your girl. Teach me the useful qualities that should be cultivated, and the errors which appear to you the most dangerous. And lastly, the manner of instruction which you think most proper. It is strange that I should not be perfectly acquainted with all your sentiments on this subject. You are wholly employed with your children, yet you never talk of them. I should be very glad to find, even in your letters, the accounts which I might have obtained from your conversation, as their being put into order, and the ideas connected, will fix them more indelibly in my mind.

Ah! my dear friend, I am but little satisfied with Flora, she will be more giddy, and more coquetish, than ever her mother was. I know not if your scholar will ever equal you. But for me, I am certain of being surpassed by mine. I laugh upon this subject at the same time it shocks and confounds me, and I assure you I am greatly affected to perceive my daughter has not those amiable qualities which are necessary to my happiness. It is true, when I was young, I was as lively, gay, and inconsiderate as she is. But at the same time I did not want understanding, sensibility, or generosity. Therefore I only was guilty of little indiscretions; and if malice sometimes endeavoured to wound my reputation, I still preserved the esteem of my friends. Was I sure that Flora had a good heart, I should flatter myself with being able to correct her faults. Sometimes I have hopes of it, and at others am absolutely discouraged. As for my little Constantia, she is my sole delight; she is possessed of the sweetest temper imaginable, and there never was a child who promised more.

And so the prudish, the formal, the learned Miss Bridget, dines at the same table with you. I really think she has reason to be proud! I have often heard her say 'she was surprized,' with such a vacant, composed countenance, that plainly proved it impossible that wonder should ever be expressed by it. But now I desire you to present my compliments to her, which I make no doubt will surprize her;

but I want to be reconciled to her, as I wish to be regarded by every one who is near to you.

I cannot end this letter without telling you a story, which will furnish you with more than one reflection. The Chevalier D. and the Count de C. had about a fortnight ago a little dispute at cards, which however was no more thought of. The next night I supped with the godmother of Madame d' Ostalis, where was a great deal of company. They talked of this affair. The men were unanimous in thinking it of no consequence. But the Ladies were astonished they had not fought. Among others, Madame de Sonanges, with that masculine voice which you know she has, cried out, 'What a strange unheard-of thing it was,' and that if the Chevalier was her brother or her friend, she should certainly give him her opinion. This discourse was addressed to the Viscount Blezac, who not chusing to say any thing on the subject, contented himself with smiling, and putting on a mysterious countenance. The company began then to repeat all the particulars of the story in whispers and exclamations of, 'amazing! astonishing!' &c. At length it was decided that the Chevalier D. must challenge the Count de C. or be for the future deemed a coward. The next day he was informed of this sentence, and he considered it, as it was, a very absurd affair. But he had no alternative, and was obliged to challenge the Count. They went together to the frontiers of the kingdom. The poor Chevalier received three wounds, which had brought him to the point of death; though he is now out of danger, and recovers fast. This is the effect of the inconsiderate prattle of three or four foolish women. They consult their own interest very little when they presume to censure the conduct of the men, who can so easily revenge themselves on them; and it is more difficult for a virtuous woman to vindicate herself against reports propagated to her disadvantage, than for a brave man to labour under the aspersion of cowardice: and indeed we ought not to be surprized at our being so frequently slandered by the men, when we treat them with so little respect. Adieu, my dear friend! We have been already separated two long months. You say very pretty things upon absence; but for my part I find it insupportable when it deprives me of you! Send me the description of your castle.

LETTER IX.

Answer from the Baroness d' Almane.

YOUR reflections on the adventure of the Chevalier are very just. It is not the first of the kind I have heard; and as you say, women, who allow themselves to criticise the conduct of men, and accuse them of playing ungenteely at cards, or of want of courage, well deserve the little respect men in general shew them.

You desire me, my dear friend, to give you a general idea of my plan of education. My first principle is to employ all my attention to preserve my girl from a fault common to almost all women, and which leads to so many others, coquetry. You say, my dear friend, that you have been a coquette. It is a character you have no pretensions to. The people with whom you have lived, custom, and bad examples, might have given you the appearance of it. But you were only so at times, and through caprice, not from your real sentiments; as you have always preserved your integrity and innocence of heart. This odious vice contracts the mind, renders it susceptible of the most ridiculous vexations. It extinguishes sensibility, and leads us into the most frightful errors. A coquette has neither principles nor virtue. She takes a cruel delight in inspiring sentiments she is determined to take no part in. To give pain to, and prevent the fortunate union of two tender and gentle lovers, is the least of her guilty frolics. She is by turns delivered up to malice, and to the meanest jealousy. She would subject every one to her humour, and would sacrifice to that desire, without remorse, both decency and virtue. This unruly passion, produced by the corruption of the heart, and the licentiousness of the imagination, when carried to excess, has no curb that will check it. By an artful dexterity, you may always lead a coquette beyond the bounds she had prescribed herself. You have only to irritate and mortify her pride, and you will conquer. But it is a contemptible victory, which is not worth the trouble it costs. There are some vices for which we must be inspired with a detestation. There are others which we must only turn into ridicule. This is the surest method of preserving people from those errors which the corruptions and customs of the age have made so common. Coquetry is of the number of those latter. Convince your scholar that the world only amuses itself with coquettes, that it despises them all the time it is flattering them, and your point is gained. Do not suffer her to be dazzled with the apparent success of the character, and she will easily be made sensible how odious it is. Above all, prevent her from thinking that beauty is her greatest charm. But take care not to inculcate this truth, by maxims which will weary her without convincing. Never praise any qualities with warmth or earnestness before her, but those of the mind and understanding, and she will be good through system and inclination. The education of men and women agree in this particular, that it is essential to both that their vanity should be placed on things of consequence, but it differs in almost every other respect.[7] We must be very careful not to inflame the minds of women, or raise them above themselves. They are born for a domestic and dependent situation, and ought to possess mildness, sensibility, and a just way of reasoning. They should have resources against idleness, with great moderation in their inclinations, and no passions. Genius is for them a useless and a dangerous gift; it lifts them out of their proper sphere, or serves to disgust them with it. Love leads them astray. Ambition teaches them to intrigue; a taste for learning makes them appear singular, and deprives them of that domestic simplicity and tenderness, and of that society of which they are so great an ornament. Formed for the management of household matters, and for the education of their children, dependant on a husband, who by turns requires their submission and their council, it is necessary they should have method, prudence, patience, and a just way of thinking, that they may be able to converse with propriety on all subjects, and possess all those talents which render them pleasing; that they may have a taste for reading and reflection, without displaying their knowledge, and that they may feel the passion of love without giving themselves up to enthusiasm.

Rousseau says, one should not correct that disposition to artifice, so natural to women, because they stand in need of it in order to captivate those upon whom they depend.[8] We might say the same of many other faults; for instance, of dissimulation, so odious in itself, and yet sometimes so necessary! Even falsehood has sometimes its use; but in one instance where these vices are of any advantage, how much more frequently are they prejudicial! There is nothing to be depended on but a constant practice of virtue. The vices, which are produced by the violence of our passions, are more pardonable than those which are derived from considerations of self-interest; these last but too plainly shew a corruption of heart, and meanness of soul, to make them at all excusable. An artful woman may be able to govern a weak and narrow-minded husband, when without that quality she could have gained his confidence; but it will never procure her the esteem and attachment of a sensible man.[9]

You ask me for the description of the castle. I shall be sure in giving it you to expose myself to your raillery; but you will have it, and I must comply. Montaigne says, 'Walking in a confined room does not tire one so much, although we take three times the number of steps as walking in the fields or road.'[10] So our lessons pass away, as if by chance, without being confined to time or place, and by mixing in all our actions, take effect without our being sensible of it, &c. &c. Remember this passage when you read my account.

We have taken up our habitation on the ground floor of the castle. The entrance leads by a vestibule to an eating parlour, which is lighted by a sky light, and the walls of which are painted in fresco, with Ovid's *Metamorphoses*.[11]

From this room we go into a very fine saloon, of a square form, having windows towards the garden. The hangings of this saloon contain pictures of the Roman History, painted in oil colours, and fixed in frames. The first contains medallions of the Seven Kings of Rome.[12] Then follow those great men who have made the republic the most illustrious, and every Emperor as low down as Constantine.[13] The opposite side of the room contains pictures of the most celebrated Roman Ladies,[14] such as Lucretia, Ælia, Cornelia, Portia, and the Empresses to the time of Constantine. The other two sides of the saloon represent some chosen passages of the Roman History. The bottoms of the hangings are painted to imitate bas relief, and produces a pleasing effect. We have only the profiles of the Emperors and Empresses, which are good resemblances, having been taken from medals which we have in our possession; round each profile is written the name of the person represented, and in what year he died. You will agree that this tapestry sort of hanging is more instructive than damask; and I can assure you it is a hundred times more agreeable; neither does it cost so much, and it will last for ever.[15] The doors are also made to represent subjects taken from Roman History. On the right and left of this saloon are two wings, which form Mons. d' Almane's apartments and mine, which is on the right hand as you come out of the saloon. We then enter a long gallery, which is painted in the same manner, to represent the Grecian History. At the end of this gallery, is my bed-chamber, where in like manner I have caused to be painted a part of the Holy Scriptures. My daughter's chamber joins to mine; it is hung with an English blue paper, ornamented with little coloured prints, which contain subjects taken from the History of France.[16] These pictures may be removed at pleasure; and I have written on their backs the explanation of every thing they contain. We have besides these, baths, a study, one half of which contains about four hundred volumes. The other is furnished with cabinets, which contain some minerals and corals, and a pretty collection of shells. This study looks towards a little conservatory, where I have a number of plants, which are classed in order, having tickets on them, of which I keep the key. Mons. d' Almane's apartments are exactly distributed like mine; so I shall only mention the paintings, which represent the Kings and Queens of France, together with all the great men and ministers, who have in any degree contributed to the glory or happiness of the kingdom. They are placed in the same medallion with the King who reigned in their time, which is an association that does honour to both. Henry the Fourth appears greater, with Sully at his side,[17] as the merit of having chosen such a Minister, would alone be sufficient to immortalize a Prince. Mons. d' Almane's, and his son's bed-chamber are furnished and ornamented with subjects relative to the military art, such as plans, fortifications, &c. and a closet which contains books, globes, spheres, &c. is the last room of this apartment. When we intend our children should survey these historical pictures in a methodical manner, we begin with my bed-chamber, which represents the Holy Scripture, from the Creation of the World. Thence we proceed to my gallery, where we meet with Ancient History; and so on to the saloon, which contains the Roman History. Then we finish our studies in the gallery belonging to Mons. d' Almane, which I have informed you is filled with the History of France. With respect to mythology, we find that in our eating parlour, and it is generally the subject of our conversation during dinner. The second story contains five or six small spare rooms, and the attics are destined for our servants. The colonades and stair-case are hung from top to bottom with large maps, which form a complete system of geography. We have fixed on the ground floor for the place of our southern maps, and the second for our northern; for by putting an attention to these things we make a better impression on childrens' minds. The whole furniture of the house is linen. The sculpture on the walls is plain white, with gilt beads. The stairs and chimney-pieces are white marble, and are every day washed clean. Over the front are written these words, *True happiness is of a retired nature, and an enemy to pomp.*[18] Besides all these representations of history, which I have mentioned to you, I have, in a closet paved with marble, six large screens, which are made to give you an idea of the chronology of the histories of England, Spain, Portugal, Germany, Malta, and Turkey. I have also a great number of little hand screens, which are all maps of different countries, and on the backs I have written in English or Italian, a clear and short description of the places they represent. With respect to our gardens, they are equally plain and simple. We have preserved a little wood and two walks of chestnut trees. But our neighbours do not admire the alterations we have made, since we have taken down our cut hedges, and above all a wilderness, which for thirty years was the admiration of the whole province, However, the above alteration is much more agreeable to us, and we have formed a delightful shade, about a hundred paces from the castle. The large grass plots and young plantations of foreign shrubs, also afford us very pleasant walks. You have often heard me condemn the custom of raising mountains in gardens: I think them very disagreeable objects, when they do not strike us by the uncommon height to which they are elevated. However, I have formed three small ones in the park; not for the pleasure of admiring them, but to make the children climb up them, which is a kind of exercise that both amuses and strengthens them.

I have not yet mentioned my neighbours. I am at present only intimately acquainted with the Countess de Valmont, who lives about two leagues from hence. She has only one son,[19] who is twelve years of age, and for whom she feels such an extreme tenderness, that I was prejudiced in her favour from the first moment I saw her. She is still young and beautiful. She has much dignity in her manner, and a negligence which adds grace to her most trifling actions. Besides this, she has wit, and an improved and cultivated mind; she speaks but little, not through timidity, but indolence, and never wishes to shine or to fix attention.

She is sister to Madame d' Olcy, whom you must have seen, and who has given so many balls ten years ago. She has another sister, who is a Nun. Her father, Mons. d' Aimeri, is a man of great learning, as Mons. d' Almane informs me. But since the death of an only son, whom he adored, he has retired to this province, and lives with his favourite daughter, Madame de Valmont. He is very absent and melancholy, but his conversation, though always serious, is often instructive and agreeable. Mons. de Valmont has neither the sense nor graces of his wife, nor the merit of his father-in-law. He understands playing at billiards and shuttle-cock perfectly, and is passionately fond of shooting and hunting. He has rather a bois- terous kind of mirth, but at the same time has so chearful a countenance, with so ruddy and smiling an appearance, and is above all so frank, good humoured, and polite, that you cannot help having a regard for him. But I begin to perceive, my dear friend, though too late perhaps for you, that I have written a volume. Fare- well. If you do not send me an answer of at least four pages, I shall not dare again to send you letters of such an extreme length; and pray do not write to me on that little paper you are so fond of; keep it for your Paris friends; for my part I am always angry when I see your writing on those little painted ready made covers which you use. I beg you will tell me something of Madame d' Ostalis; do you see her frequently, and does not my absence make her neglect her improvements?

LETTER X.

Viscountess to the Baroness.

WHAT a picture have you sent me of coquetry; it will cure me of all pre- tensions to it! I shall never again boast of being a coquette, and I shall all my life repent ever having had the appearance of one! You have really made a deep impression on me, but why did you not tell me all this when I was but twenty years old? My reformation would then have done you more honour, and would have spared me much pain. But you tell me I was only half a coquette. I used to think so myself; but are you sure of it? You have really troubled my conscience! Pray never talk to me of coquetry again. Oh, the wicked thing! If you knew the situation I was in when I received your letter! That I was on the edge of a preci- pice, which perhaps you have drawn me from! I perceive your astonishment, but I can conceal nothing from you. You will see what confidence I repose in you, but you are so indulgent, so superior to the weaknesses of our sex; you know how to excuse them all! Attend then, and by the confession I am going to make, judge of the services you have done me! You know my principles, and you are very sure, that whatever follies I may have to reproach myself with, at least my heart remains pure. I have been indiscreet enough to give the world room to say I had a lover. But it was not believed; and for some years my conduct has been thought irreproachable; for the world, a hasty judge, though an impartial one, retracts with as good a grace as it condemns. Well, my dear friend, let us come to the fact. I thought when I was one-and-thirty, I had nothing more to fear from envy, from coquetry, or from men! Is it not well, said I, that I have preserved my reputation; I have passed the age in which one is subject to such dangerous trials, and it is a happy thing to find one is no longer young enough to be in danger from them. But I was deceived. Mons. de Merville, whom you left so engaged with Madame de C— , all on a sudden, I know not how, took it in his head to fall in love with me. I never could indure this change of his sentiments in my favour. But he was young, a man quite fashionable, and he had sacrificed to me a young woman of three-and-twenty. Though my heart remained entirely free, I bore his attentions. I received him at my house; in short, I did every thing in my power to keep him my slave! This scheme was scarcely formed, when I received your last letter. My surprise is not to be told! Every feature in the picture of a coquette seemed drawn for me; every word appeared to reproach me, and this sentence more than all the rest! *To disturb the union of two tender and gentle lovers, is one of its smallest crimes.* Mons. de Merville is free, Madame de C— a widow! I represented her to myself, in despair! I saw a marriage broken, a reputation destroyed: in short, I found I was a monster. I hated myself, and detested Mons. de Merville. I lamented the fate of Madame de C— , and loved no body but you and her! I ought to tell you, Mons. de Merville had never acquainted me with his passion: these declarations are now useless, and out of fashion; one can understand without that ceremony. He and Madame de C— were one evening engaged to sup with me. But you may imagine he came before the rest of the company. I was alone, and he seized this opportunity so favourable to him, and in short, explained himself in the most earnest manner. I affected an extreme surprise, which is not difficult to put on, and by which there are very few men who are not deceived. And in order to convince him how serious I was, I mentioned his engagements to Madame de C— . I praised her to the highest degree, I even extolled her wit with enthusiasm; which you must allow was going a great length. But I had much to repair. Mons. de Merville, truly amazed and confounded at losing all his hopes, put an end the same instant to the declaration of that tender passion which he had just been describing. We made mutual protestations of friendship, and company coming in, were released from a conversation which began to be as languid as it was tedious. Once more reconciled to myself, I felt an inward satisfaction, far preferable to that foolish infatuation caused by flattery. I had more merit in this conquest over myself than I ever had had before, as I never till then had given myself up to such an excess of coquetry. Explain this to me, for I have no idea how it was. But it is certain, I now feel the consequences of this horrible vice too much, ever to fall into it again. Therefore never fear for me, be certain, I am corrected for ever.

The description of your castle delighted me much; but that of coquettes took from me for a long time all that vivacity which you seem so much to dread. So that for this time you will only receive my praises: and indeed I believe I shall never more criticize such useful inventions, which have spared your children the humble fatigue of learning a number of dates, which are all forgotten when they grow up. I apprehend this method of yours will engrave chronology on their memories; for the order in which these medallions are placed, and being constantly before their eyes, will prevent their ever forgetting them. By putting one's self to a still greater expence, I should think this invention might be brought to still greater perfection, by making every piece of furniture, as chairs, carpets, &c. to represent objects of instruction, and then replacing them by others, when they had got these by heart. There are many who could easily afford to be at this expence; certainly the idea should be adopted by all Princes, and I shall assuredly send your description to my brother, as I am certain he will avail himself of it for his pupil. I have some doubts to propose to you on that part of your letter concerning women. It appears to me, that you require a union of amiable qualities and talents, which can only fall to the lot of a very small number. You would have a woman possess solid reasoning, with all the important virtues: a general, though not a deep knowledge of the sciences; all the powers of pleasing, a knowledge of all the modern languages, without pedantry or affectation; and that, in short, she should conduct her domestic affairs like a good housewife, who pretends to no other merit. I see plainly, if your pupil is born with a superior understanding, you may make her truly accomplished: but do you expect it, if she has only a common one, and an indifferent memory? It appears to me that a plan of education ought neither to be made for prodigies or monsters. Stupidity and depravity are as rare as heroism and genius. But it is for persons of moderate talents we ought to labour, as from them we may expect most success. With regard to talents, is it not necessary the inclination should assist your cares? I had all kinds of masters. I learned Geography, Arithmetic, History, and Music. Ten years I played on the harpsichord, and learned to draw, but yet I understood nothing of all this. For dancing I had a real taste, and six months instruction made me one of the best dancers in the school. Besides, I can scarcely believe that the length of time one is obliged to give to these kind of studies, is not extremely hurtful to the production and growth of more essential qualities. I know you may be quoted as an exception to this rule; but I only speak in general. You want to cultivate the understanding, and form the mind of your daughter. How can you do this, if she learns to embroider, to draw, to dance, to sing, and to play on several instruments? In short, you propose teaching her so many things, that I am in pain for her health, and I cannot persuade myself, but that such application must be dangerous to a child.

You desire I will mention Madame d' Ostalis. I have most pleasing accounts to give you of her. She conducts herself always with the same prudence, as if she was before your eyes, and she is as much distinguished for her reputation as for her person and charms. She has an equal and unalterable sweetness of temper, and a certain serenity, which gives me pleasure to contemplate, because one feels that it proceeds from the perfect calm of her mind, and the purity of her heart. The women pardon her talents and her beauty, on account of her modesty and simplicity; and the men, notwithstanding her youth, truly respect her, because she has neither prudery, nor the least appearance of coquetry. She almost lives with me, that she may talk about you; she loves you with so much tenderness, that that alone would render her dear to me, had she no other merit.

We supped last night in a family way. There was a serious party at Reversis.[20] The players were Madame d' Ostalis, her husband, the Marchioness Amelia, and my daughter. The game, as you know, is rather noisy, and the *forced knaves*, made it much more so, that you can have no idea of the noise they made; Madame d' Ostalis, with all her mildness, laughed as much as the rest, so that she was hoarse the whole evening after. Her gaiety is blended with a frankness which makes her perfectly amiable. She is thought to be breeding, and in that case must give over all thoughts of a journey to Languedoc; which puts her quite in despair. Mons. d' Ostalis, who so passionately desires to have a son, does not share in her griefs on this account; and this difference of sentiment, has already caused some little quarrels, but you may easily imagine they are not ill-natured ones.

Adieu, my dear friend! I hope you will not complain of my paper, and that you will find this large enough. You shall have no more of those little painted sheets, which displease you so much. I know better how to dispose of them. I wanted the other day to send an answer to a Lady, to whom I had no attachment, nor she for me; and I had only some common compliments to send to her, that every body says by heart. By mistake I sealed up one of these little ornamented sheets, but without writing any thing in it. When I found it out, I thought my billet was at least as good as her's, and I wished to establish the custom of sending notes in this manner instead of returning visits one's-self. There are many of these notes, which contain little more than the name of the person, and that you may find on your visiting-list. Many women are very clever in the art of writing notes, and express themselves with great eloquence. Madame de F. for example, is persuaded her's will pass to posterity: this would be but just indeed, for it costs her great labour to deserve this honour. The most trifling subject becomes brilliant in her hands. She wrote me a most charming billet a week ago, to excuse her supping with me on account of her having a cold. But yesterday I received another from her, which surpassed all the rest. It was to borrow my box at the

Opera. The subject does not appear capable of furnishing new or lofty ideas, but in a note of eight lines, she had collected grace, gaiety, sentiment, and delicacy. I felt myself fired with a noble emulation. I was willing to try my skill. But to my confusion, though I considered and studied for a long time, nothing came into my head by way of answer, but the downright matter of fact, that I was very sorry I had already lent my box, as she wished to have had it; and this dull reply I was obliged to send her, which has certainly lowered me in her esteem.

Adieu then, my dear friend! Kiss the dear little Adelaide tenderly for me. Constantia, who is for ever talking of you, desires I will send you a kiss for her. She grows every day prettier, and more pleasing. She has been a little indisposed, but is now perfectly well again. Now I think of it, I beg you will communicate to me your notions on the medical treatment of children. I am not easy about Flora's health. I think she has been brought up with too much delicacy, and that she has had too much physic given her in her infancy. What regimen do you follow for Adelaide, and what do you think of Rousseau's method?[21]

LETTER XI.

Answer from the Baroness d' Almane.

MONS. de Merville has inspired you with stronger sentiments of coquetry, than you ever had before! This is indeed surprising! You ask me the reason of your caprices? You put me on a difficult task; but since you desire it, these were the reflections I made on your adventure. I think there is one time of life very dangerous for women, who are not entirely free from coquetry. It is when they are still handsome, but no longer possess the brilliancy and charms of youth, nor are talked of for their elegance of person, which now ceases to attract admiration. In short, as soon as it is said of a woman, she is still handsome; that *still* spoils the compliment. It begins at your age, and finishes at five or six-and-thirty, for then we are no longer regarded, and this misfortune frequently happens even much sooner. It appears to me very natural that a woman of thirty, who is no longer flattered by that eager crowd who formerly surrounded her, should set a greater value on the attentions paid her. Formerly she thought they could not help falling in love with her; at present she is almost grateful for it; as she knows it is not her beauty which is any longer sought after; the empire which she had gained over the world by her charms is gone, not to be retrieved. She is like a Queen, who being dethroned, no longer perceives her Courtiers around her, and is only the more afflicted by perceiving the neglect with which she is treated. She has renounced the glory of conquering numbers, but she is still possessed with the hope of inspiring an ardent passion. The first man who pays her any attention, she will suppose to be the object she has in view, and whatever her lover may be, she will find her vanity more gratified at this time than ever she did in her youth. But how will she reconcile herself to the vexatious idea, that he is perhaps the last she will be able to hold in her chains? What gratitude does she not owe him? It is then, that coquetry makes use of all its cunning and dexterity. It is then, that she enjoys her triumph, and makes it known to the world; and it is then, that this lover, if he is not a fool, may destroy a woman's reputation, and deprive her of happiness, even without being beloved by her. This picture is very like that of Madame ***, whom we admired so much for her beauty and elegance. She was so disdainful to her lovers, that she had the art of attracting them without appearing to be sensible of it; and after having preserved her reputation two and thirty years, lost it on a sudden, with the man in the world, least able to justify such an error! This, my dear friend, is part of my sentiments on this subject. But as I do not speak by experience, I may be deceived. You are a better judge; and from the situation of your mind, can tell me whether my conjectures are true or false; therefore I refer to you. I am not surprised that you experienced a thousand times more satisfaction in reconciling Mons. de Merville to poor Madame de C. than you had found in parting them. The pleasures of self-love, as transient as vain, cannot leave deep impressions: they are only produced by imagination, whose flame is soon extinguished, if the allurement of novelty does not rekindle it. The pleasures of the heart, less tumultuous, but milder and more lasting, can alone ensure our felicity. These things, which make but a slight impression on our minds, only leave a weak remembrance, which instead of giving us pleasure, often afflicts us. Do you think an old coquette, in tracing back the most brilliant exploits of her youth, does not experience more regret than satisfaction. Regret, which is so much the more grievous, as it is shameful, and that one is obliged to conceal it. Whilst the remembrance of a virtuous behaviour is always an inexhaustible source of self-satisfaction.

And now, my dear friend, I am going to endeavour to answer your objections on the principles of education. You cannot conceive how I shall be able to improve the understanding of my pupil, and to form her heart, and at the same time to give her every agreeable qualification. In effect, if you suppose I have any hopes of seeing Adelaide, at twelve years old, an excellent musician, playing on several instruments, understanding History, Geography, Mythology, and accounts, with many of our best Works, &c. &c. your reflections would then have been perfectly just. But if such had been my plan, I needed only to have adopted the method commonly followed. But the little success obtained by these, has well justified the necessity of taking others. Rousseau observes, that the principal fault of every Tutor is from endeavouring to make his pupils shine, more than to convince their reason. With this intention, he gives them lessons which are above their comprehensions, and so load the memory, not with useful things, but with words that have in general no sense in them.[22] Adelaide, at twelve years old, far from being a prodigy, will perhaps appear to some people infinitely less instructed than many other children of her age. She will not know a word of all those books which young people learn by heart. She will never have read Fontaine's Fables,[23] Telemachus,[24] Madame de Sevigny's Letters,[25] the Works of Corneille,[26] Racine,[27] Crebillon,[28] and Voltaire,[29] &c. Is it not absurd to put all these books into the hands of a child, who can comprehend nothing of them, and by that means deprive her of the pleasure of reading them when her judgment is riper? Adelaide, at twelve years old, will neither be capable of making any extracts, or of writing good letters, or of assisting in doing the honours of my house. She will have but few ideas, but they will be rational ones. She will read music well, and play on several instruments. She will draw in a surprizing manner for her age, without her master's retouching any of her performances; and by that means teaching her to tell a falsehood, instead of improving her in the art of drawing. She will neither understand history, mythology, nor geography, except what she has gained by our tapestry conversation, and other methods, which I shall mention hereafter. In this respect I think she will be better instructed than children in general. She will have many other accomplishments, which will only be discovered by living with her, and which she has acquired in the form of amusements. That you may be able to form some idea of these, it will be necessary to acquaint you with some of the methods we have taken for this purpose. Children in general are born with memories sufficient to retain a great deal of useful knowledge; they ought therefore never to learn things that are unnecessary or superfluous; and I know but two means of arriving at this end; which are, never to tell them what they cannot understand, and never to neglect giving them every kind of instruction within their reach. For example, it is an easy matter to render all their little plays useful. The idea of my tapestries, or hangings, have given me another, of historical magic lanthorns. I have had four or five hundred glasses made to represent subjects taken from history; and we have the diversion of the magic lanthorn four times a week. I take upon myself to shew it, and generally do it in English; by this means I give them two lessons at once; and as the pictures are often changed, I assure you Adelaide and Theodore are infinitely more delighted with our magic lanthorn, than the generality of children are with the sun, moon, and seven stars, the prodigal son, the baker pulling the devil by the tail, &c. &c. Instead of teaching my children the favourite amusement of building houses with cards, I have invented a play for them which gives them an idea of architecture. I have caused two small houses, and two palaces, to be made in pasteboard, which take to pieces; every ornament belonging to architecture are to be found in them. They are all numbered, and their names written on the back. My son has, besides these, a number of fortified castles, with which Adelaide also amuses herself sometimes, as well as with a pretty little ship, of which Mons. d' Almane explains to us all the parts of at least once a week.

When we walk out, the children divert themselves with running and skipping about, and in another year, we shall accustom them, as Rousseau advises, to measure distances by their eyes, how many trees there may be in such a walk, how many flower-pots on such a terrace, &c. &c. By this means they will learn what a foot, a fathom, or an acre means; and they will also acquire some notions of agriculture. My gardener, Mathurine, will be their chief master; he has already begun his lessons, and generally follows us in our walks; and we learn every day something new. Adelaide and Theodore have each a little garden, which Mathurine teaches them to cultivate; we accustom them to those plays which are recommended by Rousseau, to preserve them from the fears which children are so subject to, that of being in the dark.[30] Adelaide, like other children, is fond of playing at visiting. This by my attentions will become a moral progress: I invent their plans, and you may imagine the little subjects I give them, serve to inspire them with noble sentiments; and that to teach them to behave properly, is the end to be obtained. Madame de Valmont's son joins them in these plays, and I have often a part in it myself, which I endeavour to perform well. Adelaide's doll is not useless to me. Adelaide repeats to her the lessons she receives from me. I pay great attention to these dialogues. If Adelaide scolds unjustly, I interfere in the conversation, and convince her she is wrong. This amusement makes her more industrious; if she wants an apron or a cap for her doll, Mademoiselle Victoire, one of my women, comes to assist her in making them. It is the same with Theodore, if he breaks any of his toys, as a coach or a drum, we give him proper materials; and Brunel, Mons. d' Almane's footman, whose ingenuity you are acquainted with, makes whatever he desires, and by this means, he becomes industrious and patient. Thus you see, far from wearying them with too much application, we are only employed in procuring them amusements and playthings. The word study is never mentioned,[31] though there is scarce a moment in the day that they do not gain some knowledge; and certainly there never were children so perfectly happy. Adelaide begins already to have some slight notion of music, and I have placed her little fingers on the harp. These different studies, with those of reading and drawing, take up near an hour and a half of the day, which, however, is not fixed to stated times. I have a method of practicing music in two hands, which experience has taught me to be the best way.[32] To arrive at perfection either on the harp or harpsichord, you must play equally well with both hands; the left is generally inferior to the right, owing to the method which masters take. Before they learn a complete tune, they ought to practice a twelvemonth, first with one hand, then with the other; I mean if it is an infant; otherwise six months will do. They should by turns execute all the shakes and most difficult passages that are to be met with, by using the left hand, which is in fact more aukward than the right, and has less strength. This requires at the beginning so little attention from the scholar, that it cannot weary her. On the other hand, expecting her to read music, to place her hands properly to finger well, and to put treble and base together, requires much application, and is difficult and tiresome; besides, she is stopped by every cadence, and is so confounded that she plays out of time, which spoils her ear and her taste; and she very unjustly takes an aversion to a study so disagreeable and fatiguing. No master will adopt my method, because by following it they cannot make their scholar in five or six months play by rote several tunes; and I must confess there are many parents who would be very little pleased to see their daughters, after a years' instruction, only able to read their notes. But after this exercise, teach her to play lessons, and in less than three months she will surpass those who have learned three years in the common way. Nothing is more absurd than to teach children rules of accompaniment when they are only ten years old. This study is of a very difficult nature, and can only be learned by persons of fifteen or sixteen years of age. Those instructions which we cannot acquire but with great application, are unfit for infancy. This is so plain a truth, that it would be absurd to try to convince you of it by reasoning, though it is very frequently lost sight of in almost every plan of education. Is it not usual to set a poor child at six years old to learn lessons of grammar, geometry, astronomy, &c. People take great pains to teach them what they cannot comprehend, and destroy their health, and give them an invincible disgust for study. Can any thing be more ridiculous than to see a child gravely seated before a desk, employed in answering a problem or explaining a system of the world? In this case, every thing which is required of it will have a contrary effect to what the tutor expects: that is to say, the poor child gains nothing but ignorance and a distaste for labour; for if she should understand what they had made her repeat, the tender constitution of a child would sink under such an intense application, and thus her untimely knowledge would bring her to the grave. But let us return to my Adelaide, from whom these reflections have detained me so long. She learns also to draw, as it is my particular desire she should excel in this charming qualification, which suits with every age, and which offers so many resources against idleness. Rousseau will have Emilius learn drawing without a master; I shall take care, says he, to keep him from such a master, as would only give him copies to imitate, and only teach him to draw from designs.[33] Rousseau speaks here of what he does not understand. It is absolutely impossible to learn to draw without a master, and that master ought to be a very good one; for every thing depends on first principles. It is not only necessary to have good copies, but the master must understand the science perfectly; for it is by drawing with him, not by advising him, that he can make any rapid progress. It will be necessary to begin with copying: it is true you may lengthen this apprenticeship too much, which would be losing time; but in a years' time a good master will have taught his scholar to draw from nature. These, my dear friend, are part of my sentiments on the manner of teaching children, with regard to their talents for any particular instrument. I think we all have them in an equal degree, unless that the fingers of some persons are formed in an extraordinary manner. It is true a little fat hand will find it difficult to play on instruments which require strength and extension, such as the harp, the lute, and the theorbo;[34] yet with somewhat more application, they may get the better of this difficulty. Why then do you tell me that talents are so rare? It is that children are ill taught; that mothers do not direct their masters, and only give examples of laziness to their children. How can you expect a young person to have a taste for study, or to be anxious to acquire pleasing talents, when she sees her mother spend half her time at her toilet, and at public places, and the other half in knotting,[35] playing at cards, and receiving visits. You say you never could learn drawing, music, or geography, &c. But did you ever sincerely wish to learn these things? No, surely, you only was inspired with a desire to shine at a ball, and be able to dance elegantly in six months. Had your inclinations been turned on more serious objects, you would have succeeded equally well. The result of what I have said is, that the great point to be obtained in education is not to be in a hurry; to teach children what they can easily comprehend, and never to neglect an opportunity of teaching them every thing within their reach; and at first only to give them examples of morality, not precepts. I have hitherto confined myself to children, so that you are only acquainted with the least interesting part of my plan of education. But when Adelaide is twelve years old, you will find my accounts less trifling and insipid.

It remains still that I speak of the management of children with regard to their health. Rousseau, with all the attention he pays to that subject, exactly follows the system of Mr. Locke; for though he does not quote him, he copies him literally.[36] The wise Locke forbids swaddling clothes, or loading children with unnecessary clothes. He advises to accustom them to the open air, and to bathe their feet constantly in cold water. This doctrine, given from motives of benevolence, is so much the more estimable, as the author, with such superior merit, shews no desire of distinguishing himself, but only appears actuated by the wish of being useful. This book, which is translated into all languages, was in every body's hands when *Emilius* appeared, but had not brought about any change in the systems adopted. Wisdom has less influence than enthusiasm, because it is always simple in its expressions, and scarce ever assumes an imposing or authoritative tone. The English Philosopher seemed only to give his advice. Rousseau repeated the same things, but he did not advise, he commanded, and was obeyed. I have observed this method with Adelaide from her birth to three years old. She has been constantly washed from head to foot in summer with cold water; and in winter with water luke warm, observing at the same time to rub her with a spunge, to make her sleep in a hard bed without curtains, and to wear only a cap and little gown, with a single blanket in winter, and a sheet in summer. The doors and windows of her chamber were almost always to be open in the day-time, excepting in damp weather, with very little fire in the day, and none in the night. She was continually in the open air, but I was in no hurry to make her walk, thinking it better to stay till her legs were strong enough to bear the weight of her body with ease. I also paid great attention to prevent her getting wet in her feet. As soon as children are weaned, they should drink nothing but water. No thickened milk or cream; she sometimes eats an egg, some cold milk, vegetables, broth, or fruit, &c. But no sweetmeats nor pastry. No whalebone in her stays till she was four years old. At that age she began with very thin and large ones, except in summer, when she had no other dress than her shift, and a gauze or muslin frock; and she never wore stockings or shoes, except in extreme hot weather, when she walked out. People are very apt to find fault with the custom of putting on stays to children. They are indeed pernicious when they are tight, but when properly made they are far from being hurtful; the wearing them is equally convenient and healthy. By placing the shoulders in a proper position, they open the chest, support the back, and keep the stomach in a situation proper for digestion. They render falls often less dangerous; and if they are not made too tight, children feel much more at their ease in them than they do in a waist-coat. It is only the excess of heat that can make them inconvenient, and then it is a cruelty to oblige children to wear them. Adieu, my dear friend! I make no professions of the sentiments I entertain for you. I think the immoderate length of my letters will convince you of my confidence, and of my tender and lively friendship.

LETTER XII.

The Baroness to the Countess d' Ostalis.

I WRITE to you to-day, my dear child, to find fault with you. I hope this beginning will not frighten you. My reproofs you know are as gentle as your faults are small. Madame de Limours wrote me an account of a family supper at which you was present, and of a certain game at cards, which I confess a little chagrined me. I cannot figure to myself my charming daughter, who is so gentle, so humble, and at the same time so noble, giving herself up to all the extravagance of false mirth, disfiguring her sweet face by noisy and affected bursts of laughter, and making those little shrill screams, like Mademoiselle de Cerny, and Mademoiselle de Limours. Whence proceeded all these effects? Was you really vexed at the run of the cards? If you felt such an emotion, doubtless you ought to have concealed it, for it is absurd and shameful to shew it. Besides, you are no miser, nor ever play high, and it is absolutely indifferent to you whether you win or lose; consequently all those cries and appearances of vexation were only affectation. It is scarce worth while to give up your sweetness of temper, in order to gain the character of a bad player, or of want of judgment. I am sure you could not entertain so foolish an idea for a moment, but to shew your complaisance to the company you played with. But if you encourage this weakness, it will lead you farther than you imagine. When people adopt follies, either from fashion or condescension, they suffer themselves to be hurried away by still more seducing, and dangerous examples. I know the purity of your heart, your docility, and confidence in me; I know the advice of your mother can never be neglected by you, and have no fears of you for the future. Be always indulgent, my child, to those women who are guilty of such meannesses; never appear to blame or ridicule them at any time of your life, but never imitate them!

I have another cause of complaint against you, which I have scarce courage to mention, since it proceeds from your affection to me. But you ought to know I never regard my own interest, where your's is concerned. You think you are with child, and you appear to be afflicted at it, because it will prevent your seeing me this year. Now as you are not ignorant how much your husband wishes for a son, it is very wrong in you to let him see a concern which can only vex him. When complaint is useless, it only shews weakness; when it gives pain, it is absurd. The ill humour you shew justly displeases your husband, discontents the family, but cannot prevent your remaining at Paris; can add nothing to the idea I ever had of your tenderness, and only lessens the opinion I had of your understanding. So, my dear child, repair this imprudence, and never fall into it again. Adieu, my dear daughter! Write to me always with the same punctuality, and believe that I expect, with as much impatience as you can do, the moment which is to reunite us.

LETTER XIII.

Viscountess to the Baroness.

YOU have thoroughly explained to me the greatest part of my doubts. All your designs are excellent, and your method of teaching is certainly preferable to the common one. But it is necessary, according to your plan, that mothers should be capable of directing the different masters: where will you find such mothers? Where is the woman who, like you, has passed her life in cultivating her talents for instruction, that she may be useful to her children? Besides, if all mothers thought as you do, there would be an end of all society; shut up in their chambers, with masters instructing them, or flying away to their country-houses, they would be lost to the world, and Paris would become a desart. I interest myself much in your fame, but I do not wish you to succeed in making this reform. Joking apart, I have a remark to make to you. You prevent your children, till the age of thirteen, from reading *Telemachus*, Fontaine's Fables, and all such books; yet you would inspire them with a taste for reading! What books then would you give them instead of those I have mentioned? Are they only to read the Arabian Nights, and Fairy Tales, till they are thirteen?[37] Do they learn nothing by heart? I have often heard you say it was impossible to understand the harmony or sounds of Poetry if the ear is not accustomed to it from infancy. Be so good to answer me this. I write to you in great haste, as I am going immediately into the country I am waited for, and hurried. Adieu, my dear friend! Madame d' Ostalis' pregnancy is no longer doubted. I saw her husband yesterday, who told me she bears it with the best grace in the world, which was more pleasing to him, as he did not expect it. Farewell, my love. You take no journeys, therefore never write me such vile short letters as this is.

LETTER XIV.

The Baroness to the Viscountess.

I NEITHER give my children Fairy Tales to read, or The Arabian Nights, nor even Madame d' Aulnoy's Fables,[38] which were composed for this purpose. There is scarcely one of them which has a moral tendency. Love is the subject in them all. You find a Princess persecuted on account of her beauty. A Prince, handsome as the day, dying for love of her, and a wicked, ugly rival, consumed with envy and jealously! Tho' the moral of these little stories may be good, children cannot improve by them; and only struck with the wonderful, they will remember nothing but the enchanted gardens and diamond palaces; all these ridiculous ideas give them only false notions, stop the course of their reasoning, and inspire them with a dislike for instructive reading. Locke complains that there is not a single work existing proper for infancy; I know not one in the French language,[39] though it would be so useful. The fixing our first principles and turn of mind depends greatly on the impressions we receive in infancy: it is therefore necessary these books should be written with great simplicity; that they should be equally interesting and instructing, and to vary the form of these little histories will also be proper. And I believe, if the subjects were well chosen, and the charms and simplicity of Nature were properly described, it would make such works more valuable than you have any idea of: now, I hear you exclaim, and you repeat twenty times: 'Where is a book so 'useful?' 'Where can it be met with?' I will tell you, and will even produce it to you, whenever you chuse to have it. And as there is no great wisdom required in the composition, but only Nature and common sense; I will without evasion tell you I am myself the Author. We call it the 'Castle Evening.'⁴⁰ The subject of it is, a good mother retired to the castle with her three children, the eldest of whom is only seven years old, and who every evening, if they are very good, tells them a little story. These recitals are often interrupted by the questions of the children, who never let a word pass which they do not understand; without desiring an explanation. You are sensible how clear this method must make it to their comprehensions. It is only one volume, but has five hundred pages. The effect it has already produced on my children, is every thing I could wish. At each story they do not fail to ask me, 'if it has really happened!' and when I affirm it to be true, I remark an extraordinary encrease of attention and concern, which is a much greater benefit than they could possibly draw from the most moral Fairy Tale. So I engage, if ever I determine on publishing this work, to assure my young Readers, in an advertisement made only for them, that the Author has invented nothing, but that it is scrupulously and exactly true; and with this precaution, I am certain my stories will be read with eagerness, and make a deep impression. With regard to Poetry, I have collected from different Authors, the greater part of which are scarcely known by name, some extracts, which make three volumes, for the use of my children, till they are fourteen or fifteen. This little collection is really very pleasing, and most of the pieces are truly moral. But to return to prose; Adelaide will read nothing but my tales till she is seven years old; I shall then give her the 'Conversations of Emily,'⁴¹ a book you have often heard me praise. And this will employ her till she is eight. At which time you shall know the rest of my plan. You say, my dear friend, 'if all mothers were like me, Paris would become a desart!' In the first place, remember I only quitted it at the age of thirty two, and in four years I mean to return to it again. Besides, it is possible, without quitting the world at all, to be as useful to your children as I have been to mine, whatever you may say of it. Far from passing all my time in my closet, I was fifteen years in the world, and I should be very sorry not to have lived in it. For no person, who has not a thorough knowledge of it, is capable of educating her children properly. It was in the world I conceived this mode of education, which I now put in practice; and it was there, I composed these Works relative to it. If my labours have been useful, and my method should be adopted, I shall at least have spared to others the reflection, study, and trouble, which it cost me for twelve years.

I cannot finish this letter without telling you a pretty little story, which will entertain and interest you, Adelaide being the heroine of it. The day before yesterday, she asked my leave to take a walk in the fields, with Miss Bridget. I consented, and they set out at eight in the morning, with orders to return at ten: but they did not come back till half an hour past eleven. I was going to find fault, when Adelaide, blushing, and quite out of breath, begged Miss Bridget to allow her to tell me the story; and then gave me the following interesting recital: About half a league from B—, they observed a young female peasant seated on the grass, with an infant in her arms. Struck with the paleness and pretty figure of the woman, they went up to her, and learnt that she was just come from the neighbouring village, where she had been to buy some provisions, and that fatigue had obliged her to sit down. She added, with a moving air, continued Adelaide, that what gave her most uneasiness was, that her mother was ill, and would be unhappy at her staying; and saying this, 'the young woman wept, and kissed her little crying baby!' Adelaide, without hesitation, begged Miss Bridget to let her and the child get into the carriage, which followed them, and carry them home. Miss Bridget consented. The young woman told them the way, and in less than half an hour they arrived 'at the prettiest cottage imaginable,' where they found 'two charming little girls, who threw themselves on the young woman's neck to embrace her,' and 'their grandmother appears so good and so old, that indeed my dear mamma, you must see them.' Miss Bridget added more particulars to this recital; all to the praise of Adelaide's sensibility.[42] The same evening the young peasant's husband came to the castle to return thanks to Adelaide; and the next day we all went to see these good people, who are truly interesting by the extreme harmony which subsists among them. They are poor, but industrious, and appear satisfied with their condition. After making all possible inquiries into their characters and conduct, we have this morning determined to purchase for them a small piece of ground of about six acres, which was to be sold near their cottage; we shall also give them a cow or two; some poultry, clothes, linen, and some furniture.

You cannot form to yourself any idea of Adelaide's joy and transport on this determination. I have sent this evening for two sempstresses, to make clothes for the young peasant and her children; and Adelaide will herself assist in making them. Her play-things and her doll are thrown aside, and I see, with inexpressible delight, that in a heart uncorrupted, the pleasure preferred before all others, is that of doing good, and contributing to perform a virtuous and generous action. Adieu, my dear friend! I hope your next letter will make me amends for your last, which was indeed very short.

LETTER XV.

The same to the same.

WE had yesterday a charming ride. We carried to Nicole the young peasant I mentioned to you, all the furniture, clothes, &c. we intended them; Adelaide was loaded with a bundle of childrens' clothing; which, notwithstanding the extreme heat of the weather, she kept holding on her lap, the whole time we were in the carriage. She arrived at the cottage in a violent perspiration, her little heart beating, so that you could see its motion. Her cheeks flushed, and the purest and most lively joy sparkling in her eyes! Delightful, happy age, when every gesture, every action, presents an innocent and faithful picture of the sentiments of the heart! By degrees, as we lose this amiable simplicity, the silent, but interesting language of the eyes, becomes less intelligible; but they cannot quite deceive till the heart is wholly corrupted; for it is much more criminal to deceive by looks, than even by words. For he who cannot tell a falsehood without blushing, is not yet a complete liar, and whilst we preserve any traces of this sincerity, we are not arrived at the highest pitch of this odious vice. But to return to Adelaide. On getting out of the coach, she ran from us, dragging after her, in the dirt, the heavy parcel she had not strength to carry; and when we entered the cottage, we found her already employed in undressing one of the little girls, to put on a new gown, repeating every moment, 'It was I that made this hem;' 'I sewed on this ribbon,' 'and fastened on this clasp,' &c. &c. If this little picture affects you, how much more pleasure would you have felt, on seeing the satisfaction of the young peasant and her family. I have never till now found in this class of people any thing more than that kind of gratitude, which does honour to human nature. Hearts uncorrupted as theirs are, are affected with the benefit we confer on them, but are not surprised at it; while the extreme astonishment we shew at a good action, is a silent confession that we are incapable of doing it! Adieu, my dear friend! I quit you to go and read with Adelaide, who at this moment is leaning on my chair, and begging me to give her a lesson.

My sweet Adelaide has done so pretty an action, I cannot help telling it to you. And I have opened my letter again on purpose. After our reading, we went to take a walk, and amongst the chestnut trees, found a little bird just ready to fly; we took it up, and Adelaide, transported with joy, carried it to my chamber, and put it into a cage, every moment taking it out, and stifling it with caresses, and then crying over it as if it was dead. Here begins our dialogue word for word:[43]

Adelaide.   Mamma, my bird is hungry. I (writing at my desk) replied, 'give it something to eat then; you have got what is necessary.'

Adelaide.   But he will not eat.

Answer.   It is because he is sad.

Adelaide.   Why is he sad?

Answer.   Because he is unhappy.

Adelaide.   Unhappy! Oh Heaven, why is my sweet little bird unhappy?

Answer.   Because you do not know how to take care of him, and feed him, and because he is in prison.

Adelaide.   In prison!

Answer.   Yes, certainly he is: attend to me, Adelaide. If I was to shut you up in a little room, and not permit you to go out of it, would you be happy?

Adelaide.   (Her heart full) Oh my poor little bird!

Answer.   You make him unhappy.

Adelaide.   (Frighten'd) I make him unhappy!

Answer.   This little bird was in the fields, at his liberty, and you shut him up in a little cage, where he is not able to fly: see how he beats against it; if he could cry, I am sure he would.

Adelaide.   (Taking him out of the cage) Mamma, I am going to set him at liberty; the window is open, is it not?

Answer.   As you please, my dear child; for my part, I never would keep birds; for I would have every thing about me, and all that comes near me, happy!

Adelaide.   I would be as good as my dear mamma. I am going to put it on the balcony, shall I?

Answer.   (I still writing) If you please, my little dear.

Adelaide.   But first I will feed him. Oh, my dear mamma, he eats!

Answer.   I am very glad of it, if it gives you pleasure.

Adelaide.   He eats. I know how to feed him. Sweet bird! Charming little creature! (she kisses him) How pretty he is. Ah, he kisses me. How I love him. (She puts him into the cage again, then is thoughtful, and sighs. After some silence, the bird begins to beat himself again) I (looking compassionately at him) say, 'Poor little unfortunate!'

Adelaide.   (With tears in her eyes) Oh, mamma! (taking him again out of the cage) I will give him his liberty; shall I?

Answer.   (Without looking at her) As you please, Adelaide.

Adelaide.   (Going to the window) Dear little one! (the returns, crying) 'Mamma, I cannot!'

Answer.   Well, my dear, keep it then: this bird, like other animals, has not reason enough to reflect on the species of cruely you have, in depriving him of his happiness, to procure yourself a trifling amusement. He will not hate you, but he will suffer; and he would be happy, if he was at liberty. I would not hurt the smallest insect, at least not maliciously.

Adelaide.   Come, then, I am going to put it on the window.

Answer. You are at liberty to do as you please, my dear, but do not interrupt me any more; let me write.

Adelaide. (Kissing me, then going to the cage) Dear, dear bird! (She weeps, and after a little reflection, she goes to the window, and returns with precipitation, her cheeks glowing, but with tears in her eyes) says, 'Mamma, it is done; I have set him at liberty!'

Answer. I (taking her in my arms) say, my charming Adelaide, you have done a 'good action,' and I love you a thousand times more than ever.

Adelaide. Oh then I am well rewarded!

Answer. You always will be, every time you have courage to make a real sacrifice. Besides, sacrifices of this kind are only painful in idea. They are no sooner done, but they render us so amiable, that they leave nothing but joy and satisfaction in our hearts: for example, you wept at the thoughts of setting your bird at liberty; but do you regret it now?

Adelaide. Oh, no mamma; on the contrary, I am charmed at having made him happy, and at having performed a 'good action.'

Answer. Well, my dear child, never forget that, and if you are under any difficulty, in determining 'to do right,' remember your little bird, and say to yourself, There are no sacrifices, for which the esteem and tenderness for those we love cannot make useful amends.

LETTER XVI.

Baron d' Almane to the Viscount de Limours.

No, my dear Viscount, I do not at all repent the part I have taken, nor do I for one moment regret the pleasures of Paris, or the intrigues of the Court! If you knew with what an eye we consider these things at this distance, and how trifling and frivolous they appear, when they are coolly considered, you would the more readily believe me. I am however far from thinking that happiness consists only in solitude. It is certainly incompatible with vice and wickedness. But, otherwise, it is derived from various contrary causes. Wisdom and enthusiasm both equally serve to procure it; and reason and virtue will always maintain a right to create it, in every place and situation; in the midst of the tumult of Courts, as well in a cloyster, or a desart. And old people, men of the world, or those retired from it, may, by being just and good, enjoy that desired comfort, which the designing wicked man can never know! Believe me, my friend, our passions can never procure it for us. I have felt their influence, have known all the illusions of love; but in this tumultuous state the soul is agitated above its powers, and seems rather to be exhausted than satisfied, by what it experiences. These delights and transports, which almost deprive us of our reason, undoubtedly form a situation too active and violent for our weak minds; and become painful to us by their excess.

If you had not told me, my dear Viscount, a thousand times, that you had spent your life in studying different opinions, without ever adopting one, I should have been convinced of it by your last letter. You shew me in that all the advantages you have received from a good education; but you evidently prove, that you have not sufficiently reflected or meditated on that important subject, since, often praising my intentions and plans, you end all on a sudden with asking me this question: 'Do you really think that education can extirpate our vices, or imbue us with virtues; and that it is of any use to us?' I have certainly given testimony that I think so, by the sacrifices I have made in order to educate my children. But above all things consult History, and that will prove to you, that education not only improves a virtuous mind, but that (without finding even the seeds of them in our hearts) it can inspire us with the most violent passions. It was education that made such extraordinary men of the Lacedæmonians.[44] It was that, whose prevailing power was able to tear from their hearts the most tender and gentle sentiments, and to substitute those less natural passions in their stead. In short, it was education alone which could render their country dearer to them than their wives and children. Reflect how deeply engraved on our hearts are the first impressions we receive in our infancy and earliest youth. If reason, and the improvement of the understanding, has not power totally to destroy the most absurd prejudices received in infancy, how solid and lasting will be those principles which are founded on truth, and which every reflection will more and more strengthen. The essential point is, to know exactly the principles which ought first to be engraved on the minds of children, and I think we should begin by inspiring them with a contempt for every person who has not courage to execute a resolution seriously taken. Teach them then that it is not only necessary to be religious observers of their word with others, but that it is almost equally shameful to fail in those engagements they make with themselves. Weakness has a thousand times more inconvenience than obstinacy. We may esteem an obstinate man, but it is impossible not to despise a weak one. If you do not give your pupil strength of mind to conquer himself, every thing else you teach him will be useless; and the first six months he is absent from you, perhaps will obliterate for ever all the advantages you expected from eighteen years labour and attention. But you will ask, is this empire over one's self to be acquired? Yes, undoubtedly, and more easily than any other virtue; for it requires nothing more than habit. Accustom your pupil never to promise any thing slightly; but to keep punctually the slightest engagements, encourage him to it by little rewards, which by degrees you may increase as you see him improve in his resolution. But if he should fail to keep his word, you must express as much surprize as indignation; and tell him, if he was not a child, he would be dishonoured by such an action: make him feel how contemptible he must appear, and constantly add punishment to these humiliations, which at each return of his fault should be encreased: give him an example of what you expect from him, that your slightest promise should be inviolable and sacred; and lastly, when he convinces you he has gained power over himself, praise him only moderately; for nothing is more dangerous than to extol too much an action which it is our duty to perform. In shewing any admiration of it, we almost dispense with the performance of it on any other occasion. When Theodore shews me his firmness and resolution, I put on an air of the greatest satisfaction; for the other virtues that appear in him, I seem to regard him with more tenderness; but for this alone I appear to look on him no longer as a child. I reward him by an appearance of respect and consideration. I entrust him with a secret. I accustom him to feel all the pleasures of being esteemed. And I make him comprehend that the advantages they ensure to us are greater than those of even friendship itself. Theodore, like many other children, is naturally very greedy. Madame d' Almane the other day gave some sweetmeats to her little girl. Theodore also wanted some; I told him I could not give him any, as he did not deserve them so well as his sister, because he would eat them all in a quarter of an hour. But if he would promise to keep them, as Adelaide did, for several days, and to reflect deliberately on the promise he was going to make, and could assure me, after having considered of it, that he was capable of making this trial, I would rely upon him, and give him the sweetmeats. That very day, at dinner, Theodore requested leave to take a *burnt almond*, which is one of the sweet things he loves best; and instead of eating it, he wrapt it up in a paper very seriously, and put it in his pocket. At night, after supper, he approached me with inexpressible pride, and produced his *burnt almond*, telling me, 'it was yet untouched.' At the same moment, I looked out for a pretty little box made for sweetmeats, into which I put twelve perfumed lozenges, and gave it to Theodore; at the same time requesting him to promise me not to eat more than three a day, which he has performed with the strictest fidelity.[45] This example alone will give you an idea of the methods which may be taken to set children on their guard against their passions, and to put them also in a way to triumph over them. The success of these expedients, if often repeated, is infallible.

You ask me, if I teach my boy Latin? I think the knowledge of this language is useful, though not so indispensably necessary as it was five hundred years ago. They could not then have any idea of sciences of any kind, but by learning Greek and Latin. But at present, those who understand French, English, and Italian perfectly, have the opportunity of reading a great many works, at least equal to, if not superior to those which antiquity has produced. Milton, Tasso, and Ariosto, united together, may perhaps rival Homer and Virgil. And surely Corneille, Racine, Voltaire, Crebillon, Shakespeare, &c. have produced as many excellent Pieces as Sophocles and Euripides; Moliere has surpassed Plautus and Terence. Are the Fables of Phædrus better than those of Fontaine? The Poems of Boileau, of John Baptist, Rousseau, Gessert, Voltaire, Madame des Houlieres, Pope, Swift, Prior, and Thomson; are they inferior to those of Tibullus, Catullus, and Ovid? The Philosophical Works of Cicero, Seneca, Marcus Aurellus, and Epictetus, contain in general the most sublime sentiments, which we cannot too much admire. But have the Writings of Fenelon, Montesquieu, Addison, &c.[46] less eloquence or learning? With respect to Sciences, the comparison would be still more advantageous to the Moderns. I could mention several living Authors as illustrious as those I have now quoted, but this dissertation is already too long. To return therefore to my son; I intend certainly to teach him Latin. It is true, I shall not begin it till he is twelve or thirteen years old. Till then the study of it would only serve to make him weary, and when his understanding is a little enlarged, he will learn easily, and with little trouble, in eighteen months, what we could not expect to teach him in six years, by means of threats or punishments. For the present, I confine myself to the teaching him living languages by practice. He already speaks English perfectly well, and can call for every necessary in German. He has a Saxon footman, who never speaks to him in French. He will understand as much of German as is necessary for a soldier. The German literature has only been truly interesting for these forty years past. The modern Authors, Klopstock, Haller, Gesner, Gellert,[47] &c. have enriched it with Works which will make it immortal. But as it is not a language very general, and as it is scarcely possible to understand more than two or three languages besides our own, I have given the preference to English and Italian, which my children will begin to learn in six months, and in five years they will be able to read these languages with as much case as French.

Farewell, my dear Viscount! You desire me to give you an account of my avocations: let me in return, hear of your amusements, and every thing that interests you, and send me word if you have really quarrelled in earnest with Madame de Gerville? You know I shall not be sorry for it, as I can never forgive her the vexation she has given your wife.

LETTER XVII.

Viscount to the Baron d' Almane.

I REPEAT to you, my dear Baron, your plan of education appears to me most excellent, and, notwithstanding the fickleness of opinion with which you accuse me, I believe I shall always continue to think so. From all that you have said in your former letter, I am perfectly satisfied, if your son has sense and genius, that you will make a great man of him. However, permit me to tell you, I think I have remarked some contradictions in your principles. You are convinced that happiness consists only in being of a quiet, peaceful mind. And that strong passions, even when gratified, will not procure it; and yet, notwithstanding, this is your opinion. All your attentions and labours not only serve to exalt and elevate the mind of your pupil, but also warm his imagination, and kindle the fire of heroism in his heart. No doubt you will succeed, but would it not be better to make a happy than a great man? Can it be vanity which makes you prefer shining and dangerous qualifications to the more retired and milder virtues, which would ensure the repose and happiness of his life? I can scarcely believe it. And you must explain to me what I have so badly understood, or what you have not sufficiently informed me of. Your first duty and sole end is to labour for the happiness of your child. He has already obtained from nature and fortune every advantage which they can procure him; but your care and reflections will add to them all that he has a right to expect from a father, who has sacrificed every thing for his improvement.

You want to know if I have really broke off my connections with Madame de Gerville. I hope to, but ... However, I cannot answer for it. She was insupportable to me, and for a long time we have found out we did not love each other; nay, we have even discovered that we never loved. But her talents for intrigue were sometimes useful to me; and as our dispute has produced a bad effect to her, by making her lose what little consideration she possessed, I imagine she already begins to wish for a reconciliation; in which case I am sure I cannot help agreeing to it, at least in appearance. I have met with her these two days past, at a house where we visited; she played her part so well, and shewed such emotion at seeing me, that every body was duped by it except myself. But you will allow that it is necessary to submit to these indirect advances if she repeats them. One thing alone would make me hesitate; it is the certainty of giving great pain to Madame de Limours; for if I may judge by the joy she expressed at our quarrel, which she did not hear of till the day before yesterday, I should imagine she was jealous. But why should she? Has she any right to be so, considering the manner in which we have always lived together? I am as well convinced as you can be of the perfect chastity of Madame de Limours, but you know with what indifference she has always treated me. I am not ignorant that women often give themselves up to jealousy without feeling any tender sentiments; but it is not allowable for us to indulge them in such a caprice.

Farewell, my dear Baron; write to me as often as you can. Be assured, all those pleasures which you have given up, and which still remains to me, are not so estimable as your correspondence.

LETTER XVIII.

Answer from the Baron d' Almane, to the Viscount de Limours.

Y ES, my dear friend, my son's happiness is the chief duty, and sole end of my life; this dear, and sacred interest, is the only one which animates me. I am going to satisfy your friendship, and I hope clear up your doubts. I am persuaded that a reserved man, who is confined in his ideas, can never be perfectly happy. He is not to be pitied, because he has no idea of a greater degree of happiness. But it is not less true, that the situation is like that of a mere vegetable, uniform and tiresome: he is deprived of those lively and numerous pleasures, which are reserved for men of superior talents. It is much less owing to our senses that we are happy, than to our ideas and reflections. During our sleep, dreams have a natural power over our minds to affect us as much, or more, than even reality can do. But observe, it is terror in particular which makes the strongest impressions, because the stupification we are under makes us still more susceptible; and pleasing dreams make only a trifling impression on our minds. Your dreams have a thousand times represented to you enchanted palaces, and hidden treasures, &c. &c. Did those things overjoy you, or did they ever give you the pleasure you feel at the first scene of an opera? No, surely; and why? Because your imagination is without activity, and you have neither understanding, nor the power of reflection. We say every day, 'Happiness is mere matter of opinion, and he who thinks himself happy, in really so.' The Savage, reduced to live in a desart without society, pleasures, or ideas, is then as happy as the enlightened Sage; whose life is made pleasing to him by study, by friendship, and by benevolence! It would be absurd to believe on to support such an argument. Happiness, as I have said before, is offered to every honest and reasonable being; but the perfect degree of it is only reserved for a very small number of men, and even for those few is very difficult to be found. There is only one path which leads to it, and the variety of opinions, prejudices, and false systems generally conduct us to a contrary road: without ardour, and without activity, we cannot arrive at it. The Philosopher in his retreat, undeceived, and out of conceit with every thing, is only happy by these two principles. He reflects deeply, and his thoughts are constantly employed; wisdom has subdued his passions, but has not weakened his sensibility. If he had never experienced those passions which he has learned to conquer; or if his mind had been deprived of that degree of energy which made him susceptible, he would have had but an imperfect knowledge of the human heart. He would not taste the sweetest of all pleasures, that which peace and rest offer us, after a glorious and obstinate contest. In fine, he will be neither a Sage nor a Philosopher, nor perfectly happy. This is the state of happiness which I have conceived, when after an impetuous youth, after having experienced all the transports which glory, ambition, and love can inspire, one finds at length, time and age moderating this eager enthusiasm of a young, ardent, and sensible heart; and enjoys with satisfaction the tranquility which succeeds such agitation. It is thus, that the eager traveller leaves his own country, either through interest or curiosity; crosses rocks, and encounters dangers; fatigues, amuses, and instructs himself; and finds his courage strengthened, as he surveys with delight countries so new to him. In the end, when he returns back, he blesses the day which has brought him home. He finds an inexpressible pleasure in relating the history of his long journeys; he is charmed with the remembrance of them, but he does not wish to renew them. One must be possessed of a virtuous mind, to find, after moderating the passions, that peace so precious and so dear. He who suffers himself to be led into real crimes, has no right to expect it. His exhausted and degraded mind will never know any thing but remorse. Inaccessible to soft emotions, to the tender sentiments of humanity, he will in vain lament the loss of his pleasures; nothing will make him amends for them, and he will become a Misanthrope. His hatred and animosity will be extended over all nature; and, consumed with regret, disgust, and despair, he perhaps shortens the term of his deplorable life. But you will say, Is it not possible to have strong and lively passions, without their leading us astray? Yes, certainly; and this is the work of a good education, a work which consists in teaching your scholar to gain an empire over himself, and to inspire him with a desire to make himself distinguished, and with the love of glory. If these ideas are strongly engraved in a young and sensible mind, they will lay a foundation for his future conduct. Love, far from disgracing him, will only exalt his sentiments, and add to his delicacy. Ambition will never suffer him to be guilty of an unworthy action. Eager to make his name illustrious, and looking on the whole world as his judge, he will readily sacrifice, if necessary, his inclinations and his pleasures to the ruling desire of deserving and obtaining a dazzling and shining reputation. Perhaps at first he may only be virtuous by system, or by vanity, but in the end he will practice virtue by custom and inclination. In the present system, all these ideas are confounded together. Have you not seen persons at Court stiled ambitious, who are only guided by the meanest and vilest interest? Avarice and lust are the secret and shameful alternatives, by which a part of our people of rank are guided. True ambition makes Heroes and great men: she despises riches, and disdains even honours, if they are not the reward of meritorious actions. She labours for glory for the sake of posterity, and in an age where virtue is no longer loved for its own sake, she leads to those astonishing sacrifices, those unheard-of actions, which History records, never to be forgotten. Thus then, if you would have your scholar make a distinguished figure in the world; 'you must warm his imagination and elevate his mind.' But if he is confined in his ideas, if he is of a gloomy, savage, or capricious temper, you must avoid this mode of education, which will either make him a fool or a brute. For example, the education of the last Czar,[48] which only consisted in inspiring him with military ideas, might have made a Conqueror as well as a Sovereign of him, had he been born with sense and courage; whereas it only now served to make him more foolish and ridiculous. Charles the XIIth that glorious King of Sweden,[49] whose valour rendered even his follies glorious, should have possessed less ardour, or more genius. If he had had less enthusiasm, his name might not have been so celebrated, but would have been more truly great. It is necessary then, if I may so speak, to 'adapt the education' of your pupil to his character and disposition; attending only to soften his manners, and to keep his mind calm and tranquil, if he has but a moderate share of understanding; and to raise and elevate his mind, in proportion to the merit and talents you perceive in him. This is the difficult and delicate point on which all depends, and which requires the greatest discernment and constant attention. He may easily become a great man, without being endowed with superior sense and genius, provided he has courage, an elevated mind, and a sound judgement. I will explain to you in my next, the manner in which you ought to study the disposition of a child; and at what age you may begin to judge what he will be afterwards. I perceive with great concern, my dear Viscount, you are going to renew your connection with Madame de Gerville; you are sensible your wife will be truly afflicted at this news, yet you cannot sacrifice to her a friendship already broken, and which is so little necessary to the happiness of your life. Thus it is, that custom has as much power over you, as the most violent passions can have. How necessary then is it, that we should only follow those which are good! Adieu, my dear Viscount! I will not allow myself to make any more reflections at present, for I perceive they will only be at your expence.

LETTER XIX.

From the same to the same.

Y OUR last letter has so entirely put an end to the fears I had of wearying you with so many particulars relative to education, that I shall make no more apologies on the subject. I have already shewn you, of what importance it is to have a perfect knowledge of the temper, inclinations, and extent of the understanding of your scholar, so as to correct the defects he may have received from Nature, and to be in a state as much as possible to foresee to what degree of merit he may arrive: and now I am going to point out the means, by which you may acquire this knowledge. It is necessary to attend to the child's disposition, from the time he can speak. If he shews no attachment to those who have the care of him, he will afford you very few motives for hope. But we may expect a great deal from a child, who expresses sensibility, and a lively taste for the amusements procured him: follow him in his sports, and be assured, if he pursues them eagerly, and does not soon grow tired with them, that you will one day or other find him capable of great application; and you may easily give him an inclination for study. When he is five years old, often converse with him, not to instruct him, but to make yourself acquainted with his disposition. But take care he does not suspect your intentions; for then he will not answer ingenuously the questions you put to him. Seem only to talk for the sake of talking, and do not appear to pay any great attention to what he says, and notwithstanding his childishness, you will easily discover whether his ideas are at all arranged, and if he has strength of judgment. In fine, as Montaigne says, speaking of a Tutor: 'I would not have him the only talker; his scholar should speak in his turn. It is necessary to make him trot, before that the Tutor may judge of his pace.'[50]

I scarcely ever saw a child born with any sense, that is not pleased with comparing new objects with those he is already acquainted with: however trifling these comparisons may be, if they are just, they will infallibly prove, he has taste and judgment. Children are naturally talkative, which foible, according to the manner in which it shews itself, proves either that they have sense, or that they want it. A child, who cannot even by fear be kept from talking, but will converse with every body, without distinction, and never waits to be answered, will probably one day be mean and importunate. But he, who only speaks to those he is acquainted with, and is silent before strangers; prattling only to his relations and friends, and at the same time takes great pleasure in listening to others; this child will certainly have good sense. In short, I am of opinion, that after having made these observations, if one has never quitted the child, or if the discovery of the child's reason has not been delayed by illness, or by the weakness of his constitution, we may at six or seven years old begin to form a certain judgment of his temper and disposition. Rousseau has said with great eloquence, 'that a man born naturally good, if he is left to himself, will always remain so.'[51] I am not of this opinion. A man left to himself will naturally be revengeful, and consequently, will neither possess greatness of mind, nor generosity. Montaigne's sentiments are very different from Rousseau's, when he says, 'Nature has, I fear, attached some instinct of inhumanity to man; no one takes pleasure in seeing beasts playing with, and caressing each other; no one therefore should take any, in seeing them tear each other to pieces.'[52] But this is not because men are cruel, but because they are compassionate: they want to be moved, and to escape from idleness, they seek for violent agitations. This is the reason people frequent public executions, and go to see Tragedies: were we insensible, we should not go to either. Man is born with defects and vices, but he is born with sensibility; and if

Nature seldom forms a tender or compassionate heart, at least, it does not produce one which is absolutely without pity. There is no example of a child having a new nurse, who does not sensibly regret and weep for the first: therefore if the seeds of sensibility are to be found in mankind, and they become afterwards obdurate and cruel, without any particular vice either of head or heart, it is evident that this unfortunate person has been corrupted by education. In fine, it is a comfortable reflection for all Tutors, that all the bad qualities children shew in their infancy, may be of no bad consequence in future, because a good education may mend them. Whilst on the contrary, for the same reason, we may place firm dependance on the virtues they promise.

LETTER XX.

From the Baron d' Almane to the Viscount de Limours.

YOU ask me, my dear Viscount, how I shall proceed in order to give my son that true courage, which is so essential a quality in men, and above all in a soldier? Custom familiarizes one to the most frightful and dangerous things. If the use of fire was unknown to us the first time we saw it, to what a degree should we be alarmed by its destructive qualities, when we found a single spark sufficient to destroy a whole town! What precautions should we make use of to preserve ourselves in our houses, and what terror would a firebrand falling on the floor, or a lighted candle on a table covered with papers, cause in us! We feel nothing of this, however, because custom has inured us to it; though we are not so indifferent about things of infinitely less consequence. For example, the generality of women have an invincible aversion to spiders, toads, snakes, &c. whilst the sight of these creatures make no kind of impression on the mind of the most timid peasant, because they meet with such things continually. The country, where people are least afraid of thunder, is precisely that, where it does most mischief. I remember, in going from Rome to Naples, I slept in a Convent, on which the thunder falls regularly two or three times a year. That very night there was a dreadful storm, and I observed the Monks paid no more attention to it than if they had not heard it. I saw all the environs of Mount Vesuvius stripped of their verdure, and covered with lava; frightful and memorable remains of this most dreadful of plagues! Yet on this very lava, I saw a number of houses built, even at the foot of the mountain, and touching that formidable place, which carries death in its bosom. The owners of these lands trample under their feet the ashes of the unfortunate inhabitants of Pompeia. They have before their eyes the ruins of this buried city, and yet they are themselves much nearer to Vesuvius. After all these reflections, I have endeavoured, as much as possible, to familiarize my children to those things which create terror and disgust. In their infancy we accustomed them to look at, and even to touch spiders, frogs, and mice. It was only necessary to set them the example; they soon wished to have them, and to bring them up; and I have seen Adelaide weep at the death of her favourite frog, with as much grief as if she had lost the most delightful Canary-bird. When it has thundered, every body near them has cried out, what a beautiful sight! looking at the clouds, and the lightning. And the children used to go, and sit at the windows, to contemplate this 'beautiful and sublime sight; and were much pleased with it.' Since I came hither, I have placed in a gallery, through which Adelaide and Theodore pass, a glass-case, in which is placed a skeleton, and some other anatomical preparations. But I did not let them see this without preparing them for it. I thought it necessary to prevent their being terrified, as a bad impression is very difficult to destroy: this was the method I made use of; one day at dinner, I said aloud, that I had been putting in order the different pieces of anatomy, which had been sent to me from Paris. Mons. d' Aimeri (who had received his instructions) immediately began telling us, that the study of anatomy was very interesting and curious; and added, that he had such a passion for this science, that he had had for two years his 'bed-chamber entirely filled with skeletons.' The children enquired what they were, and after we had explained this to them, Adelaide said, a skeleton must be a very frightful thing: 'not more so than a thousand other things,' replied Madame d' Almane: 'For instance, the China-baboon you have in your closet;' we then dropped the subject. After dinner I was asked to shew my glass-case; we went into the gallery, and the children came of their own accord, and neither shewed surprize nor disgust at seeing the skeleton: and from this time they have continually passed through the gallery, without even imagining it possible to be afraid of a skeleton. I frequently tell them stories of travellers, for which children have a particular liking; and I give them the most superb description of tempests, in order to excite their curiosity, more than their fears. I add, that even shipwrecks are not truly dangerous to those who can swim. And Theodore says, he will learn to swim, and that he shall be very sorry, when he takes a voyage, not to see a tempest. It is impossible to conceal from children the dangers which surround mankind, in every action of their lives. Falsehood can never be of any use; for if your pupil once discovers, that you have concealed the truth from him, you lose his confidence for ever. I would have my son know, that he may be drowned in the sea, killed in battle, &c. &c. But I would not have him look upon danger with the exaggeration which fear, and an astonished apprehension give it: when one does not see the danger greater than it really is, one finds resources in one's own mind to draw one out of it. Every man, whose education has not spoiled him, has this kind of courage, which he receives with his breath, as a necessary instinct for his preservation. The coward, who loses his senses on the appearance of danger, is only a being corrupted and degraded. Nature will bestow on your pupil all that courage and presence of mind, which will be necessary for him to defend himself with, when attacked. Be it your part, to inspire him with generous sentiments, and he will defend his equal; give him a sense of honour, and he will defend his country. Locke and Rousseau, have both said, 'that you should never pity children when they fall down or hurt themselves.'[53] In my opinion, this method should only be pursued till they are three or four years old, at which time they require soothing, and without which you run the risk of hardening their hearts. I think therefore, when they suffer by any misfortune or accident, they ought to be pitied, especially if they do not complain: but if they scream and cry violently, I would appear to disregard them, and let them see, that your contempt stifles your compassion. As in every thing else, so it is in this. You yourself must set the example. If you cannot suffer pain or illness without complaining every moment; all you can say about fortitude and courage will make little impression. Madame d' Almane, four days ago, gave her children a lesson on this subject, which was of more use than all the sermons in the world. You love Madame d' Almane for that extreme tenderness she shews for her children; therefore I shall omit none of the particulars of the scene I am going to recite, which was really as alarming as it was interesting. Mons. d' Aimeri, Madame de Valmont, and her son were with us. After dinner, we were all in the saloon; Madame d' Almane, seated by Madame Valmont on a sopha, held Adelaide in her lap. When Theodore, willing to receive some of his mother's caresses, went softly behind her, and hastily seized one of her arms, which he drew towards him; at that moment a stream of blood ran from her arm, and covered Adelaide's face and her frock, who as soon as she saw it, screamed dreadfully, and fainted away on her mother's bosom; poor Theodore, drowned in tears, threw himself on his knees. We all ran to Madame d' Almane, who cried out, 'Adelaide! Adelaide! It is she who wants assistance;' and refused to give me her arm, wildly repeating the name of 'Adelaide!' The truth was, she had been blooded that morning, without telling any body of it. And Theodore, by seizing and stretching out her arm, had united the bandage, which occasioned this accident. Madame de Valmont, took care of Adelaide, whilst Mons. d' Aimeri, and I, fastened the bandage on Madame d' Almane's arm; though not without difficulty, as she had lost her senses, was pale, and trembling; agitated with the most frightful convulsive motions, had her eyes fixed on her daughter, and neither regarded our attentions nor poor Theodore, who stood, sobbing at her feet. At length, Adelaide recovered her senses, opened her eyes, and called to her mother, who flew immediately to her, took her in her arms, and embraced her a thousand times, shedding a flood of tears. We surrounded them, and listened to their conversation with as much emotion as pleasure. When suddenly, observing Theodore was not amongst us, I turned my head, and saw him standing by himself in the place his, mother had just quitted; no longer on his knees, or in tears, but fixed immoveably, his eyes dry, and having a countenance on which embarrassment, sorrow, and vexation, were equally painted. His heart, till then, so calm and innocent, received, at that moment, the first, the fatal impressions of envy and jealousy. He was no longer the same person. Injustice, perhaps dissimulation and hatred, had just entered into his mind, and had they not been quickly banished, they would have taken the deepest root there. I lost not a moment in making Madame d' Almane acquainted with my apprehensions; she immediately begged all the company to leave her; then approaching Theodore, without seeming to observe his trouble and confusion, she embraced him tenderly, and made him sit down by her, taking both her childrens' hands, and addressing herself to me: is it not true, said she, that I am a happy mother, and much beloved? My poor Theodore, what has he not suffered! But resume your gaiety, my love, added she, kissing him, your mother and sister are now perfectly recovered. At these words, Theodore, still sorrowful, though softened, leaned on his mother's shoulder, looked at his sister with tears in his eyes, and immediately kissed her, but sighed deeply at the same time; and you, my dear girl, continued Madame d' Almane, I hope when you are older, (a year hence, perhaps) you will be able, like your brother, to unite courage with sensibility. Here Theodore raised his head, as if endeavouring to find out whether she was in earnest. He then embraced her, and redoubled his tears. It is true, said I, women have long been reproached for their aptness to faint, and not without reason, as it is a proof of weakness. But, papa, it is because I love my mamma, said Adelaide, with much chagrin. I love you, my mamma, interrupted I, as much as you can do, and so does Theodore, yet we neither of us fainted. As I finished these words, Theodore threw himself on his sister's neck, crying, 'Oh, papa! how you grieve her!' At that moment Madame d' Almane looked at me, and gave me her hand, which I bathed with the sweetest tears I ever shed in my life. When we had comforted Adelaide, who had really been afflicted, the children asked their mother, why she had been blooded? Because, said she, I have had for this fortnight a most intolerable headache. This fortnight, mamma, and you never mentioned it! What good would it have done, repeating every moment 'how bad my head is!' I should have shewn great weakness, tired every body, and complaining would have done me no good: But, mamma, you did not even look as if you suffered pain; and you taught me my lessons as usual. You will never, my love, find me neglect an employment so dear to me for so trifling a matter! You see, my friend, what excellent lessons of courage were contained in those few words; and these are the kind of lessons which are really useful. After this conversation, Madame d' Almane entreated Mons. d' Aimeri, and Madame Valmont, not to commend Adelaide for that sensibility, which made her faint: for in fact, these kind of praises may, by our wishing to obtain them again, occasion affectation and hypocrisy. You should not praise children for their lively and quick demonstrations of sensibility; but for their habitual and constant proofs of duty and sweetness of temper. Adieu, my dear Viscount; it is midnight, an unlawful hour at B— Castle. I quit you to go to bed, for I must rise again before day.

LETTER XXI.

From the Baroness d'Almane, to Madame d'Ostalis.

YOU afford me great pleasure, my dear child, by the accounts you give me of the attention you pay to your health. In your present situation, it is an indispensable duty, though unfortunately at this time, is not thought so. Remember what your opinion was of a Lady who was ordered by her Physician to keep her chamber for four months, for fear she should miscarry. She declared, 'Such caution did not agree with her vivacity', and by that agreeable vivacity she lost her child. You then thought she must have a very bad heart to be capable of such imprudent conduct, and a worse understanding to suffer it to be made known. I am charmed with you for having maintained this opinion; and that, notwithstanding fashion and example, you will not set up late, or fatigue yourself by constant visiting or travelling far in a carriage. In regard to the desire you have for suckling your child, I have some observations to make, which require me to be particular. You appear to be much struck with all that Rousseau says on this subject; among other things he says, 'She who suckles the child of another person instead of her own, is a bad mother; how then can she be a good nurse?'[54] This observation of his has given you great reluctance to trust 'your child to the cares of an interested and mercenary woman.'[55] But you do not consider, this woman only deprives her infant of milk, to ensure him his bread, or at least to provide him with those necessaries, of which, without this sacrifice, he would stand in need. So far from being a 'bad mother,' she has, on the contrary, shewed herself to be possessed of real tenderness. Nature has undoubtedly convinced us of the pleasing obligations we are under to suckle our children; and we ought not to dispense with it, but when we are obliged by still more essential duties. If your husband does not oppose it, and if, without hurting his interest or his fortune, you can confine yourself to your own family for a twelvemonth, eighteen months, or perhaps for two years, you ought not to hesitate; indeed, you would be very wrong not to do it. But you will say, I see that every woman who suckles her child goes out visiting to publick places, and to Court, and weans her children at eight or nine months old. I am sensible of all this, and even know many who go to balls, and dance at them; I meet them every where dressed with large hoops, stiffened stays, &c.

&c. Do you think that the children of these elegant nurses would not be much happier in a cottage, with a good careful country-woman to attend them? You are acquainted with a relation of mine, Madame d' A—; if you wish to be a good nurse, you must imitate her. You must live a retired life, taking great care of your health, and never going abroad but for exercise; receiving no visits but those of relations or intimate friends, and determine not to wean your child till the state of its health, the advancement of its teeth and its strength, will permit this to be done with safety. I remember, one winter I often dined at a house where I constantly met with a young Lady who suckled her child; she was perfectly well dressed, and in the most fashionable style. But she scarcely was seated before she began to talk of her child. And we directly heard the shrill cries of an infant in swaddling clothes, whom they brought to her wrapt up in a rich mantle, and the mother gave it suck before seven or eight Gentlemen. I observed the men laugh, and whisper to each other. This scene appeared to me to be distressing, as well as indecent. I frequently went from thence to Madame d' A— , who fulfilled the same duty with that modest simplicity which true virtue always dictates to us, even in her most sublime actions; for we are only proud of doing what is right, in proportion to the efforts it costs us, and the little pleasure we derive from it. I have seen Madame d' A— in the midst of her family and friends; and I have experienced the sweetest emotion in seeing her with her infant in her arms: that infant, for whose sake she had sacrificed without difficulty, and without vanity, the gay world, and all the pleasures it offers us! There is certainly no sight more interesting or respectable, than to see a beautiful young woman fulfilling the first duties of nature. For what she now does for her child, who does not so much as know her, proves what she will be capable of doing one day for him, when she enjoys the happiness of being beloved by him, and when she has assured to herself more right to his tenderness. But, my dear daughter, reflect on the numerous obligations you bring on yourself by determining to suckle your child; and remember, it is better not to impose on yourself such a duty, than to fulfill it imperfectly.

LETTER XXII.

The Baroness d' Almane, to the Viscountess de Limours.

NO, my dear friend, I do not perceive the approach of winter with grief and terror; on the contrary, I thank Heaven, I shall not be obliged to catch cold in the road to Versailles, or in the streets of Paris. I shall not receive visitors, who are as tiresome as they are idle; nor shall I hear Gluck and Piccini,[56] both of whom I admire so much, continually taken to pieces! Instead of these things, I now only go abroad for pleasure and for health. I wear only a neat and convenient dress, and only associate with people I love. If you were here, who should I wish for more, or what could be wanting to my happiness? I assure you, for these eight months, that I have left Paris, I never passed a day without congratulating myself on the resolution I have taken, and at the same time reflecting with pain, that the same duties which have brought me here, will oblige me in three years to return to Paris! I have a favour to ask of you, my dear friend, I think I told you Madame de Valmont has a sister, who is a nun.[57] But before I tell you what I wish of you, I will relate to you the history of this unfortunate young Lady. Madame de Valmont acquainted me with it last night, and I am sure you will join with me in being deeply interested for her. Mons. d' Aimeri had four children. Cecilia, who was the youngest, was only three years old when she lost her mother; she was educated in a convent at Province,[58] and did not come out of it till she was thirteen, when she attended the nuptials of her eldest sister, Madame d' Olcy, who, as soon as she was married, immediately set out for Paris. Cecilia remained in the country with her father and her second sister, who was three years older than herself, and who was soon after married to Mons. de Valmont, and at the end of two years went to settle in Languedoc; she was strongly attached to Cecilia, whose amiable qualities, both of person and mind, were equally interesting; and what made her still more so, was, that she had the misfortune not to be loved by her father. On the eve of Madame de Valmont's departure, the two sisters passed the night together in lamenting their separation. When day-light appeared, Cecilia, bathed in tears, threw herself into the arms of her sister, and pressing her to her bosom, cried out, 'Oh! my only friend and support! in an hour's time I shall lose you; what will become of me in your absence? Who will excuse me to my father? Who will endeavour to conquer his aversion to me? You are the only one in the world who loves the poor Cecilia! Oh, my sister, my dear sister! when you leave me, what will become of me?' Indeed the unfortunate Cecilia had but too much reason to lament her fate. Her sister was no sooner departed, than her father sent Cecilia back to the convent where she had been brought up. She was sixteen years old when she returned to that place, from whence she was never to come back! Mons. d' Aimeri, wholly employed in the establishment of his only son, went to Paris; and some months after, Cecilia was informed she had no other alternative given her, but she must take the veil. Too gentle, and too timid to oppose the will of a father so absolute, she obeyed without resistance, and without murmuring; but her heart was no longer free. She loved; she was beloved; but still ignorant of the sentiments she felt. In giving up the world, she thought it was her sister only whose loss she regretted; her tears were given to friendship, when, alas! it was love which made them flow! A young man, called the Chevalier de Murville, a relation of Mons. d' Aimeri, was the object of this unfortunate passion; and he possessed all those virtues and amiable qualities which justified Cecilia in her choice. His mother had been some years retired from the world, and lived on a small estate about ten leagues from the Convent, where Cecilia resided. The year of her noviciate was almost elapsed, and the day was soon to arrive, when she was to make that dreadful engagement, which must never be broken!

That very day, her inhuman father had fixed upon for the celebration of his son's nuptials at Paris, where he was giving himself up to transports of joy: whilst his unhappy daughter was completeing at the age of seventeen her miserable sacrifice ... At length it was finished. Cecilia no longer lives for the world; and the gloomy walls which inclose her, are the bounds which obstruct her future felicity.

The evening after her profession, a messenger on horseback desired to speak with her from Madame de Murville, on an affair of the greatest consequence: she went to the parlour, and the man presented her with a letter, telling her, that a footman of Madame de Murville's had set out the evening before, with express orders to deliver the letter the same day; but that two leagues from the Convent he had had the misfortune to fall from his horse and to break his leg. A long fainting fit had followed this accident; but some countrymen had brought him to the farmer's house, who now informed her of this misfortune; and that the man had not recovered his senses till the next day, when he gave the letter to the farmer, who promised to deliver it. In saying these words, he gave the letter to Cecilia, who instantly flew to her chamber to read it. She opened it with the greatest emotion, which was infinitely more increased, when she saw it was written by Mons. de Murville! This letter, which Cecilia thought herself obliged to give to Madame de Valmont, and which she permitted me to copy, was written in these terms:

From the Castle of S— , the fifteenth of May.

'WHAT to-morrow! ... is it then to-morrow? ... I cannot finish ... My mouth cannot pronounce these dreadful words! ... Cecilia, it is no longer time to dissemble ... What then could you never read it in my heart? ... Alas, in happier days, I dared to flatter myself sometimes that your heart was not insensible. I opened all my soul to that inhuman father, who has sacrificed you. He deprived me of all hope, and I condemned myself to silence. Ah, if I could have foreseen the tyranny they were exercising against you! No, my Cecilia; you should not have been the victim of it. In spite of the cruel father, who banished you, in spite of the family who forsake you; nay, even in spite of yourself, I should have found means to have delivered you from the destiny prepared for you. But, far distant from you, in a foreign country, I was ignorant of the misfortune, and had no suspicion of it. I received a letter, informing me my mother was dangerously ill. I instantly left Spain, and arrived here: what dreadful misfortunes attended my return! I found my mother at the last extremity; and I was informed Cecilia was just going to take the veil ... That instant convinced me, to what a degree I loved ... Oh! victim, as interesting as dear to me, Nature and Friendship betray you, but love still remains. I alone will be your father, friend, brother; I will be your defender, your deliverer; oh, my Cecilia! Your husband ... Since you are yet free, you are mine; your relations have broken every tye that united you; you belong to no one but me ... Yes! I swear to devote my life to you: an oath, which doubtless, is as sacred, and more agreeable to the Supreme Being, than that which you are about to take ... Ah! pity me, for not being able to fly to you ... If you knew what my heart feels on this account ... But my mother is dying; and if I was capable of leaving her, should I be worthy of you? However ... if this letter cannot persuade you; if you still persist in this dreadful purpose! ... I trembler this idea alone rends my heart and overturns my reason. Listen to me, Cecilia ... I still respect the cruel author of your fate ... You are free: but if you have the weakness to obey him, from that moment, I shall no longer acknowledge him as your father: I shall only regard him as a detestable tyrant ... And, at least, I will not die without being revenged. For his own sake then, dare to resist him, or this trembling hand, that now writes to you; this hand, guided by hatred and despair, will pierce the heart of the monster that has sacrificed you. Let him keep his fortune, and reserve his affection for his son; let him disinherit you; what does it signify to me; let me but have Cecilia, and I will be the most submissive, the most grateful, and the happiest of his children. I fled from you, I endeavoured to forget you, and these vain efforts have only served to convince me that I cannot live without you. I dare believe, you esteem me enough to trust to my hands the care of your happiness and reputation. I only require from you the courage of declaring, you cannot take the vows; I will undertake the rest; and will only see you, to lead you to that altar, where the most holy and gentle tyes shall unite us for ever ... I can depend on the man, who brings this letter; I am certain you will receive it this evening. I cannot think you will be insensible to its contents. Yet a dreadful heaviness oppresses my heart; bitter tears run down my cheeks ... Oh, Cecilia, my dear Cecilia! Take pity on my situation; do not prepare for yourself eternal regrets; remember, that you are but seventeen years old. Ah! preserve your liberty: ought you not to live for me! ... I wait for your answer as for the sentence which is to fix my destiny!'

THE CHEVALIER DE MURVILLE.

Imagine, if it is possible, the situation of the unhappy Cecilia on reading this letter! She is only informed she is beloved, and this is so tender and passionate a manner, when she is irrecoverably lost! She had not till then discovered even her own sentiments; a few hours ago, she might have changed her lot; and ensured her felicity; but to receive the letter now, was only adding weight to her misfortunes! ... Surprize, affliction, and despair, made Cecilia stupid and motionless; a dreadful paleness covered her face; a death-like coldness seemed to freeze her heart. Deprived of the powers of reflection, she, however, feels all the horror of her destiny, and she knows she has no hope left but in death. At length, by degrees, recovering from the lethargy she was in, she cast wild and eager looks around her; every object which encompassed her only reminded her of her misfortunes, and of the sacrifice she had made. She cast her eyes on a table, where her long and beautiful hair, which had been cut off previously to her taking the vows had been placed.[59] At the sight of it she trembles; an inexpressible impulse of passion, mixed with terror, grief, and fury, tears her soul and distracts her reason. She rose hastily, and cried out, 'What then, is there no means of extricating myself from the dreadful abyss into which I am fallen? Cannot I fly ... Cannot I escape? But what do I say, great God! What a horrible idea! ... Oh, unfortunate Cecilia! 'It is now that you must die!" In finishing these words, she fell back in her chair, and burst into a flood of tears. She took up the fatal letter, and read it again: every line, every expression in it, was a mortal wound to her heart! How could she conquer a passion, whose violence was encreased by her gratitude. Her imagination presents to her view every thing which can add to her grief and despair. She sees her lover becoming furious, breathing revenge, and wishing only for death! She sees her father falling under his fatal stroke, or tearing from him his own life. These fatal pictures penetrate her with horror; less beloved, she would have had less to fear. Nevertheless, she could not support the idea, that the Chevalier de Murville should ever be comforted for her loss! At length she determined to answer his letter, and she wrote a billet, containing these words: 'Your letter arrived too late ... Cecilia no longer lives for you! ... Forget me ... live happy ... and respect my father.' ...

The unfortunate Chevalier de Murville received this note at the moment his mother died. He could not support so many misfortunes at once: a violent fever, attended by an alarming delirium, brought him in a few days to the brink of the grave. His illness lasted a long time; and he was scarcely out of danger, when he set about settling his affairs, in order to leave that country and France for ever. Passing through Languedoc, he stopped at Madame de Valmont's, who had always shewn him the tenderest friendship. He asked to see her in private. They conducted him to an apartment where she was alone. As soon as she saw him, she ran to him, and embracing him, shed a flood of tears. He concluded by this, that Cecilia had informed her of his passion. He was not deceived; he conjured her to let him see Cecilia's letter; she could not refuse; and you will judge whether this letter would not encrease the love as well as the grief of the Chevalier.

From the Abbey of — , 12th of June.

'I AM still alive ... But I thought I had reached the end of my troubles. I have seen at a small distance the wished-for port. I have been surrounded by gloomy tapers, and Priests exhorting me to die ... Alas! ... It was unnecessary. Why did they not rather exhort me to support life? Oh, my sister, in what a time did I know my heart! The day itself ... I tremble ... Read the letter I send you; it will inform you of every thing. This letter, which I now put into your hands, is the last sacrifice which remains for me to make ... How cruel it is ... This dear writing, which I shall never see again! ... But every word which is expressed in it, is engraved for ever in my heart! ... If you love me, my dear sister, preserve it always ... If it is not permitted me to keep it, at least let me think that it still exists. Let it be dear to you ... and think that my being deprived of it, is exactly what you would feel, if absent from the person you best love ... If you knew how painful it is to me to part with it! But, now alas! every thing is a crime in your unhappy sister; even the confession of the grief which destroys her! Insupportable restraint! Which brings on me the excess of despair. You know my heart and my disposition; you know whether I was born to cherish virtuous principles; but you would tremble with horror, was I to give you an account of all the fatal ideas, which for these three weeks past, have troubled and blackened my imagination: crimes pursue and surround me! ... I find in the most common objects, in the most trifling actions, horrible temptations ... When I walk in our melancholy gardens, my trembling eye measures the height of the walls; and a thousand times have I dared to conceive the foolish and guilty project, of freeing myself from them ... The first days of my recovery, when I sat at table, during that pensive silence, which is imposed on us, what horrible thoughts disturbed my reason! ... The knife lay near me! ... I cannot finish ... Oh, Heaven! is it possible this heart, once so innocent, could entertain such dreadful ideas? Ah! believe me, the most cruel of my torments is the remorse which tears my soul ... Sometimes bathed in tears, I implore with some degree of hope, the mercy and support of the Divine Being, not able to make to him a sacrifice of the passion which reigns in my heart. I intreat him to support me under my affliction, and to give me patience to bear it without murmuring. It is then I feel the only consolation, of which I am capable. A heavenly voice seems from my heart to pronounce these words: *Do not renounce happiness; passion troubles and destroys it. Religion and virtue alone, can ensure it to you.* At other times, I find myself too guilty to hope for pardon of so many offences ... And I again relapse into every anguish which doubt and terror can occasion. Forgive, my sister, these complainings; you will hear no more of them. I promise, hereafter I will respect the rigorous duty which condemns me to silence: I will no longer speak to you of my troubles or of their cause ...

And for you, my dear sister, never mention him to me again! ... You will see him undoubtedly, and perhaps you may see him comforted, consoled! ... Yet his letter is so passionate! Do you think that time, and the dissipations of the world, can destroy an affection so ardent and so sincere ... Ah, if you think so, do not tell me so; you will break my heart, but not alter my sentiments. The hope of sometimes engaging his thoughts, is the only thing which reconciles me to life ... Shall I own to you, the greatest of my afflictions, is the thought that he is ignorant to what degree I love him. Yes; if he knew my heart, he never could forget me. Perhaps he thinks me insensible, ungrateful ... Ah! conceal from him this passion, which distracts me! But, my dear sister, will you suffer him to accuse me of ingratitude? Oh, my God! What do I hear? ... The bell calls, and informs me that one of my companions is in the agonies of death! ... How happy is she! ... She is going to die ... Adieu! I enclose in this packet the hair for which you have asked me. That hair, which you have so frequently, adorned! You will not see it without weeping. May this sad relick recall to your remembrance my miserable fate, and tender friendship; and obtain from you that indulgence and compassion, which are the only remaining blessings left for the unhappy Cecilia.'

When the Chevalier de Murville had read this letter, he threw himself at the feet of Madame de Valmont, entreating her to give him Cecilia's hair; and to obtain this favour, he made use of the same means which he had already employed to get Madame de Valmont to shew him her letter, protesting, if she refused him this last request, he would not leave France without being revenged on Mons. d' Aimeri. His violence and threats so terrified Madame de Valmont, that she determined to let him have what he so ardently had desired; and she gave into his hands the little casket which contained the hair of her sister. The Chevalier de Murville received it on his knees; he opened it with a trembling hand; he wished, yet dreaded to see those long and beautiful tresses which he had so often admired on the head of the unfortunate Cecilia. He had no sooner cast his eyes on them, than he trembled and turned pale; then shutting the casket, and taking it in his arms, Adieu, Madame, said he, Adieu for ever. I am going to leave this abhorred country, never more to return to it; and you will never hear of me again till you receive this precious treasure which you have entrusted me with, and from which nothing but death shall separate me. When I am no more, it shall be returned to you with these words. He hastily quitted the room, not waiting for Madame de Valmont to reply. Since that day we have heard nothing of him, and are entirely ignorant of his destiny; but as Cecilia's hair has never been returned to Madame de Valmont, it is probable the Chevalier de Murville is still living, and is concealed in some corner of the world. With regard to Mons. d' Aimeri, Heaven has already punished him for his barbarity. His son, seduced by a taste for bad company and gaming, in a very short time lost his reputation, ruined his constitution, and destroyed his fortune; and three years after his marriage died without issue. Mons. d' Aimeri paid all his son's debts, and retired to Languedoc to live with his second daughter, Madame de Valmont, with a fortune which, from being very considerable, was now reduced to a very moderate one. It is imagined he intends leaving it to Charles, the son of Madame de Valmont, of whom he is passionately fond. As for Cecilia, time and reflection have insensibly triumphed over this passion, so fatal to her repose; and receiving the sublime consolation which religion affords her, she gathers at this time the sweet fruits of true piety, peace, and resignation; and she is become an example and pattern of goodness to all her companions. Such is her present situation; but the cruel disappointment she had met with, has injured her health greatly, and, together with the strict rules made use of in the convent, have almost destroyed her; and for these six months past, her life has been in great danger, Madame de Valmont is very anxious for her taking a journey to Paris, in order to consult the most celebrated Physicians. This permission has been easily obtained; and the favour I have to request of you, my dear friend, is, that you will go to Madame d' Olcy, and beg of her to receive at her house her unfortunate sister, and keep her there for two or three months. It will doubtless appear extraordinary to you, that Madame de Valmont should charge you with this message, when Madame d' Olcy is her sister, as well as Cecilia's. It is therefore necessary I should give you an idea of Madame d' Olcy's character. The immense fortune she possesses has not been able to console her for being the wife of a financier; and not having sense enough to surmount such a weakness, she suffers so much the more, as she only converses with the servants of the court; and so is continually reminded of the misfortune under which she groans.[60] They never mention the King, Queen, or the Court of Versailles, or the elegant dresses worn there, that she does not feel such inward anguish of mind, that she is obliged to change the conversation in order to conceal it. She has, exclusively of this consideration, every thing to make her amends. She lives in great pomp, has an elegant house, gives grand entertainments, and has her box at the opera and comedy. But, in short, she loves nothing; is tired of every thing, never judges of any thing but from the opinion of others; yet has considerable pretensions to wit, with a great deal of caprice and ill nature; and above all, is extremely insipid. Though she is very proud of being a woman of family, she does not shew the least attachment to her father, because he has quitted the army, and is retired from the world; and she expects nothing from him. She does not love Madame de Valmont, who she only looks upon as a downright country-woman; and she has undoubtedly forgot that she has a sister who is a nun. Thus you see your assistance will be necessary to us. I send you a letter to carry to her from Madame de Valmont; you will appear to be much interested for the two sisters, and I am sure you may obtain from her vanity, more than could be expected from her tenderness. Adieu, my dear friend!

it is time to finish this volume; but you will doubtless pardon me, on account of the interesting story of the unfortunate Cecilia.

LETTER XXIII.

Answer from the Viscountess de Limours.

OH this charming, this unfortunate Cecilia! How I love and pity her! and the poor Chevalier de Murville, how I admire him also! I am sorry, however, he is not dead. I expected that the casket, containing Cecilia's hair, would be returned, with an interesting letter written on his death-bed; this seems to be all that is wanting to complete the melancholy tale. This despairing, this passionate lover, to live so long! ... In spite of myself, I am tormented with the idea that he may be now living at his ease in some remote corner of the world. Perhaps attached to some other object; and if he has made a sacrifice of the hair! oh, the monster! ... He has no other way of justifying himself but sending it back instantly. But really now, have you not an earnest desire to know what is become of him? I have already composed ten or twelve Romances on this subject, every one more affecting than the preceding. Cecilia is going to leave the convent for some months; they will see each other again. Faintings, congratulations, &c. &c. ensue! ... or else she herself will receive her own hair with a most pathetic letter ... My opinion is, that he has never quitted France; for how could he tear himself from a country inhabited by Cecilia? He lives here disguised, concealed perhaps at la Trappe,[61] or possibly is turned hermit. In short, I cannot help thinking that we shall soon hear what is become of him. But to return to the commission with which I am charged. The very day I received your letter, I wrote a note to Madame d' Olcy, to beg a private interview with her; and the next day I went to wait on her. They conducted me through a long and superbe suite of apartments, at the end of which I found her in an elegant little room, seated on a sofa, and carelessly reading a pamphlet, which I believe she had only taken up on hearing a carriage enter the court-yard. She advanced towards me with the most obliging air, and the first compliments being over, I took from my pocket Madame de Valmont's letter, which I requested her to read immediately. You know that kind of forced smile and affected good humour which politeness spreads over the countenance. Alas! at the name of her sister, Madame d' Olcy was entirely changed, and coldness and embarrassment immediately took place; I did not appear to observe it. But whilst she was reading her letter from Madame de Valmont, I spoke much of your friendship for her, and the lively interest which we both took in the fate of the unhappy Cecilia. Madame d' Olcy answered, *That she knew very little of her two sisters; that she had been much neglected by them, but that she had not the less desire of being useful to them; yet that it appeared very difficult, in her situation, to keep a nun at her house for two months; and she had no idea where she could lodge her.* Here I could not help interrupting her, and saying, Surely, Madam, this house is sufficiently large to accommodate a person, who for ten years past has been contented with a cell. Madam, said she, I ought to lodge my sister properly, or not at all. She thought this reply so noble, and so clever, and it gave her a look of such satisfaction, that it entirely deprived me of the little patience I had till then preserved. Indeed, Madam, replied I, what appears to me the least proper, is to let your sister die for want of necessary assistance. At these words Madame d' Olcy blushed exceedingly, yet thought proper to conceal her vexation; she therefore softened her features, talked of her natural sensibility, her affection for her sisters; and ended by assuring me, if Mons. d' Olcy made no objections, she would send for Cecilia as soon as she could get permission. We then parted coolly enough. In going from her apartment, I took it in my head to ask if Mons. d' Olcy was at home. Finding he was, I went to him, and informed him of my commission. He received me with great politeness; and I was perfectly satisfied, as he shewed as much good will, as his wife had shewn roughness; but I believe she was not very well pleased, when she knew I had assured myself of Mr. d' Olcy's consent to receive Cecilia. However, she has written to me to-day, and tells me Cecilia may come towards the beginning of the winter, and may make use of the apartment they will prepare for her. She did well to give me this notice; for if she had deferred it, I was absolutely determined to have taken charge of the interesting Cecilia myself; and I should then have had the double pleasure of obliging the most amiable person in the world, and at the same time of humbling the pride of a woman, as hard-hearted as she is vain. I have not any other news to tell you, but that the Chevalier d' Herbain is at last returning from his travels. He will certainly be much concerned to find you at Paris. I dare say he will visit you, if you permit him; for two hundred leagues can scarcely appear more than a walk to a man who has been twice round the world. Adieu, my dear friend! I send you a letter from my brother to the Baron. As his letters all go through Paris to Languedoc, he thinks it better to send them in my packet, than to let them go separate; and if you will direct the Baron's answers, I will take care of them also.

LETTER XXIV.

From the Count de Roseville, Brother to the Viscountess de Limours,
to the Baron d' Almane.

YOUR letters, my dear Baron, equally interest and instruct me; you are educating your son, I am bringing up a Prince, born to be a Sovereign. The desire of being useful to the Public, can alone engage me to undertake this noble, but difficult employment. But the reflections of a good father, and such a man as you are, will be of great use to me; for paternal love must be the most enlightened upon all these matters.

Yes, my dear Baron, I have read all the books that have been written on the subject of Education in general, and that of Princes in particular; and since you desire to know my sentiments, I will tell you them with my usual sincerity. Rousseau is indebted to Seneca, to Montaigne, to Locke, and to Mons. de Fenelon,[62] for every thing that is truly useful in his book,[63] except one important truth, which he has had the merit of discovering first; it is, 'That the greatest fault we can commit in education, is that of being too hasty, and of sacrificing every thing to the desire of making our scholars appear brilliant.'[64]

It is painful to reflect, that, after giving advice so useful and so wise, Rousseau should not feel the inconvenience of falling into the opposite extreme. He will neither have Emilius taught to read, nor to write; and he proposes, on the contrary, a plan of education as defective, as the one he objects to. As to the rest, his Work is filled with pieces of sublime eloquence, declamations in a bad taste, and containing dangerous principles, failing both in interest and in action; and he offers almost in every page opposite inferences.[65] But we ought without doubt to forget his faults, on account of the superior beauties which are to be found in his book. However, it is to the Ladies that the Author of *Emilius* owes his great success; for they in general praise him with enthusiasm, although no Author treats them with less respect. He has actually denied them superior talents or genius. He accuses them all, without exception, of deceit and coquetry; in short he loved, but he did not esteem them. He has done more justice to their charms, than any other person: he has mentioned them with contempt, but with an air of passion, and passion excuses every thing. Before I quit Rousseau, I cannot forbear quoting a little paragraph out of *Emilius*, which always gave me great offence, even before I had undertaken the employment I am now engaged in. He says, 'That a Prince made him a proposal to educate his son, and that he refused it. If I had accepted his offer, added he, and that I had erred in my method, it would have been an education thrown away. If I had succeeded, it would have been still worse. His son would have renounced the title; he would no longer have wished to be a Prince.'[66] And why would he have renounced a title, which should give him power to do so much good? To make so many people happy, and to set so many great examples? Merely with a view of living independently, and without use to any one ... What false reasoning is this?

I know not whether you have ever read a little book which was published before *Emilius*, and from which Rousseau has taken some of his notions. It is written by Moncrief, and entitled 'Essays on the Necessity and Means of Pleasing.'[67] This Work is not written in the most elegant stile, but it is full of good sense, sound reasoning, and truth; and contains many new sentiments. I have remarked, says the Author, 'That two ideas, which naturally have no connection with each other, nevertheless become closely united, when they are presented at the same time. How many persons are there who cannot separate the ideas of specters and darkness? When a child, continued he, enquires what is the use of money? They tell him it is to buy sugar plumbs, play-things, and fine cloaths. This is giving him very narrow and confined notions. Money, he will say, is designed for the purpose of dressing and diverting me. Would it cost him more trouble to inform him, money was made to do good to our fellow-creatures, and to make ourselves beloved by them?'[68] Moncrief says very excellent things on the earliest education of Princes; and among others, that 'If one would inspire children, born in a superior rank of life, with the qualities which they ought to carry with them when they come into society, we should not make use of terms which only awaken their vanity. We tell them, they must be affable and obliging, &c. &c. On the contrary, we ought to make use of expressions which may render them modest, and to recommend to them, that they should entertain an esteem and veneration for men distinguished by their virtues. We should speak to them of respect, deference, gratitude, friendship, &c.'[69] I was much struck with this remark, and have frequently found an opportunity of giving my young Prince an excellent lesson on this subject. We have at this Court, a Minister who unites to the greatest talents every amiable quality of the heart and mind. I cannot do more justice to his genius, than by comparing it to his virtue. Despising intrigues, and all the little interested actions of common men, he looks forward to glory, and labours for no other end. In short, he owes his place merely to his reputation; he accepted it for the public good, and he maintains himself in it by his merit, by his services, by the esteem of his Sovereign, and that of the nation. The truth of this simple elogium cannot be doubted. It is neither dictated by gratitude nor friendship. I only know him by his actions, and I speak the more freely of him, as I shall never have any thing to ask from him. He very rarely comes to pay his Court to the young Prince, and when he does, he stays only a few moments. Very soon after my arrival here, he came one evening and found the Prince playing at nine pins. The latter having made a slight bow, smiled, and muttering something, returned again to his game. I then went up to the Minister, and said to him aloud, 'Sir, I entreat you to excuse the Prince; when he is less a child, and better instructed, he will certainly pay you the respect due to your person and character.'

I cannot express to you the astonishment which this word *respect*, occasioned in every body present; some of them thought I had been essentially wanting to the Prince; others thought that, being a stranger,[70] I did not know the real meaning of the term. But all agreed, that I was incapable of discharging the employment with which I had been honoured. As to the Prince, he was so surprized that he let the bowl fall out of his hand; and I saw I should have some difficulty to accustom his delicate ears to such unpleasant expressions. When we were alone, I expected he would have asked for an explanation; but he was piqued, and determined to keep silence. At length I began myself, by saying, 'My Lord, be so good as to explain to me the meaning of the word *respect*. 'This question made him blush, and after a moment's reflection he answered, '*Respect* is what is due to my father.' – 'You think then, that *respect* is only due to Princes? But ... Learn, my Lord, there are two sorts of *respect*: one sort consists only in little customary forms, mere outward shew; for instance, all those little ceremonies which *etiquette* requires to be shewn to Princes. The other *respect* comes from the heart; it arises from the esteem and admiration one naturally feels for every good and great man. This *respect*, far from lessening him who shews it, raises and elevates him. Because it proves that he is sensible of the excellence of virtue; and lastly, because great souls only are capable of feeling such a sentiment. But this kind of *respect* is also due to my father. Yes, because he is a good man, loves his subjects, and makes them happy; without which they would only treat him with that *formal respect* which is due to his birth. Thus the other kind of *respect*, which is only due to virtue, Princes receive in common with the rest of mankind. And this is what I require from you with regard to M. because he deserves it; and more from you than any other person, since he contributes, by his talents and labours, to the glory and prosperity of that nation, over which you are one day to rule. I flatter myself, Sir, that you will in time know how delightful it is, to feel this sentiment, and how glorious it is to inspire it ... Already I set no value on *formal respect*. – You are in the right; for it belongs only to your rank; without reference to your person. When you were only a twelve-month old, you received nearly as much honour as you receive now. The different orders of the State came in bodies, to compliment and address you, and you must have very confined notions to be proud of such things, which are only matters of mere form, and which they bestow on you even in your swaddling clothes. But if you cultivate your mind, if you acquire solid learning, if you become virtuous, and if you know how to honour and reward merit in others, all the respect paid you will cease to be vain and trifling; and will become a faithful representation of the sentiments they feel for you. This conversation has produced the happiest effects, and has destroyed that dangerous charm which is attached to those honours paid to Princes in their infancy.'

But to return to Works written on Education: I shall not speak of *Telemachus*, which is a master-piece, and equally above praise and criticism. I shall say nothing of *Bellisarius*,[71] about which we have talked so many times; and which we both so greatly admire. But, as you have not met with two books, entitled, 'The Education of a 'Prince.' One of them written by Chanteresne,[72] and the other by the Abbe Duguet;[73] I shall occasionally quote some passages from them as I find opportunity. This last Work had a great character when it first made its appearance; but tho' it was very estimable, it has since fallen into oblivion, because it is tedious.[74] If any body would take the trouble to reduce it into two volumes, it would be a very useful book. The Author has taken many of his ideas from *Telemachus*; but there are many very good ones of his own; and the following is one of them: 'Prudence, when it is perfect, is always guarded against cunning, who has not the same advantage on her side. The light of prudence elevates her above every thing which deceit meditates in darkness, and will discover at a distance the cloud under which dissimulation hides itself so closely, that for fear of being seen, she sees almost nothing.'[75]

The Abbe Duguet describes Courtiers with as much ingenuity as truth; and he also speaks perfectly well on the subject of flattery. 'The only means,' says he, 'to defend one's self against it, is to be deaf to all compliments. For the heart never rejects them, when the ears have listened to them. To be cautious in this point, will guard us against it. And we must not suppose ourselves above the attacks of the grossest flatterer, unless we repulse with severity that which is more delicate and less visible. For it is with pride, as with all other passions; it is by not yielding to it in one instance, that we can conquer it. We only irritate it by our cautions, and put ourselves under a necessity of yielding to it entirely, when we pretend to compound with it.'[76]

My pupil has already accustomed himself not to admit any kind of praise. I have so well persuaded him, that at eight years old he can have no other merit, than that of being tractable, and of applying closely to his improvements; that I have convinced him of the folly and absurdity of the praises bestowed on him: which he sees clearly are only meant to seduce persons of his rank. He has derived even from pride itself a perfect detestation of flattery, and distrusts the smallest testimony of approbation, if it is not from persons who possess his confidence, that he receives them. Some time ago, the Prince his father, performed an action, the justice and benevolence of which, one might assuredly praise without flattery. I was the only one of those who approached him without saying any thing on the subject. The young Prince remarked it, and asked me the reason. I did not praise this action, replied I, because I have a high idea of your father, and because I truly respect him. – How? – Yes: I am not surprised at any of the good actions he does; for which reason you did not see me appear with that air of enthusiasm that you remarked in others, and which is only an affectation of wonder, that pays him a very bad compliment; since it shews they did not expect to find him capable of so virtuous an action. Besides, had it been the most brilliant that had ever been performed, respect would have kept me from praising it before the Prince. – Why so? – Modesty is so estimable a virtue, that without it the brightest action would lose half its lustre; therefore I ought to suppose the person I respect possesses this amiable and indispensable quality. And if I was to praise him to his face, it is as if I would say, 'I have no kind of respect for you, and I prove it openly to you, because I believe you to be the vainest and proudest of men.' It is so certain a truth, that praise, whatever it is founded upon, becomes an insult when bestowed in this manner. Were we to tell a beautiful woman in direct terms, how handsome she is; or to say to a wise man, how virtuous you are; we should too visibly shock their modesty and offend them. And, since it is disgraceful to receive praises of this kind, we ought not to be better pleased with those of a more refined nature. For they only differ in the words, the meaning is always the same.

These are the methods I make use of, not only to guard my scholar against flattery, but to convince him of the injury it does. It was necessary to begin by this, since without doing so, all other means would have been without effect. In my next letter, I will give you, as you desire, my opinion upon the principal sentiments which a Governor ought to instil into the mind of a young Prince. Adieu, my dear Baron; let me have your reflections with the freedom I have a right to expect from your friendship, and which I deserve, by the great confidence I place in you.

LETTER. XXV.

The Viscountess to the Baroness d' Almane.

I NEED not acquaint you, my dear friend, that Madame d' Ostalis was this morning, the 4th of Jan. happily delivered of a son, because I knew before she was put to bed, she wrote you a billet to acquaint you with the news. But at least you shall hear from me, that our amiable Nun, Cecilia, arrived last night. I have seen her, I have wept with her, and I have passed an hour and a half alone with her. If you wish to know the particulars, attend to me. On getting up from table to-day, I received a letter written in an unknown hand; I looked at the signature, and saw Cecilia. I instantly rung, and ordered my carriage, and then read my letter, which was only to express her thanks, &c. But it was written in the most elegant and interesting stile imaginable. It recalled to my mind that affecting letter she wrote to her sister in the first moments of her despair. I forgot that ten years are elapsed since that time; I forgot that she was now a reasonable being, and had derived consolation from experience. My heart was deeply affected; and in this disposition I got into my carriage; during my ride, I found myself so much interested for her, that I entered her apartment with the same tenderness and emotion that I should have experienced had it been the same morning she had taken the veil. I went in hastily, and found her sitting at a little table writing, and alone. As soon as she heard my name announced, she rose from her seat, came to me, and I embraced her with great tenderness. For a few moments I was unable to speak, having an inexpressible weight on my spirits: and I found that great misfortunes inspire one with as much respect and admiration, as we feel for persons possessed of superior qualities. Nothing appears to me more noble, than a person who has been persecuted by fortune, and who has submitted with resolution to her destiny. And I assure you, few things in my life ever appeared to me so truly prepossessing, as the first view of Cecilia. Her figure is as noble as it is interesting; she is tall, and most elegantly formed, and has such eyes, as it is wholly impossible that the Chevalier de Murville can ever forget. There is in them such a sweet, yet deep melancholy; they discover wisdom and tenderness. In short, every thing amiable is expressed in them. Besides which they are of a deep blue, and are adorned with the most beautiful dark eye-lashes I ever saw. And to complete my praise of her, she has a most delicate complexion, and an enchanting tone of voice. As far as I could collect from her conversation, which was very reserved, she met with a very cold reception from Madame d' Olcy; but she speaks of Madame de Valmont with extreme tenderness; she loves you, without knowing you; and she has expressed to me much more gratitude, than my little services have merited; and all this with so much grace, and in such a manner, as could never be acquired by a knowledge of polite life only, as it must be the effect of an amiable disposition; without which, one can never possess that true politeness, which is so distinguished and so agreeable.

You wish me then, my dear friend, to speak to you about my little Constantia. I am very glad of it, for you have no idea of the affection I feel for this dear child. She has so sweet a temper, that this is alone sufficient to make her beloved; so there is no occasion for punishments or penances. When she has committed a fault, I content myself with saying, *you afflict me*, or *you will make me ill*; in short, I only attempt to awaken her sensibility, but not to excite her fears. Tell me what you think of this? I dare say you will be of my opinion. Constantia is adored throughout the house; there is not a servant who does not feel a real affection for her, because she is accustomed to treat them well; and I am continually repeating to her an excellent saying of an ancient Philosopher,[77] *That we ought to treat our servants as if they were unhappy friends*. Adieu, my dear friend. I have taken your advice, and am seriously learning English. It tires me to death. But I begin to read prose tolerably. Farewell, my dear friend.

LETTER XXVI.

Baroness d' Almane to the Viscountess.

IF you are charmed with Cecilia, I can assure you, she is no less charmed with you. She has written a very long letter to Madame de Valmont; and your charms, your wit, and your figure, fill up at least three pages of it.

I see with great pleasure, that you continue your English, and above all, my dear friend, that you employ yourself seriously in the education of our dear little Constantia. You ask my advice on your manner of correcting her faults: I will answer you without ceremony, and with my usual freedom. This method of awakening the sensibility of children, as it is called, is of no use when it is abused; or to speak more plainly, ought very seldom to be made use of. In continually repeating to your child by way of correcting her, that *she has afflicted you*, or *made you ill*; you familiarize her to an idea, which ought to inspire her with horror; that of making you unhappy: and at last, she will hear you make use of these expressions without feeling the smallest emotions; so that, far from encreasing her sensibility, you will stifle and destroy it for ever, unless you change your method. Inflict on her therefore little punishments proper for her age. Deprive her of a favourite play-thing for a few days, or of something she likes to eat; and for greater faults banish her from your own apartment, if you can be sure that her Governess will not amuse her in her own; for if she is diverted during this disgrace, every thing is lost. As for me, when I give up Adelaide to Miss Bridget, I am sure that she will not speak a word to her; that she will scarcely answer a single question; and in short, will treat her with the greatest disdain. Besides this, Adelaide knows, that though I suffer a great deal, when I punish her in this manner, yet she is convinced I shall always persevere in it; because I regard it as my duty, and because nothing prevents my doing it with the most scrupulous exactness. When she is received again into favour, I express the greatest satisfaction, by which I excite her sensibility and gratitude, without diminishing that necessary fear, which gives me so much command over her. That kind of fear, is the only esteem children are capable of feeling; for if they do not fear those on whom they depend, they will despise instead of loving them. This kind of fear never destroys confidence. But take care never to inspire it by your presence, or by putting the smallest constraint on their diversions. You ought never to restrain them, but when they commit a fault; and not in their gaiety. And by this means, you may assure yourself, that the affection of your child will equal its respect for you. But if you are peevish, and check her in the midst of her amusements, you will inspire in her the same fear which a tyrant would excite; and that can only produce aversion.

We are then only truly noble, when we know our real situation. Insolence, so far from exalting us, in effect only disgraces us; even when it seems to succeed the best. This is so true, that a woman who rules her husband, a son who governs his father, make themselves despised, if they do not carefully conceal the power they exercise: all usurpation is naturally odious to us, and the love of order and justice, is found in all hearts which are not entirely corrupted. Therefore do not destroy that fear in your child, which I have just described to you; she ought to feel it, and you to cherish it. Let us respect and acknowledge the rights of others. But never let us be base enough to renounce those which Nature has given us; for this would be to reverse the order of things, and take from us all the merit of paying a proper regard to those on whom we are dependant.

Locke says, 'Children should be always commended instead of punished, when they confess a fault, be it what it will.'[78] This does not appear to me to be right. When Adelaide accuses herself of a small fault, she is pardoned with a short exhortation, constantly attended with the praises due to her candour, and her confidence in me. If it is only a confession, that is, an answer to my questions, I punish her in proportion to her fault. If she comes to me, and owns she has been guilty of a serious fault, she is then punished, but in a less degree, than if I had discovered what she has acknowledged of her own accord. We come out of the hands of our Tutors with such false notions, that it is not astonishing we should stand in need of the experience of the world to rectify them. If our education has been a good one, experience would convince us that we have imbibed right and just principles; and they would be the rule of our future conduct. Instead of which, the first thing we learn on our entrance into company is, that all we have been taught relative to morality, was either false or exaggerated: and this discovery gives us great satisfaction, as it allows us to look on all principles as prejudices, and permits us to deliver ourselves up to our passions. When a child, who has owned itself guilty of a fault, receives more praise by so doing, than if it had not committed it, it is very natural that she should imagine she may behave ill again, if she is but honest enough to confess it. This is the reason we see so many people boasting of their faults, and saying, with a ridiculous vanity: 'I confess myself peevish, capricious, and passionate;' as if these words would excuse and make amends for all their follies. Persuade your child, that it is right and noble to confess her faults freely; but that it is infinitely more so, never to be guilty of any. When a girl is arrived at the age of fifteen or sixteen, what stories is she not told with the laudable intention of inspiring her with a horror for vice! People fancy they do wonders, in telling her, 'that a woman who is not virtuous, is regarded by nobody, is banished from society,' &c. &c. At the same time they will see in the most polite circles, 'women of little virtue, who are very much taken notice of.' They immediately conclude, their mothers or their Governesses are all lyars; and that there can be no harm in their having an intrigue. This is all that is gained by not adhering to the truth. Virtue is so amiable, that it is unnecessary to employ artifice to make it esteemed. Let us leave falsehood and dissimulation to vice: which has need of it to conceal her deformity. But if we wish to succeed in our instructions let us always adhere to truth.

You must excuse my being 'a little tedious' in this one letter, as it is necessary above all things, that I should express myself clearly. What I understand by principles, is to have a just idea of right and wrong; and I understand that what is meant by virtue, is to acquire a taste for that right, founded on principle, and strengthened by the custom of doing well. It is evident that education gives us these principles; and I think I have proved to you in some other letters, that it also gives us virtues; but you will doubtless tell me, all this is not sufficient to make us truly good. Experience is still necessary to give us a knowledge of our own strength, and to know how to use it; 'to have had experience,' is in a length of time to have felt all the temptations of which we are susceptible; it is to be convinced that we cannot be happy or esteemed, but in proportion as we are virtuous; and as we have the *fortitude* to resist our passions. If you content yourself with only saying all this to your pupil, you give her only a lecture, and not that knowledge, which is to be gained solely by facts. Produce events; throw temptations in her way; and repeat these trials, encreasing their attractions, as her reason gains strength. If she yields to them, let the punishment spring from the cause itself. For instance, if she tells a lie, punish her for it, as for any other fault; but, besides that, let her feel for a long time the great inconveniencies attending this vice. Appear to have lost all confidence in her, distrust every thing she tells you, &c. &c. In short, prove every thing to her by actions and situations, instead of lectures; and your daughter at sixteen will have as much experience, as the generality of women at five-and-twenty.

It is necessary, that I make you a reply on a subject, which I consider, my dear friend, as a very important one. You tell your daughter 'to regard servants as unhappy friends.' I never admired this idea, as it is not founded on truth: we cannot regard persons without education as our friends; as to any thing else which is meant by this maxim, it is very allowable, as it proceeds from goodness of heart. But I know nothing more dangerous for a young Lady, than familiarity with servants. I would recommend it to her always to treat them with civility; but would expressly forbid all conversation with them: for she can only learn trifling and absurd expressions, low sentiments, and a taste for bad company; which generally proceeds from peoples' not being able to bear restraint, and preferring the society of persons beneath them, to that of whom they are obliged to treat with respect and deference, which will always be disagreeable to such as love to take the command. Adieu, my dear friend. I greatly fear this letter will tire you to death. But if you will consider this matter, you will perceive that it is necessary for me to acquaint you with the whole of my plan of education.

LETTER XXVII.

Answer from the Viscountess Limours.

So then my ideas of education, which I thought so good, are all worth nothing; I cannot even deny it, since *experience* has already convinced me of it. I have been three months trying to break my little Constantia, of the unpoliteness of answering 'Yes,' or 'No,' without the addition of 'Sir,' or 'Madam,' which children have such an aversion to repeat. All my sufferings, all my maladies, were of no effect. At length your letter determined me to punish my girl for this fault; and for these four days past she has never omitted saying Sir, and Madam, very distinctly, which has persuaded me that your method is better than mine.

I had a very serious dispute yesterday about you: they were talking of you and Madame d' Ostalis; and they thought it very strange that you did not come to see her in her lying-in, as you affected to love her like your own child. I said, Madame d' Ostalis was one-and-twenty, had an excellent state of health, and this was not her first lying-in; and it would have been very simple in you to have left your children to take a journey of two hundred leagues, to be present at an event which could not occasion you any apprehensions. They persevered in saying, that you could not love Madame d' Ostalis; that you had only sacrificed so much of your time to her, and educated her so well, in order to establish her advantageously in the world. Through vanity, in this country essential benefits go for nothing; and praise is only given to trifles. It is because we praise with reluctance what we cannot imitate; and for this reason we do not so much admire sensibility for its great sacrifices, as when it shews itself by attentions, visits, and those little acts of friendship, in which we take so much pleasure, because the most trifling people can give the same testimonies of regard.

Notwithstanding your predictions, Mons. de Limours is more closely than ever engaged to Madame de Gerville. She has perfectly regained the empire over him, which for a short time she had lost. Mons. de Limours now almost lives with her, and their reconciliation has put me so much out of temper, that we live infinitely worse together than before their quarrel. I have two daughters, the eldest will probably be settled in less than two years, as she is now fifteen; and I have the pain to reflect, that the most intriguing, and the most ill-bred woman in the world, will chuse a husband for her. For Mons. de Limours, though he is sensible of her faults, suffers himself to be entirely ruled by her; and is so very indolent and careless, that he is pleased when any body will take the trouble to consider and determine for him, and by that means save him so much labour. Yet he does not want sense; he has naturally penetration, acuteness, and a just way of thinking. Ah! if I had but ... If I could have followed your advice! ... I should not now have been so unhappy, ... Yes: unhappy I am; I know all my follies, all my caprices; I have passed fourteen years without reflecting one moment on the advantages which might have resulted from making a friend of my husband. It is scarcely eighteen months since I began to think about it. Since which time I have seen him with other eyes; or, to express myself better, have observed him, listened to him, and have learned with inexpressible surprise, that if I had not loved him before, it was merely from inattention, and because I was taken up with other things. When one is past the age of thirty, and has renounced the airs of coquetry, and finds one's self tired with dissipation, one can do nothing better than love one's husband, if it is in one's power. Whilst I was making these prudent reflections, Mons. de Limours quarrelled with Madame de Gerville. I felt a joy on that account, which he easily perceived, and I thought he seemed flattered by it. He dined more frequently at home; did not seem tired when he was there, and every thing went on as I could wish. When all of a sudden he met with Madame de Gerville again. They were reconciled, and again he abandoned his house, so that I have not seen him for fifteen days together. This conduct gave me a concern which at first I ingenuously discovered; but finding Mons. de Limours was more perplexed, than afflicted by it, I changed my behaviour, and treated him with the greatest contempt. Bitter reproaches succeeded; and in short, we now live a thousand times worse together than ever. How much do I feel at this moment the want of such a friend as you are! ... Adieu! I am too gloomy to converse with you any more at present; I will not disturb the peace you enjoy ... What a difference is there in our situations! ... You married a man of a most resolute, and even imperious temper. He despised women, and made you suffer the greatest injustice, from his absurd jealousy, at the very time that he had conceived a violent passion for another woman. You have found means to detach him from your rival, to obtain his esteem, his tenderness, and his entire confidence. And as to me, they married me to a man the easiest in the world to manage, to govern; and I have never acquired the smallest power over his mind. I am not able to separate him even from a woman whom he does not love, and whom in fact he despises. Ah! I see now too plainly we are the cause of our own unhappiness. Had you been in my place, you would have been happy; was I in yours, I should have been the most wretched of all creatures. Adieu, my dear friend! At least pity me, and write to me. Point out to me all the faults I have been guilty of; shew me the consequences of all the mistakes I have made, and which have occasioned me so much grief. I have only a confused notion of them myself, and wish to have them better explained, not on my own account, for my fate is fixed; but that I may better describe to my children those dreadful inconveniences; and that at least the sad experience I have gained may be useful to them; and this will console me for the uneasiness it has occasioned me.

The Chevalier de Herbain is at last arrived; he is just as chearful and as amiable as you ever saw him. He pretends, that in five years we have absolutely changed our fashions, our customs, and our manners; and that he is as much a stranger here, as he should be at Constantinople. The astonishment which he affects at every thing he sees is very droll, and sits very well on him. He has charged me to lay his compliments at your feet, and intends writing to the Baron next week.

LETTER XXVIII.

From the Baroness d' Almane to the Viscountess.

How much you afflict me, my dear friend, by the account you give me of your situation. And you wish me to have the cruelty to place before your eyes, all those little faults which have produced such great misfortunes! Did you not make this request to me merely to affect me, and to take from me the power of reproaching you? It would not be the first time you had made use of this artifice. But, my dear friend, do you not know it is impossible for me to let an opportunity escape of preaching to you? Besides, I am well persuaded it is still in your power to change your present uneasy situation, and make it perfectly happy. But for this end you must have great perseverance, and a resolute and determined mind. Your first fault proceeded formerly from your thinking it perfectly genteel, to appear cold and disdainful to your husband; he was very nearly of the same opinion; and this conformity of sentiment ought to have prevented your coming together. With regard to the vexation his attachment to Madame de Gerville has caused you, it is but too true, that you in great measure owe it to yourself. I have kept all your letters, and have this morning found one which you wrote me on this subject twelve years ago. It is now by me on the table, and I will copy it exactly.

'At length, my dear cousin, all my wishes are accomplished; I have no more fears nor uneasiness for the future. I am now sure of being for ever at liberty, and enjoying my own ease. Mons. de Limours is fallen in love with a woman of intrigue. They assure me it is a real passion; that it is natural, and that it is an engagement entered into for life. Now, if you wish to know the name of the object, it is Madame de Gerville; and as you do not know her, I will give you a description of her. She is four years older than me, consequently is four and twenty. She is one of those sort of women who are only handsome three or four hours in a day, when she is full dressed, and by candlelight. She has a very disagreeable air of coquetry, which consists in making faces, and affecting to be gay. Her character is at least doubtful; for it is said, Mons. de Limours is not the first engagement she has entered into of this kind. At present, she has what is called many friends, which only means that she keeps a great deal of company. In short, she is the most bustling, most visiting, and most intriguing character in the world. To consider this in a political light, a woman of her temper and turn of mind might be useful to Mons. de Limours; she could transact all his business, and inspire him with that quickness which he has not at present; she would also be a means of leaving me entirely at liberty. It is true that Mons. de Limours has not hitherto been very troublesome to me; but how can I tell from one minute to another, that he may not, for want of other employment, take it into his head to pay attentions to me! Thank Heaven, Madame de Gerville delivers me from this fear; therefore, out of gratitude, I ask her to sup with me; lend her my box at the opera; and let no opportunity escape of praising her figure, her dress, her graces, and her wit. Oh! she has not obliged one who is ungrateful! ... Adieu, my dear cousin! Quit the melancholy country where you are, and return quickly hither; for I have no real joy without you.'

Well, my dear friend, what say you to this letter? What a surprising revolution have twelve years made in your ideas, and in your heart? When our happiness is not founded on reason, how subject it is to decay! That which transports us to-day, will perhaps torment us to-morrow. You know the poor Countess de L—, who, by her jealousy, made herself so insupportable to her husband. She was undoubtedly to blame; but her fault could not injure her reputation; nor was it sufficient to deprive her of her husband's friendship for ever. By your shewing so much joy, my dear friend, at what ought to have afflicted you in secret, by seeking after and receiving your rival at your own house, you have fastened the knot higher, which you now vainly endeavour to divide. This imprudent conduct was a breach of decorum, and you know the pretences it gave afterwards to Madame de Gerville to blacken and injure your reputation to Mons. de Limours. But let us say no more of the past. It is the present and the future which ought to engage our attention. It is necessary that we obtain from Mons. de Limours the sacrifice of a connection so unworthy of him; and in which he has not found, even in his fortune, those advantages which you expected. For his attachment to a woman so dangerous, and of such an intriguing spirit, only served to lead him into errors, and to render him often suspected, though unjustly; and it has deprived him of that esteem to which he was otherwise entitled. Is it possible, my dear friend, that with the desire you have to bring him back to you, you should take it into your head to treat him with the greatest contempt? He might excuse passion, petulance, even though unjust; but contempt and disdain he can never pardon. Let him see your grief, your concern; take the first opportunity to explain yourself to him; then confess your faults with freedom, and this will make him sensible of his. You may not be able to bring about a reconciliation perhaps in a day, but by persevering in this conduct, be assured, before a twelvemonth is elapsed, he will bestow on you all his tenderness and confidence; since he has nothing of real consequence to reproach you with, and that he certainly has an affection for you. Adieu, my dear friend! Do not conceal from me any thing which interests you; and above all, let me know whatever relates to Mons. de Limours.

LETTER XXIX.

From the same to the same.

I SEND you, my dear friend, a letter from Adelaide. You will certainly be satisfied with the writing, but perhaps will be astonished to find in it many faults in regard to the spelling. But when I give her leave to write to you once a month, I told her I should neither correct her stile, nor the spelling. She has just brought me her letter; I have pointed out the faults to her, and she wanted to write another, which I would not allow; so that she saw this sent away with great concern, and waits with impatience till 'the twelfth of April,' in the hope of doing better, and of sending you a more complete letter. This is the kind of emulation I wish to inspire her with. Apropos, of writing; I will now tell you the manner in which Adelaide has been taught to write, and which I advise you to follow for Constantia. I have observed, the most fatiguing of all lessons to children, is that of writing; for, indeed, nothing can be more tiresome, than filling a large page by repeating one or two phrases, which contain only two lines. I therefore had extracts taken from some instructing and amusing books, and written by an excellent master; which I made nine or ten volumes of, to serve as copies for my children. Some of them are written large for their first lessons; others in a small hand, for the ages of twelve or thirteen, &c. They are all written on single sheets of paper; and when one volume is finished, they begin another. By this method Adelaide finds her lessons agreeable. She is instructed while she writes; and as she finds in the same space a greater number and variety of words, than other children who only copy a single line, she will certainly learn to spell much sooner.

No, my dear friend, Adelaide is not already perfect. Nature has formed her with many great faults; and I have as yet only been able to repress them, not to destroy them entirely. She is violent, giddy, and heedless; and of course not able to pay close attention with people of whom she is not afraid. She is impatient, and even passionate; but, like all other children, she knows perfectly well how to submit to necessity; and being convinced I have the power, as well as the will to punish her, she is extremely submissive to me. She has two or three times played tricks with Miss Bridget; but at last, finding her as inflexible as I was, she now respects and obeys her, as well as me. We should indeed think her perfect, if I did not watch her narrowly, when she is not aware of it. Whilst she is learning to draw, I either write or read; and frequently surprize her in making faces, or mimicking Dainville; and I see clearly, that if I was not present, she would be both impertinent and perverse to him. Nothing is more easy than to prescribe rules to children; but when you have forced a mind, naturally imperious, to submission, you must never leave her to herself a single moment; for if you once lose sight of her, you may be sure that she will make herself amends the very first opportunity, for the constraint you impose on her. The more submissive she is with you, the more untractable she will be with others; and then, instead of curing her of one vice, you only make her guilty of more. The mildness she shews you is only the effect of her submission, and in time will become deceit and hypocrisy; therefore never put her into hands on which you cannot depend, as well as yourself. Keep your eyes on her, till time, reason, and habit, shall have absolutely changed her disposition. As to other matters, Adelaide has many amiable qualities, she has an extreme sensibility; is generous; incapable of envy; never out of temper; and certainly has a very good understanding.

It is very necessary to accustom children to treat all their masters, not only with politeness, but with respect; for they ought to be persuaded they are under obligations to every body who teaches them any agreeable or useful knowledge. This sentiment of gratitude will do honour to the parents who have directed the education of their children, and they will take their lessons with greater advantage. Adelaide, thinking I did not see her yesterday, snatched a pencil out of Mons. Dainville's hand, which he had not cut quickly enough for her. I obliged her to make excuses for it, which I dictated to her in the most humble terms. This went much against her; and when we were alone, she told me she did not think she owed so much respect to a young man like Mons. Dainville. But, said I, does he not instruct you in a most agreeable science, and devotes his time and attention to you? He is one of your benefactors. Benefactors! ... A master! ... Ah! well, but do you not mean to tell me, he is paid for all this, and that it is his duty? If this reason excuses your gratitude, you will be ungrateful to all the world; for example, to me, who in educating you, rewarding, or punishing you, only do my duty, and so you are not obliged to me for it ... Oh! mamma, how can you compare yourself ... I know very well, you owe much more to me than to Mons. Dainville; but there are different degrees of gratitude; and if you are not sensible of small obligations, you are incapable of feeling great ones as you ought to do. If you have no gratitude towards Mons. Dainville, that which you owe to me will be very weak. This way of reasoning made a very lively impression on Adelaide; and I am very certain she will make a point of appearing to shew great gratitude to Dainville, in order to convince me, that what she feels for me is without bounds; she has thus perfectly understood that every body who does not fail in the duties they owe us, contribute all in their power to promote our happiness; and for that reason, ought to inspire us with gratitude in proportion to the pleasure or comfort they procure us; and she has even felt, that if these duties are discharged with exactness, our affection ought to be the reward.

And now, my dear friend, I must talk to you a little of our amusements. We have had very brilliant ones this month. For instance, we have acted comedies, and my children were our principal actors. I see here your astonishment. How! *Adelaide has played the part of a girl in love! Does Adelaide know already what it is to be in love? to have a lover, violent passions,* &c ... Lay aside your fears, my dear; Adelaide knows nothing of all this. We have played two comedies, in which there is no love, no lovers, no violent passions. But I will explain this riddle to you: you must know I have composed '*Dramas for the use of children, and young persons.*'[79] I have already said, that children must have natural and lively images before them, which may strike their imaginations, touch their hearts, and be engraved on their memories. On this principle I have planned my Work, and these little comedies form a collection of lessons on morality. I have endeavoured to point out those irregularities and faults which are ridiculous; but in general have avoided representing characters that are truly odious.

They are very dangerous parts to be acted. Children may forget the unravelling of the plot, and the moral to be drawn from it; and the bad part only will remain in their heads; that is, they will adopt, what they have been taught to represent. I have composed plays, both for Adelaide and her brother. The persons in the former are all women, in the latter they are men. This was the more easy for me to do, as I banished love from my theatre; and thus I avoided that familiarity, which the rehearsal of their parts necessarily occasions between actors; which would not agree with that strict delicacy, so becoming young people. It appeared to me, that these new kind of plays might be useful in the education of youth; so that children, by amusing themselves in this manner, may exercise their memory, improve their pronunciation, acquire grace in their speaking, and lose that foolish kind of embarrassment, to which they are so subject. When they have acted a part, filled with goodness, delicacy, and generosity; they will blush to be perverse, or insensible. In short, they will love and cherish that virtue which they see so amiable and so much admired. But I repeat, that it is absolutely necessary the pieces should be composed on purpose; for the best of our theatrical compositions would be dangerous, and at the same time, above the capacity of the most sensible child, who is only ten years of age.

On the first of March, we had two of our little Plays acted; the first was called the *Flaggons*, and the second the *Dove*. Madame de Valmont and I, took the parts of the Mother and the Fairy. Adelaide performed the principal parts, and two pretty little girls, daughters to Madame de Valmont's waiting-women, formed the rest of the company. Four days after, there were two other Pieces performed by the men, at which we were only spectators. The actors were Mons. d' Almane, Theodore, Mons. de Valmont, his son Charles, who is thirteen years old, and a most elegant figure; Mons. d' Aimeri, Dainville, and two of the footmen. The plays were called the *Traveller*, and *The Ball for Children*.[80] Charles was very successful in the first, and Theodore performed very well in the second. There was great emulation between our two companies. But our best Actors are Charles and Adelaide, who are really surprising for their age. Our Plays have succeeded so well, that we shall act the same over again in the course of this month. We have a very pretty play-house and a hall, which will hold two hundred people, and which is completely filled by our neighbours, our own family, and the country people round us; which altogether forms an audience very respectable; but they treat us with great indulgence. Adieu, my dear friend. If you wish to have tickets for our next performance, let me know. Oh! I wish you could see our little Dramas. I should enjoy them as much again, if you were here; and perhaps they would interest you more than you imagine; for the affecting and innocent graces of infancy add to these inexpressible charms inconsiderable productions.

LETTER XXX.

Answer from the Viscountess de Limours.

'IF I want tickets for your next plays, you will send me some!' Do you think this a pleasant jest! Or that it is generous in you to insult the grief I feel at being separated from you? I am very sure I should prefer your childrens' plays to the greatest part of those amusements I see here; for instance, to one I was present at yesterday. Mons. de Blesac, gave a very grand entertainment at his country-house. He had collected together about fifteen Ladies of the best quality, the greater part of whom were very young. It began by a beautiful illumination in the garden, and ended by acting two Comedies of a very different nature from yours'; you may have heard of them, because they are reckoned good ones of their kind; but are so indecent, that ten years ago, no woman of any delicacy would even confess she had read them. Ah, well! we saw them, at this time, performed before a hundred Gentlemen without any difficulty; and have even desired Mons. de Blesac to let them be played again. I confess to you, I had no idea of such licentiousness; and I wondered at the intrepidity of all these young Ladies, whilst the play lasted; who at other times affect to be so fearful and bashful even on entering a room. If I could, without an appearance of prudery, have declined going a second time, I certainly should have broke my engagement; for really my mind is not so corrupted as to make me prefer such pieces to French Comedies.[81] Madame d' Ostalis was invited to this entertainment, but would not go, which I very much approved of; and certainly, had I been only twenty years old, I should have done as she did, in spite of fashion, or the power of example.

I tell you, my dear friend, I make great progress in the English language, and begins to read prose very prettily. Apropos, do you know any thing of an English book on Education, written by Lord Chesterfield, in *Letters to his Son*?[82] This Lord Chesterfield is an impertinent Author. Listen, I entreat you, to the manner in which he treats us, and see whether you could know yourself in this gallant picture, which I translate literally: 'Women are only children of a larger growth, they have an entertaining tattle, sometimes wit; but for solid reasoning, good sense, I never in my life knew one that had it, or who acted or reasoned in consequence of it, for four-and-twenty hours together. A man of sense only trifles with them, plays with them, humours, and flatters them, as he does with an engaging child. But he neither consults them about, nor trusts them with serious matters.'[83] Do you, my dear friend, approve of a father's giving such an opinion of women to his son? For, besides that it is false and unjust, it appears to me to be dangerous; for the man who despises women, is not more secure from their seductions than others, though he thinks he disgraces himself by loving them. But for the rest, I, who am more just than Lord Chesterfield, agree that there is much good sense in his letters. But I think in general he sets too much value on what he calls the *graces*, and *Bon ton*. When his son first appeared at Paris, Lord Chesterfield was afraid he would conduct himself aukwardly, and takes much more care of his manners than of his temper and disposition. His letters are filled with the most trifling particulars relative to the customs of the polite world. He teaches his son how to blow his nose gracefully, tells him never to spill the sauce at table, never to spit before company, and never to laugh loud, &c. &c. – In short, he has such a desire to see his son fashionable, that he even sacrifices his principles to that vain fancy: and he advises him to keep two mistresses at a time! Besides, though he valued himself on his fashionable and polite air, he really was not polite in reality. There are often in his book letters consisting of whole pages written in French. I will only copy one of them. He informs his son, that a woman of fashion undertook to form him, and that one day, in a large company, she said to several people, 'Do you know that I have undertaken this young man, and that you must help to polish him. He must necessarily have an attachment: and if I am judged worthy to be the object of it, we must find him another. But do not go and disgrace yourself by keeping company with opera girls, who will not put you to the expence of sentiment or politeness; but will cost you much more in every other respect. I repeat it, my friend; if you associate with these women, you are lost; they will ruin your health and your fortune: corrupt your manners, and deprive you of that true politeness, which can only be acquired by keeping good company.'[84]

I know very well, that among polite people, one sometimes meets with a Lady, who undertakes to form the minds of young men; but I do not believe they ever expressed themselves in such a manner. Lord Chesterfield's Letters are written in Four Volumes; I have read them through; you see I attend closely to my English. – I begin also to devote a great deal of my time to Constantia. I make her read to me, and she gets by heart the little tales you sent me. I keep her almost the whole day with me. In short, I imitate as well as I can all that you do for Adelaide. I begin already to reap the fruits of my attentions; my own house becomes more agreeable to me, dissipation is less necessary to me, and my health is much better. Constantia is equally sensible, mild, and obedient. But since I have punished her faults, she has told me several lyes in order to keep herself from these little corrections which I have given her according to your advice, when she confesses her fault. How must I remedy this? How prevent a child from telling lyes, when she thinks herself sure of not being discovered? In short, how must I act to make her sensible of the crime of telling lyes? Answer me this in the most particular manner; for, in my opinion, it is the most important of any thing.

The day before yesterday, I spent the whole morning with Cecilia, whose health is almost perfectly re-established. She told Madame d' Ostalis and me, that from what she had seen of the world, she found she had no reason to regret it; that she had formed a very different idea of it in her solitude; and that her opinion of it was much more pleasing than she had found it in reality. 'I meet with nothing,' said she, 'but constraint and dependance. It is in vain that I seek for freedom and happiness; I see only ridiculous connexions, opposition, and the most changeable whims and caprices.' She added, that she should return to her Convent with no other concern, than that of leaving Madame d' Ostalis and me, for whom she had a sincere friendship; which I am sure is mutual on all sides. For these two months past, Madame d' Olcy has behaved very kindly to her, and values herself much on the affection she has for her. As she sees we pay great attention to her, and that we go to breakfast with her three or four times a week; she has done the same thing, and has introduced her to several of her own friends. Cecilia is so interesting both in person and mind, and has so many amiable qualities, that every one who sees her is charmed with her; so that in short she is quite the *Ton*, as far as her situation will admit. And the Ladies, who cannot well be jealous of a nun, are all desirous of seeing her, and being acquainted with her; and they talk of her with a degree of enthusiasm. Which has made Madame d' Olcy pretend to have a violent affection for her, which does her great honour in the opinion of the world; but it does not hinder her from hinting to Cecilia, that she would not wish her to prolong her stay at Paris. Cecilia would have gone immediately, but as her physicians desired her to stay five weeks longer, I have made her promise to remain here till the month of May, though she did it with great reluctance.

Adieu, my dear friend; do not forget, when you give my dear little Adelaide my answer to her letter, to embrace her for me as tenderly as you would do for yourself. And now I think of it, let me beg you to be very particular in giving me your opinion of Charles, Madame de Valmont's son. I already know, that he is thirteen years old; that he has a fine person, and that he acts his part in Comedy to a wonder; which plainly proves him to have wit, and graces innumerable. Besides these, what is his disposition, what his birth, and what will be his fortune? I have the most earnest desire to be informed of these particulars, because I foresee, that this little Charles, so amiable, so near you, so often with Adelaide, may perhaps in the end act a still more interesting part than those you have hitherto given him. Adieu. Remember, if you do not answer me very clearly and particularly on this subject, I shall think you mean to conceal some of your intended schemes from me.

LETTER XXXI.

Answer from the Baroness.

I AM not at all surprised, my dear friend, that Constantia, who has never been accustomed to be punished for the faults she has committed, should have recourse to telling lyes, in order to escape punishment. What can hinder us from doing a bad action, which may be useful and agreeable to us, when we are almost certain we shall never be discovered, and when it does no harm to any other person? Conscience! and pray what do you mean by Conscience? It is a sentiment in our hearts which, by the remorse it occasions, punishes us for our fault. This remorse would have no existence in our minds, if virtue was only a thing talked of: that is, if it was not to receive immortal recompence in another world. In short, if every thing died with us, Heroes, who devote themselves to the good of their country, and who sacrifice their own interest for that of others, would act the parts of mad men; whilst the wisest men would be those who gave themselves up to every passion they could gratify without incurring the punishments inflicted by the law. Conscience is a guide little to be depended on, unless accompanied by religion. Give then to your scholar religious sentiments. Persuade her, that in every moment of her life the Divine Being sees and hears her: impress her mind with this sublime and important principle. Set her the example of piety; let her often surprize you praying to God, that she may be convinced you find in this duty all the consolation you stand in need of, and that you take pleasure in fulfilling it. Make her admire the works of God, the heavens, the earth, the verdure, the fruits she eats, and the flowers which she gathers, every thing will serve to make her sensible of the power and goodness of God, who has created every thing for our use. Let her learn short, simple, and affecting prayers, of which she may understand and feel the use. I have made some on purpose for Adelaide, which she repeats with respect, and in a manner which always affects me; I frequently speak to her of her guardian Angel, whom I describe to her beautiful, as it is possible to be, crowned with garlands of never-fading flowers, having wings of the most dazzling brightness, and hovering always round her. This sweet and smiling picture affects her heart, and seduces her imagination. She knows, that this charming being is as innocent as he is lovely; that he detests lyes, artifice, gluttony, and passion. And that every good action pleases and delights him. She fears to afflict her good Angel, and when she is very good, she says to me with inexpressible pleasure, God protects me, and my guardian Angel is satisfied with me. I also often speak to her of the evil spirits, made so by pride and ingratitude, whom the Divine Judge precipitated from Heaven to the bottom of the dark abyss, a frightful gulph, the eternal abode of the wicked! Adelaide knows, that this infernal spirit is only employed for our destruction; that he caused the first fall of man; and that it is he who prompts us to the crime of failing in our engagements and resolutions; and teaches us to be vain of the gifts of Nature, which Heaven has bestowed on us. Teach Constantia all these things in conversing with her; for this kind of instruction ought to precede the Catechism, which you thought it your duty to teach her, when she was only six or seven years old. Let her know, in reading the Catechism to her, that the mysteries there mentioned are above human understanding. That God has made us *to love him, but not to comprehend his greatness.* That we are too limited in our ideas, to dare to maintain, that every thing we do not understand is false; since throughout human nature all is mysterious, and appears a prodigy; and as Montaigne says, speaking of our incredulity on indifferent things, 'That it is a dangerous courage and may be attended with bad consequences, besides the absurdity, which it draws one into, of not believing what we do not understand.'[85]

These are the methods I have taken with Adelaide to awaken, as you say, her conscience. I have also made use of other means to produce this effect, which perhaps may appear to you to be trifling, but of the success of which I am certain. It is ridiculous to tell children, that a little finger can inform you of every thing they do in private, because it is both folly and falsehood. But I tell Adelaide, when she does not answer me with sincerity, I see it plainly in her countenance; and in truth it is so, for, when you know children thoroughly, it is very easy to read in their eyes all that they think. By this means she is never tempted to disguise the truth from me, certain that I should always penetrate through it. Besides by means of repeating to her, that I am sure she would not commit a real fault, even if she was certain I should not discover it, I persuade her, and it is really true, that she is not guilty of any without feeling a desire to communicate it to me. The reason for which is very plain, exclusively of those I have already given you; she thinks this lessens her fault in the eye of Heaven, and is a proof of her confidence in me which she supposes will attach me still more to her. In short, my dear friend, let Religion be the foundation on which you build, or you will have no lasting effects. Endeavour at the same time to give your scholar a command over herself; you will then succeed to your utmost wishes; and your labour will not be destroyed by passion, or by bad examples.

I have read those letters of Lord Chesterfield's, and think the remarks you have made on them are perfectly just: but, if he had not been so severe on the women, you would have praised many things in his book, which now you have not mentioned. Is it not striking, for example, that a man like him engaged in the service of his King and country, employed by the State, and given up to ambition, should write such long and interesting as well as instructive letters, to his son, who was only eight years old: containing abridgements of Mythology, and History, very well written: and that this correspondence, during the course of twenty years, should be so punctually kept up, and so well connected? I agree with you, it would have been better for him to have educated his son himself, and not to have been separated from him so long. But this son was illegitimate, which adds more merit to what Lord Chesterfield did for him; besides this, we find in his Letters many excellent sentiments, a perfect knowledge of the human heart, learning, wit, sense, and found reasoning. In short I think it ought to be looked upon as a Work valuable in many respects, and an affecting proof of paternal tenderness.

How was it possible, my dear friend, you could go to the entertainment given by Mons. de Blesac? And how could you resolve to see a second performance of such plays? You, who I always thought was so remarkable for your love of decency? Is it possible that you could sacrifice your inclination and principles to that trifling and ridiculous fear of being called a prude by people whose reproaches are rather to be considered as praises? *You are thirty-two years old, and your reputation is established!* In the first place, you are not past the age, in which you may lose it; and have you obtained it merely to free yourself from your attentions to that kind of behaviour, which ought most to be respected? On the contrary, reflect that, in order to preserve it, you must act in the same manner you acted to obtain it: and remember, that bad examples set us by those we esteem, are the only ones which are really dangerous. If Mons. de Blesac had only invited women of doubtful characters, there certainly would not have been a second representation of these plays; a general cry would have been raised against such an indecency, and they would have been thought what they really were. But when it was known, that some persons of unblemished character were present at these performances, the world would form a very different opinion. Thus you have contributed a great evil, that of rendering indecency less disgusting and less odious: that is, in the general opinion; for there are still remaining many good minds, who judge of actions as they really are, and not by the people who do them. In short, what an example is this for your daughter, who is going to be introduced into the world? When you recommend prudence and discretion to her, with the most scrupulous attention to decency and modesty, of what weight will your admonitions be on these articles? ... Forgive me, my dear friend, these reproaches made with so much severity. I look forward with grief to all the consequences of your indiscretion, and I am too sincerely concerned to think of my expressions. Friendship betrays, when she flatters on subjects of such importance; and I had rather run the risk of displeasing you, than conceal from you these useful truths. And, now after having preached a long sermon to you, I am going in my own and Madame de Valmont's name to thank you for all your goodness to Cecilia; and to ask of you a new favour. We read to Mons. d' Aimeri that paragraph of your last letter, in which you mention the impression which seeing the world and being introduced to company has made on Cecilia. This account gave great pleasure to Mons. d' Aimeri, who, since the death of his son, has constantly reproached himself with having sacrificed the unfortunate Cecilia. He is so severely punished by this reflection, that it is impossible not to pity him almost as much as the poor victim herself! and the more so, as he speaks himself of this error, never to be remedied, with a frankness and penitence which renders him as interesting as is possible for any one to be, after having committed such a fault. Since his misfortune he has devoted himself to religion; and his piety, which is solid as it is sincere, adds still more to the remorse, by shewing him the injustice of which he has been guilty. He is not ignorant, that Cecilia loved the Chevalier de Murville; he thinks of her continually. He paints her to himself, as she was when he sent her back to the convent, possessed of all the charms of youth and beauty. This affecting image, he tells me, pursues him in all places, and at all times; and inspires him with such tender pity, that he declares he feels the same affection for Cecilia, that ever he felt for Madame de Valmont. Nevertheless he has not been able to resolve to see her, since her profession; although he has a thousand times intended it. But he writes to her; he doubles her pension, and sends her every year, in the greatest plenty, every present that can be useful or acceptable to a nun. Cecilia, whose gentle heart only wished to attach him to her, feels the tenderest affection for him, which she shews in all her letters to him, and in the most affecting manner possible; which cannot but aggravate the grief and repentance of her unhappy father. She has concealed from him with the utmost caution her bad state of health, and did not inform him of her journey to Paris, till the moment when she was going to set out. This news overwhelmed Mons. d' Aimeri with grief, as well on account of Cecilia's illness, as from the fear which he conceived, lest the slight knowledge she was going to acquire of the world, and the seeing her sister possessed of riches, magnificence, and prosperity, might make her more sensible of her own misfortunes. Your letter, having put an end to these fears, has redoubled his esteem and affection for Cecilia. He is no longer torn by remorse, since he finds his daughter is at last contented with her situation; and he now passionately wishes to see her. So that, my dear friend, if you could obtain for us five or six months more liberty for Cecilia, instead of returning to her Convent she might come here, and spend the summer; and you would thus be the means of conferring great happiness on her father and Madame de Valmont. Adieu, my dear friend! Let me have an answer on this subject as soon as you can. Just as I was closing my letter, I very fortunately recollected the questions you asked me concerning Madame de Valmont's son. Since I have not mentioned him to you in a particular manner, you ought to conclude that I had formed no particular scheme for the future. In point of fortune, my daughter has a right to expect a better match: in other respects, though Mons. de Valmont does not go to Court, yet he has every qualification necessary to his being presented. His family, though not noble, is very ancient, and cannot be accused of having demeaned itself by improper marriages; a merit, which at this time of day few families can boast; and which at least proves that their ancestors thought nobly. To return to Charles, he is really an elegant youth, and I think I can give you some idea of him by telling you, he is extremely like Cecilia. Above all he has great good sense, much sensibility, a lively imagination, and judgement far above his age. Yet he appears at first to be reserved; and is serious in his manner. He has had a very good education from his grandfather. But he is only thirteen years old, and has very strong passions; and if he should lose Mons. d' Aimeri, before he comes into the world, he may perhaps disappoint the hopes his friends have conceived of him. Adieu, my dear friend! I intreat you do every thing in your power to send Cecilia to us, and you will greatly oblige me.

LETTER XXXII.

From the Viscountess, in Answer.

AH! my dear friend, I am so afflicted, so agitated, that I can only hope to compose my spirits by writing to you. I have just had such a dreadful dispute with Mons. de Limours ... I have already told you that I was sure Madame de

Gerville would endeavour to marry my daughter to whom she chose ... And who do you think they have proposed to me? The son of her friend; of a woman, if possible, still more contemptible than herself: in short, it is Madame de Valcy, disgraced by so many bad actions, whom they would make the mother-in-law of my daughter! ...

Mons. de Limours began the subject by mentioning the family of Mons. de Valcy, which is indeed honourable, and boasted of his fortune, his person, &c. &c. I at last replied, But, Sir, do you not imagine, that my daughter has a hundred times heard of the shocking behaviour of Madame de Valcy? ... We are not obliged to take our mothers-in-law for patterns; and we should often succeed better, if we did not follow the example of our mothers. This ill-natured reply vexed me beyond all expression. The conversation grew warm; and I declared I would never give my consent to the marriage; and that this was my determined resolution. At these words Mons. de Limours rose up very coolly, and said, 'I was not absolutely fixed on this marriage; but now I shall certainly give my consent to it. I came to consult you about it; but, since you have so perfectly forgot that I am the master of my own child, I ought to prove it to you; and to-morrow you shall be convinced of it.' He then went out, and left me in a passion not to be described. Oh! what tyrants men are! and how soon may the weakest of them become formidable even to the most haughty woman! ... At length, after having uttered many imprecations against the men, after having wept plentifully, rung the bell for all my women, and taken a glass of orange flower-water, I determined to write a letter to Mons. de Limours, to acknowledge my fault, and to intreat him to take some time to reflect on so important an affair. He has just sent me an answer by his Valet de Chambre, that he will see me to-morrow. This must be submitted to; I must wait for to-morrow with patience and submission; and must receive him with mildness and composure ... I am humbled, mortified, and quite confused ... But let us talk of something more pleasing: I have executed your commission, I have obtained liberty for Cecilia till the month of January; she is transported with joy, and sets out on the ninth of May for Languedoc; that is, twelve days hence. Adieu! my dear friend. I am not at this time worthy to hold a longer conversation with you. I send for the Baron a letter from the Chevalier de Herbain, which he read to me yesterday, and which I thought pleasant enough. Though an Epigram of twelve pages appears to me to be rather long, in other respects it must be owned his Criticism is very just, and at least it is impossible to accuse him of exaggeration.

LETTER XXXIII.

From the Chevalier d'Herbain, to the Baron d'Almane.

M Y Voyages are at last finished, my dear Baron; and after five years travel and fatigue I am glad to find myself once more at Paris. But perhaps I shall surprize you by telling you, I find every thing as strange, and as new here, as I should find them at Stockholm or Petersburg; but you shall judge.

I left the men all engaged in gaming, hunting, and their little country retirements.[86] The Ladies I left taken up with the thoughts of their dress, and the arrangement of their suppers: and I find on my return the women all scholars and wits; and the men are every one turned Authors.

Is not this a wonderful change in five years? I did not expect it, I confess to you; and, to give you an idea of my first surprise, I must acquaint you with my adventures the day after I returned. On Monday I went with great eagerness to see my old friend Madame de Surville,[87] who, to be plain with you, I always thought, till now, had much more goodness than understanding.

She received me very politely, and told me I was come quite apropos; for, said she, we are going to have a reading to day ... a reading, replied I; and of what? ... 'Tis a Comedy ... And of whose writing? The Viscount's, answered she, coldly. Now, my dear Baron, I must tell you, when I went to Italy, this Viscount was forty years old, and scarcely knew how to write a letter.

Whilst I was seriously reflecting on this matter, I saw near sixty Gentlemen and Ladies arrive at the house. – Thought I to myself, if the Viscount has been so unlucky as to write a Play, the most he would risk would be to read it before five or six of his intimate friends; but surely he is not going to expose himself to the ridicule of this numerous assembly. Madame de Surville is in jest, she has a mind to impose upon me. But I see by the Ladies dress and their feathers, that we are going to have a ball. I will humour Madame de Surville however, and appear to believe what she says. Presently they brought a large table on which they laid an immensely large green silk bag; good, said I; while they wait for the violins, they are going to play at Biribi.[88] I was mistaken, it was Madame de Surville's work-bag.

The Ladies sent for theirs, and in a short time every body was at work; very soon after the Viscount de Blemont is announced; the Ladies are agitated; they rise to meet him, and overwhelm him with caresses and compliments; they seat him in an arm-chair near the table, on which is placed a large decanter of water. They shut the windows, let down the curtains, stop the pendulums of the clocks; and seat themselves round the Author; who, with a serious and commanding air, cast an eye of self-satisfaction on his audience, took his manuscript out of his pocket, and began. I thought I was in a dream, but my astonishment was to be much more increased. Unfortunately for me the best places were taken; and I was separated from the Reader, by half a dozen Ladies, whose repeated exclamations and sobs absolutely prevented me from hearing a single word of the performance. But I could easily judge the prodigious effect of it by the confused murmurs of applause, and the admiration painted on their countenances: I found the Piece was very pathetic, for every body was in tears, and particularly the Ladies, among whom I was placed. They threw themselves back in their chairs, raising their hands and eyes to Heaven, and the youngest Lady of the company was so violently affected, that she was really quite ill; so that Madame de Surville, who was herself in a dreadful state, ran to her assistance, and was obliged to unlace her. The Viscount, accustomed doubtless to produce similar effects on his audience, only smiled, and continued reading. The Play went on in the same manner; and you may easily conceive the despair I laboured under, at not being able to share in the transports which appeared in every countenance; I was actually in the situation of Tantalus.[89]

When the Viscount had finished, the Ladies all rose and got round him; their passionate gestures, the piercing tone of their voices, the volubility of their speeches, expressed the enthusiasm they were seized with: as for myself, who had nothing to say, having heard nothing; I was much confused, and did not dare to appear before the Viscount with dry eyes and an indifferent countenance: I therefore made my escape, and went into Madame de Surville's apartment, where I purposed staying till the Viscount was gone.

But I was destined this day to meet with things unexpected and surprising. The first thing that struck me on entering the room was a desk covered with books and papers. How, said I, a desk with books in Madame de Surville's apartment! But, however, since it is so, I shall not be tired with staying here alone. The first book I looked into was *A Treatise on Chemistry*, and, as I am no Chymist, I took up another, which was *A Treatise on Philosophy*; finding that too abstruse for me, I opened a third: alas! my dear Baron, it was *A Dictionary of Natural History*. Mortified, and confounded, at not being able to find in the house of a woman (and that woman, Madame de Surville) a book to my mind, I rose from the desk quite out of temper; when I cast my eyes on a small piece of sculpture, which stood on one side of me. It was an altar, raised to *Benevolence*, and ornamented with verses on that subject, which appeared to be full of sentiment.

Turning about, I perceived another group of figures in marble, still more interesting. It was an altar to *Friendship*; and one of the figures, which I knew to be Madame de Surville, was placing a Crown upon it. Oh, my God! cried I, how little did I know Madame de Surville? I was far from thinking her so sensible, so learned, so wise. It is her modesty then which makes her conceal so many amiable qualities, for who that sees, or hears her, would suspect her of possessing them! As I ended this exclamation, the door opened, and in came a large man in black, whom I had observed at the reading, and who, I remarked, was the only one who had neither wept, nor extolled the performance. He had an air of chagrin and moroseness; but we entered into conversation notwithstanding.

This is a charming room, said I, and the more so, as it gives one such ideas of the person to whom it belongs. The black man shrugged up his shoulders, saying, from whence do you come Sir? From Moscow, Sir ... From Moscow! Oh then you are my man, I will instruct you. This apartment, which you may well imagine to be a Temple consecrated to Friendship, to Study, and Meditation, is only a room for parade; all these books spread on the desk are merely designed for ornament, like china on a chimney-piece. Moliere ridiculed the learned women of his age,[90] who were to be sure very absurd, but at least they knew something. Instead of which, ours, at this time, pretend to great knowledge, when they labour under the most profound ignorance. By this discourse I suspected the man to be an original, a kind of satirical, whimsical jester; and I was not deceived in my opinion. But, Sir, answered I, the Ladies of our time, though it is true, they cultivate the Sciences, yet they cannot be accused of pedantry. They make use of no learned expressions, they do not make a parade of what they know ... But Sir ... once more, they know nothing. That sort of pedantry, of which you are speaking, at least supposes some degree of knowledge. But none is necessary to go and see Experiments in Electricity, to attend a course of Chymical Lectures, and to be infinitely amused by it: in short, to listen with an appearance of understanding, and at the same time by now and then putting in a word, to discover their total ignorance. They have in general received very indifferent educations; and, as soon as they are their own mistresses, they read nothing but foolish pamphlets and plays, which completes the corruption of their taste. They lead the most dissipated lives, and pretend to universal knowledge. They affect to understand painting and architecture. They suppose themselves judges of the principal Opera-singers, or performers, without knowing a note of music. They go to Court, ride on horseback, play at billiards, go out hunting, drive about in their carriages, spend the night at assemblies, or playing at Pharo,[91] write at least ten billets in a day, receive a hundred visits, and shew themselves every-where in the space of twelve hours; at Versailles, at Paris, at the milliners, the Minister's levee, the publick walks, at the shop of a statuary, at the market, the academies, the opera, and the rope-dancers; equally delighted with, and applauding Reville, and Jeannot; d' Auberville,[92] and the Little Devil. Doing so many things, pursued he, how would you have them succeed in any one? Nevertheless they are peremptory in their decisions, and particularly Madame de Surville, who knows not the measure of a verse; and is even ignorant of grammar, or spelling; yet she gives her opinion on Works of Literature; and is vain enough to imagine, the letters she writes to her friends will descend to posterity, like those of Madame de Sevigny.[93]

With regard to their sensibility, it is true, they have ornaments made with their friends hair; they have galleries with their pictures; they have altars and odes dedicated to Friendship; they are continually embroidering cyphers, they talk only of love, friendship, gratitude, and the charms of solitude, &c. and they every one fancy themselves possessed of superior talents.

But do they employ themselves more in the education of their children? Do they live more retired lives than the women of former times, are they more useful, more sensible, or more amiable, than des Houlieres,[94] the Sevignys, the Grafignys?[95] Have they fewer whims, or are they less extravagant, since they are become so benevolent and so learned? You may compare the irregularities of their conduct to those hypocritical devotees, whose religion consists only in out-side shew, who keep an oratory, and relicks, and pray to the Saints, without any love for the Divine Being; who preach to others without correcting their own faults, and blame with great severity those who do not imitate their examples.

During this conversation I stood immoveable, struck with indignation and astonishment, but at last broke silence, and said with an ironical air, The Ladies, Sir, are much to be pitied, having so eloquent and so dangerous an enemy in you. I, their enemy! replied he with eagerness. How ill you judge of me; I naturally esteem and love them. You love them, Sir! I should not have suspected it. Yes, I do love them, and much more than those who flatter and praise them.

In truth, Sir, replied I, they cannot accuse you of flattery or of indifference towards them. I only hate in them, replied he, that which does not belong to them. I would run the risk of displeasing them, to be able to inform them of their real interest. They are formed by Nature to seduce, to interest, and to charm us; and they owe to her those innocent and affecting graces which are embellished with a delicacy of wit and sentiment far superior to ours. If they would give themselves time to reflect, and not prefer to such estimable and natural qualities these vain and ridiculous pretensions, their society would be preferred to any other. They would be able to give their opinions on works of taste; and their approbation would reward the Author for his labours.

May I venture, Sir, to ask you one question? You say you are a zealous friend to the women, and yet you inveigh bitterly against them. It appears to me, in the first part of your discourse you spoke against Plays. But perhaps you may not like them the less for what you said. That is quite another matter, said he; for I am out of all patience with theatrical performances; and have been so for these last two or three years. Before that time, I used to go to the Theatre on those nights when they acted good Pieces; but now the Drama pursues one every-where. We meet with it in all societies, and all families; for every body think themselves able to form a dialogue out of any novel, or even out of a common anecdote;

nor suppose it at all requisite, that they should possess any superior talents, or knowledge of the human heart, or even of the Theatre itself; in short, every body is employed in this way; and I have two sisters, who at this time compose Comedies with the same ease, with which two years ago they made purses. I thought, said I, that *plays* were rather out of fashion. Not at all! but, as they have been much ridiculed, the title is banished: but as that species of writing is convenient, they will always subsist, and are composed more than ever; only they call them by the old name, Comedy, which indeed is much better.

What, Sir, was this then a Play, which was read to us to-day? Why, now do you think, replied he, that a man of the world, who has the duties of his station to attend to, who has neither renounced gallantry, ambition, play, nor amusements, can find time to compose a Play that is tolerable? Why had not people in Moliere's time this passion for writing? Because this dramatic taste was not then in existence, and because it was thought necessary to have genius, united with deep study, in order to produce a good Comedy; and neither the one, or the other, are now made use of to produce an unformed collection of little romantic facts, full of repetitions, without plot, without character, and wholly void of probability. In short, if Moliere had been either a soldier, a magistrate, or a courtier, he would not have presented the world with his Theatrical Works; or, if that employment had been an agreeable one, he would not have produced his *Tartuffe*,[96] or his *Misanthrope*.[97] What causes this universal pretension to wit, which we have all acquired? Half the world write, and read their Works to the other half, who, pleased by this confidence, blindly bestow their approbation. We are to conclude all these Works are perfect; for I have never seen one of them, which fell under the hands of criticism. The hearers are always satisfied; and the success of these readings is certain. Men in these times judge only of living Authors, and scarcely approve of any other, but those whom they can imitate, which insensibly vitiates their taste. This is so true, that the greatest part of those valuable Works which were written in the age of Louis le Grand,[98] are no longer esteemed; and if Telemachus, or the Poems of Madame des Houlieres[99] were new productions, they would be found very insipid. We can no longer perceive the beauties of a deep, though simple plot, of a style pure and natural; and verses, full of harmony, softness, and sensibility; but, devoid of points and metaphysics, appear insipid, and tiresome.

Out of all patience, my dear Baron, with these foolish declamations, I again interrupted my severe critic, and said to him, with some earnestness. What signifies the Sheep, or the Pastorals of Madame des Houlieres? Let us come back to the present times: tell me, if you please, what you think of the Viscount's Play? I can only, said he, speak about the first act, as the other four drew me into the sweetest sleep I ever had in my life. Sir, said I, in an ironical tone, this is a new, and remarkable method of criticising indeed. – Alas! it is no criticism; it is the real truth, I assure you. I shall depend much on your opinion, replied I; when I saw sixty people in raptures, and bathed in tears, and you the only person dissatisfied with the performance: you must permit me to conclude your judgment none of the best. Besides I flatter myself that the Viscount will soon have his book printed, and then perhaps the opinion of the Public ... Have it printed, interrupted he? Do you think a man of his rank would have his Work printed? Oh fie! this would indeed be setting himself up to ridicule. But, Sir, when a person reads his performance to an audience of sixty persons, I have the honour to inform you, Sir, that, should he be foolish enough to read them to a hundred of his friends, he would not be prevailed on to print them ... But why, Sir? said I ... Ah; why! said he, smiling: it is because we always have a secret instinct in our hearts, which, in spite of false opinions and unjust flattery, tells us when we have done wrong; and this sentiment the Viscount feels too strongly to suffer his Works to be printed.

As he finished these words, I found myself out of all patience; and quitting him very abruptly, I went to rejoin Madame de Surville, whom I found alone, and at her toilette. She thought I was gone home, and was surprised to see me. I told her all that had happened to me; and you will naturally suppose, I did not spare the unmerciful critic, who had provoked me so long. He is a Misanthrope, said Madame de Surville, and tires one to death; he is dull, tedious, obstinate, full of whims, and besides has not common sense. But, added she, rising, I must go out; when shall I see you again ... To-morrow morning, if you will give me leave. Ah, to-morrow! that is not possible, I am going to the academy, to hear there my brother's speech on his reception there ... How, the Marquis de Solanges received into the French academy? Yes; and I assure you he has not solicited this honour: you know his disposition. No one will accuse him of having any pretensions; he is simplicity itself. I think you will be very well pleased with his speech. Well then, Madame, to-morrow afternoon, replied I, leading her out ... No, said she; I shall then have my English master. Wednesday, the Author of a new Play, has desired me to be present at the rehearsal. Thursday, I go to Greuse's, to see his Danaë.[100] Friday, I attend some experiments on fixed air; but on Saturday I shall be at liberty ... After having given me this invitation, she got into her carriage; and I returned home, amazed and confounded at every thing I had this day met with; in order that I might reflect on it at my leisure.

At seven o'clock I went to the French Comedy; I was in Madame de Semur's box, whom I found just going out, as the fifth act of *Rodugune*[101] was beginning. She told me she was going to see acted *Les Battus payent l' Amende*, as were also three or four persons who were with her. I asked if it was a Play. At this question they all cried out, What, do you not know *Les Battus payent l' Amende*! Come with us, you will be charmed with it. At these words, they took me with them, and conducted me to a horrid kind of Theatre; but, where the best company in

Paris were assembled. They played a little Farce, which was agreeable enough, and was called *Le Cafe des Halles*.[102] I confess I could not enjoy all its pleasant-ries, because the language was entirely new to me. Yet I found that the actress, who personated the principal low character, performed it in a very superior man-ner. But the *Battus payent l' Amende*, quite confounded me. The contents of a certain utensil[103] thrown on the head of Jeannot, the hero of the Piece, produced the most striking effects I ever saw, and the moment when Jeannot smells his sleeve, and says, ''tis so,' is not possible for me to describe, as it excited transports and applause for near a quarter of an hour. This Piece has already been acted a hundred and fifty times, and is now as much crouded as on the first day. Let them after this say the French are changeable. I have many other things, my dear Baron, to tell you; but I reserve them till I have the pleasure of paying you a visit; and believe me, they are not less interesting or curious, than those I have already related; but I think it not prudent to trust them by the post.

LETTER XXXIV.

Baroness d' Almane to the Viscountess.

CECILIA arrived here yesterday; I found her exactly what you described, ami-able and interesting beyond all expression; and it is very true that her nephew Charles is extremely like her. The whole family are come hither to stay a week with us. I was very desirous of being present at the first interview between her and her father; and I never saw any thing which affected me more. Mons. d' Aimeri wished for, yet dreaded the moment. He rose yesterday before day-light; and, when he came to our house, I could easily perceive by his countenance what a dreadful night he had passed. After dinner, we got into our carriage, Madame de Valmont, Mons. d' Aimeri, and I, in order to meet Cecilia. Mons. d' Aimeri was pale and trembling, he appeared to labour under the most cruel constraints; he avoided our looks, and seemed to wish to conceal the dreadful emotions which tore him to pieces. I saw he dreaded the impression which he feared the affecting sight of his poor victim would make upon us; and that he feared the presence of Cecilia would destroy all the compassion we had felt for him. As long as he could flatter himself with our being deeply interested for his sufferings, he spoke of them very freely; but now, having lost his hope, he endeavoured to dissemble, persuading himself that, in finding his remorse, he should conceal some part of his fault. We had scarce gone two leagues, when Madame de Valmont, on seeing a carriage, cried out, 'Here comes my sister.' Mons. d' Aimeri alternately turned pale and red; and, seeing that Madame de Valmont wept, he said to her, with a very angry and tremulous voice, *What, Madam, are you going to act a scene in a Tragedy*? Surprized at the manner in which he spoke, and more so with the wild, fierce, and gloomy air of his countenance, Madame de Valmont wiped away her tears, without being able to account for his sudden ill humour. By this time the other coach had stopped. I immediately drew the check-string of mine. Mons. d' Aimeri, who was scarce able to stand, got out; and at that instant I heard a most affecting scream, which undoubtedly must have pierced the heart of Mons. d' Aimeri. Cecilia, the lovely Cecilia, had thrown herself into her father's arms, and fell fainting on his neck. At this sight Mons. d' Aimeri saw nothing but Cecilia; he even forgot his grief. Nature resumed all her powers over his mind, a flood of tears fell to relieve him. He called his daughter by the most tender names. He pressed her to his bosom. His knees trembled, and bent under him. He almost lost the use of his senses. Madame de Valmont and I wanted to assist him in supporting Cecilia. He pushed us away; he snatched a smelling-bottle out of Madame de Valmont's hand which she held to her sister for her to smell to. He would take the whole care of her himself. He watched for the moment when she would open her eyes. He sent every one away from her who came near her. In short, he seemed afraid any one should rob him of her first look ... I cannot undertake to paint to you the affecting scene which followed on Cecilia's recovering her senses; and you will much better imagine than I can describe her joy and transport, in finding herself in the arms of her father and sister. The painful and melting sorrow which oppressed her father, the tenderness of Madame de Valmont, the share I took in every thing that concerned them all three, and the curiosity with which I observed their emotions. Above all, I admired the delicacy of our amiable Cecilia. She saw the remorse which rent her father's heart; and she took the utmost pains to lessen it, by affecting to appear chearful, by speaking of her taste for solitude, which she says is much increased by the little she has been able to judge of the world. In short, by praising her Convent, and the friends she has there. Mons. d' Aimeri eagerly listens to her conversation; it is easy to perceive he tries to persuade himself she is sincere in what she says; and he then seems to be a thousand times more affectionate, as if he wished to shew his gratitude to her, for endeavouring to justify his conduct in our eyes, as well as in his own.

For my part, I am convinced Cecilia has made up her mind, and that she is entirely resigned to her fate. Yet she is only seven-and-twenty years old; so beautiful, and still so young, with a heart so tender, and an imagination so lively, how can one hope she will be entirely free from every kind of regret? ... I walked with her a little while alone this morning; we talked of indifferent things, among others of the beauty of the present month. She sighed, and said, to-day is the sixteenth of May; it is just ten years since I took the vows. These words were accompanied with a look which penetrated my heart, especially the words *six-*

teenth of May, on which she laid such an emphasis. There was something in her manner which was truly affecting! However, she soon changed the conversation, and seemed to resume her accustomed tranquility. Madame de Valmont and I agreed it would be right, if possible, to procure her some kind of amusement for the rest of the day, in order to banish from her mind the dreadful remembrance of the *sixteenth of May*. In consequence of this, we are all to go, after dinner, to the house of Nicole, the young farmer, of whom I have spoke to you so frequently. This is one of our favourite airings. The house is really delightful, both from its situation, and the particular neatness with which it is kept; and the garden is well worth seeing at this season. You who love natural rivulets, flowers, and grass walks, would find it a thousand times more agreeable than all those gardens formed after the English fashion, which are found within the walls of Paris.[104]

My children are both very proud of the compliments you pay to their drawings; and you may be very sure neither of the heads they sent you were ever retouched by their master. We have established a little kind of drawing academy here, which greatly excites emulation in Adelaide and Theodore. One of our neighbours, who lives only half a league from hence, sends his three children here every day, and Dainville teaches them to draw. A grand-daughter of one of our servants learns also; and Charles attends our little academy at least three times a week. They all meet together in a room appropriated for the purpose, and with Adelaide and Theodore all receive instruction in this art from Dainville, who takes great pains to improve them. We call it our academy, and I am the President of it; and have instituted rules which are to inforce application, attention, and silence. This assembly is open to every body who has any inclination to see them at their work; but it is expressly forbid that any one of the pupils should either look at, or speak a single word to those who enter into it.

Adelaide does not accompany us to-day in our visit to Nicole. She is doing penance, and I will tell you the cause. Dainville has taken it into his head, that Miss Bridget is like the Emperor Vespasian[105] one of the medallions in the saloon, where the Roman History is represented. In fact there is striking resemblance; but Miss Bridget did not approve this comparison, and is very angry with Dainville, who, to revenge himself, has made a copy of the Emperor, and placed upon his head a large bonnet, which has made the picture so exceedingly like Miss Bridget, that it was known by every body in the house. Adelaide asked for this drawing, and fixed it against the hanging. Miss Bridget, coming into Adelaide's room this morning, saw this unfortunate profile, which she immediately tore in a thousand pieces; and, taking Adelaide by the hand, brought her to me. She was in so great a passion, and stammered in so strange a manner, that she could neither in French nor English make me comprehend the cause of her anger. I begged her to leave me alone with my daughter, and then Adelaide explained the whole affair. When she had finished, I said to her, 'Is it out of regard to Miss Bridget that you have placed this drawing in your own chamber? At this question Adelaide blushed, cast down her eyes, and said very softly, 'No, mamma.' – Then you did it out of ill-nature? – But why should Miss Bridget be so angry that she resembles Vespasian, who was so good an Emperor? You have told me, mamma, that we ought never to mind what people say about our persons. – But, if Miss Bridget should have this weakness, ought you to let her see you ridicule her? I think Mons. Dainville much to blame for having continued a joke that was so disagreeable to Miss Bridget; for Madame de Lambert, in her *Advice from a Mother to a Son*, has said very justly, 'That the person we attack has the sole right of judging whether we are in jest; as soon as one feels one's self wounded, it is no longer raillery, it is offence.'[106] No joke can be innocent that is offensive. Therefore Mons. Dainville is much to blame; but can his fault be compared to yours? You, who owe friendship, respect, and gratitude to Miss Bridget, you make her uneasy, *you* laugh at that which gives her pain, and *you* wish to make her appear ridiculous. If you was a few years older, this fault, which is a very serious one, would prove at the same time that you had a bad heart, and that you wanted understanding. At these words Adelaide burst into tears. – Ah, mamma, how shall I repair my fault! ... In shewing Miss Bridget a sincere repentance. However, do not flatter yourself with gaining her pardon in one day. She had a very sincere affection for you; but you have just given her so bad a proof of your disposition, that she is well authorized to doubt whether you have any regard for her, and ... Oh! she knows very well that I love her ... She cannot read it in your heart; she can only judge from your actions; and you have treated her with so much ingratitude! ... But I am only a child ... So far she will judge you as such, and not without forgiveness; but she will entertain doubts and suspicions, which you may easily put an end to in time. And, if you was not a child, you would this day have lost for ever the affection both of your mamma and Miss Bridget too. – Oh, my dear mamma, you then have doubts of me? ... I confess to you, your behaviour has both surprised and afflicted me, I had an opinion so different of you! ... I should not have supposed Miss Bridget would have been offended at Dainville's pleasantry, because that which neither affected her character nor disposition ought never to make us angry. But, as soon as I saw it had had such an effect on her, I should have endeavoured to conceal it from every body; I should have shared her uneasiness, though it was not well grounded; because every body who think themselves ill-treated have a right to the compassion of good people. For instance, there are persons who have been allowed, by the negligence of their parents, to take the most absurd and uncommon prejudices; and I know a Lady who fainted away at the sight of a cat! ... A cat! ... Yes, it was really true: and she was much to be pitied, for two reasons; first for the pain she suffered, and next for having been so badly brought up. I have often thought, if I had had no better education than she had, I should have been guilty either of that, or of some similar folly; and I was not weak enough to suppose I had more sense than she had; on the contrary, I thanked Heaven, who had given me parents that were attentive, sensible, and affectionate; and I pitied this poor Lady from my heart. I ended this conversation, which I have greatly shortened by telling Adelaide she must not go with us to Nicole's house, and that for three days she must dine and sup in her own chamber. She received this severe punishment with great composure and perfect submission; for she well knew that the smallest murmur would prolong her punishment, therefore she heard it with as much mildness as concern. I have settled it with Miss Bridget, that it shall be at least six weeks before she treats Adelaide in the manner she used to do. She is to tell her, she has no anger remaining against her; but that it is impossible to rely on the affection of a person who has treated her with so little regard. And I, on my part, shall tell the poor guilty but repenting Adelaide, 'you see what this giddiness has cost you.' For the sake of a joke, which could only afford you half an hour's diversion, you have lost the affection of a person who ought to be very dear to you; altered the opinion which I entertained of you; and in short have rendered yourself suspected by every body; and have brought on yourself a punishment, which is to last three days.

LETTER XXXV.

From the same to the same.

I HAVE been a long time, my dear friend, without writing to you; but, since my last letter, I have been witness to a most melancholy scene, the dreadful consequences of which, affected me so much, that I have not been in a capacity to inform you of what you will be very anxious to hear, when I inform you it is relative to the unfortunate Cecilia. Alas! how much is she to be pitied at this time! ... And, you shall judge, whether, at any time of her life, she was more worthy of exciting your compassion. I told you in my last letter the expression which escaped Cecilia on the subject of her profession, which was made on the sixteenth of May (a day, which has now proved itself doubly fatal to her repose!) and that we purposed, in order to divert her thoughts from this melancholy reflection, to carry her to the house of Nicole. We set out about five o'clock in the afternoon, Mons. d' Aimeri, Mons. and Madame de Valmont, Cecilia, Mons. d' Almane, Charles, Theodore, and myself, all in one carriage. I perceived Cecilia took very little share in the conversation, but she appeared to take great pleasure in admiring the beauties of the country, and the different prospects which offered themselves to her view. A sigh now and then escaped her, and seemed to say, how happy are those who are not deprived of the liberty of contemplating so beautiful a sight! ... When we came within a short distance of Nicole's house, Madame de Valmont proposed our walking the rest of the way, in order, she said, to surprise these good people in the midst of their employment. We got out of our carriage, and, having crossed a large meadow, and passed through a double row of willows, we arrived at the house. This little habitation is thatched with straw, and is situated in the midst of a tolerably sized garden, surrounded by a hedge of hawthorn in full bloom. The fruits were beautiful, the prospect delightful, the air was perfumed with sweets: little streams of transparent and running water crossed in serpentine forms the walks of turf, which were full of violets and wild thyme. Every thing conspired to make this little country dwelling the most delightful habitation in the universe. When we got to the house, Theodore went forward and opened the door, and we all went in. We found the young farmer Nicole seated between her mother and her husband, with her youngest child in her arms, her eldest girl was on her knees before her, caressing her little brother, who was standing with his face carelessly leaning on his father's shoulder. We could have wished for a few minutes to have continued viewing this delightful picture of conjugal love and happiness. But, as soon as the family perceived us, they rose up; and the young woman sent her husband to gather us some flowers. The good old woman went to get some milk and cream, and to spread the table. Whilst this was doing, we admired the order and neatness of the house, took notice of the children, and the farmer's wife talked to us of her happiness and her affection for her family. Her husband soon returned with a basket filled with nosegays. They presented us with fruits, flowers, and the produce of their dairy. And, while these good people were anxiously and busily employed about us, Mons. d'Aimeri perceived that Cecilia was no longer seated near him. He found her retired to a distant corner of the room: he approached her; the unfortunate girl turned her head ... He looked at her; she was pale and trembling, and her face was bathed in tears; she would have spoke, but her sobs stifled her. Madame de Valmont ran to her; and Cecilia, in the utmost confusion and despair, said, as well as she could, but in a voice scarcely intelligible: Oh, my sister, take me from hence or I shall die ... Madame de Valmont, as much astonished as afflicted, was wholly at a loss to penetrate the cause of Cecilia's present unhappy situation. Her father had but too easily guessed the truth; and, not being able to support the dreadful sight, he on a sudden took Charles by the hand, and drawing him along with him; he went out of the house in great displeasure. Monsieurs d'Almane and Valmont followed him with the intention of overtaking him, and of returning back to the castle on foot. At length we took Cecilia from this house which had proved so fatal to her, and got into our carriage; she did not speak a word the whole way, but rested her head on her bosom, and her eyes were half closed. Penetrated with grief at her situation, I attempted to take her hand and kiss it; but she kept it still, with a gloomy pensive air, and remained motionless, regarding nobody. One of the most fatal effects of despair is that of hardening the heart, and making it insensible of the compassion it inspires. However, Cecilia's is naturally so tender, that she soon repented the indifference she had just shewn me, and, when we arrived at the castle, she pressed my hand, and embraced me with the greatest tenderness. As soon as I left the two sisters alone, and at liberty to converse with each other, Cecilia, guessing the curiosity of Madame de Valmont, threw herself into her arms; saying, 'Learn, my dear sister, all that has passed in my heart, and that it is pierced with a dart which death only can remove! ... I saw in that cottage the picture of happiness, which I could not keep myself from envying; in that moment a vile sentiment of bitter jealousy poisoned my mind! I saw you smiling at the felicity you was witness to. But this sight, so pleasing in your eyes, served only to make me more sensible of the horror of my destiny, and to convince me still more of the extent of the cruel sacrifice I have made. Alas! this woman is in the midst of her children, in the arms of a tender mother and beloved husband! ... And I, unhappy as I am, was deprived of my mother almost at my birth, banished by my father, torn from all I loved, condemned to oblivion, to slavery, and forced to renounce the sweetest sentiments of Nature! ... Oh! my sister, whither did you carry me? Ought you to have shewn me this delightful image of happiness, which I am so wretched, that I can never enjoy or even hope for! ... Ah! why was not I born in an inferior rank, like this happy woman? ... I could also have loved ... This unfortunate heart would have been as innocent, as it is affectionate; and then, remorse, frightful remorse, would have been unknown to me, and all those sentiments, which now destroy me, would have contributed to my felicity!'

Madame de Valmont could only reply with her tears to these affecting and just complaints. But, when she saw Cecilia appear a little more calm, she seized that moment to say every thing to her, which her understanding and her affection dictated. Cecilia heard her with mildness and attention, and expressed the most anxious fear of afflicting her father; she promised to banish these dreadful reflections, if possible from her mind, and endeavour to submit to her destiny, with the resolution and fortitude she had hitherto shewn. When Mons. d' Aimeri arrived, she went to meet him, she had even resolution enough to talk to him, almost jokingly of the scene they had been witness to, and attributed it only to her being suddenly taken ill: Mons. d' Aimeri who was brought back by Mons. d' Almane almost in despair, began to recover himself, and to believe at least, that the impression she had received would soon go off again.

At night she sat down to supper, eat as usual, and talked a great deal. She put such a constraint on herself, that every one, except myself, was deceived by her. I had much rather have seen her melancholy and silent, than so lively and animated. I was convinced she did great violence to her feelings; and the redness which coloured her cheeks, the vivacity which appeared in her eyes, and a certain eagerness that I perceived in all her motions, made me certain she was then in a fever. We went to bed soon after supper, and I had not been there above an hour, when I heard somebody knock gently at my door. I rose instantly, and found it was Madame de Valmont, who, drowned in tears, told me her sister had a violent fever, and was in a frightful delirium. I immediately sent to Carcassonne[107] for a physician; who did not arrive till five in the morning, at which time we called Mons. d' Aimeri, not chusing before to disturb his rest, and dreading the effect which the sight of Cecilia in such a situation would have on him; for, besides her dangerous illness, the unhappy Cecilia, in her delirium, was continually repeating the name of the Chevalier de Murville, and with tears intreating him to come *once more to see her before she died!* At other times, when she seemed less distracted, she asked her sister what was become of him; and, obtaining only tears for answers, she cried out in the greatest terror, *He is dead, he has been killed, and, no doubt, my father has done it!* ... At these words, the most dreadful convulsions agitated and disfigured her countenance, and seemed as if they would put an end to her miserable life. In short, while she was under these shocking deliriums, she discovered all the sentiments and ideas which she had concealed in her bosom for these ten years past. You may judge of the state of her father on hearing them. It affected him so deeply, that he appeared quite insensible. Grief, when carried to the highest excess, seldom discovers itself by any outward appearances. It is silent, it overwhelms, it oppresses, and, not hoping for consolation, it avoids making complaint. At present the physician declares that Cecilia is in very great danger; and that it will be necessary, the moment she recovers her senses, for her to receive the Sacraments. On hearing this, Mons. d' Aimeri turned pale, and cried out, 'recover her senses! ... And, if she should die without recovering them!' ... It is impossible to give you any idea of the horror and affliction which was painted on his countenance, when he repeated these words ... The unhappy man, penetrated with the sublime truths or religion, saw himself at this moment the author of his child's death, and perhaps the cause of her eternal condemnation! ... Terrified, and almost out of his senses, he sent for a Priest, and made him stay in an adjoining room! ... In the evening, Cecilia all at once became more calm, and by degrees perfectly recovered her senses. Mons. d' Aimeri approached, and embraced her; Cecilia looked around her with astonishment, and said, I have been very ill ... Am I out of danger? We do not fear for your life, we only fear for your peace of mind, said her father, and we have sent for a Priest ... A Priest! ... Ah, am I in a situation! ... No, I will not see him ... How, my child, reflect on your danger! ... Ah, my father, if you knew my heart! ...No ... I have lost all hopes of pardon. At these words, Mons. d' Aimeri trembled; and looking at his daughter with a countenance, in which terror, astonishment, and tender affection were united: oh! my daughter, cried he, you pierce my very soul! ... And, what have you to fear? ... Be composed, God always pardons involuntary errors ... No; you have nothing to reproach yourself with ... You, alas! are an innocent victim, and I am the guilty! ... Yes, continued he, throwing himself on his knees, thy unhappy father ought alone to experience such terrors. It is he that will be punished for every sigh which escapes thee, and for the despair which fills thy broken heart; in short, every error of thine will fall upon my guilty head. As he finished these words, Cecilia, almost choked with her tears, threw both her arms around her father's neck, and laid her face close to his. Oh, have done, said she, with this fatal discourse. Lament no more on my account. My father, my dear father, you love me; you have made amends for every thing. Pardon a moment's distraction ... This heart, returned again to itself, shall be devoted only to God and to you ... The Priest ... where is he? Let him come ... Assure yourself, my father, he will find me full of confidence and resignation ... It is upon this dear hand, my father's hand, that I now swear it ... Compose yourself ... If you will snatch me from death ... I will be content to live ... I will live for your sake ... When Cecilia had ended these words, she addressed herself to Madame de Valmont, to send her Confessor to her, and we all left the room. She received the Sacraments the same day; and the night after she slept tolerably, and in four-and-twenty hours was out of danger; so that by the end of the week she was able to return home to Madame de Valmont. She has now been gone a fortnight, in which time I have seen her frequently. She is very much altered, and extremely thin. But she says she is very well. You can perceive no alteration in her disposition. She is perfectly chearful in company. But I know her resolution, and the command she has over herself so well, that I greatly fear she is in a much more dangerous state than people imagine. Mons. de Valmont alone his recovered his chearfulness, since Cecilia has been growing better; not that he has an unfeeling heart, but because he does not yet know the real cause of his sister's illness, or the affliction of Mons. d' Aimeri. He never supposed any other reason for Cecilia's being ill at the cottage, than that she had a violent pain in her stomach. And it never entered into his head, that the presence of Nicole could make her weep or give her a fever. With this superficial manner of viewing things, you may easily imagine, that there are many circumstances in which he appears equally imprudent and troublesome: so that, for this last fortnight, Mons. d' Aimeri, Mons. d' Almane and I have been provoked with him a hundred times, without his ever being able to guess the cause. As to Madame de Valmont, she never appears to take any notice of his folly. I admire her conduct extremely in this respect. She takes the only method which a polite and sensible woman ought to follow, which is that of not appearing to be distressed, at what such a husband does that is wrong; in this case, disimulation is justifiable, and to appear blind is also a proof of merit, which demands respect. So that, though we often were very angry with Mons.

de Valmont, we never expressed it before his wife. Every body respects the good opinion she appears to have of him, therefore she never has the pain of seeing him ridiculed or ill treated; for doubtless, if she appeared to suffer by his absurdities, every body would take the liberty of laughing at him, and even before her face, and she would every day be told how ridiculously he behaved. Thus it is, that women take away all their husband's consequence, and at the same time lose great part of their own. Adieu! my dear friend, let me know if your daughter's marriage with Mons. de Valcy is still in agitation? From your last letter I flatter myself the treaty is at an end; for, if Mons. de Limours promised to take time and reflect on it, I doubt not but you will easily prevail on him to renounce it.

LETTER XXXVI.

The Count de Roseville to the Baron d'Almane.

I THANK you, my dear Baron, for the obliging reproaches you made me on my long silence; I have not been ill, nor have I had any particular business. But I wished to write you a very long letter, and I have not had two hours at my own disposal for these three months past. I can neither rely on a Sub-governor nor Preceptor, therefore never quit my pupil. It is true, I get up two hours before him, and I go to bed an hour after him; but in the morning I prepare his lessons for the day, and in the evening I write a very exact journal of every thing he has done amiss throughout the day, and enumerate every opportunity lost or neglected, when he might have done a good action or have said an obliging thing. As the greatest part of his faults are committed before company, I very seldom take notice of them at the time, which makes him often flatter himself, not having been reproved throughout the day, that the journalist will have nothing to say; I leave him in this uncertainty when he goes to bed: so that he wishes for to-morrow, that he may be satisfied. As soon as he gets up, and is dressed, which he is very little time about, as his curiosity makes him eager to hear, he comes into the room and asks me for my journal, I give it him, and he reads it aloud, which I insist on his doing from beginning to end, and without making any comments as he goes along; for it is a very right thing to accustom him to read an account of his own faults. I then read it a second time, and we communicate to each other the reflections we have made upon it. Thus I not only familiarize him to hear the truth, but to desire it, to like it, and to listen to it quietly, without its having been at all disguised. That you may judge of the manner in which it is presented to him, I will transcribe the journal of the day before yesterday. This is it:

'My Prince at dinner appeared absent, and embarrassed with the persons who made their Court to him. He contented himself with asking them two or three questions, without waiting for their answers. The Prince imagines, that the moment he smiles every body must be delighted with him: but an affected smile, which is nothing more than grimace to which he has used himself, would become very pleasing and agreeable, it he had really the desire of being so, and wished to make himself beloved, without which it appears tiresome and ridiculous. The Prince has forbid Roland, the son of one of his valets, to touch any of books which are in our Study, and this morning, walking on the terrace, we saw young Roland reading very attentively a large book bound in red Morocco; the Prince said to me, I lay a wager, Roland has got the book of your writing which you gave me yesterday. I am sure I know it again. Do not judge too rashly, I replied; let us be certain of it before we accuse him; remember, that in losing your favour this man will lose his fortune, and consequently you would be equally cruel and unjust, were you to judge him merely by appearances. The Prince on going home looked for this book, and could not find it. He sent for Roland, and questioned him about it. Roland blushed, turned pale, and was confused. However, he protested he had not touched the Prince's book, and that which he had been reading was sent him by a relation, to whom he had just returned it, as he was then going back to his own province. This account appeared to the Prince to be nothing more than a made up story, Roland was treated as a deceiver, and was banished the apartments; I suffered this sentence to pass in order to convince the Prince of the consequences of his petulance and rashness, But now I inform him, that the poor disgraced, banished, despairing Roland, is entirely innocent. Every thing he said is exactly true. It was I, who this morning took the book, in order to add some notes to it. So that the Prince has cruelly and falsely accused the unfortunate Roland. It is true, that appearances were against him, but, when the happiness of a man is in question, ought one to judge by appearances? Before you had determined on any thing, you should have enquired the name of his relation; you should even have sent into the country, and have written to him. In short, reason, equity, and humanity ought to have put the Prince on making the most particular enquiries into the truth of this affair.'[108]

I promised you in my last letter to give you my opinion, what are the first principles which ought to be instilled into the mind of a Prince, and what are the chief qualities he ought to be possessed of. I think one cannot too soon inspire him with sentiments of true religion, of the most tender humanity towards his people,[109] and aversion to flattery, and an inclination for truth; and that it is essentially necessary to make them early accustomed to application; and never to judge lightly, or in a hurry, either of good or bad actions.

Yesterday, when the Prince had turned away Roland, he told me he had a great desire to put another young man named Justin in his place; and he added, that he was certain of his being perfectly steady, exact, and prudent, 'And how have you acquired this certainty? Have you studied the character of this young man? Have you put him to any proofs? ... Oh! no, but ... But pray then do not say you are certain, since you cannot bring any proofs; this is talking like a child. – You do not then believe the good qualities of Justin? Who, I? I do not say that I know nothing of him, I never observed him; I am entirely ignorant whether he is worthy or unworthy of your confidence; for, as I am not so weak as a child, I never form an opinion of persons I do not know. But every body speaks well of Justin. – One ought certainly to be prejudiced in favour of a person who is so universally well spoken of, and that of itself is a sufficient foundation for your esteem, yet it would be absurd to depend on that, and to grant him your entire confidence merely from report. No man of sense will do this, till he has proved it by his own particular observation. Never say then, my Prince, I believe, or I do not believe such a thing, because I have been told so, or because it is probable; which is only the language of credulous, trifling, and ignorant people. Always learn to judge for yourself, and never depend on the opinion of others.'

It is impossible that a Prince, thus accustomed from his infancy to examine into the truth of every thing, and not to believe common report, should not acquire at the same time a just way of thinking and acting, together with that kind of judgment which is so necessary to our gaining a knowledge of the human heart. Thus you see how important this principle is; yet it can be of no use to a Prince who is indolent, and will not learn to think for himself. Idleness is more pernicious than even ill-nature, or want of understanding. It is therefore an essential point to use every means to preserve a young Prince from this so dangerous and common a fault, by accustoming him very soon to examine into every thing himself; for it would be a thousand times better he should be distrustful, and have an active mind, than be credulous and indolent. I would also use my utmost endeavours to cure him of that bashfulness and fear which are but too frequently observed in persons of his rank, and which can only be conquered by appearing and speaking frequently in public, and by a desire of appearing amiable. The Prince receives visits twice a day; I never direct him what to say. But, during the time which his company are with him, I fix my eyes on him, and observe him strictly, in order to familiarize him to it. If he speaks ungracefully, or makes use of improper expressions, I reprove him gently, either when we are alone, or in his journal. But, if he does not speak at all, I shame him before every body, and ridicule him in the most striking manner. By this means I engrave a very good principle in his mind, that it is much better to treat your friends with civility, though you do it is an aukward manner, than not to take any notice of them; because at least one should suppose you meant to be polite, however you might fail in the attempt. I have observed that Courtiers are afraid to shew their affability, for fear of appearing to want ease and grace in their manner, and had rather

pass for unpolite, absent, or proud, than be accused of aukwardness. Nevertheless nothing can be more aukward than this way of acting; for, if one tried for six
months to get the better of it, one should very easily acquire those graces which
are so highly valued. We should gain the reputation of being as obliging as amiable; and we should obtain the esteem of every body. 'Few Princes, says the Abbé
Duquet, know what may be done by a kind word, a look, an air of complacency;
and few are acquainted with the effects of the slightest marks of inattention,
in-difference, or coldness. But a wise Prince will know how to distinguish both,
and will never mistake in the use he means to put them to. He will give to his
people every mark of affection and goodness. But, besides this general method
of treating them, he has another which he must proportion to their birth, their
employment, their services, and their merit. He does not treat all alike without
distinction, nor is he prodigal in rewarding those who have not deserved it; neither does he disgrace those who ought to be treated with distinction.'[110]

The same Author says, 'He should wish that a Prince might have eloquence.
Virtue and truth, says he, would receive new lustre from it; it would support a
just sentiment; it would persuade, instead of commanding; it would render every
thing amiable which he proposed; and he would be listened to in his Councils
with admiration, &c.'[111]

Nothing can be more true than this; but, if your scholar absolutely is without
understanding, do not aim at making him eloquent, for you will only render
him pedantic, talkative, and absurd. As to mine, he shews as much sense as it is
possible for a boy of ten years of age to have. I already exercise him in speaking
in his turn without preparation. Every day, after dinner, the persons employed in
his education meet together in his apartment, and every one is obliged to repeat
two histories: one of invention, the other is either taken from Ancient or Modern History. Every fault in the language or pronunciation is a forfeit, and draws
on a punishment which makes this an amusing game to the Prince, especially as
the subgovernor and myself are never spared. We let nothing escape us; if I let fall
a single note, or a reflection which is not perfectly just, the attentive preceptor
immediately interrupts me, and with great politeness makes me remark my error.
Sometimes I do not submit at the first word, but defend myself with mildness,
give them my reasons, and explain myself. The Prince listens attentively to this
dispute, which is very interesting to him, as he is at a loss to know whether I shall
be punished or not; and at the same time he profits by the argument, and sees at
the same time a perfect model of the manner in which one ought to dispute; for
we always keep our temper, and argue with great politeness. In short, we support
our opinions as long as we think proper, and, when we find it of no consequence,
we give it up with great good humour and freedom, which pleases every body
present. The Prince for these three months past has preferred this diversion to
any other; and he reaps all the advantage from it we can desire. He has learned to

express himself much more fluently, and he relates his two histories in a surprising manner, considering his age. With regard to the kind of instruction a Prince should receive, I think he ought to have a general knowledge of History, and particularly that he should understand that of his own country. He should have a clear and distinct idea of the Constitution of the State which he is to govern, that he may know the extent of the rights which he will have over them, to the end that he may support them, and not usurp others. I would have him acquainted with every part of Administration, that, when his education was finished, he should know as much of Military Arts, as Books and Masters could teach him; and he should not content himself with only superficial notions of Navigation or Sea Engagements. In short, I would have him well acquainted with the riches and resources, the necessities and the strength of his kingdom. This you will tell me is requiring a great deal. However, I am of opinion there is nothing superfluous in all this. But it is true, that, if we join to it all the different studies of music, drawing, and ten years of Latin, what I propose would be impossible. With regard to languages I have adopted your method. He learns the living ones by custom; and will only be taught Latin when he is from twelve or thirteen to fifteen or sixteen years old. He shall learn enough of drawing and geometry to inable him to make plans. But he shall never learn a note of music. I would not have him without learning, because it will be right for him one day or other to protect and countenance men of letters; but books of Morality and History will form our principal and most serious study.

I am quite of your opinion, that it is important to inspire Princes with sentiments of benevolence and compassion for the unhappy. All you say on the subject is as true as it is affecting; but, as you observe one cannot teach one's scholar to be charitable by lessons or phrases, it is in this matter above all, that one should convince them by producing examples. My young Prince has not a bad heart, but he has no great sensibility; besides, the words poverty and miserable are scarce understood by him, because he is too young and too giddy to have any idea of things so melancholy, and which he has never been witness to. But he has understanding, self-love, a lively imagination, and a good temper. It is requisite therefore that his vanity should be directed to objects worthy his attention, and to make him feel compassion, which is a sentiment he is almost a stranger to, merely because it has never been awakened in his heart, by presenting to him affecting pictures of distress which will excite it. I have been some time preparing a scene of this kind for him as new as it is affecting; and which I am certain will never be effaced from his memory. You shall have the particulars of it in my next letter; for even to you I have reserved the pleasure of a surprise. Adieu! my dear Baron, I have no journal to write this evening, my young Prince has behaved admirably all this day; and I have received double pleasure from it, as it has procured me the pleasure of conversing with you.

LETTER XXXVII.

The Baroness to the Viscountess.

IT is true, my dear friend, as you imagined your letter would surprize me, your daughter's marriage with Mons. de Valcy is not concluded; but I see clearly it will be, and that Mons. de Valcy will get a title ... And so you consent to receive him at your house, and you want to be acquainted with him, although you already know that he is a gamester and a coxcomb, which appears to me to be sufficient knowledge of him. In short, you are almost reconciled to Madame de Gerville, who you say has behaved very well on this occasion by making Mons. de Limours treat you with respect and attention ... But cannot you see that these pretended regards are only shewn with the desire and even certainty of winning you over to their party? This marriage should have been disapproved, because your daughter, with the name she bears, and the fortune she will have, ought not to be dazzled with a fortune; and, besides that, it is very shocking to give your daughter to the son of a woman of bad character, and who is himself but a very inferior kind of man. I know very well that Mons. de Limours is master; but, with prudence and resolution you might have dissuaded him from his purpose; or at least, if he had persisted in his design, by yielding with repugnance and concern, you would have made Madame de Gerville's part appear truly odious; you would have had a right never to admit her to your house; and you would have discovered her behaviour to the world in general; and no one could have reproached you with having sacrificed your daughter through vanity or weakness.

Though you have told me some time since you are infinitely more satisfied with Flora than you used to be, yet I cannot conceal from you that the description you give me of her disposition afflicts me much. You allow that she might have had a better education. But that which comforts you is exactly that which gives me most concern. She has no superior qualities, nor any very great faults, except that of extreme vanity; and you are sure she has no strong passions. Ah! how easy and frequent it is for people to be led astray without having violent passions! and this it is which disgraces us most. Believe me, in general, the vanity of little minds causes as much ill conduct, as is frequently attributed to those who are possessed of the strongest passions. A woman, prepossessed with the ridiculous idea that the happiness of her life consists in surpassing all others in charms and in beauty, sacrifices every thing to this extravagant fancy; at first her delicacy, and afterwards her honour. You will see in her all the fury of jealousy, the height of rage; and, in short, you will think she is agitated by a violent passion; but these are great events produced by little causes. There is nothing in her heart. All the evil arises from the idea which solely employs her thoughts, that the felicity of a woman consists in being beautiful and admired. You will often meet with this principle. You know the Count d' Orgeval, he is said to have violent fiery passions, which education has not been able to conquer, or even moderate. The world believes him wicked, dangerous, and an Atheist. Nothing of this is true. He has very little sense, though he knows how to express himself with tolerable ease and grace; he has spent his youth in bad company, surrounded by vile flatterers, whose interest it was to corrupt him; they praised him for the facility they pretended he had of saying *bon mots*. This made him impudent. They praised his good fortune and inclination for gallantry; and this made him a coxcomb and a debauchee. They admired the strength of his mind; and this made him be looked on as an Atheist. The truth is, that he is vain, weak, and confined in his notions, and the desire of being celebrated has ruined him. This desire is only dangerous to fools and people of moderate understandings. But happy is the noble and sensible heart that is inflamed by such a sentiment! It then changes the name as well as the motive. It is no longer vanity or self-love; it is an enthusiastic passion for glory; it is, however, founded on the same principle, but the one produces nothing but vices, the other heroism and virtue. Flora now reaches her sixteenth year, and so young, so little formed, you are going to marry her, and to give her in your place as a mother, a woman you have so much reason to despise! ... Ah, my dear friend! at least wait a little. Think how much the virtue, the happiness, and the fate of your daughter depends on this choice, which you are going to make. What a terrible and affecting day is that in which a mother conducts her child to the altar to put her into the hands of a stranger, and give her a master who perhaps knows only the right he has over her to make an ill use of it. In short, if he becomes a tyrant instead of a friend and protector, or, if wholly neglecting the mild and sacred authority her parents have given him over her, he abandons to herself her whom he ought to lead, to advise, and to govern. The parents alone are answerable for the misfortunes and ill conduct which may result from such an ill-concerted union. But you will say, with such fears one may hesitate for ever, and never be able to establish one's daughter. Ah! do not marry her to get rid of her, neither for interest or ambition; and be first certain that the choice you will make will insure her happiness.

LETTER XXXVIII.

Viscountess to the Baroness.

YOUR letter has affected me exceedingly; I am perfectly convinced of the strength of a part of your arguments. I will delay as long as I possibly can the settling of Flora; and I flatter myself the choice I shall make will render her happy. But I must confess the manner in which you have described marriage makes me regard it as a cruel and heavy bondage. I should fear to let her see it in such a light; I should also fear to deceive her, by pointing out to her such severe duties of obedience as do not exist. But, to grant you something, I will acknowledge she should not aspire to the government of her husband; let them, however, at least be on an equal footing. Love, which is capable of uniting all states and conditions, can never admit of those shocking distinctions which you wish to make, and which would absolutely destroy the sentiment. I would have Flora's husband her lover at the same time, and then she can never experience those uneasinesses under which I have always laboured. She will have no master to fear. I would have him amiable, because it is necessary she should love him, and that she should do her duty at the same time that she follows the dictates of her own heart. For these two months past I have had many conversations with her on this subject; and have endeavoured to convince her, that marriage is an engagement which ought to be as delightful as it is sacred; and to this idea she listens with great pleasure, as I tell her continually, that the greatest happiness she can enjoy is to find in her husband the object of her tenderest affection. I also represent to her the dangers she will meet with in the world, and the rocks that she may chance to encounter; and here perhaps I may exaggerate a little, in order that she may have some distrust of it; and that his distrust may give her that pleasing timidity so necessary and so agreeable in all young persons to preserve them from the heedlessness and imprudence of acting improperly. This is my system, it is plain matter of fact, and well known but, if it is a good one, why should we seek to refine upon it? I have always thought the plainest path was the most eligible. I conjure you, my dear friend, to read my letter attentively, and to answer me very minutely I make objections to your opinions, and lay my doubts before you; but my confidence in your judgment is not in the smallest degree lessened.

Madame d' Ostalis has at last determined to accept the employment her husband has so long wished her to take; and I fancy you are the person who has prevailed on her. She has been the more fearful of attaching herself to a Princess, left she should not acquit herself to her own satisfaction, or take on herself a task which she was afraid of not discharging with propriety. Adieu; my dear friend, send me an account of Cecilia. She writes to me frequently, but she says not a word of her health, which I am very uneasy about.

LETTER XXXIX.

Answer from the Baroness.

IF I am not able to convince you of the truth of my arguments, I shall at least fulfil the duty of a sincere and affectionate friend in telling you all my thoughts. Perhaps I may not have done well in straying from the *beaten path*; but I am sincere, and, if I have gone a little way from my point, it is because I thought I should the more certainly arrive at it. Love, you say, puts every thing on an equality. Yes, that momentary passion, which is disapproved and destroyed by reason; but not the sentiment of reflection, which is founded on esteem and confidence; which is agreeable to the laws of society, and formed by Nature. These are the sentiments which give to men power and authority. You have given your daughter a very unjust and dangerous representation of this matter. You have described love to her in such a manner, that now she wishes to have a lover, or, to express myself better, she wants to govern, and will esteem him; a Tyrant who will not submit to be her slave; and if she should not have such a husband, as you have given her the idea of, if he should not answer expectations, do you think she could consent herself with regarding him as a friend; when a wife fulfils her duty, and knows her dependence, if her husband has the least delicacy, even without a violent affection for her, he will never treat her with so much severity or opposition, as to make her feel her inferiority. Though we are jealous of the rights which are disputed with us, the more are granted to us, the more generous we are. And where is the heart which has not experienced this truth? I must also confess to you, that I do not better approve what you have said to your daughter concerning the dangers she may meet with in the world. I know it is generally the first thing young women are taught, and by hearing it often repeated they believe it; and, when they first go into the world, they are so ill able to defend themselves against these ideal dangers, which have been described to them in so dreadful a light, that they must be above human nature, to be able to avoid falling into them. Let us suppose, a beautiful and amiable young woman, without experience or advice, married to a man she does not love, and appearing for the first time at Court. Here is every sort of danger united together. I only wish, to preserve her from them, that she should have good sense, a little penetration and reflection; and, with this disposition, she will begin to make observations, she will see with what respect and attention women are treated whose characters are without spot; she will even see, that vice itself does homage to virtue; or at least that it never ridicules or speaks ill of it, but, when it is thought to be only pretended, she will see coquettes in the midst of their triumphs meeting with the contempt which is due to them; she will be struck with the humiliating part a woman of forty is obliged to act, when she has lost her reputation; she will be obliged to listen to the stories of her youthful misconduct, which are related with reproach and infamy: she will see the contrast of so disgusting a picture, and from this moment her resolution is fixed; you will perhaps tell me that in first coming into the world, it is almost impossible for a young person, intoxicated with dissipation, to observe or reflect. But, how ever, it appears to me to be very easy to look round and observe with attention things which are quite new to us, and to form our opinions from these observations. The world does not charm us at the first sight; every thing appears too strange to afford us amusement, and the fear and diffidence we carry with us prevents us from taking pleasure in it; so that the first year is always tedious, disagreeable, and fatiguing; let it then be usefully employed, while, the head is cool, the manners simple, and the heart innocent. Wretched will those be who suffer this precious moment to escape them, without reaping the advantages it offers. But you must be sensible, my dear friend, that if your scholar has only had a common education, if her inclinations are confined to a ball or the choice of a new gown; if you marry her at fifteen; or if, before that you introduce her too soon into company. If she has, in short, seen every thing before she was capable of forming a right opinion, her reason will never be able to make any new discovery, nothing will surprise or affect her; and she will consequently follow the stream. Adieu, my dear friend. It is with real concern I make these me melancholy reflections with respect to a child, who I assure you is as dear to me as to yourself: the affectionate interest I take in her may perhaps make the danger appear greater than it really is. But I have laid my heart entirely open to you, and have disguised nothing from you. Cecilia's health continues much the same; but her tranquillity seems quite restored, and she never appeared more calm and easy. The Physician from Carcassone, who is a man of great merit, came yesterday to see her, and spent an hour with her in her apartment. When he came away from her, his countenance really terrified us, as it appeared he had been weeping; However he assured Mons. d' Aimeri, Cecilia was then very well, and that he had no fears on her account. But I must own I have a great many, and I shall never be free from them till the Autumn is over.

LETTER XL.

The same to the same.

YOU still have some doubts, my dear friend; and you think it would be useful to give a young and beautiful woman some idea of the number of lovers she is likely to meet with on her entrance into the world. They are neither graces nor beauty, which attract the croud you speak of; it is merely coquetry, which allures them. You remember Madame de Clarey, the most beautiful woman in our time, and without doubt one of the most available. Did you ever hear of any one's being in love with her? Every one admired and respected her, but nobody followed her; because she was truly virtuous, modest, and reserved: while her cousin Madame de Clevaux, with a very indifferent person, was continually surrounded by all the young men of fashion. Love never can subsist without hope; and, let a women be ever so charming, you may be sure, if she inspires any one with a serious passion, that she meant to do so; and that she is not entirely free from coquetry. A sensible man never loves passionately, but when he thinks he is beloved again; and a vain man would never subject his vanity to the contempt he might meet with; he depends always on being successful. Why then should he run the hazard of being humbled? Examine your heart thoroughly, my dear friend, and you will perhaps acknowledge I am in the right. Do you remember the poor Chevalier de Herbain, whose brain you almost turned, and to whom you was for ever saying, Indeed, I can never feel a mutual affection for you, and I must absolutely put an end to your addresses, but you continued to receive them; you suffered him to entertain you with his passion a thousand different ways, and you allowed him to follow you every-where, so that you took up all his attention. Was not this giving him encouragement? You are sensible how this conduct hurt your character, and that, when I spoke to you so seriously about it, you told me it was not in your power to cure him of his folly I undertook the cure myself, provided you would only second me: and in one single conversation we convinced him, he had not common sense in loving you so tenderly. You may not perhaps have forgot, that he told you, a little angrily, your explanation came rather too late; and that, if you had told him so six months sooner, he should never have been so much in love with you. He spoke truth, and you would have been much more sensible of your fault, if he had been a vain, impertinent coxcomb, instead of being a virtuous and good man; for then he would have revenged himself by speaking ill of you; and be assured, after such conduct, however innocent you might be, many people would have given credit to his assertions.

We will now come to what you say with regard to love. You seem to think a woman, who has no affection for her husband, can scarce live without having a lover. If this is not exactly your expression, it is at least the meaning of it. You repeat, 'The heart is made for love:' I agree, that there must be a passion to agitate and employ it. But why must that passion be love? It is a general notion, that every body in the course of their lives are under the impulse of a violent affection. There are scarcely any young persons, who have not admitted this absurd idea. Formerly young people were told ridiculous stories with good intentions, which were listened to with credulous simplicity. But, now their minds are more enlightened, it is not the mind, but it is the heart which is deceived. By talking upon sentiment they have formed a false definition of it, as far from Nature as it is contrary to reason. The language of men and women are quite contradictory on this subject; one party exhaust themselves in making dissertations on the violence of their passions, while the other, when among themselves, deny its existence, on one side it is the most sublime philosophy, and on the other the direct contrary. One may conclude from hence, that one ought equally to distrust a pompous display of extravagant sentiments, and the affection of a vain boaster. In the present mode of education, a mother thinks she does quite right in suffering her daughter to read what are called moral novels or romances. For instance, the *Princess of Cleves*,[112] where they say you will find such beautiful examples of virtue; where the Heroine resists with so much strength and resolution a most violent passion. In seeing the excess of the affection which governs her, and the dreadful struggles she has with herself, if one is to believe this a faithful representation of the human heart, we must also believe, that love is totally independent of our will; that it is useless to oppose it in its progress; and that virtue is only a torment to us. This is a very moral and satisfactory conclusion! A young woman, instructed in such reading, married to a man she does not love, but fancying, that she is to be violently in love some time or other, waits for the fatal moment with anxiety, it soon arrives: The first person who speaks of love is exactly him whom Heaven has predestined to inspire her with a sentiment, which is to be the torment of her life. No more repose, no more sleep, sweet liberty is gone for ever; a gloomy melancholy succeeds to all her chearfulness; in short, she is herself the Princess of Cleves; and she then begins to think she loves still more than the Princess, or that the Author perhaps has rather exceeded the truth, in the account he gives of her resistance, which indeed appears to be probable. A tender and ardent lover at length obtains from her the confession which he solicits: in the first moments of this weakness which is new to her, she afflicts herself, sighs, and submits to her destiny; but, as soon as the veil is fallen aside, these romantic notions grow weaker: the Heroine perceives with surprize, that she loves no longer, or rather that she never has loved: she finds herself deceived, and that she has not found this ideal object, which was to inspire her with so tender a passion. At first she waited for the moment to arrive. But now she seeks for it without being happier, and will not be discouraged, till amidst repeated errors the pleasing days of her youth are vanished like a tiresome dream, which only leaves behind it confused and vague ideas of a thousand follies as strange as they are absurd. It is then she makes bitter reflections: the past humbles, the future terrifies her. The illusion is totally destroyed! Abandoned by the croud of flatterers who surrounded her, she finds herself neglected, and a stranger in the midst of her family and children. She reads in their faces the frightful sentence which condemns her, contempt pursues her, sorrow and repentance consume her, and, to compleat her misfortunes, her race is not yet half run. I believe it is infinitely more easy to find a woman who never had a lover, than to meet with those who never had but one. The first step is the most difficult, when that is passed, the rest of the way is very smooth; nevertheless I know there have been instances, but they are so rare they can only be mentioned as exceptions. Love at the beginning is never very ardent. It is at first only a sentiment of preference, of which it is very easy to stop the progress, by ceasing to see the object who has inspired it. This is the most certain means; and the remembrance will be effaced with very little trouble. But if a woman hesitates, if she will blind herself on this attachment which she has formed, or if she will exaggerate the degree of it, resistance will become more painful and victory more difficult. There is no sensible woman who has yielded to this weakness, but has for a long time foreseen her defeat. She who maintains her cause with resolution, will never be conquered. The determinations of a virtuous and serious mind cannot be destroyed in a moment; in that case virtue would only be a vain and chimerical idea. Now it is that you must examine the very bottom of your heart; question it, and its answer will be worth more than a treatise on morality.

A singular reflection is just come into my head, Paris is the center of tumult and dissipation; the confusion of ideas which arise from so many different objects must ill agree with love; which is always described as preferring concealment and solitude; and yet it always appears here under many and various forms. Whilst in the country, far from noise and bustle, we see no woman retired to her country-seat, who falls desperately in love with her neighbours. In general, she is attached to her husband, and the life she leads prevents her from entertaining romantic ideas. In coming still nearer to Nature, we do not see among the peasants any other than moderate sentiments, which can scarcely be called passions, although they are affectionately attached to their parents, their wives and their children. Ought we to believe, that our improved understandings are the cause of these contrary effects? Ought we not rather to search for them in our hearts? Adieu! my dear friend. Cecilia, to whom I have given your last letter, has answered it, as you will see. She is truly affected with the proofs of friendship you have give her. We talk of you continually. And, if she had no other merit than that of knowing how to value you, I find it would be impossible for me not to love her with the greatest tenderness.

LETTER XLI.

Same to the same.

At length you say your daughter's heart is engaged; she loves Mons. de Valcy, and prefers him to every other man; you have therefore given your consent. You are to blame, my dear friend, any longer to fear my censure. It is very natural to make reflections, when one fancies they may be of use; but it would be very absurd to persevere in condemning an affair which is determined on. That would be merely to shew my opinion without proving my friendship. I beg therefore you will be assured I am greatly interested for Mons. de Valcy; and that in future I will only look forward to the advantages which may arise from this union. Your daughter is not to leave you; she will live with you; this is a very lucky circumstance. You may watch over her actions, and gain the confidence and friendship of her husband, and, at the same time, keep her from the counsels of her mother-in-law. In short, she will be under your eye, and I shall have no more fears for her safety.

You think, what I said in my last letter upon the subject of reading novels is too severe. You think forbidding young people to read them is the only way to make them more earnest to get at them. I am of the same opinion; for, as soon as ever a young woman comes to be her own mistress, she will make herself amends for the constraint she had laboured under, and she will read every novel she can lay her hands on, What I object to is their being allowed to read novels, just at the time when they are most likely to make impressions on them; that is, when they are about sixteen or seventeen. I know but of three novels which have any morality in them; *Clarissa*, which is the best, *Grandison*, and *Pamela*.[113] My daughter shall read them in English, when she comes to be eighteen; as to the generality of all the rest, I shall begin to let her read them when she is a little older. By the time she is thirteen, she will read a very small number of these Works, the best of their kind; and reading them with me, at that age, will do her no kind of harm, but on the contrary will help to form her judgment, in letting her see the faults and ill consequences, as well as the improbability of the greatest part of these books, even of those that we reckon the best. After this time she will never see me read them; she will not even meet with them in my library. And she will never hear me speak of them without contempt. With these precautions, I am very certain, when she is twenty years old, she will never have an inclination to amuse herself in so trifling a way with books, which are only calculated to corrupt the heart, as well as mislead the judgment.

You desire me to be very particular in my account of Adelaide's improvements. She can draw a head very prettily; she knows all our Historical Pictures by heart. The copies, from which she writes, have made her acquainted with the Scriptures: she speaks English as well as Miss Bridget; she begins to read very well; she understands singing tolerably; and she can perform the most difficult lessons on the harp in a very pleasing manner. She has at present learned only the first rules of Arithmetic, but she can calculate amazingly well. For her writing and spelling you yourself can judge; and I think, in this respect, very few, if any, children exceed her. As she will be eight years old the tenth of next October, which is three weeks hence; I intend to make her read an Historical Work, which I have written for her, and which is called *Annals of Virtue*,[114] and is written in six volumes. It contains a particular account of all the great actions, together with the singular and memorable events, taken from the publick and private History of People of all Nations, from the Creation down to the present time, in Chronological order; and contains also an abstract of the best laws made use of in different Governments; extracts from the sentiments and morality of the most celebrated Philosophers; and a short, though tolerably exact account of the manners of the manners and customs of the Ancients. I have placed each History according to its degree of antiquity, or rather according to the connection between countries, as China and Japan, France and England, &c. &c. Each History begins by a Chronological abridgement, which precedes the separate events; and to this abridgement I have added a short Geographical Description of each country, its extent, situation, &c. &c. As I wrote this Work for the use of children, I was particularly desirous it should improve their understanding and their hearts at the same time. A child, from eight years old to twelve, is not capable of making reflections unless they are assisted, and, even then, I think it is dangerous for them to read those Histories which we esteem the best. This History, so proper for us to read, because we can understand and reflect on it, is useless to children, who, by being dazzled by every appearance of grandeur, do not perceive the cruelty or injustice of an action which appears glorious and is attended with success. How many young Princes heads have been turned by reading the life of Alexander the Great![115] It is well known, what an effect it had on the mind of Charles the Twelfth, when a child.[116] The chief point, which I have kept to in this book, is not to judge of persons and things, but as they really deserve; never to praise those who do not deserve praise; and, in short, to make such reflections on each character and event as may inable Adelaide to form a right judgment of them, by the time she comes to read our best Histories.

LETTER XLII.

Viscountess to the Baroness.

OH, my dear friend! What a day is this, which has just past! ... It is done! Flora is married ... At length she has pronounced the dreadful word which engages her for ever ... Her fate is fixed, independent of me for the future ... and it is for ever! ... There are circumstances, without which we should not know the excess of our sensibility. She who has never seen her daughter married, or at the point of death, can have no perfect idea what it is to be a mother ... I cannot describe to you all that has passed in my mind since yesterday. Certainly I see with different eyes, I have a different heart and another way of thinking; I am no longer the same person! ... In one moment I have discovered my daughter dearer to me than any thing on earth, and that all my happiness depends on our future fortune. I have no idea how it should happen, that her education has not always been the principal concern of my life. I am continually reproaching myself for having neglected it, and for suffering her to marry so young; and above all with having made a choice, which at this time appears to me full of inconveniences. The conduct of her mother-in-law comes back to my memory under the most odious colours. I blush to hear my daughter call her mother ... If I had been my own mistress this morning, if I could have broke the engagement, my child should have been free; she should still have been mine ... Mons. de Valcy appears to me nothing more than a coxcomb, without sense and without character ... Add to all these painful ideas the presence of Madame de Gerville, who has been here all day, and who triumphs in her own power, and the vexation she has given me ... Ah! it is at this moment that I feel, in the anguish of my heart, how happy I might have been, had I followed your advice! I should then have gained the confidence of Mons. de Limours. My daughter would have had a proper education. Vanity and folly would never have led me into such imprudences; and I should not now be a prey to useless remorse! ... For these four and twenty hours I have not had a moment's peace; it is now one in the morning. The company are in the saloon; they are all at cards; and I at this hour of midnight have escaped from them to shut myself up with you! ... With you! ... I may say so; but, alas! you are two hundred leagues from me! ... My dear friend, you have forsaken me ... But I have still some friends left who see my grief and pity me, though their compassion humbles rather than comforts me; it appears as an indirect reproach on my conduct, since it is but too true I am made unhappy by my own fault; and this kind of pity is always mixed with a contempt which makes it insupportable. I want none but yours; whatever it may be, it is necessary and valuable to me. Ah, do not refuse it! I weep while I am writing ... Never, never, have I been so deeply afflicted ... so melancholy, so apprehensive! ... And on the day on which I have married my daughter! the day which ought to be the happiest of my life! ... But it appears to me as if I was not in my own house, but in that of a stranger! ... Only think of Mons. de Limours! he has not for these two days had a wish to see me alone, that he might speak to me of his daughter. This evening they were talking of her being presented. Her mother-in-law was for having it done the day after to-morrow, or this evening at eight, leaving Mons. de Limours to determine. I told them I should have preferred a more distant day; but Mons. de Limours did not seem to hear me, and it was fixed for the nearest. A thousand other little things of this kind have contradicted and vexed me to an unreasonable degree. But you know my violence, and that I am extreme in every thing. I have no patience, no consideration. I am not apt to fancy grievances, they are actually before my face. I do not concern myself in a moderate way; I am absolutely in despair. Adieu, my dear friend, adieu! pity me, love me, write to me, and remember that you only can console me, or at least mitigate my sorrows! I have a dreadful head-ach. I almost wish it was a dangerous illness. I should hope then you would return hither to take care of me. As for any thing else, I assure you I should leave this world very willingly; for there is nothing in it very agreeable to me.

LETTER XLIII.

Madame d' Ostalis to the Baroness.

Do not alarm yourself, my dear aunt, for Madame de Limours. I am not at all surprized, that, having wrote to you on the day of her daughter's marriage, she shall have made you so uneasy, for she was in a dreadful situation; but, happily for her, she is as easily calmed as she is irritated. The morning after the wedding I went to see her; and found her spirits extremely low. Going out of her apartment, and knowing Mons. de Limours was alone in his, Mons. d' Ostalis and I went to see him; we both spoke to him on his behaviour to Madame de Limours. He smiled and asked me if you had appointed me your deputy to preach to him. I told him I should never have sense enough to be able to take your place; and that I was much too young to venture to give advice, if the tenderest friendship did not allow me such a liberty. At these words he quitted the tone of raillery, and we entered into a serious explanation. He complained with some reason of Madame de Limours's capricious temper, but he did justice to the rest of her amiable qualities; and, when I informed him she was really ill, he appeared disposed to do every thing which I should judge necessary to make her mind easy; and he intreated me to return to dinner, in order, as he said, that I might judge of his behaviour. And indeed he treated her with the utmost kindness, which made the more impression on Madame de Limours, as there were forty people at dinner. By degrees she grew chearful; she forgot her headach and her nervous complaints; and never was more amiable in her life. You know, my dear aunt, how charming she is when she wishes to please; so that, in short, she gains the attention of every body, as if they had never seen her before. And the Chevalier d' Herbain is in the right when he says, that, *when she chuses to make herself agreeable, it is impossible any other person can be taken notice of.* He has, however, great merit in never speaking of her, and in endeavouring to make her esteemed by other people. Madame de Gerville was there at dinner, and made but a poor figure; for all her smart, studied, little expressions appeared very insipid, compared with the natural wit of Madame de Limours, who is never more generous than when she conquers. Madame de Limours tried all in her power to keep her in good humour and satisfied with herself. But Madame de Gerville, governed only by her malicious spirit, received all her attentions with such a ridiculous coldness, that Mons. de Limours himself was shocked at it, and treated Madame de Gerville with that kind of raillery of which you know he is capable. Madame de Gerville enraged, and disconcerted, would have acted a curious scene, if Madame de Limours had not taken her part; and, with a chearfulness and grace which it is impossible to describe to you, turned every thing which had been said into pleasantry. What a pity that, with so many charms, so much wit and liberality of sentiment, Madame de Limours has not her ideas better connected and more steadiness of opinion! However, she is at present perfectly satisfied, delighted with Mons. de Limours, charmed with her daughter, her son-in-law, and even Madame de Valcy. You ask me, my dear aunt, to give you an account of Flora, or, to speak more properly, Madame the Marchioness de Valcy; I will tell you freely what I think of her. She is grown very much since you saw her. She has a very good shape, because she is laced very tight, which makes her waist appear slender; she has not a good complexion; but her eyes are almost as beautiful as Madame de Limours', though she has not her lovely countenance or her graces. The fear of disordering her head-dress, or rumpling her gown, gives such a stiffness to her motions, that it makes her quite disagreeable. As to her talents, or other qualifications, one word expresses the whole: she dances perfectly well. In short, I think she has very little understanding, and, what is much worse for her, I fear she has not a good heart; and I am sure she has a great deal of cunning. For example, she affects to be artless and innocent, with such as degree of cunning as quite shocks me, who have known her from infancy; but deceives many other people, particularly the Chevalier d' Herbain, who has a collection of her innocent sayings, which he repeats with a satisfaction that always puts me out of temper. Upon the whole she is pretty; her youth makes her pleasing, and she is generally admired. As for Mons. de Valcy, he is a mere nothing. He gives himself many airs, and has not one single idea; he pretends to be inattentive and absent, and his conversation consists only in repeating with an affected air what other have just said. There is but one opinion concerning him: he is equally trouble some, free, and talkative; besides this, he has the *Anglo-manie* to a great degree.[117] He unfortunately spent fourteen days in London, and speaks of it incessantly; is always boasting of the learning and genius of the English; he despises the French from his heart. He keeps English horses, reads the English newspapers, makes his morning visits with boots and spurs, drinks tea twice a day, and thinks himself as wise as Newton or Locke.

Now, my dear aunt, allow me to talk to you of my own affairs: I have left my little twins for in twelvemonth with my mother-in-law. As soon as they are five years old, I shall take them with me. I am told this is a very absurd scheme, and that, being wholly employed in my attentions on the Princess, it will be impossible to educate my children. It is very true these little journeys carry me from Paris for near two months in the summer, which will prevent me from taking care of them for that time; but then I shall intrust them to a Governess on whose fidelity I can depend; and, when they are older, I shall send them to a Convent for those two months. In short, I shall make fewer visits; I shall not go to balls or any public places, but when I am obliged to attend the Princess; and I am certain I shall find time enough to fulfil all my duty towards her, and the same time attend to the education of my children. The only concern I have is the thoughts of not being able to come to Languedoc; and, when I reflect that it will still be eighteen months before I shall see you, I am then convinced that Prudence herself does not make us amends for the sacrifices she requires of us. Adieu, my dear aunt! Do me the favour to send me the little Tales, and other Papers relative to Education, which you have promised me; for what can I do without you? ...

LETTER XLIV.

Answer from the Baroness to Madame d' Ostalis.

I AM entirely of your opinion, my dear child. When we make a point of doing our duty, there is no situation in which we are unable to attend to it. When the inclination leads us, we shall always find time.

I am told since your last lying-in you have learned to ride on horseback. I must own I have very little right to condemn this exercise, which I have been very fond of. But, however, you are sensible I renounced it entirely, when my attentions to you became really of use. I do not know an amusement more dangerous in every respect for women than this is, or which leads them to waste their time more. In the different rides about Paris you meet all the young men of fashion, and you know how often those meetings have been taken for assignations, and that this very circumstance ruined the character of Madame de Tervure. Besides, how is it possible you can employ yourself with your children, improve your understanding, or fulfil the duties of your station, if you ride on horseback three or four times a week? That is to say, if you pass those three days in the Bois de Boulogne,[118] and in dressing and undressing yourself. I cannot finish this letter without adding some remarks on the manner in which you ought to conduct yourself in your new situation. First, you must never forget that your family desired and sollicited this place for you; and this remembrance will preserve you from the absurd custom of complaining of the duty imposed on you. It is a piece of affectation much in vogue to appear dissatisfied with the society of Princes, and to complain of the obligation we are under to go to Versailles. Although, by an inconsistency as striking as it is absurd, people would be in despair, were they to give up this task, which they pretend to be irksome, for that liberty which they boast of with so much emphasis. Besides, remember that every chain which it is possible to break becomes disgraceful, when those who carry it appear to do it with regret, which is saying in plain terms, I sacrifice my pleasures, my inclinations, the happiness of my life to my interest and ambition! For you, my dear child, I hope that you have sentiments too noble to suffer yourself to be misled by such examples. Never allow yourself to make the smallest complaint on this subject; and, as affection alone will make every thing appear in a more dignified light, love the Princess sincerely to whom you are attached, as she merits your affection by the qualities she possesses. I am certain she will very soon distinguish you. When she learns the integrity of your mind, and the goodness of your heart, then you will be so much the more to be envied, as you are young, beautiful, engaging, and have a character without blemish. Many efforts will be made to injure you with the Princess;[119] every body will speak ill of you, some openly, and others with more art and finesse. To all this make no other opposition but that of innocence and generosity; be always open, true, and disinterested. Never employ your own credit to hurt that of your enemies; appear to know them, but at the same time do justice to their good qualities, and never complain of them. On the contrary, if the Princess should be angry with you through their base endeavours, try all in your power to soften her; and, if they should afterwards ask a favour which she seems unwilling to grant them, intreat her with earnestness, and enjoy the noble pleasure of obtaining it for them. This, my dear child, is an art infinitely superior to intrigue; an art of which common minds are ignorant, which will revenge you even of your most dangerous enemies, and will give you a triumph over even envy itself. Adieu! my child, I send you all the papers you desire, and I expect with impatience the miniatures you promised me. I am told, that, since my departure, you have made an astonishing progress, and that you are quite a proficient in painting. Adieu! Cultivate your genius, and remember your success in every particular, will contribute to the pleasure and happiness of my life.

LETTER XLV.

The Baroness to the Viscountess.

AT length, my dear friend, there are no longer any hopes of our amiable Cecilia. She is nearly arrived at the end of her long sufferings, and, in a few days, will perhaps be no longer in existence. It is now two months since she has known her danger; she obliged Mons. Lambert, the Physician from Carcassonne, to inform her of the truth, at the same time forbidding him to acquaint her family with her real situation. Yesterday morning I received a note written by herself, desiring me, if possible, to come and see her immediately; I obeyed her summons, and found her alone in the castle, as Mons. d' Aimeri and Madame de Valmont were gone to make a visit in the neighbourhood. She was seated in a great chair, for as yet she has not kept her bed a single day. I was shocked at seeing her so pale and weak; nevertheless she appeared to recover herself on seeing me, and made me sit down by her. I know, my dear Madam, said she, your sensibility; therefore allow me, before I explain myself, to assure you, that it is impossible for any body to be more perfectly happy than I am at this time ... This beginning prepared me but too well for what she was going to tell me. Ah! what, cried I! ... What has Mons. Lambert said to you? ... I saw him this morning ... Ah! what? ... He has told me, I ought to bid you a last adieu ... At these words some drops moistened her eye-lids; as for me, I was drowned in tears ... we were a moment without speaking ... at last Cecilia said, What, Madam! does my happiness afflict you? ... Ah, Cecilia! interrupted I, you deceived us when you assured us you would wish to live! ... No, replied she, I did not deceive you; if the Almighty had prolonged my pilgrimage, I should have submitted to his will, not only without repining, but without concern. Since my last illness he has changed my heart: this heart formerly so weak! – It was in the cottage of Nicole that I received the stroke which deprives me of life ... What I suffered at that time can neither be conceived nor expressed: I abhorred my existence, and yet I looked upon death with inexpressible fear and terror; and I experienced in those dreadful moments, that, without innocence and purity of heart, there is no true courage. In short, when I was thought to be out of danger, I was convinced I was only snatched from death for a short time: I made use of the delay which was granted me. I reflected on my errors and the guilty illusion of all the passions to which we are subject. I ventured to address myself with confidence to the Divine Being; he heard my prayers, and restored me to peace and tranquillity. He raised my soul towards him, and became the sole object of all my affections and my dearest hopes. She had scarce finished these words, when I saw her paleness vanish; her eyes were animated, and her countenance was brightened by the most striking and noble expression. The firm tone of her voice, the sweetness of her looks, the majestic serenity of her countenance, made me change insensibly from grief to admiration! I thought I saw, I thought I heard an Angel. I looked at her with eagerness; I listened to her with respect; and, when she had ceased to speak, I regarded her with rapture, and I was affected in a manner too extraordinary to suffer me to break silence. At length she explained to me her reasons for wishing to see me alone. She intreated me gently to prepare her father and sister for the event, which, she said, she felt must be extremely near ... You may guess with what reluctance I charged myself with this commission, and with what grief I performed it! Mons. d' Aimeri and Madame de Valmont saw nothing in Cecilia's situation but that weakness which is generally the consequence of severe illness. They had flattered themselves from her youth and her air of content, and they were absolutely quite ignorant of the symptoms which rendered her situation so dangerous. However, as one lively sentiment is often replaced by another, Mons. d' Aimeri, from the first words I uttered, was sensible of all his misfortune. But, as if he wished still to encourage a ray of hope, he all at once ceased to question me, and, a moment after, went and shut himself up in Cecilia's chamber. As to Madame de Valmont, she had so much pain to understand me, that I was obliged to repeat to her almost all Cecilia had said to me. I staid with her till the evening. It is now three days since I saw her; she writes to me that her sister is in the same situation; that Mons. d' Aimeri is overwhelmed with grief; and that the perfect resignation and angelic piety of Cecilia procure him the only consolations he is capable of receiving. Adieu, my dear friend! These things have so troubled and distressed me, that I have been really ill. I shall go the day after to-morrow to Madame de Valmont, and I will write to you the same evening, before I go to bed.

LETTER XLVI.

From the same to the same.

ALAS! ... She is no more! ... Oh, to what a dreadful sight have I been witness! ... It is the unfortunate Mons. d' Aimeri, it is he alone, who is at this time to be pitied! ... Ah! if for one fault, though in truth an irreparable one, yet expiated by ten years repentance, Heaven punishes with such severity; what is there which unnatural parents have not to fear, who seek to blind themselves on the heinous crime of their injustice? ... My mind is so taken up with what I have this day seen; my heart is so much affected by it, that I can speak of nothing else; hear then this melancholy recital, it shall be faithful and true; and it appears to me, that I am too much affected not to communicate to you a part of those deep impressions which I have received myself. I came to Madame de Valmont's to-day at dinner time. I found all the family in great consternation, and they told me Cecilia had been so ill in the night, that they had sent for the Physician; that she had received the Sacrament; but that at present she was better, and that she had just got up. I went into her chamber; she was seated on a sopha between her father and sister, and the Physician was offering her a medicine. As soon as I appeared, Madame de Valmont came to me, and said, with an air of satisfaction which shocked me, she has had a dreadful crisis, but is better; she is surprisingly better now. At these words, I cast my eyes on the Physician, as if to know his opinion: and he gave me a look which made me tremble. My heart beat in such a manner, I was obliged to sit down ... At this moment Mons. d' Aimeri began to speak; certainly, said he, as she has had the strength to go through the crisis of this night, we have all the reason to believe, that she is now entirely out of danger. Indeed, added Madame de Valmont, looking at the Physician, to think otherwise would be very absurd ... Ah! my sister, my dear sister! you have little reason! ... Mons. d' Aimeri, who till then had kept a profound silence, cast his eyes, which were filled with tears, on Cecilia; and, seizing one of her hands, ah, why, said he, with a voice scarce intelligible, why would you deprive us of our hopes! ... All the reply Cecilia made was to throw both her arms round her father's neck, and to keep them there for some minutes without speaking. Afterwards, addressing herself to Madame de Valmont, she asked her where Charles was, and appeared desirous to see him. They sent for him, and, when he came, Cecilia made him sit down at the foot of the sopha, and, observing that his eyes looked red, Charles, said she to him, you have been weeping too! Charles, at these words, kissed her hand, and rested his head on his aunt's lap, not daring to shew his face, as he still continued weeping. Cecilia perceiving her hand wet with his tears, Charles, said she, if you were not quite so young, you would learn, that, after a life well spent, this moment, in which you now see me, is the most delightful, the happiest of my days ... My body is very weak and languid, but my mind is quiet and content ... I feel such delightful sentiments ... I am sure, Charles, that you will add to the happiness of my father, and that you will love him as tenderly as I do ... As she finished speaking, Charles got up hastily, and, bathed in tears, threw himself into the arms of his grand-father ... I cannot express to you the grace and sensibility with which he performed this action. Mons. d' Aimeri pressed him to his bosom with the most passionate tenderness, and, taking his hand, led him out of his daughter's chamber, in order, without doubt, to give himself up to all the grief with which he was penetrated. A moment after Cecilia intreated us all to go to dinner. You will suppose we were not long at table. Madame de Valmont persevered in keeping up her hopes. For my part, I had none: for the Physician told me absolutely, that Cecilia could not live twenty-four hours. When we had dined, we returned to her chamber, and found her quite composed; and the Priest, who had not left her, told us she appeared better than she had done the evening before. We seated ourselves round the sopha, and, a moment after, Cecilia said, she had a desire to try if she could walk. Her father and the Physician helped to lift her from her seat, and supported her by her arms: but she had scarce taken five or six steps, when, stopping suddenly, she cried, oh, my father! ... At this plaintive and piercing cry, Mons. d' Aimeri, almost distracted, took her in his arms; she leaned gently on him, with her eyes half closed! ... The Physician seized her hand, and after feeling her pulse, made a sign to the Priest, who at the same moment took a Crucifix, and, approaching Cecilia, said with a loud voice these dreadful words: *Recommend your soul to God!* On hearing this, Cecilia opened her eyes, and, raising them towards Heaven, pressed the Crucifix to her bosom; and in this attitude her whole person and countenance had an expression and majesty which gave her beauty the appearance of something celestial. After having said her prayers, all at once she threw herself on her knees, saying, 'My father, give me your blessing!' Mons. d' Aimeri threw himself down by her, his arms trembling, once more unfolding themselves to receive his beloved child ... Cecilia fell on the bosom of her unhappy father; ... it was then all over ... She expired! ... After this melancholy story, you will not expect any other particulars. It is sufficient for me to tell you that Mons. d' Aimeri's grief is far above any thing that can be felt by those who have no children. I obliged him to come with me to B— the same evening, with Madame de Valmont and Charles; and, when he is in a situation to receive our friendly advice, we mean to persuade him to travel with his grandson: for that will be the only method of supporting his spirits in his present situation. Adieu, my dear friend! Write to me; I am very melancholy; you know, that I am not lightly affected on these occasions; you know how dear my friends are to me, when I see them afflicted and distressed: so you may judge, how much I am concerned, and how necessary your letters will be to me.

LETTER XLVII.

Count de Roseville to the Baron.

I PROMISED, my dear Baron, to send you an account of a truly interesting scene, which I was preparing for my pupil. I could not satisfy your curiosity sooner, as I was willing nothing should be wanting to my History; and it has cost me six months search to find what I desired.

I have already told you, my young Prince promises to be possessed of very brilliant qualities; he has good sense, a lively imagination, and a happy disposition. But I observed in him a certain degree of insensibility which afflicted me, though I only attributed it to his want of experience. When one has never been unhappy, nor a witness to scenes of distress, it is not possible to be truly compassionate. It is not bare recitals that can impress our hearts with sentiments, which will be opposed by all those factitious but dangerous passions, to which the corruption of the times give rise. It is not words but examples, which are necessary for this great work; and, above all, affecting scenes, which will leave an indelible impression on a young and innocent heart. Persuaded of the truth of this, I determined to search the city and suburbs for some unfortunate family ready to sink under the weight of their affliction; and, in order to succeed better in my search, I applied myself to a Gentleman who bestows on the poor more than three fourths of a considerable fortune gained by his own industry in trade.

He is a stranger in this country, and is called Mons. d' Anglures; his country and his birth are unknown. He speaks several languages equally well. He has lived here about ten years, in a small house, on the borders of the lake – The singularity of his way of living attracted our Sovereign's curiosity, who desired to see him. One should imagine that Mons. d' Anglures had related to him some very affecting story, for the Prince, from that moment, has shewn a particular regard. for him, and soon after employed him in different negociations, which, by their consequences, have gained the Prince's confidence, and he has loaded him with kindness. For these two years past, Mons. d' Anglures has retired from Court, and lives in peace and solitude at his own house, which he has made one of the most delightful places in this country. I went to him about three months ago, to tell him of my scheme. He gave me all the intelligence I could wish; but I was too difficult to determine hastily. I considered I should lose my object, if I only made a slender impression; and, when I had succeeded in the choice of my object, I found all the preparations, which I am going to relate to you, were necessary before-hand. Our young Prince, like all other children, is extremely curious. I therefore affected frequently to speak low, and with an air of secrecy, to Mons. Sulback, his Sub-preceptor. The Prince did not fail to question me about it. I told him, I was employed about an affair, which interested me beyond all expression: and I added, if you was a few years older, I should trust you with it, but at present you are too much a child. At these words you may imagine how much I was intreated; but I was steady, and the Prince could only draw from me some vague answers, which augmented and inflamed his curiosity. At night he was still more uneasy, when he found Mons. Sulback's son was let into our secret; he made heavy complaints to me: I contented myself with only saying, Young Sulback was no longer a child. He is thirteen years old, and is remarkably sensible for his age: and then I changed the conversation. The Prince was out of temper and sullen. I told him, that was not the means by which he would gain my confidence. It is not a distrust of you, said I, which prevents me from acquainting you with the affair we have in agitation. It is, because I think you are too much a child to take any part in it. Yet it is very possible for children of your age to understand and even feel things that are interesting and distressing. If you had not shewn so much curiosity and ill humour, and how little power you had over yourself, I should certainly have told you what you wished to know: but now it will be difficult for you to obtain this favour, and I give you notice, if you do not repair your fault by an extreme prudence, gentleness, and mildness of temper, and if you ask one more question on the subject, you never will possess my confidence. When you promise, as a recompence to a child, the very thing he wishes for, you may make your own terms. The Prince immediately smoothed his brow, and came to me with a mild and fond countenance, promising I should see that he had command over himself; and he kept his word. The next day after dinner, we were together in his room, when Mons. Sulback and his son entered in a great hurry, and the former, coming up to me, cried out, at last we have found what we sought. I affected the greatest joy, and bid, let us go then immediately! What, said the Prince, with an air of surprise and anxiety, are you going out? Yes, answered I, for two or three hours. Shall my son go with us, said Mons. Sulback? Oh, I intreat that you will let me, interrupted the young man; I shall be wretched, if you deprive me of this happiness! During this conversation, the Prince looked at us all by turns, and did great violence to himself to conceal his vexation and grief. I took my hat and sword, and prepared to go out. I sent for the people to attend on the Prince in our absence. He came to me, and I embraced and took leave of him. He could not any longer contain himself, and not daring to speak, burst into tears. I appeared much concerned at it, and asked him what was the matter? He acknowledged to me, that he was quite in despair; Mons. Sulback begged me to tell him the interesting tale! The Prince intreated ... I hesitated ... but at length I yielded. We sat down, and I took the Prince on my knee, and, addressing myself to him, being very certain of fixing his attention, Mons. Sulback and I lay aside every month, said I, a part of our yearly income, for the support of unfortunate people, who are oppressed with poverty; and we both make diligent search, that our money may be well disposed of and given to persons who are as honest as they are unfortunate; about six weeks ago, we bought some tickets in the lottery, and we won thirty thousand livres; we immediately formed a scheme, in consequence of this success, to employ half the money in making one whole family happy; and we purchased, about three leagues from hence, a neat little farm, provided with all necessaries, and have furnished the house in a plain and neat manner. We have been ever since searching out for a proper object to give it to; and at length we have found a family, very poor, and very honest! They live in the suburbs of the city, and we want to go and find them and conduct them to their charming little farm: Mons. Sulback here joined in the conversation, and said to me, what pleasure will it give you to see wretched Alexis Stezin enjoying peace and happiness, with an aged father, and a wife, and four beautiful children, who this morning, when our messenger arrived there, were all ready to expire with hunger! At these words, the Prince seizing one of my hands, and throwing his other arm round my neck: Oh, my dear friend! let me go with you, that I may see all this. His eyes were filled with tears, when he said this. I embraced him tenderly, and told him, since he had sensibility, I should no longer regard him as a child. You shall go to Alexis Stezin's; you are worthy of such a sight, said I to him. The joy and transport the Prince expressed at this is not to be described: he loaded me with embraces and thanks, and was impatient to be gone. While we were preparing for our departure, he walked about the room, holding young Sulback by the hand. He had an air of triumph, which seemed to say, 'What, if I am not thirteen years old, I am no longer treated as a child.'

We went down the back stair-case, got into a hackney-coach, and, attended only by two servants in plain cloaths, we set out, the Prince, Mons. Sulback, his son, and myself. It was not five o'clock; but, being in the midst of Winter, it was quite dark; and we suffered more from the extreme cold, as the coach-windows did not shut close, and we had no carpet at the bottom. The Prince took notice of it without complaining. Judge, Sir, said Mons. Sulback, by this little proof of the bad effects of cold, what this unhappy family we are now going to relieve must have suffered, having lived all this Winter in a garret, without cloaths or fire, as you that are covered with a warm dress, a long fur cloak, and a large muff, find the weather insupportable. The Prince only answered with a deep sigh, which expressed the greatest humanity. I enjoyed with delight my own work, and I was so much affected I could not speak. In about half an hour we entered into a very narrow street, and the coach stopped. The Prince cried out 'This is the place, doubtless, we are arrived!' – And in his eagerness he tried to open the door and get out. I stopped him, and said, I lay a wager your heart beats! – Yes, indeed, it does very much, said he. They brought us a flambeau, and we went into a house which was, in appearance, ready to fall. We ascended near a hundred and twenty steps; and, after that, climbed up a little, dark, narrow, wooden stair-case which led us to the garret inhabited by this miserable family ... In a room, lighted by one dismal lamp, we found a man about thirty years of age lying on-straw. He was just recovering from a fainting fit. A young and beautiful woman supported him in her arms, whilst a venerable old man made him smell to some vinegar. Three little boys were at his feet, and a lovely girl about nine or ten years old, who had no other covering than a ragged shift, was on her knees before him, praying to God for his recovery, and shedding at the same time a flood of tears! ... This sight, which was quite unexpected, surprised and affected me equally. When the sick man had recovered his senses, we found this accident had been occasioned by the nourishment we had sent him, and which was the first he had taken for three days, as he had persisted in eating nothing for that time, in order that his family might have a little more bread. I made him drink a glass of cordial water, which revived his spirits; and we then presented him with a purse of fifty Louidores. At this sight he cried out, 'Oh, my children! thank these generous strangers; and you my wife, my father, fall at their feet!' The whole fam-ily surrounded us, bestowing on us the most affecting marks of their gratitude, except the little girl, who, being ashamed to appear before so many strangers almost naked, crept into a corner, and did not venture to approach us. You may be certain nothing could divert my attention from my pupil: he observed every thing that passed with as much curiosity as emotion, and even wept at what he saw, without being sensible of it; he kept leaning on my arm, and scarce allowed himself the liberty of breathing, that he might not lose a syllable of what was going forward. He observed the modest distress of the unfortunate little girl, and, quitting my arm, advanced towards her, took off his fur cloak, and, throw-ing it over her shoulders with a faultering voice, said, 'I give you this cloak, now you may come forward.' It is impossible for me to describe the joy I felt at this action. I ran to the Prince, and taking him in my arms, 'Oh, my dear child, cried I, I am now well rewarded for all my tenderness and care.' I could say no more; tears stopped my speech! At this moment one of our servants arrived with a large bundle containing some common fur cloaks which I had ordered for the family. The Prince having given his own to the little girl, there was one more than was wanted; I gave it to him, saying, 'Keep it for ever, though it is neither so fine nor so warm as your own; for with what pleasure will you wear it, when it brings to your remembrance an action which does you so much honour.' The Prince put it on immediately; and never did he feel such joy and satisfaction on wearing the most elegant dress as he felt in this coarse and heavy cloak. During this time we were busied in getting Alexis Stezin removed to a convenient apartment in the first floor of the house. His father, wife, and children followed him; and, when we had fixed them in their new habitation, we left them saying, As soon as the poor man was well enough, we would conduct them. We did not arrive at the palace till past eight o'clock, and sat down to our fire-side again with a double pleasure, reflecting on the happiness we had procured for these miserable people. We sat up much later than usual. The Prince not being at all inclined to sleep, he found great pleasure in recollecting the most minute circumstances of this affecting evening; and I am very certain the remembrance will never be blotted from his memory. However, I would not have these kind of scenes too often repeated; for it would be very dangerous to accustom him to see such instances of wretchedness and misery. This weakens and destroys that sensibility which you should awaken in such a manner as to make a lasting impression. Thus you see bad effects might arise from good causes; where is the mind enough enlightened to stop at the exact point beyond which it ought not to go? At least this is what we should be aware of, in order to act with caution and prudence.

But to return to my pupil; before we went to bed, Mons. Sulback and I intreated him not to mention this adventure to any body, 'Because we did not chuse such a common act of humanity 'should be known, as vanity had no share in it.' The Prince promised to tell no one but his father, who you may suppose had already been acquainted with the story, and who had furnished us with the means of giving him so magnificent a lesson on benevolence. For it has cost more than twenty thousand livres; but it is a sum well spent, and what a powerful Sovereign and a good father can never regret. The next day the Prince, who was all impatience to see Alexis Stezin settled in his farm, sent to know how he did; and we heard with extreme satisfaction he was up and perfectly recovered. It was immediately settled that we should send them a carriage that very day to conduct them to the farm, and that we should go there also. We set out after dinner, and got there a little before their arrival. The Prince, of his own accord, carried them several presents, and waited their coming with the utmost impatience; as soon as he heard the carriage, he ran out hastily to meet it, and he afterwards followed them about to enjoy their surprize and happiness with a pleasure in his countenance which almost arose to transport. Before we went away the Prince came to me, and, throwing himself into my arms, cried out, 'Oh! my friend, how much I thank you for shewing me such a sight as this! how happy must you be in reflecting on the satisfaction of these honest people!' – 'Yes, said I, I am indeed happy beyond expression, that I have made you acquainted with this delight, and, when you thoroughly enjoy it, it will afford me greater felicity.' One morning, about a week after this, Mons. Sulback and I being alone with the Prince, a person came to tell me that a very ingenious artist, whom we had heard of, desired to speak with me. I went to him, and returned immediately with a large drawing in crayons very elegantly framed. 'Ah! cried I, our secret is betrayed, here we are all represented at the house of Alexis Stezin's, pray look!' ... At these words the Prince, amazed, looked at the picture, and saw, with emotion, that they had fixed on the moment when he was throwing his cloak over the little girl's shoulders ... He blushed, and told me, indeed it was not owing to his indiscretion. I told him I believed it; nor had any of us mentioned it, yet I was not surprized at its being known. Why so? ... Because you was one of the party. – Well! – It is very true, the actions of Princes can never be concealed, too many people know them, and look out for them. I am not sorry the secret is discovered, as you have done a good action; had it been a bad one, it would have been equally known. This remark appeared to affect him; yet I saw he was much flattered with the painter's chusing the incident of the cloak for the principal subject of the picture. He looked at it with great satisfaction, and was much pleased with me for intending to send it to the Prince, his father, as he was then certain all the Court would see it. I the more readily forgave him this little piece of vanity, as it was the first he had shewn since this adventure. This, my dear Baron, is the History I had to give you. I make no apology for the prodigious length of my letter, because every thing you have done for your own children convinces me that whatever concerns Education must be interesting to you.

I have with great concern heard of the marriage of my niece! What a mother-in-law have they given her! ... You will judge whether I have not reason to grieve, knowing that Lady as I do, and recalling to my mind her dangerous and despicable qualities. But I flatter myself, my dear Baron, my sister will at least have the happiness of marrying her youngest daughter to her own satisfaction, and that I shall return to my own country to the wedding of Constantia and Theodore. Ah! if I can but see this so much wished-for union; and if the Prince should confirm the hopes I have entertained of him, what mortal on earth will be able to compare his happiness with mine?

LETTER XLVIII.

Baron to the Viscount.

IT is very true, my dear Viscount, you would not know Theodore again. He has no longer that fair and delicate complexion which children in general have who are brought up at Paris. He is a head taller, and grown strong in proportion; and this alteration in him is not only owing to the pure air of this country, but to the active life he leads. He is equally accustomed to heat and cold, to sunshine and rain, without being incommoded by either, as we use him to these things by degrees and in moderation; for I have not had the cruelty to make him hazard the loss of his life, in order to strengthen his limbs. Rousseau is for taking no precautions of this kind with children, but allows them to fall and hurt themselves, and would expose them to the severity of the coldest weather. In doing thus, he runs into the very evil which he so strongly recommends you to avoid, that of making children unhappy. He says, afterwards, 'What can be thought of this cruel method of education, where you sacrifice the present to an uncertain future?'[120] – In the same book, he also says, We should guard mankind from unforeseen accidents: let Emilius run about every morning in the coldest weather without shoes or stockings, either in his chamber, up and down stairs, or in the garden, and, far from being angry about it, I would imitate him,' [121]&c. &c.

This imitation is not so easy. For my part, I confess, I would not imitate Theodore, if in the month of January he chose to walk in my park, without shoes or stockings. Rousseau, always desirous of 'guarding his pupil against any sudden accidents,' disturbs his rest, interrupts his sleep, and wakes him abruptly, to make him get up in the middle of the night.[122] In short, Emilius appears to me to be the most tormented and the most unhappy child possible. Another of Rousseau's sentiments to me appears still more dangerous: 'Never permit your scholar,' says he, 'to value himself on his birth, his birth, his health, or his riches: but humble and alarm his vanity by shewing him the dangers by which mankind are surrounded; let him hear and attend to your description of the rocks against which he may be driven, and he will rely upon you to preserve him from them.'[123]

All this is in order to make him mild and compassionate! But for that purpose let us take another method; this will only make him a coward. In teaching him neither to value his health nor his riches, shew him the resources, which in the most dreadful reverse will remain to a man who has resolution and virtue. Describe this man to be brave, patient, and superior to his destiny; he will be so much more interesting, and your pupil will feel more compassion for him; but this pity, far from being contemptible, will give him more dignity and greatness of soul: his pity will become sublime, when it is united to admiration and esteem. In short, by this means your scholar will be deeply affected with the situation of the Hero, but he will not be terrified by it, and he will promise to support a similar fate with the same virtue, if he should ever meet with it. Adieu, my dear friend! I assure you, notwithstanding the happiness I enjoy here, I think, with great pleasure, that in another twelvemonth we shall go from hence, and that that period will again unite us. Mons. d' Aimeri went from hence yesterday with his grandson. He begins his journey to the North, where he has not been, and goes directly to ***. I have given him letters to the Count de Roseville, who I am sure will esteem him; for these two Gentlemen have both too much merit not to entertain a friendship for each other.

LETTER XLIX.

Baroness to the Viscountess.

ADELAIDE and THEODORE, for this fortnight past, have been put to hard trials; but at length they have conquered them to my satisfaction. They have both been taught for a long time, how important it was to have a command over themselves, and how contemptible it was to fail in their promises. – Adelaide being nine, and Theodore ten years old, we thought that, after having tired them with several little matters, in almost all of which they behaved very well, we might risk one which was more serious, and now begin to make experiments on their virtue. It will be necessary to tell you, that, for these two or three months, the appearance of enmity between Miss Bridget and Dainville seemed to be greatly lessened. Dainville made the first advances, and Miss Bridget received them with proper dignity, but with complaisance; and their former quarrels seemed entirely forgotten. In short, Dainville declares publickly, that Miss Bridget is a person of real merit, and Miss Bridget acknowledges that Dainville is a good young man in the main. It is from these circumstances that we formed our plan. You have not forgot Adelaide's putting the profile of Vespasian in a part of her chamber, in order to ridicule Miss Bridget; and that this had in appearance greatly diminished her affection for Adelaide, as well as her confidence in her: and you ought also to know, that Theodore on his part had given Dainville much cause of complaint. Now I begin my story:

Adelaide observed one morning, that Miss Bridget was exceedingly grave and absent. She asked her the reason of it; Miss Bridget sighed, blushed, turned pale, appeared confused, but remained silent. The questions were repeated on one side; the confusion increased on the other. Adelaide's curiosity was raised to the highest pitch. She begged, intreated, conjured. Miss Bridget hesitated, and said to her, Ah! if I could depend on your friendship, your discretion! ... What then? You fear me! ... I am very young, it is true; but I would sooner die than betray a secret. My dear Miss Bridget, you think me then a monster? ... Well then, I will tell you every thing this evening, if we are alone! ... Why not now? ... I cannot now: What I have to tell you will take up too much time ... Oh, Heaven, must I wait till evening! ... You must indeed; and let me caution you, that from this moment, if you are guilty of the smallest imprudence, that is, if you betray any sign of wishing to be alone with me, or any other mark of impatience, I will not tell you a single word of the matter. Does mamma know it? ... No person in the world knows it. I shall certainly acquaint your mamma with it, but not these two or three months yet: so you see you must not even mention it to her. You know she has often told you you must never betray, even to her, the secrets of another person. It is true, she has said to you, that any thing intrusted to you, which she is not to know, does not look well, and you should be in doubt ... But you, Miss Bridget, that she esteems so much! ... It is certain this makes a difference; besides, I assure you she shall know it one day or other ... To every body else I will refuse to listen to a secret which mamma is not to know; but ... You except this of mine, and is not that your meaning? I think I may without scruple. – Well then, you give me your word to keep it faithfully? ... I promise you ... That is sufficient ... At this instant the conversation was interrupted to the great concern of the impatient Adelaide. A servant came to tell her I wanted her, and she left Miss Bridget with an emotion which was still visible on her countenance, when she entered my chamber. During this time, Dainville had exactly the same conversation with my son, and received from him the same promise, you may therefore suppose, that Adelaide and Theodore waited impatiently for their hour of walking; but they were deceived in their hopes, we never left them a moment, and they went to bed without knowing the secret. Adelaide, while undressing, desired her maid to fetch Miss Bridget to her for one moment only. She returned for answer she could not come; and poor Adelaide went to bed very melancholy. The next day Miss Bridget made her many reproaches. 'You have been guilty,' said she, 'of at least ten indiscretions. You sent for me last night, and you, who are always so happy with your mamma, had such an appearance of trouble and impatience; you looked at me so earnestly! In short, you seemed to think of no one else! and every body observed that you did not behave as usual. I am therefore determined to try you still more, before I trust you with my secret; so that you will not know it till eight days hence, if, at the end of that time, I shall have no more cause to reproach you.' You may imagine this determination appeared very cruel, but there was no remedy; and Theodore was obliged to submit to the same law. At last these eight long days were passed; Adelaide and Theodore received the reward of their patience and discretion. The great secret is revealed; and they have been informed, that Miss Bridget and Dainville have been privately married these two months! You may easily guess the astonishment they were under at this intelligence. The only sensation they felt at first was the joy of being thought worthy to be told such an important secret; but they presently found out, that some secrets are very difficult to be kept. The same evening, when I was alone with Adelaide, I want to tell you something, said I, which will interest you. I am very busy in making a match for Dainville, which will be a good establishment for him. On hearing the word Match, she changed colour, which I did not appear to remark, but went on: I am going to marry him to a rich widow who lives at Carcassone. I have no doubt of his consent, and therefore I shall reserve the pleasure of surprising him with the news of it, when I have settled every thing. So that I desire you will mention it to no one, not even to Miss Bridget ... Why do you blush, Adelaide? ... Who me, mamma? ... Yes, you have blushed every time I mentioned Miss Bridget's name ... it is that ... You imagine perhaps, that Miss Bridget has still the same aversion for Dainville ... Oh no, mamma, on the contrary! ... How on the contrary! What would you say? ... Nothing, mamma ... Do you know any thing particular on that subject? ... But ... as to me, I am convinced that Miss Bridget still retains some resentment against Dainville; but, whatever be the case, I forbid you to say a single word about this intended marriage. After these words I changed the conversation. Adelaide fell into a deep reverie, and, under some pretence or other, I sent her to Miss Bridget. She did not tell her of our conversation, but she intreated her with the greatest earnestness to inform me of it, and she offered her service to prepare me for the news. All this Miss Bridget absolutely refused. The next day, I was walking alone with Adelaide; I expressed a concern for her health. My dear child, said I, you are melancholy; what is the matter? ... Nothing, mamma ... Your thoughts seem much taken up, you are absent, what are you thinking of? ... Mamma! ... How, does this question confuse you? ... You have frequently assured me, and in this very garden, that you would never hesitate to tell me your most secret thoughts, let them be what they would, if I asked you ... Without an entire confidence, there can be no real affection ... So I would, mamma; I would tell you all my secrets ... Well then, what was you thinking of just now? ... Why don't you tell me? ... But what do I see, you weep! ... It is because I am not able to tell you ... Yet! ... But I must not tell you a lye ... What then is it? ... Mamma, ought I to tell you the secret of another person, when you ask me? ... Another person's secret; what then you know a secret which I am ignorant of? ... Yes, mamma, and a very great secret ... I suppose it was by chance you discovered it? ... No, mamma, it was intrusted to me, and I gave my word of honour not to tell you of it. – And how could you engage to do so? ... You was not sensible, that you either would be obliged to break your word, or to deceive me in not answering my questions with truth! Therefore you see how dangerous curiosity may prove! ... Mamma, may I hope, that you will not ask me any more questions about it? ... Then it is necessary, with this curiosity, that you have more command over yourself, and that you do not appear so absent and your thoughts so much taken up. For, if you had the greatest prudence imaginable in this respect, how could you escape the single question which I asked you so often. Adelaide, what are you thinking of? You would always have deceived me by your answers. Deceive your mother! Your only true friend, or break your word and discover your secret! – I thought, mamma, I might have been excused, if I owned I had a secret; and that, when you knew I had promised to keep it, you would not insist on my telling you. – But merely to confess you have a secret is always betraying half of it, and very frequently the whole. For example, how are you able to keep an important secret? From your father it cannot be, since he keeps nothing from me. As to your maid, I have forbid your ever talking to her on any subject; and it is impossible that it can be any man who has trusted you with a secret. Therefore it is very easy to discover that it can be nobody but Miss Bridget who has placed this confidence in you: and, having found out so much as that, the rest I may learn before the day is out. Thus you have not kept your promise, never to conceal any thing from me; you have unthinkingly given your word of honour. You have for several days been guilty of a hundred indiscretions, and at last you discover the secret which has been deposited with you! See how many faults are united! And all for want of reflection, and because you could not resist the emotion of a foolish curiosity. This conversation ended by my positive order not to acquaint Miss Bridget with what had passed. I left her for eight days in an uncertainty, which was painful enough to a temper so curious and impatient as her's, whether I had come to an explanation with Miss Bridget, or whether she knew that I had got the secret out of Adelaide, or whether I was acquainted with the secret marriage, not daring to ask a question, and not being able to find out by our conduct she was in an uneasy suspence, which she could not very easily tell how to bear. But, having felt the force of her first faults, she had power enough over herself to be silent, and to appear with a calm and serene countenance. The time arrived, when the secret was to be made known. Miss Bridget took Adelaide by the hand, and, embracing her, said to her, the secret I confided to you is now no longer to be kept so, and I am going to acquaint you with the truth. As you had given me reason to doubt your friendship for me, I was desirous to put you to the proof, before I bestowed all mine on you: and therefore I intrusted you with an imaginary secret. You have kept it very well in some respects. You have not told your brother of it, nor have you given Dainville any suspicion of your knowing such a thing. You avoided telling your mamma of it; at the same time you have carefully concealed from me, that she had forbid you to tell me what she said, and you have convinced me that you are really interested in my happiness. All this is acting very nobly at your age, as you are not yet ten years old. I perceive you have a good head, and that you will be very prudent, when you are less governed by your curiosity, and have learned to have more command over yourself. What! cried Adelaide, are you not married then to Mons. Dainville? ... How could you suppose, if it was so, replied Miss Bridget, that I should have confided the secret to you in preference to telling it to your mamma? ... I have often told you, Adelaide, said I, that you should always be suspicious of any information you received which I was not to know; and with a little more reflection you might have guessed Miss Bridget only did it to try you, and that she knew too well the duty you owed to me to be able to endeavour to make you fail in it. Do you not see plainly what you was ignorant of before? And why? Because you was so much taken up with the desire of learning the secret: because you suffered your curiosity to get the better of you sense; and because that every passion, to which you give yourself up, takes away your judgment and makes you blind.[124] I hope, my dear friend, you will forgive my troubling you with this long, and, in appearance, trifling account: but it will not be useless to you, if you really wish to adopt my method. This is the only certain way of succeeding in your lessons, and I shall put my child to every proof of this kind, in order to form her character, and strengthen her understanding. When she comes into company, she will know by her own experience, and without having learned it at the expence of her happiness or reputation, all the inconveniencies of giddiness, eagerness, indiscretion, curiosity, weakness, &c. in short, she will know how to conquer her passions. Theodore will receive the same instructions: he has gone through all the same trials which I have told you of Adelaide, and has behaved still better than she has, for he never gave the least cause of suspicion, that he had been trusted with a great secret. But he is a year older than his sister, and, when children have a good education, a year makes a great difference.

LETTER L.

Madame d' Ostalis to the Baroness.

I AM this day, my dear aunt, three-and-twenty years old; and I cannot celebrate my birth-day better than in conversing with you; but, when I think, that for these three long years I have been separated from you, and that I shall still be deprived of the happiness of seeing you for another twelvemonth, my heart is very melancholy ... The only thing which I receive consolation from is the thought of having conducted myself at this distance from you in the same manner as if you was always with me; in short, the having exactly followed the rules you gave me, and the advice which you have constantly pointed out to me in your letters, those dear letters in which I find so much to make me amends for the distance which is between us. You will never be told on your return to Paris, that your child is guilty of coquetry; this odious vice, for which you have given me so just and so serious an aversion. I have never turned the brain of any one, and I can even boast, that it has never been said, that any person has fallen in love with me. It is true, I have followed your advice, and always preserved a proper behaviour, with that mild tranquillity which you recommended to me; that I have made use of no arts, and have never gone into company by myself, that is, without my mother-in-law, till within these two years; and almost always with Mons. d' Ostalis: that I never received company at my own house till last year, and that those I associate with are very sensible as well as reasonable people;

that I neither go to Balls nor Operas,[125] nor ride on horseback: and therefore it is not astonishing, that I should have preserved my reputation without blemish. This is a cause of great happiness to me, and I value it at too high a price not to endeavour to keep it.

I have no satisfactory intelligence to give you of Madame de Valcy. Madame de Limours is blinded towards her in every particular. She is persuaded that she loves her husband tenderly, but I do not believe a word of it. She is already the greatest coquette you ever saw, and, when her mother is not present, she boasts of it: and is weak enough to think that this confession is infinitely graceful, and that it shews her to be possessed of a most amiable frankness. I think, my dear aunt, you will not find this frankness much to your taste; in my opinion, it appears both indelicate and absurd. She has altered that stiff formal appearance she put on, on her being married. She is now frisking and fluttering about, seems to be all life, and her head appears to be the perpetual motion. I think, if I was inclined to coquetry, I should rather attempt to please by my understanding and conversation than my person. But Madame de Valcy takes a quite contrary method. To give you some idea of it, I will relate to you an account of a breakfast which we had yesterday at Madame de Limours'. There were only four Ladies of us, Madame de Limours, Madame de Valcy, myself, and Madame de Germeiul, a young woman about my age, married about four years, neither beautiful nor amiable; but she has an elegant figure, and has some gracefulness in her manner, though very inconsiderate and giddy, and full of affection. Madame de Valcy is intimately attached to her, for these six months past. We were moderately gay at breakfast, when Madame de Limours received a letter which called her out of the room. She desired me, in her absence, to be her daughter's Chaperon. The moment after she was gone, the Marquis de L— and the Chevalier Creni were announced – It is reported, that the latter is in love with Madame de Valcy, and that the Marquis is likewise attached to Madame de Germeiul. I was seated between these two Ladies, and immediately took notice of their behaviour which was wonderfully changed. Madame de Valcy appeared all at once to have a violent affection for me! She embraced me, affected to whisper in my ear continually, as if to tell me a secret, when she only said things of no kind of consequence, and then burst into violent fits of laughter. All this was accompanied with such motions of the head as is impossible to describe, but from which I suffered great inconvenience, for every moment I found her feathers and her braid in my face. At length, seeing that I was very cool, and did not return her great and sudden friendship, she rose from her seat with Madame de Germeiul, and they walked arm in arm up and down the room, for six or eight minutes, with great carelessness. They then seated themselves on a sopha in a studied attitude, in order that it might be said, that they formed a most beautiful picture.

At length I returned home without being able to comprehend how people can be so stupid as to suppose they can make conquests by such ridiculous means. I should rather prefer the coquetry of an English Lady, whom Mons. de Herbain met with in his travels; she was very beautiful, but through a strange caprice she disdained a conquest which was only obtained by her person: and, when she wished any one to fall in love with her, she renounced dress, and concealed her fine hair, and half her face, under a large hat; and, covering herself with a cloak, she hid from their sight the most elegant shape in the world. But she took care to display all the charms of her mind, and by the insinuating graces of her conversation, and the delicacy of her wit, she triumphs over the most beautiful or best dressed rivals in the world. By this means, added the Chevalier de Herbain, this dangerous coquette was not content with slight attentions, but inspired her admirers with serious and lasting passions. Adieu, my dear aunt! I am going this moment to Versailles. I shall return the day after to-morrow, and will then write to you again, and send you the little box of Music which you asked me for – They send for me, they wait for me. Adieu! your child embraces you as tenderly as she loves you.

LETTER LI.

From the Viscountess to the Baroness.

I AM every day more pleased with my situation, my dear friend; at least I am so with my daughter, for my happiness depends on her conduct and her affection for me. I told you all the little causes of complaint I had against her, on her first being married. But those little clouds are now vanished, and I begin to believe, that, in doubting her sensibility, mine has often made me unjust. She loves her husband passionately. In general, all the emotions of her heart are violent; and tho' these tempers may be more dangerous than others, you must agree that they are the only ones that are formed for attachments. I ought to applaud myself for having given her to the man of her choice: a person so impetuous, open, and with such lively passions as she has, could never have supported an engagement contrary to her inclinations. She, who could never bear the slightest contradiction, even in the most trifling matters! She has many faults, I confess, but they are chiefly owing to her vivacity and the little dissimulation of which she is capable. You have known me suspect her of falsehood on some occasions, and it gave me great affliction. Thank Heaven, I was deceived; and, as she herself tells me, what I was inclined to attribute to artifice was merely owing to her being inconsiderate and giddy; and, in fact, these are her principal faults; and, her heart, besides, is very susceptible of good impressions, and will yield to them. She has made choice of a friend, and loves her to excess. This friend is a few years older than herself, has been married about four years, and is equally distinguished by her birth, situation, and agreeable behaviour. It is with great pleasure that I observe my daughter giving herself up to all the enthusiasm of a first friendship. But at present let us talk of an object which is still more interesting to you, since you mean one day or other to adopt her for your own: Constantia will not have the striking charms of her sister; her beauty is of the softer kind; her gentle and ingenuous disposition, together with a constant sweetness of temper, makes every body delighted with her: her understanding is infinitely above the age of seven years. She has great sensibility, but is timid and bashful, always the same, always serious, fearful, and submissive; so that, in spite of her beauty, she seems more formed to be loved than admired. I think her temper and disposition would suit you exactly; and that you will find her an artless, sensible, and amiable girl; which appears to me to be all we wish. May she insure the happiness of our beloved Theodore, and we shall then be still more united than ever, applaud ourselves, and enjoy together a general felicity! Ah, my dear friend! these happy days are still at a distance! ... And, waiting for their arrival, what sacrifices have you made! I admire them, but I sigh and complain of them more and more. I have neither your courage, your enthusiasm, nor your philosophy, to inable me to support myself properly. Adieu! forgive me this weakness, on account of the tender affection which occasions it.

LETTER LII.

Answer from the Baroness.

I CONGRATULATE you, my dear friend, on the happiness you enjoy at this time. Certain of possessing your daughter's affections, I think with you, that you ought to bear with and excuse her faults; her loving you will be sufficient. When she grows older, her temper will insensibly improve. You tell me she has made choice of an intimate friend. Allow me to give you some remarks on that subject, which I formerly made, when I had opportunities of observing what passed in society. This part of your letter brings it back to my mind, and perhaps it may be of use to you. It is by lavishing the sacred names of friendship and confidence, on all those transient and trifling attachments we are continually forming, that we are come almost to doubt whether such a sentiment as friendship exists at all. This rapid succession of lively and tumultuous emotions exhausts and hardens the heart, without being able to affect it. Fickleness proceeds from want of affection; we wish to attach ourselves, we change with the hope or prospect of making a better choice, and our lives pass away, in seeking, what at last we imagine is no-where to be met with, because we have not found it. These errors proceed from our own prejudices, and are every day increasing. One real attachment is sufficient for our hearts. But people persuade us we should have several at the same time. So, to make happiness more uncommon, they establish differences which do not exist, and give to the same sentiment an infinity of names. They divide it also into many branches, and they assure us, that perfect felicity consists in finding objects to fill this numerous list. I am going to make you a calculation according to these received notions. A young woman, taught to think in this manner, knows, if she does not love her husband, that she ought to be in love, and therefore she looks out for lover; she also knows, that she should feel a tender affection for her relations, which is a different sentiment from that of friendship; she visits them, and pays them all proper attentions, which is the whole of what they expect from her. She has brothers and sisters; the affection she feels for them is called by a particular name, but all these are not sufficient; she must, besides, have a faithful friend. Sympathy comes to her assistance, and, at the end of six months, she perhaps meets with this person worthy to possess all her confidence. But, not contented with one, she must have what are called *friends*, for they distinguish between your particular friend and your friends. The latter are only intitled to half your confidence, or the secrets of the moment. If they are ill, you must go and shut yourselves up with them, to take care of them. There ought to be five or six of them, all equal both in rank and privileges, and inferior only to your particular friend. So you see there are two sorts of friendship distinct from each other, without reckoning the ties of relationship, or the passion of love. Your affection for your intimate friend is to last for ever. You must wear her picture, and have bracelets with her hair. You are never without three or four secrets to whisper in her ear, whenever you meet, even if you have not left her a quarter of an hour: and you are never invited to a supper, unless she is of the party. But, as to your other friends, you only feel for them a kind of a tranquil and tender regard founded on esteem and convenience, which has nothing violent in it. If one should chance to be possessed of a little cunning, there is another sentiment, which is called interest. This may fall on about a dozen people of our acquaintance, whom we select on account of their superior rank or fortune: and this will require us, during their absence, to write a letter to them once a month, or, if they are sick, one must send to know how they do, two or three times a day; and, in case of their death, one must absent one's self from public places, for at least the remainder of the week. All these ceremonies are marked so exactly and followed so strictly, that it is easy to see they have been learned from infancy, and that education and custom have fixed them in the memory. Is it not as strange as it is ridiculous, that a young person, who finds in her own family objects which ought so naturally to engage her affections, should go among strangers, to form those idle and trifling connexions, which, without having power to make her amends, by degrees insensibly estrange her for ever from all those persons whom she ought to love best? ... Believe me, it is not a friend, that people seek for at eighteen: it is not a guide and adviser they wish for, because they may find those in a mother or a husband. But these they neglect. They only wish to form a connexion that may be taken notice of: they chuse a person most admired and most in fashion to fix their affection on. But, above all, they want a kind, complying confidant, and this it is that makes people suspect, when they see two young women so very intimate, that they are concerned together in some imprudent affair.[126] They begin by communicating to each other all the little secrets of their passed life, till by degrees their imaginations are heated, and, to shew they have the strictest confidence in each other, they betray their inmost thoughts, particularly on the subject of love: and their communications are generally exaggerated, and give false ideas of the conquests they have made. In these little Histories their vanity frequently alters the facts, and often conceals the truth. They acquire a taste for intrigue and a habit of telling lyes; and they use themselves to this practice, in order to give their friend, whom they care for no longer than she will listen to them, all these proofs of their lively and passionate attachment. From what I have observed, I should think it right to point out to young people, by mild and gentle means, the folly and absurdity of forming such attachments which they are so fond of. Adieu, my dear friend! A letter from you is just brought me; I shall therefore finish this without regret, as I am not going to quit you altogether.

LETTER LIII.

From the same to the same.

WHAT attention ought one to pay to children, even in the most trifling things! ... Adelaide almost always tells truth. Education has confirmed this virtue in her, she never attempts the smallest disguise to try to hide any of her faults; and yet, notwithstanding this, I have found her, for some days past, making stories from the gaiety of her heart; and, to amuse herself, Dainville last week was relating to us a very comical dream which he had, and at which we laughed very much. The next day Adelaide dreamt also, and acquainted me with her dream, to which I paid little attention; and, two days after, she had another: and, in short, this morning, she has related so pretty a tale, that I am convinced she composed it at her leisure, and she has since acknowledged, that she invented them all. I had no great difficulty to make her understand, if it is wicked to tell lyes for the sake of interest, it is still more inexcusable to do it without any motive. I have often told you, said I, what a mean and detestable vice lying is, and how much it is despised. I must tell you yet more, that those who are guilty of it can never be esteemed, nor thought amiable. There are numbers of people who amuse themselves by composing Histories, which without any scruple they pass off for truth, because they do no harm to any body. These people have no other intention in exaggerating and in telling lyes, but to entertain their acquaintance, and make themselves agreeable in company; but they mistake the matter, and dishonour themselves by it in the most ridiculous and foolish manner: and a man, who tells lyes in this way, for his own pleasure, is never believed in any thing. Whatever he says, let it be ever so agreeable, can never interest you, because he never can raise your attention or gain your confidence; and he is, indeed, scarcely listened to. While persons of veracity, supposing even they have not much understanding, if they have any thing extraordinary to relate, are always listened to with attention, and heard with pleasure. Besides, the esteem we have for such characters, the certainty that one may believe all they say makes their conversation interesting, and their company agreeable. And, were they only possessed of this single virtue, they would be esteemed and sought after. After these observations, I requested Adelaide to compose no more dreams for the future.

I have just received a letter from Madame d' Ostalis, in which she speaks of nothing but our charming little Constantia; she tells me she is amazingly improved, and that she is beautiful as an Angel. I am almost sorry for it. To be sure extreme ugliness is a real misfortune, but perfect beauty is a gift of Nature, always dangerous, and frequently pernicious and fatal! A person of perfect beauty, who draws all eyes upon her, is judged with the greatest severity, even when jealousy is out of the question. Curiosity, which is natural to us, seeks to find out, if this object who charms us so much possesses other qualities which we wish to find in her. Even a good and gentle mind will experience this sentiment; the beauty, which charms us so much at the fight of it, will give us a desire to know more of her. This disinterested idea keeps us from distrust. We do not consider, that love and hatred are equally blind, that indifference examines nothing, and that benevolence alone is just and clear-sighted; and that this is the general opinion. Therefore it is, that an advantage, so valuable in appearance, is in fact very dangerous. It is much the same thing in another way, as with a man in a humble situation raised to superior rank. Every eye is fixed upon him with the intention of discovering his most trifling faults; and, while flattery is paying homage to him, hatred and calumny endeavour to blacken and dishonour him and truth itself unveils and accuses him. All his faults are observed, repeated, and exaggerated. Take from him this shining title which has decorated and exposed him, and half of his faults will be unknown; nobody will give themselves the trouble of discovering his vices, they will remain secret in his heart, and the actions he wishes to conceal will never be brought into day-light. It is very seldom that a woman perfectly beautiful is in other respects amiable. She thinks Nature has done every thing for her; that it is sufficient for her to be seen, in order to enchant and reduce; and that no other qualities are half so estimable. With these sentiments she goes into company, and all her success depends on the impression she makes at first sight; these uncertain effects, which cannot be lasting, only leave behind them indifference, insipidity, and often disgust. With her the mind has no employment, the heart is cold, and it is a very true observation, 'that the most tender attachments are seldom inspired by the most beautiful persons.'[127]

A figure which has nothing disgusting in it, a countenance which marks the character, and points out sense or good humour, these are the most desirable qualities; and add to these the graces of the mind, gentleness of manners and sense, without affectation, and you will see whether beauty alone will ever be able to dispute the prize. Therefore, my dear friend, redouble your attentions to Constantia, be sure to convince her, that beauty can never supply the place of other amiable qualities, when she comes into company. That it will only expose her to the cruel envy of women, and the impertinence of the men; and that, in attracting the general notice, she will only be a means of drawing on herself observations on her errors and foibles which would not otherwise have been seen: but that it is in her power to make modesty still more interesting, and to give to virtue a still more brilliant appearance. Do not endeavour to conceal from her that she is beautiful; it is a thing impossible to hide. Talk of it with coldness and indifference, without appearing to set any kind of value on it. At the same time tell her, if she should preserve it, which is very uncertain, till she is five-and-twenty, that she will see a hundred in that space of time, that may not have such regular beauty as she, who will be greatly preferred by being more in the fashion and taste of the world. Did we not see that Madame de Gerville passed at one time for the prettiest creature in the world, in spite of the song which criticized so dreadfully, but, at the same time so justly, her shape, her teeth, her complexion, her mouth, and her nose? – As nobody is absolutely perfect, when you do not conceal from her that she is handsome, tell her also as freely, the faults which may be found with her, that she may not look upon herself as a miracle of beauty: and let her be used to hear herself criticized, without shewing spite or vexation. And to effect this, make your remarks on her little imperfections, not with an air of concern, but as if it was a matter of indifference. Adelaide is really very pretty, and she knows it, but never seems to think about it. Some days ago, I gave a dinner to almost all my neighbours. The company was very brilliant, Adelaide was well dressed, and looked remarkably handsome. All the guests cried out, how beautiful she was! and that they had never seen any thing so lovely or so agreeable. In the evening, when we were alone, Miss Bridget asked me the name of the Nobleman who sat on my right hand, and whose conversation appeared to interest me very much; I answered, he was called Mons. de Lorme; that he had travelled a great deal, and was very sensible and agreeable. But a little severe, said Miss Bridget; and there happened to me a droll adventure, which I shall tell you of without hesitation, before Mademoiselle Adelaide, who I am sure will be the first to laugh at it. I lay a wager, added Mons. d' Almane, you heard him say he did not think Adelaide pretty. Oh! that, said Miss Bridget, would not be worth relating, for every one to their taste; and, if Mademoiselle were as beautiful as an Angel, she would not please every body; but that Mons. de Lorme should have selected me for his confidant on this subject is very remarkable. He took me for one of the neighbouring Ladies, and, half an hour before dinner, while the company were all in the Saloon, I was walking on the terrasse, where he joined me, and entered into conversation. I asked him what he thought of Mademoiselle Adelaide's explanation of the Historical Pictures in the Saloon and other rooms? I think it wonderful, said he, and what I have admired above all is, that she explains them without any affectation of learning, and only speaks when she is questioned. She will do well to preserve this modest simplicity, for, without these qualities, let her have ever so much knowledge, she will only appear troublesome and tiresome, and at the same time ridiculous. This, continued he, is what I would have wished they had found in this young person to applaud, instead of admiring her person, as they did; which, in my opinion, is nothing extraordinary. Indeed, said I, they give her very trifling praises: it is true, that she is very pretty; but, ... Pretty, – interrupted he, I do not think so at all. She is a little figure, without any regularity, with a pleasing look, which is, however, very common; and I do assure you, the greatest part of the company, who have declared her so lovely, do not think so in reality. I am above this ridiculous flattery, I assure you; and I much wish this child, whom I really admire, on account of her education, should know how little truth there is in such compliments as they have paid her, and how injurious they are to the person to whom they are addressed, for they must suppose her very vain, and very silly to believe it, and be delighted with it. This discourse appeared to me to be very sensible, and I should have liked to have prolonged it; but Mademoiselle Adelaide came to tell me dinner was on the table. By the manner in which she spoke, Mons. de Lorme found I belonged to the family; and Mademoiselle Adelaide might perceive that he appeared much confused, and that I spoke very softly to him, because he begged me not to betray him, which I promised I would not. So then he thought, said Adelaide, if I knew he did not think me handsome, I should be grieved. I wish he was to know the truth of this matter! ... Adelaide is much in the right, said I. But how can it be done? He will not come here again, and he leaves the country in two days. Miss Bridget, said Mons. d' Almane, must write him a letter, and, as he is a man of great merit, and is besides fifty years old, Adelaide may, if her mother will permit her, add a few lines from herself in the letter. I approved of this scheme, but Adelaide had some difficulty to consent to it, as she was afraid of not spelling quite properly. However, at last, Miss Bridget prevailed on her, and when she had wrote her own letter, in which she acquainted Mons. de Lorme that she had found his remarks so very just, that she could not help telling them to her young friend. Adelaide shut herself up in her closet to add her few lines. She staid there a long time, and, when she came out, she blushed exceedingly, and brought us the letter in her hand, which was extremely well written, and was as follows: 'It is very true, Sir, I am neither surprised, nor angry, that you did not think me handsome; this might very well happen, and, when I am flattered, and told I am pretty, I often think it is done to make a joke of me. I had much rather be praised for the little knowledge I have gained, and for the qualities of my mind, because, that is praising my mamma, as well as me. I intreat you, Sir, not to think me a young girl of an absurd and frivolous turn. With such a mother as I have, I can never be either one or the other.'

I approved this billet very much, and we sent it immediately by a postilion, with orders to carry it to Mons. de Lorme, who was to spend a day or two at a friend's house about two leagues from hence. Adelaide was impatient for his return, which he did about nine o'clock with Mons. de Lorme's answer, which I send you:

'Madam, I cannot believe that Miss Bridget has told you I thought you plain. I think I could never have made use of such an expression. I do not like to exaggerate any thing, and especially when it would be unpolite and disobliging. I even think your person may be called very pleasing; for taste and opinions have not settled ideas relative to beauty or ugliness; persons judge variously, and frequently the most indifferent face is preferred to the most beautiful; and this proves, that those who wish for general admiration, merely on account of their beauty, are equally absurd and ridiculous. But you, Madam, will never be one of these: it is by the sweetness of your temper, by your mildness, your steadiness, your sense, and your talents, that you wish to please; and, if you go on improving with the education you will have, you will make one of the most distinguished as well as one of the most pleasing persons in society: and perhaps, in eight or ten years, chance may procure me the happiness of meeting you, when I shall with great pleasure see my predictions verified.'

Adelaide was very well satisfied with this letter, which she said she should keep and read over from time to time. She added, Mons. de Lorme was not a very polite man, but that he had a great deal of prudence and good sense. You cannot think, my dear friend, how very amusing this kind of lessons is. Instead of preaching long sermons, which tire both the speaker and the hearer, we invent these pretty plans, which we bring into action, and perform the principal parts without the trouble of getting them by heart; and, I assure you, these little

Comedies, which sometimes engage us for ten or twelve days, both interest and entertain us more than you have any idea of.

LETTER LIV.

The Count de Roseville to the Baron.

I AM going to inform you of such an extraordinary event, my dear Baron, that I would not delay a moment writing to you, particularly, as Mons. d' Aimeri is the principal person concerned in my History. The friendship you have for him would have been sufficient to have made me regard him. But his great merit, and the dreadful misfortunes he has met with, have given him a right to my most tender friendship, which he will ever possess. I guess what your curiosity must be, and I will satisfy it. Mons. d' Aimeri arrived here about ten days ago. After what you wrote to me about him, I took a lodging for him at a friend's house, and, the evening he came here, I went to make him a visit. A slight indisposition obliged him to keep his chamber a few days, at the end of which he went over the city, and saw every thing that was curious in it; people mentioned to him the house of Mons. d' Anglures, as being well worth his seeing. He wished much to go there to visit this extraordinary and benevolent man, whom I have already mentioned to you. As I am very intimate with him, I promised Mons. d' Aimeri to carry him thither. We went the next day, as soon as we had dined, Mons. d' Aimeri, Charles, and myself, in the same carriage. When we had got there, we were told Mons. d' Anglures was gone to take a walk in the fields, but that he would certainly be at home presently, and we were desired to walk into his apartments. About half an hour after, finding Mons. d' Aimeri was much engaged by a Cabinet of Natural History, I offered to conduct his grandson into the gardens, which were well worth viewing, and of which I will give you an account in my next letter. We had scarce left the house, when a servant came to tell us that Mons. d' Anglures was returned from his walk, and was looking for us. At that instant we saw him coming to join us. He had no sooner cast his eyes on Charles, than I perceived a great alteration in his countenance; he looked at him with an air of astonishment and tenderness, and, after a moment's silence, he cried out, My God, what a likeness! ... And, turning his head, he wiped his eyes, which were filled with tears. He then came up to Charles, and, taking him by the hand, pardon, said he, my curiosity, but ... How old are you? ... Fifteen years and a half, replied Charles ... Oh, Heaven, said Mons. d' Anglures, the very sound of her voice! ... Ah, Sir, said he, addressing himself to me, who is this young man, what is his name? ... The Chevalier de Valmont ... I had no sooner mentioned his name, than Mons. d' Anglures took Charles in his arms, and pressed him to his bosom with such transport as would have made me easily guess the cause, had I known more of Mons. d' Aimeri's story; but, not being acquainted with any of the particulars of it, I regarded this scene with inexpressible surprise. When Mons. d' Anglures turned to me, and said, you shall know this very day, the cause of the situation in which you see me; you shall learn it, and you will pity me: I am sure you will! ... But who does this dear child travel with! Is it with a Governor? No, said I, with his grand-father ... His grand-father, said Mons. d' Anglures, with a frantic air! ... Yes, Mons. d' Aimeri ... What do you say, interrupted he, is Mons. d' Aimeri here? Is he now in my house! ... He pronounced these words in so loud a voice, and at the same time so faultering, and with anger so strongly painted in his eyes, which were still filled with tears, that I plainly saw, if he had met with an interesting and beloved object in Charles, he had also found a detested enemy in Mons. d' Aimeri. I hope, said I, to him, you will remember the rights of hospitality, and that you will do nothing contrary to the high opinion I have of your sense and virtue. Ah! if you knew, cried he ... He stopped, appeared to reflect a moment, and, turning his eyes on Charles, his rage, instead of lessening, seemed to collect new strength; and Charles, who till then had remained motionless, at last broke silence: Sir, said he, do you know my grand-father, and can you have any complaint against him? If so, I am ready to offer in his name any satisfaction which you can desire ... Generous boy, interrupted Mons. d' Anglures, embracing him! But let me ask you once more, said Charles, do you know my grand-father? ... Mons. d' Anglures took a moment to reply, then, assuming a milder air, he does not know me, said he, as you will find. But, by a strange fatality, his name brings to my mind the most dreadful events: I wish to see him instantly. Wait for us in the garden. No, no, interrupted Charles, with great quickness, you shall not see him but in my company ... Young man, replied Mons. d' Anglures, with a little severity, I forgive the unkind fears you entertain of me; it is a respectable cause which inspires you with it. But remember, I consent that the Count de Roseville shall be witness to this interview; besides that, I am in my own house, and, supposing it to be true that Mons. d' Aimeri is my enemy, he would always find here a sacred asylum. Mons. d' Anglures is right, said I, and I think Mons. d' Aimeri himself would blame you for the words you have just made use of. Stay here, therefore, and in a quarter of an hour we will return to you again. At these words we quitted Charles, who was not yet intirely freed from his tears. For my part, I was surprised and confused at every thing I had seen and heard, and waited with some concern, and extreme-curiosity, to see how this affair would end. I did not venture to ask Mons. d' Anglures any questions. But, on entering the house, he said, go, my dear Count, and see for Mons. d' Aimeri; I only request you will not say a word to him of what has passed. I will not, said I. Then, said he, wait, till I send for you. He then left me without giving me time to answer him. I found Mons. d' Aimeri where I had left him in the room, and he was so busily employed with the study of Natural History, that he did not even perceive that I was returned without his grandson. In about ten minutes a servant came to inform us that Mons. d' Anglures waited for us in another room. This invitation gave me some pain; but Mons. d' Aimeri, always absent, did not take notice of it. I took him by the arm, and we followed the servant, who led us through several apartments, and came at last to the door of another, where he stopped, gave us the key, and then left us. I immediately unlocked it, and went in first. I thought I had been acquainted with all the house, which I had been over fifty times. But I saw with astonishment, that this apartment, as remarkable as it was magnificent, was intirely unknown to me; the walls and the floor were marble of the most dazzling whiteness, and, at the end opposite the door, were four grand pillars of porphyry, supporting a canopy of silver stuff, ornamented with silver fringe, before which were fastened curtains of gauze, which, being then drawn close, concealed the whole of the pavilion. But, the moment Mons. d' Aimeri appeared in the room, the curtains were drawn up, and we discovered Mons. d' Anglures, who, addressing himself to Mons. d' Aimeri, said to him in a dreadful voice: Lift up your eyes, barbarian, and contemplate the work of your hands! ... Mons. d' Aimeri trembled, and cast his eyes on the affecting object, which was to tear open all the wounds of his heart ... He saw, standing on a pedestal of white marble, a statue representing Fidelity[128] bathed in tears. She held in one hand some long and beautiful ringlets of flaxen hair, and in the other a letter half folded, of which no words could be seen but the name, written in large letters of gold, of Cecilia. At the sight of this, your unhappy friend, petrified with astonishment, and overwhelmed with grief, remained a moment quite motionless. Then casting his eyes towards Mons. d' Anglures, he trembled, he shook, and supporting himself against one of the pillars: What, said he, the Chevalier de Murville! ... Yes! himself, interrupted the Chevalier; I am that unfortunate man, thy most implacable enemy ... Oh, my daughter! ... cried Mons. d' Aimeri! He could not say more, his sobs deprived him of speech. *Inhuman!* replied Mons. d' Anglures, *of what happiness has thy execrable ambition deprived me!* It is just, that this ambition should at length serve to double your confusion and remorse. Think of the fortune I posses, of these riches which I despise, and which I could never know the value of, but in sharing them with the object I adored. The innocent victim of thy cruelty, as sensible of her misfortune as I was; for, alas! if you are still ignorant of it, learn now, that she loved me! ... Yes, barbarian, Cecilia loved me, and in spite of thy unheard of cruelty, It is she who ordered me 'to respect thy life!' It is she alone who could have kept back this wretched arm ... I abandoned my country; I came to the farthermost part of the North, to seek in vain the repose which you have taken from me for ever! ... One only friend, that I have left at Paris, every year gives me an account of Cecilia; I know that she still lives ... return thanks to Heaven ... For, as long as she exists, you have nothing to fear from my resentment; but ... Ah! then, interrupted Mons. d' Aimeri, satisfy your revenge ... Your friend deceives you ... Cecilia is no more! ... She is no more! cried the Chevalier de Murville; Cecilia dead, and you still breathe! ... At these words, astonished, and almost frantic, he advanced fiercely towards Mons. d' Aimeri ... I threw myself between them at this moment. Charles, led by his anxiety, entered suddenly, and, seeing me holding the Chevalier's arm, cried, why do you deceive me? What is the meaning of this furious passion! ... If my grandfather is the object of it, it is I that demand the cause of it ... These words brought the Chevalier de Murville again to himself. The countenance of Charles, and the sound of his voice, was to him an irresistible charm. Tenderness took place of his rage; his eyes were filled with tears, and turning towards Mons. d' Aimeri; ah! cried he, give me this child, and I will forgive you the evils with which you have imbittered my life! ... Mons. d' Aimeri, far from being able to answer him, did not even hear him. Plunged into the deepest reverie, his eyes fixed on the hair of his unhappy daughter, he was wholly taken up with that melancholy object. I approached him, and seizing hold of his arm: Come, said I, let us leave Mons. de Murville to his own reflections, doubtless he will soon reproach himself with having aggravated grief, a thousand times more painful than his own. Yes, Sir, continued I, going up to the Chevalier, I was ignorant both of your name and your passion for the unfortunate Cecilia; but, I know, that it was in the arms of her father that she gave her last sigh: and that this unhappy father, inconsolable for her loss, weighed down with sorrow and regret, could not have supported life, but for the sake of this young man ... The nephew of Cecilia, and the only son which Heaven has left him ... What then, replied the Chevalier, his son is dead! ... And he laments Cecilia! ... Ah! if he is unhappy, I am the only person guilty! ... Cease to reproach yourself, cried Mons. d' Aimeri, for an anger which appears to me to be the effect of the wrath of Heaven which pursues me ... It is true, that strong resentments last for ever in generous souls. You ought never to pardon me, and I should excuse every thing you have done. At these words, Mons. d' Aimeri, leaning on Charles's arm, and supported by me on the other side, left the house. You will easily conceive the deep and melancholy impressions this scene produced on Mons. d' Aimeri; I brought him back to *** in a situation truly worthy of pity. I spent the evening with him, and he related to me, before the Chevalier de Valmont, all his History; and ended by this advice, which he addressed to his grandson: 'You may one day be a father, said he. Take care never to prefer one child to another, as an object of greater tenderness; restrain yourself from a sentiment of preference, which soon will plunge you into a fatal blindness, for the errors and vices of this favourite child, and will make you cruel and unjust to all the others.'

The next day, I returned alone to the Chevalier de Murville, whom I found in the greatest grief, and reproaching himself with his behaviour the night before. I made him still more wretched by the account Mons. d' Aimeri had given me of all that had happened. He was drowned in tears at the recital of what passed at the cottage where Cecilia received the fatal impression which cost her life. And you may easily suppose what he must feel, on hearing the account of her sickness and death! After answering all his questions, I asked him some in my turn. He told me he had changed his name, and quitted his country, in order that Cecilia should never hear of him; and also that he might never meet with Mons. d' Aimeri. That he kept up a correspondence in France with only one person; but that he had intreated him never to mention the name of Mons. d' Aimeri. That time and reflection, though they had calmed the tumults of his despair, had not abated his passion; and that Cecilia would live for ever in his heart. That, in short, the desire he had to appear worthy the goodness and confidence of a great Prince had given birth to some seeds of ambition in his heart; but that he had only received true consolation in solitude, study, and in the pleasures of benevolence. Before we parted, he wrote a letter to Mons. d' Aimeri filled with the most affecting excuses for his conduct, and desired me to deliver it. Mons. d' Aimeri received it with kindness. That very evening, we heard Mons. de Murville was very ill, and had sent for a Physician. He is much better to-day. When he is quite recovered, and in a situation to receive us, I intend to carry my young Prince thither, to see his house and gardens; and Mons. d' Aimeri has desired I will at the same time take the Chevalier de Valmont. So that I flatter myself there will be no longer any animosity between them either on one side or the other. Mons. d' Aimeri, knowing I have been sending you the particulars of this affair, bids me tell you he will write next post, and will send you his journal, as he promised you, once a month. I cannot conclude this letter without mentioning the Chevalier de Valmont. I never saw a young man of his age so polite, so well improved, and, at the same time, so artless and so amiable. He is continually talking to me of you and your agreeable family; and he assures me there is not a girl in the world equal to the lovely Adelaide. The young Prince has conceived a great friendship for him; and I shall take advantage of this attachment, which I greatly approve, in order to establish a correspondence between them, which will more assuredly contribute to the improvement of my pupil.

LETTER LV.

Viscountess to the Baroness.

I AM vexed and out of humour, my dear friend. For some days past, little quarrels and domestick concerns have seriously troubled me, and I am going to ease my mind by telling you of them. Mons. de Valcy had hitherto conducted himself intirely to my satisfaction. He appeared very fond of his wife, but, at the same time, left her quite at liberty, and nobody ever appeared to be more free from jealousy, or a greater enemy to restraint; than he was. Last Monday my daughter was engaged to a ball; her mother-in-law came to call for her; Flora was in her bed; she pretended to have the head-ache; the party to the ball was put off. As soon as I heard of this sudden resolution, I went into her apartment, but, before I had entered it, I heard such loud and repeated bursts of laughter as fully satisfied me that I had nothing to fear on account of her illness. I found her alone, with the friend I mentioned to you, Madame de Germeuil. As soon as they saw me, they both assumed an air of gravity, and there was a profound silence, for a minute or two, occasioned by their confusion; I began to inquire after her health, and my daughter told me she was perfectly well, but very much disappointed at not going to the ball; that it was a whim of Mons. de Valcy's, who had obliged her to put off her engagement. I asked her what was his reason? Ah, my God! said she smiling, do not you know his strange humour and his violent jealousy? ... I have tried to conceal it, said she, assuming, as long as I was able, a more serious countenance; but the proofs he gives of it are now so ridiculous and so frequent, that it is impossible to hide it any longer. During this discourse I stood motionless with surprise! What, said I, is Mons. de Valcy jealous, and you make so light of it! Is it in this manner you speak of the greatest misfortune which can happen to a virtuous and sensible woman? Why should I vex myself, said Flora, for his madness? I forgive him, I pity him, I submit to his humour; but I do not see that I am to make myself miserable about it. This answer, which appeared to put an air of ridicule upon what I had said, quite confounded me; I then talked to her more seriously. But she made use of so much sweetness and so many graces, in order to soften my anger, that I could not resist her. She told me her husband was engaged to the ball before she was invited, and that afterwards he was much out of humour, and said he would not go; and, that all this day, he had treated her in a very cruel manner; which Madame de Germeuil confirmed, as she had been witness to it; and added many circumstances too tedious to mention. I made my remarks, and gave the advice I thought necessary, and then went to bed. The next morning I sent for Mons. de Valcy, and talked to him of his jealousy. He fell a laughing. It is Madame de Valcy's folly, said he; she will insist on it that I am jealous, and every day reproaches me with it; she not only makes her friends believe so, but she appears convinced of it herself. However, I protest to you there is not a word of truth in it. I do every thing in my power to remove this notion; she is intirely at liberty to receive whatever company she pleases. I never watch her steps, nor follow her, and I am never out of temper, but when she accuses me of errors I never was guilty of in my life. Yet, said I, she did not go to the ball last night, because she would not displease you; and this was a great sacrifice for her to make. Yes, answered he, and, if I was jealous, as she pretends, I should not have been the less so on that account, as she spent the night at the Masquerade, where I also was, where by chance I saw and knew her. But, added Mons. de Valcy, seeing astonishment painted on my face, I do not altogether disapprove of these things. She is very young, and she thought it more agreeable to go to a masqued ball with her friend, than to a dressed ball with her mother-in-law. This appears to me the plain case, and you should not be more severe than I am. Put yourself, my dear friend, one moment in my situation; and imagine, if possible, the grief this explanation gave me, which proved the sincerity and indulgence of Mons. de Valcy, and discovered in his wife a series of falsehood, artifice, and intrigue. Grieved to the heart, and in a violent passion, I went to her, and we came to very high words; she wept very much, and protested to me, when she saw me, she had no thoughts of going to the masqued ball; that it came from Madame de Germeuil, who had pressed her so much, that at length she yielded to her intreaties. She still insists on it, that her husband is jealous, but that his pride will not suffer him to own it, for fear he should appear ridiculous.

I have laid down a plan for her conduct, which she has promised me she will follow exactly. She gave me such assurances of her affection and confidence, and confessed her faults with so much candour and concern, that whether from being convinced of the truth of it, or whether from my own weakness, she has quite satisfied me. But I could not help observing with some concern, that she was scarce able to conceal her ill humour towards her husband. However, for these two days past, she seems in perfect good temper, and they are to all appearance very good friends. What vexes me is, that this story is got abroad, and is told much to the disadvantage of Mons. de Valcy, who they pretend is very unjust and tyrannical. They think my daughter is very unhappy; they pity and lament her fate; and I cannot help thinking these false notions are circulated about by herself and her friends. This, my dear friend, gives me the greatest concern. I still hope my daughter deceives herself, and that she has not yet learned her husband's disposition; but this appears incredible with the sense of which she is possessed, and yet it seems as if she was not sincere, as if she was acting a part to make herself interesting, and as if she wanted to find a lawful pretence for no longer loving the husband she preferred to every other man ... This thought afflicts me; it is dreadful, and fills my heart with grief. It is supposing her capable of more art and cunning than one could imagine possible in a young woman of nineteen. Adieu! my dear friend. I stand much in want of your remarks, of your advice, and your friendship. Advise me, teach me how to act; on your counsel I depend. Adieu! Let me have answer as soon as possible.

LETTER LVI.

The Baroness to Madame d' Ostalis.

I FLATTER myself, my dear child, you will receive this letter with pleasure, since it is written to acquaint you, that your mother will have the happiness to embrace you in a few days. I shall set out next Friday, and, though I know all your tenderness for me, yet I must tell you it is impossible for you to form a just idea of the pleasure I shall have in seeing you again. No, my dear child, there is no sentiment to be held in competition with the affection of a tender mother! If Nature has not made you my daughter, are you not the child of my adoption? And do you think I can ever love those more whom chance has given me? In short, I am going to receive the reward due to my fortitude and resolution, which have so long resisted your pressing intreaties, so often repeated, to let you come to Languedoc. It was of too much consequence to your husband's affairs, and the happiness of your own life, that you should remain at Paris, and that I should give up the ardent desire I had to see you to such prudential reasons. It is thus, my dear child, we ought to shew our affection. And now I may tell you, that for this twelvemonth past I have earnestly wished to return to Paris; and that it has cost me more pain to consent with a good grace to stay here these last six months, than the whole four years we agreed upon. But Mons. d' Almane thought with great reason, that we should not leave the country till the month of August, the season of the vintage being a great amusement to the children; and, besides, it would give them more cause to regret the pleasant country life they had led, and the situation where they had received their improvements. Adieu! my dear child. This is the first adieu that I have bid you without pain, since our separation. You will find me, no doubt, as the Viscountess says, very old, and very much tanned, with our fine Sun of Languedoc, for which she has taken such an aversion. As for you, my dear, I am sure that four years and an half will have only improved the charms of your elegant and agreeable person which I so much admire. Adieu! once more. My heart palpitates, when I think that another fortnight will bring me to you.

LETTER LVII.

The Baroness to Madame de Valmont.

Paris.

I ARRIVED here, Madam, yesterday noon, and, about twenty-five leagues from Paris, I met Madame d' Ostalis and Madame de Limours. So that you will easily guess, notwithstanding my aversion to travelling, that the last part of my journey appeared very short. When I arrived at my own house, Madame d' Ostalis conducted me to a little room she knew I was very fond of. I saw with astonishment she had new furnished it in a very different manner from its former state. I wish to convince you, said she, that I have not been idle in your absence. All this is my work. I have embroidered this furniture, have drawn these landscapes, and painted these flowers, fruits, birds and miniatures. This pleasing attention in Madame d' Ostalis was still more valuable, as she had many other avocations, such as taking infinite pains with her children, and fulfilling the duties of her employment, which she does with the utmost exactness. But one has no idea of what may be done, when one is not inclined to idleness, and when one does not lose a moment from some useful or agreeable work. With regard to her person, she is beautiful as an Angel. Her mind is all purity and innocence. She keeps good hours, she never intrigues, she drinks no tea nor coffee with cream, and therefore she will for a long time preserve her charming state of health, her beauty, and her complexion.[129]

Adelaide and Theodore already regret Languedoc. They have been to-day to walk in the Palais royal, and complain much of the croud and the dust. They find it a sad thing to have only a little garden, which they can go round in ten minutes. Miss Bridget agrees perfectly with them in their opinions, as the eating her meals alone in her chamber makes the residing at Paris extremely disagreeable to her.

Mons. d' Almane has just received a letter from Mons. d' Aimeri, who tells him he means to remain in *** till November, when he intends going to Russia, and will return to Paris next June. He will stay here three months, and then conduct Charles to his Garrison. Adieu, Madam! Let me hear from you. You may judge, by my eagerness to write to you, the value I shall set on your punctuality.

Billet from the Viscountess to the Baroness.

AH my dear friend! if you have a moment to spare, come to me ... pray come ... I am miserable ... quite miserable ... The adventure of the Garden is but too true ... She will be lost ... Come, for Heaven's sake; I must absolutely speak to you.

Billet from Madame de Valcy to Madame de Germeuil.

OUR midnight walk is no longer a secret ... You may imagine the consequences! What scolding, what sermons, I have been obliged to listen to! ... I cannot come out. But do you go immediately to Madame de Gerville, and acquaint her with our disaster. Tell her they put the worst construction on that which was in reality nothing but giddiness ... She will manage the affair for us ... Adieu, for I am afraid of being surprized.

LETTER LVIII.

The Baroness to Madame d' Ostalis.

I KNOW not, my dear child, if the adventure of Madame de Valcy is talked of at Fontainbleau, but this is the true story: Last Monday, the 20th of October, Madame de Valcy told her mother she should sup at the Palais royal, and about half past nine, she and the Countess de Germeuil sat out, and did not return till half past Three in the morning. The next day she told her mother she had supped there, and that, at Twelve o'clock they heard, from the room they were in, some delightful music; that Madame de Germeuil would not let her rest, till she consented to go down to the garden, where they staid about a quarter of an hour, and then they both returned home to Madame de Germeuil's house, where they drank tea together, while Madame de Germeuil undressed herself; and that in short they forgot the time till it was Three o'clock. The next evening the Chevalier de Herbain told Madame de Limours, that it was reported her daughter had been seen, with Madame de Germeuil, walking with Mons. de Creny and Mons. de L— from One o'clock till Three. Madame de Limours would not believe it, but the next day one of the servants, who attended Madame de Valcy, being much pressed by Madame de Limours, confessed that his Lady returned from the Palais royal at Eleven o'clock; that they went and undressed at Madame de Germeuil's, and then returned to the Palais royal, where they staid three hours in the garden. This affair has been made public by Mons. B—, who has been in love with Madame de Valcy these six months. He also supped at the Palais royal, and pretends to have heard Madame de Valcy make the appointment with Mons. de Creny. Mons. de B— went into the garden with two of his friends, and there saw the two Gentlemen, after waiting half an hour, joined by Madame de Valcy and Madame de Germeuil, and walk with them till the hour I mentioned.

Mons. de B—, to revenge himself for the coquetry of Madame de Valcy, and for the false hopes she had given him, has been so uncivil as to divulge this adventure, and unfortunately with such circumstances as leave no room to doubt the truth of it. Madame de Valcy has suffered the reproaches of her mother, and sees her grief with so much coolness and indifference, that I have no hopes of her ever being cured of her imprudence. What appears to me most extraordinary is, that her father does not take notice of it properly, but treats it as a childish folly. He has even quarrelled with Madame de Limours on the subject. Unfortunate mother! ... How much I pity her ... She is now undeceived; she knows her daughter but too well. She sees no prospect of amendment; she is truly in despair ... If you should hear of this affair, deny the truth of it,[130] say you are certain Madame de Valcy has not set her foot in the Palais royal; that she returned the same evening before Twelve o' clock. There is no other means of defending a bad cause; for, if you admit the truth of one circumstance, you must own the whole. Adieu, my dear child! return to me as soon as you can.

I open my letter to tell you, that Mons. Creny and Mons. B— have fought this morning; the last is very well, and the first has only a small scratch on the hand. If the duel did not end tragically, at least they give the finest description of it; and the Seconds declare they never saw such generosity, presence of mind, delicacy, &c. in short, every thing but wounds and bloodshed; and the two rivals, charmed with each other's bravery, embraced, and are now perfectly reconciled. But what gives me stronger proofs of the truth of this adventure is, that Madame de Valcy is more afflicted than ever.

Billet from Madame de Valcy to Mons. de Creny.

T HINK no more of coming to me; that is impossible; but, since Madame de Gerville has sent to know how you do, you may avail yourself of that, and visit her. Make friends of her, and of my mother-in-law, let it cost you what it will: it is the only means by which we can see each other as usual. Praise and flatter Madame de Gerville upon her beauty, her youthful appearance, and talk to her about being at Court. Play at Quinze[131] with my mother-in-law, and all will do well. I say nothing of my attachment to you, you know it but too well. Let me at least have yours in return, to make me amends for the sacrifices I have made you, in order to convince you of my affection.

LETTER LIX.

Madame de Valcy to Madame de Germeuil.

REALLY, my dear friend, you have not common sense; you are in despair; you can never console yourself for a conduct which nothing can excuse the illusion is vanished, &c. &c – These are fine expressions! ... What words, what a romantic style! and all this to say you have a lover, and that you do not feel for him that extreme tenderness which only exists in imagination. You prefer him; you love him better than any other. But this is not the kind of love we admired so much. in *Cleveland*,[132] or *Zaide*;[133] but such as it really is. Ah! do you reckon as nothing the charms of being beloved, obeyed, and the pleasure of commanding? You shall always you say be unhappy, because you have an extreme delicacy and a steady mind. What can there be worse? We are never satisfied, and we cannot deceive ourselves. As for me, I have the happy talent of pleasing myself, at least for some time; and, when one fancy is at an end, I repair the loss by forming another. And therefore you see me, by turns, indifferent in love, a coquette; and always what I appear to be; because, when I undertake a part, I go through with it. My inclinations yield to it, and it appears as if it were my real sentiments. This is all the artifice I make use of. I leave you to judge whether it is excusable, since, instead of deceiving others, I begun by deceiving myself.

I agree with you, if one could dive into futurity, one never would encourage a lover. If one was but sensible, that the pains and the emotions we experience before the fatal confession were the principal pleasures of love, and that the moment we deviate from the path of rectitude, we find the sweet enchantment to be broken for ever, we should never wish to be under such delusions. For my part, I was a thousand times happier six months ago than I am at this time. Prejudice and repentance out of the question, one moment's conversation, a word said to me unperceived, even a look, an accidental meeting in the street or at the Opera, was inchanting! The habit and certainty of being beloved have made me infinitely less sensible to these little incidents. I have nothing to look forward to; every thing is settled; my heart is at rest, and I honestly confess to you vanity engages me much more than love! – Vanity! ... Yes! it is that alone which determines the destiny of a woman. If it had not been for the fear of a rival on the most trifling matter imaginable, I should never have had a lover, or at least I should have made another choice; an Assembly determined my fate. Madame de *** danced better than me, but my beauty was more admired than her's; this celebrated evening made us enemies: you know the triumph I have since gained over her. She laments the lover I have robbed her, of and I regret the tranquillity I have lost. See what an effect a dance had over *three* persons! But, if vanity leads us astray, at least it affords us consolation. We do not chuse to look forward to futurity; the prospect is too frightful! To be admired, to be in the fashion, to be successful in our pursuits, and to amuse ourselves, will keep us from remorse and melancholy ideas. You ask my advice, my dear friend, and I recommend it to you to renounce the folly of keeping a secret which already is known in the Polite World; to own it publicly would be indecent; but to acknowledge it to some particular friends, on whom you could depend, would be one of the best means to attach them to you, and to interest them in your fortune. You appear to me to regret most dreadfully what you call your former character; they could never, you say, accuse you of having a lover: this is true; and, supposing you to be thirty years old, I should think your concern well grounded. But in short it was not, that your character was perfectly established; only, that you had not yet got a lover. However, they may still quote you as an example of having but one; and though this glory is not so great as the other, yet it is almost as singular, and indeed I am not much surprised at it; for a first lover is almost a husband; and such are frequently engaged so young, that it is less owing to the choice of one's heart, than to vanity and giddiness: and how is that likely to last? ... Adieu! return from the country; I must see you and talk with you. Your letter, your complaints, your difficulties, all give me pain, in spite of myself, and put me out of humour. Happily for me, I am to sup this evening with a Lady who loves her husband, who has never had a lover, who is yet beautiful, though she is more than thirty years old. You know whom I mean: in truth in the humour I am in, her presence will disgust me more than ever. Apropos of women of unblemished character, I have much to say in praise of Madame d' Ostalis. She has defended me with great warmth in the world, as you have heard. Since that, she has taken great pains to reconcile me and my mother, and even now she is doing very kind things for me; the particulars of which I will tell you when I see you. Indeed I reproach myself greatly for the dislike I had taken to her. Adieu! return quickly, you are more necessary to me than ever. I shall expect you on Monday to supper.

LETTER LX.

The Baroness to Madame de Valmont.

Y OU desired to know, Madam, what effect an evening ball would have upon Adelaide, and I can now satisfy your curiosity. I carried her and her brother to a ball last night, for the first time. You know they have had a dancing-master for these six months past; and that they are as able to acquit themselves properly as any other young persons of their own age, and the more easily, as they have been accustomed early to run and jump with the greatest dexterity: Adelaide, prepossessed by the little Comedy of the *Dove*,[134] had no great desire to go to a ball; and her cap, and high dressed head, and gown ornamented with flowers, &c. &c. appeared to her as an attire ill calculated for dancing. When she was dressed, I led her into the Saloon, where we found Madame d' Ostalis, and some other friends, who had dined with us. Every body praised her dress, but did not say a word of her person; and Madame d' Ostalis said, Adelaide is very well dressed; but do you not think she looks a thousand times better in the white frock she wears every day, than in this fine coat? Every one was of her opinion, and agreed that an elegant neatness was always the most pleasing! This conversation made Adelaide still more displeased with her dress. She complained that the wires, which fastened on the festoons of flowers, scratched her arms; and that the weight of her head-dress gave her an intolerable pain in her head. In the midst of these complaints, the clock struck five, and we set out: as we were crossing the anti-chamber, Brunel stopped us a moment, because he wanted to see Adelaide in her new dress; but he had scarcely cast his eyes on her, than he burst into a loud laugh. Adelaide, a little disconcerted, asked him the reason of this incivility? Excuse me, Madam, said he; but the rouge and the dress altogether make Mademoiselle look so droll ... At these words he laughed again; and we continued our way, vexed enough at the impertinent gaiety of Brunel, and got into the coach in a very indifferent humour to go to a ball. We were scarce arrived at the place, and Adelaide seated in her place, but she begged me to take a fly off, which had settled on her cheek: you must bear with it, said I, or you will rub off the rouge, and make your face all in streaks. Adelaide complained much of the rouge, and, not being able to bear the tickling of the fly, she put her hand cross her cheek two or three times, and by that means painted her nose and eyes. I made her observe herself in a looking-glass, and she was not very well satisfied with her appearance. However, she behaved very well. I do not think, said she, that any dancer will like such a figure for his partner. Well, said I, if you do not dance, you may talk. For instance, what do you think of that little girl who dances with Theodore? Oh, I have been looking at her this long time. – Well, what do you think of her? I think, Mamma, she appears as if she was mad. Pray look at her, when they stand still, how she is agitated; with what a familiar air she talks to all the young men! What faces she makes! Her head turns round like a weather-cock ... Ah, now she dances ... My God! How she jumps and turns about! This is very droll, but it is very ugly, is it not, Mamma? – Yes, she pretends to be extremely light and nimble, but she appears quite ignorant, that above all she ought to be genteel and modest: besides, one may surely dance very lightly, and much more gracefully, without twisting one's self about, or jumping so ridiculously ... But, Mamma, I see this manner of dancing is quite the fashion: do you see those two young Ladies, one in the rose-coloured silk, the other in white ... They do the same thing ... Yes, I see it is the reigning fashion, and it is natural it should be so; all that is best to be done is generally uncommon. The number of sensible people, and those who have a good taste, are very few, and this makes persons of this class so much admired; for, if wit, virtue, and knowledge, were united with the graces more frequently than they are, one should find infinitely more pleasure in such society. But, mixed together in the croud, one has but little opportunity of acquiring esteem or of meeting with admiration. – Yes, I understand you, Mamma; good things are always scarce; and this is the reason why there are so many coquettes, lazy, idle, ignorant people, and little girls who are so giddy-brained, and who make such a whirling and capering about in order to appear nimble. One must be a very absurd, however, to place one's self in such a croud as this, instead of chusing the pleasing few which are so agreeable! ... Where one shall be distinguished, admired! ... Adelaide was in the midst of this conversation, when a young man came to ask her to dance. She quitted a discourse which amused her; she was sensible that her dress did not make her appear to advantage; besides, not being used to such a habit, she was much distressed, and did not dance well; so that she saw people criticized her, and that nobody took notice of her beauty; and she soon returned to her seat, fully resolved not to dance any more. From time to time, there passed before us large baskets full of refreshments, and tartlets, which tempted Adelaide very much. Accustomed only to eat fruit or bread at her supper, she did not attempt to take any thing. But I perceived the baskets drew sighs from her, and that she looked very earnestly at them. Adelaide, said I, you are not now such a child; you are now eleven years old, you may eat if you are hungry, and of what you like best, provided it is not too much. I leave it to your own judgment, and I shall not even look at you.[135] Adelaide took advantage of this permission with great joy. And, every time I saw the baskets pass by, I turned my head another way and talked to my friends. Adelaide, thinking I did not observe her in the least, eat all the tartlets they brought her. I was going to leave the ball, when Theodore came up to me in great concern, to tell me 'he had had the misfortune to break a looking-glass, as he was playing by himself in an adjoining room; and intreated me to go and tell the mistress of the house, that no one should be accused wrongfully.'

You will guess the pleasure this delicacy and candour gave me. I embraced Theodore, and acquainted the mistress of the accident. I then took him and his sister, and we came away. Adelaide was silent and melancholy. I asked her the reason of it. She told me she had a pain in her head. It is because you have surfeited yourself. – Me, Mamma? Yes; you have eat ten tartlets, six biscuits, and taken two glasses of ice cream, therefore it is not at all surprising that you should be sick. – I did not think I had eat so much – nor that you had been so narrowly observing! This will teach you two things: First, that temperance is a virtue as useful as it is estimable; and secondly, that nothing can prevent my attention to you, and that, when I seem not to regard you, I see every thing you do. Besides, Adelaide, when one is generous, you should never abuse the confidence reposed in you ... Oh! Mamma, I see my fault, and will take care to mend. – I hope so; but, my dear child, was it necessary you should learn by so sad an experience what you might have been perfectly convinced of, had you paid a proper regard to what I told you? ... Oh, Mamma, I believe every thing you say to me ... Why then did you not prove it on this occasion? For instance, putting the tartlets out of the question, your dress at the ball; I should have advised you to one much plainer. My little Comedy of the *Dove* I thought had given you an aversion for a dress so ornamented. And yet, when you saw at Mademoiselle Hubert's a robe trimmed with flowers, you desired to have such a one. You see the success it procured you, and also the enormous quantity of rouge which you put on ... Oh, it is enough! I will never again have a robe trimmed with flowers, nor ever will put on any more rouge ... Do not go to extremes in any thing. It is right to follow the fashion, but always with moderation. I wish you to have a proper taste, to prefer in general a modest simplicity, with elegance and convenience, to a shining dress overloaded with ornaments. As I finished these words, the coach stopped. Poor Adelaide, scarce able to support herself, got out with great difficulty, and, as soon as she got to her chamber, she was ill, and vomited very much; and had not even the consolation of finding any of those who surrounded her pitied her; on the contrary, she heard every body saying they were surprised at her intemperance, and testified a great dislike for the kind of illness she suffered. And, in short, the word *surfeited* was pronounced with great contempt by every body but me, who was silent, and who carefully watched over Adelaide with pity and concern. She was very grateful to me for this kindness, and shewed a true repentance for her fault, declaring she would never have a surfeit again of her own causing.

All these things have made me sensible of the advantages of our method of education. It is certain that the best child in the world would not have been able to support herself under a trial so new. For example, you have seen Adelaide in a room filled with sweetmeats and sugar-plums, and, thinking herself alone, she has not attempted to touch them, because she has given her promise not to eat any. You also know it was necessary to punish her and put her to trials, in order to bring her to this degree of probity at which she is arrived. But, as hitherto she was only temperate through obedience and a principle of honour, so, as soon as she was left to herself, she forgot all the praises she had heard of this quality, and she eat to excess. If one should forget conversations on these subjects, one always remembers facts, especially when they are accompanied by such disagreeable circumstances. It is therefore indispensably necessary to instruct children on all these points, not only by lessons, but by experience. I do not mean to exclude reasoning, but I repeat that they will learn more by experiments. To return to Adelaide, she had still a pain in her head this morning, and found herself much fatigued. Madame d' Ostalis has preached a good deal to her, at last she added: You see I have a fresh colour and have very good teeth. Madame de Germeuil does not appear handsome to you, because she has not these advantages; and yet she is younger than I am by two years. – But she never had your complexion or your teeth!... Pardon me; when she was married, she had a beautiful complexion; but she was a glutton, she eat numbers of tartlets, and often had indigestions, and now you see what a pimpled face she has. Adelaide appeared much struck with this discourse, and after two days living on plain diet, she will be able to make still better reflections than she has yet done on the subject. Adieu, Madam! You see how punctually I obey you; it is necessary I should depend on your friendship, as well as your partiality to Adelaide, when I venture to talk to you so much about her.

LETTER LXI.

The Baroness to Madame d' Ostalis.

I CAN easily conceive, my dear child, that you are vexed at being obliged to stay two day longer at Versailles, only on disagreeable affairs. But your husband is absent, and you must take care of his interest. Besides, do you remember the excellent advice of Madame de Lambert?[136]

'Whilst you are young, form your character, establish your reputation, settle your affairs: when you are older, you will find more difficulty in doing it. In youth, every thing assists you, every thing offers itself to you. Young people rule without knowing it. At a more advanced age, you meet with no help. You are no longer possessed of that seducing charm which diffuses itself over every thing. You have nothing left you but reflection and truth which do not often govern mankind.'[137]

I spent a delightful evening last night with Madame de Limours. The Ambassador from – whom I do not know, is arrived there, and, almost as soon as he came in, asked if you was returned from Versailles. You became the subject of general conversation: every one praised your conduct, your talents, your person, your mildness, and that natural and lively chearfulness, which so well becomes you, and makes you so amiable. Oh! how pleasing to the heart, and how flattering to one's vanity, is it to hear it said it is to you she owes these principles, those virtues, and this character. One is not obliged to conceal this kind of pride; on the contrary, one may avow it, and even boast of it openly, and prove that one is susceptible to it. Of all the compliments paid you, none have flattered me so much as those of the Ambassador ... because he did not know me, and was insensible of the interest I took in the conversation.

Yes, my dear child! I with great pleasure see the time arriving, when we shall return to Languedoc. What can I regret at Paris, since this time I take you with me? I think, that we shall not go directly to B—, our intention is to pass a month in Bretagne. I will tell you the reason; it is a long History, and will surely interest you. Adieu! my dear child. I expect you on Saturday.

LETTER LXII.

Madame de Valcy to Mons. de Creny.

Y OU desire me to explain myself. *You see plainly I am discontented. In vain you seek to find out the reason.* Since you are neither delicate nor penetrating enough to divine it, I am going to tell it you. You love me, I have no doubt of it: but it is in a manner I do not approve. Incapable of feigning, detesting art and constraint, I have neither been able to disguise nor conceal the sentiments I had for you. Nobody is ignorant of it. You ought at least to justify by your conduct the preference you have obtained from me, but you take a directly contrary method. When we are alone, you speak to me of your passion, of the excess of your love, which forms a conversation with little variety, and which at the end of a twelve-month might weary the most constant woman. Sure of possessing your heart, all these protestations are useless; the repetition tires one; the very idea makes one melancholy. When you talk of your happiness, it is with so serious a tone, that really by your appearance and manner of speaking one would think you was in despair. For Heaven's sake, let me have a little variety, for I cannot bear this any longer. But, on the other hand, when we are in company together, you pursue other methods which are still more insupportable to me. You scarcely seem to look at me; then every thing employs you, every thing pleases you, except me. In your general conversations, love, according to your opinion, is only imagination and folly. You speak of it with a degree of raillery, which would make one suppose, you did not believe there was such a sentiment; and you call this ridiculous affectation, prudence, and discretion: for my part, I cannot bear it. It is known that I love you; and people would be persuaded from your discourse, that I have only yielded to an imaginary passion; so you deprive me of the only excuse I could make, that of a mutual and ardent attachment. I declare to you, I cannot support this opinion. My heart, and my pride, are both equally wounded. I would have every body see, that you love me and prefer me to all others: at the same time I forbid you ever shewing the smallest degree of freedom with me, or any of those little attentions, which belong only to gallantry, and which I disdain being the object of. To be attentive, with reserve and respect is to be your part in public. When we are alone, you may be trifling, inconsiderate, and if you please, a little more chearful; it will not alarm me, and I shall like it much better. Adieu. I have told you my sentiments, and disposition: after this, you see, you must follow my advice exactly, if you mean to preserve me yours.

LETTER LXIII.

Madame d'Almane, to Madame de Valmont.

IT is true, Madam, that we are determined to go into Bretagne before we return to Languedoc: and what has determined us, is the desire of seeing two persons as extraordinary as they are interesting; they are Mons. and Madame de Lagaraye. This is their history:[138] Mons. le Marquis de Lagaraye, was thought to be the happiest man in Bretagne; beloved by an amiable wife; considered in the province where he lived as a man of the greatest personal merit. His birth, and his fortune, collected together all the respectable families in the neighbourhood. There they acted Plays, gave balls, and every day brought with it a new entertainment. Madame de Lagaraye partook of the same amusements with her husband. When in the midst of gaiety, at one of their entertainments, the sudden and extraordinary death of their only daughter[139] produced in their minds as sudden a change, as it was unexpected. A dislike of company, a detachment from the trifling amusements they had been used to, made them turn their thoughts to the sublime principles of religion; and at the same time gave rise to a design, which was never before thought of. Mons. de Lagaraye communicated his intentions to his wife, and nothing prevented their putting them into execution. They went to Montpellier, and staid there two years, employing themselves in every thing relating to physic and surgery. They went through several courses of Chymistry,[140] Anatomy, &c. learning to bleed and dress wounds, and uniting to this study all the application necessary to effect their purpose, which their charitable motives and enthusiasm led them to; and they both made an astonishing progress in the profession. During this time, they had given orders for their Castle at Lagaraye to be transformed into an Hospital, containing two wings, one for men and the other for women. And this beautiful situation, which once was the habitation of joy, pleasures, and magnificence, is now become a Temple sacred to Religion and Humanity. As soon as Mons. and Madame de Lagaraye left Montpelier, and arrived at their own Castle, Mons. de Lagaraye being then forty-five years of age, put himself at the head of the hospital for men, and devoted his life and fortune to the service of those poor, to whom this house is dedicated. Madame de Laga-raye, ten years younger than her husband, imposes on herself the same duties in the part of the house belonging to women. Still young and beautiful, she leaves with delight the gay apparel of vanity, and takes the humble and modest vesture of a nun, whose business it is to take care of the sick. This establishment, this example of every virtue, beyond what has ever been seen worthy of admiration, is still subsisting, and has subsisted for these ten years. This, Madame, is what we are going to see. Adelaide and Theodore will take their first Communion in six months; and I cannot better prepare them for it, than in letting them take a jour-ney to Lagaraye. It is so charming to behold Virtue in its true light! the respect paid to it is the first step towards acquiring it. Madame d' Ostalis goes with us to Bretagne, and returns with us to Languedoc, for three months, therefore I shall only leave Madame de Limours behind me to regret.

You ask me for some account of the amiable child, who is one day to be my daughter in law, if her heart does not make any objection to it. She is indeed charming both in person and mind. Theodore finds her very gentle and very beautiful, and Adelaide loves her passionately; Constantia has not the genius of Adelaide, but she is sensible, prudent, mild, and obliging. Madame de Limours has brought her up very well, and has given her excellent principles. This child, notwithstanding, has an extreme sensibility, and a disposition to melancholy, which by its effects, if not guarded against, may make her very unhappy. Adieu, Madam. We go to-morrow to Languedoc, where we shall stay three weeks; we shall then return for some days to Paris; therefore in about six weeks I hope for the happiness of seeing you again; and I flatter myself you have no doubt of the impatience, with which I wait for the moment, which is again to unite us.

END OF THE FIRST VOLUME.

ADELAIDE AND THEODORE;

OR

LETTERS ON EDUCATION:

CONTAINING

All the Principles relative to three different
Plans of Education; to that of Princes, and
to those of young Persons of both Sexes.

*Translated from the French of Madame la Comtesse
de Genlis.*

VOL. II

LONDON

Printed for C. BATHURST, in Fleet-street; and
T. CADELL, in the Strand.
MDCCLXXXIII.

ADELAIDE

AND

THEODORE.

LETTER I.

The Count de Roseville to the Baron.

YOU cannot imagine, my dear Baron, the pleasure your letter gave me: I am really flattered by what Mons. d' Aimeri tells you of my young Prince; for it is indirect praise alone that can make an impression. Mons. d' Aimeri is particularly surprised at his attention, and ease of expression. You know how I taught him to speak, and that he contracted this habit in his plays and amusements. As to his activity, he owes that principally to some little care of mine. When I arrived here, he was seven years and six months old; I found him indolent, lazy, and diverted with nothing; yet I remarked in him a natural life and spirit. I attributed therefore his laziness to some particular fault of education, and soon discovered it. The Prince's apartment was filled with toys; the child in the midst of all this treasure not knowing how to chuse, and desirous to enjoy all, in reality enjoyed none; and was accustomed to inconstancy, which always fatigues and never satisfies. The young prince was likewise attended by five or six low people, whose sole business was to invent amusements, and fetch any play-thing he wanted; or pick up his shuttlecock, ball, &c. The Prince was so accustomed to this servility, that if what he held happened to fall, he never made the least motion to take it up, knowing six persons were ready to strive who should do it for him. I presently banished all these slaves, and replaced them by one child of his own age, sending away at the same time all these toys, reserving only what were really necessary for his amusement. At first he looked on this as a barbarous reformation; but in a very short time he lost his indolence, and assumed all the activity which was natural to him. We had a very serious discourse the day before yesterday. I entered his apartment at eight o'clock, dismissed his valets, and embraced him, saying, you are this day thirteen; your education cannot be finished, nor your understanding, or character formed, but still you are no longer a child; and the rank you bear will henceforward make all your actions interesting. Behold, my Lord, here are eight volumes of my writing; they are the journals of your childhood. You will find some reflections, that even now will not be useless to you; accept this present as a proof of my attention to you. – Oh! surely it is very dear to me, interrupted the Prince; I will read it again and again with avidity, and preserve it all my life; but, continued he, will you then not go on with the journal? – Pardon me, I replied; I shall now write it with still more care and circumspection; for this will be done for posterity ... How? – My Lord, I again repeat, you are no longer a child; the journal of your life will now become a history: and as the historian will be exact and faithful, keep a strict guard over yourself; and remember you will make me very happy every time you give occasion for praise. – But this journal will never be printed. – Certainly it will; my writing of it is known, and surely after my death the manuscript will be made public. – And if I should be so unhappy to do any thing very blameable, would you write that? ... No; the journal would finish there; but I should leave you. – Oh! you will go on with it, I promise you, for I will believe you always, so I shall never commit any great faults. At these words we were both softened; the Prince has made me promise never to quit him, and I really feel, that if he answers my expectations, he will dispose of my destiny; and can compensate every sacrifice I make him, notwithstanding the tender attachment I preserve for my country, family, and friends.

A very critical and important period, my dear Baron, approaches; that, wherein my pupil's passions are going to display themselves: he will certainly have very lively ones. He has the most ardent desire to distinguish himself; is active, sensible, grateful; not easily led to think ill of any one. He must have evident proofs of their faults; but he thinks well of people too readily; a very dangerous failing in a prince: and yet I shall not attempt to correct it in mine but with the greatest precaution, fearful of impairing the goodness of his heart. Every amiable person he thinks perfect; but judges of people, who are indifferent to him, with discernment far surpassing his age; while he becomes blind to those who please him; and as soon as his heart is touched, examines no more; or to express myself with more propriety, loses a part of his natural penetration. Having great taste and delicacy, the graces make a deep impression on him; and he is easily seduced by a noble and animated discourse. The Abbe Duguet says with reason, 'Princes, having commonly an exquisite taste and elegant manners, are more exposed than others to be deceived; as they feel, but do not see, the whole. They are allured or offended by things that deserve it, but which frequently are far from the most essential matters; they quickly form a judgment, and generally with great exactness, of what is before their eyes; but that which is visible is rarely decisive; and they readily dispense with experience, where there are certain engaging qualities.'[1]

My Prince has been educated with young Sulback, the son of his under governor, who, though but sixteen, shews all the virtues of his father, (one of the best men I know;) but the Prince has more esteem than affection for him, because he wants the graces, and has nothing striking in him, though he abounds in discretion and good sense: on the contrary, the Prince has the greatest affection for Count Stralzi, sole heir of the noblest house in this kingdom, who is seventeen, has a very fine figure, a superficial understanding, much cunning and pliance of disposition. His birth, and the rank of his father, give him a right to pay his court here frequently; and the Prince receives him far better, than in my heart I could wish; for I look on this as a very dangerous connection. Yet I take great pains to disguise my sentiments, knowing remonstrances would not detach the Prince, and only make him suspect me of unjust prejudices; which would entirely prevent the execution of a plan I have formed to open the Prince's eyes by degrees. The arrival of the Chevalier de Valmont has made a great diversion in the Prince's sentiments; the Chevalier's accomplishments are much superior to the Count's, and he has sense, education and modesty sufficient to gain every heart. If he was to remain here, I am very sure that he would supplant the young favourite, even without attempting or wishing it; but unfortunately he leaves us in a month.

I have not, my dear Baron, forgot the promised description of Mons. de Murville's gardens. His illness was very long; and when he was recovering, Mons. d' Aimeri and his grandson were in Russia, so that I have not yet taken the Chevalier de Valmont thither, but we shall go in a few days, and I will assuredly write to you on our return. I shall be much obliged to you to communicate this letter to my sister, for you know how anxious she is for all particulars that relate to Mons. de Murville. She has filled six pages with questions on this subject; and wants me, to give her an exact detail of all the Chevalier de Murville's thoughts and actions, since he was compelled to relinquish Cecilia and his country. If you are still in Paris, please to tell her, that he has quitted the name of Anglure, and resumed his own; that he is forty years old, still handsome, and without grey hairs, that his air is very melancholy, that he has very bad health, and has never loved any but Cecilia. These are the principal among a thousand questions my sister wrote; adding, that she should have no rest till I answered her; and if satisfactorily, that she should have but one wish remaining, namely, to have a good portrait of this rare man, a 'hero and martyr to love and constancy.' Farewell, my dear Baron! remember your promise to send me from Lagaraye a copy of the account you write to my brother-in-law.

LETTER II.

The Baroness to the Viscountess.

Y ES, my dear Friend; we arrived at Lagaraye the night before last; Mons. d' Almane, Dainville, and my son having made most part of the journey on horse-back; poor Theodore was extremely fatigued. You will be much surprised that we have not yet seen Mons. de Lagaraye; but every thing we hear augments our desire to be acquainted with this truly incomparable man. As you insisted on a very exact recital, without the omission of a single circumstance, I must begin my narration from Saturday, the day of our arrival. We alighted at a pretty good inn, and in half an hour a venerable old man, of the most interesting appearance, came into our room, and intreated us to dine with him the next day. We accepted the invitation; and the old man resumed his discourse by saying, you are come to see two angels sent from Heaven to bless this country ... They not only attend the sick, but feed the aged and infirm, employ the young, and make all happy. With your permission I will be your guide to morrow; and I am certain that all you see, will make you revere a thousand times more a character which fame can but imperfectly paint; it is only by having access to him, hearing him, witnessing his actions, that you can give him due praise. During this discourse, which raised our curiosity to the height, I considered attentively and with astonishment the person who delivered it, and could not dissemble my surprise at finding his man-ners and expressions so far superior to his appearance, which was only that of a peasant. He replied, with a smile, my history is really singular, and if it excites your curiosity, I will relate it to-morrow, with double pleasure, as it will be at the same time a tribute of gratitude to Mons. and Madame de Lagaraye. I live and am happy, and entirely through their munificence. He finished these words with eyes swimming in tears; we surveyed each other, and a sentiment of tenderness inexpressible made ours also overflow. I asked if we could see Mons. L— to-mor-row; he replied that that gentleman was gone six leagues from hence to comfort and assist the inhabitants of a farm, which had been burnt down, but that we should be introduced to him as soon as he returned.

The next day we were all up and drest by day-break, our good old man break-fasted with us; and then said, if you will follow me, I will conduct you to the manufactories; hospitals are all you have heard of, but you will be convinced that Mons. de Lagaraye has formed establishments of every kind: At these words we all set out, and our guide led us directly to the great street of the village; there he stopt and said, you see these plain rustic houses; they are filled with immense numbers of persons; most of these cottages are new. The stranger and the wretched, drawn hither and entertained by Mons. de Lagaraye, have for ten years been crowding to inhabit these mansions of peace and happiness. Each unfortunate being finds here a friendly country, which offers him the honourable resources of labour, and the means to accomplish his schemes, or to establish himself elsewhere. People of every country are found at Lagaraye; it is the sure refuge of laborious misery; the idle and vicious alone are banished and treated as strangers. Heaven, which blesses this place, grants to its happy inhabitants health, strength, and industry; and in no part of the world is population so extensive. In truth, the first view of this street offers a most interesting and agreeable picture; a multitude of little children meet you at every step; the houses, all open, display the most charming neatness; numbers of women of all ages, and young girls, are seen spinning and singing by an husband or father's side, who is working at his trade of carpenter, hatter, wheelwright, &c. &c. In short, every thing breathes an air of gaiety, plenty and content.[2] From this street we entered another rather less, where we saw a great many women, but not one man: surprised, I asked our guide the reason, who answered, the street you have left contains the artisans; part of its inhabitants, as I have already told you, are strangers, unfortunate artificers without bread or means, when they came to establish themselves here; the remainder were their apprentices, who preferred settling here to carrying their talents elsewhere. That street alone contains men of sedentary lives; this and all the rest are occupied by labourers, who work on buildings, repair the great roads, or till the earth; at night, their labour finished, they return apparently without fatigue; and perfectly happy in the idea, that their work is not for the benefit of others, but secures a subsistance for their wives and children. As the old man ceased speaking, we perceived a vast brick edifice, of a long and irregular form; it was the manufactory: we were led into a large hall, where twenty-six girls were making lace with four elderly women to overlook them: You see, said our old man, those four young women at the end of that little table; they are my daughters; above I have three sons; and all these, the delight and comfort of my age, live and enjoy their existence solely by the generous compassion of Mons. de Lagaraye. After this speech, which brought on many still more interesting, he conducted us into a little gallery, where we found twelve spinners. We then went up stairs to the mens apartments; and you may easily believe chose to begin by that, in which his sons were employed; there we saw twenty-six weavers; and in the last room found a cloth manufactury, in which were forty workmen, not including those who directed it. Now, says the old man, if you are not fatigued, I will shew you the plantations; we consented; and he took us quite across the

village, and stopt in the open field, desiring us to observe those long and beautiful avenues of young trees opposite to us, those fertile fields, rich meadows, and
luxuriant harvests; this land, heretofore uncultivated and abandoned, offered to
view only a vast morass, whence noxious vapours spread sickness and death on
all around. Admire this blissful change, and recognise in it the author Mons.
de Lagaraye. You cannot take a step here, but it reminds us of and proves his
beneficence; we owe him every thing, even the pure and healthy air we breathe.
You may conceive the number of hands employed for such works; he has made
skilful labourers by good pay and constant work; and the earth rendered fertile,
by augmenting his riches, impowers him to maintain and extend these immense
undertakings. Whilst the good old man was talking, I contemplated with much
emotion this happy and living soil; and said to myself, if the will of one can give
birth to so much happiness, can produce so many useful things, how is it possible such models should be so rare? Ah! if the sight of ill is dangerous, if its
example is contagious, how touching and persuasive is that of virtue? Vice may
well assume the most seducing form, but she has always some side that discovers
her, and gives distaste even to those she misleads; whilst the charms of virtue are
pure and unmixed, like herself. But let us then return to Lagaraye. After having
walked till noon it was time to go in. We dined with the old man, who according
to promise recounted his adventures, which appeared to me so interesting and
singular, that I returned immediately to the inn, that I might write them whilst
the impression remained.

I left Adelaide in the care of Madame d' Ostalis, and Miss Bridget, and passed
the rest of the day writing the enormous packet I now send you. This morning
we are told Mons. de Lagaraye does not return till night, so we shall not enjoy
the happiness so earnestly desired till to-morrow, and it is Mons. d' Almane who
is to write the Viscount the particulars of that interesting interview; in short,
our heads are all turned with what we have already seen. Theodore and Adelaide
wept much during the good old man's narration; they talk and think of nothing
but Mons. de Lagaraye, and have really a passionate desire to see him. In short,
I am delighted to observe in their young hearts an enthusiasm for virtue, consequently they will draw from this journey all the fruit we could wish. Farewell, my
dear friend: do not lose our old man's history; it is Adelaide who lends it you;
for I have promised to sent it on condition, that you return it to her, as we pass
through Paris.

The Life of St. André.[3]

The name of this excellent old man's father was Vilmore, a man of low extraction; who had amassed an amazing fortune very rapidly, and whom you must
recollect hearing your father-in-law (who was born in the same province) fre-

quently mention. Mons. de. Vilmore had several children, of whom St. André was the youngest. Mons. de Vilmore, anxious to marry his daughters nobly, that he might be aggrandised by alliances, and desirous to secure a vast estate and brilliant fortune to his eldest son, sacrificed the young St. André to these ambitious views. He had him brought up at a distance, on a very small income, where his education was totally neglected; but the goodness of his disposition and understanding made him exceed the expectation of his masters. When he attained his sixteenth year, he was informed that he had no other choice but the church. A lively fancy, strong passions, and the knowledge of his parents riches, all conspired to give him an insurmountable disgust to that profession. He desired to see and speak to his father, in hopes of making him change his design. Mons. de Vilmore, not knowing his intentions, granted his request; and he arrived at his father's house, when they were celebrating his sister's nuptials with the Marquis of C— . He found his father, brother, and sisters in the midst of grandeur and opulence; they looked on him as a stranger, and his father treated him with disdain and indifference. He discerned and felt all the misfortunes such a reception indicated; however he spoke, and with as much firmness as respect. Let mediocrity, said he, be my lot; I can be content; but do not debar me of my liberty, nor force me to engage in a profession, for which my aversion is invincible. Mons. de Vilmore, rendered furious by resistance, overwhelmed him with the most cruel reproaches. Your obstinacy, said he, would ruin you, did not my goodness still leave you time for reflection. I will send you for six months to one of your aunts in Flanders, when, if you are not intirely resigned to my will, I shall employ the most violent means to make you know your duty. The hapless St. André set out for Lisle in despair; but fixed in his resolution. An interesting figure, an amiable character, with manners mild and noble, made him soon taken notice of in his exile; whilst the charms of society softened its rigours. Unsuspecting and inexperienced, he was easily led away by every one, who approached him. The regiment of – was then at Lisle; the officers gamed very high, and knowing the immense riches of Mons. de Vilmore, engaged his son in their dangerous parties. He began, as is generally the case, by winning; and which is still more inevitable, ended by losing. The hopes of recovering his money led him on, until he had lost upon honour 24,000 livres: reduced to despair, he wrote to his father, confessing his fault in the most pathetic terms. His only answer was an arrest; they confined him in the castle of Saumur. He submitted to this punishment with a gentleness not to be expected from a character naturally violent. Knowing all his debts were paid, gratitude made him bear with patience a treatment, he could not imagine would be of long duration. Notwithstanding, contrary to his expectations, he remained a prisoner two years: this barbarous usage soured his temper, and made him lose part of those sentiments of moderation he had till then preserved. At length his prison doors were opened, and this sentence pronounced, 'You must give your word and honour either to become an ecclesiastic, or go a volunteer to India.' My choice is made, cry'd St. André; and I shall be happy to leave a country foreign to me, since I have neither father, relations, not friends. This answer fixed his fate; he was sent to Brest, and two days after embarked. Thus did an unnatural father drive beyond the seas a youth of eighteen, of the most promising genius, without succour, money, rank, or establishment; and perhaps in hopes that, surrounded with perils, oppressed with misery and poverty, he might put a period to his unfortunate life.

His youth however made him support the most excessive fatigues; and his courage rendered him superior to his fortune. He distinguished himself, and being promoted, soon emerged from misery and oblivion; these successess led to many still more advantageous; having gained reputation and friends, they joined with him in commercial enterprises, which in a country so fertile in resources, procured him in less than five years happiness and independence. Content with a moderate but honest fortune, raised to an honourable rank, he began to turn his thoughts towards his country. Still young, he was not insensible to the vain desire of exhibiting to his family the rapid fruits of his industry; resolving however to return to the Indies, but not as driven thither by necessity, but as led by ambition and glory. His father, informed of his good success, had for two years before condescended to acknowledge him; and to write to him; and appeared cured of his prejudices.

A truce concluded for a year promised him a security which was not to be forfeited by a delay of his voyage; and he embarked with his whole fortune in paper. This imprudence was the cause of all his misfortunes; for scarcely was he at sea, but the truce was broke, his vessel attacked, taken by the English, and himself carried prisoner to Launceston,[4] a town in the west of England: thus were all his hopes blasted, and he lost at once his liberty and his fortune. He wrote to his father, who filled up the measure of his woes by returning a letter full of reproaches. At the end of six months he was released, approached the coast of France and beheld that fatal shore, and arrived at Brest nearly in the same miserable situation in which he had left it six years before. Without hope or money, entirely destitute, he recollected a surgeon, named Bertrand, with whom he had lodged, and from whom he had received many marks of friendship; and soon found this honest man; who offered him his house, purse, and every service in his power. St. André accepted without blushing the courtesies of friendship; and wrote to Mons. de Vilmore demanding his portion, which he had never received, and even forgot during his prosperity. The answer contained a promise of money on condition only of his reembarking for India in a vessel ready to fail: such inconceivable severity alienated an heart long since soured. Resentment and despair deprived him of courage. He fell dangerously ill; and was soon reduced to the last extremity. Bertrand watched him night and day, and paid him every attention the tendrest friendship could exact. Bertrand had a daughter of the age of eighteen, who, thinking only to follow the impulse of a laudable compassion, remained by the hapless St. André's bedside, and shared with her father the employment of his nurse. Bertrand related his unfortunate adventures, told her of his successes in India, extolled his preservance, courage, and accomplishments, of all which there were several witnesses at Brest; and they both bewept a lot so unmerited and deplorable. St. André, delirious from the beginning of his illness, was incapable of enjoying such affecting care; and being before opprest with affliction, and always shut up in his room, Blanche (for that was the name of Bertrand's *daughter*) had been scarcely seen, and never remarked by him. This young woman, notwithstanding the obscurity of her birth, was known and celebrated in Brest for a superior education, behaviour replete with modesty and sweetness, and still more for her personal charms.

One night when St. André's life was despaired of, Blanche, seated sorrowfully by him, observed with unusual tenderness the unhappy object of so much care and anxiety. A deadly paleness seemed to overspread his features, rendered still more affecting by the graces of youth yet visible in them. He lay with eyes apparently closed for ever, with one hand extended on the bed, on which Blanche (impelled by an irresistible impulse) let fall one of her's, and finding it immoveable and cold she thought him dead: Oh heaven! exclaimed she, all is over; unfortunate young man! terror, pity, and a sentiment still more tender, prevented her saying more, and she fell down by the bedside without sense or motion. At that instant St. André, recovering from his trance, opened his eyes, and the first object which struck them, was Blanche in a swoon by him: it was youth and beauty surrounded by the shadow of death. He uttered a piercing cry; help arrives; and Blanche is speedily restored. The affecting scene is explained; and St. André recovers only to receive into his soul emotions of the most passionate gratitude. Thus, in the midst of agonizing horrors and on the brink of the grave did love unite for ever to unfortunate hearts, fixed his shafts indelibly, and proved that his power was irresistible even under the most dreadful and affecting form.

St. André, quickly convalescent, gave himself up entirely to the dangerous impression of a passion, which he experienced for the first time. He easily obtained that confession, on which depended his happiness. Blanche had betrayed herself, even before she was beloved, and now happy and tranquil, confirmed by transports of joy, what despair had already declared. Bertrand himself, seduced by pity, affection, and perhaps ambition, consented, after a slight resistance, to the joint request of St. André and his daughter, and approved of a secret union, which took place six months after St. André's illness, and raised him to the height of his wishes at the age of twenty-five. Not desiring or expecting any assistance from his father, he resolved to conceal his marriage, and to seize the first opportunity of returning to India, with his wife and her father. He made several applications; and by the help of his reputation and friends soon saw a possibility of being constantly employed in a very advantageous manner. During these transactions Blanche became pregnant; he pressed his solicitations in hopes of getting to India in time for his wife's delivery; but his affairs not keeping pace with wishes, they perceived it would be impossible to elude the discovery of a secret, already well known in the city. He therefore took the resolution of informing his father of it by letter; and wrote to him in these terms.

'Sir, can you recollect the name and existence of a wretch so long forgotten; I ought to believe you have renounced for ever the rights which nature gave you over me. I know what were my first errors: if my youth could not then excuse them in your eyes, six years exile, passed in useful, and I will be bold to say, glorious pursuits, might, I sometimes flattered myself, have obliterated them. But cruelly abandoned in my last misfortunes, I found in a stranger the compassion, assistance, and tenderness of a father. Without renouncing him rejects me, I thought myself at liberty to adopt one, who by his beneficence and virtue proved himself worthy of so sacred a title. Obscure, poor, without rank or fortune, but honest and sensible, is the father I have chosen. By accepting his favours, residing in his house, and marrying his daughter, I am become his son: and the felicity that it has procured me, exceeds if possible all the misfortunes I have endured. I have a due respect for the distinctions established in society; and had I been born in a rank, that such an alliance would have dishonoured, my courage would have enabled me to sacrifice my passion, and with it the whole happiness of my life, to the honour of my family. But, thank God, no such obstacle existed; my wife's birth is equal to mine, as is her fortune; her father is poor; there is the only difference between us; therefore no reason could or ought to have impeded me. I am bound by a tie which love and honour renders equally dear and sacred to me; and I beg you to believe, that ambition, authority, and even the laws themselves would in vain attempt to dissolve it. I am going to India to begin a new career; I entreat you not to trouble my destiny by clamours which cannot change it. I desire nothing but tranquility, and forgetfulness of a country which I abandon perhaps for ever. This is the only favour I dare ask, I ought to hope, and do expect it from your justice.

I have the honour to be, & c.'

This letter produced the most terrible effects in Mons. de Vilmore; it hurt his pride too much, not to inflame his anger to the height; the comparison between his family and Bertrand's appeared to him the extreme of impudence. He procurred at the same time two warrants. St. André was torn from the arms of his distracted wife, loaded with irons, and cast into a dungeon: and Blanche, notwithstanding her youth and condition, experienced a similar treatment; it was there this unfortunate woman brought into the world the unhappy fruits of their deplorable passion. They wanted to rob her of her infant; but her resistance, sobs and tears, touched their hearts, and made them sensible of pity for the first time; so that she retained her child, and to preserve his life was careful of her own. In the mean time St. André, drove to desperation, distracted, furious, invoked vengeance, and demanded Blanche or death. Three months passed in this dreadful way; when he was told that a man desired to speak with him from his father. My father! cried he, I have none. At that instant he beheld a person, whom he knew was Mons. de Vilmore's steward. Oh! says St. André, does the barbarian, who sends you, grant my prayers? Do you bring me death, for that is the only favour I can expect from him? – Compose yourself, Sir, replied the man; I come to announce to you a fortune, to which you durst not pretend. Whilst you are accusing fate, she is labouring for your welfare. Your brother is dead, and you become the natural heir to a father, who can still pardon, and receive you with open arms. – What do you say? interrupted St. André, my brother dead! Heaven is just; it takes from my persecutor the object his pride rendered so dear to him; and I, victim sacrifice to his cruel ambition, have not invoked vengeance in vain. – Hear me, said the steward, and rather merit by your repentance the favours offered you. Mons. de Vilmore, founder of his own fortune, is at liberty to dispose of it; he has two daughters whom he might enrich at your expence, but having no grandchild of his name, and compassionating your faults and misfortunes, he invites you to the succession from which death has taken your brother. His dignities and fortunes await you. You may easily imagine, by what blind submission such favours are to be purchased; – Speak, Sir, returned St. André coldly; a father, who will again receive me, and calls for my hand to wipe away his tears, is doubtless incapable of imposing dishonourable terms; therefore speak, I listen without fear. – You must, Sir, abjure for ever a disgraceful as well as an unlawful marriage. A competent fortune will console Blanche for your mutual error; your consent alone is wanting to dissolve these shameful bands; every other step is already taken; and it is at this price alone you can pretend – Enough! interrupted St. André, I foresaw from the beginning of your discourse this odious proposal, yet had the patience to hear you: Attend in your turn to my answer. I may be persecuted, opprest, robbed of my wife, child, and life; all these cruelties are possible to tyranny armed with power: but honour is a good they cannot take from me; and I will preserve it pure and spotless, happy to suffer for the objects of my love and esteem. This is my final and irrevocable resolution: violence, torments, and even death itself, nothing in the universe shall make me change it. – The steward would have replied; but St. André refusing to hear any more, he left with the shame and regret of having vainly attempted to seduce an incorruptible man. Blanche in her prison experienced a persecution still more odious and unjust. She was prest to relinquish her rights, and her title of wife to St. André. They made her very advantageous proposals for herself and child; and by turns employed prayers and menaces. Her constant answer was, that she expected from her husband the example she ought to follow. She hoped for one of courage and fidelity; but that in every case she was resolved to make his conduct the model for hers. Mons. de Vilmore, despairing to conquer so firm and settled a resistance, gave himself up to all the fury pride and resentment could inspire in a cruel and implacable soul. They snatched from the wretched mother's arms her dear child, the only hope and comfort of her life: they loaded the unhappy couple with heavier chains; augmented the horrors and cruelty of a prison; and, to compleat their misery, assured them this treatment was to continue for life. Four years passed in this horrid situation; yet St. André made it a duty to live and suffer for that love which had sustained him. By indefatigable pains, and perseverance, he corrupted one of his gaolers; and unable to obtain his liberty, he prevailed on this person to procure him pens, ink, and paper, with which he wrote a true history of his life, and concluded it by demanding his liberty, his wife, and child; without pretending to his father's goods, or even to his just inheritance. This petition was inscribed *To my Country*, and began thus: 'I have shed my blood for her; I am an obscure citizen, but innocent, and persecuted: my cause is that of all virtuous and feeling hearts. Loaded with chains, dying and forlorn in an infamous dungeon; as father, husband, and son, equally unfortunate, I cast myself into the arms of the first of my countrymen, who shall read this history; and I conjure him to have the generosity and compassion to protect and defend and unhappy man; enslaved for near five years by violence and tyranny. May a good and virtuous hand deposit this writing at the foot of the royal tribunal which protects the innocent! and may I in embracing my wife and son forget for ever the torments I have suffered.

The man whom St. André had gained, got this history secretly printed, and distributed several copies. An advocate, celebrated for his talents and his virtues, moved by so mournful a detail, was desirous of the glory of supporting so singular and interesting a cause: and notwithstanding the credit and opposition of Mons. de Vilmore, he soon made all the tribunals resound with the cries of the wretched St. André. He enquired the fate of Bertrand, and learnt that grief had put a period to his days within six months. He had the young child delivered into his hands; and at length obtained liberty for St. André and his wife. When he went to her prison, Blanche was ignorant of all these circumstances; and utterly in despair, expected from death alone and the end of those cruel pains, which rent her heart. The generous advocate, led by humanity, penetrated the dreary abode, where youth, beauty, and virtue in distress displayed a most affecting picture. He held the child in his arms; and entering a most dismal dungeon, he saw by the glimmering of a melancholy lamp, Blanche laying on straw, with dishevelled hair, clad in miserable rags, her face overflowed with tears, and her beautiful hands raised to heaven, tho' loaded with irons. He stopt to contemplate with a mixture of pity and admiration, her charms, her youth, and the horrors that surrounded her. Blanche, imagining she heard the gaoler, raised her pensive head, and asked with a weak and dying voice, what he wanted. – I come, cried the advocate, to do homage to suffering virtue, and to terminate its sorrows. On concluding these words he prostrated himself at her feet, and presented her child; Blanche recollecting him, exclaimed, Oh! if he be restored me, I can support life. She strove to embrace him, but extacy and transport increasing her weakness, she fainted in the arms of her deliverer. What words can do justice to the emotions of surprize and rapture, which filled his sensible and compassionate heart? When she regained her senses, she learned that the goodness of an utter stranger was going to unite her for ever to her husband. Come, said the advocate, quit this frightful dwelling, which has but too long echoed the groans of innocence; come! that I may deposit in the arms of a father and a husband two objects so dear. But, continued he, you must not go out in so shameful a condition; I have foreseen every thing, and have brought in this parcel, all that is at present necessary: dress yourself, whilst I go and shew the keeper my order, and in a quarter of an hour I will return and fetch you. He left her without waiting for an answer; and Blanche found in the bundle linen and a compleat dress, in which nothing was omitted; she sprinkled with tears these precious pledges of a beneficence at once so delicate and so attentive; and her heart, again open to happiness, was overcome with gratitude.

The advocate returned, as happy and as much moved as Blanche. He led her with a trembling hand, assisted in carrying her son, and snatched her with transport from that dreary abode of bitterness and horror. A coach waited, and quickly conveyed them to St. André's prison; they are admitted, and Blanche clasping her son in her arms, ran and threw herself into those of her husband; and at that moment they experienced all that love and joy could inspire in two fond hearts, raised suddenly from the depth of despair to the height of happiness. The advocate stood opposite them, contemplating with delight so sweet a scene, saying to himself, this is my work; and doubtless was not the least happy of the three. Blanche tore herself suddenly from the arms of her husband, and threw herself at her benefactor's feet. Here, says she, is the guardian angel, the beneficent God, who restores your wife, your child, and your liberty! She could not proceed, sobs stopt her words. St. André flew, and cast himself on his knees by her, saying, Alas! my heart empoisoned during five years by hatred, relinquishes for ever every sentiment of anger or revenge; gratitude and love will henceforward occupy it entirely; yes, I forget my persecutors and my misfortunes; I renounce the torment of rage, and consecrate every emotion of my soul to the dear objects restored to me, and to the most generous of men.

From this pathetic scene, the life of St. André describes nothing but a long series of misfortunes, of which I shall only give you the most interesting parts. His generous benefactor received them at first into his own house; then settled them in a farm, where they dwelt peaceably during two years, engaged in husbandry; his diligence nearly doubled the revenues of the land, and procured him the pleasure of being useful to his patron. He made many unsuccessful efforts to get into the army; but Mons. de Vilmore's hatred, ever active and vigilant, constantly prevented him. He had the misfortune to lose his son, and a short time after his benefactor and sole support. Overburthened with sorrow, he removed with his wife to the extremity of a distant province, resolving to subsist there unknown, by the work of his hands. It was in Auvergne that he fixed his unhappy fate; his talents for husbandry, and his courage as well as hers, procured them the means of life; they both entered into the service of a rich farmer. St. André cultivated the earth, whilst Blanche, occupied in the work of the house, overcame by these hard employments her disgust and delicacy. During six years passed in this manner St. André had several children, to whom he gave an education suitable to their condition; and accustoming himself to this laborious but quiet life, he at length became possessor of a small spot of ground, which by cultivation was sufficient to maintain his family. Thither they retired, and during ten years tasted all the sweets of peace and happiness. Content with his lot, he forgot in the embraces of his wife and children the difference of this fortune, from that to which he seemed entitled at his birth. An unexpected event came to destroy the fruits of time and reason; and to replunge him into a dreadful abyss of cares and misfortunes. Mons. de Vilmore having been attacked for almost a year by a slow but mortal disease, felt some remorse for his unnatural conduct towards his son. On the brink of the grave, his troubled conscience made him look forward with horror to the formidable moment of an approaching dissolution. Religion, so consoling to those who have lived well, could only add to the secret terrors that haunted him. He strove in vain to banish the cutting remorse that pursued him; he drew to that period, when the most perverse mortal has no longer the pernicious faculty of deceiving himself. Truth, so dreadful to the guilty, came to dazzle and to confound him; and determined him at last to get information of the situation in which his son was. He spoke to his steward, who being a man of probity, and interested for the happiness of St. André, after many fruitless researches discovered his retreat, and wrote him the following letter: – 'Mons. de Vilmore is dying, and wishes for you. His oppressed heart is again awake to tenderness; do not therefore hesitate; fly into the arms of a father, who daily reproaches himself with all the misfortunes under which you have so long groaned. There is yet time; profit from these moments; his vain desires of pride and ambition are now annihilated. He wishes to see you, but has not courage to ask it. He is surrounded by your enemies, who already devour his substance and yours. I advertise you of their secret dispositions. Appear; conduct to his feet your unfortunate family; and you will recover all your rights. But make haste; all depends on your activity and diligence.' – St. André hesitated not; the interest of his children outweighed every other reflection. He sold at an under price his little inclosure, and set out with his family. On quitting this loved place a confused emotion made him shed tears; he regretted his humble cottage, and could not tear himself away without feeling grief and trouble inexpressible. To expedite their arrival he was compelled to buy a carriage and travel post; and the expences of this journey nearly consumed the fruits of sixteen years hard labour. At length he descried the walls of Paris, and presently after the splendid habitation of his father. – At this sight Blanche threw herself into his arms. – Here then, said she, would have been your abode without me; and yet you can regret that we have now left. St. André wept and embraced her: and this instant, which brought before her eyes the full value of those sacrifices, with which he had never reproached her; this moment, so affecting and so flattering, was perhaps one of the sweetest of her life.

But alas! what grievous news awaited them! the friendly steward ran to him, and informed them, that he had in the night informed his master of their approach, but that these tidings did not at the time determine him: that he had passed a most dreadful night; and in the morning feeling himself near his end, he desired a confessor to be called; and after two long conferences he resolved to make a new will. Thus far all was favourable for you, continued the steward; the worthy priest spoke with so much energy of his proceedings against you, that, penetrated with awe and remorse, he did not hesitate about sending for his notary; but at that minute your courier arrived with intelligence, that you would be here in two hours. Mons. de Vilmore at that moment experienced an emotion, which produced the most fatal effects: he instantly lost the use of speech, a circumstance rendered still more terrible to him, as he retains his senses and recollection perfect. In fine, he knows you are here, and manifests the greatest desire to see you. The physicians say, that your presence may occasion another change, and restore to him the faculty he is deprived of. Come, Sir, let us lose no more time. – At these words St. André, followed by his family, went into his father's apartment; who on seeing him raised his eyes to heaven, and stretched out his arms to him. St. André ran, and threw himself on his knees by the bed-side; Mons. de Vilmore regarded him with the most pathetic expression in his eyes, and the name of St. André burst from his lips. On this the confessor ran to him, and said, make one effort more, your lawyer is here; one word, a single word will confirm the fortunes of a wretch, which your silence and death will doom for ever to the most frightful poverty. Implore the Almighty for grace, in these last moments allotted you, to make reparation for the sufferings of innocence. At these tremendous words, Mons. de Vilmore lifted his clasped hands to heaven, opened his mouth, attempted to speak, but could only articulate a few interrupted and confused sounds. Grief, terror and remorse were painted on his countenance. His arms stiffened, and the paleness of death overspread his features. The priest approached, and offered him the crucifix; but this miserable dying sinner, raving with agony and despair, cast a dreadful look on his son, and beholding with a wild and furious air the proffered crucifix, pushed it from him with horror: the most shocking convulsions at this instant ended his life. The bare recital of so terrible and insupportable a death makes one tremble, and is a lesson for ever useful and striking for fathers (if there remain any such) who are capable of hating and of abandoning their offspring. He died without making any provision for St. André; there was no will but such a one as hatred had dictated. Thus his irresolution and late remorse served only to make his end more agonising and dreadful, without altering the condition of his unhappy son; who was now infinitely more to be pitied than ever, and reflected with dismay on all the woes to which this last reverse had reduced him. He had still some money remaining. He retired with his family to a remote suburb, where he hired an apartment to reflect at least during the night on the course they should pursue. The children, fatigued with their journey, and still too young to feel the torments of disappointment, soon fell asleep, and peaceably enjoyed the most profound repose. One melancholy lamp gave light to this gloomy retreat. St. André, now dumb and motionless, sat with wandering eyes, then started up and traversed the room with hasty steps, and discovered by every gesture the cruel agitations of his soul. Blanche, till then overpowered by grief, looked up, sighed, ran and threw herself at his feet. – Alas, miserable man! said she, into what an abyss have I plunged you! without me, without this fatal love, you would this day be happy, and your life would have been as fortunate as it is now deplorable: but if you still love me, your courage will not abandon you. – Let the voice of your wife and the sight of your children revive you. – My children, replied St. André, my children! I could support thy misery and my own, but these unfortunates! have they thy reason or thy strength? See them lament and suffer! No, no; it would be better – At these words he paused, and went to the other end of the room, and threw himself into a chair. – Oh, heaven! exclaimed the affrighted Blanche, what do you make me imagine? What horrid design? – She could say no more; sobs stopt her speech; and St. André came to her with a fierce and gloomy air. – Believe me, Blanche; dry your tears; we have endured life long enough; our talk is ended; one moment will set us free; and I have courage to give you the example – This terrible speech re-animated Blanche, who collecting all her fortitude, with a firm voice exclaimed – Who I! shall I thus offend heaven and nature? I abandon my children? I should be altogether wicked and barbarous. Alas! I am only unfortunate; innocence is left me; and I can support it all. – Yes, if you condemn me to the agony of surviving you, I shall have the courage to endeavour at least to prolong so cruel an existence. I will live for thy children, those hapless children, whom you would betray and abandon to misfortunes, which you yourself have not the courage to endure. – At these words some tears fell from the eyes of St. André; and his wife seeing him softened, seized that favourable moment to melt and draw him back to virtue. St. André having recollected himself, acknowledged, detested and abjured his ill conduct; was convinced, that religion, honour and nature equally required him to live. But his body sunk under these violent agitations; he was seized with a burning fever, which soon carried him to the brink of the grave; and reduced Blanche to the utmost extremity of grief. She beheld on one side her dying husband, and on the other her dear children famishing with cold and hunger. In this distress she invoked heaven to terminate by one blow the miserable existence of so many innocents. One morning, mournfully seated by his bed, she considered his visage disfigured by the shades of death, which recalled to her remembrance that period of her youth, when, in a situation nearly similar, she felt the first impression of a passion, since so fatal to both. This thought reanimating her tenderness, she seized one of his hands, and bathing it with her tears – Oh, dear spouse! said she, falling on her knees, can you pardon me the torments with which my luckless love has poisoned all your days? – Alas! replied St. André, my last moments are doubtless terrifying, since I leave you and my children in the depth of misery; but if this dismal and painful race was to be run over again, I would endure it all to possess you. – These words were scarcely uttered, when the door flew open on a sudden, and a sight the most unexpected rivetted the eyes and attention of the unhappy pair. A young lady of about twenty-five years of age, of a charming figure, appeared, leading a little girl seven years old,[5] and advanced with an affectionate air towards the bed, where she stopped and dismissed her attendants; and causing the door to be shut, addressed herself to Blanche in a soft voice and asked her name. Blanche confused and abashed, hesitated and trembled. St. André conquered his weakness sufficiently to raise himself, and in a few words delineated their wretched situation. I see, said the lady, they told me true; God grant I may not be too late; and you, my child, said she, turning to her daughter who was weeping, observe well this room, and the affecting objects it contains, and never suffer the idea to be erased from your memory. – Take this purse, and deposit it at the foot of the bed; approach with respect; we owe that to the unfortunate; and by never forgetting it, you will one day become worthy the sacred trust, with which I now honour you.

You surely wish for the name of this charming and generous unknown; and you will be still more interested, when I tell you that it was Madame de Lagaraye in the bloom of youth, with that daughter she has since lost, that only child who died at fifteen, and who, blessed with such an education and example, might justly be the delight of so virtuous a mother. But to return to St. André: Mons.

de Lagaraye hearing his history, was so sensibly touched by his sufferings, that he offered him an asylum on his estate; and at length placed him at the head of his new establishment, which he has now directed six years. Mons. de Lagaraye provided for all his children, and crowned all his favours by the gift of a charming house, surrounded by an immense garden. It is in this delightful retreat, that St. André passes in sweet repose the relics of a life heretofore so turbulent. It is there where the praises of Mons. and Madame de Lagaraye resound every hour, and where their respectable names are written on all the walls, and celebrated every instant by the voices of sentiment and gratitude.

LETTER III.

The Baron to the Viscount.

AT length I have this morning enjoyed the happiness of seeing and admiring the most respectable and interesting of human beings. During the three days we have been at Lagaraye, I have had time to inform myself thoroughly of all he has done. I desired to know him perfectly by his actions before I saw him; and beyond all I wished, that my son (previously to that moment he so anxiously waited for) might be circumstantially acquainted with the degree of admiration which Mons. de Lagaraye merited from him, in order that I might observe the impression, which the first interview with so extraordinary a man produced on Theodore. It was not sufficient for me that my son should behold him with emotion; I would have him unable to approach him without transport; and said to myself, 'If Theodore is not beside himself at the sight of St. André's benefactor, and of the founder of all these works, I have deceived myself; my system of education is of no value, and I have done nothing worthy of praise.'

This morning my son, awakened by his impatience, rose before day; and all of us were drest and assembled by six o'clock; and conducted by St. André took the road to what is here from habit still called the Castle. It is a quarter of a league from the village, through an avenue of ancient elms. Adelaide and Theodore, though naturally so lively, walked quietly by us, keeping a profound silence, instead of skipping and chattering incessantly, as is their practice when animated by any thing interesting: the truth is, they were really struck. A common sentiment is exprest by lively and quick motions, but a deep impression even produces a kind of oppression and recollection, which renders us at once equally serious, attentive, and sedate. We were all on foot, and after a quarter of an hour's walk we perceived at the bottom of the avenue a castle, whose elegant and noble architecture displayed grandeur and magnificence. Here St. André made us stop, whilst he told us, that this splendid edifice was the work of Mons. de Lagaraye's father: Vanity laid the foundation, and could not foresee the use it would this day be put to. As the apartments are spacious, Mons. de Lagaraye only changed the partitions to make it suitable to his design. It is there he lives, and there is the hospital for men. Turn your eyes to the right, and you will see a large new building quite unadorned; that is the hospital which Mons. Lagaraye has built for women. When St. André ceased speaking, we quickened our pace, and soon reached the gates of the Castle. It was seven o'clock; a porter drest in grey asked our names, and admitted us. We crossed two immense courts, and on entering the house were told, Mons. de Lagaraye was in the chapel, where mass was going to begin; and thither we desired to be conducted. St. André told us, he should not present us till Mons. de Lagaraye came out of the chapel; we went in, and seated ourselves on an empty bench near the door. You will easily imagine how eagerly I cast my eyes around to discover Mons. de Lagaryae; St. André whispered me, No seat or distinction will point him out, but he is in sight, seek and guess. At this moment my son struck my view, and I must own he alone fixed my attention. He was on tiptoe, his neck stretched out, his mouth half open, his breath appeared oppressed, and in this attitude his looks, blushes, and every action was expressive of the most lively emotion and curiosity. There were, exclusive of ourselves, near fifty people, part convalescents, and the remainder servants, and workmen; but all drest in one uniform of coarse grey cloth. Thus it was very difficult to distinguish Mons. de Lagaraye wearing the same dress with the others, and seated accidentally. On a sudden my son, quite transported, caught hold of my arm, crying out – See, there he is, that surely must be him— and pointing to a man of a noble and striking figure, and whose long white hair, though he was not very old, spread over his shoulders, gave to his whole countenance a most venerable air, which commanded respect. The fervour of his devotion distinguished him, and all eyes were turned towards him. – Yes, it is he, says Theodore; see, all eyes are fixed on him. – Indeed my son was not mistaken; and doubtless these were the features, by which he most deserved to be known. Mass being ended, every body rose, and made way for Mons. de Lagaraye, who went out followed by the crowd blessing him as he passed. St. André then went up to him, and announced in a low voice the intent of our journey; which done he presented us, and Mons. de Lagaraye received us with a politeness full of ease and sweetness. – He embraced Dainville and I, and was going to do my son the like honour; but Theodore, forced by an impulse (which filled me with delight,) put one knee to the ground, and kissed his hand, which he wet with the sweetest tears he will perhaps ever shed. Mons. de Lagaraye, surprized and moved, lifted him up, and took him in his arms, asked the motive of an action, which his modesty and simplicity prevented his comprehending. Madame d' Almane took upon herself the task of explaining it: Mons. de Lagaraye listened with a mild and serene air, embraced my son, and said – 'I do not deserve to be admired; I am satisfied; the manner of life I have adopted constitutes my felicity; and you see in me only a happy man.' – Then, turning to us, proposed our seeing his house; and offering himself for our guide, conducted us first to the Infirmary, an immense room containing sixty-two beds, disposed in a stile of neatness and even elegance that surpasses all conception. But what appeared to us the most pathetic, was to see Mons. de Lagaraye speak in the most affectionate and consolatory terms to all the invalids, and to hear them bless and thank him with the most lively expressions of tenderness and gratitude. At the sound of his voice we beheld all the curtains half undrawn, and every head throughout the hall raised and bent forward to enjoy the happiness of seeing him. He appeared like a divinity, who deigns to dispense his blessings in person in the temple where he is adored. This hall is lighted by four windows of Bohemian glass, and has two large doors and two chimnies. Testifying my admiration of its grandeur and regularity to Mons. de Lagaraye, he replied, – It is not my building: I made use of it as I found it. – I expressed my surprise at what could have been its former use. He simply answered, – it was a theatre; but being the most spacious, dry and healthy place, I preferred it for my invalids. – Those words, my dear Viscount, *it was a theatre*, what a crowd of reflections did they not inspire! a theatre converted into an hospital! what an astonishing change! This man, who was talking to me, clad in coarse raiment, and surrounded by these direful and loathsome objects, I figured to myself as the person, who formerly in this very hall had engaged in the sweetest and most elegant pleasures, and in the midst of a brilliant and numerous society. I said to myself, it could have been only the enthusiasm of an heated imagination, or the boundless ambition of raising a name, that could have induced him to make such sacrifices; but yet simplicity of manners, and an air of calmness, modesty and peace announce neither fanaticism nor pride. Mons. de Lagaraye appears happy, and a munificent philosopher. Is it possible, that these mild virtues could produce alone such extensive designs, and so singular a conduct? These ideas occupied me deeply, and I anxiously wished, if it was possible, by a particular conversation to investigate his system, and his most secret sentiments. In the mean time we left the infirmary, and were conducted by Mons. de Lagaraye to the apothecary's apartment, whom he presented to us as a man of distinguished merit and education. Here is a compleat surgery, disposed with that order and elegance, which is so conspicuous in this mansion. From thence we proceeded to the opposite extremity of the house, into a very large room, heretofore a saloon, whose beautiful carving, gilding, and wainscot, painted white, yet remains; but it is now furnished with small tables and forms set in rows, round a kind of pulpit, somewhat raised, and placed in the centre of the room. – This, said Mons. de Lagaraye is my school; here all the lads of the village, from ten o'clock till noon, and again from three to four in the evening, are taught to read and write; and at seven every night I read a lesson of morality, which I composed and had printed expresly for these children. This work is in two parts; the first for infancy, and the second for youth. Madame de Lagaraye has formed an establishment exactly similar for the girls. After this interesting explanation, Mons. de Lagaraye proposed our seeing his apartment, which consisted only of a small bed-chamber, a charming cabinet, a library, and laboratory. – You have seen, says he, what are my occupations; reading, chymistry, the study of physic, and botany, are my amusements; and I protest to you, that during twelve years I have not experienced a single moment of weariness. St. André whispered me – Could you have had any idea of what you have seen? – No, surely, replied I; to be known, he must be both seen and heard. He speaks of all he has done with a plainness, which takes away all surprise; and one is even tempted to believe, whilst he is speaking, that it would be easy and pleasant to imitate him. He seems purely only a philosopher; nevertheless I own to you, I cannot reconcile such unprecedented sacrifices with a cool brain, and an imagination so little inflamed. – I had foreseen your astonishment, returned St. André, and was willing to leave you the pleasure of hearing from his own mouth, by what chain of ideas he was conducted to that point of perfection, at which it is impossible for any one to arrive without a piety equally sublime. When you are master of that interesting part of his history, I doubt not but your surprise will end in the highest admiration. As he finished these words, Mons. de Lagaraye advanced towards us, saying, the clock strikes; nine is our breakfast hour; will you be of the party? At this instant a female, dressed in the Lagaraye uniform, entered the room and saluted us; Mons. de Lagaraye embraced her; I need not tell you this was Madame de Lagaraye. He presented her, and she received us with that ease and politeness which characterizes both; and already prejudiced by Blanche in our favour, honoured Madame d' Almane and Madame d' Ostalis with expressions of particular friendship. She is still a regular and striking beauty, and preserves, notwithstanding her age, which is forty, a most extraordinary bloom; her countenance is equally mild and chearful; and her person is so noble and distinguished, that her dress appears only a disguise: she is lively, free, communicative, talks well, and with an earnestness which attracts attention, and gives to her expressions a particular air, that in any other person would seem the height of affectation, but in her is pure nature; and makes her conversation equally animated, agreeable, and interesting. She admires and loves her husband to a degree bordering on enthusiasm, and listens to all the eacomiums bestowed on him with eagerness and transport. In half an hour I defined all this, and readily conceived, that loving Mons. de Lagaraye so entirely, a lively imagination would easily lead her to comply with every thing he proposes; but he was still an enigma; and every moment increased my curiosity. We were informed breakfast was ready. Mons. de Lagaraye's apartment is on the ground floor; and he led us through his closet into a little grove, where we found a table loaded with fruit, and the produce of the dairy. The whole society met at the same time, consisting of the two surgeons, the curate of Lagaraye, Blanche, and the chymist, whom we had already seen. – Behold, said Mons. de Lagaraye, the companions of our retirement. Their sense, knowledge, and better than all their friendship, have for ten years been its chief charm. During the repast the conversation became general, and was both agreeable and lively. Breakfast ended by a walk in the garden, which was all dedicated to the use of the kitchen, excepting a great walk of chesnut trees. Madame de Lagaraye resumed the discourse, and pointed out the beauty of the trees and fruits. – All you see, said she, all these useful productions are Mons. de Lagaraye's work. Those orchards of various fruits were formerly groves of myrtle and roses; those espaliers were covered with jasmine and honeysuckles; that vast field of herbs was formed into parterres enamelled with a thousand flowers; here we were lost in the mazes of a labyrinth; there lofty hornbeam hedges were reaching to the clouds; nature, every where useless and constrained, presented only the works of art. A wise and good hand destroyed all these monuments of luxury, fit only for the effeminacy of sloth. The enchanted gardens of Armida[6] disappeared; and in their place arose peace, order, plenty and happiness; an abode worthy of the master who inhabits it. Whilst Madame de Lagaraye was speaking I admired the fire in her eyes, the varied and expressive turns of her countenance. You must allow, that women of real sensibility exceed us by a delicacy, of which we are not susceptible; they have a certain ingenuity in extracting enjoyment from numberless little incidents, which escape or make no impression on our minds. The pliability of their organs make them experience passionate emotions, which we can scarcely comprehend. They have a manner of loving peculiar to themselves: and she, who on her lover's departure, proposed to him to look every night at the moon at a particular hour, enjoyed surely by this engagement a most delicious sentiment; and I am persuaded that hour alone compensated for all the trouble of the day. Talismans, cyphers, and hair bracelets, all these delicate inventions are theirs; whilst we, who are capable of sacrificing our existence, and too often our glory for their fakes, set little value on what gives them such delight. Our passions are perhaps stronger and more fervent: but, their sensibility being moved and attracted more easily, and being more continual and uniform, must certainly procure them enjoyments unknown to man, and happiness preferable to any we can taste. I shall not apologise to you, my dear Viscount, for this digression; your love for woman will insure its pardon. But let us return to Lagaraye. St. André, as he walked by Mons. de Lagaraye, made him partly acquainted with my astonishment, and the difficulty I found in fixing my opinion of him. Mons. de Lagaraye turning to me, said – If you can spare me a few moments, I can perhaps satisfy your curiosity. Madame de Lagaraye joining in our conversation, indicated him to give us not only a circumstantial account of his life, but of his sentiments also. He consented, and seated himself on a green bank, shaded by trees, between Madame d' Almane and me; the rest of the company surrounded us, and my children took care to place themselves so as to see his face. We were all silent, whilst Mons. de Lagaraye, whose every word is engraved on my memory, addressed us in the following terms:

'I spent the greatest part of my life in tumult and dissipation. Master of my liberty at the age of twenty, and of a considerable fortune, neglected in my education, ignorant how to employ or to conduct myself, I fought for happiness where it never can be found, that is, in vain and frivolous amusements. My heart was cold, or, to express myself more properly, my natural sensibility was stifled by the life I led; yet my brain inflamed me, and led me more astray. I wished to be happy; but having no idea of those pure and tranquil joys, which alone are permanent, I despised and left the advantages I possessed, to search after imaginary delights. At length my eyes began to be open: being weary, disgusted with every thing, having enjoyed nothing, I felt satiety without having experienced those tumultuous pleasures which commonly precede it: I reaped from all these illusions only an importunate remembrance of them, attended by a cruel uncertainty. I searched to the bottom of my heart; and questioning it, I found it feeling; and at length discovered, that to taste of happiness it was that alone which I must consult. A new world seemed opened to my view. Until then discontented and selfish, I quickly flew from one extreme to the other. To love, and to live alone for the sake of those objects which were become dear to me, such was the new plan of felicity which I had planned. I was a father; I resigned my heart up to the sweetest and most natural affections. I doated on my daughter; till then I knew not happiness. But this happiness brought with it fears and agitations, of which till that moment I had had no idea. At that time, when my daughter by her virtues and her tenderness filled my soul with the most delightful sensations, a horrid thought would poison all my joy; the bare possibility that so pure a delight might be ravished from me; that accident or sickness could in one moment destroy all my present and future happiness. This cruel reflection harrowed up my soul, even in the instant in which I felt myself most blessed.' – Here Mons. de Lagaraye paused, remarking without doubt Madame d' Almane, who, with eyes fixed on Adelaide, could not restrain her tears. – After a moment's silence he proceeded. 'Yet my ideas expanding by degrees, I felt all the sweets of benevolence by dispensing happiness around. At first all was pleasing; but soon the impossibility of relieving to the extent of my wishes, caused me to make bitter reflections on luxury and vanity, which robs wailing misery of succour, and compels us to let it implore in vain. Thus was I situated, when an event the most horrid and unforeseen, by taking from me my chief happiness, hastened to accomplish a total change in my mind. My daughter, so worthy of our tenderest affection, on account of her virtues, accomplishments and beauty, that dear child, the amiable object of all our cares and hopes, in the midst of a grand entertainment made for her, suddenly fell as if thunderstruck, and expired in our arms ... Imagine, if it is possible, the grief, consternation and terror spread through the hall by this dreadful catastrophe ... Whilst we surrounded the innocent victim, the songs and shouts of joy of the croud, celebrating at a distance the festival, resounded in our ears ... Horrid contrast, which by making this event appear more extraordinary, rendered it still more terrible!

Relieved from the stupidity a violent despair at first occasions, I abandoned myself to new reflections. What! said I, are these the precious fruits of that sensibility I held so dear? One moment may annihilate all the bliss it gives! ... Yet without it this life is only a tiresome and cold vegetation; there is no real good but what flows from the heart; but to attach oneself passionately to place all one's happiness on a single object, is to expose oneself to griefs and troubles, which carry horror in the very thought; love and good works are necessary to our existence; but why confine all our affections to one or two weak and frail creatures? Universal beneficence! that is the virtuous sentiment which inspires the sage; who by strengthening and preserving in his heart this sublime passion, prepares consolation, which will enable him to support the sorrows his particular affections may cause him. It is true, he will weep for the loss of his friends; but he will not despair, nor think himself left destitute on earth, whilst there remain misfortunes which he can relieve. Shall life be a burthen to me whilst I can extend protection to the helpless orphan, raise the courage of virtue sinking under oppression, extricate from despair wretches delivered up to misery, vice, and death; and change such horrid destinies for pure and serene days; and having it in my power to run an useful, nay glorious career, shall my heart blasted by vain regrets consume in melancholy and despondence the residue of a weak and blameable sensibility? Oh my daughter! you are no more! never again shall I hear from your dear mouth the sweet name of father! nor my eyes be blessed with your sight! I shall no more press you with transport to my breast, that breast agonising which received your last sigh; you are torn from me for ever! but my heart is left me; by consulting that I can still be happy; I shall hear the wretched bless me, as I wipe away their tears and dry up their source; and I shall feel satisfaction and delight in the gratitude, and joy I occasion. These salutary reflections reanimated and eased my spirits; my soul reassumed its former vigour, and rose by degrees to enthusiasm. With a lively fancy united to reason, I at length formed the project of devoting myself entirely to those sacred duties, to which my life has ever since been dedicated. To execute the plan I meditated, it would not be sufficient to renounce the world, its luxuries and vanities; self must also be entirely forgotten and neglected, and the whole of a large fortune, together with my time,

attention, and study, appropriated to the relief of others. I wished to be legis-
lator of a community made happy through my benevolence. Vain of so new a
project, I was not insensible to the glory it would bestow; I thought of making
great sacrifices, and perhaps a little pride mingling with enthusiasm helped
to confirm my resolution. Assured of the heart of Madame de Lagaraye, and
knowing her love for virtue and for all its dictates, I communicated my ideas to
her, in which the strength and sensibility of her soul made her acquiesce with
transport. We set out for Montpellier, after having written to our relations and
friends our fixed resolves. You know the rest, and I have nothing further to
acquaint you with, but the real state of my heart at present. In speculation my
projects appeared to require vigorous and even painful exertions, and doubtless that pride I mentioned was necessary to enable me to bear the idea. I am
not ashamed to acknowledge, that I expected more glory than happiness: but
there is in good works an inexhaustible spring of pure felicity, which imagination alone can never reach, and which I have experienced. Deeply occupied in
the necessary cares of agriculture, of my manufactures, my inhabitants, and my
patients, these objects alone filled my mind and engaged my affections, made
me forget the world, and the frivolous ambition of being admired. I turned my
thoughts to that supreme judge, who can alone set a just value on man's works;
and presumed to believe, that some of mine were an homage not unworthy
even of him: – This thought exalting (as I may say) my mind above the world,
rendered me insensible to the deceitful allurements of restless vanity. I proved,
that it was from religion alone I could derive courage joyfully to persevere in
the enterprize I had formed. But how shall I describe to you the happiness,
almost without allay, I have experienced for ten years past; since it is beyond
the power of words to delineate it? Judge, if it be possible, from the retrospect
of all I have done; I will begin by the manufactures. As there is no trade which
may not be acquired in three years, I have already seen my manufacturers thrice
renewed; there are in all one hundred workmen employed; by trebling this
number you will have three hundred, their labours are either consumed in the
hospitals, or sold, and the profit added to my income. In improving my lands,
which step has answered amazingly, and in building, I have engaged near two
hundred and eighty more; add to these sixty strangers, who have been received
and settled at Lagaraye during eleven years. The stewards, nurses, and servants
to the hospitals amount to seventy persons more; I keep an exact account of
all the sick cured to this day; there are nearly nine thousand, including those
from an hospital of inoculation, not yet mentioned, but which I erected about
a quarter of a league from hence. These numbers united comprehend a total
of nine thousand seven hundred and ten. My first establishments were certainly very expensive, but the sale of all our furniture, plate, jewels, trinkets,
wardrobes, &c. brought the necessary sum, and in ten years my revenues are

increased more than a third. Although I have attained my fifty-seventh year, I may expect to live still ten years; and then you must nearly double the calculation just now made, which is far from being exaggerated. Should I reach seventy-seven years, it will be trebled: how dear and precious does this idea make life to me! Thus having multiplied the bands which tie me to this world, I do not look forward without concern to the awful moment when, by my death, so many will lose their sole support.

I owe my successors the fortune I inherited, and can only dispose of the increase, a sum too inconsiderable to maintain these establishments. Moreover leaving hospitals to the care of interested persons, is frequently doing more for the advantage of the trustees, than for the poor. I only order by will, that the sick in these hospitals, on the day of my death, shall remain till they are cured, and a certain sum of money to be given them at their dismission; and also that the workmen shall be suffered to finish their apprenticeship, I provide for some who have served me faithfully, and leave the rest to Providence. I have nothing left to entertain you with, but a summary account of the inhabitants. In return for procuring them ease and happiness, I require them to be industrious, orderly, and peaceable. I adjust their disputes; for some will always exist in large societies. My decisions have ever met with respect and obedience. – I rebuke with severity all kinds of disorder; and never suffer idleness. I will have even the amusements active and manly. In Lagaraye there are wine merchants and inns; but not one alehouse, that is to say, no houses open to the idle and intemperate. They receive and lodge strangers; but clubs are strictly forbidden. Those who infringe this law, by admitting the inhabitants and selling them wine, are banished for ever. On Sundays and holidays, the young are encouraged to amuse themselves in various games, such as cricket, swinging, &c. &c. but, it is my absolute command, no money shall ever be played for. Wine and cyder are provided at my expence; and not unfrequently, seated with the old men, I am a pleased spectator of these sports. Bows and arrows are one of the amusements I have introduced: I give a prize yearly to the most dexterous. In the village are two large spots appropriated to this use; where, beneath trees disposed in the form of an amphitheatre, are benches for the spectators. The old men occupy the first row, and behind them are placed the wives, maids, and children. I have prohibited music and dancing; and this severity, which perhaps will appear unreasonable, has greatly contributed to that perfect purity of manners I so much desired. The lads live separate from the girls; they do not so much as join in their diversions; so there can be no improper familiarities. The young women sometimes dance in circles to the sound of their own voices; they sing and recount ancient ballads, and are present at the public games. Such are their pleasures; knowing no other, they do not think it possible to find any more delightful. I had a great deal of trouble in bringing them to this degree of innocence and simplicity. It was necessary to reform the manners of the common peasants, rendered brutal by idleness, misery, and debauchery: but I was insensibly gaining my end, by patience, firmness, exhortations, and reward, when Madame de Lagaraye thought of a quicker and a more expeditious means, that of emulation, which is only a desire to distinguish one's self, a sentiment found in every heart, and which leads to virtue, and can sometimes even supply her place. Reason convinced Madame de Lagaraye, that purity of manners would ever dwell in well-regulated families; she therefore proposed I should give an annual prize to good fathers and good mothers.[7] It was a woman who merited the first prize, and a man gained the next; so it has now been given alternately for six years. The prize is 300 livres and a silver medal, presented with a great deal of pomp and ceremony. You cannot imagine how sudden and miraculous a revolution it produced; alehouses from that moment ceased to be regretted; husbands and wives became assiduous in their household duties; both became tenderly attached to their children, reformed themselves by their endeavours to instruct, and set their offspring good examples; gained to themselves love and respect, by forming a virtuous generation; and found happiness at home, by fulfilling the most sacred and pleasing duties.' Thus, my dear Viscount, did Mons. de Lagaraye open to us a soul intoxicated with the love of virtue. I had still some questions to ask him – Without doubt, said I, your sensibility and benevolence procure you a felicity the most enviable, but still it cannot be without alloy; every condition has its troubles: for example, that duty to which you particularly devote yourself, attendance on the sick, the dismal sight of their sufferings or death must give you the most cruel pangs. – 'Those are in fact the only sorrows of my life, yet they are not so poignant as you imagine; the hopes of curing, on at least of relieving their pains, occupy and sustain me. An inactive pity racks the soul, but when we are employed in the hopes of being useful, it becomes a sentiment, which redoubles our strength and reanimates our courage. I strive as much as possible to soften the horrors of death, by proscribing all that mournful pomp which usually precedes it. My mouth never pronounces the fatal sentence. I engage them to fulfil all the religious rites before they are in danger; nor have I the cruelty to strike consternation and dismay into weak minds. I discourse with them on the power and goodness of God; I dispose them to love and not to fear him; I offer them only sweet and consolatory ideas, and flatter myself that peace and security follow them to the grave. How is it possible that a man without education or philosophy, when weakened by pain, can hear with patience the rough exhortation of a priest, who comes to alarm his thoughts and trouble his conscience? Can we believe he will support, without terror and despair, all the mournful preparations for death? those dismal tapers set round his bed, and those agonising prayers* sounded in his ears?[8] No; his senses are bewildered, his heart faints under the black ideas engendered by fear; they poison his last moments; they make those moments dreadful and terrible, and even accelerate them. Is it possible that a religion, the moral of which is as mild as it is pure and sublime, can inspire such madness, and cruelty so absurd? But to finish my answer – From what I have been saying you will understand, that the sight of death is less grievous here than any where else, and consequently that it moves and affects me less than you imagined. Moreover, my sensibility for these unhappy sufferers is unconfined, universal, and includes the whole; no choice or preference binds me to one more than another. I love and take care of all, because they suffer; and that same reason consoles me for their death. Then if I am so fortunate to save and to restore one to perfect health, it gives me a thousand times more satisfaction, than the loss of the others can give me grief.' – By this answer Mons. de Lagaraye satisfactorily removed all my doubts. I was as perfectly acquainted as himself with his sentiments and situation of mind. The result of this knowledge compelled me to deem him the most astonishing, the most admirable, and the happiest man on earth. Why should such a man be born in a rank to display only an abridged and small pattern of all the moral and legislative virtues? He ought to have been successor to an Alexander,[9] who, after ravaging and subduing the universe, would have compensated all by leaving it in such worthy hands. What delightful days of peace and felicity history would have transmitted to us! It would at least have given us the idea of perfection, and have assured us of its reality. But other circumstances, and another condition, might have made even Mons. de Lagaraye a different man. All those events he has related, were requisite to raise him to that point of perfection, and produce that crowd of ideas which depended on each other. Although he has a soul full of greatness and passion, he does not appear ever to have felt love. He past those days, when the impressions are most lively, in error and extreme dissipation. This time being over, other sentiments filled his heart. But let us suppose he had loved his wife passionately; that that union had never been interrupted by any disaster; his daughter living; he would have been without doubt an affectionate and faithful husband, a tender and anxious parent, busied in his family, in his fortune, and his preferment, assisting his friends and neighbours, a worthy and a valuable man; but he would not have been Mons. de Lagaraye. After these reflections, it is not be wondered at that great men are so seldom to be met with. Genius, deep

---

* All these customs are observed still in all the villages and most of the little cities in the provinces. I myself have seen a father by his expiring daughter's bed-side, reciting aloud the prayers for the dying, which begin and end with these words: 'Christian soul, leave the world.' What words for the mouth of a father! What horrid madness! ... It is equally offensive to religion and to humanity. Besides all this thocking apparatus, which can only inspire terror in the dying person, excites also in the attendants the fear and horror of death; a weakness very inconsistent with Christianity, which particularly recommends courage, and prescribes a contempt of life.

and just designs, a vast and cultivated understanding, the fortunate union of all these virtues, would produce nothing really useful, without an happy concurrence of circumstances, and the advantages of rank and fortune. Here, my dear Viscount, is the account I promised you, which I am persuaded will make a deep impression on your mind. I feel that Lagaraye will be ever present in mine, nor can time blot from my memory any thing I have here seen. We are to-morrow to be present in the school, when Mons. and Madame de Lagaraye instruct the children. I shall write to you again on Friday: Saturday we set out for Brest, there to remain some days. But I shall certainly be at Paris towards the end of the month; and as I shall only stay a short time, I hope I shall find you and all your family there, and that you will not begin your little journies till after my departure for Languedoc.

LETTER IV.

The Baron to the Viscount.

WE were yesterday and the day before with Mons. and Madame de Lagaraye, whilst they fulfilled a duty, which appeared to us not one of their least interesting or useful occupations. In a word, we saw Mons. de Lagaraye surrounded by children, reading moral instructions on the duties of men in general, and of those in their situation in particular.[10] This course of morality, comprised in one little volume, is written with as much clearness and exactness as simplicity. It is divided into chapters, of which he never reads more than one at a sitting, making frequent pauses, either to question some one of his auditors, or to explain any part he thinks beyond their comprehension. It is really very pathetic to see with what kindness he answers or questions them; and that he may be more clearly understood, adapts his comparisons and expressions to their capacities. The children listen to him with an attention that nothing can disturb. Mons. and Madame de Lagaraye gave me a copy of their respective lectures; I spent a night in reading these two little volumes; the truths and good sense I found there not suffering me to quit them. These works, though extremely simple, appeared to me both interesting and useful. Their value is increased by being made for an obscure class, forgotten or disdained by all former writers. The children are admitted into these schools at twelve years of age, and remain till fifteen, the priest having previously instructed them in their catechism; so that a fresh set of twelve, taking the places of those who are fifteen, the school is renewed every three years. During the first six months Mons. de Lagaraye reads to them his work, which is succeeded by the Gospel, which takes up eighteen months; they then return to Mons. de Lagaraye's lessons. Madame de Lagaraye follows the same process exactly with the girls. I was curious to know whether, in such a number, Mons. de Lagaraye had not found some of distinguished abilities. – 'I have, replied he, met with many who gave hopes of wit and knowledge, but I resolved to draw none from their proper sphere, unless possessed of superior and very striking talents. Of such I have found but two in all this time. As there are many capacities, which the simplicity of my school would suit infinitely better, than one where the beauties of Homer and Virgil are displayed, so these two young men were absolutely misplaced among their companions: I therefore procured them a more distinguished education. One was born with a remarkable genius for the mathematics, and is now become a great geometrician, and settled in a foreign land. The other, named Porphiry, son to a labourer in the neighbourhood, was one of my first pupils. I was attached to that child by his meekness and sensibility, and soon discovered in him a most astonishing understanding and memory. He profited so much by the particular pains I bestowed on him, that I determined to send him to finish his studies at Paris. He is now twenty-two years old, and merits, by his virtue, wisdom, conduct, and gratitude, the parental tenderness I feel for him. He possesses as much wit as learning, is passionately fond of poetry and letters, and I am sure he will one day cultivate them with success.' – I need not tell you, my dear Viscount, how eagerly I enquired for this young man's direction. I find he spends every winter at Paris, so that I shall certainly see him on my return from Languedoc; for I must be acquainted with the beloved pupil of Mons. de Lagaraye. We set out in an hour, and shall sleep at —. Our children are quite in despair at leaving Lagaraye. My son this morning imparting his grief to me, I said, 'Persevere in this admiration, which does you honour. Never forget this great man; and let the recollection of his sublime virtues ever remind you, that it is religion and piety alone that can inspire so perfect a neglect of one's self. A noble pride, the love of glory, often produces great actions; benevolence and compassion make one perform good ones: but worldly motives never raise us to this degree of heroism and perfection. Instinct teaches us to expose our life to preserve that of a fellow-creature: but it is above human nature to devote ourselves for ever to these duties, which Mons. de Lagaraye has imposed on himself. Man is born good, his first emotions are generous; but his reflections cool, change, and make him selfish. He is inconsistent, because he is naturally an imperfect and confined being. It is religion alone that can give him a constant taste for virtue, and a perseverance in well-doing. In a word, my Theodore, if ever you hear religion condemned, recollect Mons. de Lagaraye and all you have seen here.'

We dined with Mons. de Lagaraye; and, on taking leave, Adelaide and Theodore could not refrain from tears. For my own part, I must own I never experienced a more sensible regret than in quitting them; and left with pain this blest abode, where the good genius of one man has restored the golden age, where every step discovers the prints of goodness and virtue, and the image of innocence and peace. – The thought, that I was probably embracing Mons. de Lagaraye for the last time, that I should never see him more, affected me beyond expression. The admiration he inspires is very tender, because he is truly good, indulgent, and sensible, free from pride or prejudice, and because his virtues are more affecting than dazzling. Farewel, my dear Viscount! My fellow travellers are waiting for me. Adieu.

LETTER V.

The Baroness to the Viscountess.

Yes, assuredly, my dear friend, I am pleased to find myself in Languedoc. I was happy to see Madame de Valmont. My walks in my park, between Adelaide and Madame d' Ostalis, are delightful to me; but yet my heart is not fully satisfied; I am not perfectly happy; and should be still less so, if I thought it possible you could believe half you say on that subject. I am not apt to be out of humour, but I own your letter has made me so; and therefore you will not now have the account your politeness made you demand: and I shall only acquaint you we are all perfectly well, and that Adelaide cried for joy when she beheld the turrets of the castle, and said that true happiness was only to be found here and Lagaraye; that Madame d' Ostalis rose by break of day to draw the landscape from her window; that Theodore, impatient to see all his former walks, went three leagues this morning on foot with Dainville; that Miss Bridget has left the spleen at Paris; and that I am very seriously angry with you. Adieu, my dear friend! If you wish for more particulars, write me a letter kind enough to make me forget the one I have just received.

LETTER VI.

The Viscountess's Answer.

No, you do not understand all the privileges of friendship. It even possesses that of being sometimes unjust, and then its vivacity is best expressed. Oh! if it was always reasonable, could it be a passion? It is cold, when never in the wrong ... You say my letter put you out of humour. You boast without foundation, my dear friend; for, in the number of years I have loved you, it has never been in my power to excite in you the least degree of indignation or ill-humour. Take not this as a compliment, for it is a very just and serious reproach. It is not consistent with true sensibility always to preserve that equanimity and superiority of reason, for which doubtless you ought to be admired, but by which friendship has often a right to be hurt. Besides, I am sufficiently miserable for you to excuse all my caprices. You have again left me, and what comfort have I when you are away? You know all the uneasiness my daughter and Mons. de Limours give me. I feel my sorrows more poignantly, as you are not here to share them. My little Constantia remains, but she is still such a child. Apropos, I have many questions to ask about her. Pray tell me what books of prayer you give Adelaide; likewise the name of her confessor at Paris. I am dissatisfied with Constantia's and intend changing. Let me know also in what manner you prepare Adelaide to receive the sacrament. You have so thoroughly convinced me how important it is to instil true piety into our children, that it now employs all my thoughts and care. I regularly send Constantia to mass every day: she follows exactly all the rules for Sundays and holidays; and confesses every three months. She spends Lent in retirement; that is to say, without dining at our table when we have company, or coming into my apartment at visiting hours. Adieu, my dear friend! I am going into the country, to spend two days with a woman who is very prim, very formal, scrupulously polite in her own house, but very arrogant every where else; who thinks it impossible to be fashionable, or have common sense, without the advantage of being admitted into her coterie. She is, in short, as tiresome as she is insipid, vain, and calumniating. As I give you her picture, her name is unnecessary. Before I finish my letter, I must say a word of Porphiry. I thank you for introducing him to me; he is really both amiable and interesting, and worthy in every respect of all Mons. de Lagaraye's affection. He lives with that Madame de M—, who has so much wit, and receives so many men of letters. Porphiry extols her so highly, that I long to visit her. Besides, I am weary of myself, and have an inclination for wit, which I shall meet with at her house. I have always observed, one may be witty when one will; and I am precisely of the age when such a fancy generally takes our sex. Therefore expect to find me, on your return, a wit, and perhaps an author. Adieu, my dear friend! and be assured I can never assume any form that will alter my heart in respect to you.

LETTER VII.

The Baroness's Answer.

WELL! I do not possess true sensibility, because I am neither sickle, unreasonable, peevish, nor spiteful; because I place implicit faith in you; and you, my dear friend, because you pout without occasion, an scold without reason, it is you only that know how to love – this is a fine description of friendship. But since caprice is one of your proofs of sensibility, I ought not to flatter myself with being your only friend; for surely you lavish that testimony on many. It is thus, that we often attribute to the strength of our sensibility and passions, faults which proceed only from our dispositions. I never saw a lover, who was always jealous without reason, that was not naturally suspicious in mixed society. Friendship occasions no caprices; but you are a proof that it does not cure them. Trust me, we had best have done with this quarrel, and love one another as we are, relinquishing the hope of a mutual reformation. We are born never to resemble each other, but always to agree.

So you are going to attach yourself to Madame de M— . I am curious to know, what impressions a society so different from what you have always lived in, will produce on you: but I beg you will not give me any account till after the third or fourth visit, that your opinion may be fixed.

Let us now talk of Constantia. Without doubt, by bringing her up piously, you secure the happiness of both. But it appears to me that the means you employ, are absolutely contrary to the end you propose. In all education, let us first remember to what kind of life the child is destined. Your daughter is born to shine in the great world, at Paris, and at court. When she is eighteen and her own mistress, do you think it will be possible for her to go every day to mass, to confess every three months, and to live in retirement all Lent? Certainly not; but, accustomed from her infancy to look on these practices as essential duties, she will relinquish with them all her religion. Have you remarked, that those young people who are brought up in this manner, (as they are in all convents) continue more devout than others? Let us always revert to our most useful principle, never to give our pupil a false idea: let us not suffer them to confound perfection with simple duty. Besides, is it reasonable to exact from a child of nine years that universal rectitude? Do you think that Constantia, so often obliged to pass two hours at church, will be always collected and attentive? Sure I am, that more than once she has envied her mamma, who during that time was in bed, or making visits. On the contrary, you should set your daughter the example of what you make her practise; at the same time you should only require from her the duties which are really essential to religion. I am convinced that is not the most convenient method; for it is much easier to send a child to mass, than to go every day ourselves, particularly when one goes to bed at two in the morning. I only advise you what I have constantly done myself by Adelaide: she knows she can never lessen what she now practises, without failing in her duty, and giving a bad opinion of herself. The dissipation and amusements of the world will never prevent us from fulfilling our indispensible obligations; and which do not take up more time than any station in life will allow. You are in the right to be particular in the choice of a confessor; it is a point too often neglected, and yet a most important one; for a confessor without understanding can easily spoil the best teacher's work. I inclose the direction to mine; but advise you to have some conversation with him before you put Constantia under his care, and to acquaint him with all her little faults, and her disposition. In regard to the books of devotion you ask about, I cannot satisfy you; and shall again occasion that wonder and shew of anger you always put on, when I own myself authoress of any treatise on education. I must answer you nevertheless, and tell you that, after having read all the books of this kind, I found with surprise that there was not one 'adapted to young people.' You will readily conceive, for example, that there are many books of prayer that you would not only not give your daughter, but be very sorry she knew them; particularly those in which the 'cases of conscience' are very prolix. I have already spoken to you of some prayers I composed during the infancy of Adelaide. But besides these I have still another for her youth; it contains the mass, the psalms, and the church prayers, besides those for morning and evening, confession, communion, self-examination, &c. I know not a single book, where one can read these kind of prayers without being continually shocked by false grammar or ridiculous expressions in them. I will, if you desire it, send you a copy of my work, and in it you will also find what I have often heard you wish for, namely, prayers for every interesting situation in life; and I am sure you will be tenderly affected when you read that for a mother imploring God's blessings on her children. You can have but half the volume of prayers, till my return to Paris: the other half contains sentences and detached maxims, extracted from the writings of the fathers. Adelaide has had this work in her possession near two years; I gave her at the same time the Gospel and the Imitation of Jesus Christ: and these are all the books she will have till she is fifteen. – You ask how I prepare her for receiving the sacrament. The first step, you know, was taking her to Lagaraye; and she is come back with so profound a respect for Mons. de Lagaraye, so fervent an increase of piety, that I thought I never could seize a more favourable moment to imprint on her mind all I had to say on that subject. Therefore, the morning after our arrival at Brest, I spent two hours with her alone; when, after much conversation on Lagaraye, she begged to know when she was to be admitted to the communion – The day you are twelve years old: in six months, if you conduct yourself till that time in a manner to convince me you are no longer a child; for as soon as you have received the sacrament, you will enter into society, and I shall begin to look on you in the real light of a friend, and place confidence in you. But you well know I am not hasty in my judgment, and that to obtain such a happiness, you must merit it. – Oh! mamma, I shall make myself worthy of it, I dare hope; I am sure, I so much with it. – I give you notice, it will not be slightly granted; and before you are allowed to partake of the most holy and awful of all the sacraments, I must be very well assured that you will never oblige me to treat you as a child. If, during these six months to come, you are guilty of any one fault for which I am under the necessity of punishing you, or of imposing a penance on you, I shall think you do not feel its importance, nor the value of the promised reward; and I shall defer it for a year. – A whole year! oh Heaven! and for one single fault, my dear mamma? – Yes, for one serious fault. – There is justice in that; but I will conduct myself to well, that I am sure I shall not henceforth be guilty of a serious fault. Since this conversation, I have remarked in her a very visible alteration for the better; and I am persuaded there is not a moment in the day, when the fear of committing a 'serious fault' is not before her eyes. The great art is to promise children such rewards, as will engage them to a constant self-attention; it is teaching them at the same time perseverance and the command of their passions, the two great means of attaining perfection. For one cannot, during six months, obtain from a child a conduct free from essential blame, without eradicating at the same time all her faults. The choice of the promised rewards is really difficult: promise none but what are interesting, noble, or useful; such as some mark of confidence, your picture, an instructive book, a new master, &c. Do not teach your pupil to desire any thing but what she ought to love, or what deserves to be esteemed.

LETTER VIII.

The Baron to the Viscount.

YESTERDAY, my dear Viscount, my life was in manifest danger. I will give you a recital of this little adventure, as I am sure it will please you, since the conclusion afforded me the highest satisfaction. The river Aude, you know, forms a canal in front of my house. I have had a large tent pitched on the bank, and we frequently go and bathe. My son learns to swim; he comes on surprisingly, and it is one of his greatest pleasures.

Yesterday, the heat being excessive, my son, Dainville, and I, repaired to the river, followed by my water-dog, that faithful Mouche, that you well know. I swam as usual; and after some time told Dainville and Theodore to return to the tent, and dress themselves, and that I would follow them presently. After they left me, I delivered myself with my dog; when all on a sudden the blood flew violently into my head, and I felt myself fainting. I strove to regain the tent, but my strength intirely failed; and I had only time to cry 'Here, Mouche,' before I lost my senses. On my recovery, I found myself on shore, and in my son's arms. He was half drest, dripping wet, his countenance changed, pale, and disfigured. The instant I opened my eyes, he seized both my hands, with a transport, beyond description, and pressed them to his breast, cried, sobbed embraced, and asked me a thousand questions in a breath. He was so distressed and trembling, that my dread of the baneful effects of so violent an emotion made me feel, at first, but imperfectly the joy that his sensibility caused me. When we were dreft, and returning in the carriage, I desired to be informed of particulars. – 'Scarce had you (said Dainville) uttered that dreadful cry, *Here, Mouche*, when Theodore, who was dressing, burst from the hands of Brunel, plunged into the river, exclaiming *'Alas! why did he not say, Here, my son?'* Those were his very words. I threw myself in after him, and catched him in my arms, in spite of his cries and resistance; at the same instant a boatman, by my order, flew to your rescue. We saw you floating, and the dog drawing you by the hair towards the side. The boatman reached and brought you on shore; and all this past within a minute.' Observe, interrupted I, how natural, or rather instinctive virtues are courage and generosity. Judge by the intrepidity of my dog. If the world is to blame in attaching infamy and dishonour to cowardice; and if any one who refuses to risk his life to save his fellow-creature, does not prove himself a thousand times inferior to Mouche. And you, my dear Theodore, continued I, have done an action I shall always recollect with pleasure. – The action of Mouche, replied he, is alone to be admired; mine was only duty. – This idea I perceived was a little painful to him, but I did not let him know it, and continued the conversation: – If you had attained your full strength, and knew as well how to swim as Mouche, your observation would be just; but, on the contrary, you are but thirteen years old, and have learned to swim scarcely six weeks; therefore I ought too be very gratefully affected by what you did for me.

I was blooded yesterday, and am perfectly well to-day; and have been bathing and swimming this morning with my son, who would not leave me an instant, least I should be again taken ill. How delightful it is to be so beloved by the child, on whom the happiness of my life depends! But there is no father who may not enjoy the same satisfaction, if he will fulfil the sacred duties which nature imposes.

Yes, certainly, my dear Viscount, my son is learning mathematics. At twelve he began the first volume of Mons. Bezout,[11] which treats of arithmetic. In a few months we shall get to the second; at fifteen he will study the third; and at seventeen the fourth, which treats of mechanics. As I think the study of mathematics should employ six years, three hours in a week is sufficient to dedicate to it. By this method children cannot be fatigued; and let their understanding be never so weak, it is hardly possible they should not learn enough for any station.

I intend also to teach my daughter as much geometry as is indispensably necessary towards raising a plan, and drawing a landscape from nature, and in which the perspective is strictly observed. Latin my son will begin learning this autumn: and I shall use the *Cours de Latinite* de Vaniere,[12] which appears to me a most excellent work; for it has a perfection, wanting in all other rudiments, that of being always intelligible. I am very certain he will understand Latin at seventeen much better than the generality of the world, not excepting those who are esteemed very good scholars. I find another, and in my opinion a very great advantage in my method, that of not disgusting my pupil with works, which are really worthy of admiration. A boy who begins learning Latin at six years old, and cannot read Virgil at twelve, has lost his time; yet at that age it is impossible for him to feel its beauties: still he learns it by rote; and when he is eighteen, he will know the *Eneid*[13] is a masterpiece; but he will feel it weakly, or at best without enthusiasm. I have made rather a singular remark, that the men who love reading the least, are those who are commonly esteemed to have received the best education: yet it is reasonable it should be so; for at fourteen they have read all the best books without being sensible of their beauties, and only preserve a tiresome remembrance of them, which naturally leads them to imagine, that they dislike reading; they therefore renounce it entirely; or if they do read, it is only inferior works, which have at least the pleasing charm of novelty to them; they think themselves acquainted with all others, having learnt them by heart in their infancy. I recollect feeling in my travels a prince only eight years of age, who talked to me an hour together of *Telemachus*; and his governor assured me, that the Prince was passionately fond of that work, and had made notes on every part with his own hand. So much the worse, replied I, this poor child will never have read *Telemachus*. Theodore, it is true, is only beginning mathematics, and has not had one Latin lesson; but he is well acquainted with the principles of our own language, without the fatigue of having learnt it out of a grammar; but was taught verbally by me in correcting his spelling. He reads and speaks English and Italian perfectly well, understands a little German, has a general idea of geography, and already knows as much chronology as he will ever want. Besides the magic lanthorn, and various other of his infantine plays, together with Madame d' Almane's abridgments, have imprinted on his memory a prodigious number of historical facts; and what surpasses all, his judgment is as solid as his heart is pure. He has clear and distinct ideas on all the principal points of morality, and knows by experience that the most honest and virtuous path is ever the wisest; – that our inclinations lead us astray; that reason alone should be our guide; and that it is through her alone, we can be esteemed, be loved, or be happy. But the bare repetition of all these known truths will make no impression; we must give proofs to fix them on the mind, and then they will never be eradicated. As to accomplishments merely elegant, Theodore, only possesses that of drawing, which he has a great taste for; and already begins to copy very prettily from nature; as does his sister. Madame d' Ostalis renders our little academy very brilliant at present: she is extremely assiduous, and Dainville, you may be assured, has yielded to her the president's chair. Adieu, my dear Viscount! pray inform me, if Mons. d' Aimeri is arrived at Paris, you will find him very melancholy, but he has so much merit, that you certainly will be happy in his acquaintance. Give me your opinion of the Chevalier de Valmont; it is near two years since I saw him, and that time may have made a great alteration at his age. My friendship for his parents interests me much in his well doing.

LETTER IX.

Count de Roseville to the Baron.

AT last, my dear Baron, I am going go give you the promised description of the Chevalier de Murville's gardens, which my occupations during the last three months have hitherto prevented; – You will not lose by the delay, it being all present to my memory. Three weeks before Mons. d' Aimeri's departure I took the prince, accompanied by the Chevalier de Valmont, to Mons. de Murville's, who you will easily believe did not receive the nephew of Cecilia without manifest emotion. After surveying the house, Mons. M— conducted us into the garden*, where he has collected an exact representation of all the most interesting things he has seen in his travels. We went out of the house on to a large irregular lawn, formerly an immense parterre, but now filled with status and antique monuments faithfully copied, (but in less proportion) from the best ruins in Italy. Amongst others the magnificent temples of Seraphis,[14] of Minerva Medica,[15] Trojan's pillar,[16] &c. Various foreign plants of different shapes and colours are artfully interspersed among the ruins. Willows and cyprus shade the tombs; majestic pines and palm-trees surround the temples; laurels grow at the foot of the Apollo of Belvedere;[17] myrtles and roses encompass the Venus of Medicis.[18] To the right of this kind of museum, there is the grotto of Pausilipo;[19] which is a long passage built with brick, but so covered with rock and verdure, that it appears hewn out of the solid stone, like the cavern it represents. – At the bottom of this grotto, one discovers a charming perspective, which conducts you to

---

* This idea, so beautiful magnificent, is not new; for the Emperor Adriana had a garden of this kind.

the lake of Agnano, one of the most delightful views near Naples; and very easily imitated in a garden, being entirely surrounded by trees, which hide the rest of the country. On the other side of the park, you travel in Spain. After seeing all the Gothick ruins which ornament this part, we entered a meadow, divided by a stream, over which he has built a bridge, of a plain but elegant architecture; and here the Chevalier de Murville[20] made us stop. – observe, said he, this bridge; no monument in the garden better deserves to fix your attention, or retain a place in your remembrance. It is called the Widow's Bridge.[21] A woman of St. Philip's, in Spain, having had her son drowned in a flood, caused a bridge to be built across the fatal torrent, that for the future no mother might mourn a similar misfortune. Thus, by a sentiment truly angelic, the derived consolation from erecting an edifice, the fight of which would have redoubled the grief of any other person. There are many actions which appear more brilliant, but none more generous. In short, my Lord, continued the Chevalier, when you read this maxim of Mons. de Rochefoucauld,[22] 'in the adversity of our best friends we often find something not displeasing to ourselves;'[23] when you hear human nature aspersed, recollect 'the Widow's Bridge.' After this discourse, he led us to the bottom of the garden, where he has a village built in imitation of Broek, in Holland.[24] You will easily believe, that this is not so spacious as the original; it only consists of fourteen houses in one little street. In the first there is a delightful hermitage and dairy; four others are inhabited by gardeners; and the rest by old servants of his, or poor families which he has extricated from distress, and given an asylum to in this charming retreat. The Prince and the Chevalier de Valmont left this delicious abode with regret, where taste has assembled such a collection of interesting and instructive objects. Mons. de Murville was much affected by the adieus of young Charles, and begged permission of the Prince to embrace him; when clasping him in his arms with inexpressible tenderness – Oh Charles! cried he, may you be ever happy! Love virtue; and preserve your heart, if it be possible, from a dangerous passion which perhaps will embitter your whole life! –

The sun was set before we left the Chevalier de Murville; and being very near the house of Alexis Stezin (the unhappy father of the family whom we settled on the banks of the Lake ***), the Prince desired to go there, that he might see if the good people continued happy. Since the affecting scene, which I recounted to you, my dear Baron, three years are past, and in all that time I had not once found a leisure hour to visit them. The Prince's curiosity appeared so natural, that I consented to gratify it. When we reached the house, it was near dark; and we found the family in the lower room, sitting in a circle (without a candle) amusing themselves in singing romances. We stopt to listen to a voice, which was finishing a stanza, and sounded as young as it was melodious. The singing being over, we opened the door; but the darkness prevented our distinguishing objects. A servant announced us; at the name of the Prince they all started up in the greatest agitation. Alexis called for lights; his wife and children ran to fetch them; and a moment after our eyes were riveted to one object; it was a young woman of thirteen who entered precipitately with a candle in her hand, which she set on a table. Imagine all the ingenuous graces of childhood united to the bloom and beauty of youth, a noble and slender shape, features equally delicate and regular, an animated countenance full of expression, a smile all innocence and sensibility: figure to yourself this seducing assemblage, and you will yet have but an imperfect idea of this bewitching form. Alexis took her hand, and presenting her to the Prince, said, this is Stolina, my eldest daughter; that child, to whom you, Sir, gave your cloak. These words made the Prince and the girl both blush; and he changed the discourse by asking, if we had not heard her voice as we entered. It was indeed hers. The Chevalier begged her to sing again; and Stolina, with a modest confusion, which added to her charms, in a trembling voice, sung two verses; which were thought much too short by the Prince and Valmont. I believe, was my pupil two or three years older, this visit would have been a dangerous one. Be that as it will, I left Alexis Stezin's house, fully resolved never to take the Prince there again, who could talk the whole evening of nothing but Stolina, and the next day was thoughtful and melancholy to a surprising degree for a child of thirteen and a half; but fortunately at that age such impressions can be neither deep nor lasting. Adieu, my dear Baron! and be assured, I highly approve the reasons, which determine you on travelling with your children, and the preference you at this time give to Italy beyond all other countries; but I hope a day will come, when I shall have the pleasure of seeing you in this. – Were it not in itself interesting and curious, you would here find a great King, gloriously reigning over a virtuous people; a sight far exceeding all the temples and ruins about Rome.

LETTER X.

The Viscountess to the Baroness.

OH the charming creature! ... so interesting a figure! so modest an air! ... a countenance all sweetness! I lay any wager you guess who I mean: – Well, yes, it is the Chevalier de Valmont. Now it will be in vain for you to deny your designs; he must be Adelaide's husband; I saw that clearly on the very first visit. I questioned him very much concerning his travels. All his answers were short, plain, and modest: and then he blushes with so much grace! without being disconcerted at blushing; he is timid, but never embarrassed. Besides, he is so like our amiable Cecilia! In short, I am quite infatuated. As to Mons. d' Aimeri, you may say what you will, my dear friend, but I feel that I can never esteem him; my memory is too faithful to poor Cecilia. He may well weep for her, but he is not the less guilty of her death. His sorrows grieve, but can never interest me: however, I desired him to look on my house as his own; and I believe he was satisfied with my manner of receiving him. He goes in a month to conduct his grandson to his garrison; but they will return hither towards the end of December; therefore you will see them this winter. I positively will be present at Adelaide's first interview with the Chevalier. I am certain, sympathy will be visible the first moment; they are made for each other; and will love one another passionately. – Remember this prediction.

Well, my dear friend, I have made an acquaintance with Madame de M— ; have already been with her thrice, therefore I can now satisfy your curiosity. You insist on a true and circumstantial account: – Listen then; this is what happened on my first visit. I got there at half an hour past eight in the evening; was conducted into a dismal saloon, very ill lighted, where I found a very solemn circle: – the mistress of the house seated me by her; I cast my eyes on all the company; and saw only two women, and ten or twelve men; and could not find a single face I knew, except Porphiry's, whom I call to inform me of the company. He whispers all their names; amongst them three or four, who are equally known and esteemed by their works. I immediately looked on those celebrated persons with an admiration, which inspired me with so extraordinary an emotion of self-love, that it suspended my curiosity; for instead of listening to the conversation, I only felt the desire of being heard myself, and of drawing the attention of those, who ought naturally to have fixed all mine. Here was I then solely employed in seeking an opportunity of saying something witty; I thought a long time, and at last hazarded a very abstruse reflection; and then another still more far-fetched; I grew bold, vehement, and fell into a dissertation; was dull, and all at once found I had not common sense, and that I was compleatly ridiculous. Very much disconcerted at this discovery, I could think of nothing better than to retire; and I went out with the double regret of having been very absurd myself, and of not having heard a word of what others said. I reflected on this accident, and concluded I should never succeed in pretending to wit and a desire of shining. I resolved for the future to be always simple and natural; and I returned to Madame de M— 's with this intention. – But scarcely was I seated, when the frenzy of shewing my wit and knowledge seized me with redoubled fury. At first I courageously resisted all temptation; at length I yielded, and succeeded no better than the first time. – I left the house absolutely enraged with myself; and with a firm resolution to observe a strict silence for the future, since it was impossible for me to talk there, as I did elsewhere. Behold me then making my third visit. This time I did hold my tongue: I observed and listened with extreme attention. I heard the company speak sensibly, and remarked several strokes which deserved to be remembered and quoted: – Yet I found the conversation in general languid and heavy; and when it was animated by discussions, it seemed to me degenerating into disputes. In short, it frequently astonished, but never charmed me; and I said to myself, every one of these people have more wit than I, but I am certainly more amiable than them. What mismanagement then is it that deprives them of the advantage they ought to have over me? After having reflected on this singularity I discovered, that they had precisely the same madness, which had inspired me the two first days; that they knew not how to attend to others, and instead of wishing to please, sought only to be admired. I also observed them often guilty of little inattentions and rudenesses, either from self-love ill understood, or the want of a knowledge of the world, which alone can teach us to be observant of others, never to be angry, and to maintain one's opinion without peevishness or pedantry. From all these observations I infer, that men of letters should mix more in society. They only go into three or four houses, where they engross almost all the conversation. Mildness, complaisance, delicate attentions, in a word the graces, are not to be acquired where they preside; and this is the reason learned men are so often reproached with an arrogant and supercilious manner;[25] if they were more at large, they would lose many of their little failings; they would then be met with pleasure, and sought with eagerness. Instead of producing pain and constraint, they would be the delight of society. A thorough knowledge of the world would enable them to describe it; and to give faithful and striking pictures of our faults, our vices, and our manners; and we should find their works replete with wit and modern sentiments. But I will dwell no longer upon these reflections, as Porphiry has had a letter from Mons. de Lagaraye, in which that subject is much better explained than I can pretend to explain it. I have leave to send you a copy, which I am sure you will read with pleasure. Farewell, my dear! embrace Madame d'Ostalis for me, and tell her I am no longer jealous of her; but I am of Madame de Valmont; yes, still more since I saw her son. As the mother-in-law of Adelaide, how you will love her! – At least own to me the truth; I am sure you are not sincere on that score. – Alas! you have not that confidence in me, which I have in you. I cannot think, why I love you so much; – I ought only to esteem you. Notwithstanding your easy, natural and unaffected air, you are in reality very proud, and very reserved; reserved beyond expression. Oh you are! and you are even vain of your reserve. You call it prudence and discretion; but if you do not confess, that in the bottom of your heart you have destined Adelaide for the Chevalier de Valmont, I shall think you never loved me, and only have that kind of sentiment for me, that one feels for a child which amuses one.

LETTER XI.

The Copy of Mons. de Lagaraye's Letter to Porphiry.

WELL, my dear Porphiry, you are going to profess yourself a man of letters! I certainly shall not oppose that design. False devotion or bigotry can alone condemn it. You have learning, a feeling heart, and have read a great deal; – leave then your closet, shut your books, and study mankind; unless you acquire a perfect knowledge of the human heart, you will write nothing but what is trifling or imperfect. See men of all ranks; examine them in all the different situations, from the humble labourer to the exalted courtier. Know them accurately; and do not despise amiable infants. As a painter, copy the striking and natural features they present; as a philosopher, observe the seed, from which spring all the virtues and passions of man. Be particularly assiduous in separating our natural faults and inclinations from that croud of irregularities and vices we derive from education. A mere scholar should remain in his study: an author should live in the great world. – If he dedicates to society four hours of the day, there will still remain time enough to reflect on what he has seen. But all this is insufficient; – you, my dear Porphiry, must still preserve your sensibility and your principles – if your heart and manners be corrupted, you will never produce a work of genius. From wit alone may slow amusing things, those works of a moment, made to dazzle but not to last; read with eagerness, praised and quoted during three months, and then consigned to oblivion. It was not to his wit, that Pierre Corneille[26] was indebted for his fame; – it was his greatness of soul, that acquired him his surname, and the admiration of his contemporaries, and of posterity. Oh, my Porphiry! be honest, indulgent, and beneficent, that thy writings may inspire men with the love of virtue. There will then not be found (in them) exaggeration nor inconsistency; for he who is inspired by love of truth, can never contradict himself. Would you give useful and moral lessons, begin by reforming yourself; subdue your passions, shut your heart against hatred and resentment; learn to forgive: you will then know how to bestow eloquent praises on greatness of soul and generosity. For what a delightful career are you destined; to what a noble vocation your taste and genius call you; if you are sensible of all its dignity! but alas, if you should be led astray; if, too weak to resist the vain desire of temporary fame, you should prove an apostate to truth, and to your principles; if you should suffer yourself to be misled by the spirit of party and faction! ... Oh, my son! those talents which which you possess, they were given you by heaven; they were cultivated by me, not to flatter vice, to amuse the immoral, or to seduce the ignorant; but to obtain the approbation of men of taste and virtue. In fine, my dear Porphiry, remember that the season, in which we can work and write, flies rapidly away. When that is past, what happiness will be yours, if you can say, 'I have never written any thing, but in conformity to reason and truth: humanity and the love of order and of virtue inspired me. I sought only pure and spotless glory: at least in the hour of death, at that awful moment, when the recollection of one good action yields a thousand times more satisfaction, than the most brilliant successes, how sweet will be the thought, that my works will never be productive of dangerous consequences; that a young man at his first entrance into the world may read them with advantage, and that the enlightened and tender mother will be eager to give them to her daughter.' This, my dear Porphiry, is what ought to be your ambition, if you would answer my expectations, and justify the tenderness I feel for you. Farewel! I expect you towards the end of the month.

LETTER XII.

The Baroness to the Viscountess.

I THANK you, my dear friend, for the accounts you have given me of our little Constantia. I am sorry she is slatternly; it is a fault too little attended to. Yet it occasions a great loss of time, and is frequently the cause of more expence than prodigality itself. I have corrected Adelaide of this fault, natural to all children, by punishments, provided the thing lost was absolutely to be replaced; or if it was a thing of entertainment rather than of use; a play thing for instance, by making her long wish for such another, before I gave it her; and at last by giving her a large chest of drawers, in which she might lock up and set all her things to rights. But read Mons. de Fenelon * *sur l'Education des Filles*, and there you will find all the advice necessary on this subject.

I shewed my children a melancholy sight this morning; and I will presently give you my reasons for so doing. My gardener's daughter died last night; she was pretty, and only twenty years old. I was told of it, when I was getting up, by Mademoiselle Victoire, who added, that she was just come from sprinkling her

---

* Make your daughters observe that nothing contributes so much to œoconomy and neatness, as keeping every thing in its proper place. This rule appears trifling, but would be very efficacious if strictly attended to. You never lose time in seeking any thing you want, there is neither trouble, dispute, nor embarrassment; whatever you want will be ready to your hand ... Add to these advantages, that of removing from your servants the spirit of idleness and confusion. – Moreover, it is a great thing to render their services quick and easy; and to free ourselves from the temptation of being frequently offended by the delays occasioned from things being in disorder, and consequently long in finding

Education of Daughters by Mons. de Fenelon.[27]

with holy water, that she had seen her face, and that it was not in the least disfig-ured. This particularity being confirmed by many people, I resolved on shewing her to my children. When we were all met for breakfast, the gardener's daughter was talked on, and Miss Bridget said she had never seen a corpse; Theodore and Adelaide repeated the same; – I proposed our going to the gardener's as soon as breakfast was over; we went; on entering the chamber, I observed Adelaide's countenance change; we all knelt down; and our prayers ended, I approached the bed, lifted up the cloth, entirely uncovered the face of the deceased, which I could not look on without feeling an inexpressible anxiety of mind; from the thought, that she was an only daughter, and that her parents survived her. – Tak-ing Adelaide's hand, I said to her – See my child that affecting object; it can only inspire compassion. – Really, she replied, there is nothing hideous in it; I had formed quite a different idea; but I now see that many disorders are more disfiguring than death itself. After some reflections on this subject we returned to the castle. I have forbid all farther mention of the deceased before my chil-dren, and took care to entertain them that whole day in the most lively manner. – I remembered in my infancy having heard many stories of ghosts, &c. I was absolutely frantic with that kind of fear, which, altho' the most absurd of any, has the greater effect on the imagination. At thirteen or fourteen I determined to see a corpse; unfortunately it was that of an old man, horridly disfigured. This hideous object made such an impression on me, that it was more than a month before I could get it out of my thoughts. Age and reason at last cured me of those ridiculous apprehensions, which had but too much influence on my health, and brought on that nervous disorder which still affects me. Adelaide, thanks to my care, never had any idea of those vain terrors. But as she had not seen a dead person, I was fearful her imagination might represent it as much more terrible than it often really is; I therefore determined to shew her the corpse of this young woman; and I applaud myself so much the more, as Adelaide, before she saw it, was agitated and trembling; and that she looked upon it without alarm, because she found it infinitely less frightful than she had imagined. Adelaide and I often walk in the envirous of the castle; and generally in the dusk of the evening return across a church-yard, where we sometimes set and rest ourselves; and converse (at least Adelaide does) with as much case, as if we were in a meadow. – Great address and apparent simplicity are necessary to accustom a child to all these things; for they will be most afraid, when they suspect you mean to embolden them. Therefore you must use the utmost precaution; but, above all, every thing must appear the effect of chance. – Adieu, my dear friend! Adelaide makes her first communion in a fortnight. Madame d' Ostalis sets out towards the end of the month, and I shall soon follow her; for we shall certainly be at Paris by the beginning of November at farthest.

LETTER XIII.

Madame d' Ostalis to the Viscountess de Limours.

CERTAINLY, Madam, I am here as much instructed as entertained. I learn of the best of mothers the value of those duties, which she fulfils with so much delight. Living with her, and observing her in the midst of her family, we see her so perfectly contented, that all our astonishment at the sacrifices she has made, in order to arrive at such pure felicity, entirely ceases. Such is the power of true virtue! At a distance her brilliancy strikes, and excites astonishment and admiration; but near us, she is so beautiful, so affecting, and so persuasive, that her dictates cease to appear difficult. She does better than dazzle; she engrosses, she charms, she attaches.

Adelaide and Theodore this day received the sacrament for the first time. After our return from church, my aunt retired with Adelaide and me into her closet, and, seating herself between us, she took one of her daughter's hands, and putting it in mine, said, – Now I flatter myself you will look on Adelaide as your friend. It is true, she has neither your experience nor your understanding; but you well know she would not have been admitted to the sacrament, was I not perfectly sure she is no longer a child; therefore we can now talk before her without constraint, and trust her with our most secret conversations. At these words Adelaide, quite softened, leant gently on her mother's shoulder, and tenderly clasped my hand, which she still held: my aunt continued her discourse, thus – I am now going to reap the fruits of those cares I dedicated to you, my dear Adelaide. I shall never more be compelled to impose penances on you, or humiliating punishments. You will now become my most pleasing companion, and my tenderest friend. On pronouncing these words, my aunt could not refrain from tears. Adelaide threw herself at her feet; and with an expression and sensibility as earnest as it was natural and affecting, said to her happy mother all that the best-founded gratitude could inspire. Although you, Madame, accuse me of envying Adelaide's destiny, yet this kind of jealousy does not prevent my asserting, that there is no child of her age to whom she can be compared; and in these last six months she has made a most surprising progress, which ought entirely to be attributed to that extreme desire she had to take the sacrament. What I can never sufficiently admire, is the manner in which my aunt knew how to gain her affection; though overlooking nothing, but punishing her severely, and reprehending her before all company; and yet, in spite of this apparent rigour, she is passionately beloved by her daughter, who places an unlimited confidence in her. She is never perfectly happy but with her mother; and I always observe, she prefers conversing with her to every pleasure accommodated to her age. This is without doubt the great secret in education and never to be obtained by spoiling a child, and indulging all its whims. Adelaide being now admitted into the 'company of rational people,' the is for the future to assist my aunt in all family affairs, the maitre d'hotel and cook are to bring their account book to her every morning. This will teach her (let her fortune be what it may), never to look on these very necessary cares as below her notice; which most women neglect only through idleness, or want of abilities. Ignorance is commonly envious and slanderous; and would, if it were possible, vilify every thing which shows its inferiority; it strives to conceal its shame under the appearance of carelessness, and even often of disdain. This is the reason why we frequently see learned and reasonable persons derided by fools: and this is the cause that Madame de G..., who never knew one rule in addition, makes such a joke of women, who are so unemployed that they can find amusement in casting up their servants bills. Adieu, madam! I depart in eight days. I do not expect to find you at Paris; but, I flatter myself, you are assured my first care on my arrival will be to seek you, that I may inform myself of your health, and give you an account of my aunt's.

LETTER XIV.

The Baroness to the Viscountess.

N O, my dear friend, Adelaide does not yet read any of the books you mention. Although she has as much sense and reason as is possible at her age, yet there requires a great deal more to make her feel the merits of the good authors of the age of Lewis XIV.[28] As yet she has read very little but what I have composed for her. But now we are going into longer and more instructive lessons. She has begun Rollin's *Ancient History*;[29] which will be succeeded by those of Rome and France; then the *Age of Lewis XIV*[30] and some English historians; and this will finish our course of history, containing in all fifty volumes. As to works of amusement, we are at present reading some plays. In three years we shall have read Campistron,[31] Lagrange, Chancel,[32] Lachaussee,[33] Destouches,[34] Marivaux,[35] Les Poesies de Fontenelle,[36] de Pavillon,[37] de Desmahis,[38] &c. All these pleasing, but second-rate authors, will amuse her, till an age in which her taste will be sufficiently formed to read, with transport, books of true genius. We last night finished the tragedy of *Andronicus*;[39] and, in spite of my commentaries and criticisms, Adelaide was drowned in tears, and asked me if it was possible to form a more interesting and affecting piece. – Yes, doubtless, replied I, you yourself will be convinced of that when you come to read those immortal authors, Corneille, Racine, Voltaire, Crebillon, & c. who are at present known to you only by name. -But, mamma, since a moderate performance makes such an impression on me, what pleasure would a tragedy of Corneille's give me! and why deprive me of it?-It is precisely the transports and admiration you profess for *Androni-cus*, which proves you not yet worthy to read *Cinna*.[40] Was you sensible of the faults of *Andronicus*, you would be scarcely affected by what has made you shed so many tears; and for the same reason *Cinna* would not move you, because you could not feel his sublime beauties. – But, mamma, *Les Horaces*;[41] I am sure I should be struck with the beauties of that. – How so? – The day before we left Paris, Madame ... came to see you, and brought her daughter, who is exactly my age. – Well. – Why, mamma, this young lady made me a visit in my room, and told me she was just come from the play; it was *Les Horaces*, and she spoke of it with delight. – So much the worse for her; since it proves only that she unites affectation to ignorance. – At what age then may I read Racine and Corneille? – When you have understanding sufficient to discover the faults of those we now read. – I perfectly comprehend all those in *Andronicus*. – Yes, because I pointed them out to you: that will not do: you must know and be struck by them, without my being obliged to explain them. – Oh! how impatient am I to read those charming works, which I hear spoken of with so much applause! But, mamma, you surely have all these books: I have even read their titles in your catalogue, but I do not see them in the library: where then are they? – In the presses in my room: I took them out of the library, when I gave you the key. – Would it not have been sufficient to have forbidden me to read them? – Certainly, you are convinced I depend on your obedience and integrity. If I doubted it, Adelaide, could I love you? I was only desirous of sparing you the mortification of having daily before your eyes so just a subject of regret and curiosity. – But, mamma, you have promised to take me this winter to the play sometimes: I shall then see some pieces of Racine's and Voltaire's. – Not at all; I shall not go on those nights. – You will then chuse only the indifferent ones. – Yes, all those which are in your own list. – How sad this is! So we shall not see any new plays: I shall never be at a first representation. – Be comforted: I may take you sometimes without inconvenience. You see, my dear friend, from this conversation, the desire Adelaide has to know all those interesting works, which it is necessary she should read with attention. Judge, then, if she will not read them eagerly, after having wished for them so long; and how I shall enjoy her surprise. All you tell me of Constantia's sensibility does not surprise me; I have in myself a proof how susceptible she is of tender attachments: but permit me, my dear friend, to repeat to you, that instead of endeavouring to render her sensibility more lively and passionate, you should strive to suppress it. You had a slight fever, and did not see her for two days. She was in despair, cried, and would not eat: they were obliged to bring her to you; and she was quite sick with grief: yet you had the cruelty to applaud yourself for having inspired such an unreasonable tenderness, and which might have had the most dismal consequences to that charming child. Suppose you were to have a tedious and dangerous illness, what would become of her? Were you to be separated for months, how would she bear your absence? And you neglect correcting a weakness, that may make her life miserable, because it flatters your vanity. Is it thus a mother ought to love? Oh! it is from the virtues and felicity of Adelaide, that I expect my happiness! The maternal should be the most disinterested of all affections, since it cannot expect an equal return. For that same reason it ought to be more lively than friendship, more powerful than love; that alone can suffer, and sacrifice all, with the certainty of being rewarded but by halves. Brothers, friends, and lovers may feel a mutual affection; but did ever the best-educated daughter love her mother to the degree she was beloved? The disproportion of age alone, and the idea that the child will of course long outlive the parent, ought to make a prodigious difference in their sentiments. Let us not require from our children a tenderness equal to that we feel for them. I possess at present the first place in Adelaide's affections: but she will one day have a husband, children, a daughter ... What then would be my folly to expect to maintain that preference! I would have her feel for me the same affection now, which I may reasonably expect from her always. I wish her to leave me with regret, but without tears; see me in a slight fever, and not fall sick of sorrow. In short, that her tenderness, being founded on gratitude, should be deep and unalterable; but that reason should guide all her thoughts and actions. And you, my dear friend, by allowing your daughter to love you without measure, and almost to folly, soften her heart, and dispose her to abandon herself blindly to those dangerous passions, from which it is your duty to guard her. You instil excellent principles; but what will they avail, if she does not at the same time acquire an empire over herself? Are we not agreed, that a woman of strong feelings can never be happy? Vehement passions will lead her astray, or make her miserable through life. Teach then Constantia not only to oppose, but to conquer, hers. You will say, she will have no unlawful ones. Alas! can you answer for that? I hope and believe so. She will love her husband passionately; but who can assure you she will be as passionately beloved? But if that is the case, will she not feel all the fears and horrors of jealousy, justified sooner or later by a change which will reduce her to desperation? Recal to your mind all we have said heretofore on this subject. Constantia, I aver, is inexpressibly dear to me; her disposition is as engaging, as her person is charming: but if you do not moderate her sensibility, her virtues will depend on chance and circumstances, and she will never enjoy pure and permanent felicity.

LETTER XV.

The Viscountess to the Baroness.

OH, my dear friend, how I want you! my situation becomes every day more painful: – my daughter! – But you shall have all these melancholy accounts when we meet; it is impossible to write them. Mons. de Valcy too gives me all the uneasiness in his power. I now see him very seldom; but I am assured, he is ruining himself by gaming and foolish expences; and that he is passionately in love with a dancer just come on the stage. You will feel into what difficulties the taste will lead him, and what a prospect I have for my daughter! – and what encreases my trouble, is, that she appears absolutely insensible not only of her husband's conduct, but of the loss of her own reputation. It is true, all circumstances seem to unite in prolonging her errors and her blindness. Notwithstanding her glaring imprudencies, she is sought after and well received; without doubt they abuse her when absent, but she is not less in fashion; and this makes her think, that her birth and accomplishments allow her to act with impunity. We must admit one thing, namely, that in our time, that fifteen years ago the world was infinitely less dangerous than it now is. A beauty must then have been very strict in her carriage to be received in it. – What formerly would have cost a young person her reputation, is now scarcely taken notice of. A woman appears alone at twenty, receives all the young people of that age at their houses, has her little boxes, where she is alone with men, or at least without a *chaperon*; and the same is allowed at the balls after the opera, where they are sometimes accompanied only by a female attendant. Any one of these things in our day would have dishonoured and made a young woman the town talk.[42] Custom familiarises every thing. Then there was no having a lover without exposing oneself to a thousand dangers; to receive them at home was impossible; and very difficult to make an assignation elsewhere. It was then necessary to have recourse to means, which required more assurance than the generality of women are capable of. Thus bashfulness and fear frequently stopt those, whom virtue alone would not have withheld. At present there is no such thing as being talked of, or disgraced; and it appears to me equally difficult intirely to preserve, or to lose one's reputation. Thus liberty, degenerating into licentiousness, manifests itself in every action and discourse; our taste is as much corrupted as our manners. We see young people, who have been in the world six or seven years, boating publicly of their irreligion; considering impiety as a good substitute for wit, and atheism for philosophy. Modesty is now esteemed only a ceremony, required in a circle, but utterly renounced when one is not surrounded by fifty people. In a word, this revolution is remarkable even down to the female dress. I cannot bear to see them on the public walks, and at exhibitions, with their naked throats, hair flowing on their shoulders, disordered and without powder; that dress at once so negligent, and so studied; and all this after spending three hours at a toilet. – I think the men ought to be less attracted by these affectations of negligence, and abandoned airs, than by those noble and decent dresses we were obliged to wear in our youth. Oh, my dear friend! what a cruel thought it is, that Adelaide and Constantia are on the eve of entering a world so full of dangers! How shall we arm them against all these perils, or how prevent them from availing themselves of the ready path to error and destruction? Can I behold with indifference what passes in the world? All that I observe, affects me; and I bear a part in all, since it is here that Constantia is to spend her days. Trifles, follies and singularities are no longer subjects of derision and pleasantry to me. I am now really afflicted with what used to divert me: I have also lost all that gaiety, for which I was so envied. Reason is of no value to me, since she has robbed me of the graces; she is only becoming to those, who have always been guided by her; and thus it is, that she fits you so well, and sets so aukwardly on me. Adieu! my beloved. Madame d' Ostalis arrived in perfect health last Monday; she assures me, that you will be here towards the end of November: but I dare not flatter myself, and will not expect you till December.

LETTER XVI.

The Baroness's Answer.

ALL your observations, my dear friend, are perfectly just. It is very true, that the world is infinitely more dangerous now, than it was in our day: but I think a young woman well born and educated may very easily avoid all the rocks it presents. The greatest is certainly, as you remark, the excessive liberty which custom has granted to all young women for some years. But when my daughter enters into company, she will certainly possess a clear understanding, sound principles, purity of heart, discernment, noble sentiments, and a great desire to distinguish herself by her conduct and virtue. I will then give her this picture of the world, which you have drawn so correctly, and will say to her, 'Remember that the liberty young women now enjoy, prejudices their reputations much more, than it can assist their pleasures: never avail yourself of it, if you would wish to be esteemed irreproachable.' But, you will ask me, are you very sure, that in spite of fashion and example Adelaide will have the courage to follow this advice? Doubtless she will; or all I have done for her, will be lost and useless. I will go farther and assert, that she will follow this advice without constraint, and even with delight. When one is truly virtuous, and firmly resolved to continue so; in short, when one is totally free from coquetry, one pays a due respect to all the laws of decency, because none of them will then appear troublesome. Did you ever see a beauty dread the clear light of the sun? Neither does unsuspecting innocence avoid witnesses, or shrink from observations. Therefore my daughter will not go secretly to the balls after the opera with her chambermaid; at twenty she will have no little boxes; she will never go unaccompanied by a woman older than herself; nor will she be met on horseback, attended only by a groom, &c. When one has no intrigues, it is very easy to make such slight sacrifices to reputation. Besides, do you set no value on those noble and satisfactory enjoyments of distinguishing oneself, and being never confounded in the senseless croud of flirts and coquets? To conclude; the contagion is not so general, but we may still name many examples, and models worthy of imitation. I dare boast of Madame d' Ostalis as one. Madame de L... yet older, (but still young) has she ever made one false or imprudent step? With so noble and engaging a figure, so much life and bloom, has she even given room to say any man was in love with her? Her modesty has so many charms, that all the young women at one time attempted to imitate her timidity; – but unfortunately 'Blushes are not voluntary:' so that this fashion was of very short duration. There are many other young women as conspicuous for their conduct as their accomplishments; amongst others Madame de P ... who with the most seducing wit, the most charming countenance, and all the sprightliness of youth, has nevertheless established a reputation, which envy itself never dared to attack. These examples ought to convince you, my dear friend, that it is very possible with a good disposition to escape all the dangers you dread so much for Constantia. Educate her well, continue your attention to her, and have no fear for the future.

LETTER XVII.

Madame d' Ostalis to the Baroness.

I HAVE already told you, my dear aunt, that I had seen the Chevalier de Valmont, and how amiable he appeared to me; but I can now speak with more certainty, as I supped with him yesterday at Madame de Limours's. Madame de Valcy was there; and I never saw her more adorned, lively, and brilliant; all this was not without design, and perhaps not without success ... The Chevalier is very young, and inexperienced ... Yet I thought I could perceive he was more astonished at, than seduced by her coquetry ... Ah, if he could but look into futurity, and foresee the happiness designed for him, if he knows how to deserve it! ... He would I am sure escape all the snares preparing for him! ... He drew near to me after supper, and made enquiries concerning you with an eagerness, that affected me. He asked two or three questions about Adelaide; and when I told him she was prodigiously grown and improved; indeed I believe he blushed, but I am sure he sighed. Madame de Valcy came and interrupted us, offering him a card for whist; and he left me, to play with her, all the remainder of the evening. – I could not discover, if Madame de Limours sees into her daughter's schemes. She has naturally a great deal of penetration; but then she must be quite unbiassed; the least degree of interest will blind her. There are moments, when she even persuades herself, that Madame de Valcy has only imprudencies to reproach herself with; – for example, she firmly believes her as well received in the world as ever. With high rank, youth, and an husband who will be offended at nothing, we are not wholly banished from society. Madame de Valcy is pretty; she dresses well, dances admirably, and graces an assembly; she is invited to all the balls and suppers: this will last, till age obliges her to leave off feathers, flowers, and dancing: – On these depend all her consequence. Besides, she continually experiences all those humiliations, to which bad conduct exposes itself. There is not one new-married woman, who will appear with her in public. Even those women who receive her, carefully avoid every advance towards intimacy. In short, all the mothers-in-law, and mothers who dread that kind of connection for their daughters, treat her with a disdain frequently amounting to rudeness. She is perpetually seen making advances, either coldly received, or openly rejected; bearing all these slights without daring to complain, and seeking to revenge herself by scandalising all the women, who enjoy an unblemished reputation. She has just lost (at least for a time) her friend, Madame de Germeuil, whose husband, less careless than Mons. de Valcy, is out of humour; and, after exposing himself and making a great clamour, has taken her to an estate sixty leagues from Paris. He (it is said) intends returning towards the end of the winter; but will leave her in exile at least two years.

Adieu, my dear aunt! I have begun the portraits of my two girls, and you will certainly find them in your closet. Seraphina is a little spoilt by my mother-in-law, who was too much diverted with her frolicksome disposition; and this has greatly increased it: but Diana continues all mildness and good humour. I myself teach them music and drawing. Being both of an age, and learning together, they have a great deal of emulation; – a sentiment I shall encourage as much as possible, as it is very useful in proper hands.

LETTER XVIII.

The Baroness's Answer.

I SHALL be at Paris within three weeks, my dear child; and I write by this courier to inform the Viscountess of my intentions of travelling into Italy this spring. I beg you to wait on her and explain my reasons, for it is impossible to make her comprehend them by letter. Let us now talk of your children. Use your utmost endeavours to correct Seraphina of that frolicksomeness and spirit, which may so easily degenerate into downright malice.

Montaigne has said, 'and what father is so foolish to take as a good omen, his son's striking a servant or peasant, who does not defend himself. This is the real seed and root of cruelty, tyranny, and treason.'[43] Rousseau, in the first volume of his *Emilius*, makes a similar observation; 'if a child dares give a serious blow to any one, be it a servant, or any very inferior person, make them return his blows with interest.'[44] I have seen simple governesses animate the fury of a child, encourage it to fight, suffer themselves to be beat, and laugh at its weak blows, without thinking that they were so many bruises in the little fury's intention; and that he who strikes in his childhood will grow up an assassin. Therefore punish Seraphina severely for the very first malicious act; be particularly careful never to laugh at any of her tricks, or repeat them sportively before her; for self-love is more powerful than the fear of punishment. The pleasure of amusing others, and of being talked of, will make her brave all the chastisements in the world. It is of great importance to convince children, that what is bad is hateful, and can only inspire disdain. But when you punish, and at the same time laugh at their fault, they may reasonably believe there are deceitful vices, which can even contribute to make persons liked. This pernicious idea has spoilt more than one character. You know Madam Clarence; she owes all her faults to the desire of appearing keen; because she is persuaded, that a mild person is always insipid. One must have very little sense to believe, that beauty, meekness, and complacency, are incompatible with other accomplishments; and that bluntness, caprice, and contradiction, can be graceful, and supply the place of understanding.

I also recommend to you, my dear, never to avail yourself, but with the utmost precaution, of the dangerous stimulus of emulation. Take great care of making them envious of each other. If ever they are infected by that dangerous sentiment, their hearts will be corrupted without remedy. To preserve them, be you always just. A merited encomium excites envy and hatred only in hearts that are intirely perverted. For example, if Diana discovers that you think she does not love you as tenderly as Seraphina does, she will certainly feel a jealous sorrow, which will make her dislike her sister. There is no child in whom this idea, with or without foundation, does not inspire an extreme jealousy; even in those who can hear their brother or sister praised for accomplishments they do not possess without envy. Natural justice persuades us, they bestow on us only that degree of affection they think us capable of feeling; and at that innocent age we prefer the happiness of being beloved to the vain pleasure of being applauded: for this reason the child who would enjoy the commendations given to her sister, cannot support the thought of that sister's being more beloved. Convince your daughters, that your heart knows no partiality, and that you believe them equally affectionate. Be equally just in your praise and blame, and your decrees will never produce animosities. Should you be weak enough to shew the slightest preference on account of trifles or personal advantages; if, for example, you should caress Diana most because she is prettiest, or appear to delight most in Seraphina's conversation because she is wittiest, you would raise a jealousy, that would annihilate all the qualifications they derive from nature and your attentions. I see clearly from the accounts you send me, that the Chevalier de Valmont will be enamoured of Madame de Valcy. From the opinion I had formed of his heart and understanding, I could not have thought he would have been so easily ensnared by a coquette. Alas! if he is vain, if he is weak, all is over; nevertheless I must own to you, I shall not relinquish, without regret, a plan, which, in spite of me, has engrossed me ever since I have known him: I studied him well in his infancy, he was so promising! ... His grandfather and the Count de Roseville's letters were so full of encomiums! ... His person is so pleasing! ... In short, I shall see him, I shall observe him myself; and assuredly I shall be able to form a decisive opinion before I set out for Italy. – To conclude, be particularly careful, that Madame de Limours does not perceive the interest you take in him; for she will easily guess the reason, and it is a secret I shall never confide to her. Even if the Chevalier answers my expectation, if I carry into Italy the hopes I have conceived, I would not have my daughter entertain the slightest suspicion of my designs. The thoughts of matrimony should not only never occupy for a moment a young woman's thoughts; but she should be inspired with a belief, that it is very possible she may never be married. A condition ceases to be loved, which we know we are soon to change. Moreover to make known to your daughter the husband you design her, is authorising her to place her happiness on a project, that a thousand events may defeat; but even supposing it should be realised, such a confidence would always be imprudent. It must naturally inflame her imagination, raise her ideas, and give her up to the seducing illusions of the most dangerous of all passions. You know Madame de Limours; she is a real friend; but she is only capable of keeping those secrets, which do not concern her; and it is impossible for her not to betray every secret that interests her. She has so much sensibility, that it is impossible not to be attached to her; but she is too imprudent to inspire confidence. When her heart takes but little part in what is told her, she gives proofs of discretion and reserve that can withstand all trials; she is then impenetrable; but when the secret gives her either grief or joy, it is so legible in her eyes and countenance, that the least clear-sighted person may discover it. Thus by a most uncommon caprice, of all her acquaintance her intimate friend is the only person who should not trust her. Has she been able to keep the secret of the intended match between Theodore and Constantia? I am certain that even her child knows it. Thanks to my precautions, Theodore is still ignorant of it; but I may perhaps not be able to conceal it from him as long as I would; however, such as discovery is attended with much less inconvenience to a man than to a young woman. Farewell, my dear child! I will write to you again before I leave this place.

LETTER XIX.

The Baroness to the Viscountess.

I HAVE, my dear friend, something to tell you, which I own hurts me much; and I even feel I shall not have resolution to talk to you myself of a scheme, which, believe me, will cost my heart as much as yours. I am again obliged to separate myself from you, and for a long time. I shall spend the winter at Paris; but we set out in the spring for Italy, not to return for eighteen months. You will doubtless say, that my children are very young to travel; yet you must allow their reason far exceeds their years. Moreover, it is neither men nor laws that we are to study in Italy: my children will acquire a taste for the polite arts, and perfect themselves in drawing. Whilst they amuse themselves in admiring the monuments and ruins of Roman grandeur, they will gain a complete knowledge of that interesting history. In short, my son, conducted by a father, whose tenderness can only be equalled by his knowledge, will learn to write a good journal, and in it nothing frivolous; in a word, reap all the fruits of travelling. I shall bring back Adelaide at fourteen, an excellent musician, an adept in drawing, talking and singing like a native Italian; and intirely divested of all those little feminine delicacies, which nothing but travelling can radically cure. She will neither fear the sea, nor bad roads; sleep as well in an alehouse, as in her own apartment. She will learn to be contented with a bad supper, and to do without a thousand things she now looks on as absolutely necessary. I also see in this project many more advantages than I can enumerate in one letter, but which you shall be informed of, and I am sure will feel their importance. Do not, my dear friend, add to the grief I experience in separating myself from you, the chagrin of seeing you fretful and unjust. Do you think I have not occasion for all my courage to resolve to leave you and

Madame d' Ostalis? But can I refuse any thing to my children? ... Farewell, my dear, my real friend! for Heaven's sake, do not write during your first emotions: spare me those reproaches, which will afflict my heart, without relieving yours. Adieu! I set out in a few days: write not to me, I beg; wait my arrival; hear me before you complain or accuse me.

LETTER XX.

The Chevalier Herbain to the Baroness.

I MUST absolutely, Madame, ask you the reason of Madame d' Ostalis's conduct and behaviour. I can no longer bear it; she is become quite unsociable. I allow she has still many good qualities: she has sense and sweetness; she speaks ill of nobody; she seems to blame nothing she sees; but there is vast hypocrisy hidden under that apparent mildness, or, to speak more properly, she has a manner of criticising still more severe than detraction; for she censures not by her words, but by her actions. I am going to relate a few anecdotes, that will convince you to what a height she carries her dissimulation and malice. It is about three weeks ago, since I took a little trip into the country to visit Madame de R— , where I found a good deal of company, and Madame d' Ostalis: She behaved pretty well for the first twenty-four hours. After dinner the men went to billiards, and the ladies retired, and shut themselves up in a little closet, to untwist gold at their ease. Madame d' Ostalis's complaisance made her quit her embroidery to read aloud foolish novels, which must have tired her, and which none of the rest attended to. One day, that we were all assembled in the hall before the hour of walking, Madame de R— suddenly observed, that the fringe on my dress would be excellent for untwisting; at that instant her sprightliness induced her to cut off one of my tassels. I was directly surrounded by ten women, who with an enchanting grace and vivacity, stripped me, ran away with my dress, and put all the fringes and gold bindings into their work-bags. Madame d' Ostalis alone did not condescend to take the least bit, alledging, that she did not understand untwisting; but she laughed heartily, and seemed to think it a very good joke. I own to you her deceit exasperated me, and I resolved to unmask her. I immediately dispatched my valet de chambre to Paris; who brought me the next day a superb cloak for a woman, full trimmed all round with an elegant gold fringe. I carried it into the hall. At the sight of the cloak, all the women arose. I avoided them; and approaching Madame d' Ostalis said to her, Madame, as you are the only one who has not robbed me, nor would have any hand in the plot on my fringes, I give you all this gold as a reward for your honesty. At these words

I presented her the cloak. Madame d' Ostalis, looking on this pleasantry as a severe reproof on the rest, blushed, and told me, laughing, she did not understand untwisting, therefore my present was of no use to her ... Nay, Madame, I have seen you an hundred times untwisting Mons. d' Ostalis's shoulder-knots, and your own trimmings. This reply embarrassed her still more, as she clearly discovered my intention of giving a public proof of her nonconformity with the manner of thinking of all the world, even in the most insignificant things. Her situation was distressing. One of her whims is, never to accept (particularly from a man) either gold or silver, under whatever form it could be offered; yet she did not chuse to affect a delicacy that might offend ten women. At length recovering from her distress, and resuming her open and lively countenance: I tell you once more, said she, I no longer untwist; I have intirely quitted that work for embroidery; therefore I will not accept a very pretty thing, which would give me little pleasure: but sell it us, that is to say, let us raffle for it. This proposition, which pleased the whole assembly, confounded me. Madame d' Ostalis, without deigning to listen to me, valued the cloak, had the lots made, took one, and distributed the rest; put the money into my hat, and settled the raffle. Fortune gave the cloak to Madame de R—, who was perfectly satisfied with the conclusion of this adventure,[45] and found this joke just as good as the preceding. The next day I desired an explanation from Madame d' Ostalis: wherefore, says I, do you refuse a present, which every other woman not only would accept but solicit? Madame de L—, whom you meet perpetually, does she not make all the men of her acquaintance present her with golden dolls, dogs, laces, and even new gold thread? The Ladies G—, de C—, de R—, &c. have not they all the same madness? – Very well; but I have not. – Do you then blame those women? ... Me! not at all; I have, on the contrary, a very good opinion of all those you have just named, particularly Madame de R—, for whom I have a great friendship, and believe her possessed of the noblest sentiments. – And you think it *very noble* to be continually asking presents, for no other intent but to sell them? For example, yesterday, instead of pulling off my gold, would it not have been more honest, natural, and sincere, to have asked for ten Louis d'ors? ... Believe me, if Madame de R— had thought a moment, she would not have subjected herself to your censure; and I might have been guilty of a similar solly, had I received a different education. This last reply, I own, touched me; for I ought to allow, that by excusing in others the faults she herself is incapable of, Madame d' Ostalis displays a frankness which convinces one she thinks as she speaks, and that the indulgence she grants is as sincere as it is estimable.

But it is far from my intention to commend her; so let us resume the subjects of my complaint. On my return to Paris, I supped with her at Madame de Limours's. Madame de Valcy and two more women came in at ten o'clock, and told us they were come from the Variétés Amusantes; that they had seen *Jerome*

Pointu, Eustache Pointu, and *Le Fou raisonable.*[46] The world is full of the fame of these pieces; and every one in the party extolled them with enthusiasm, except Madame d' Ostalis, who was perfectly silent. At last we questioned her, and she was obliged to own that she knew none of them. Although these plays are new, yet all Paris knows them by heart already: it is as shameful not to have seen them, as it would be extraordinary never to have been present when *Phædra* or *Cinna*[47] was performed. She was laughed at by the whole company. We unanimously intreated her to go the very first opportunity. Two or three women pressed her to fix the day, and engaged to secure a box. Madame d' Ostalis, to rid herself of our importunities, promised to attend them in two days, 'provided she was not obliged to go to Versailles' on that day. But on that day she did go to Versailles; and at the instant I am writing to you, Madame, she knows no more of *Jerome Pointu, le Fou Raisonable*, &c. than what she has learned from common report, which can convey but a very imperfect idea of them; for the most brilliant sallies are precisely those which cannot be quoted in conversation. I thought myself obliged to talk to her again on this subject. Acknowledge, said I, that you will not go to the Variétés Amusantes, because you have been told they are not strictly decent. Yet you are fond of the French comedy, and there you often see acted such pieces as are very free; all Dancourt's, for example[48] ... Did they act only those, I should not go; for then this diversion would be disgraced, and one could not appear there without incurring a character, which of all others a woman should avoid, that of indelicacy. Besides, do you think the most licentious comedy so indecent as the master-piece of the Variétés Amusantes? – Oh! certainly not; but all the world goes there ... I could name several women, who have not been seduced by example; the Ladies de L— , de Cr— , and doubtless many more whom I know not. Moreover, should it be absolutely a universal fashion to go, I should only be still more tempted to restrain, as I should distinguish myself the more by not following it. What, Madame, do you think of this excessive vanity, in a young person apparently so unaffected and modest? Such pride is still more disgusting, as it is by no means the fault of the present age. One may assert, without flattery, that excepting a slight pretension to particularity in dress, their humility is striking; they have not the least desire to distinguish themselves. All women are alike, speak and act in the same manner; and surely, if one may judge by their conduct, they are not desirous of admiration. As for Madame d' Ostalis, I must own she gains her end; she distinguishes herself; she enjoys a great reputation; she is so mild, consistent, and obliging, that those who envy, cannot hate her. She has sincere friends; she is adored by her husband and family: but in spite of all these apparent advantages, the singularity of her conduct exposes her to all the bitterest strokes, with which detraction and calumny can oppress a young woman. For example, they accuse her of wanting wit, because she is neither scornful, coquettish, nor capricious. They set no price on her attachment to you, to her husband and children; and they assign her having no lover to her want of sensibility. These outrages extend still farther: although the men think her both beautiful and charming, the women only say *she has beauty*; an expression which malice has invented, signifying, *regular features without the graces and allurements*. Others maintain, that she has no elegance nor ease in her shape, &c. In short, Madame, you cannot conceive how they ridicule her; and this, you must allow, she draws on herself by affectation, which become every day more absurd and insupportable. My attachment for you, and my liking for her, have engaged me to speak to you with a freedom, which, I dare flatter myself, will not be displeasing. Farewell, Madame! let us know if your return hither is put off, or if we may still hope to see you towards the end of the month.

LETTER XXI.

Madame d' Ostalis to the Baroness.

THIS letter, my dear aunt, may perhaps never reach you; as I suppose you are already on your journey. But in case you should not, I cannot help writing some anecdotes in which you are interested. Madame de Valcy has broke intirely with Mons. de Creny: she has all at once made an acquaintance with Madame d' Olcy, the Chevalier de Valmont's aunt. She sups there three times a week, and all the world says, it is solely to meet the Chevalier. In short, her attachment to him is known to every body but Madame de Limours. Mons. d' Aimeri perceives it, and has spoken of her coquetry to Mons. d' Ostalis. The Chevalier has hitherto behaved surprisingly well: I believe he thinks Madame de Valcy very pretty; but her advances certainly shock him, for he does not return them in the least. She begins to assume a different character towards him: she has quitted that gay air, and jesting manner: she affects a soft melancholy, and an inattention to all around. These manners are more dangerous, and may very probably seduce an inexperienced youth of sensibility. But you, my dear aunt, are coming; and my uncle can give the Chevalier the best advice, which I hope will prevent him from being duped by all those artifices, which are set at work to deprive him of his liberty. You will not find him here on your arrival: Mons. d' Aimeri hurries him from Paris, designedly no doubt. They set out to-morrow on a visit to a relation in Picardy, and intend staying a fortnight. I must own to you, he appears to leaves Paris with regret. He dined today at my mother-in-law's: his departure was talked on, and I was sorry to observe the conversation seemed to give him pain.

I was yesterday, for the first time in my life, at a party at blind-man's-buff, at Madame de Clarence's; for it is proper you should be informed, my dear aunt, that for six months past, instead of giving balls after supper, it is the fashion to play at blind-man's-buff, traine ballet,[49] &c. You will naturally imagine, that these childish amusements are unpremeditated, and that they only spring from the sprightliness of a small and select company: no such thing. You receive a card of invitation to Traine Ballet a fortnight before-hand, and frequently from a person with whom you have no particular connection, as in the instance of me and Madame Clarence. I went yesterday to her house at half past nine, drest for blind-man's-buff, that is to say in a Levée. I found eight or ten young ladies, as many young men, and five or six mothers-in-law: all this company, seated in a dull circle, appeared to wait without impatience the appointed hour for playing, which is not till after supper, for they cannot resolve to discompose their dress till near midnight; a disposition which ill agrees with the mirth, which ought to belong to these parties. Madame de Valcy and the Chevalier de Valmont were at this supper; she affecting to mind nothing, but sunk in a profound reverie; yet from time to time seeking him with her eyes, and casting looks at him equally mild and deceitful ... At length it strikes eleven; the mothers-in-law sit down to whist, and the romps begin. Then were several attachments revealed, which were hitherto unknown, or merely suspected. The blinded person is seen to attempt catching only her, who engrosses his affections. Feigned or real embarrassments on one side; eagerness, folly, and coquetry on the other: all these hasty emotions discover, to the least discerning, all the little intrigues of the party. The game was very animated; all ran and screamed, except two or three indifferent persons. But innocent mirth is the only mirth that is true and sociable: by making a vast noise, and playing the fool, it may be counterfeited, but cannot be inspired. To Mons. d' Ostalis, the ladies of S— , and myself, the entertainment was intolerably dull; and Traine Ballet, which you have seen us enjoy so much in the country, could not enliven us an instant. I own to you, I was insupportably distressed every time I was compelled to hunt five or six young men, whom I scarcely knew; and I certainly struck them very aukwardly with the handkerchief, and I received their blows with still more disgust. A general riot concluded this charming evening: the tables, chairs, &c. were overturned: twenty bottles of water were thrown over the room. In short, I retired at half past one, sinking with fatigue, benumbed with blows, leaving Madame de Clarence absolutely hoarse; her gown torn in a thousand pieces, the skin stripped off her arm, and a contusion on her head; but applauding herself for having given so gay a supper, and flattering herself it would be all the talk next day. I trust my dear aunt is assured, I shall be no more seen at these noisy assemblies; and that I should not have appeared at one, had I been two or three years younger. Adieu, my dear aunt! Be so good as to send faithful Brunel to inform me of the day you propose to be here, that I may meet you.

LETTER XXII.

The Baroness to Madame de Valmont.

— Paris.

I ARRIVED the day before yesterday, Madame; and can as yet give you no intelligence of Mons. d' Aimeri, nor of the Chevalier de Valmont; but I this day received a letter from Mons. d' Aimeri, which informs me I shall have the pleasure of seeing them in four or five days at farthest. But every body, that knows the Chevalier, is delighted with him; and they praise him equally for his accomplishments, understanding, sweetness, and good conduct. It is much to be wished, that Mons. d' Aimeri may not leave him to himself for two or three years to come; that is to say, that he may attend him till that time as he has hitherto done. Mons. d' Aimeri does not love company; but we are not permitted to follow our own taste till we have fulfilled our duties; and we cannot think of living for ourselves, as long as we can be useful to our children.

I received a visit yesterday from Madame d' Olcy. The Chevalier's success in the world insures to him, from her, not only the affections of an aunt, but those of *a mother*; that was her expression. She gave me to understand, that she had already a view to settle him. It seems to me very early for her to busy herself in that matter; and, I own, it would not be Madame d' Olcy who should determine my choice; for I imagine she sets very little value on personal merit, and none at all on the advantages of a good education. In an affair, on which depends the happiness of one's life, it is my opinion, we ought not to consult those who would be led and determined by vanity alone. I send you, Madame, the books you desired; and add a new one, which is much admired. It is the first production of Porphiry, that young man you have heard me mention so often, as educated by Mons. de Lagaraye. This work appears to me worthy your attention; and although it is modern, you will read it more than once with pleasure. The stile of it is pure and natural; there are no obscure, far-fetched, and ambiguous phrases; nor those striking inaccuracies, which at once discover the bad taste of an author. It is well known, that the best works have their faults and weak parts; but an author, who knows how to write, will always posses clearness, truth, and the stile which suits the subject of which he treats.

LETTER XXIII.

The Baroness to Madame d' Ostalis.

ALAS! my dear child, notwithstanding the wish of us both, you were not witness to Adelaide's first interview with the Chevalier de Valmont! Mons. d' Aimeri, who was not to leave S— till the 20th, arrived here last night, and visited me this morning. Adelaide had just left me to go and write. I was alone in my closet, when, all at once, Mons. d' Aimeri and the Chevalier were announced. This last name raised in me a kind of emotion, which must have discovered my secret to Madame de Limours, had she been present. We must not value ourselves on our prudence, for there are moments when the most cautious women are very indiscreet. – But to return to the Chevalier; I am equally pleased with his deportment, his countenance, and his manners. After a quarter of an hour's conversation, Mons. d' Aimeri asked me to let him see Adelaide: I rang directly, and ordered her to be called, and she came running in directly: but perceiving Mons. d' Aimeri and his grand-son, she stopped all on a sudden with an embarrassed air, made a low curtsey, looked simple, and blushed in a very particular manner. What emotion was it made her blush? was it shyness, surprise, instinct, or foresight? This is what perhaps we may never know. You will readily imagine my looks were directed to the Chevalier at that instant, and I was very well satisfied with the impression I saw on his countenance. He looked on Adelaide with as much pleasure as curiosity, and I am certain he was charmed with her. Madame d' Almane came into my closet, and pressed Madame d' Aimeri to stay dinner. When we rose from table, Mons. d' Aimeri went up to Adelaide, and told her, the Chevalier de Valmont, recollecting the taste she shewed in her childhood for natural history, made a collection of choice pebbles during his travels; 'and my grand-son,' continued he, 'not daring to presume to offer them to you himself, has intreated me to present them.' At these words, Mons. d' Aimeri took a large box from the Chevalier; containing a most beautiful assortment of the rarest stones, and besought Adelaide to accept them. My child, at a loss, sought counsel in my cyes: I made a sign of approbation, and the box was received with a little confusion, and much gratitude. I repeat it again, I am quite enchanted with Charles. It is impossible, at eighteen, to be formed more amiable, and at the fame time to have more reserve and simplicity; but his heart is no longer his own, I am certain. He is melancholy, and inattentive; he is thoughtful, and sighs. In short, he is passionately in love; and I am sure, from all you have told me, and from what I have seen myself, it can be only Madame de Valcy. I own I am more afflicted at the choice than at the sentiment! – Alas! if he is really in love with Madame de Valcy, he never can love Adelaide! – I am indeed too sure Madame de Valcy has infatuated him. I was dying to talk to him of her; and I found a very natural opportunity. You know, that one of the prettiest miniatures you gave me represents Madame de Limours and her two daughters. Painting was the subject of conversation; and I said, that the likest portrait I had ever seen was one you drew of Madame de Valcy. This speech made him blush, and put him quite out of countenance; I appeared not to take notice of it. When he was a little composed, I sent for the picture. Mons. d' Aimeri applauded it highly: as for the Chevalier, his admiration deprived him even of the fear of betraying himself. He contemplated her image with a rapture which (I will not hide it from you) occasioned me as much surprise as displeasure. I cannot conceive how so manifest a coquet, with such free behaviour, so moderate an understanding; a woman, in short, whose whole merit consists in an agreeable figure, could inspire so deep an impression. A young man's first attachment generally decides his character and his principles. What then must we think of the delicacy of his heart, who makes so despicable a choice? Moreover, a man always judges of all women from one, that is to say, from her he has most loved: and it is usually the object of his first affection which fixes his opinion in this respect. I should be much concerned, if my daughter's husband had an ill opinion of women in general. Therefore you see, that if Charles is really attached to Flora, he will cease to be suitable to me. I shall regret it much, I confess, but we shall see. I will not relinquish a hope, which is become more dear to me, since I have seen him a second time. Adieu, my child! Mons. d' Ostalis told me to-night, that you may perhaps stay at Versailles till Thursday. I beg you to send me word what day you positively will return.

LETTER XXIV.

Mons. d' Aimeri to Madame de Valmont.

At length, my dear daughter, I am acquainted with Charles's sentiments. His 'secret' is no longer such to me; and assuredly your surprise will be as great as mine at the unexpected avowal. You was informed of the real motive for my journey into Picardy. I was desirous of separating him from Madame de Valcy for a short time, flattering myself, that the necessity of talking of her would induce him to lay open his heart to me; but my hopes deceived me. Charles, melancholy and thoughtful, sought solitude, avoided me, and, for the first time in his life, seemed to fear being alone with me. Walking with him one day alone, I began talking of Madame de Valcy, and I mentioned her with contempt. Charles did not betray the least emotion. So profound a dissimulation afflicted, as much as it surprised me: but wishing to see to what a length he would carry it, I resolved to urge him no farther; and returned to Paris without having obtained the confidence I so anxiously desired. The day after our arrival, that is last Monday, we waited on Madame d' Almane; and there it was Charles betrayed himself intirely. She shewed us a picture of Madame de Valcy, painted by Madame d' Ostalis. His confusion at the sight of this picture was so visible, that it certainly could not escape the penetrating eyes of Madame d' Almane. I felt the necessity of an immediate explanation. I went into Charles's room the next morning, as he was rising; I sent away his attendants, and sat down by his bed-side. 'Charles, says I, it is time to break a silence which afflicts and distresses me. As your governor and your father, I come to demand a secret, which I could not obtain as your friend. It is no longer a confidence I require; you have lost the opportunity of bestowing that. I have, in spite of you, read your heart: now at least I expect sincerity. But remember, that in this instance the slightest dissimulation will rob me for ever of the only hope of happiness Heaven has left me.' At these words Charles was too much affected to be able to speak, seized my hand, and pressed it between his. He trembled, and I myself was greatly moved. – We were some minutes silent: at last Charles resumed the discourse. – I might fear to own a folly to you; but could you think me capable of dissimulation with you? – Nevertheless, I have had cause to accuse you of it more than once: but be that as it may, you are in love; you have delivered up your heart to a passion the most criminal; and what conflicts have you sustained to defend yourself, or overcome it? – In never seeking, and even avoiding, the object which gave it birth. – But you meet her every-where: hitherto, indeed, you have received her advances with proper reserve. – Her advances! what say you? of whom are your speaking? – Of whom! why of Madame de Valcy. – At these words his face flushed with anger and disdain. Madame de Valcy! who, me! what, I love so despicable a woman! Ah! cease to deceive yourself: the sentiment I feel is more excusable; but it is yet more dangerous. – Ah! who is then the object which inspires it? What! can it be Madame d' Ostalis? At these words he cast his eyes down and blushed; and by that tacit avowal filled me with an astonishment, which you no doubt will share. I felt at the same time a secret joy, which I concealed with difficulty. I interrupted a pretty long silence, with saying, Well, what hopes have you? – I have none. – If you think so, my child, you deceive yourself: love never exists without hope. I can easily conceive that you are a little frighted by Madame d' Ostalis's reputation; but you have a kind of flattering hope, that a sincere passion, an unshaken constancy, meet their reward at last, especially in a form like yours. – No, no; I have too high an esteem for Madame d' Ostalis. – Well then! are you firmly resolved never to mention your passion? Have you promised yourself to leave her ignorant of it for ever? No such thing: on the contrary, at the bottom of your heart you have perhaps fixed the moment to declare your sentiments, and you think she will give you credit for your discretion in concealing it so long; but this pretended discretion is only an artful policy, an additional snare, which you prepare in order to surprise her the more readily. Such are the chimeras which seduce you. Ah Charles! should you be so unfortunate not to trust in virtue? – Alas! I believe that of Madame d' Ostalis to be as solid as sincere. – Why then would you wish to corrupt it? – I only desire her compassion. – Vain error! you disguise your real intentions even to yourself. Search the bottom of your heart; examine it strictly, and you will be terrified at its situation. I have but one more reflection to make: if Madame d' Ostalis is (as I firmly believe her) truly virtuous, the delusive hope you have nourished can only serve to render you miserable: if, on the contrary, she owes the preservation of her reputation to circumstances rather than to principles, you may possibly destroy it; but in this supposition can you look forward, without trembling, to the dreadful abyss into which you will plunge her? Reflect on the happiness she now enjoys, admired by all her acquaintance, cherished by a virtuous husband and family, who look on her as their glory and felicity. Are you capable of the cruel design of robbing her for ever of a bliss so pure? You love her to distraction: well then, if that is true, reverence her duties, her reputation, and her happiness; conquer this mad passion, which, if known, can only make you ridiculous. – Ridiculous! is it possible to be so by loving the person in the world the most worthy to be adored? – By daring to appear in love with her, you will display a rashness which no man has hitherto shewn. Besides, recollect the disproportion of age; she is twenty-six, and you only in your nineteenth year; she is a mother of a family, and I cannot yet even think of settling you. This idea alone ought to convince you of the folly of an attachment, which your reason would readily cure, if you sincerely desired it. – Our conversation ended with Charles's reiterated protestations to follow my advice with a scrupulous exactness. To deal sincerely with you, my dear daughter, an attachment for so estimable an object cannot give me any serious uneasiness: the disproportion of years necessarily opposes its duration. Madame d' Ostalis is still in all the bloom of beauty; but in four or five years she will cease to rank amongst the young. Oh! if our hopes do not deceive us, before that æra Charles's heart will beat with a more fortunate passion! – From the knowledge I have of Madame d' Almane's character, I am convinced she has turned her thoughts more than once on Charles; and I am very certain that education, conduct, and personal charms, will take the lead in deciding her choice. If it be true that she has formed any such designs, I am persuaded nothing will more effectually destroy them than the idea of your son's feeling a real passion for a woman of Madame de Valcy's disposition. Therefore I think it absolutely necessary, for Charles's sake, to own the whole truth, and undeceive her in this respect. Was the charming Adelaide but two years older, Charles would soon experience inconstancy. He was so struck with her grace and figure, that it would be very easy for me to turn his heart to love. Oh! could my eyes, before they close for ever, but behold this desirable union, I should die contented with my fate, notwithstanding all the woes I have suffered. Farewell, my dear child; I shall talk to Madame d' Almane tomorrow, and give you an account of our conversation.

LETTER XXV.

Count de Roseville to the Baron.

I WILLINGLY subscribe, my dear Baron, to all you have advanced concerning the female sex. I believe I could name more than one mother, who could educate her son as well, and perhaps better than the best father,[50] or most able governor. What man durst pretend to equal them in delicacy and art, whilst women elevate themselves to virtues which ought to characterise us, courage and greatness of soul? I agree with you, that no education can be perfect, which they have not either directed or polished. But this rule holds good only in some cafes; and here is doubtless the most striking difference, remarkable in the two plans of education, for a subject (let him be of ever so exalted a rank) and for a Prince who is born to reign. It is of consequence to your son's happiness, that he should have an advantageous opinion of womankind in general. It is particularly the desire of pleasing them, that will make him appear amiable; it is their good opinion alone that can make his life agreeable, and retain him in good company. The wife you choose for him will certainly merit his affection; it is therefore necessary he should have a great esteem for, and an intire confidence in her; but a monarch is not born to live in what we call the great world. Women cannot contribute to the success he ought to desire; his glory and happiness depend solely on the esteem of the warrior, of the magistrate, of the virtuous citizen; on the voice of the nation and his people's love. The wife that will be given him, will not be chosen for personal qualifications; political motives alone will be preferred. She may be, perhaps, rough, cruel and imperious; perhaps may add a vain desire of governing, to the greatest imbecility. It is therefore necessary for a Prince to be resolved never to be governed by her. – In fine, I do not attempt to inspire my pupil with a disdain for women in general; but I would have him know how to distrust them, and that he should be convinced of a truth, (of which I myself am convinced) namely, that they should never be admitted to great affairs. They may equal us in sense, but very rarely in prudence. Endowed with less sensibility than they are, after our tender years we are secure from those sudden and violent emotions, which the female sex so often suffer; causing faintings and hysteric fits, by which they instantly discover the most important secrets. The weakness of their constitutions, the flexibility of their features, the expression in their eyes, the

involuntary blush raised by the least surprise, the delicacy even of their complexions, which makes those blushes still more visible and remarkable; everything
in short conspires to make their first emotions known. In a word, I cannot look
on them as more designed by nature as the depositaries of state secrets, than to
command armies. I know that women have gained battles, and reigned as gloriously as the greatest Kings: But I only speak in general, and am ready to admit
many exceptions; the history even of our own times would furnish more than
one example. The Abbe Duguet, in his *Institution d'un Prince*, judges infinitely
more severely of women than I do; and I even deem his picture of them an unjust
satire, dictated by ill humour rather than truth. This dissertation, which is as long
as ungallant, finishes thus:

'The court, where they have power, insensibly degenerates into a palace of
pleasures, diversions, frivolous occupations; where luxury, gaming, love, and all
the consequences of those passions reign. The city quickly imitates the court,
and the provinces soon follow the pernicious example. Thus a whole nation, tho'
formerly ever so courageous, is weakened, and becomes effeminate; avarice and
the love of pleasure supplant the love of virtue. It is therefore necessary, in order
to discard all favour, cabals, venality, interest and passion, never to grant to the
women the least share in government. They will be modest and reasonable, when
they are commanded; but they corrupt both court and state, where they command.'[51]

You will without doubt ask me, how I propose to preserve my pupil from
their seduction. I do not flatter myself with the expectation of securing him from
the power of love: but I am sure, that this dangerous passion will never govern,
tho' it may sometimes lead him astray. He agrees with me, that no woman can be
so prudent as a man; he will retain all his life this idea, which I have imprinted
on his mind, not only by reasons, but by all the proofs I could collect. I found
means to inspire him with two causes for mistrust instead of one. I did not content myself with telling him, that women in general were fickle, indiscreet, that
they loved talking, and boasting of secrets confided to them. I added, there are
nevertheless some irreproachable in all these respects; but still they are women;
and consequently liable to all those indiscreet emotions, which astonishment,
fear, grief, or joy ever produce in them. They will not tell a secret consided to
them; but they involuntarily betray it. Thus tho' the cause is different, the effect
is always the fame. Similar discourses, repeated from his earliest youth, could
not fail producing the most deep impressions; particularly when they were eluci-
dated by examples; and such are not scarce in a court. An event has just happened
here, which has furnished us with many reflections on this subject. A lady of the
court, equally celebrated for her behaviour and beauty, dined at the Count de
*** with fifty people; her husband came in just as the company were fitting down
to dinner, and said aloud, that the Baron de L— had just fallen from his horse,

and broke his leg. – As he finished his recital, he cast his eyes on his wife, and saw her turn pale, change countenance, and at last faint away. This fatal imprudence of a too sensible heart deprived this hapless woman of her reputation, the esteem and friendship of her husband, and all the tranquility of her life. Many people pretend that she is innocent, and that the secret she has betrayed is unknown even to the object of this violent passion. This adventure has struck the Prince very forcibly, and confirmed him still more in the opinion I have given him of women. This brought on a long conversation on love. – It is a very dangerous passion, said the Prince. – Yes, replied I, for weak characters; therefore its empire is so great over women. – Has it most empire over the women? – Certainly; for they frequently sacrifice their honour at its shrine; whereas a man of the least delicacy would not hesitate a moment to sacrifice love to honour. – But amongst us this alternative is very rare: – Not so much as you imagine; I, for example, have been in this situation. – Oh! do tell me. – I was in love with a charming girl – Was she fair or brown? – Her hair was bright chesnut – a fine complexion – a beautiful shape? – Yes, she was a perfect beauty; we were both at liberty; we loved each other. Our parents approved and fixed the day, which was to unite us for ever. I was then in the sea service. War was declared. I instantly flew to Versailles, asked for a command, obtained it, but on condition that I set out without delay, that is to say, the next day. This was imposing on me a cruel sacrifice. I must defer for four or five months a marriage, on which depended the happiness of my life. I was obliged to go, to embark, and to leave my love a prey to despair. – Yes I did not hesitate; I accepted the command; and promised to depart at day-break. – And did you see your mistress? – It was necessary to tell her the fatal news. She vainly employed tears, intreaties, convulsions, and faintings to retain me. I left her, set out, and embarked. – And what became of her after your departure? – She consoled herself; and at my return I found her married. – I did not expect such a conclusion. – Was you older, it would surprize you less. – But your behaviour does not astonish me in the least. – In truth it was very natural. – I am sure I should not hesitate a moment between love and duty. – Neither is love a passion made for you. – How? – None but a madman would give himself up to it, unless he could flatter himself with a sincere return. – Well then? – Well then, consider your rank; and what assurance can you have, that you do not owe the preference shewn you to secret motives of ambition. – That would be a sad idea; I must then relinquish all hopes of possessing friends. – Oh! that is quite another case: a man will shew his attachment for you by real services and virtuous actions, and such proofs ought to obtain your confidence and esteem; whilst no woman but your wife can manifest her affection for you, but by rendering herself despicable, even in your eyes. Suppose that a man, entrusted with a secret, should reveal it to you, telling you that he can hide nothing from you; that he is only guilty of this treachery from his friendship to you; would this pretended proof affect you?

Would you be persuaded that he really loved you? Certainly not; – because a dishonourable person never deserves to be trusted: – Even the action, which she looks on as a mark of affection, will only serve to make her suspected. – There are nevertheless men, who think themselves really beloved by women, who are not estimable – assuredly. When a woman sacrifices her reputation, ease, and honour for a man, one ought to believe it is love alone that seduces her; but in your place, my Lord, how can you ever ascertain that? – But if a Prince should be beloved by a disinterested woman, who apparently despises riches and honours? – And who will affirm, that this woman may not be at the bottom of her heart as ambitious as she appears the reverse? But supposing her to persevere in such conduct, still a Prince would have reason to suspect the sincerity of her love; for there has been many instances of people, who could despise money and preferment, yet were very susceptible of that sort of respect which attends authority and favour. I will go further: he, who as a private man would never have inspired this passion, as a Prince has frequently been very successful. – But why so! for my title is in effect nothing to my person. – Very true; but rank has a great sway on the imagination; and imagination alone is the mother and nurse of love. This weak and imperious passion requires equality; it can never exist with ambition; and a lover, from whom we expect, or receive a great fortune, should never flatter himself with inspiring a great passion. – All this is very true; I feel it; but yet history celebrates many great Princes, who have loved passionately. – They had been much greater, could they have defended themselves from the seducing power of love; but you ought likewise to observe that it was very rare, that these king's mistresses governed them, or obtained any secrets of state. – State secrets! Why a man must be mad who trusts a woman with them. – Most surely; for exclusive of their imprudence, woman understand nothing of that sort. A Prince is convinced of the understanding and integrity of a man, before he places any confidence in him; and how is it possible to judge of a woman's, since she can be employed neither in council nor embassies? – Is it possible there should ever have been a Prince so thoughtless as to consult women on important affairs? – To such an excess of blindness love may lead them, if they have the frailty to allow themselves to be enslaved; judge then if it is not necessary for a Prince to know how to resist it at all times.

This conversation, my dear Baron, ought to satisfy your curiosity, and answers your questions better, than a long string of arguments. Finally, it makes you perfectly acquainted with the ideas and opinions, I would instill into my Prince relative to love and women.

LETTER XXVI.

Mons. d' Aimeri to Madame de Valmont.

AT length I have obtained a private interview with Madame d' Almane; I have made a free confession, and applaud myself for so doing. She told me without disguise, that she was delighted at Charles's proving himself more sensible to the charms of modesty and accomplishments, than to the allurements of coquetry. All my hopes are confirmed by the interested and even affectionate manner, with which she spoke of him. She was of opinion, that I ought to enjoin Charles to conquer his passion entirely; that is to say, to go away with me directly without seeing Madame d' Ostalis, and for us not to return to Paris of a year. But this seeming to me too severe, we agreed that I should remonstrate very strongly, and make him promise to avoid her as much as possible. The very day I had this conversation, I took Charles to a little ball; Adelaide was there; my grandson had never seen her dance, and seemed charmed with her graceful figure. – To day he heard her sing, and saw her draw; he told me to-night, that he was convinced she would one day possess all the talents, accomplishments, and virtues of Madame d' Ostalis. As to Madame de Valcy, she persists in her scheme, and the behaves so very imprudently in this respect, that every body is convinced Charles has supplanted Mons. de Creny: for they do not imagine a youth of eighteen capable of resisting such advances. We supped last Sunday at Madame d' Almane's, and there met (for the first time these three weeks) Madame d' Ostalis. Charles could not conceal his emotions, and found means to seat himself next her at supper. I was too far from them to be able to observe him; but after supper sorrow was so visible in his countenance, that I was quite alarmed. I inquired the cause. He pressed my hand without being able to speak, and I saw his eyes filled with tears. Equally disturbed and surprised I sought an occasion to depart, and took him away immediately. When we were alone, he broke through all constraint, and gave free vent to his tears. I entreated him, but in vain, to let me know the motive for so violent a grief; I could draw from him only incoherent words. At last, becoming a little calmer; I am, says he, the most wretched of men; I have broke my resolutions and promises. – Madame d' Ostalis will despise me; and I am unworthy of your favours. – But what then has happened to you? – I have broke silence; I have declared myself, or at least I have made known those sentiments, which I promised to conceal. – What! you have then dared to declare your passion to Madame d' Ostalis? – Intoxicated with joy at again seeing and setting by her, I forgot every thing, even the fear of disobliging her. I do not know what I said, but too well remember the look she cast on me – that look which manifested so cold a disdain, and such scornful pride – and which imposed on me such absolute silence! – This confession afflicted me very much; I knew that Madame d' Ostalis would not fail informing Madame d' Almane, and I resolved to go and talk to her myself; which I did the next day. She seemed affected by the confidence I placed in her. After having thanked me, she said, you see I was in the right, when I advised your going away directly; violent measures are always the most efficacious: the Chevalier de Valmont would then have made an entire sacrifice of his passion. You did not insist on what you have a right to expect; and you have obtained nothing. You have increased his weakness by humouring it; you would have given strength to his resolution by appearing to rely on it. These reflections made a deep impression on me; but the time for departure is lost; Charles will not consent, but with despair. Besides, he is at present much less occupied by love, than by the desire of regaining Madame d' Ostalis's esteem. He feels, that he cannot obtain that but by avoiding her in earnest, and convincing her he is radically cured of a sentiment which offends her. I therefore see no inconvenience from our staying here till May. Finally, my dear daughter, if I change my plan, you shall be informed directly; and I shall not leave Paris but to come to you.

LETTER XXVII.

The Baroness to Madame de Valmont.

IS it possible, Madame, that you should ask me seriously, if Adelaide is present, when I receive my evening visitors? Can you figure to yourself my little Adelaide, seated sorrowfully on the edge of her chair, in the midst of a circle, listening to a very unconnected and frivolous conversation, and making all the little customary compliments? – No, no, Madame, Adelaide is charming child, but she is still but a child; and she will not see the world, till she is of an age to see with her own eyes, and judge for herself. I have a new anecdote, which will serve to add to the collection you make of 'the trials Adelaide has sustained.' This course of artificial experience will not end these two years. When Adelaide is above fourteen events will naturally arise, and I shall be no longer compelled 'to create them.'

But let us return to the trial of the day before yesterday. – You must know that for these last four months she has received two guineas a month by way of pocket money; out of which she is obliged to find herself in pins, powder, pomatum, shoes, gloves, and writing paper. The first month the whole sum was wasted in three days in superfluities; and she was forced to wear ragged shoes and dirty gloves. She felt the necessity of order and œconomy. She keeps her accounts exact, and has already learned to suit her expences to her income. Adelaide came into my closet yesterday noon, just as I was going to a cabinet-maker's to buy some furniture I was in want of; she intreated me to let her go with me. I have, says she, some money remaining of my monthly allowance, and I wish to buy a little table. – I consent, replied I, and the more readily, as I wish you to begin to know the price of those things you must one day purchase; which cannot be learnt but by going sometimes to the shops. We set out, and went into a very fine shop. She inquired for tables, and they shewed her a charming one, in which was inclosed an inkhorn and desk; but unfortunately it came to twenty-seven shillings, and she had but twelve. This is unlucky, whispered I; if you had not spent eighteen shillings last month in cut paper, straw boxes, Bergamot toothpick-cases, toys in short, all of which you have already broke or lost, you could have bought this pretty table. Adelaide sighed; I left her to reflect on this misfortune; and when I had made my purchases, called her, and we went away. When we were in the carriage, I perceived a large box of rose wood under her arm: what, says I, have you bought that? – Yes, mamma; – and for how much? For my twelve shillings. – But it was a table you wanted? Yes; but I could not find a pretty one for my price – And for that reason you bought a thing you did not want, nor have any use for – Would it not have been wiser to have reserved your twelve shillings to assist in raising a sufficient sum to pay for such a table as you saw? – That is true; I was to blame. – Besides, we ought never to divest ourselves entirely of money to please our fancies. Things may happen, which will make us regret it. – But I shall receive my allowance in three days. – It is very possible you may wish for money within that time. The day after this conversation, a footman came into Adelaide's chamber, and delivered a letter which was directed to her, saying, a woman, who appears very pale, and ill dressed, had just brought it. Adelaide, surprized, gave the letter to Miss Bridget, who opened it directly, and read aloud what follows:

'Mademoiselle,

I implore your compassion; I have seven children which I have just left in a garret, almost dying with hunger. Acquainted with your mamma's charitable disposition, I came to beg her to relieve me; but hearing that she is not yet awake, I address myself to you. I am writing in your kitchen, where I see a fire for the first time these eight days. But, alas! my poor children are at this instant perishing perhaps with cold and hunger! – For Heaven sake have pity on them!

Marianne, the wife of Durand.'

Oh, great God! exclaimed Adelaide, bursting into tears, what shall I do? – How! Mademoiselle, returned Miss Bridget, can you hesitate about giving this unhappy woman money to buy bread? Send her a crown; that relief will suffice for to-day; and you cannot doubt your mamma's extricating her utterly from so deplorable a state. – A crown, replied Adelaide, sobbing, a crown! Alas, I have it not! – Oh had I but my twelve shillings! Detestable box! Oh, Miss Bridget!

I conjure you, my dear Miss Bridget, to lend me twelve shillings! – What is it you say, Miss? How! have you nothing remaining of your monthly allowance? – Ah! do lend me twelve shillings! – I cannot; your mamma has expresly forbid my ever lending you money. – Alas, Alas! and this poor woman! – Be easy, she shall be relieved; – I for my part do not spend all my money in trifles: it is not requisite for me to see distress, to remember and pity it. Thus saying, she went hastily out of the room, leaving Adelaide absorbed in confusion and remorse. A little while after Mademoiselle Victoire went into her room. Oh, Miss, cried she, weep no more at this poor woman's misfortunes: she is now quite happy; the guinea Miss Bridget gave her has restored her to life. Oh, how you would be moved could you be witness to her joy! – She knelt to Miss Bridget! – She is so grateful! – Oh, Miss, what a good action you have just done! – Me! – what are you talking of? – Why, that guinea you charged Miss Bridget to give her. – What has Miss Bridget said? – That it was from you. Oh, heaven! I ought not to suffer it – follow me, Mademoiselle Victoire. Adelaide rose, as she finished this speech, took her rose-wood box under her arm, and desired Mademoiselle Victoire to conduct her to the poor woman. They went into the kitchen, where they found Miss Bridget, surrounded by the servants, by the side of the poor women. This last hearing Adelaide named, came and prostrated herself at her feet, all in tears. Adelaide weeping bitterly, raised her, saying, 'I have not been so happy as to be able to give you the relief you have received. You owe it intirely to Miss Bridget: – but take this box, sell it to-morrow, that I may at least flatter myself with being useful to you in some respect.' The woman refusing to take the box, Oh rid me of it, added Adelaide; that alone was the cause of my not assisting you; let me never see it more. After this action Adelaide returned to her own apartment, far less discontented with herself. A moment after Miss Bridget went to her, and told her that the woman was gone in a hackney coach with Brunel, who had undertaken to see her home. Adelaide asked why Brunel followed her. Because, answered Miss Bridget, I was desirous of knowing the truth of her assertions. I could not refuse this assistance to a person apparently so unfortunate; but in general I do not give alms, without first obtaining all the information which prudence and even well-directed humanity exacts. In order to be able to alleviate as much as possible the distress of the truly indigent, one must strive not to be the dupe of idleness and knavery. When I awoke, my daughter and Miss Bridget attended me; and the former related this story with tears in her eyes. I did not allow myself to make a single reflection; her own heart dictating all that a similar adventure could inspire: a useless remonstrance is as disgusting as it is tiresome, and frequently choaks the source of the most repentant tears. I contented myself with pitying Adelaide: my poor little dear, what must you have suffered, said I! what a cruel morning! Alas, replied she, I shall never again feel this grievous pain; I am cured for life of those whims which can alone produce them, and deprive me of the happiness Miss Bridget this morning enjoyed. – Hear me, Adelaide, said I; I will not have you carry any thing to extremes. Take Reason for your guide in forming any resolution, and she will not exact the absolute sacrifice of your fancies; she will limit herself to requiring you not to indulge them all. That graceful virtue, Moderation, is good and even necessary in every thing. We abuse our privileges, when we enjoy them in their full extent. If you walk as much as you can, you will be overcome with fatigue; so if you employ in superfluities all the overplus fortune has allotted you, you will want moderation, and lose that satisfaction and happiness you cannot taste without it. Therefore, for the sake of humanity, and to enhance your pleasures*, you ought not to spend all in baubles, but reserve half for charitable uses. – But how am I to know the exact sum which will remain? – There is nothing more easy. You receive two guineas the first day of the month; buy nothing but what is absolutely necessary; and unless such an occasion as that of this morning should offer, keep the rest of your money till the last day of the month; then that sum will be your overplus, divide it into two equal parts; the one for the poor, and the other for fancies. – But, mamma, you give all your overplus to the poor; I cannot recollect any one whim of yours. – In some years you will have fewer; at my age you will cease to have any. You have thrown aside the toys of infancy; you now amuse yourself with those adapted to youth. There will come a time, when you will care no more for china, monkeys, or little tables, than you now care for dolls. We grow tired of fine houses, beautiful gardens, jewels, magnificence, a throne; every thing in short disgusts us but the pleasure of doing good. – Yes, Kings, Queens, and Emperors have abdicated, in all ages; and Mons. de Lagaraye, for example, finds his felicity increase daily, in the manner of life which he has adopted. Doubtless this is the case; for it is so delightful to dispense happiness, that the man who would resolve to be charitable for six months, would continue so to the end of his life. – Although I am but a child I feel that – Oh, mamma, from this hour I will give all my overplus to the poor. – No, you are not yet worthy; limit yourself to what I have said. – On the contrary, I desire you for some years to amuse yourself in making a collection of all the pretty baubles which tempt you, that you may the sooner known how easily they disgust us. – Most assuredly, I, for instance, shall never again buy a rose-wood box; I have taken such an aversion to theM— and the little tables of twenty-seven shillings value! – Twenty-seven shillings! – Oh that I had but such an overplus! I would send it to the poor woman![53]

When Adelaide retired that same night, she saw the charming little table she had cheapened at the cabinet-makers by her bedside. After having expressed her joy: This, said she, ought to satisfy all my fancies for three months: therefore

---

* Montaigne says, speaking of virtue: 'She is the mother and nurse of the pleasures of life; by making them just, she makes them certain and pure; by moderating, she keeps them in breath and appetite; by diminishing those she refuses us, she makes those she leaves us the more desirable.'[52]

during that time I shall not divide my overplus 'into two equal parts:' it will be all for the poor. You will judge, Madame, if such a resolution, the result of the first emotion, and which I am sure will be adhered to faithfully, is not a sufficient reward for all my care.

I do not mention the Chevalier de Valmont; for he told me yesterday he should write to you this morning. So I shall content myself with telling you, that he spends his days with us, that he does not appear tired, that I love him now, Madame, not for your sake, but very sincerely for his own.

LETTER XXVIII.

Madame de Germeuil to Madame de Valcy.

OH! my dear friend, what a dismal winter have I just passed! I own to you that the probability of my exile lasting another year distracts me. – To live sixty leagues from Paris, is it life? – Shut up in an old castle, with a mother-in-law who detests me, and who is as tiresome, as she is godly, deaf, cross, and quarrel-some; and to all this 'the torment of neighbours;' such shocking men! – Women so dressed! – Such behavior and fashions! – The least insupportable amongst them calls her husband *my friend* before all company. Judge then of the rest. Moreover, the fashionable amusements here are walking, fishing, reading, and playing at Loto.[54] You see how well this suits me, and how I must be diverted. I am so altered, so horridly thin – If they will force me to spend another winter here, I declare to you there are no extremities, into which I shall not be ready to run. – My debts in two years, it is true, amounted to forty thousand livres, but did I not bring Mons. de Germeuil fifty thousand livres a year; and has he not himself gamed away upwards of five hundred thousand? Does he think, he alone has the right to ruin himself? He has just treated me in a manner, which raises my resentment to the height. I thought proper to write, and inform him it was my desire to have my daughter taken out of the convent, and sent to me. He answered me bluntly, that I ought to give up that fancy; that *his daughter* would be much better educated in a convent, than with me: in a word, he flatly refused me. You know I am not naturally fond of children. Besides, a little girl of six years old could not be any great resource. Therefore this refusal affects me slightly in regard to the object. But you will allow, that the reason is very offensive. – It is plain from that, that I shall not only never have the disposal of my daughter, but I shall not be even permitted to preside over her education. I would lay any wager, at fifteen she will neither know how to come into a room, nor to dress herself gracefully, nor even to put a flower in her hair; for how is it possible for a man to bring up a young woman, and take the place of a mother?

Would you believe, my love, that it is above three months since I have heard of a 'certain person.' He is nevertheless in a great measure the cause of my slavery. Oh! if I could but have foreseen! – You prohibit recurring to the past – Of what then must I think? The present is insupportable; I durst not look forward; indeed I never could conceive the pleasures of futurity. It contains two ills, the bare idea of which chills me; old age and death – Particularly old age; what an horrid thing! – Only figure to yourself, what it is to be forty, and a grandmother! You see, my dear friend, what pleasing thoughts solitude inspires. I do assure you if it lasts, I shall die of a consumption. Adieu, my dear life: for heaven sake inform me, if levees are still fashionable, and if they wear sacks. If so, I shall beg you to send me two.

LETTER XXIX.

Madame de Valcy to Madame de Germeuil.

OH! my dear friend, how I pity you! I am sincerely affected by your sorrows! – But the idea that you may pass another winter sixty leagues from me, is insupportable. I stand in need of you every moment; and more than ever during these last three months, when I have experienced a succession of difficulties, which I feel myself no longer able to resist. Madame d' Almane is here: that is saying every thing. You will readily believe she dictates at least five or six sermons a day to my mother, which I am obliged to listen to; and all to engage me to adopt the manners and behaviour of Madame d' Ostalis. If they look on her as so perfect a pattern, why did not they educate me as they did her? – We are both 'just as they made us.' She is very prudent, very reasonable; I am very giddy, very trifling; she knows how to employ herself, to paint, and play on the harp; I know how to dance. We have profited alike, each of us, of the examples, attentions, and education we have received. Notwithstanding my detestation of lectures, I could submit to hear them from those who have a right to preach. – But I would have people just and consistent; I shall never be converted by any preacher, who does not possess these two qualifications. For example, my mother came into my apartment the other morning, and found on the table two volumes of plays, 'a little free,' which brought on some remonstrance of half an hour long, a most eloquent panegyric on decency, modesty, taste, and propriety, &c. &c. In short, this dissertation perhaps might not have been finished by this time, had I not suddenly interrupted it by saying, very plainly, 'these plays are truly very free, but I did not think there was any more harm in reading than in seeing them acted.' Now in order for you to feel all the smartness of this reply, you must know, that these very plays were acted some years since at Mons. Blesac's, and my mother attended every representation. I owe this information to Madame de Gerville, and cannot doubt its truth; for my mother took me in an instant: she blushed extremely, put herself in a passion, and quitted me in a fury. In fine, she will revenge herself on my sister; she will make her 'a prodigy.' In the mean time, she is the most insipid little creature you ever beheld. Apropos of prodigies and 'perfection:' we have, just arrived here, a young man, who fascinates every body; he is called the Chevalier de Valmont. Madame d' Almane patronises him extremely; and was he richer, I should think she intended him for her daughter. Finally, he is really very pleasing; but he has the most dismal grandfather, and the most tiresome imaginable: besides, he is a pedant, a man of learning, a devotee, a philosopher; in short, a man as unfit for the world, as he is vexatious to his grandson, whom he watches, harasses, and follows like a shadow. But to return to the Chevalier: they pretend that he is in love with me. I should be sorry if he was; for he interests me, and I would not inspire him with a sentiment of which my heart is no longer susceptible. – I will not lose again that sweet peace, I have at last found means to recover, after so much agitation. If we are really doomed once in our lives to be violently in love, my tribute is not yet paid; for you know how I deceived myself. Oh! was I to love truly, it would be without bounds; I feel it – But I will not love at all. I will fly from the slightest emotion of preference: I will seek you, confide to you my weakness, and you will make me conquer it – If there are any antidotes to love, friendship alone can administer them. Farewell, my dear creature. Oh! why are you not here? How dear may your absence perhaps cost me!

LETTER XXX.

Madame d' Almane to Madame de Valmont.

YES, Madame, the adventure of the poor woman has been followed up: we have learnt her history, and we know that she has told nothing but the truth. She has seven children; that she is in the utmost distress; that she was formerly a milliner; that the immense credit she gave many young ladies occasioned her to become a bankrupt; that she divested herself of every thing for the sake of her creditors, &c.

This recital of Miss Bridget's, on her return from the poor woman's, has sensibly affected Adelaide. But, said she, all those young people who bought on credit, finished by paying? Not at all, replied Miss Bridget; the major part are unable. – But how so? – A tradesman who sells on credit charges higher, that he may receive interest for his money; which is but just. A woman who buys in that manner has no right to cheapen, and commonly receives the goods without asking the price; which causes her, at the end of a year or two, having frequently no more than six or seven thousand livres a year allowed her, to have bills amounting to fifteen or twenty thousand; consequently she cannot pay them. – Does not the tradesman summon her? – Her husband is obliged to pay her bills, but he has them taxed; he obtains a long delay, and in all this time the unfortunate dealer, pressed by his own creditors, unable to gather in his debts, is quickly ruined. – It is nevertheless shocking for a woman to be the author of such a calamity! For instance, you know Madame de Germeuil? – Yes. – She is in Provence, and yet her husband is here, which appears very odd to me. The reason is, they have quarrelled, and on account of the enormous debts she has contracted; for she paid nobody. – But how is it possible to carry extravagance to such an excess? – When ladies want honesty and consideration, and foolishly accustom themselves to yield to all their fancies, they have the ridiculous ambition of outshining all other women by the elegance and expensiveness of their dress: this brings on great milliners bills. They are cheated and robbed, ruin and dishonour themselves, and barter the confidence of their husbands, the sweets of domestic felicity, and the approbation of the world, for some pieces of gold stuff, some feathers, flowers, gauzes, and ribbons. – Oh! gracious Heaven, what a frightful picture! How is it possible, that so frivolous a temptation should induce any one to engage in such misfortunes? For my part, the fear of contributing to a bankruptcy will preserve me for ever.

Thus the dangers attending bills, the necessity of learning to resist our fancies, and of being an œconomist, if one would be benevolent, are maxims indelibly engraven on the heart and understanding of Adelaide.

Mons. d' Aimeri has informed you, Madame, that the proposed alliance of Theodore and the little Constantia is known to all Madame de Limours' acquaintance. Notwithstanding all her resolutions to the contrary, she talks openly of it. Her manner of caressing Theodore, and her behaviour to him, would alone suffice to discover this secret, which she has promised me so faithfully to keep. I am most pained by her indiscretion in revealing it to her daughter, a child of eleven years. – Madame de Limours, ashamed of her weakness, tries in vain to deny it; but I saw it too easily, by the extraordinary affection Constantia already betrays for Theodore. She blushes the moment he appears; never talks to him but in a low, and almost a trembling voice; if he leaves her or is absent, she is melancholy, thoughtful, and distracted. Thus it is, that her young heart feels the pains of a dangerous passion, the very name of which she ought to be ignorant of! Had not an imprudent confidence set her up, and inflamed her imagination, she would now enjoy that amiable and soft tranquillity suitable to her age, and she would see Theodore without observing him more than any other person. Alas! who can tell to what a depth of misery this imprudence of her mother may lead her! – Adieu, Madame! I shall have the pleasure of seeing you again in a month; but, unfortunately, it will be for a very short time; for Mons. d' Almane will positively have us at Toulon by the end of April.

LETTER XXXI.

Mons. de Lagaraye to Porphiry.

HOW! Porphiry, after your great success, are you astonished to have found enemies, and to have lost the friend whom you most confided in? This astonishment, however, does you honour – Go on, and never abandon those noble sentiments which occasion it. Oh! may increase of years, and the woeful experience of riper age, never rob you of that extreme surprise, which envy, breach of faith, injustice, and malice, cause in you! Be, if it must be so, the victim of hatred. What does it signify, provided, while you suffer by it, you yourself feel not the torments of that detestable passion! If ever you should come to have a bad opinion of mankind, throw away your pen, and lay aside your studies: to be able to instruct and inform mankind, you must love them too. Works, produced under the influence of that sublime sentiment, will have a just claim to immortality. Why should you hate the rivals that envy you, and the enemies that persecute you? – Because they are worthless? – Proud boy! Are you very sure that you are naturally more worthy than they? If they have been misled by education, if they have never been restrained by the persuasive voice of a faithful friend, tell me which they deserve most, your hatred or your compassion? – And *you!* do you imagine that you owe to nature only the good qualities you possess? – Ungrateful youth! have you already forgot the happy days of your infancy? – Ah, my son! call to mind the school of Lagaraye, and you will be modest and more indulgent. – Ten anonymous pamphleteers have taken your work to pieces, and endeavoured to ridicule your person. A set of *periodical writers* have amused and diverted themselves in burlesquing you,[55] though very aukwardly; like professed story – tellers, whose insipid, threadbare, and often-repeated stories provoke nobody's laughter but their own. – What! do you then pretend to universal empire? – In vain do you hope to please both wise men and fools. Make your option between them; for you will never persuade them to entertain the same opinion of your productions. – If you despise not all these petty attacks upon you, you will multiply them; your notice will give them importance, and you will thereby discover a weakness unworthy of your character.

Imitate M—, who published a useful work, and consequently a valuable one. Mons. de V— criticized it unjustly and without foundation, but at the same time with much wit and humour. A friend of the author going one morning to see him, overheard him laughing in his closet alone. Surprised at the novelty, he stopped at the door, and saw M— reading a pamphlet, and from time to time ready to burst with laughter, and crying 'What a comical rogue! how lively!' This pamphlet, which so diverted him, proved to be Mons. de V— 's satire. – He that can laugh heartily at a criticism upon his own works, must certainly be a man of no common turn of mind. You, it is true, are not likely to be put to this test; for there are few critics now-a-days who can write like V—.[56] Never answer any of them, except they attack the moral principles of your works: then, indeed, and then alone, you should defend yourself; but still it should be done with a clearness and dignity, void of irony and ill-humour. – Take care, however, my dear Porphiry, to distinguish partial satires from just criticisms, which never adopt the insulting stile of burlesque and banter. Dictated by reason, taste, and truth, they will afford you new lights, and teach you how to put a perfect and finishing hand to your works; and you should read them, not only without peevishness, but with gratitude. As a man is very apt to be partial in his own cause, send *me* all the criticisms they have made on your work; I will read them carefully, and tell you sincerely what I think of them. Were a friend of no other use, no author should be without one. – Happy the man, whose pride prevents him not from consulting his friends, and following the salutary advice which friendship alone has courage to give!

LETTER XXXII.

The Baroness to Madame de Valmont.

I LEAVE this place to-morrow, Madame, and shall stop at D— till the seventh; but shall certainly have the pleasure of embracing you in less than ten days. Madame de Limours is less affected at our parting than you can imagine, because she herself is leaving this place for four months. She follows Mons. de Limours, who is to command this year at —, and being about to make a journey of fourscore leagues from Paris, and for the first time, she is so taken up with the preparations for her own departure, that she has no time to think of mine. The Chevalier de Valmont came this afternoon to take his leave of me. Having pressed my hand and killed it, he quitted my apartment without being able to utter a word. He has an excellent heart; it will be a great pity should he do otherwise than well! You can have no conception how it would grieve me. – Adieu, Madame! I hope you will be so good as to give me a dinner the 14th or 15th.

LETTER XXXIII.

The same to the Viscountess.

Antibes, 1st May.

W E arrived at Antibes yesterday, my dear friend, and perhaps shall not leave it to-morrow; for the winds are quite contrary. Adelaide began yesterday to familiarise herself with precipices. We were seven hours and an half in performing the twelve leagues between Frejus and Antibes; for the roads are equally bad and dangerous. The mountain of *Estrel, among others, is really frightful on account of its precipices. I observed Adelaide, astonished and pale, often fix her eyes upon me, as if to ask me if there were any danger. She would have been glad had I discovered her fears, but durst not confess them to me. I affected not to take notice of her emotions, and even contrived, by some indirect conversation, without her discovering my intentions, to create a desire in her to conceal her feelings; for the care of hiding our fears occupies the mind, and diminishes the excess of them: so that by degrees Adelaide recovered herself, and at length became tolerably composed. Upon the whole she is enchanted with travelling. All she sees astonishes and charms her; and nothing is comparable to the pleasure she takes in writing her journal; but, if she does not acquire a little more precision, this same journal will amount to thirty or forty volumes. Antibes already takes up eight pages of it; it is true, four of them contain a catalogue of flowers and plants in this neighbourhood; for we took a long walk this morning, and Adelaide was astonished to see the fields full of flowers, rosemary, thyme, marjoram, and bushes of althea, myrtle, yellow jessamine, and honeysuckle, &c.

You ask how we travel. – We, that is to say, Mons. d' Almane, Miss Bridget, Dainville, my children, and myself, are all in my great coach, which you know; and we have a second carriage, in which are my women and Brunel. We always stop four hours a day, to dine and give our children various lessons. Adelaide writes and draws: in the mean time I tune her harp, after which she plays an hour. In the carriage, we contrive that our conversation may not be useless to them. The great art of instructing young folks, without their suspecting it, is by talking familiarly to them; those important means, so neglected in common educations,

---

* This mountain is four leagues long, and affords many admirable prospects.

are perhaps the most efficacious and most useful of all. How happens it, that we see so many people, who do not want parts, who yet know neither how to talk themselves, nor how to listen to others? It is because they are brought too early into the world. A young person, fourteen or fifteen years of age, hears nothing talked of, in the circle he frequents, but frivolous things, which leave no impressions at all upon his mind; or such only as raise false and dangerous ideas. If the conversation falls upon interesting and solid subjects, they are treated in a manner above the comprehension of a person of fourteen years old, who would be horridly tired by them, and from thence acquire a lasting habit of inattention; and every serious conversation would appear to him cold and insipid, and he would carefully avoid it; or, rather, his indolence and inattention would prevent his bearing a part in, or even comprehending it. Make a young person read books above his comprehension, and he will never love reading; and if he often listen to the discourses even of persons of understanding, who converse for their own pleasure, without a view to his improvement, he will never love conversation; and yet this is the method followed by the most intelligent mothers and the most able directors of youth!

To return to our employments in the carriage: we frequently tell stories, sometimes repeat verses, make reflections on poetry, and criticise the verses we have recited: we talk alternately English, Italian, French; then each of us has a book, and, at different intervals, we all read three or four hours a day, and mutually give an account of what each has read, which furnishes new matter for conversation.

Now, my dear friend, I have answered all your questions, let us talk of Madame de Valcy, and let us discuss the matter minutely. – *She is in despair*, you say, *on quitting Paris for four months, because she leaves her friends and her society.* – She is twenty years old, and goes with her husband, to follow her father and mother; and yet she weeps and is in despair on *quitting her friends and her society.* Alas! ought she to have any society but yours? – The whole mischief comes from Madame de Germeuil, from that *first* friend, against whom I declared myself so roundly from the very commencement of the connection. Madame de Valcy adopted *the friends and the society* of her intimate friends, and immediately ten or twelve strangers introduced themselves into your house, and robbed you of the predilection, the confidence, and the heart of your daughter! – I observed Madame de Valcy continually giving breakfasts to *her friends* without you, and going out alone to sup with them. Imagine to yourself, what passes at those dangerous assemblies! Be assured that they there contrive every method of estranging Madame de Valcy from her most important duties, those of loving her husband, and revering her mother. – *There* she is pleased, because she is *there* praised, approved, and admired. *There* they turn into ridicule every society but their own; and certainly they do not spare yours, composed in general of persons of knowledge, and of a mature age. This kind of liberty passes under the name of confidence and unreserved friendship; but from ridiculing their friends and acquaintance, people too easily pass on to turn into ridicule the most respectable, and sometimes even the most sacred things.

I think it better to apply to the understanding than to the heart of Madame de Valcy. – I advise you to observe her carefully, and, the first occasion of discontent she gives you, speak to her with the greatest firmness; and when you leave — , carry her with you for six months to your estate in Anjou, where, you know, Mons. de Limours has long wished to pass an autumn.

Besides, such a party may serve you to regain the affections of your husband; and certainly it will be serviceable to Madame de Valcy. – You will at first find her sorrowful and dejected; she will think herself unhappy; she will treat with disdain her country neighbours, who strive to please her; will look upon them as a species of creatures unworthy to judge of her merits, and set a just value on them; she will think it a pitiable case to be obliged to live with ill-dressed women, and men who have not the *ton* and manners of the court. But by degrees these ideas will grow weaker; she will become more tractable, more just, more obliging. At length she may find out that good-sense and good-nature are of all countries; that *forms*, which always vary in various places, are also always frivolous, and of no account in the eye of reason. Nothing is more irksome, for a continuance, than disdain to her who uses it; and in the end she will be tired of it. Pride, which causes, will also correct it; for one cannot be always out of humour, without being disagreeable, and that reflection may cure it. In short, Madame de Valcy, in that retreat, separated from *her friends*, and given up entirely to you, will have time to make some useful reflections: you will bring her back to Paris cured, in part at least, of her errors; she will be certainly less capricious, and less perverse; she will make fewer enemies; she will be more prudent and reserved; and, if she has any sense, she will see how much her happiness depends upon preserving your friendship, and regaining the affections of her husband. – This, my dear friend, is the method I should pursue, were I in your place. As soon as you are come to a resolution in this affair, pray acquaint me with it. Adieu! I will write to you from Nice. – Direct your letters to me at Genoa.

LETTER XXXIV.

The same to the same.

Nice.

WE travel slowly; for since my last letter we have advanced but *four leagues. We have all been horribly sick at sea, except Mons. d' Almane and Dainville. Adelaide and Theodore suffered cruelly; but they, as well as myself, were sick without complaining. Matrasses were provided in the felucca for the sick to lie on. In about half an hour, Mons. d' Almane observed to his son, that such delicacy was ridiculous in a man, and that he might vomit as well sitting as lying. Theodore immediately got up; and I did the same, saying, that courage was as *necessary* in a woman as a man, though perhaps less *useful:* but still it was a virtue, and we ought to blush to be one moment without it. At these words the dejected Adelaide crept towards me, and sat down by my side. – This piqued Theodore, who, resolving to surpass women in courage, began chatting in the most free and easy manner; and, though frequently interrupted by sickness, he resumed the conversation as though he had been in perfect health. Mons. d' Almane triumphed; his eyes sparkled with joy, and seemed to say to me, *this is beyond the effort of one of your sex.* I leaned towards Adelaide; and whispering in her ear, said to her, have you a mind to shew your father, that you have as much resolution as Theodore? Let us sing a duett. She pressed my hand, and in an instant we began a duett, which we sang, a little out of tune indeed, but with all our force, and with a chearful mein. Mons. d' Almane came and embraced his daughter: Preserve, my children, says he, this laudable desire of equalling each other in virtue; such an emulation cannot produce a rivalship between you; for endeavouring mutually after perfection, you will render yourselves more worthy of our affection, and of that love you have for each other. As Mons. d' Almane finished these words, Theodore came, and falling on his knees before me, took one of his sister's hands and one of mine, and joining them together, he kissed them with that ingenuous and tender air, which you know him possessed of, and which renders all his actions so obliging and so agreeable. – We have however resolved to go to Genoa by La Corniche,[57] that is to say, by land, in a sort of litters carried by men. This little journey will take us up four or five days. Mons. d' Almane says, it is very interesting and little known, and, in short, will quite harden the children against precipices and bad accommodations. We are to set out to-morrow morning at six o'clock. – Nice is a very pretty town, and its air so wholesome, that invalids come hither from far to breathe it, without using any other medi-

---

*   From Antibes to Nice.

cines. The mountains, that surround Nice, produce many plants and simples. We botanized yesterday and to-day. Adelaide has drawn and coloured many plants, and among others *the wild asparagus*; a shrub whose leaves are prickly, and of an emerald-green, its shape and delicacy are charming. She intends the little drawing for you, and I shall send it you from Genoa.

LETTER XXXV.

The Baron to Mons. d' Aimeri.

Nice.

Yes, Sir, the confidence you repose in me, does me honour at the same time that it obliges me. *Your* frankness ought to excite *mine*, and I shall answer you without reserve. – The match, which Madame d' Olcy proposes to you for the Chevalier de Valmont, is too advantageous, in point of fortune, to leave you in the least doubt of my sentiments on the subject: so that I must confess, you are not out in your conjectures: for it is very true, if the Chevalier de Valmont should answer the pains you take with him, and the hopes he gives, Madame d' Almane and I should prefer him to any other. But I must at the same time inform you, that we would have this project, which can be but very uncertain as yet, absolutely unknown to my daughter: so that you must promise me not to communicate the confession I now make to any one, no not to Madame de Valmont herself. I know your prudence and discretion, and I have not the lease doubt of your keeping this secret, which I look upon as a very important one. You know this union, however desirable it may be to us, depends entirely on the conduct of the Chevalier de Valmont. Adelaide is no more than twelve years and an half old; and Madame d' Almane had determined not to marry her, till she is eighteen. Between this time and that we shall be able to judge with certainty of the character and principles of the Chevalier de Valmont; and, if during that time he does nothing to forfeit the good opinion we now have of him, I am very certain that Madame d' Almane will give him her daughter with the greatest pleasure: Madame d' Almane, I say; for on her alone shall the destiny of Adelaide depend. This right she has a claim to from me, both from justice and affection. Her behaviour to me, and the pains she has taken with her children, deserve this proof of my acknowledgment and esteem. Besides, can I better consult my daughter's happiness, than by leaving the disposal of her to so affectionate and intelligent a mother! – Consider, Sir, whether such a conditional engagement ought to make you decline the proposal of Madame d' Olcy. – Mademoiselle de V— , it is true, is not a person of quality; but she is a greater fortune than

Adelaide will ever be. Do not refuse her, therefore, till you have well considered the matter; and pray take your time to answer this letter. I feel, as well as you, all the uneasiness the two approaching years must cause in you, on account of the Chevalier de Valmont. They will decide, perhaps absolutely, what he will be for the residue of his life. You must not judge by the last winter, what he will be the next. He then was but eighteen years old, and he thought it nothing extraordinary to be still in a state of dependence. He was but just entering the world; and his inexperience and timidity made him every instant feel the want of a mentor and a guide. He was in love too with a woman as virtuous as she was charming; which made him insensible to all the arts which coquetry employed to seduce him. But next winter he will be a year older; he will know more of the world; he will see all the young men of his own age become their own masters; he will be cured of his passion for Madame d' Ostalis; for love without hope cannot long subsist. To how many dangers will he then be exposed? – If you abandon him, he will yield to them; if you follow him without his consent, you will not preserve him. It is *he* that must retain *you*, must with for you, and not be able to do without you: but this is not to be expected, except in a case where two persons have an unbounded confidence in each other, which is become habitual from their having been ever inseparable. But you have not had the care of the Chevalier de Valmont from his infancy. And since he came to years of discretion, you have been separated for many months. You have not accustomed him to think, that, except on extraordinary occasions, you were born to be ever together. It will be no wonder, therefore, how good soever his natural dispositions may be, if he should long for independance. It is what you must expect; he will certainly slip thro' your hands: but, if his heart be good, he will return and seek you; you will easily regain his confidence, and at least you will preserve him from those grosser errors, which repentance can neither repair nor expiate. We must overlook some failings, provided he keep up a regard to decency and morality, a sensibility of mind, and good principles. – You ask me, how you shall secure him from the love of *play*. He has sense, knowledge, and education; idleness therefore, and want of employment, will not drive him to commit follies; and this is saying a good deal: but still opportunity and example are always to be dreaded. – I dare not advise you to make use of the means I should employ with *my* son, to snatch him from this danger; because it may be attended with the greatest inconveniencies, if your pupil has not a command over himself, and if you are not sure, that he is incapable of breaking a reasonable resolution, when he has once seriously made it. For my part, when Theodore goes into the world, I shall require his word of honour never to play at games of hazard, and I am certain he never will. I should rely much less upon his discretion, if I required less of him; I mean, if I only requested a promise of him never to play *deep*. An absolute sacrifice is easier to make than a partial one, which neither takes us out of the way of temptation, nor from the danger which opportunity may lay in our way: for it is easier to renounce things which give us pleasure, than to enjoy them moderately. But if you are not perfectly sure, that the Chevalier de Valmont has resolution enough to keep such a promise, do not exact it of him; leave him rather to learn wisdom from experience, and correct himself at his own expence, than expose him to forfeit his word. – When I have your answer to this letter, I will communicate to you another method, which you may employ without inconvenience; and which may serve as an excellent preservative against all the dangers that threaten the Chevalier de Valmont. – Adieu, dear Sir; permit me again to desire you would not answer me, till you have very maturely reflected on the proposal of Madame d' Olcy.

LETTER XXXVI.

The Viscountess to the Baroness.

WHILE you ramble up and down in search of great adventures, traverse the seas, enlarge your ideas, and acquire knowledge; whilst you lie on hard beds, eat tough chops, and onion soups; I dully vegetate in the midst of fifty persons who think of nothing, talk of nothing but common-place topics, knot, play at *loto*, and sit three hours at table. – You know how desirous I was to follow Mons. de Limours; I had formed a delicious idea of this excursion. – First of all, I was to act the governor's lady, and I imagined I should do it with a good grace; and the part did not displease me. Then I flattered myself that four months spent fourscore leagues from Paris, and from Madame de Gerville, might produce a great change in my situation, and in the sentiments of Mons. de Limours. Besides, carrying Madame de Valcy with me, I still hoped to regain that place in her heart, which I could not renounce without extreme regret: but these hopes, so agreeable, are absolutely vanished. I was very happy the first fortnight I passed here. I had the greatest desire to please and be popular. All the officers of the garrison, all the gentlemen of the neighbourhood, and all the ladies of the place, vied with each other who should most praise *my grace, my politeness*, and *my evenness of temper*; and even Mons. de Limours himself deigned frequently to commend me for the manner in which I did the honours of his house. I was in this situation, when one unlucky morning comes Madame de Gerville from Paris, under pretence of visiting an aunt of hers, who has been settled here these twenty years, and to whom she has not perhaps written four letters during the whole time. Her sudden appearance disconcerted me the more, as I understood at the same time, she intended not to return to Paris for two months. – She comes regularly to dine with me every day; gives balls, and fetes, and is the delight of the town. – Mons. de Limours makes no secret of his attachment to her; and Madame de Valcy herself professes the most tender friendship for her. All this increase of intimacy arises from her having persuaded him, that, he owes his government to her solicitations; and therefore it is but just he should pay, in estèem and tenderness, what he has obtained by her rare talents at intrigue. – You may well imagine, that all this has hurt my *evenness of temper, my grace*, and even *my politeness*. – At first I was out of humour; afterwards I had the ambition of forming a party against her, and began to succeed; for a reasonable number of persons preferred my house and society to that of Madame de Gerville: but all on a sudden I became tired of my party, and did what I could to get rid of them. At present I am quite abandoned; I see no company except at meals, and I pass the rest of the day with my little Constantia, my only resource, and my sole consolation. – After having undergone much vexation, chagrin, and ill humour, I find myself, at last, in a situation of mind tolerably easy. I have taken my resolution like a philosopher. – A perfect indifference has restored my repose, and even a part of my gaiety. – I am charmed with myself; my resignation, and my sweetness of temper. – I am much to be pitied, and yet I am calm and reasonable! – Trouble is good, at least it is so for me. It discomposes me at first, but afterwards it cures me: for I can neither hate nor despond for a long time together. – Ah! certainly, were I capable of hating any one, I should hate, not Madame de Gerville, I should not do her that honour, – but Mons. de Limours. – Let us talk no more of it; were I to dwell on that idea, vexation might again take hold of me. – I am mortally tired of this place, I confess, and long to return to Paris, and most certainly I shall not very soon take a fancy to *ramble* again. Adieu, my dear friend; write to me; tell me minutely every thing that is interesting to you; speak of your amiable children, the places you pass thro', the people you see: think of me, and continue to love me. Alas! your friendship is become so necessary to me! – Believe me, I am really more unhappy than I appear, or than you can imagine me to be. My heart, at bottom, is much smitten and much afflicted. Adieu; I enclose a letter from my brother to the Baron, and, according to the direction in your journal, I address this packet to Nice: acquaint me exactly with your route.

LETTER XXXVII.

Count de Roseville to the Baron.

YES, my dear Baron, my young Prince has still the same prepossession in favour of Count Stralzi, which I mentioned to you: and since the departure of the Chevalier de Valmont, that attachment seems to be augmented. The Count was ill; the Prince testified great uneasiness at it, and sent ten times a day to enquire after his health. One evening, as he talked to me of him in a very affectionate manner: I did not think, says I, you loved him to that excess. – He is amiable; I believe him to be strongly attached to me, and it is very natural that I should have a friendship for him. – And what proof has he given you of his attachment? – He visits me often, and never flatters me. – Are you very sure of that? – Oh! very sure. – He has sense, and he knows you do not want it, he knows likewise that you are well informed and instructed. He will not therefore flatter you openly: but he has a certain manner of listening to you, and such a smile of approbation, that *I* should distrust were I in your place. I should distrust likewise those general encomiums he bestows on all those qualities, upon which you value yourself. – Must a Prince then live in a perpetual state of diffidence? – He should guard himself against deceit; because a whole nation will be the victim of his error. He ought not, therefore, to take any man into his friendship and confidence, till he is perfectly acquainted with his character. – I have a good opinion of Count Stralzi, and I have an inclination for him; yet, if I had any secrets, I would not trust him with them, nor repose any confidence in him, till time and circumstances had informed me whether he were really worthy of it. – But why should you expect *that* from time and chance, which you might yourself discover more certainly? – How so? – I will furnish you with the means if you desire it, and will in a few months acquaint you with the particulars.

I have long since given the Prince to understand, of what importance it is to him to acquire an exact knowledge of the general state of the kingdom, of the particular provinces, and even of the persons of merit they contain: and I have advised him to send young Sultzback secretly thro' all the provinces, with orders to make the most minute observations upon the state of them. He will set out in a week, will travel under a feigned name, and in taking his public leave of the Prince, will give out that he is going to pass six months in France. After his return, I shall engage the Prince to propose the same tour to Count Stralzi, who will certainly accept the commission the more readily, as he will be ignorant of the Baron de Sultzback's having been already charged with the same. You may well imagine, that on the Count's return we shall compare his memoirs with those of the Baron, and we shall certainly find but little conformity between the relations of the two travellers. Then, in order to know which has made the best observations, and told the truth with most exactness, the Prince and I will make the same tour; and he will see, with his own eyes, to which of the two he ought to give his esteem and confidence. I have spared no pains, as you may easily believe, my dear Baron, to inspire into my pupil 'an aversion for taxes.' I began with exciting his compassion for the poor; and having endued him with humanity and pity, I now furnish him with information, without which those precious virtues can neither contribute to his own glory, nor to his people's happiness. The present circumstances of the state have obliged the minister to raise a new tax; but such a one as by no means falls upon the common people. However, the very word *tax* made an ill impression upon the Prince, and he told me so; but I easily convinced him that the minister had not, on this occasion, belied his usual sagacity and moderation. In short, added I, there are cases in which the best of Princes is obliged to levy new duties, and then nothing can be more equitable, than that he should lay them on the rich; for it is better to take a small portion of the superfluities of the few, than a part of the necessaries of life from the wretched multitude. – Nevertheless one sometimes sees the latter method preferred to the former. – Oh, Heavens! – for what reason? – Because the complaints of the rich make a great noise in the world, and the groans of the poor are not heard. – And how can a Prince prevail upon himself to deprive his subjects of their subsistence? – His ignorance alone is the cause of this great evil. He is told, that the tax proposed will not only *not* take from the labourer and artisan, what is necessary for his subsistence, but will still leave him at his ease. He believes it, and is deceived. – A young Prince ought then to know exactly how far his people may be taxed without ruining and rendering them miserable; and this is what I burn with impatience this moment to learn. – I can teach you nothing more truly useful. To acquire this knowledge you must enter into many small and very minute details; but the motives which animate you, will make them all interesting. Two days after this conversation, as we were talking on the same subject, the Prince suddenly casting his eyes on the clock, cried out, 'It is eleven o'clock; I am this moment fifteen years of age; embrace me, and remember your promise? – What do you mean? – You always told me, when I was fifteen, if you were pleased with my conduct, you would give me the book I have so long desired. Are you satisfied with me? – Yes, very much so. – Well then give me *Telemachus*. – *Telemachus!* What already! – If you would wait another year, you would do me a pleasure. – A year! Oh Heavens! – Come, do not vex yourself; to-morrow, when you rise, you shall have *Telemachus*. The next day the Prince rose before seven o'clock: I entered his apartment with *Telemachus* under my arm; and approaching him— Here, Sir, says I to him, this is the immortal book, in which you will find all your duties traced by a man, who, tho' living in a court, dared to speak the truth, and feared not to unmask the deepest artifices of intrigue and flattery. If you read this work, as affecting as it is sublime, without being moved, without being melted at every page, ah! return it to me, do not proceed, you are not yet worthy to read it. – Ah! replied the Prince, give it me; if sensibility alone is wanting to make me set a just value upon it, what do you fear? Can an heart of your forming be ignorant of its real worth? – At these words, as you may very well imagine, my dear Baron, I gave him up the *Telemachus*, which was received with as much joy as it had been desired with *eagerness*.

I expect with impatience the accounts you have promised me of your voyage. Adieu, my dear Baron; do not forget the little journal of La Corniche; for I am quite unacquainted with that part of Italy.

LETTER XXXVIII.

The Baroness to the Viscountess.

W E left Nice this morning at five, Adelaide, one of my women, and myself, in chairs carried by men. Mons. d' Almane, Dainville, my son, and Brunel, upon mules. Miss Bridget prefers going by sea to Genoa in the felucca, with the rest of my family. – Leaving Nice, you pass the old castle of Montalban, taken by the French in 1744.[58] Two leagues from Nice, Dainville desired me to stop at the tower of Eze,[59] whose situation is admirable, and commands the sea. He, Adelaide, and Theodore, have taken a view of it: during which time Mons. d' Almane and I read, and talked alternately, and in about an hour we resumed our march. – This road is very properly named La Corniche: it is like a real Cornish, and in many places so narrow that one person can scarce pass. On one side, enormous rocks form a sort of wall, which seems to reach the skies; and on the other are precipices five hundred feet high; at the bottom of which the sea, against the rocks, makes a melancholy and terrifying noise. At every pass that was really dangerous, Mons. d' Almane made us alight, and handed us over. From Monaco to Manton we breathed a little, for the road is very good. – This last town is agreeably situated on the banks of the sea, and affords a quantity of citron and orange-trees, which perfume the air. After leaving Manton, the road again becomes terrible. We begin, however, to accustom ourselves to it, and the view of a number of beautiful cascades, formed by nature, charmed Adelaide in such a manner as almost to make her forget the precipices. When we arrived at Bourdequierre, a little town; where we found some superb palm-trees dispersed among very picturesque ruins, we were tempted to stop and make a drawing of the most beautiful point of view we had yet met with. At seven o'clock, night coming on, forced us to stop and sleep here, only twelve leagues from Nice. It is called Hospitaletta; but is a most unhospitable place: for the poor people, with whom we now are, being unaccustomed to *lodge* any one, have neither beds nor supper for us. Adelaide and her brother were famished with hunger; and Brunel, having with some difficulty procured a few eggs and some rank butter, made an omelette of it, and brought it, with an air of triumph, up into the garret, where I have been writing ever since our arrival. The flavour of the omelette, which was smelt at a good distance, filled Adelaide and Theodore with transport: but the sight of it soon changed their joy into sorrow; not because it was very black and burnt: hunger is not delicate, and appetite is blind; but because if consisted of five of or six eggs only. I observed their uneasiness; and tho' I had likewise a mind to the omelette, I said I should eat no supper. Mons. d' Almane said the same, and for the same reason. Adelaide and Theodore immediately fell upon the omelette, and ate it with an eagerness that caused in me one of the most singular sensations I ever felt in my life. I beheld my children in a garret, lighted only by a pitiful lamp, eating as if they were famished; and I said to myself, How many unhappy mothers are there in the world, who this very moment suffer that horrid fate, of which the idea alone makes me tremble. – And who see their wretched children partake of a slender repast, insufficient for their subsistence. – Such calamities exist, and unfeeling mortals are regardless of them!' – These reflections filled my soul with inexpressible anguish: fixing my eyes on Adelaide and Theodore, I felt a tenderness and compassion that rent my very heart; my tears flowed, and I perceived it not: so absorbed was I in that afflicting reverie. At length Adelaide, turning that way, observed me, trembled, and flew to me; Theodore did the same, and I folded them both in my arms. Never did I feel more, than at that instant, how dear they are to me. I would have answered their questions, but could not. My tears redoubled; they likewise wept both of them. Mons. d' Almane, confounded at the scene, in vain asked an explanation of it. It was more than a quarter of an hour before I could satisfy him. – After a conversation which carried us on to nine o'clock, Mons. d' Almane, with his son and Dainville, retired to a chamber next to ours. They then brought straw, and made up three beds for Adelaide, Mademoiselle Victoire, and myself. We spread sheets upon the straw; and Adelaide laid herself down as gaily, and slept as soundly, as if she had been in the best bed in the world. While she sleeps, I am writing this journal. It is now eleven o'clock, and time I should repose myself likewise.

Continuation of the Journal of the Baroness.

St. Maurice.

THIS day has been very fatiguing, tho' we have advanced no more than five leagues and an half; but we found the roads so bad, that we have performed almost the whole journey on foot, continually coasting the sea, as yesterday, sometimes on the top of a precipice, and sometimes in a narrow pass at the foot of the rocks by the sea shore, and upon sharp pointed flints; the whole country indeed is barren and frightful. Our porters are the vilest fellows in the world; they understand neither French nor Italian; they talk a jargon unintelligible to every body but themselves; they get drunk, swear and quarrel perpetually. It is difficult for those they carry, not to interest themselves in their disputes; when they see them, all on a sudden, tremble with anger, agitate themselves, totter, and carry the chair with only one hand, that they may be at liberty to gesticulate and menace with the other*. These chairs are not at all like *sedans.* They are narrow and long; the seat has a kind of cradle over it covered with oil-cloth, to keep off the rain; and ones legs are extended forward, so that one cannot bend them; and as I am tall, my feet reach beyond the chair. We are tolerably lodged at St. Maurice, a small seaport; and we shall sleep to-morrow at Pietra.

Continuation of the Journal.

Albenga, Tuesday.

AT length my journal becomes interesting; and surely, my dear friend, I can send you nothing from Venice and Rome, which will give you so much pleasure, as the relation I am about to make to you. But I will not anticipate; that in reading this journal you may share the surprize, which I myself felt on the occasion. – The road from St. Maurice to Albenga is full of very frightful passes: but it affords admirable prospects, and among others, that which is seen from the top of the mountain which commands the town of Languella. The descent of that mountain is very steep and very dangerous. We walked down it, and, one may even say, barefooted; for the rocks we had been climbing for three days, had so worn our shoes, that the soles were almost entirely gone; and as we had not foreseen that we should walk so much, we had not taken the precaution to provide ourselves with a proper supply. At ten o'clock in the morning we made our chairmen halt on the summit of a mountain, from whence we discovered the town of Albenga, in the midst of a delicious plain; which is a remarkable singularity on this coast, where all the other towns are situated upon rocks. We descended the mountain, and advanced into an immense and fertile plain, surrounded with rocks and majestic mountains, some of which were covered with ice. The barrenness of the rocks, and solemn aspect of the mountains, form a striking contrast with the smiling beauty and fertility of the plain. The meadows are enamelled with pansies and lillies; and the rose-laurel grows here without culture; all the fields are senced round with vines, formed into arches; and thro' these long,

---

*   The chairmen have shoulder-straps: but it is necessary likewise to hold the poles.

charming, and open arbours you discover the verdure, the flowers, and the fruits, which these light arcades enclose; every arch of which is ornamented with a festoon of the elegant and flexible branches, which wave to the gentlest gale. In this delicious abode the earth seems cultivated, not for use, but for pleasure only. Every object you meet is agreeable; and it is here, my dear friend, you may see real shepherdesses, instead of those country-dowdies, whose night-caps offend you so mightily. All the young girls wear their hair without caps, and place a bouquet of natural flowers on the left side of the head. They are, almost all, pretty, and particularly remarkable for the elegance of their shape*. Figure to yourself the transports of Adelaide and Theodore on seeing objects so charming and so new. They asked permission to ramble into the plain, and to walk under the arcades; and in an instant they had got an hundred yards distant. Theodore stopped to gather a bouquet; and his sister, pursuing her course, entered a small path, where I lost fight of her. I called to her two or three times, but she was too far off to hear me. I sent Dainville in search of her, who soon came back without her; but informed me he had found her, and that she would return presently. I redoubled my pace, and Dainville approaching me with a smile, said, we shall not leave Albenga without an adventure which will make a figure in our journal. But where is my daughter, cried I? Hard by, replied he, with a lady beautiful as the day. – As Dainville was speaking, Adelaide appeared; and running, soon rejoined us: but so fluttered and out of breath, and so transported with her *adventure*, that she stammered, and could only answer in monosyllables. When she had, at length, recovered herself, we sat down on the grass, and she informed us, that soon after she had lost sight of us, she perceived at a distance, in a kind of grove on the left hand of the path she was in, a woman sitting alone on the ground. Curiosity led her nearer, and she saw plainly a beautiful woman reading with a good deal of attention. She was dressed in a robe of white gauze, and had a sorrowful countenance; but a physiognomy full of sweetness and majesty. A young person, who seemed to be her woman, was sitting at a little distance from her. The *heroine* lifted up her eyes at the noise Adelaide had made, and seemed surprized to see her; she made her a profound curtsy, and stopt short, not daring to advance. The incognita fixed her eyes upon her, and smiled. Encouraged by this, Adelaide approached, and the stranger said in Italian, you are a charming creature; *but most certainly you do not understand me*. Adelaide's answering her in Italian, was matter of fresh surprise. She asked her some questions, embraced her tenderly several times; then rose, called her woman, and left her. Adelaide adds, that the unknown lady, tho' not in the *flower of youth*, is a perfect beauty; and Dainville said, tho' he had seen her only at a distance, her figure was remarkably

---

* This description is not exaggerated; it is literally time, and taken from the author's own journal written at Albenga.

striking. After this relation, Adelaide begged of me to sleep at Albenga, instead of going to Pietra, as we had designed, and Mons. d' Almane contented to it. – We are here settled in a tolerably pretty house; we have informed ourselves concerning the *incognita*; and from Adelaide's portrait of her, we are assured, that it can be nobody but the Dutchess of C— , a person as distinguished and as extraordinary for her virtues and her misfortunes, as for her birth and beauty. – She has been four years at Albenga, and lives retired in an house she had caused to be built in the most solitary part of the plain. She lives in the most recluse manner; and they add, her beneficence and piety render her the admiration of the whole country. As to her history, it is known but confusedly; and the particulars, which I have been able to collect, are so extraordinary and so improbable, that I shall not yet commit them to paper. You may easily believe that we are curious to know something more particularly of the Dutchess of C— . Adelaide desires it with more warmth than any of us. Not knowing how to prevail on her to receive us, we have at last followed the opinion of Mons. d' Almane, that Adelaide should write to her on the subject; and we hope for some success from the infantine grace and simplicity of her billet. It has been sent near an hour, and we have as yet no answer.

Good news and great joy! The answer is just arrived; the Dutchess will see us; she has asked us to supper. As she tells Adelaide she sups at seven o'clock, and it is now near six, we are this instant going.

Ah! Dainville had good reason to promise us a charming adventure! – We no longer know when we shall leave Albenga. We shall stay till we have been able to obtain a more perfect knowledge of the history of the most interesting person I ever saw. Judge yourself, from the particulars of our first visit, if our curiosity be not well founded, and whether it ought not to be very much raised. At a quarter after six we arrived at her house, which is finished with the most elegant simplicity. After passing through two antichambers and a pretty long gallery, we were shewn into a little cabinet. Adelaide, seeing the Dutchess, quitted me and ran to her.

The Dutchess embraced her two or three times. I approached, and desired Adelaide to *present me*; and Madame de C— received us very graciously. We sat down; and while Mons. d' Almane was giving her an account of our journey and answering her questions, I examined her with as much pleasure as astonishment. She is thirty-eight or forty years old, and is really a regular and striking beauty. Her eyes are black, and in size and shape would be much like yours, were they less languishing. Her shape is exactly proportioned; and though by habit she stoops her head a little, she has a most noble air; and when by chance she turns her head, or draws herself up, she appears truly majestic. She has nothing of the Italian vivacity; all her motions are slow; she speaks softly, and even expresses herself with some difficulty. It is soon perceived that she is very absent. All of a sudden she falls into a *reverie*, which has something in it melancholy and striking; and when she comes out of it, she looks with a stupid astonishment on all around her. Her physiognomy is at the same time sweet, interesting, and sorrowful: she has by habit acquired the air of a person who has suffered much; her manners are affectionate and insinuating; and, as much as one can judge from a two hours visit, her sensibility is excessive, her imagination lively, and she has a good share of sense. During supper she asked many questions about my daughter; said she had one likewise which was her greatest happiness, and that I should see her at Rome. When I testified my surprise at the distance which separated them, she replied, that her daughter came every year, and absent two or three months with her; after which she sighed, and changed the conversation. On getting up from supper, I observed that the house was rather illuminated than lighted; for all the apartments were filled with lustres, flambeaux, and girandoles. Ah! Madam, said the Dutchess, if you knew what reason I have to value light, and to hate obscurity and darkness! – As she spake these words, her eyes were filled with tears, and she fell into the most profound reverie. We left her about nine o'clock; and as I took my leave, she said it gave her pain to think I should depart to-morrow. To which I answered, if she would permit me to wait on her again, I would stay. She pressed my hand, and, embracing me, said, Albenga attracts but few travellers; and though within these four years several strangers have stopped here, I refused to see them; but I wish, Madame, it was in my power to fix you here: promise me, however, that you will dine with me to-morrow. – You may easily judge that I accepted the party with pleasure; and that I did not fail to be exact to the appointment. Oh! that I could obtain from her some particulars of her history! – It is most certain, I shall not leave Albenga without doing my utmost to gain that point.

Continuation of the Journal of the Baroness.

Albenga, Wednesday evening.

I HAVE it at last – I am possessed of this history, so desired, so interesting, so extraordinary! – This precious manuscript, written by the very hand of the Dutchess de C— ! I am trusted with it for four-and-twenty hours; and am permitted to translate and take a copy of it! – I have read it – and I shall not, without inexpressible regret, leave the heroine of such a history – This woman, as virtuous and interesting as she is unfortunate – Oh! what a destiny is hers! – But, to return to my journal – While Mons. d' Almane and Dainville are shut up translating the Dutchess's story, I will relate the transactions of the day which procured us so inestimable a present. – We waited on the Dutchess at eleven o'clock. She proposed a walk before dinner, and conducted us to a little seat, which afforded so delightful a prospect, that my children and Dainville were desirous of taking it. They presently made a slight sketch of it; and the Dutchess expressing a desire to see some of Adelaide's performances, I sent for her portfolio. She was surprised to find a child of twelve years and an half old able to speak several languages, and draw so well after nature. She sings too, says, I, and plays upon the harp. The harp was sent for, and, as Adelaide had a great desire to please, she succeeded; and really the Dutchess seemed to be charmed with her. – After dinner she proposed another tour, that is to say, just out of the house; for she can neither walk much at a time, nor fast. – We sat ourselves down on a green bank, and she made Adelaide again the subject of our conversation. She seems to me, said she, to have great sensibility. – Yes, replied I, very great. – Ah! Madame, rejoined the Dutchess, do your utmost to guard her tender heart from the deadly impression of love! May she never feel that fatal passion, which is capable of producing so many misfortunes and so many crimes! – She pronounced these words in a tone of voice, that made me shudder. She perceived it and taking me affectionately by the hand, I know not, says she, whether you have heard my story. – Ah! replied I with eagerness, how happy should I be to hear it from your *own* mouth! – From *my* mouth, cried she; ah, Madame! It is so dreadful, that it would be impossible for me to have resolution enough to relate, though I have had sufficient to write it. I was desirous of leaving to my daughters, still in the tenderest infancy, a relation which may one day be useful to them; a striking lesson, which may teach them two important truths: the first is, that the passions are capable of precipitating us into the deepest abyss of human miseries; and the second, that there are no evils so great which religion cannot enable us to bear. – Oh Heavens! interrupted I, is there them such a precious manuscript? and shall Adelaide never read it? – No, Madame, replied the Dutchess, – to such a mother as you I cannot refuse it. Stay here two days longer, and I will put it into your hands. – At these words I felt so lively an emotion of acknowledgement and joy, as was impossible for me to express, otherwise than by embracing her with a transport, that made her sensible of the very great value I set upon such a favour. – I do not offer it you, says she, as a mark of confidence, but as a proof of friendship. My story is known to every body: at Rome they will tell you all the particulars of it; but I alone can inform you of my own sentiments and reflections; and these no doubt will be the most interesting to you. – After this conversation we returned to the house. The Dutchess conducted me into her closet; and taking, from a small cabinet, two thick paper books, closely written, – Here, says she, take this manuscript, and if you think it worth copying, present it to the charming Adelaide in my name: I am sure she will not read it without some tears. May it prove a useful lesson to my young friend, and add, if possible, more strength to the good principles you have implanted in her tender mind!

In fine, at five o'clock I quitted the Dutchess, to go and read the treasure she had entrusted me with. I forbear to say what impression the perusal made upon me. You yourself shall judge. For whilst I have been writing to you, Mons. d' Almane and Dainville have translated more than half the story: they will finish it to-morrow; and then Brunel shall make two copies of it, one for Adelaide, and the other for you, which I will send with this journal, as soon as I come to Genoa.

Continuation of the Journal.

Albenga, Thursday.

W E supped last night with the Dutchess. With what heart-felt compassion did we meet so interesting a person! – She had desired us not to mention her adventures; but Adelaide could not refrain from melting into tears when she embraced her. And we were so taken up with looking on her, and thinking on her misfortunes, that she herself was obliged to find conversation the whole evening. This morning she made us promise to pass to-morrow with her; so that we shall not leave this place till Saturday afternoon. I have returned her manuscript, and Brunel this instant brings me the copy I design for you, which I shall place at the end of my journal.

The History of the Dutchess of C—, written by herself*.[60]

H OW shall I have courage to recal particulars of misfortunes, the mere remembrance of which has excited in me such dreadful agitations for so long a time! – How can I write this deplorable history! – O my daughters! you will read it; it will afford you useful and striking lessons – that idea will support my courage. – And thou, who wast made the arbiter of my fate by an unfortunate and sacred tye, whose ashes I am reluctantly going to disturb by relating thy passions and thy crimes, forgive me! – Thy enormities and my misfortunes are but too well known; if they were not, I should have learned how to respect thy memory, and impose on myself an eternal silence. If this writing renews the remembrance of them, at least I shall not dissemble the imprudence and the faults which plunged me into that depth of misery, and drew on me such cruel

---

* The foundation of this history is perfectly true. The nine years of confinement in a cavern, where the sun never penetrated, the pretended death of the Dutchess, the manner in which she lived and received nourishment, her deliverance; all these particulars are exactly true. The only invention in this history is love, and the characters of the lover and the friend. The author, in 17—, saw at Rome the Dutchess de C—, and every day dined with the father of that interesting person.[61]

punishments. – I was born at Rome, sole heiress of an immense fortune, and of one of the most illustrious families in Italy. I received an excellent education; brought up by the best of mothers, cherished by a tender father, and a family, of which I was the only hope; fortune and nature appeared united in my favour. – I attained my fifteenth year, without having experienced a single sorrow, without having been once ill, without having shed any tears but those of tenderness or joy. I loved to recall the past, I enjoyed with transport the present, and I only saw in the future as bright and happy a condition. I had had for a companion, in my infancy, a young lady, the daughter of a friend of my mother's. I contracted for her a violent friendship. She was ingenuous, had sensibility, but no experience: she could neither advise nor direct me; yet I had an unlimited confidence in her. I loved and respected my mother; but I did not look upon her as a friend, because she had permitted me to take another; she was even pleased at my forming so dangerous a connection. That imprudence cost me dear, and was the principal cause of all my misfortunes. My friend married the Marquis de Venuzi, whom she had been in love with for a year. I was in the secret, and my acting as confidante had but too much raised my imagination, and softened my heart. My friend, two days after the wedding, set out for the country. The Marquis took her to a delightful villa, thirty miles from Rome. My mother was of the party; I went with her. The Marchioness de Venuzi was three years older than me; she appeared equally prudent and sensible. Though she was only in her nineteenth year, my mother left us entirely at liberty to see each other alone at all times. One evening after supper the Marchioness proposed our taking a walk in the park. We went by ourselves: on entering a little wilderness, in a turn of the walk, we saw a young man sitting on a bank: on perceiving us, he arose: the great surprise he shewed caused in us the same emotion. We were very near him; the moon shone on his face; we were equally struck with his graceful figure and noble air. After a moment's silence, as he did not retire, the Marchioness asked him who he was; he answered her with as much respect as gallantry, but refused to tell his name, and immediately went away. Very much surprised at this adventure, we directly returned, and trusted the Marquis with it. He smiled, and left us to suppose the young man was not unknown to him. As I shewed a great desire to be further informed, all I can tell you, said he, is, that his birth is noble; he has long ardently wished to see you; if he will consent, to-morrow I will tell you his name. I renewed my questions the next day, and I only received unsatisfactory answers. At night, when my mother was gone to bed, I went down to my friend: we shut ourselves into her closet, and talked of last night's adventure, when, all at once, the door opened, and the Marquis came in, holding a dark lantern in one hand, and conducting with the other the same young man that I had so great a desire to know. I remained immoveable with surprise; the Marquis, approaching me, I present to you, said he, my prisoner, to whom I believe, continued he, laughing, since he has had the imprudence of determining to see you a second time, it will no longer be in my power to give liberty. At these word I blushed, and felt great confusion. In spite of my youth, I had some faint idea of the consequences of such an adventure. I was one moment tempted to go and find my mother, and own all to her; but curiosity restrained me, and I forgot my duty. The Marquis, assuming a more serious air, told us, he was going to trust us with an important secret. I know, added he, the discretion of you both; I am sure you will justify the confidence which you are able to excite. After this preamble, the Marquis made me promise an inviolable secresy. The young man then told us, he was called Count de Belmire; that his father, the Marquis de Belmire, was brother to the Duke de C—, one of the greatest families in Naples; that the latter, head of his house, having quarrelled with his brother, found means to ruin him at court, and persecuted him with such cruelty, that he forced him to leave his country and settle in France, where the Marquis de Belmire had an affair of honour four years afterwards, which obliged him to seek another retreat; that the Marquis de Venuzi, his intimate friend, then in France, just returning to Italy, determined him to come secretly to the neighborhood of Rome, by offering him a retreat at his country-house; that he had been concealed for three months in the house we were in; that the young Count, having heard often of me, could not resist the desire of being introduced to me, and, after the transient glimpse by moon-light, he had been more urgent with the Marquis to procure him this delightful interview, on which he set so high a value; and that he was to depart to-morrow with his father for Venice. After having listened to this recital, I got up, and, notwithstanding the entreaties of the Marquis, retired. I returned to my chamber, overwhelmed with sorrow. I dared not reflect on what had just passed; I was afraid to interrogate my heart, or examine my conduct; I could not conceive how I had been able, in the middle of the night, unknown to my mother, to listen to a young man, and a stranger, who had dared to talk to me of love. I saw clearly that I ought to have no confidence in the Marquis; even his wife was not in a situation to advise me; I shuddered at the danger of my situation; a prophetic horror seemed to tell me, I was going to lose my reputation irrevocably, my repose, in short, all the happiness I had enjoyed till then. – The Marchioness de Venuzi too soon regained her influence over me; she incessantly talked to me of the Count de Belmire. These dangerous conversations did not soothe my melancholy, though they perverted my understanding. We staid three months in the country, when we returned to Rome. Towards the end of the winter, there were many entertainments given; the Marquis gave a masqued ball; I went with my mother. At two in the morning, the Marchioness proposed my going into her room to change my dress. We went out of the hall, and in crossing a little gallery, almost dark, I observed a man following us: how great was my surprise, when the mask approaching me, and falling on his knees, made himself known to be the

Count de Belmire! Notwithstanding my astonishment; and the secret joy I felt at seeing him again, my first impulse was to endeavour to escape. He held my gown, begging me to grant him a moment's conversation: he conjured the Marchioness to beg me to hear him; she united her entreaties, and I had at last the weakness to consent. The Count told me his father's affair was happily settled; that he had been for six weeks at Naples; that he had again seen the Duke de C— his brother, to whom he was sincerely reconciled. 'My father,' continued he, 'sets out in a month for France; some interest concerning his fortune recals him; but he is absolutely determined to return again to his own country. And I, before I follow him in this last journey, determined to known my fate. I came secretly from Naples to learn if the tender vows I presume to make are entirely rejected! Speak, Madame! if you hate me, I shall have you for ever – If you despise me, I am determined: – I renounce Italy; I shall never be seen here again – Speak! You can restore me to my country, or banish me for ever.' As the Count pronounced these last words, I could not restrain my tears: that answer was but too well understood; the Count asked for no other. A thousand times he assured me of his eternal love. Certain of my affections, and of returning to Rome in six months in a condition to demand me in marriage, though his fortune was not so considerable as mine; all appeared to justify his hopes; and yet my heart could not anticipate. Two months after this interview, which deprived me of all the tranquillity of my life, the Duke de C— came to Rome. I saw him at an assembly[62] at the French ambassador's. When he was introduced to me, I felt an extraordinary sensation, and which perhaps proceeded only from the bad character the Marquis de Venuzi had given of him, who, in speaking to me of his proceedings with the Marquis de Belmire, had represented him as equally vindictive and dissembling. The Duke was about thirty-six years of age, perfectly handsome, yet in his eyes and eye-brows was marked an inauspicious gloom, which struck one much more at first than the noble symmetry of his figure. He had a look that was severe, piercing, and wild: when he wished to soften it, he made it ambiguous and deceitful. His manner was in general disdainful; and although he was not deficient in politeness in some respects, his stile of behaviour was as decisive as it was imperious. Proud of his birth, fortune, employments, and interest at court, and of his success with the women, he thought nothing was ever to resist his inclinations, or oppose his will. Passionate, violent, spoilt by pride and prosperity, he knew not how to conquer his passions, or suppress his resentments. Implacable, through weakness and vanity, he gloried in never forgiving. He hated with fury, and sacrificed all for the horrid pleasure he found in being revenged. Such was the Duke de C—. I felt an invincible aversion for him from the first moment I beheld him. Unfortunately for me, I inspired him with a very different impression. He got introduced at my mother's: a fortnight after, my father told me, the Duke had demanded me in marriage; and that I must prepare for the ceremony in a month. My father added, 'I have given my word without asking your consent; for I doubted not your accepting with pleasure the greatest match in Italy; a man who adores you, and whose person is so agreeable. I received this declaration (which appeared the sentence of my death) without being able to utter a word. My father loved me, but was absolute; therefore what could I say? could I have the comfort of complaining to my mother! with what face could I own my faults! or dare confess that I had disposed of my heart without her approbation! It was then I experienced the full force of the fatal imprudence of my conduct, and the greatest misfortune that could happen to a young woman, that of not having looked on her mother as a true friend and confidante. Not being able to speak or complain, burying in the bottom of my soul all my sorrows and misfortunes, I avoided the Marchioness de Venuzi, whose dangerous advice I dreaded. I thought obedience alone could expiate my faults. I submitted to my fate, and sacrificed my happiness to the respect due to the will of my parents. I married the Duke de C— , and set out almost directly with him for Naples. When we arrived in the city, and entered the palace where I was to spend my life, separated from my mother, from my friends, from my family, I suffered emotions of despair bitter beyond description. The Duke attributed my profound melancholy to my affection for my parents, endeavoured to soothe me by protestations of an affection, which it was not in my power to return. I appeared at court, and I soon found the Duke was excessively jealous. It gave me but little vexation; I should have preferred retirement; but the Duke's vanity retained me at court, notwithstanding my taste and his jealousy. I had been married seven months, when I heard the Marquis de Belmire had died in France; that he had in his will appointed the Duke guardian to his son, who was only eighteen years of age; and that the latter returning to Italy, was taken ill at Turin. A fortnight after, the Duke coming into my room, said, he had just heard from his nephew, whose health was re-established. He will return no more to Naples; he writes to you, to entreat you to solicit my permission for him to travel for two years. Here is his letter. At these words, the Duke gave me a letter, the seal broken. I took it trembling, and read aloud, with a faltering voice, what follows:

'Madame,
Although I have not the honour of being known to you, I have hopes that my miseries are sufficient to inspire you with some compassion! – I have lost the tenderest and best of fathers. – Grief and despair had almost brought me to the brink of the grave! – The unkind assiduities of cruel friends have recalled me to life! – But to what an existence am I restored. – I have lost all that could make it valuable. – Forgive me, Madame, for troubling you with a sorrow, to which you are a stranger; my heart overflows! – Oh! will you at least condescend to excuse, to pity me! – The last will of my father has made me dependant on my uncle;

'but I cannot obey his orders to return to Naples. – My father was born and lived there twenty years. – Every thing will recall the most cruel ideas! – No, I will never go! – I am sure, Madame, you will approve this delicacy; and that you will persuade my uncle to revoke an order, which I have not power to obey. Obtain for me, Madame, the permission of travelling – of flying – of banishing myself from Naples. – In a word, the liberty of carrying far from Italy the sorrows and misfortunes I shall retain to my last breath. I am with respect, &c.

The Count de Belmire.'

I can give you no idea of the dreadful uneasiness I felt in reading this letter. I was afraid it was impossible not to understand the double meaning of it – Besides, the Duke was of all men the most jealous and suspicious; but still ignorant that his nephew had been at Rome, convinced I never could have seen him, he had not the slightest notion of the truth. As for me, unable to keep those sentiments to myself which rent my heart, I wrote the next day to the Marchioness de Venuzi a letter, in which I had the audacity to complain of my fate, and lament the fatal passion I could not overcome. The Marchioness, in her answer, questioned me on the Duke's conduct. I answered her freely; and did not conceal from her, that every day I discovered in the Duke faults, vices, and a determined violence of temper, which too much justified the antipathy I had for him. It was thus by fresh imprudencies I dug a pit for my own destruction. About this time I enjoyed the happiness of seeing my father and mother again; I was near lying in; they came to Naples to be with me. I was brought to bed of a daughter. I asked, and obtained permission to suckle her. This tender employment, during the time it lasted, suspended my sorrows, and made me insensible of the Duke's ill treatment, who for a long time had ceased to restrain the impetuosity of his temper before me. The day after I had weaned my child, the Duke came to me, and said, we must immediately set out for an estate he had twelve leagues from Naples. My daughter was with me; I took her in my arms; and without uttering a word followed the Duke. We got into the carriage; I held my daughter on my lap; I caressed her; the Duke was silent; during the journey he appeared absorbed in thought; when we arrived at the castle, we crossed a draw-bridge; the rattling of the chains made me shudder; at this moment I looked at the Duke. What is the matter with you, said he? The ancient appearance of this castle seems to surprize you. What! do you think you are entering a prison! He uttered these words with a forced and malicious smile, and I observed his eyes sparkling with an inhuman joy, which shocked me. – Wishing to conceal my terror, I leant my head on my daughter's, and could not restrain my tears. My child feeling them trickle down her face, began to cry; her cries pierced the very bottom of my soul; I pressed her to my bosom with the tenderest affection, and my sobs redoubled. Thus I got out of the carriage. The Duke snatched my daughter out of my arms, and gave her to one of his attendants; and seizing one of my hands, he led, or rather dragged me towards the castle, made me go up a flight of steps, at the top of which was a long gallery. The evening came on; the gallery we crossed was very large and dark; the Duke walked extremely last, when stopping all at once; you tremble, said he; what occasions this fear? Are you not with a husband whom you love, and who ought to cherish you? – Oh, Heavens! cried I, what means that gloomy and disturbed look, that terrible voice – Come, come, replied he; we are going to finish the explanation. At these words, almost carrying me in his arms, for I could neither follow him or walk, he took me out of the gallery into a large bed-chamber. I flung myself into a chair, and gave a free vent to my tears. He went out, and soon returned, holding a light, which he set on a table opposite to me, and seated himself by it. I dared not look at him; I waited, trembling, with eyes cast down, scarce fetching my breath, sinking with terror, for his breaking silence – My memory recalled at once all my faults; I had a confused idea that the fatal secret of my heart had been discovered. That heart, filled with a criminal passion, beat with fear, and trembled before an irritated judge. – Oh! what courage innocence would have given me! – But I felt myself culpable, and I had not courage to support those horrid thoughts which my remorse occasioned me. At last the Duke spoke: Enough of enjoying the secret reproaches of your conscience – It is time to fill up the measure of your confusion. – Read those letters, that I have copied myself. – He then gave me a packet of papers; and seeing I hesitated about taking them, he took out one, and read aloud. From the first words I knew it was one of the letters I had written to the Marchioness de Venuzi, in which I spoke without disguise of the sentiments which filled my soul, and of my invincible aversion for the Duke. Oh! I am undone! cried I. – Perfidious woman, replied the Duke, could not I make you happy! – I chose you, I preferred you, I adored you; and you hate me, and deem yourself unhappy – I inspire you with *an invincible aversion!* – Ah! I will justify your dislike – You shall have just cause to hate me! – Betrayed, dishonoured by you, do you think I will suffer such outrages with impunity? – Stop, interrupted I, you may accuse and punish me without aspersing me. I am really culpable; but if I could not overcome an unhappy passion, at least your honour and mine are without stain. I have only to reproach myself, that friendship drew from me such an imprudent confession. Perjured woman, the Duke replied with fury, taking up one of the letters, listen to your condemnation. He then read the following sentence: 'That object that nothing can erase from my heart. Alas! he is as much to be pitied as I am! Does he not know, to what excess I love him! – Does he not know, to what excess I reproach myself for a confession, that renders me every day more culpable and miserable!' – I but too well recollected this sentence in one of my letters; I also remembered, I had not mentioned the name of the Count de Belmire in any of them. I had spoke of him in so indirect a manner, that it was impossible to fix the date of the passion I acknowledged: the

Duke, violently jealous of two men at the court of Naples, who had shewn evident marks of admiration as soon as I appeared, fixed upon one of those as the object of my love. That supposition rendered me truly criminal in his eyes; for, after the sentence he had just read, it seemed to prove I had confessed my sentiments since my marriage. It was (to justify myself,) necessary to declare, that when I gave him my hand, I had not a heart to give; but I was not ignorant of the despicable opinion he had of women, and the odious constructions he formed; after that knowledge, my daughter's interest silenced me. I did not leave Rome till six weeks after my marriage; the Duke was but too capable of conceiving injurious suspicions on the birth of my daughter, if he knew I loved before I saw him. – Besides, that confession would have led to the discovery of the whole truth. He would have recollected a thousand circumstances to confirm it; the letter I received from his nephew; my confusion in reading it; my blushes every time his name was mentioned; he might discover the connection, that the Marquis de Venuzi had with the Count de Belmire's father. In one word, removing all his suspicions, which he had fixed at Naples, was risking a secret, which it was impossible to betray without exposing the object of my affections to all the fury of his resentment, rendered more formidable as the Count de Belmire depended absolutely upon him: he was not nineteen; the Duke was his uncle and guardian. All these reflections at once presented themselves to my imagination, and plunged me in the greatest embarrassment. Not being able to justify myself, I dared not answer. The Duke construed my silence into a tacit avowal, which confirmed his dishonour and my shame. His passion then knew no bounds; he arose, and approaching me with a face enflamed, and his eyes sparkling with fury; then, said he, you have nothing to alledge in your defence? – Alas! answered I, are you in a condition to hear me? – I call Heaven to witness, I am innocent. – You innocent! interrupted he; dare you maintain that? Have you not written yourself, that your lover *knows to what excess he is beloved:* – and yet, replied I, shedding a torrent of tears, I am innocent; yes, I am. – Hypocritical monster! cried the Duke; tremble at the vengeance ready to overwhelm you. – At these words, pronounced in a menacing and terrible voice, I expected to hear the irrevocable sentence of my destruction. I threw myself on my knees; and lifting my hands to Heaven: O God, cried I! God, my sole resource, protect me! Rise, said the Duke, in a softer voice, sit down, and listen to me. I obeyed, with a timid and supplicating look. He was some moments without speaking. At last, fetching a deep sigh: you ought to know, said he, how greatly I am offended! – You, who accuse me of being furious and vindictive! You, ungrateful, to whom I have given every proof of love, you have reason now to dread the effects of so just a resentment. – Yet – it is possible for me to forgive you. – Your sincerity alone can mitigate my anger; remember that: henceforth the least disguise will be your ruin. – I can be satisfied with one victim. – But one I will have. – Name, without hesitation, the villain who seduced you from your duty, and made you break your vows. – No, interrupted I, no; I have neither broke my vows, nor been seduced from my duty. – I will, replied the Duke, raising his voice, I will know the name of your lover: I command you to tell me. At that instant, I felt all the horrors of my destiny: but with my danger I felt my resolution increase: preferring even death to the baseness he proposed, If you must have one victim; replied I, sacrifice that you have in your power. Let fall on me all the weight of your vengeance; for the name you demand, you shall never know from me. Astonished, confounded at my courage and resolution, the Duke remained immoveable for a moment; he could not find an expression to describe his rage and indignation. At last, eagerly exclaiming: Unhappy woman, said he, I shall never know it! – Ah! I see, that you have no idea, how far my rage will carry me; you do not yet know me! – I expect every thing; I am unfortunate enough to brave death. – Death! – Cease to flatter thyself; go, it is not death I design for thee – My hatred and my fury have been buried in the bottom of my soul for a year; that time I have been meditating the punishment of thy infidelity, and dost thou think that my vengeance can be satisfied in a moment! – No, thou shalt not die. – Indeed thy grave is prepared; but thou must descend into it alive, and there thou wilt not find that death thou desirest. – At these dreadful words I felt all my blood freeze in my veins; my eyes closed, and I entirely lost the use of my senses. When I recovered, I found myself in the arms of my women. I asked eagerly for her who was the most attached to me, the only one I had brought from Rome. They told me, she remained at Naples. I apprehended it was by the Duke's orders, who was afraid without doubt of a witness so attentive and watchful; that circumstance raised my terror to the utmost. I spent the night surrounded by my women, constrained by their presence, and dreading to be alone, not daring to complain before them, nor to send them away, suffering all the torments occasioned by remorse, fear, and the expectation of a dreadful catastrophe. About six in the morning I desired them to conduct me to my daughter's apartment. She was still asleep. I sent away her women. I sat down by her cradle. The sight of her, far from mitigating my sorrows, augmented them. Alas! dear child, said I, thou sleepest in peace; thou tastest the sweets of repose; thou canst neither feel nor partake the bitter sorrows of thy unhappy mother! – I see thee perhaps for the last time! – O receive my most tender blessings! – O God, pursued I, throwing myself on my knees, I resign myself to my horrid fate; but may my daughter be happy! – May she live in peace and innocence! – If they have the cruelty to take me from her, great God, protect her, be a mother to her! – At these words my sobs redoubled, and stopped my utterance. In that instant, the door suddenly opened, and the Duke appeared. I shuddered at the sight of him; my tears stopped. I arose; unable to support myself, I fell into the great chair. Well, said the Duke, has reflection made you more reasonable? Do you feel the consequence of opposing my will?

A deep sigh was all my answer. – That name I have demanded – are you still determined never to tell me? I lifted my eyes to Heaven; I persisted in my silence. – I will have a positive answer. – Will you, or will you not, tell the name? I cannot, answered I. – Ah! cried the Duke, thou passest thy own sentence! Look at that child, and take your leave of her for ever. – No, interrupted I, you cannot have the cruelty to separate me from it. – Oh! leave me my child, permit at least that I may sometimes see it, and I will support without murmuring all that your hatred can inflict. – Alas! is your heart really inaccessible to pity? – Ah! if it is, whatever destiny you have prepared for me, you will merit more compassion than I! – But I cannot believe it. – No, you will not deprive me of my child for ever! – That moment she awaked; the opened her eyes, and smiling on her father, lifted up her little hands, almost joined, towards him. Alas! said I, she seems to plead for me! Oh, my child! my dear child! why canst not thou speak? Thou wouldst soften thy father! – Then I would have taken her in my arms; but the Duke seized her: Leave her, said he, she is no longer yours. – Oh! cried I, take my life, or restore my child! – Must I, to appease you, fall at your feet? – Behold me. – In saying these words, I cast myself at his feet; I bathed them with my tears; I embraced his knees. – My pride felt no condescension, as I was begging for my child. – The barbarian appeared to enjoy my humility; he gazed on me for a moment; then pushing me away with fury, he made some steps towards the door. I followed him on my knees, crying, my child! my child! – The child, quite terrified, gave a plaintive cry, stretching out her arms to me. She seemed to take a mournful leave of me. – Alas! at the same moment I lost sight of her, the Duke burst out of the room, and left me in the height of despair. He returned a moment after, and compelled me to go to my apartment. Then composing his countenance, You think, said he, my heart unfeeling, and yet – He stopped, and cast down his eyes, those furious and inauspicious eyes, which might have discovered his horrid artifice. – I was in his power; I was ignorant of his dreadful intentions; I saw no interest he could have in dissimulation; I was only eighteen; I thought he must reproach himself for the excess of his cruelty; and that at least the first vengeance he had meditated would be softened. A ray of hope reanimated my heart: I again talked of my daughter; the Duke listened, with a gloomy air, but without shewing any anger: he even pretended to feel a tenderness for me, which he endeavoured to hide. He gave me to understand, that his love for me was the sole motive of his violent conduct: he finished by saying, if I took care of my health, I might see my daughter again. So dear a hope, made me forget all my sufferings. Seeing the Duke less cruel, I thought myself more culpable; I felt that he ought to hate me, and that after my letters he might think me really criminal. I excused his fury; I was deeply affected with the compassion I perceived he felt for me; and whilst the most sincere repentance caused my tears to flow, the cruel author of my misfortunes secretly applauded the success of his black artifices, and every thing was prepared for my destruction.

A violent fever, occasioned by my extreme sorrows, obliged me to go to bed. The Duke appeared then to feel the greatest uneasiness; he sent a courier to Naples for two physicians; he never quitted my bed-side; before my women he testified the greatest tenderness; said every thing to persuade me his love exceeded his resentment; and positively assured me, that as soon as I had lost my fever, I should see my daughter again. At this promise I forgot all he had made me suffer: I took one of his hands and pressed it between mine; I bathed with tears of gratitude that barbarous hand, that in a few hours would drag and throw me into the bottom of a horrible dungeon. The physicians assured him my illness was not dangerous; and desiring to return to Naples, they went in two days. The morning of their departure the Duke affected more anxiety on my illness; and although my fever was gone, he obliged me to keep my bed. As he made all my women watch me the three preceding days, they were overcome by fatigue; he sent them to rest themselves for the whole day; saying he would watch me, with one of his valets and an old woman, keeper of the castle. These two witnesses were not chosen without design. He gave them the preference to all the others, because he knew them both to be as credulous as they were ignorant. The curtains of my bed were drawn; I thought my women were still watching me: at noon I perceived that I had only in my chamber those two people, whom I have just mentioned. I expressed my surprize. The Duke approached my bed, saying I should not be the worse attended, and that he would not leave me. Ah! why, replied I with emotion? – I am no longer ill. – The only answer he gave me was, begging me not to speak; and endeavouring all he could to quiet me, he set down by the side of my bed. Without knowing why I felt uneasy, my eyes were filled with tears. The Duke appeared distressed, agitated; and I observed an extraordinary alteration in his countenance. About three in the afternoon, he desired me to give him my arm; I gave it trembling; he felt my pulse; and directly he went to the two attendants, told the valet-de-chambre aloud to run to the stables, and send an express to Naples for a physician; and the old woman to go and fetch the chaplain. After having given these orders, he added, with a despairing voice, *She is dying! She is dying!* – Conceive, if it be possible, the excess of my fright and surprize. – My first thought was to get up and fly; but I fell again on the bed without strength, with a beating heart which deprived me of breath, and a cold tremor which rendered me motionless. My two attendants, after having received each a commission, that at least would take them three quarters of an hour, went and left me alone with the Duke. Then he came to me, and giving me a cup; Take, said he, with a low voice, swallow this draught.

At these words my hair stood an end, a cold sweat ran down my face. I thought I was come to the last moments of my life; for I doubted not of his giving me poison. – Drink then, replied he. – Ah, answered I, what do you give me? – What you must take. – Give me then time to implore everlasting mercy. – What! do you dare to suspect me? Do you accuse me of a crime? – Alas! it is fate and my own imprudence I most accuse. – O my God! continued I, clasping my hands, pardon me, forgive my persecutor, comfort my father and mother, protect my child! After that short prayer, I felt all my coverage revive; I dared to hope that my resignation made me worthy to appear before God. I cast on the Duke a confident look: he was pale, trembling, and astonished; he stammered out some broken words, and with one hand lifting up my head, with the other he put the cup to my lips. Then, without resistance, I drank all the liquor he gave me, thinking I had received my death. I fell back on my pillow, having resigned my life to God. Some minutes after my eyes grew heavy, and closed; a total numbness entirely deprived me of speech and thought; I sunk into a lethargic slumber. In about half an hour the old woman and valet returned. The Duke, his hair in disorder, and his face bathed in tears, ran to meet them; and said, I had just expired. He brought them again into my chamber, in order, added he, to acquire a confirmation of his misfortune, or to assist me if I had still any remains of life. He approached my bed; having had the precaution to shut the curtains, and make my room extremely dark, he pretended to give me all imaginable assistance: afterwards he appeared to give himself up to the most violent despair. The chaplain arrived: he ordered him to read the prayers for the dead. During this time my women awaked, and all the servants came running. The Duke was on his knees at my bedside. My two attendants recounted to the whole house all they had done to endeavour to recall me to life. After this account, the Duke half opened for an instant my curtains: I was pale and motionless, and nobody doubted of my death. The Duke ordered all the people to go into the next room; he remained in mine, and kept the chaplain with him, an old man of eighty. He made him continue the prayers for the dead till midnight. Then he sent all his people to rest. He declared he would not have me buried till the next evening; and that he should pass the remainder of the night there, not being able to tear himself from me. He shut all the doors of my apartment. He placed the Chaplain and my two attendants in an anti-chamber, separated from mine by three large rooms. He told them he should not leave me till seven o'clock in the morning; that he would remain alone with me, that nothing might disturb either his sorrows or his prayers. All the house, exceedingly fatigued with watching, readily availed themselves of the permission to go to their repose. All the people were in a profound sleep at four o'clock in the morning, when, by degrees, coming out of my lethargy, I awoke. Opening my eyes, and recovering the use of my senses, I perceived the Duke standing by my bed-side. The sight of him startled me, although I had no remembrance of what had happened to me. Then, looking at him stedfastly, I had a confused recollection that he was irritated against me; I felt an emotion of fear; I turned away my head; endeavouring to recover myself, and recall past ideas, a thousand vague and fantastic forms arose in my imagination; I fell into a stupor, which was followed by a kind of fainting. The Duke made me smell at some sal-volatile, and swallow some drops, which entirely revived me. I raised myself up; I looked around me with astonishment. My ideas growing by degrees less confused, I recollected that I had thought I was taking poison; and I almost doubted my existence. – O what miracle has saved my life, cried I, at last! You have only felt a vain terror, said the Duke; be calm, banish those injurious fears. I dared not answer; I half opened my curtains; I looked round the room; and seeing I was alone with the Duke, my fears increased, as I had entirely recovered my senses. Why then do you alone watch me? – You shall know; get up directly. At these words he gave me a gown; he helped me to put it on; and supporting me in his arms, he conducted, or rather carried me into a great chair. As he saw me weak and trembling, he gave me more of the draught that I had taken before. And after a moment's silence; I shall now hide nothing from you. – The draught you took yesterday was a sleeping potion. – And wherefore? – Listen to me without interruption. You have betrayed and dishonoured me. I have offered you forgiveness, you have refused it. Convicted of infidelity, you still nourish a criminal passion at the bottom of your heart. Neither my displeasure nor menaces could make you declare the name of your lover. You perhaps thought that my consideration for your family would prevent my taking your child from you, and depriving you of liberty. You think, without doubt (for your hatred will judge me capable of any crime) that the only means I had for revenge, was secretly to attempt your life; and that invincible aversion that you have for me, determined you to die! – But know, that you shall live, and be for ever separated from your parents, your friends, servants, and the whole world! – O Heavens! cried I, and do you think, barbarous man, a tender father and the best of mothers will not demand me of you? – They will receive to-morrow, replied the Duke, the false account of your death. – Great God! – And how could you? – I have already announced your death in the castle. During your profound sleep, all my people came to see you. – Alas! interrupted I, bursting into tears, I no longer live but for you? – Ah! I see all the horrors of my fate! – You do not yet know all, said the Duke; learn that I have in this castle vast subterraneous places, unknown to all the world, and where the light never penetrates. – O God! it is then all over; I am lost without redemption! – No, replied the Duke, your fate is still in your own hands; I can go in a moment, and wake my people, and declare to them you were only in a lethargy. I have not sent my letter to your father. I can forgive, and restore you again to the world. – I only exact from you one word, one single word. – I have told you, I must have a victim. Name your lover, and I will grant you life; I will restore you to your rank and to the world! – What do you propose to me? To deliver up to your resentment an object, I repeat to you, has never injured you. Ah! I should be unworthy to live, if I had the baseness to consent to it! – Consider it well, said the Duke, darting at me a furious look; another refusal, and I drag you to that dark abode from whence nothing can release you. To-morrow your father and mother will mourn your death, or rejoice at your recovery. To-morrow you will again see your daughter, and the sun; or for ever be deprived of light, groaning at the bottom of a horrible dungeon: in short, to-morrow we shall see you in this castle enjoying perfect health, or be attending your funeral. Reflect; this moment passed, no hope of pardon remains. Your repentance may implore in vain; I shall have no longer the possibility of granting it.

At this urgent and dreadful speech I rose up dismayed. I turned my eyes fearfully towards the door, and, giving a lamentable shriek, Ah! why am I then abandoned by the whole world? My daughter! I shall live, and I shall never see thee more! My father! my mother! to-morrow you will weep my death! My child! oh let me once more see my child! – Say one word, replied the Duke, and in a quarter of an hour your child shall be in your arms. At these words I felt my heart torn to pieces. I remained silent for a moment; I thought the Count de Belmire was absent; that he was not to return for a year; during that time, I could easily inform him; besides, an ingenuous confession would make known my innocence. But the cruelty of my persecutor came all at once to my remembrance, and I quickly rejected this ill-grounded temptation. Who could assure me that such a confession would restore to me my daughter or my liberty? Ought I not to think, on the contrary, that the Duke, certain of my hatred, would not renounce the vengeance he had meditated, or content himself with softening the inhuman rigour? And in that doubt, could I be tempted to give up to his fury the object of my love? All these considerations presented themselves to my imagination with the greatest rapidity. The Duke thought I wavered. He urged me again; adding, that the day would soon appear, it is time you determine: I go and awake my people, and tell them that you live; or go and conduct you to your tomb. Speak – Will you name the author of your misfortunes and mine? At that question, I lifted up my eyes to Heaven: recalling all my strength, I replied, I cannot! – What do you say, unhappy woman! interrupted the Duke. – No, give up that hope; I will never tell you. – Perfidious! cried the Duke, then thou preferrest thy lover to thy child, liberty, and life! – To the whole world! – Henceforth tremble! The moment of vengeance is now come! – As he finished these words, he endeavoured to seize me by the arms. Penetrated with fear and horror, I escaped. I ran to the other end of the room; and casting my arms round one of the bed-posts, I kept fast hold. In this agitation my night-cap came off, and my hair fell on my shoulders. The Duke came to me; he stopped; he appeared surprised, struck, observing me a moment in silence. Then pulling me from the bed-post, he carried me over against a glass. Unfortunate woman! contemplate for the last time that beauty, which is going to be hid for ever in perpetual darkness! Lift up those eyes; look at thyself. Do not be more cruel than I am. Think of thy youth, thy charms, compassionate thy own fate: thou canst still change it. – I could not then forbear casting a timorous and languishing look on the glass. I presently shut my eyes, and I felt some tears steal from my eye-lids. – Well, replied the Duke, are you still resolute? – Oh! have you not offered me the sight of my daughter in vain! – Scarce had I uttered these words when the Duke, transported with rage, caught me in his arms, and carried me out of the room. I made no resistance; the violence of my fright made me dumb and motionless. After having crossed two or three rooms, he made me go down a little private stair-case and I found myself in a large court: at the end of it there was a door, which the Duke opened; we went out, and I saw we were in a garden. That instant the Duke perceiving day appear; It is the last time, says he, thy eyes will ever behold the sun rise! – I threw myself on my knees, and raising my eyes to Heaven, O God! God who knowest my innocence, wilt thou suffer me to be buried alive, and deprived for ever of the light of heaven? – As I said these words, the Duke dragged me about twenty paces to a rock; and putting a key behind a large stone, a trap-door opened directly – I shuddered – The Duke stopped: this moment is still left you; this is your tomb; it is but half open. Repent at last; convince me of your remorse by a sincere acknowledgement, and I am ready to pardon you. Perhaps you think, that at the instant of accomplishing my just vengeance, I may dread to put it in execution; but I have long mediated it; all is foreseen; and nothing can stop me. He then recounted all the dreadful precautions he had taken: he told me he had a wax figure made, pale and livid, which he should put in my bed; and that, under a pretence of fulfilling an act of piety, he should bury it himself, with the assistance of the old woman, who would be a spectator and witness of this action, without his being obliged to place any confidence in her. Finally, added he, will you accept the pardon I again deign to offer you for the last time? Speak; sacrifice your lover to my resentment; tell me his name, or renounce for ever light, liberty, and the world. At these words, raising my arms towards the rising sun, to take an everlasting leave of heaven, whose bright and majestic clouds presented the most glorious sight; that contemplation elevated my soul, and restored all my courage. I cast with disdain my eyes on the earth: turning towards the Duke, Take your victim, said I with a firm voice – At the same instant he dragged me in; my heart beat violently; I turned my head once more to behold the light of the sun, which I abandoned for ever. We descended into a dark cavern; my legs trembled so they could not support me. Agitated by dreadful convulsions, I struggled in the arms of my barbarous persecutor, and I fell at his feet without sense or motion. I know not how long I remained in that condition. Alas! I came to life again only to abhor my shocking existence! How shall I describe to you the horror which seized me, when, on opening my eyes, I found myself alone in those vast dungeons, encompassed with impenetrable darkness, and laying on a straw mat! – I made a plaintive scream, and from the bottom of the cavern the echo repeated it. It made me shudder, and redoubled the fear and terror which oppressed me! – O God! said I, is this the only voice which will answer me! the only one that I shall hear! That idea made me shed a torrent of tears. – At this moment I heard the door of my prison open, and the Duke appeared with a lantern in his hand: he set down by my side a pitcher full of water, and some bread. – Here, said he, is your future nourishment; you will find it every day in the *wheel you see opposite to you; I shall bring it you myself; I shall put it in this wheel, and I shall never re-enter this horrid dungeon†. At these words I looked about me; I saw an immense cavern, the extent of which the eye could not penetrate. The part I was in was hung with coarse straw mats, in order to keep it from the cold and damp; for the barbarian who threw me into this dreadful abode, had taken every precaution to preserve my life. – After having considered with trembling all that surrounded me, I turned towards my cruel jailor; and discovering a hatred so long concealed and so well founded, I dared in that moment to reproach him with the severity of his cruelty, and painted to him all the horror and detestation he had inspired me with. He listened to me for some time with a settled fury in his eyes; then, not being able to contain himself, he fell into the most terrible passion, and all at once hastily left me. From that day he entered my prison no more. When he came to bring me my food, he always knocked till I answered him, and then went without uttering a word. I soon repented having augmented, if it was possible, by my reproaches, his hatred and resentment. I recollected that he was the father of my child, and that dear child was under his care. Notwithstanding the horror of my situation, hope was not yet absolutely banished from my heart. The more I reflected on it, the probability appeared less, that he really meant to detain me for ever in that dreadful captivity. I even flattered myself that he had not announced my pretended death, either in his house, or to my family; that he had found some other means to elude their enquiries; and that he would reserve the possibility of making me appear when he chose. How could I imagine he would impose on himself the painful necessity of bringing me, every other day, the necessaries of life? And that he would be consequently obliged to the slavish task of not quitting his castle more than two or three days, since he was my only jailor; for he had not intrusted any one with the secret? – Alas! I did not think that hatred, to satisfy itself, was capable of imposing chains the most passionate love would carry with regret! – After my reflections, I persuaded myself he had fixed a term to his

---

*   The wheel, or turning box, in a nunnery, is a machine by which they received and give out provisions or any thing else, without seeing or being seen.[63]

†   The unhappy Dutchess de C— received also regularly, in the same manner by the wheel, linen and some garments, when she indispensibly wanted them.[64]

vengeance. Full of this idea, every time he knocked at the wheel, I spoke to him; and although he did not answer me, I implored his compassion, and assured him of my innocence. As I was absolutely deprived of light, I could not tell how many months I preserved this hope; but at last I lost it. Then, reason entirely abandoning me, I accused Providence, I murmured against its eternal decrees, My soul, dejected, wounded by grief, lost its courage and principles, and I fell into the most dismal and gloomy despair. I dared to think, that the excess of my misfortunes gave me a right to dispose of my life; as if one could break the most sacred tie, because it ceases to be agreeable! – Determined to die, I was near two days without taking any nourishment, or fetching it from the wheel. The Duke in vain knocked and called me; I obstinately refused to answer him. At last he came into my prison: when he appeared, with his lantern in his hand, in spite of the horror his presence inspired me with, I felt an emotion of joy in again seeing light; but I did not speak to him. He offered to soften my captivity, to give me a light, books, and better food, if I would at last tell him the name so often demanded. At that proposal I fixed my eyes upon him with the greatest disdain. Now, said I to him, that you have broken all the fatal ties which united us, my heart is at liberty; it owns without remorse those sentiments that in vain it formerly struggled with. – That object, whose name you only wish to know to sacrifice him to your resentment, I love more than ever; my last sigh shall be for him: judge if I will now declare him! – Then all religion, replied the Duke, is extinguished in your soul: you nourish at the bottom of your heart an adulterous passion, and you renounce life. – Monster! interrupted I, am I still your wife? Dare you say it? You, who have plunged me in this abyss? You, who are even now in mourning for me? It is true, I have no longer courage to support life; but that God, who hears and judges us, will punish you alone for the despair you have reduced me to. In my situation, if I commit a crime, you only will be answerable. No living creature can hear my complaints and my cries! But what deep dungeon, what thick walls, can hide from the Almighty the groans of the weak unjustly oppressed? Tremble! he sees us; he excuses me, he is ready to pardon me, and his avenging arm is lifted over you! – At these words the Duke shuddered, and cast on me a look of distraction. I enjoyed for a moment the pleasure of striking with fear and remorse a soul equally weak and cruel. Pale, astonished, perplexed, with downcast eyes, for some moments he kept a sullen silence. Speaking at last, – Impute not to me, he said, but to yourself, the misfortunes you lament. You are criminal; I have undoubted proofs; you have not disowned it; and yet I did not punish you before I had offered you pardon a hundred times. I again propose to soften your punishment, and you refuse it! Notwithstanding your infidelity, and your hatred for me, if you pleased, you should be still in my palace, you should again see your daughter. – O my daughter! interrupted I, alas! is she still alive? What is become of her? – She is with your mother. – Is it true that she is no longer in your hands? – Then the Duke, seeing that this idea revived me, took out of his pocket a letter from my mother, and permitted me to read it. That letter, which I bathed with my tears, contained the following words:

'My grand-daughter arrived yesterday evening – Oh! how shall I describe all the sentiments that rent my heart in embracing her! – You have given her to me; she is mine. I feel that I already love her to excess: she can attach me to life, but not console me. – Alas! how can I, without feeling the most dreadful uneasiness, enjoy the happiness of being yet a mother? After the loss I have had, is there on earth a felicity I can rely on? I will come and see you next summer, and bring your daughter; we will spend two months with you. Since you cannot tear yourself from the melancholy habitation your grief has rendered so dear, I will have the resolution to come to you. – I shall see that superb monument your love has erected to the memory of an object so deserving of our sorrows! – Perhaps I shall there find an end to all my troubles! – Ah! then will it be possible that a mother, without dying, can embrace the tomb of her daughter? – Yet I will live – Religion commands me, and nature enjoins the same law. I will live for the child you have deigned to trust to my care. Oh! how shall I ever acknowledge such an obligation, such a sacrifice! How dearly you ought to love this child! Alas! she has all her mother's features, she has all her charms; my daughter in her infancy is given me again! – O too flattering illusion! Unhappy mother! thou hast no longer a daughter, and the violence of thy grief cannot restore her to life.' –

Hardly had I finished this letter, when, falling on my knees, O God! cried I, my daughter is in the arms of my mother! that tender mother consents to live for my child! – O God! I will bless thee, thou hast afflicted me only! Contented, I will now submit to my fate! Pardon my distracted complaints; give happiness to all those I love; my painful existence prolong at thy pleasure! – In ending these words, I fell back on my straw, for I was so weak I could not support myself. The Duke seized that moment to offer me some food, which I took directly. He then left me, and from that time I never saw him. Yet, faithful to the vow I had made, I took care of my life. The idea, that my prayers and resignation would draw on my mother and daughter all the blessings of Heaven, consoled, revived, and supported my courage. The recollection of my faults became my greatest affliction. – Alas! all my misfortunes proceed from myself! I wanted confidence in my mother; in ceasing to consult her, I was led astray. Ungrateful and guilty daughter! Heaven, to punish me, blinded my parents in their choice: the husband they gave me, could not make me happy. Yet, without fresh faults, maternal affections would have made me happy; but, far from trying to overcome a criminal passion, I secretly nourished it. I even dared, in the imprudent letters which have been my ruin, to describe all it violence, and to complain at the same time of a husband I abused! – These reflections made me shed torrents of tears. Nevertheless I felt a soft melancholy pleasure in weeping for my faults; I loved to have rather a lively sensation of them; to lament over them, is to expiate them. Remorse for a crime wounds the soul; but repentance for an involuntary weakness has nothing cutting or bitter in it. These virtuous sentiments console us for our faults, and reconcile us to ourselves. Every bond of society broken, separated from the world, my heart, formed for love, soon gave itself up to the sublime passion, which alone could render life supportable. Religion made me know and taste all the inexhaustible consolations that she is able to give: insensibly she banished from my heart that unhappy attachment, my greatest misfortune; she gave me at last what human wisdom and mere philosophy could not procure; courage to support, without despair or murmuring, nine years of captivity in a dungeon impenetrable to the sun! – I will confess, however, that I suffered, in the two or three first years, sorrows, the bare remembrance of which now makes me shudder. The time when I supposed (according to such a calculation I had been able to make) that my mother and child were to be in the same castle where I was a prisoner; this time passed with me in the most dismal manner, and was the most cruel part of my captivity: my heart was rent in pieces with thinking that my mother and daughter were so near me, without the possibility of entertaining a hope of ever seeing them again. – O my mother! cried I, you mourn my death and I exist! And what hand, great God! have you chosen to wipe away your tears? It is in the bosom of my persecutor, my executioner, that you shed them! – Ah! it is not my tomb that he carries you to – Alas! you tread me under your feet without knowing it: you will with dry eyes look on these rocks that cover me! – Perhaps, in the silence of the night, not being able to taste the sweets of sleep, you will wander around my cavern! Perhaps, at this very instant, you are sitting by that horrid trapdoor, which will never again be opened for me! Ah! if it is so, you think without doubt of your unhappy daughter; you weep for her; and cannot hear her cries or her voice, which calls you! – These dreadful ideas pierced my soul, and often disturbed my reason. To these cruel fits of grief succeeded a kind of stupid insensibility more frightful than even despair itself: but in proportion as piety strengthened my heart, these violent transports diminished; I found in prayer inexpressible consolation. All the meditations, which commonly afflict men, were to me the most agreeable contemplations. With what pleasure did I reflect on the shortness of life! I looked forwards to death with the greatest serenity. – Is the happiest being, said I to myself, ever fully satisfied with the weak and frail pleasures this world affords? His mind is less occupied with present than future blessings. In this deceitful felicity, his imagination delights to wander into futurity: but what avails it, whether his fate be happy or miserable? what signifies the completion or destruction of his hopes? will he not be for ever forming new desires? can he enjoy the present, can he be contented with it? Why then do I so severely regret the good fortune I am deprived of, since it cannot procure happiness? I am, it is true, to pass my life in this horrible darkness;

the future offers nothing to my depressed imagination but a long and sorrowful night. – Well, let us think only of the awaking! Let us forget this perishable life; let us fix our eyes on eternity; let us despise a momentary grief, which will be succeeded by an immortal felicity; let us bring all our desires, all our hopes, towards the only object worthy of fixing and possessing the human heart! – It was thus, by these salutary reflections, I rose superior to my fate, and at last attained an entire resignation. Restored to reason, to myself, my sorrows were not only assuaged, but I became accustomed to darkness and to my captivity. I formed for myself employments; my prison was spacious; I walked a great part of the day (or night); I made verses, which I repeated aloud. I had a fine voice; I was perfect mistress of music; I composed a sort of hymns, and one of my greatest pleasures was to sing them, and listen to the echo which answered me. My sleep became peaceable; agreeable dreams represented my father, mother, and daughter; I always saw those dear objects satisfied and happy. Sometimes I found myself transported into fine palaces, or charming gardens. I saw again the heavens, trees, flowers. In short, these sweet illusions restored me all the happiness I had lost. I awaked fighting, it is true; but I slept with pleasure. Even waking, joy ceased to be a stranger to my heart; my imagination was exalted. Under the eyes of the Supreme Being, I dared to flatter myself, that my patience and resignation did not present an unworthy object to his view. Witness of all my actions, he heard me, he spoke to my heart, he re-animated it, he raised it up to himself, and I did not feel alone in my cavern. After being deprived of the objects I loved, the only thing I regretted still, in spite of myself, was the light, and the sight of heaven. I could not comprehend how any one could give himself up to despair in the most dismal slavery, if he enjoyed a window that had a prospect of the country. At last I was so used to my situation, that, far from desiring death, I found more than once that I still feared it. – Often I wanted nourishment: the Duke sometimes brought enough for three or four days. I imagined he was then compelled to go a short journey; and when my provision was nearly exhausted, I felt much uneasiness. The death of my tyrant would cause mine: and that cruel thought obliged me to pray for his health. In reality I had no longer an aversion for him: religion had made me easily renounce hatred. Could this weak effort be painful to me? Had I not already triumphed over my love? – I pitied my persecutor; I represented to myself the horrid state of his soul, his passions, his fears, his remorse; and I found myself but too well revenged. In the beginning of my captivity, I never heard him come without being ready to faint with terror. By degrees these violent agitations grew weaker. He always inspired me with a kind of emotion mixed with some fear; yet I wished him to come, not only for the preservation of my life, but because he interrupted the frightful and profound silence of my solitude. He made me hear a noise, and something move; in fine, he procured me a kind of variety, which was never agreeable, but became necessary.

I cannot explain to you how very lively and singular my desire was to hear some sound. When it thundered violently, I heard it; to express what I then felt is impossible: I did not think myself in total solitude; I listened to that awful sound with as much joy as attention; and when it ceased entirely, I fell into the deepest melancholy. Such was nearly my situation for six or seven years. During that time I was only really concerned for my absolute ignorance relative to the fate of my mother and daughter: in vain I questioned the Duke, whenever he knocked at the wheel; I could not obtain a single word in answer; for since his last appearance in my prison, he had never spoke to me. All my courage was necessary to support that cruel uncertainty on so interesting a subject. – Often, when I invoked Heaven for my child, for my mother, all at once my heart was oppressed, my tears flowed. Alas! cried I, do they still live? I pray for their happiness, and perhaps I have the dreadful misfortune to survive them! – In other moments, hope was so strongly imprinted on my heart, that I did not feel even the slightest uneasiness, on that account. In that happy disposition of mind, I flattered myself that it was not impossible an extraordinary event might snatch me from my prison. That idea was so fixed in my heart, especially during the last year of my captivity, that I made a vow to God, if ever I recovered my liberty, to consecrate my life to him in retirement far from Rome, and there to spend the remainder of my days, as soon as my daughter should have no occasion for my care. I am now come to the most interesting period of my life. I approach the moment of my deliverance; and soon the Divine goodness was going to recompence me amply for nine years of misery and grief. The Duke for some time, I imagined, constantly inhabited the castle, because he regularly brought my food: but one day he failed coming at the time; I waited impatiently for him; he did not come, and I had entirely finished my little provision. I slept peaceably enough. The next day I waited in vain for the relief, which every moment made more necessary for me. The time passed; uneasiness, as much as hunger and thirst, deprived me of sleep; and I remained in that situation near another day. Then, absolutely exhausted, I thought the end of my life was approaching. I considered death with tranquillity; yet the remembrance of all that was dear to me occurred to grieve and affect me. – Unhappy daughter and mother, cried I, must I pass my last moments in this fatal solitude! Dear authors of my life, must I then die without receiving your blessings! O my daughter! I cannot give thee mine; I shall not enjoy the indulgence of dying in thy arms! – My daughter! thou canst not even regret me! – In that moment, when thy unhappy mother is expiring, thou art enjoying, without doubt, amusements and pleasures suitable to thy age! – Dreadful thought! I die; and all those I love have long been consoled for my death! – But what do I say? Unreasonable that I am, I complain, I murmur, when all my misfortunes are going to end! – Great God! forgive me this criminal weakness – My heart rejects and disowns it. O my Judge and my Father! design to call me at last to thyself! – Full of hope and confidence, sure of enjoying eternal happiness, I expect death with security; I should even call it to my aid, if thou didst not forbid me to desire it! – Intending these words, I fell back almost lifeless on the straw, which served me by way of bed – I felt in the bottom of my soul a serenity, a tranquillity, the charms of which I had never tasted till that moment. A salutary balm appeared suddenly to heal all the wounds of my heart. My ideas were soon confounded with the excess of my weakness. I gently fell into a wandering and delicious reverie, a sort of sleep, during which the most delightful forms successively offered themselves to my imagination. I thought I saw my bed surrounded with bright angels of light, and celestial figures: I heard at a distance harmonious voices, divine concerts: I saw heaven half opened, the Almighty, on a shining throne, calling me, and stretching out his arms to me. – In reality, he was then watching me; his paternal hand was going to break my chains – All at once I awake in a palpitation; I think I hear a knocking at the tower; I listen – they knock again – my heart beats – But, O surprise! O unheard-of transport! – transport impossible to be described! – I hear a voice, and that voice is no longer my tyrant's; it is a new voice – It sounded to me like that of an angel descended from Heaven to deliver me. – Distracted, amazed, I clasped my hands with the most passionate emotion and the most lively gratitude. O God! cried I, it is a deliverer that thou sendest me! – Ah! I accepted death with joy; and thou givest me life! – Life is one of thy blessing; I am permitted to cherish it! – In saying these words, I endeavour to get up to go near the wheel; I am not able, my strength fails me, and I fall back upon my bed. – At this moment my door opens, and I perceive a light. One comes in; I raise myself; I wish to look; I distinguish nothing; my eyes, so long deprived of light, cannot bear the faint glimmer of a lamp, and shut in spite of me. – Yet something approaches. – O! who are you? cried I, with a faultering voice. At these words, I again with difficulty open my eyes, still dazzled. I see a man on his knees before me; he puts his arm under my head, he supports it, and presents me with some food, then famishing with excessive hunger, I have only one idea, that of satisfying that imperious want; all my other thoughts are as it were suspended, and I seize with avidity the nourishment that is offered me. At last, feeling my strength revive, I turned all at once towards my deliverer. His face was in the shade; I could not distinguish his features. – O speak to me, said I; are you the accomplice of my persecutor, or do you come to deliver me? – O Heaven! interrupted the unknown, what voice! Where am I? O God! – In concluding these words, he hastily rises, and taking the light, he returns to me; he looks at me with an attention mixed with tenderness and horror. I fix for a moment my eyes on his face, enlightened by the lamp. His hair seemed to stand an end; he was pale and trembling – but I could not mistake him. I wish to speak; my tears stop my utterance; I am only able to pronounce the name of the count de Belmire – It was really he – he falls at my feet; he bathes them with his tears; he still looks at me; he stammers out some confused words; he accuses and blesses Heaven; the violence of his compassion gives to his joy the appearance of madness and despair. We both speak at the same time, without hearing or answering each other – The cavern re-echoes with our cries. At length the Count, getting up with an air of dignity, O most barbarous of men! cried he, execrable monster! is there a torture sufficient to punish thee for thy crimes? And you, continued he, assisting me to rise, you, unfortunate victim of the fury of a relentless tyger, come; you are free. – At these words, my first motion was to rush towards the door; but stopping myself directly, Oh! said I to the Count, you are my deliverer; I owe to you my life, my liberty! But these benefits which you have restored me, can they now give me happiness? Alas! I dare not interrogate you. My mother, my father! – They live. – Heaven! And my daughter? – She is at Rome; she will be soon in your arms. – O God! cried I prostrating myself, what gratitude can ever acquit my obligations towards thee! This single moment has already paid me for all my sufferings! – O you, my generous protector! pursued I, addressing myself to the Count, now, for your recompence, learn that I am innocent: but before I tell you the melancholy circumstances of my history, allow me to ask you one question – Doubtless the Duke is ill? – Attacked with a dangerous disease, he is on the brink of the grave, and cannot live more than two days, – Come, quit this horrible dungeon, that the monster, before he expires, may know you are at liberty. – No, interrupted I, it is my father, my mother, who must take me out of my prison; it is only guided by them that I can go out. – I then intreated the Count to send an express immediately to my father. He promised me; and giving me a pencil and a piece of paper, I wrote without delay a note, which contained these words: 'O my father! my mother! I exist, I am innocent! – Come, by your presence restore me really to life! – Come, take me out of a horrid dungeon, and make me forget all the misfortunes I have endured.' – This note was scarce legible: I was near a quarter of an hour writing it; for I did not know how to form a letter, and spelling I had totally forgot. – The Count, seeing I was irrevocably determined to stay in my prison till the arrival of my mother, gave me the keys of all the doors, and left me with an inexpressible regret, after having promised me to dissemble with the Duke, if he should still live, and to come again the next day, as soon as the dusk of the evening should come on. When I found myself alone, I was seized with a terror almost as violent as that I experienced in the beginning of my confinement. Yet I had light; the Count had left me a lamp and a dark lantern. I had also asked him for a watch, that I might count all the hours; for I did not expect it was possible for me to sleep a moment. Immoveable at the place the Count de Belmire left me, with difficulty I breathed; I dared not lift up my eyes, and yet I could not help by stealth casting a look around me. The light, far from encouraging me, added to my fears, because it made me distinguish my melancholy and sad habitation. At last, not being able to bear myself, I got up, I took my light, I opened my first door, I went out; I came into a kind of long gallery, on the side of the cavern where the tower was placed. I already felt a great relief in seeing myself in a new place; it brought me to the last door of my prison. I quickened my steps to the end of the gallery; I opened the door of entrance. Then I found myself at the bottom of the stair-case of the cavern; and being no more shut in than by the double doors that led to the garden, I shut those of the gallery, to separate myself from my horrid dungeon. Then, going up the stair-case with rapidity, I seated myself on the last step, and I then began to breathe. After such an event, so happy, so unexpected, it might seem I should have felt the most lively and pure joy. But I had suffered too long, I had been too unhappy, for my heart to dare to give itself up to the seducing charms of the sweetest hopes. I thought, it is true, with transport, that all I loved existed. Nevertheless, when I considered the inexpressible delight I should feel in finding myself again in the arms of my mother, in embracing my father and my child, I could not flatter myself that so great a felicity could ever be my lot! A thousand destructive ideas arose to trouble and blacken my imagination; and in that dejected and melancholy state, all my most chimerical fears I looked upon as predictions. That interesting period of my life, the day when the Count de Belmire entered my prison, was the 3rd of June, 17—. He left me at midnight; till six in the morning I remained in the situation I have just described, when all at once I thought I heard a gentle noise: I listened with the greatest attention at the door of my prison; and in spite of its thickness, and that of the rock which covered it, I heard distinctly enough the chirping of the birds, waked by the appearance of day. The impulse of joy which I felt at that instant, is not to be described or conceived. All my melancholy vanished, my heart was again opened to hope and happiness. The sweetest tears flowed from my eyes, although my ideas were still extremely confused, and though I was not in a condition to reflect on the unexpected change of my situation; for I was entirely engrossed with the desire of hearing what passed in the garden. My ear fixed to the door, holding my breath, I listened with an attention which no other thought could divert me from. I heard the dogs barking, men walking, and even talking confusedly; and all these different noises gave me inexpressible pleasure. Yet, towards the end of the day, I eagerly wished for night, that I might again see the Count de Belmire, and question him upon a thousand things I ardently desired to be informed of, and which presented themselves successively to my imagination, as my ideas got into order. For instance, I wished to know how long I had been confined in my prison; before I had seen the Count, I though I had been near fifty years. The youthful appearance of the Count de Belmire proved to me, that grief and sorrow are bad calculators of time: I did not even know, within four or five years, what was any age. The Count came exactly at midnight. I easily perceived by his pale countenance, how deeply he was affected with sorrow and compassion by the event which changed my doom. Through respect for my situation, which obliged me to receive him alone, in the middle of the night; through respect for the fatal knot, ready to be broken, but which was still binding to me, he never mentioned either the sentiments which I had dared to acknowledge in happier times, nor those he still preserved towards me. After he had told me that he had written to my father when he sent my note, and that the Duke was at the point of death, I begged him to tell me the reasons which had made the Duke confide in him so important a secret. – Then the Count satisfied my curiosity in the following words:

'I had been a year on my travels, when I heard the news of your death. At the same time I learnt the Duke was inconsolable for your loss: that circumstance greatly weakened the natural antipathy I had for him. – I travelled two years more; recalled by my affairs, I returned into Italy. Obliged to see the Duke, he made me come to this castle; for he very seldom left it, and then only went to Naples to spend two or three days. I here saw your tomb; I saw your picture, placed in almost all the apartments. I attached myself to the habitation, and even to the inhuman monster who had made you his victim. He discovered such a violent grief, so deep a melancholy, that I soon preferred his society to all others. I came every year, and spent five or six months in this castle. A year ago, the Duke was seized with a dangerous disorder; ignorant of his state of health, he still made little excursions to Naples. Last winter he left off entirely going to court, and wrote to me at Rome, desiring me to come and see him. I arrived about the end of January, and found him dying, though he did not keep his bed, and always walked about. I even thought that I perceived at times he was not entirely in his senses. Consumed by remorse, his life for nine years has been an insupportable burthen to him; and yet he could not look on the end of it without horror. At last his weakness increased every day; he fell all at once into convulsions, so that he was obliged to be put to bed. He remained there three days, when one of his valets-de-chambre came to tell me, at nine o'clock at night, that he wanted to speak to me. The man added, the Duke, that night and the preceding one, had sent his servants away, in order to endeavour to get up by himself; but not being able to support himself, he had rung for them; and that they had found him out of his bed, and half dressed. I went directly to his room; he sent away his physician and his people; and telling me he was going to trust me with an important secret, he made me swear to keep it faithfully. Then, looking at me with timidity, – Family reasons, said he, oblige me to keep prisoner in this castle a guilty woman, and one who deserved death – She must want food; go, carry her some. Knock at the wheel, which serves for that purpose; if she does not answer you, go into her prison and succour her: but I give you warning that the woman is mad; do not listen to her; give her some nourishment; return again immediately. I promise you one day to tell you her history and her name.

The Duke then taught me the secret of his caverns; and taking from under his pillow a parcel of keys, he gave them to me, desiring I would execute his commission without delay. – The barbarian, supposing I had never seen you, thought he could not place his confidence better, and delivered into my hands your fate and mine.' When the Count de Belmire had finished this recital, he intreated me to tell him my history. But as I could not relate it without speaking of the sentiments which I had had for him, I declared I would not tell him, but in the presence of my father and mother. The Count de Belmire had calculated that my father must arrive, at the latest, in less than two days. Less agitated, and more in a condition to reflect, I tasted, during twenty-four hours, all the happiness so dear an expectation could procure me. My impatience then augmenting as the hour of my deliverance approached, soon it knew no bounds, and became an insupportable torment. I had never felt any thing I can compare to the violent agitations I experienced the night that preceded the happiest day of my life. My eyes fixed attentively on the watch, I mournfully considered the slow motion of the hands. Every instant I thought I heard a noise; I shuddered; I felt my blood boiling in my veins; and all my arteries beat with violence. These lively emotions still increased, when the singing of the birds announced the dawn of day, the fortunate day, when I was to be born again, and take the dear and sacred title and rights of daughter and mother! – That moment made to compensate an age of misery! that moment so passionately desired! – it approaches! – it comes at last! – Cries redoubled, tumultuous voices, are heard – Soon I distinguish a confused noise of carriages, of horses, of armed men – The noise increases, it draws near. – I tremble, I shiver – O God! – what voice strikes my ears, and re-echoes at the bottom of my soul! – O my mother! – she calls her daughter! – my heart rushes towards her! – Good God, who gavest me strength to support my misfortunes, O do not let excess of joy overcome me! – I feel that I am fainting – Must I expire at the feet of my mother! – As I ended these words, my door opened; I precipitately rush out of my cavern. In spite of the bright glare of day which strikes and hurts my dazzled eyes, I see, I again recollect my mother, my father; I give a piercing shriek; I throw myself into their arms, and there fall down in a fit. – O! who can describe the joy, the transports, I felt when I recovered my senses!

I found myself on the bosom of the tenderest of mothers, my face bathed with her tears. My father on his knees before me, pressing both my hands in his. – I again saw the day, the sun! – Nay, I was certain of soon seeing my daughter – That instant realized all my dearest hopes, and satisfied all the wishes of my heart. I can give no account of my thoughts in these first moments; I felt too much to be able to think, or to express the violence of my joy, otherwise than by my sobs and my tears. At last my father, raising me in his arms, Come, my dear child, said he, quit this dreadful abode, where vice has so long oppressed innocence – Come. – At these words I arose; I looked around me, and I saw we

were surrounded with a numerous troop of armed men, among whom I recollected a great many relations, and some friends of my father's, who told me he
had assembled them before he left Rome, he had conducted them directly to
Naples, where, throwing himself at the feet of the King, and shewing him my
note, he not only obtained permission to come and take me by force, if force was
necessary, but even troops to second him. When I arrived here, continued my
father, I learnt that your infamous persecutor had just expired. Thus this happy
day restores all that love you, delivers you from an execrable tyrant, and secures
to you perfect liberty. All the answer I gave to this discourse, was embracing my
father with tears. At the height of happiness, having nothing to fear, I could not
help pitying, at the bottom of my soul, the fate of the unhappy Duke de C— .
Alas! said I to myself, if I had loved him, he would not have polluted his life
by such criminal passions; he would now be alive and happy! – That thought,
whilst it excited my compassion, made it painful and melancholy; and during
some moments impressed my heart with a cruel sorrow, and corrupted all my joy.
At last we set out; and the next day, fortunate as a mother as I had been happy as
a daughter, I found again that child so passionately beloved; I clasped her in my
arms; I saw her shed tears; I heard her call me her mother! – I was in a kind of
delirium the two first days of my arrival at Rome, stunned with noise, astonished
at every thing, and enjoying nothing thoroughly but the happiness of seeing my
daughter again, and finding myself between my father and mother. Then, my
heart being fully satisfied, I began to feel the value of all the happiness that had
been restored to me. I found enjoyments, as agreeable as new, in the most common things of life; all were sights for me. The first time I walked by moon-light,
I felt an admiration, an extasy of joy, not to be expressed, in beholding again that
clear and soft light, and the heavens spangled with stars. I could not walk in the
country, or in a garden, without stopping at every step to examine particularly
all the objects that came in my sight. I contemplated the flowers, the fruits, the
trees, the grass, the clouds, the rising and the setting sun, that delightful and
sublime sight. O God! exclaimed I to myself, what wonders does thy goodness
create for our use, what treasures does it lavish upon us! and ungrateful man is
capable of disdaining them; and when he enjoys so many blessings, can think
himself unhappy! – It was thus my heart gave itself up with transport to the felicity which it had been so long robbed of. I also felt an extreme pleasure in finding
myself again in the palace where I was born, and where the happy years of my
infancy and early youth were spent; but I own I could not see the Marchioness
of Venuzi, that old friend, again, without feeling some pain: she was the first
cause of all my misfortunes. The Count de Belmire soon followed me to Rome;
and in the presence of my father, my mother, the Marchioness de Venuzi, and
some relations, I told him my history. Scarcely had I finished when, throwing
himself at my feet, he expressed in the most passionate terms the excess of his

compassion and gratitude. What! cried he, you could, by naming me, have prevented that horrible doom! It was I who plunged you in that abyss; and whilst you groaned there, I lived; I saw light, which you were deprived of for me! – May I be permitted to flatter myself, that love can recompense you for all the terrible calamities it has caused you? – That heart, so noble and so tender, can it be faithless! Have your misfortunes made you abjure those sentiments, without which I am unable to live? My father at this discourse affectionately embraced the Count de Belmire, and by that action made me know he approved his sentiments. But for me, having almost lost the very idea of a passion which formerly had such an ascendancy over my heart, I could no longer even conceive how any one could devote himself to it; and still less the possibility that I could be the object. After a moment's silence, I spoke; and, addressing the Count, I described to him so naturally the situation of my heart, that he instantly lost all his hopes. He left Rome for some time; but the sentiment which made him fly brought him back again; and consoled by the friendship I shewed him, he fixed himself there entirely.

For my part, far from losing my relish for the good fortune which I tasted, every day seemed to make me more sensible of its value. How delightful were my first thoughts every time I awoke! – In casting my eyes around me I felt the purest joy, in seeing my daughter's bed by the side of mine, in finding myself again in my paternal dwelling! I could not comprehend, how I had been able to support myself without that felicity I now enjoyed, or even without those comforts and conveniences which use began now to make me think absolutely necessary to life. These ideas inspired me with the tenderest compassion for all the unfortunate. I had lain upon straw for nine years; I had suffered hunger, thirst, and cold. – I owed at least to my misfortunes the sentiment, which brings us the nearest to the divinity! – I did not listen with inattention to the lamentations of the poor imploring my compassion. Their fate made me recall mine; I conceived them as of the same species with myself; and I found the most delightful satisfaction in consoling and relieving them! To receive, to entertain them, was not sufficient for me; I went to seek them. – Ah! who deserves to have the first advances made to him, if it is not the wretch that is in pain, and who often dares not ask for the feeble succours which would save his life? – This desire to find the unfortunate in order to change their condition, was no virtue in me; it was the most pressing exigence of my heart, and the sweetest of all my pleasures. But the more I grew accustomed to the case which was restored to me, the stronger impression did the remembrance of my captivity make upon me; and soon it was not in my power to talk of my misfortunes, nor even to listen with tranquility to the recitals or discourses, which could recall them to my memory. That weakness gave me a great many more. I could not bear darkness, or total solitude, were it only for a moment. I remember, that one night my light went out. I opened my eyes, and finding myself in a profound darkness, I felt an horror that my reason could not conquer or moderate. I gave a piercing cry: they came, and found me pale, disfigured, almost without my senses, and agitated with the most frightful convulsions. These vain terrors, these involuntary weaknesses, melancholy fruits of my misfortunes and captivity, were not my greatest afflictions. I found myself absolutely incapable of directing the education of my daughter. I was forced to learn again to read, write, and cast accounts: but by a singularity remarkable enough, I had hardly forgot any thing I had read in my youth; for having had, during nine years, no kind of amusement to engage my attention, I had looked for one in the past, by recalling frequently and circumstantially what I had learnt from books and conversation. Thus all those things were imprinted in my memory, perhaps better than if I had never quitted the world. I was twenty-seven years old when I came out of my confinement, and my daughter was then ten. Entirely occupied with her, living in the most secluded retirement, always shut up in my apartment, seeing only my father, my mother, and sometimes the Count de Belmire, I lived thus for five years. My daughter at last attained her fifteenth year; and being the greatest match in Italy, all the families of distinction at Rome made proposals to me. My choice had long been made at the bottom of my heart. I consulted my daughter; she acknowledged her sentiments coincided with my wishes; my father and mother gave their approbation. I did not delay executing my intention. The Count de Belmire, still young, a captivating figure, virtuous as amiable, possessor of a considerable fortune, had constantly refused the most advantageous and splendid establishments. It was to that too faithful lover, that dearest friend, my deliverer, to whom I offered my daughter. I give her to you, said I to him; she is yours. She loves you; she is fifteen, the age I was the first time you saw me; she will recall all that I was then, both by her figure and her sentiments. Fate gives you back to-day, what it formerly deprived you of. As I was not born to make you happy, nothing but seeing you happy with my daughter can give me consolation. At these words the Count de Belmire seized one of my hands, bathing it with tears; and as I was pressing him to answer me: Ah! said he, at last, have you not a right to dispose of my destiny! – The same evening this conversation passed, the marriage articles were signed; and eight days after the Count de Belmire married my daughter. I remained at Rome another year. Then seeing my daughter settled and perfectly happy, I now only thought of retiring into solitude, and performing the vow I had made in my prison. Besides, the air of Rome being very prejudicial to my health, the physicians had ordered me to go to Nice for some time. I undertook that voyage by La Corniche. I was so much charmed with the situation of Albenga, that I resolved to fix myself in that agreeable place. I had a plain and commodious house built, in which I took up my abode, when I returned from Nice. It is here, for four years, I have recovered perfect health, and my life glides away in the most delightful repose. It is here, that I have had the resolution to write this history, which I design for my grand-children, when they are of an age to reap advantage from it. In abandoning the world I have not renounced those objects that were dear to me. Since I have been at Albenga, I have already made two journies to Rome to see my father and mother; and every year my daughter and my son-in-law come and spend three months in my retirement. In short, it is impossible to be more perfectly happy than I am. I bless God every day for the happiness I possess, and even for the misfortunes I have suffered, since they have expiated my faults, purified my heart, and have taught me the full value of the felicity which I now enjoy.

Continuation of the Journal of the Baroness.

Pietra, Sunday.

WHEN you have read the story of the Dutchess de C— , you will easily conceive the pain we felt in quitting Albenga. We could not prevail upon ourselves to leave it till this afternoon. We were obliged to perform a good part of the journey on foot, and our conversation turned perpetually on the beautiful and affecting Dutchess. We observed that all her misfortunes arose solely from her want of confidence in her mother; and that without the aid of religion her cavern had been her grave, or would have rendered her stupid and senseless. So that Adelaide and Theodore have now a more enlarged idea of religion. They have seen it at Lagaraye, great, beneficent, heroic; they have just now seen, that there are no accidents in life, no misfortunes, which it cannot enable us to support with courage and resignation. – They will never forget, that it is as comfortable as sublime; that it imprints on the heart virtues, which by nature we have not; and that it inspires us with a courage, that unassisted reason cannot pretend to.

Savona, Monday.

To avoid an horrible and dangerous mountain, we embarked this morning at Pietra, and went three leagues and an half by sea to Novi, where we again took to our chairs. From the top of the mountain, which overlooks the towns of Anvaye and Savona, is the finest view in the universe. This is all we have found remarkable since our leaving Albenga. Savona is a pretty town, agreeably situated, and but twelve leagues from Genoa. We have already ran over it and its environs. After having finished our journey by La Corniche, we found great pleasure in getting into our carriages once more, and in seeing horses again. – We are just returned from visiting Abbissola, a village one short league from Genoa, in which are the two magnificent palaces of Novere and Durazzo. – The gardens are extensive, but in a bad taste. I observed, which is singular enough, that none of the charming flowers which grow spontaneously in the fields, except the orange-tree, are admitted there; whilst the box is cultivated with the greatest care; and the superb vases, which ornament the terraces, are filled with it. Adelaide testified her surprize at it, and said, the master of this palace seems to have very little taste. – It is certainly, replied I, a very frivolous vanity, if he takes any notice of his garden himself, and does not abandon the care of it entirely to his gardener: for this nasty box is placed in these beautiful vases for no other reason, than that it is *here* more scarce than myrtle, jessamin, and the rose-laurel. – But, mamma, does an agreeable thing become less so for being common? – No, surely! not in the opinion of persons of sense and taste: but a rich man, with much vanity and little understanding, thinks of nothing but displaying his wealth. He lavishes his money, not to procure what he likes best, but what makes most show; not to conciliate the esteem of persons of worth, but to raise the admiration and envy of fools; and sacrificing to that absurd vanity the most rational pleasures, he has no enjoyments of his own; and thinking to dazzle all eyes by his magnificence, he only shews his folly and absurdity.

LETTER XXXIX.

The same to the same.

Genoa.

WE arrived at Genoa, my dear friend, in the morning of the day before yesterday. As I this day met with a safe conveyance for my little journal of La Corniche, and the history of the Dutchess de C—, I made use of it to send them to you. And now I am going to make a *real journal*, which you will not see till my return. I shall write it with care, because it is to serve as a model: for my daughter is to write one, and I to write another; and every night she is to communicate *her* observations, which I shall correct by mine. – As we shall both write on the same subject, and as I shall not shew her my journal till I have seen hers, this method will serve to form her stile, her judgment, and her mind at the same time. But, however, that my letters my appear less insipid to you, I shall enliven them from time to time with some particulars relative to the manners and customs of the countries we pass through. – For instance, I can inform you already, that what they say of Cicisbeo's*,[65] is literally true. – It is absolutely necessary for a lady to have one after the first year. He is the choice of the parents and the husband, so that you may easily guess, whether she always keeps to him alone. His business is to attend upon his Cicisbeo[66] every where; to be of her party at cards; to walk by her chair; to open and shut it for her; to carry her cloak, her fan, &c.

---

* The word Cicisbeo is Greek, and signifies, they say, whispering in the ear.

Except the new street, and that of Balbi, which are broad, all the rest are very narrow; so that there are scarce any carriages kept at Genoa, and every body uses chairs. All the women of inferior rank appear to be pretty; they wear a sort of English dress, with long trains that sweep the streets, long muslin aprons, and a mantle of Persian, which they wrap round their heads in such a manner, that one seldom discovers the whole face at once, but the different features one after another; sometimes the mouth, sometimes the eyes, and sometimes the nose; and this manner of exposing themselves, as it were by retail, and discovering whilst they conceal themselves, becomes them, and appears very alluring.

Yesterday we were at a grand assembly, which they call Veilla delle quarante;[67] because forty noble Genoese ladies give these assemblies by turns. Adelaide, who thought the ladies not dressed in taste, gave Miss Bridget a description of them droll enough, but satyrical. On hearing this, I turned coldly to Miss Bridget, and shrugging up my shoulders, surely Miss, says I, you must have had a better opinion of the sense and character of Adelaide. – Really, Madame, *I am surprized at it.* – How do you mean, Mamma? – I did not think, Adelaide, you would have so soon forgot what I said to you on this subject, when you criticised the ladies of Languedoc. – But, Mamma, the Genoese ladies are a thousand times more ridiculous. It is impossible not to be astonished at their head-dresses, so flat, so frizzed, so powdered! – Your astonishment is very absurd, and you would have greater reason for it, were the Genoese ladies dressed exactly in the same mode as those of Paris and Versailles: for it would indeed be very surprising, if in such frivolous matters there should be a general agreement, and one exact model for all countries. – After this short lesson I changed the discourse. This morning Adelaide and I went a shopping, and as we speak good Italian, we were advised not to pass ourselves for foreigners, that we might get better bargains. So we went out in the morning dresses of the Genoese ladies. As we were coming from a shop where they sold artificial flowers, and were getting into our chairs, my Genoese footman proposed to us to go to a print-shop just by. I at first made some difficulties; but yielding to the solicitations of Adelaide, I went in. The master of the shop, a fat, good-humoured man, shewed us some prints, and asked, with a laugh, if we had seen *La Bambolina Francese* – *The French Puppet.* What is that, says Adelaide? It is a coloured drawing, which a young painter made last night at the Veilla delle quarante. – And what does it represent? – You must know first of all, Ladies, there are two French women come to Genoa, mother and daughter. – Here Adelaide and I looked upon one another with some emotion; and the man pursued his discourse: The mother, continued he, has nothing extraordinary; but the little girl is a fine caricature indeed! – Here, Lawrence! where are those little drawings? – Lawrence answered, they are all sold except this, which he brought. The painter has not lost his labour then, says the master. He passed the whole night, with two or three of his friends, in making a score or two of them, and they are all gone but this. Here – observe, Ladies, how very comical! – Adelaide blushing, and very much confused, cast her eyes upon it, and immediately turned her head away with a forced and disconcerted smile. – You will agree with me, that it is an excellent figure! – Observe this mass of hair floating all over the shoulders, these enormous curls falling down and covering the neck and breast, and this basket of flowers upon the head. Oh! what an excellent caricature! what an excellent caricature! – And did the painter, says I to him, tell you that it was like. – Oh! he did not much attend to the likeness; and yet two ladies of the Veilla delle quarante, who were here this morning, knew it instantly, and laughed heartily. – Do they say this young French woman is pretty? – The painter says, she would be very well, were she not trussed up in so extraordinary a manner. As he finished these words, I arose, purchased the *little French puppet*, and went out. At our return home, Well, my dear Adelaide, said I, what think you of this adventure? – Why, Mamma, I see that when we ridicule others for trifles, they may be retorted upon us. I was very foolish, I own; but the ladies of the Veilla delle quarante were as silly as I; for they likewise laughed at my dress, and they are older than me. – And for that very reason you may be assured, that many of them had sense enough not to be surprized, that a French woman was not dressed like a Genoese. – Now you have bought this wretched little drawing, what do you design to do with it? – Whatever you please. – It is fit for nothing, but to burn. – Why so? – This little figure is droll enough; besides, it is like you. – Oh, Mamma! – I have not this nose, I hope. – They have not flattered you in this portrait; but, however, it resembles you. – Thus it is, that *they* paint us who love us not; but unfortunately, tho' they make us ugly, they do not disfigure us entirely, but maliciously leave some feature by which we may be known. – But, to return to your caricature; Why would you burn it? – Mamma! – Do you know that the only method to defeat such a jest as this, is to appear neither shocked nor embarrassed at it? – If evil-minded people sought to wrong you, or blacken your character, you would have had reason to be afflicted: but this jest does not attack your reputation; and if you have the good sense to be the first to laugh at it, far from setting you in a ludicrous light, it will turn to your advantage by shewing, that you are above the childish vanity of being vexed at trifles, and that you will not, by your notice of them, give importance to things beneath the consideration of persons of sense. – Well, Mamma, that is the method I shall observe in future. – I applaud your resolution, as it is a proof of your good sense. – Well then, I am resolved to be vexed at no *ill-natured jests* whatever, that do not attack my *character*. – *Ill-natured jests*. – You look upon *this* jest then in that light. – Certainly; for it has given me uneasiness. – That is a good reason indeed! But, however, what you call an ill-natured jest, because you are the object of it, is in truth nothing more than a little raillery, a joke by no means so severe as that you formerly put upon Miss Bridget, when you stuck up in your chamber a profile of the Emperor Vespasian; for *there* the whole ridicule fell upon the person, not the dress of Miss Bridget. – Oh, Mamma! what an old story have you brought up! – If what *then* passed had entirely cured you, I should not have mentioned it. It taught you indeed to respect your friends; but it has not corrected your satirical turn. No longer ago than yesterday, that ridiculous description you gave Miss Bridget of the Genoese ladies – I protest, Mamma, I now abhor raillery; and you shall never see me fall again into that low and despicable fault. – Well, I believe you. Let us say no more about it. – I expect company to dinner; let us go and receive them. – I will bring my portrait, and shew it to every body. – Very well! Come, then. – She entered the room with an easy air, holding the *Bambolina Francese* in her hand, and told our morning's adventure and our conversation at the print-shop with a good grace. The whole company, prepared by Mons. d' Almane, commended very much the manner in which she took the jest; and Adelaide, charmed with her success, has had the drawing framed, to hang it up in the saloon. So that now I am sure of two things; that she will take a jest with good-humour, and never make a severe one. Adieu, my dear friend; I am already two hundred and seventy-four leagues from you and Madame d' Ostalis, and am still going farther from you. How afflicting is this calculation! – I confess, three months before my departure, I never thought on my journey but with delight; and now my heart is much oppressed, when I think on the distance that sepa-rates us! How much does the imagination seduce and deceive us! True and solid pleasures are those of the heart; such, for example, as I shall feel at my return.

LETTER XL.

The Baron to Mons. d' Aimeri.

Genoa.

Y OU have at last decisively broken the treaty of marriage proposed by Mad-ame d' Olcy. I cannot say, that I am sorry for it; for I still adhere to the project, which I have communicated to you. Let us now come to particulars with regard to the Chevalier de Valmont; and let us see how we can preserve him from some of the dangers, which will surround him this winter. I have already said, if he quits you, he is lost; if you follow him against his will, you will be of no service to him. Confidence is your only tie upon him. A young man, naturally well disposed, ought to feel that kind of attachment to a person, whose wisdom and experience he is acquainted with; of whom he thinks himself beloved, and whom he has been accustomed from his infancy to consult. And yet very few fathers, very few preceptors know how to inspire this confidence into their sons and pupils. I have sought the reason, and believe I have found it. There are two sorts of confidence: the one founded on esteem, and the necessity of sometimes consulting, in matters of importance, a person more knowing and experienced than oneself: the other comes from the heart, and from a conformity of opinions and sentiments. This kind of confidence we repose in a man disinterestedly, and without having need of his advice; we find an inexpressible pleasure in talking with him of whatever is uppermost in our thoughts, of whatever amuses us; in telling him the little secret of the moment, and in throwing off all disguise before him, and appearing what we really are. The first sort of confidence is more flattering; the second more engaging. The one without the other always leaves friendship feeble and imperfect; but both of them united form those deep and durable attachments, which nothing can destroy, and of which so few examples are to be found. It is not often that a person loves to talk of his feelings, his pleasures, his occupations, except to one who seems to interest himself in the detail. If you never listen to your son with attention, but when he asks your advice, he will have no other confidence in you, than such as we repose in a steward, or a lawyer whom we consult. Persuade your son, therefore, that his conversation is always interesting to you, and he will prefer your company to any other. Different ages will necessarily be different in taste, and see things in different lights: but this is the very thing that must be concealed. When Theodore, even in his childhood, talked to me for hours together of his cart, his playthings, or his garden, he was persuaded that his conversation was infinitely interesting to me; and finding nobody but me, who could listen to him so long without being tired, his most agreeable recreation, his greatest pleasure was to amuse himself tête-à-tête with me. If any one came in upon us, this charming conversation was disturbed; for we both of us knew, that the things we were so fond of talking about, were interesting to nobody but ourselves. But when we were interrupted, I failed not to let him know by a significant nod or whisper, how much the interruption was impertinent and disagreeable to me. I have hitherto constantly followed this method; and the fruits I reap from it, the intimate confidence Theodore reposes in me, makes ample amends for the trouble it has sometimes caused me. I am certain that my son will never have more confidence in any one than in me. Accustomed from his infancy to conceal nothing from me, but to open his whole heart to me, it is now become necessary to him. Brought up by me from the cradle, he has no opinions, no principles, but what I have given him. Consequently we shall always have a great conformity of character, we shall have the same manner of judging, and shall see things in the same light. Our taste alone will be different, but Theodore shall not perceive this. I love solitude; but I shall follow him into the world, and appear to amuse myself there. If I go with him to an horse-race, I shall seem to interest myself for *Glow-worm*, or *King Pepin*. In short, I shall always endeavour to persuade him, that I participate and relish his pleasures as long as they are innocent and reasonable. This is the way I advise you to follow with the Chevalier de Valmont. Consider, that austerity startles youth, and keeps them aloof from us; and that we cannot allure them back, but by appearing to think them agreeable; consider also, that we justly render ourselves insupportable, when we censure their innocent actions.

In my former letter I entered into a detail of the method I thought necessary to be taken to guard him from the epidemical passion for play. I am now to speak of a danger perhaps still greater. Next winter his heart will be disengaged: and what will become of an heart naturally so tender? He admires talents, and he is fond of the theatres. You are sensible, whither that taste leads most of your young men. The Chevalier de Valmont is decent and delicate; and errors of this sort will in him be but of short duration; but how short soever they may be, they always leave bad impressions. Besides, should your son escape this rock, how will he defend himself from a propensity, of which he has hitherto felt only the pains, and of which he longs to taste the pleasures? I see but one means to secure him from it; it is to offer to his imagination an object, to which he may direct his vows, his desires, and his hopes. He thinks Adelaide amiable; he seems convinced she will make the man happy, who shall be destined for her: she is still too young to create a passion: but an imagination of nineteen may easily represent to itself an idea of what she will be two years hence. Besides, the Chevalier de Valmont has a real affection for Madame d' Almane; and surely he will not be insensible to the prospect of being so nearly allied to her, and of being adopted into a family he has known from his infancy. In short, even with regard to interest, he cannot find a better match; for, since he resolves to marry a person of quality, he cannot find one, in whom more advantages are centered: so that I have no doubt but our project will be conformable to his inclinations. Conceal from him the conditional promises we have made to each other; but acquaint him with part of the truth: tell him, from your knowledge of my character you are certain, were his conduct irreproachable, I should prefer him to any other. But, for his own sake, he ought not *soon* to know that in reality I design my daughter for him. The good one is sure to obtain, soon ceases to appear in an advantageous point of view. *Certainty* will cool his ardour; but *hope* will make him enterprising, and enable him, if necessary, to undergo the most difficult trials. But if his imagination be enflamed, if that sentiment encouraged by you becomes a passion, never fear that he will lose himself, that he will stray from you; you will become his friend, and his confidant; all your advice will be attended to and followed. In short, you risk nothing in inspiring him with a passionate attachment to my daughter. If he truly loves her, he will obtain her; for he will learn to deserve her. Adieu, Sir; I shall stay six weeks longer here, after which I shall go to Venice, where I intend to pass the winter.

LETTER XLI.

The Baroness to the Viscountess.

Genoa.

TOMORROW we leave Genoa, and we do it with pleasure; for we have, all of us, a great desire to see Venice. Genoa is a fine city; but it is seen with admiration, and quitted without regret; because there are no charms in its society to attach one to it. Luxury *here* affords no agreeable enjoyments: it consists in mere outside shew; and displays itself only to dazzle, to astonish the stranger, and to attract his eyes as he passes. – Genoa is adorned with sumptuous palaces, superb marble colonades, and immense galleries of pictures; but the rooms of these vast houses are very inconveniently disposed. You must ascend a very steep stair-case, and always seventy or eighty steps at least, before you reach the best apartments. On the days of assembly, these palaces are lighted up with an extreme magnificence. For instance, one lustre commonly holds one hundred and twenty or one hundred and thirty wax-lights. – The Genoese see company perhaps four or five times in a year, and then receive two hundred persons. They give *magnificent entertainments,[68] but never little †social repasts. – Curiosity led me yesterday to a masked ball: Never did I see any thing more dull and more silent. The dancers are obliged to dance in turn minuets for half an hour; and then English country-dances for half an hour; and lastly, Genoese dances for half an hour; these last are exceedingly slow and ‡lifeless. After the Genoese, the minuets recomence; and so on for ever in the same order. I am persuaded that the French alone know how to amuse themselves. Upon the whole, Adelaide and Theodore are very well pleased with their stay at Genoa; they carry away with them a superb collection of designs, and each of them a very pretty journal. Adelaide would have torn some pages of hers, at which I had laughed a little; but I would not permit her; and, according to my promise, you shall see it without correction or retrenchment. Adieu, my dear friend. I hope to find a letter from you at Venice; and for my part, on my arrival there, my first occupation shall be to write to you.

---

* Des fêtes.
† Des petits soupers.
‡ Monotone.

LETTER XLII.

The Viscountess to the Baroness.

Paris.

WOULD you believe, my dear friend, that I received but the other day, that is four months after the date, your journal of La Corniche, and the history of the Dutchess de C— ? The man whom you charged with the packet, fell ill on the road, and arrived at Paris only last Thursday.

I shut myself up with Madame d' Ostalis and the Chevalier D' Herbain, in the little closet you know; and there we read, with inexpressible pleasure, that terrible and affecting story. The Chevalier D' Herbain says, the Duke de C— is like Blue-beard;[69] but not withstanding this piece of wit, he wept as much as we. He thinks the Dutchess has painted the various emotions she felt in her very extraordinary situations, with a truth that carries conviction along with it. – Oh! what a monster of an husband! – Shall *we* now complain of ours! – Shall *we* think much of any little contradictions that may fall out, after such an example of patience, resignation, and courage! – I feel myself humbled in thinking, how far I am from that degree of human perfection! Oh! surely *I* should have gone mad in that vault; I should have died, or rather, I should never have entered it; for I should have told all; I should have declared every thing. – At least I fear I should. – I am not very well pleased with the Count de Belmire. I can very well conceive why the Dutchess, coming out of the cavern, should not love him. Nine years of such confinement might well cool her passions; but her lover ought ever to have adored her; he, who had neither fasted, nor laid upon straw. He is to blame not to love her still. – To become all at once the son-in-law of his mistress, is a strange thing. I can excuse him, however, if the Countess de Belmire perfectly resembles her mother. You will let me know how this is, when you come to Rome; and pray be very circumstantial.

I have nothing new to tell you in regard to my situation. By turns I am tired, and I amuse myself; I grieve, and am comforted; I cry, and I laugh; things go on in the old train. To kill time I have taken a physician. He neither cures my headachs, nor my nervous complaints; yet I am mighty fond of him. This appears to me so singular, that I have given myself the trouble to reflect upon it; and I have discovered, when one is not sick, and has that sort of affection for a physician, that the sentiment arises from the same cause which most commonly occasions our taking a lover. Mons. de Rochefoucauld says, *What prevents lovers and their mistresses from being weary of being alone, is because they always talk of themselves.*[70] A physician then is much more amusing, and much more amiable than a lover; for he never talks of himself, and he listens to you continually with an air of concern, and with the greatest attention. This is, no doubt, the reason I am so fond of mine, and I shall keep him till you return. When *you* are here, I shall have no need of him; for I feel, that I shall with the greatest sincerity prefer the pleasure of listening to you, to the vanity of talking of myself.

The son of Mons. de Blesac is, after all, going to be married; his bride, Mademoiselle de R—, is the most charming little creature you ever saw. She has been brought up by an old aunt, in a secluded castle in the country. She knows nothing, no not how to make a curtesy. She has seen nothing; but she has as much natural wit, as a girl of fifteen and an half can have. Her aukwardness is full of grace, and she is beautiful as the day. Since the death of her old aunt, she has been three months in a convent here, and to-morrow she leaves it to be married. As her mother-in-law goes no more to court, and as Mons. de Limours is pretty nearly related to Mons. de Blesac, I shall present her. I have been to see her several times; she astonishes me. Her candour, temper, and frankness make her both interesting and poignant. She has an excellent heart; and still laments her old aunt, tho' she consesses she was something of a scold; and she is in despair at quitting her convent, because she has strongly attached herself to a nun, to whom her guardian had particularly recommended her. She is tender and ingenuous; has no idea of any thing; she is not sixteen, and is going to launch into the world. Poor thing!

A propos of *innocence:* Constantia took it into her head the other day to ask me, what a lover was. The question embarrassed me, and I believe I did not make her a very good answer: but what is one to do in such a case? Must one make a silly answer, or say something *pretty near the truth?* – I know not; pray inform me. The Chevalier de Herbain, to whom I shew your journals, tells me you will yet find very dangerous roads from Venice to Rome. Now Adelaide is *familiarised with precipices,* if you can avoid them, you will do me a pleasure. I am afraid in a carriage on the road to Versailles; judge then what uneasiness you give me. Your journal of La Corniche made my hair stand an end; and your passage by sea from Antibes to Nice, and your barbarity in making Adelaide sing in the very moment of suffering – All this appeared to me as cruel, and as terrible as the story of the Dutchess de C—. Adieu, my dear; I will always endeavour to imitate you as much as I am able. But I declare to you, my only voyage with Constantia shall be upon the Seine, and the only mountain I shall make her climb, shall be that of Bons-Hommes.[71]

LETTER XLIII.

The Baroness to the Viscountess.

Venice.

WHAT a singular and dull place is Venice! One is astonished on entering it; and you can have no conception of its appearance. A great city in the midst of the sea, all its walls bathed in water, and canals instead of streets! Nothing truly is more extraordinary. In most of the streets, particularly in that where we lodge, there is no passage between the houses and the canal; consequently no foot passengers, no cries in the streets, not the least noise, for the Gondoliers make none; so that you might fancy yourself in a desart, or in the cavern of the Dutchess.[72] If you look out of the window, you see nothing pass but Gondolo's covered with black cloth, which look like coffins; and you have nothing under your eye but dirty water; and old Gothick houses, blackened by time, present you with a most woeful and disagreeable prospect. Add to this, if you go out of the town to amuse yourself, you are not sure of getting back again; for it is very possible the weather may prevent you. This happened to us, who were obliged to sleep in an horrible inn at Fussina, a small league from Venice, because the bad weather prevented our getting further. This city, nevertheless, is well worth a stranger's curiosity. It has not its fellow in the world, and its affords some very fine buildings, and some excellent pictures.

I am obliged, my dear friend, to own to you *another new work* relative to education. It is upon Mythology; or Poetic History;[73] which I have endeavoured to render more agreeable, and, above all, more decent than those already published. – Adelaide had only a general idea of fabulous history; and as for the understanding the pictures and antient monuments, of which Italy is full, it is necessary to know it as perfectly as the Roman history, I have composed this work for her use. I put it into her hands on our arrival at Genoa, and she is now reading it the second time.

How! my dear friend, does Constantia already ask what a lover is? – It is early! – for my part, I think one should not, in these cases, give a foolish answer; *you* can follow this advice better than any one. Say something, then, *pretty near the truth.* Innocence and ignorance are two things very different, and yet they are often confounded. *One* is the most alluring charm that can embellish youth, the *other* does not embellish, and cannot but be hurtful to it. Let us then leave them no more ignorance, than what is necessary to preserve their innocence. It is true, there are questions one cannot answer *pretty near the truth*, without impairing or destroying innocence. I would not lie, nor answer absurdly. What is to be done then? I have long reflected on this difficulty, and have found the way never to be embarrassed with it. Adelaide has never been accustomed to believe me obliged *always* to answer all her questions. On the contrary, I have used her to have her curiosity frequently repressed by this answer. *What you ask, is not worth the trouble I must take to explain it to you.* – Or this. – *It is not necessary for you to know this; the explanation of it will be tiresome to you as well as to me.* You see, that in refusing to satisfy her curiosity, I endeavour at the same time to diminish it as much as possible, by assuring her that what she desires to know, has *nothing interesting* in it. So that she never repeats her question, nor seems vexed with my refusal; and I take care to make this answer very often to questions the most indifferent; which gives me an opportunity of doing it without suspicion, when in reality I could not give an explanation. By this means she is never surprised when I will not answer her. She believes I only spare her the trouble of a tiresome detail, and thinks no more of it. Besides, she is so occupied, her life is so active, and all her time so filled up, that there is scarce a possibility of her dwelling on dangerous objects. When her reason advances, she will find, no doubt, there are things which are mysteries to her; but she will at the same time feel, that she ought to be ignorant of them; for I am sure the purity of her mind and her modesty will guard her innocence. Adieu, my dear friend; I am called upon to go to St. Mark's Place. I will write to you again after to-morrow; for this letter is too short for me.

LETTER XLIV.

Madame d' Ostalis to the Baroness.

Paris.

MADAME de Limours is very unhappy at this instant, my dear aunt. Her daughter and her son-in-law vex her cruelly. Mons. de Valcy soft the other day eight thousand guineas. This news getting abroad, his creditors and those of Madame de Valcy went to Mons. de Limours; and in short, debts have come out to the amount of twenty thousand pounds, contracted in four or five years. Mons. de Valcy is sent to his regiment for a year; and they are about selling one of his estates. Mons. de Limours has paid all his daughter's debts, which amount to thirty-six thousand pounds. She shews great gratitude to her father, and seems to love him passionately: but behaves to her mother in such a manner, as to bring into doubt the grateful sentiment she possesses. She is entirely estranged from Madame de Limours; and tho' she lives in the same house, scarce sees her for a quarter of an hour in a day; and, in short, has no society but that of Madame de Gerville. You know, doubtless, that she is breeding;[74] but she does not seem to partake in the joy, which so desired an event has given her father and her husband's family. She must have a soul of a different stamp, before she can feel the happiness of having children.

Mons. d' Aimeri came not to town till late in the last month; having been six weeks in Languedoc. Since the return of the Chevalier de Valmont, Madame de Valcy has often supped at his mother's; which has been remarked. I was there one evening, and I observed them with all the attention I was able. – Madame de Valcy seems to me still to pursue her point. So much perseverance merits some success; and I believe the *virtue* of the Chevalier is in a tottering condition. – I think Mons. d' Aimeri follows him too openly; he has an air of severity which gives me pain. Fear is sometimes a powerful restraint; but it is always a precarious one. Tyranny gives occasion to great revolutions; and I very much fear, an approaching revolution will soon ravish from Mons. d' Aimeri, at least for a season, the power he abuses.

You have heard of the marriage of Count Anatolle, the son of Mons. de Blesac; his wife is really charming, upon all accounts. Madame de Valcy says, she resembles *Ninette a la Cour*,[75] which is not ill imagined; for she has ingenuity and ignorance, grace and aukwardness; but at the same time it is impossible at the age of sixteen to have more wit, to be less taken up with the prettiest person in the world, and to shew a better disposition. Her relations seem to me not to know her value. Her father-in-law laughs at her; Madame de Blesac feels deeply her want of breeding, and scolds her perpetually; her husband looks upon her as a child, and shews an indifference towards her, nearly approaching to contempt. All this must turn out ill. – What a pity!

Adieu, my dear aunt; eight months are already elapsed; and ten more! – What a long while! You have promised me you will never travel again. – Alas! if, as you say, I have no longer occasion for a guide, have I not still need of a friend, whose place in my heart nobody can supply?

LETTER XLV.

Mons. d' Aimeri to the Baron.

Paris.

I Promised to be sincere, and I keep my promise; but remember, Sir, you promised likewise to excuse some *short errors*. – You shall know all. Depend upon it, I will be ingenuous with you; and indeed you ought to depend upon it: for friendship, gratitude, probity, all equally lay me under the obligation of concealing nothing from you.

As you had foreseen, four months absence has absolutely obliterated the inclination of my grandson for Madame d' Ostalis. He saw her again, not indeed without some confusion and some pleasure; but, being destitute of hope, he is also void of passion. I then observed his looks and attentions turn towards Madame de Valcy, who, making the same observation, has played off every art in the science of coquetry to seduce him. One evening as we returned from supping with her, the Chevalier expressed a very great desire to go to the ball at the Opera House. I answered, I would carry him thither some other time; he said no more, and I went to bed. His chamber is next to mine, separated only by an anti-chamber, which opens to the stair-case. About an hour and an half after I had been in bed, hearing somebody stirring in his room, I called Placide, his old valet-de chambre, whom you know. When he came, I asked if his master was in bed. – Ah! good God! is he not with you? – What then can be become of him? – These words made me tremble, and Placide informed me, that my grandson had gone out of his chamber, saying, he was going into mine, and advised him to go to sleep, for he had many things to say to me, and the conversation might last a long time. Whilst Placide was giving this account, I dressed in haste, and ran into the anti-chamber. The door that leads to the stair-case was fastened; but I found the window open, and perceived that my grandson, at the peril of his life, had escaped by the leads, (which are excessively narrow, and in some places without ledges) and in that manner had got into the next house, where, no doubt, he had maintained some correspondence: and I was not deceived in any of these conjectures. I called up all my people; I made them search all the leads; and I myself went into the street; and after having satisfied myself, that at least he had escaped without accident, I returned to my chamber to reflect on what was to be done; and after much uncertainty, I determined to wait his return. I fixed myself in my armed chair, and in that manner passed the whole night, which, you may well imagine, must have appeared long to me. When day appeared, I opened the window, and shuddered at the sight of those leads, over which my grandson had passed; with precipitation, no doubt, and in a very dark night. – At last, about seven o'clock, a Savoyard brought me a letter. I knew the hand of my grandson, and read as follows:

'I dare not appear before the eyes of a father, whom I respect and love. I am forced to avoid him, and conceal myself. I fear all the weight of his anger; and yet, what is my crime? – The having, *at nineteen years old*, gone *alone* to a ball. – Permit me, Sir, to say, if you had deigned to have allowed me half the liberty, which I see all the men of my age enjoy every day, I should never have concealed from you the least of my proceedings.

Will you permit me to come and ask your pardon? – There is nothing I will not do to obtain it.'

When I had read this note, I wrote in my turn, and sent this answer.

Whilst *you* were at the ball, your father, seventy years old, was in the streets, covered with snow, half naked, and agitated with the most fearful uneasiness. He was examining whether his son, his only hope, had not broken his neck in escaping from his paternal mansion! – Whilst *you* were at the ball, your father was watching alone in his chamber, counting every hour, groaning in a state of desertion, and thinking of nothing but the *ingrate*, who abandons and forgets *him!* – You ask, what are your crimes; they are these – O, Charles! Thou knowest *mine*, and the remorse which overwhelms me. Thou knowest, if the unfortunate Cecilia be not ever present to my thoughts! – Wilt *thou* turn out a fatal instrument of the divine displeasure towards me? – Ah! my son, cruel as such a destiny would be to me, I would submit to it, if thou couldst punish *me* without ruining *thyself.*

A quarter of an hour after I had dispatched this answer, my door opened hastily, and Charles appeared, pale, out of breath, and with his face bathed in tears. He sprang towards me, and threw himself at my feet. After a long pause, caused by our mutual relentings, he broke silence, and made me the most affecting protestations of repentance and tenderness, mixed, however, with some artful and guarded complaints for the little liberty I had hitherto permitted him to enjoy. It is true, replied I, I had flattered myself, after having consecrated the remainder of my life to your service, you would have suffered yourself to have been guided by me, at least for a year or two, after your appearance in the world. – All the young men of your age enjoy you say, an entire independence. But observe, what are they? – I wished you other sort of enjoyments. – I was preparing for you an happier lot. – Ah, Charles! had you seconded my views for you, what a felicity might you have pretended to! – Here I stopped; and seeing in my grandson's eyes an eager curiosity; I have hitherto, continued I, deferred acquainting you with a project, I have much at heart: I waited till you should, as formerly, seek my company, and wish to be alone with me, that I might have an opportunity of communicating it to you. But for three months past you take every occasion to avoid me. In the evening, when we return home, you seem sleepy; you hear me without attention; and you never talk to me but upon indifferent subjects. – And may I not now know this secret? – Without hesitation, I then entered into the particulars, which you advised me to acquaint him with. – At the name of Adelaide he blushed, and I observed a visible emotion in his countenance; and he asked her age. She is now thirteen, replied I, and when she returns from Italy, she will be fourteen, and will then no longer be a child; her talents will be greatly improved; and her person will certainly eclipse hers, whom you now think so charming. You will then be in love with her – and perhaps it may then be too late: for if you are not worthy of her, your passion will be vain. In fine, speak; what are your sentiments on the subject? Do you desire this project to be realised? – Yes, earnestly. And I will confess, thinking that Mademoiselle d'

Almane would one day have the charms, the talents, and the virtues of Madame d' Ostalis, this very idea has more than once presented itself to my imagination. Besides, even in Languedoc, in my early youth, I felt an extraordinary interest in the charming little Adelaide; especially since the day she swooned away, when Theodore inadvertently untied the bandage of Madame d' Almane's arm. That picture will never be effaced from my memory. – So then, *your* sentiments, I find, agree with *mine*: but do you think, Madame d' Almane would chuse for her son-in-law a young man, thoughtless, insignificant, immoral; or even one of moderate attainments? – My conduct hitherto ought not to make me despair. – Harkee, Charles, one may confess one's own weakness, without divulging that of another person. A man of honour ought to have a regard for a lady's character, tho' she has none herself. I do not therefore ask *your* secret; I have told you *mine*; reflect upon it. An error of a few hours may be overlooked; but if you are capable of forming a permanent connection with a despicable woman, whose indecent advances ought to have inspired nothing but disgust; that Madame d' Almane, prejudiced in your favour, should not be deceived in your character, and persist in the good intentions I suppose her to have towards you, I myself will be the first to acquaint her with your irregularities. But she is too well informed, to lay me under the obligation of accusing you myself. If she has the views, I suppose her to have, I do not doubt but she will be instructed, in Italy, of your conduct here; and that from Rome and Naples she will have an eye upon you. Be consistent, that is all I ask of you. If you really feel all the advantages of so desirable an establishment, conduct yourself in such a manner as to be worthy to aspire after it. This conversation has done wonders. Charles, repentant, grateful, and docile, has voluntarily thrown himself wholly into my hands. He consented to set out the very next day for Picardy, where we passed a week, and returned the day before yesterday. We have heard that Madame de Valcy has miscarried, and, it is pretended, thro' her own fault, by going to the ball at the Opera House one night, when there was an excessive croud. My grandson has received two or three notes from her, which he has not shewn me. I fancy, I am but roughly handled in them; and that Charles, on his part, accuses me, without scruple, of tyranny in his answers, and throws the whole blame of his conduct on me. But, in truth, his heart has no share in this intrigue: he speaks of Adelaide with extreme pleasure; the hopes of being one day allied to you, wholly possess him; and I am very sure *that* idea will produce all the salutary effects we expected from it. – Adieu, Sir; let me have your thoughts on all these particulars; continue to give me your advice, and address your letters to me at Paris; for I shall not leave it till towards the end of May.

LETTER XLVI.

The Count de Roseville to the Baron.

I AM now arrived at that dangerous period, at which the preceptor should redouble his care and vigilance, if he would not run the risk of losing all his labour. My pupil is but fifteen and a half, and he is in love. I have long foreseen that his passions would be strong, and would shew themselves early: but he has a command over himself; he has a friendship for me; and his young heart is already filled with the love of glory.

You have not surely forgot Alexis Stezin and his daughter, the young and charming Stolina, to whom the Prince formerly gave his *pellise. We saw her again two years ago, and I thought her so handsome, that I resolved with myself to make no more visits to Alexis Stezin. But notwithstanding her retreat and obscurity, Stolina is but too well known by her charms. Her mother, two months since, coming to town to consult a physician, brought Stolina with her. The physician's son-in-law, an excellent painter, saw her, and drew her picture clandestinely, without either the mother or daughter perceiving the theft; and a fortnight after Stolina's picture was to be sold at all the jewellers. The Prince was soon apprised of it; and from that moment was very curious to inspect all the shew-boxes that were brought him. At length he found what he sought; he met with the portrait of Stolina; he knew it in an instant, and examined it with much attention and disorder. The day after, going through a long gallery leading to the apartment of the Princess his mother, he stopped at a jeweller's shop, telling me his watch was out of order, and that he would have another. I thought he only wanted to see if the portrait of Stolina were in that shop; and endeavoured to engage him to pursue his way, by offering him my watch. He answered he had a mind to buy one: and at the same time, without looking into the shew-glasses, he asked to see some watches. The jeweller offered him one; he took it hastily, and walked on. As we were going, he gave it me to look at: I examined it on all sides, and returned it him again, without being able to comprehend his design; not doubting, at the same time, but his sudden desire of having a new watch proceeded from some secret cause, of which I was ignorant. At night I observed the Prince put his new watch at his bed's-head: I had a great desire to take it for a quarter of an hour, while he was asleep, but the fear of waking him prevented me. The next day and the days following he wore the same watch, and I thought I could perceive some slight signs of a secret intelligence between him and Count Stralzi. Being willing to get farther information, I behaved in such a manner as to persuade him I had no distrust; reckoning that a perfect security would put him

---

*   A cloak lined with fur.[76]

off his guard. In short, a few days convinced me of what I had at first but a vague suspicion of. I eagerly wished for an explanation; but felt how much I risked in being hasty, and in taking an improper time. If I obtained not a sincere concession; if the Prince, already in a course of dissimulation with me, could resolve to tell me a determined untruth, all was lost. I resolved then to wait a favourable opportunity; and chance very soon offered me such a one as I had wished.

One of the great lords of the court is just dead. The places he possessed were asked for, even during his illness. All his spoils are already dispersed and given away, except one dignity he was invested with, and which the sovereign destined for me, though I had by no means solicited it. – One morning the young Prince and I were tête-à-tête, and he was communciating to me his reflections on *Telemachus*, which he is now reading the second time. I stopt him in the midst of it; and why do you not mention, says I, the isle of Calypso, and the growing passion of young Telemachus for Eucharis?[77] – At that question he blushed, and cast down his eyes. I confess to you, replied he, *that* episode is not the part of the work I like best. – At the first reading, however, you were very much pleased with it; you admired the penetration and firmness of Mentor. – Upon second thoughts, I find his conduct too rigorous and too authoritative. – I understand you; you do not approve his pushing Telemachus headlong into the sea. – True; I think the pupil of *wisdom* should have been persuaded by reason, not subdued by force. As he finished these words, a note was brought him from the Prince his father. He opened it eagerly, and, after reading it, embraced me, and informed me that the Prince had granted me the favour I just now mentioned. I kept silence a moment, and then said, I am sensible of the joy this news seems to cause in you: but I am not desirous of this favour; it may make some other man happy; and therefore shall not accept of it. – Why so? – Do not imagine, Sir, that money, places, or honours, can repay the cares I have consecrated to you. Neither the state, nor the Prince your father, can recompense me; you alone are bound to pay that debt; and you have acquitted it hitherto, as far as you are able to do it: I am satisfied, and I ought to be so. If you had exhibited a common genius only, I should, perhaps, seek these vain honours, which I now disdain. But how can so frivolous an ambition seduce me, when your virtues promise me such brilliant and solid glory? – Oh my friend! interrupted the Prince, taking my hand, and pressing it affectionately between his own, my friend! how can I acknowledge so real and so disinterested an attachment? – By conducting yourself, replied I, as you have hitherto done, by loving me, and by letting me always read your noble and grateful heart, which never has concealed any thing from me. This is my real recompence, and, I dare say so, one of your most sacred duties. – Ah! this is too much, cried he, melting into tears, I can no longer resist the remorse which oppresses me. – At these words I affected the greatest surprise. He threw himself into my arms, and I pressed him to my bosom. – Ah! said he to me, I ought to throw myself at your feet. You! my friend, my guide, my father! I have deceived you. I am senseless, but I am not ungrateful. You shall know all – I am ready to obey you – to sacrifice every thing to you.

Put yourself a moment in my place, my dear Baron, and figure to yourself the joy, the transports, which so much candour, so much generosity, must have caused in me! – Oh! cried I, nothing is now wanting to my happiness, but to see *you* feel, as I do, the whole value of this conduct. Ah! I allow you to be proud of it; since it fills up the measure of my felicity, by justifying all the tenderness I have for you! – These words caused the most sincere satisfaction to take place of grief and remorse in the Prince's breast. – He sat down by me, and, after a moment's silence, drew out his new watch, and giving it me, blushing, – Know, then, says he, my faults and my folly! That watch has a portrait in it. – A portrait? – He then shewed me the secret spring, and I opened it. Well, resumed he, do you know that figure? – It is Eucharis. – Ah! the comparison is weak: Telemachus's was a recent passion; he did not love Eucharis from his infancy. – But tell me, Sir, how happened it that, seeming to take a watch by chance, this very individual one should fall into your hands? The jeweller was certainly prepared, and consequently you must have had some confidant in this business. – That is true: I had confessed to *some one* a very earnest desire to have this portrait, and that I dared not ask you for it. Two days afterwards I was told I should find it in that shop I stopped at, and that it would be enclosed in the watch which the master should have in his hand. – And what opinion have you of the person who has done you such a piece of service? – Don't ask me his name; it is the only thing I cannot possibly tell you. – You will give me your word, then, that it is not one of your own people; for I would not suppose that any person, concerned in your education, could be capable of so base an action. – It is a person who does not belong to me. – And one who, I am now sure, will never be your friend. But let us drop the subject: I am now under no uneasiness about your future conduct; having restored me your *confidence*, you will not reject my *advice*. – Alas! what do you require of me? – Promise me to renounce an inclination which will dishonour you, if you have the weakness to yield to it. – Which will *dishonour* me! – Yes, Sir, dishonour you. There have been princes, I know, whose brilliant actions have rendered such errors excusable; but you! what have *you* done to excuse your want of *morals*, and your yielding *basely* to a passion, from which a prince ought, above all things, to guard himself? Besides, what is the object which inspires so criminal a passion? A young person raised by you from the depth of misery; who owes her all to your bounty. What! from a benefactor, from a protector of innocence, will you become a vile and base seducer? Will you lose all the merit of the first good action you have ever done; of that very action, which then gave you so much satisfaction, and made me so happy? No, Sir, I am very certain, the slightest reflection will soon cure you of an inclination which will debase you. – I will promise you to do nothing without, at least, acquainting you with it. – I ask no more; I am satisfied: but what will you do with this watch? I imagine you will be so good as to give it me. – I consent, but on one condition; it is, that you leave Alexis Stezin and his family in the house they occupy on the lake – .

I easily perceived the real fear of the Prince was, lest Stolina should be sent away to some distant province; nevertheless, after the ingenuous confession he had just made, I could not refuse promising what he asked. I was unwilling to discover my fears to him; for every thing that looks like diffidence, mortally wounds a generous heart. But you may well imagine, that in less than a year Stolina shall be well portioned, and advantageously married. With regard to Count Stralzi, I have found means to remove him, for some time at least. Young Saltzback is returned from the expedition he made, by the Prince's order, into all the provinces of this country; and has brought back with him memoirs very well composed, and, I suppose, very faithful. The Prince, by my advice, has just given the same commission to Count Stralzi, who, thinking himself the first employed in it, has accepted it with great pleasure. He set off yesterday, and is to return in six months: I will then inform you what use I intend to make of all this. Adieu, my dear Baron! Let me know your progress exactly; since my young Prince so much interests you, as to make you earnestly desirous of being informed of all particulars relating to him.

LETTER XLVII.

The Baroness to the Viscountess.

FROM Rome! – You, who suppose I date with so much pride from Venice, will, I imagine, think me more proud to be able to write from Rome. But happy those who, like you, my dear friend, date always from Auteuil and from Pantin.[78] You cannot conceive to what a degree one loves one's own country when separated from it far, as I am at present from mine. I meet no Frenchman who does not appear amiable to me. I saw two at Venice, whose company was become necessary to me, and who probably would have tired me at Paris. In short, every thing that recalls France to my mind, is truly interesting to me. But let us return to Rome, since I came thither last night. You may well believe my first care was to send to the daughter of the Dutchess de C— , that Countess de Belmire, whom I so much wished to be acquainted with. Prepared by her mother, she came to me, with her husband, that very evening; and I found in her all the politeness, all the graces, of the Dutchess. She is as like her too as you can desire, though not so regular a beauty. I am sorry to tell you, the Count de Belmire seems to love her in such a manner, as to make one fear the remembrance of Albenga is not always uppermost in his thoughts. However, he has a melancholy air; and when the Dutchess is mentioned, he sighs and is thoughtful. But I was so very much fatigued, that I could not observe and examine him with all the attention necessary to give you a very exact account of him. But I shall dine with him to-day, and in my first letter will fully satisfy your curiosity. – It is true, the journey from Venice to Rome, by Bologna and Loretto, is very fatiguing. The Colfiorite is a *Corniche* extremely dangerous, being as narrow for a coach as La Corniche of Genoa is for a sedan. The mountain, known by the name of *La Cartiere de Foligno, is also a passage very frightful, on account of its precipices, five hundred feet perpendicular, which range along the side of the road, almost the whole length of it. We were obliged to do without our women, almost the whole journey; and very often content ourselves with bread and a few stale eggs for our dinner and supper. On these occasions Adelaide every instant felicitated herself on her abstemiousness, on her not being delicate, and on her having accustomed herself, for a year past, to undress herself and go to bed without the assistance of her woman.

Yes, no doubt, my dear friend, I did not enter Rome with indifference; nay, not without emotion. Rome! that famous city, the country of so many illustrious persons, and, for so long a time, the sovereign of the universe! – But I am wholly taken up with a sentiment, too deeply rooted and too habitual, to permit me to receive very lively impressions from any other objects. Wholly employed in looking into, and reading the deepest recesses of the hearts of Theodore and Adelaide, *that* occupation absorbs me entirely; so that I have but a faint and confused idea even of my own sensations; when at the same time I could give you an account of whatever Adelaide felt on entering Genoa, Venice, and Rome, and of what she felt and thought in admiring the different pictures we have hitherto seen.

I cannot finish this letter without communicating to you an idea, which is originally your own. You know, in talking on education, we have long agreed, that experience is absolutely necessary to the preceptor and to the mother of a family; that we ought to have made children our study, to be enabled to bring them up well, and consequently ought to have educated more than one.[79] I have a letter of yours by me, of an old date, on this subject;[80] in which you say that, according to this principle, the younger daughters will be better educated than the elder; adding, this is a very affecting circumstance for the elder; and you exhort me to seek a remedy for this inconvenience. I have sought long without success; for very often the simplest ideas (almost always the best) are the last which present themselves, because one often rejects and disdains to attend to

---

*   So called from the *paper-works* in its neighbourhood. These mountains afford admirable prospects, natural cascades, springs, torrents, & c.

them. But at last I have been obliged to have recourse to them, and have sound what you required of me. I have arranged my plan, and am now about to put it in execution.

This morning, in the presence of Adelaide, I desired Dainville, who is of this country, to look me out a very poor family; adding, I would take one of the daughters, and bring her up to some business. He is to give me an answer in a fortnight. You must be so good as to wait till then, my dear friend, for the explanation of my project; for, till then, I cannot make you perfectly comprehend all the advantages I expect from it. Adieu, my dear friend! Madame d' Ostalis tells me you are grown astonishingly thin; let me have an account then of your health. Can you entertain me with any thing in which I am more interested?

END OF THE SECOND VOLUME.

ADELAIDE and THEODORE;

OR

LETTERS on EDUCATION:

CONTAINING

All the Principles relative to three different
Plans of Education; to that of Princes, and
to those of young Persons of both Sexes.

*Translated from the French of Madame la Comtesse
de Genlis.*

VOL. III

LONDON

Printed for C. BATHURST, in Fleet-street; and
T. CADELL, in the Strand.
MDCCLXXXIII.

ADELAIDE

AND

THEODORE.

LETTER I.

The Baroness to the Viscountess.[1]

TWO day ago, being alone in my apartment with Adelaide, Miss Bridget entered hastily, and, calling to me from the door, said, she was certain I should be satisfied with the manner in which Dainville had executed my commission – At that instant he came in, leading the most charming child I ever saw; it was a beautiful little girl, of six years and a half,[2] who, on perceiving me, ran to me, holding out her hands – I set her on my knee, and asked Dainville, who she was – he replied, it is a little orphan; she has lost her father some years, and her mother is just dead – Ah! Mamma, said Adelaide, you will take care of her! It will be a good action, said Dainville, for she is with an old woman who cannot afford to keep her any longer – I will, interrupted I, with pleasure accept the charge; but what shall I do with her till we find a proper situation to place her in? Oh! Mamma, let us keep her! She is so pretty, and looks so mild! – That is impossible! – But at least keep her here for some days – Well, I consent to that; and you, Adelaide, shall have the care of her; I have so many other employments ... With all my heart ... Mamma, she shall sleep in my chamber ... Oh! the charming little creature! I will be her Governess! ... I must talk to her in Italian. In short, as all this discourse had passed in French, the child did not understand one word of it. – Adelaide, embracing her tenderly, said, I am going to be your Mamma. – Shall I? At the word *Mamma*, the poor little thing wept bitterly, and cried, I have none! Adelaide fell on her neck, and, taking her in her arms, my Mamma will be yours, she said – The child then looked at me, her eyes still full of tears; is it true, said she, that I shall remain with you always? ... She asked this question with so much simplicity, so tender an air, and sweet a tone of voice, that I felt it to the bottom of my heart – Yes, replied I, you shall never leave us. – These words made Adelaide as happy as the child, and more so, when I added, that I was really determined to keep her, because she appeared to be as sensible as she was pretty. – But, Mamma! said Adelaide, you have promised also, that I shall be her Governess – We shall see that, answered I, we will talk about it in the evening. – At half past eight, when the child was gone to bed, I had a long conversation on the subject with Adelaide. – Was you serious, said I, when you desired to have the care of this little girl? – Yes, indeed, Mamma, I doat on children, and – But you are yourself little more than a child, you are but thirteen years and an half old. – My dear Mamma has sometimes said, that I have a good deal of sense for my age. – That is true; but do you think that you are capable of educating a child? No, Mamma, I am not so vain; but I think, that with your advice and assistance there is nothing one cannot do – if I had a sister of that age, surely I could be of some use – for my own amusement I should teach her some things; I would make her read – I would tell her little stories – and, if she was inattentive, I would rebuke her mildly – for instance, if she should be inquisitive – I know by heart all that I should say to her – I would tell her all that has happened to me – and the Veillée des quarante – and the *Bambolina Francese*.[3] – All that would avail nothing, if you did not set her a good example ... How would she know that she ought to be attentive, if she see you draw without attending – and play on the harp without looking at your notes? – Mamma, in general, I do attend ... Yes, in general, I own you do; but good examples must be shewn constantly to have a proper effect ... The fear of spoiling a child by setting a bad example will be a sufficient reason for me to conduct myself well ... That may be, and I am rather inclined to let you make the trial – Oh! Mamma, do, I conjure you! – It is very likely, that you will some time or other be married and the mother of a family; if that happens, you will then have gained experience, which will be very useful to your children. – You have goodness of heart and generosity; – I am certain, therefore, that, though you are very young, you are convinced of the important duty of a Governess. – I repeat to you, that it is all comprized in this one point, *always to set examples of those virtues you require in others* – I shall be watchful of myself – You will do right, for nothing is more shocking than to spoil and corrupt a child born with natural good dispositions. – The bare idea makes one tremble. – You will one day be accountable to God for the unhappiness of that child; he will say, 'I *created* her good, and *thou haft made her wicked:* at the *same time, barbarous, impious, and sacrilegious, thou hast spoiled and dissigured my work:* there is no *punishment too severe for thee.'* Oh, Heavens! – but at the same time, there is no reward that a mother like mine has not right to expect; in saying these words, Adelaide gently touched my face with her's, and I felt her tears run down my cheeks. – You frighten me, Mamma, said she; I dare no longer wish to be concerned in the education of this charming little girl. – You are too sensible how sacred this duty is ever to neglect it. – Mamma! you really think so! – What joy you cause me? – Besides, if this child should become dear to you ... Oh! I shall love her passionately! ... Well, it will cost you nothing; in endeavouring to make her perfect, you will insensibly correct your own faults – and the desire of deserving your confidence, and of contributing to your happiness. – I understand you; I will watch over your conduct, I will give you advice, and I deliver the care of this child intirely to you. – Intirely – Oh! my God! – Yes, that is to say, she shall sleep in your room, she shall not quit you, she shall play in the closet where you study; at your leisure hours you shall teach her those little things she is capable of comprehending. – You shall in time procure for her those matters that you think necessary; and you will, in short, be her mistress, her Governess, and her mother. – Her mother! poor little thing, can I deserve the name of mother! – Yes, without doubt, if you supply that place. – She will then call me Mamma, Oh! I wish it were to-morrow that she could say so! – Mamma, you must tell her that she must obey me, and call me Mamma; for perhaps she will not believe me. – I am sorry I am so little of my age; if you would let me wear heels, I should appear more respectable. – It is true, you have not a very striking figure, but reason, application, and mildness will gain you as much respect as high heels.

After this conversation Adelaide went to bed, but not before she had looked at her little charge, (who was in a profound sleep) at the risk of wakeing her, she embraced her several times, and doubtless dreamed of her during the night. – Early the next morning, even before I was up, she came to me leading her child, and told me she had given her a new name, as she did not like her own. – She calls her Hermine, because she is extremely fair, and her manners extremely mild. – Hermine is already accustomed to her little Mamma, and obeys her strictly. – Adelaide, on her side, thinks of nothing but setting her good examples; she makes her read, she translates my little stories into Italian that she may understand them; and she has desired Dainville to teach her to draw. – Such, my dear friend, are the simple means I take to render Adelaide capable of bringing up one day or other her eldest daughter. She will pass this important apprenticeship under my own eyes; and it will not interfere with any of her other employments, because she has only to attend to a child, whose age requires no other care than to correct her if she speaks amiss, or if she fails in mildness and docility. – Hermine draws by the side of Adelaide, who will not suffer her to look off, and piques herself on setting her an example of attention. – We are determined, that Hermine shall not learn Musick; we would have her know all sorts of work; write and cast accounts perfectly; understand French as well as Italian, and have a competent knowledge of History. – As she will not play on any instrument, she may always follow her studies in Adelaide's apartment, without disturbing her – Adelaide, by observing her with care, will learn to know children, their inclinations, their little tricks; in presiding over her studies she will be accustomed to be diligent; she will become more attentive, more sagacious, more patient; in short, the desire of being well thought of and esteemed by her pupil will make her correct many little faults in herself, and ripen her understanding.

The Roman Ladies, my dear friend, are in general neither handsome nor well dressed; they use no rouge, nor white and yellow powder, as I had been told – they have a strong dislike to perfumes, and never use any; and, as they know the French women are always very much perfumed, when they think they shall meet any, they fill their noses with little green leaves to prevent them from smelling – I own, I was a little, surprized the first time I saw this green appearance half out of the noses of all the women – Adelaide did not shew the least astonishment at this custom, for, since the Veillée des quarante, nothing seems to surprize her.

At Rome, it is a great mark of politeness to place the most considerable person backwards in your coach. – *You* would be unhappy here, because it is not customary to drive fast; they think it beneath their dignity; and they never stop in the streets, if they have any orders to give to their footmen, they receive them as they walk slowly on. – When the manners are corrupt, fashion must necessarily feel it. I cannot give you an idea of what is her called gallantry, nor of the general manner in which they express themselves. – The man of fashion, speaking of a woman, describes her very familiarly – as *la Marsescotti – La Palestiane – La Barberina*, &c. – Wit is perhaps more common here than in France, but there is no civilized country where education is so neglected, and ignorance so profound. Besides, as, in all parts of Italy, all the great Lords, whose Palaces are so sumptuous, live like little citizens. It is true, that they are fond of ostentation, and that on particular occasions they display great magnificence; but, otherwise, they have a scarce a dinner or supper; no establishment; and think themselves well lighted by a single candle; and think themselves well on half a crown a day.[4] – With regard to jealousy, they pretend, that it now exists only among the lower people, who possess it to a terrifying extreme; for here they stab, instead of boxing as at Paris. – You cannot imagine how common murders are at Rome. The assassin is always favoured by the people. All the shops and houses are open to him; and he saves himself in one of the Churches, where he finds an asylum as safe as it is sacred. – Are these the Romans which History celebrates? Is it the climate which produces these manners? – It is the form of Government which does every thing.

Adieu, my dear friend, embrace Constantia for me, and tell her that I will certainly answer her pretty letter by the first post.

LETTER II.

The Viscountess to the Baroness.

I AM also going to commence travelling, and set out on Monday for Spa;[5] my Physician wished to send me to Plombieres,[6] but I assured him that place is so tiresome it would be death to me; and that I had a great desire to spend some time at the Spa; which he not only consented to, but ordered me thither immediately. I propose taking Madame de Valcy with me, whose health is really much impaired since her miscarriage; otherwise I should not have thought of indulging the extreme desire she has of taking this journey; for her late proceedings have intirely overcome the blind affection I once had for her. I expect to meet many acquaintance at the Spa, particularly the Chevalier d' Herbain, who set out for that place yesterday, and took Porphiry with him, as they are now inseparable; also Madame de Blesac, and her daughter-in-law the little Countess Anatolle, Mons. d' Ostalis, and Madame de Germeuil, who has been returned only three months to Paris, but says her regard for Madame de Valcy is her only motive for going to the Spa, as she must be near her; so that connexion is again revived. But never was divine friendship so much in fashion as at present; for the women are always together; even at supper, they run and place themselves next each other in order to avoid the men, and, if one unfortunately slips among them, the whole set are disconcerted, and shew visible marks of displeasure in their countenances; however, some people will maintain, that they are as envious and satyrical as in our time; and that the men are not essentially worse treated than they were eighteen years ago. – Oh! but, my dear, have you heard that the pretty, the grave, the insipid Madame de N— has a male friend? Undoubtedly you will be surprised to hear me so positively accuse a person who has always had a good reputation; but one may without scruple mention Madame de N— 's conquest, as she talks of it herself to every one who will attend to her; otherwise, no woman, in my opinion, has a right to attack the character of another, even to her most intimate friend. This free confession, however, is supposed to do infinite honour to Madame de N— , and renders her perfectly engaging; all the world commend her sincerity, and think her integrity and honesty ought to excuse every fault; in short, this lover has gained her admiration and friends innumerable.

Upon my word, this is an indulgence which puts one much at one's ease, and will establish an universal freedom, as people will now honestly avow their faults and follies; and I hope, in a short time, the dread of telling a falsehood will be so great, that villains and cowards will no longer conceal their cheats or their fears. And, from the appearance of things at present, there is a prospect of this happy revolution in our manners taking place. I heard the other day, a man with whom you are acquainted, presumptuously boast, that he had *taken in* two men at billiards; he undoubtedly did not say *I robbed*, but as *taking in* is a synonymous term for cheating, there is all the reason from this example to believe, that the men will very soon equal the women in sincerity. Farewel, my dear friend, my health is already mended; the very idea of going to Spa has revived me, judge then the benefit I must receive from the waters themselves.

LETTER III.

The Baroness's Answer.

Rome.

So then, now one is to confess without reserve that one has a lover, and this assurance is to be looked upon as frankness and sincerity! – Formerly, decency would scarcely tolerate a weakness, and now imprudence excuses vice. – 'Why do you say (says J. J. Rousseau) that modesty makes women false? Are the most abandoned more sincere than others? Quite the contrary, they are a thousand times more false, they acquire this height of wickedness by the vices which they cannot divest themselves of, and which exist only by intrigue and falsehood.' – 'I know,' says Rousseau again, 'that women, who openly give themselves up to gallantry, make a merit of this frankness, and swear that, independent of that, nothing is to be found in them but what is praise-worthy. But I know also, that on that head none but fools will believe them – The greatest restraint on their sex taken away, what can deter them? And what honour will they value, having renounced that which particularly belongs to them? Having made themselves once easy with regard to their passions, they have no occasion to resist them.'[7] – Who can help being struck with the solidity of reasoning in this fine passage in *Emilius*?

Adelaide becomes every day more sensible; Hermine contributes infinitely more than I do towards forming her. The other day, Adelaide, for the first time since Hermine has been here, did not draw well, and all the time of schooling seemed absent and careless. When her lesson was finished, I said to her very low, you are negligent, you are going to set your daughter a bad example. – At these words she looked up, and then seemed very thoughtful. – A moment after she came to me and said aloud, Mamma, this is my play-time, I beg you will permit me to employ it in drawing – Why? You have drawn your two hours. – Yes, my dear Mamma, but I have been unfortunately inattentive to-day; I ask you a thousand pardons; and I will repair my fault. – Observe, Hermine, said I, what a charming example your little Mamma gives you. – Adelaide is too young yet not to commit faults sometimes, but you see how she makes up for them, and therefore she will certainly soon be without any.

During this discourse joy sparkled in the eyes of Adelaide, and she immediately brought her porte folio, and for a whole hour applied to her drawing with the most steady attention. – You may suppose, my dear friend, that I am not a little pleased with myself for having found so simple and easy a way to improve her. – Besides, I also enjoy the satisfaction, which results from doing a good action, in prefering from misery a poor little orphan, whose fate, without my assistance, would have been so unhappy. – She was selected from an hundred others: – she is really charming both in person and disposition. – Her first education was very good; she was not even born in the situation in which I found her. – A variety of accidents ruined her family; and the death of her mother, who had no subsistence but a small annuity for life, completed her misfortunes. – I preferred an Italian child, because it must accustom Adelaide to that language. – The only person in our house, who is not very fond of Hermine, is Miss Bridget,-who holds the Italian[8] in high contempt, and has no idea of wishing to speak it, when one has the happiness to understand English; so that she does not know one word of it, which makes the journey to Italy not very agreeable to her. – She is always angry with the servants on account of their ridiculous jargon. – Her natural aversion for Dainville is increased, since we have talked so much Italian; but we must overlook all these little oddities, on account of her excellent qualities, and the exact manner in which she seconds my plan. – Adieu, my dear friend; I wait with impatience for your account of Spa. I am sure you will recover your health, and am charmed with the life you lead.

LETTER IV.

The Baroness to the Viscount.

Naples.

A KIND of epidemical disorder has hastened our departure from Rome, and I shall pass the months of August and September here. – You desire me to send you some account of the women. I am surprised you have not already received a letter I wrote to you from Rome, wherein I mentioned the Roman Ladies. – It is said that their manners are still more corrupt at Naples; however, I was at a ball yesterday, and I returned even edified by the constancy of the Neapolitan Ladies. – They chose a partner for the whole year, and during that time never dance with any other; yet they are said to shew their fidelity in no other kind of engagement.

– There is a woman here, of whom they tell you adventures that appear incredible, if they were not confirmed by people of probity: she was at the ball yesterday, and spoke several times to my son. – I observed that Theodore did not answer her with great politeness – to-day I reproached him for it; he replied, Madame de D. is so despicable! – and, because she is despicable, would you appear to have received an imperfect education? besides, in shewing disrespect to Madame D. you fail in that politeness you owe to more deserving women. – How? – Certainly – since Madame D. is admitted into company, you cannot be uncivil to her without being uncivil to all the Ladies of the party. – Always remember, that a man of sense and delicacy should appear to behave with respect to all women; and that he can never have the air of a man of distinction, if he takes any liberty even with the least amiable: – he should never seek the company of those he believes unworthy, but in public he should ever treat them with deference – this conduct will gain him the esteem of those whose interest and acquaintance he ought to cultivate; – in short, believe me, it never becomes a man to appear to despise the other sex. – For example, what do you think of that young Frenchman whom we saw at Rome, and who has followed us here? – The Marquis de Hernay. – The same; does he seem amiable to you? – I would not wish to be like him, though he has wit, is not ignorant, and behaves well; but he is ridiculous – infinitely so; that is true, because he is always treating women lightly and contemptuously. He thinks that kind of familiarity gives him an air of ease, and that disdain is a mark of superiority; he is mistaken, it only proves that he is a fool, and has been ill educated – yet he has sense, is not that surprising? – a bad education destroys the sense, as it corrupts the heart – he has good parts; his conversation is even sometimes solid. The artists at Rome say, that he is a judge of pictures and statues; or at least he talks well on those subjects. – He seems to be acquainted with history; – how is it then that his company is so little desirable. It is, because he is so important, and he spoils all the good things he says by a severity of manner, a self-sufficiency which is intolerable in most people, but in a youth of twenty is absolutely absurd, impertinent, and ridiculous.

You see, my dear Viscount, how much I endeavour to disgust Theodore with pedantry; for, as you justly observe, the more particular an education is, the more necessary it will be found to attend to this point; and be assured, that Theodore at the age of twenty years will be as modest and unaffected as he will be well informed. – Our young men of this age are in general either completely ignorant, or insupportably pedantic; – they are first-rate wits and philosophers, or, knowing nothing, they deliver themselves up to the most disorderly lives: – this is the fault of their parents, who instil no principles into them, or inspire them with a foolish pretension to wit. – I have seen a father, sensible in other respects, distribute copies of a letter from his son of eighteen, written from his garrison upon a work of morality lately published; which so elated the unhappy young man as to deprive him of his senses. – In like manner a father sends his son at sixteen into foreign countries; he bids him, 'Go, get instruction, and study mankind.' – He goes, – returns – and says, 'I am instructed, – I know the world.' His own family believe him: he repeats with vanity and confidence all the commonplace observations his Governor has taught him. – He asserts, that 'The English are deep; the Italians ignorant and superstitious; the Spaniards barbarians: he extols English liberty;[9] and exclaims against the Inquisition.' – His parents listen to him with amazement; they admire, quote, praise, and in short render him for life an absurd tiresome blockhead. Will education never be improved on? and will the best dispositions and natural parts be for ever given up to the vices and irregularities occasioned by a neglect of it?

LETTER V.

The Baron to the Viscount.

Naples.

THEODORE to day gained some credit, which was very flattering. We dined at the French Ambassador's, where one meets the best company; there were seven or eight people, three or four of them of distinguished knowledge and wit; of whom two were Englishmen. I had business with the Ambassador, who took me after dinner into his closet. I left Theodore for near an hour with the company. At our return the conversation was animated, and on the subject of literature: the Englishmen maintained, against the Marquis d' Hernay, who pretended to understand, and against two Italians who really did understand English, that the *Paradise Lost* was the finest poem in any living language.[10] They told us, that to support their opinion they wished to quote many passages in the first and fourth books, but their memories failed them: they asked if the Ambassador had a Milton? No, said he; but Monsieur d' Almane used to have it by heart: he, perhaps, can assist you. My memory, replied I, is not so good as it was; my son must make up for it. Every eye was now turned with surprise on Theodore, who had hitherto listened in silence to the debates; no one having applied to him. They exclaimed, Does your son understand English? – From his infancy, replied I: the lines you allude to being very remarkable, I am sure he recollects them. Theodore endeavours to repeat them! He, blushing, recited near 200 verses without a blunder, and with a just English pronounciation. Much praise was given to his memory, and more to his modesty. When alone, embracing him, I said, You have given me great pleasure: I could not be vain of your repeating Milton; a fool, had he learned it, would have done the same:

it was your reserve of modesty that gave me such satisfaction: preserve these valuable qualities, they will increase your success, and disarm envy. That merit which is boasted of will be ever questioned; that which others discover will insure praise: for our own sakes, we should endeavour to get the better of the vain wish of displaying our abilities and knowledge: without our taking any pains there will be opportunities enough of their being made public. Theodore agreed to the truth of this reasoning, and frankly owned the satisfaction my approbation of his behaviour gave him. Modesty is the only virtue in a young person to be praised with safety; other commendations serve to render men vain and affected. How many are there, who by being extolled for their sincerity, ease, knowledge, and politeness, become blunt, forward, pedantic, and coxcomical? Modesty cannot be made too much of; nor is it possible, since in the greatest extreme it cannot degenerate into a vice: place her in the most amiable light to your pupil, and never fear that he can follow her too far.

I am determined, my dear Viscount, to stay six months longer in Italy, and not return to France this autumn. I spend the winter at Rome, and leave it by the end of February; pass a month at Florence, the same at Turin, and I shall be in Languedoc in April: where I shall reside seven or eight months: come to me there, if you can, according to our old engagement; if you cannot, I will seek you at Paris. After an absence of two years, I cannot resist the desire of seeing you, and of presenting Theodore grown, well formed, and as amiable as possible for one of his age. This dear son! – Who, I hope, will one day be your's. –

LETTER VI.

The Viscountess to the Baroness.

OH! this charming Spa! I shall be ill every year, in order to be sent hither; every thing is here to be met with; variety of company, play, entertainment, dissipation, or retirement; in short, perfect liberty: was you here, nothing would then be wanting. In the mean time I have got a new friend; for how is it possible to appear at the waters without one? She is a person I was acquainted with about fifteen years ago; but at that time I had not an idea I could ever like her: 'tis Madame de L— and now we agree perfectly: I never question any of her pretensions, which, by the bye, do not at all interfere with mine. Her great pleasure is to disconcert modest people, or those who are just entering the world; she is delighted at having a harsh voice, which is really enough to frighten the most courageous; and from inclination she has adapted a blunt manner of expressing herself, and at the same time a pouting, angry countenance; and her great joy is to find that she distresses people, and that they fear her. Now, as I wish to please, rather than produce all these grand effects, we suit each other perfectly: but, in truth, notwithstanding all her odd ways, she has many amiable qualities; for she possess a great and feeling mind, is extremely frank, and has a fine understanding; she is a person you would avoid, were you only to have a transient view of her; but she attaches you, when you know her better.

WE have also another French woman, Madame de Rainville, but I have no acquaintance with her; she neither attracts you at first sight, nor attaches you on a nearer acquaintance; she is never one instant free from affectation, is naturally insipid, trivial, and silly; but has undoubtedly been told, that, when people are tired themselves, they are sure to tire others; and she is so deeply struck with this maxim, that she appears eternally entertained; consequently, she is passionately fond of every thing: music, dancing, public diversions, walking, family parties; in short, any thing delights her; she sets up to be an epicure, and not to have a single liking in a moderate degree; she is all *fire* and *enthusiasm*, and disputes with warmth and vehemence. She is an eternal talker, never listens, understands nothing; foolish, puts herself on the rack to persuade you she has feeling and a ready wit; and only is able, after all her endeavours, to convince you that she is troublesome, ridiculous, and indeed insupportable: she tires me to death, and makes me almost take an aversion to those things I like best: the other day we dined at the water-fall of Coo; Madame de Rainville was in such an extacy, and praised with so much energy the water, the verdure, and even the sun which burnt us; and accompanied her words with actions so *expressive* and *animated*, that she has given me an aversion, which perhaps I shall never get over, to rivers, cascades, and dinners on the grass.

Mons. d' Ostalis arrived last week at the Spa, and dines most days with us: I spend my time also with Madame de Blesac, the little Countess Anatolle, the Chevalier de Herbain, and my new friend Madame de L.... . I often go to Vauxhall, and I carry Constantia to dance there: we walk on the mountain of *Annette and Lubin*;[11] but it hurts our pastoral ideas to find Annette very plain, and Lubin selling beer.* I return home at nine o'clock, my little society are then assembled, and we converse till midnight; for I have not the simplicity to go to bed at ten, and rise with the sun, in order to drink the waters, which I like much better to have before I am up. – They tell me, indeed, they are more wholesome at the fountain: now, in my opinion, nothing is wholesome that thwarts my inclination.

I am less dissatisfied with Madame de Valcy, since I have been here; that is, with her outward appearance and behaviour. – As to her affection, – I ought no

---

* This mountain so called after two peasants, who were united about fifteen or sixteen years ago by a Frenchman, who named them Annette and Lubin, and built for them a pretty little farm on the top of one of the hills which surround Spa.

longer to reckon upon that; – but, however, she is only two and twenty! – she is still young! – Oh! how the heart of a mother is ready always to forgive!

Farewell, my dear friend, you will be equally happy in Adelaide and in Theodore; and you deserve to be so. I envy your felicity, but at the same time believe me it lessens my afflictions. Yes, I enjoy your happiness, as much as I pride myself in your virtues and your friendship.

LETTER VII.

The Viscount to the Baron.

YOU will now be satisfied, my dear Baron: I have at last for ever broke with Madame de Gerville. She had deceived me in an affair in which she appeared desirous of serving me, and she sacrificed me in the most shameful and ridiculous manner. I confess I find myself at a loss, as, for at least seven years I have had, in fact, no other society than her's. I know what you will say, *return to your family again, and reconcile yourself with your wife.* I know the amiable qualities of Madame de Limours; but I am deterred from doing this by the trouble of *getting acquainted with her*; for we are become absolute strangers to each other. However, I promise you to try what can be done.

All the world are returning from Spa. It is said Mons. d' Ostalis has shewn a great affection for the young Countess Anatolle; but they do not think she returns it; she is very young to determine so quickly; she is only seventeen; but they say that part of her acquaintance very much approve this arrangement, and employ themselves in trying to dispose her to a choice which appeared to be the best she could make of this kind. She loves her husband; but she is treated in such a manner by him that she cannot long preserve those sentiments she has for him. The Count Anatolle disdains the French; he only loves Foreigners, and they to please him must be Russians, English, or Polanders. My charming little Theodore will not have, thank Heaven, any of these sentiments. How impatient I am to see him again! he approaches his fifteenth year; at that age I was already in love; my head was turned by one of my mother's women, Mademoiselle Adrieni, whom I have since raised to the degree of Chorus-singer at the Opera. By the time I was fifteen, I had scaled the walls of my father's garden ten times to go and see a little country girl, whom I almost loved as much as Mademoiselle Adrienne, notwithstanding I had a very severe Governor; but fortunately he was deaf and a little inattentive. I escaped without his being able to hear me, and I deceived him without his suspecting. In short, whatever precautions he had taken, I am sure I should have found the means of escaping his vigilance. How then do you do with Theodore, that child so sprightly, so lively, so ingenious? How is it that he is still innocent; in short, how have you conducted yourself to as to be master of his inclinations, and always to be watching him without becoming troublesome to him?

LETTER VIII.

The Baron to the Viscount.

Rome.

IN the first place Madame d' Almane has no handsome maids, nor am I either deaf or absent. One is not necessarily in love at fourteen, fifteen, or even sixteen years. At that age you say you was in love; but you had equally a liking for Mademoiselle Adrienne, and for your little country girl, which proves you had no real affection for either. Love depends chiefly on imagination; the idea we form to ourselves of this passion gives it the power and influence it has over us. If we look upon it merely as a temporary intoxication, affecting the head and not the heart; beauty alone will seduce us, and the illusion will not long continue. This was your case: your imagination was heated, before you knew how to love. The first experience persuaded you, that thinking one woman handsomer than another was to be in love. The consequence was your giving yourself up to a thousand temporary raptures; a great many intrigues, and not one settled attachment. On the other hand, I would have my pupil be convicted, that, when beauty, accomplishments, sense and virtue are united in the object of this passion, this will create the happiness of his life. I would have him believe, that it should last for ever; or, at least, if time should diminish it, that so tender a friendship, so sweet a remembrance, would be implanted in the heart as to leave no regret at its loss, nor desire of experiencing it again. With its opinion, my pupil will not be fond of two persons at the same time; and he will be in love but once in his life. He will be difficult and nice in his choice; but he will be invariably fixed. Love being a natural illusion in our youth, the preceptor ought to make this passion serve to the happiness and honour of his pupil. A liking may be violent enough to lead one astray, to disgrace, to ruin one; a proper passion may lead one to great actions. The one will make us do extravagant things; sacrifices of the first impression: the other can alone lead us on to deeds which require perseverance. That woman, who said to her lover *be silent for two years*, and was obeyed, had inspired a passion, and not a liking only. Every thing is to be expected from a sentiment of which we are only susceptible in the flower of our age. A sentiment produced by a warm imagination, which esteem and friendship should render as sweet as it is solid and violent. I well know that one may passionately love a contemptible object; but this is the misfortune of those who are weak, narrow-minded, and despicable themselves, or who are misled in their choice. It is of consequence for a young man *not to begin* with a *liking*, which will rob him of his principles and prudence. A virtuous passion should force him from insensibility, of which he will not be susceptible till he is eighteen. How can he be preserved till that time from little flights which do not touch the heart? Watch him attentively, guard his innocence, do not suffer him to be one moment idle, and believe that this imagination will not figure to him any thing you would with concealed. You will say, is it possible to preserve a young man innocent to the age of eighteen? I am sensible it is not the present custom, though it was the custom formerly; and even now Princes, more assiduously looked to than other young men, come out of the hands of their Governors without the knowledge of love, or any thing resembling it. You ask me, how I contrive to be thus watchful over my son, without disgusting him? Because he is not conscious of being more strictly attended to than he was at six years old. He has always slept in a closet within my room, and even in it, when on a journey. This is no constraint on him; I have even made it agreeable to him. He is by nature communicative; he likes talking; he has an unbounded confidence in me; but he has so many studies, particularly for these last two years, that we seldom have in the day-time any opportunity of a regular discourse. I have promised to converse with him every night after we are in bed. Theodore, having always a number of things to talk to me about, waits for that time impatiently; and with the greater eagerness, by my telling him often in the day, that I have some few secrets to impart. I never fail to add, 'There is not time now to inform you to them; at night you shall know them.' Theodore is delighted with bed-time; half undrest, he whispers me a question. I refuse to hear it, prudence not permitting me to talk of things of that consequence before my Valet de Chambre. Theodore with a grave air gives me a sign of approving my discretion, but hastens me to bed; when we are there, lighted by a small lamp which gives the appearance of twilight, our secrets begin: it is then we indulge the pleasure of a free conversation. We often speak both together, or mutually ask each other questions with equal earnestness and curiosity. This is the more agreeable, as we have no reason to fear interruption. Besides, I take care always to appear at this time more gay, more easy, and more affectionate than at any other part of the day. If he has any thing to accuse himself of, he chuses this time. In short, these nocturnal entertainments are so delightful, that he often declares his extreme regret at the thoughts of sleeping in another room at our return to France. He talked of it yesterday. I told him, that I too should be sorry to be deprived of them, but we must contrive to discourse in the day, O! Papa, what difference? – You do not find me then so good-humoured, is not that it? – I am convinced, Papa, that you are always kind, but in the night! You appear then to love me best. You make me more your equal. No doubt, when you have behaved well, I must like you better at the end, than at the beginning or middle of the day; you have given me twelve satisfactory hours complete. Dear Papa, let me lay in your room at B— at Paris? – You make there a very reasonable request: you would have me go to bed at your hour. – True, but you have done as much for me before; besides, I am almost fifteen; when we leave Italy, we shall go to Languedoc, and stay six months there. In the country, as well as on our travels, you always went to bed when I did. – Very well, but at Paris? When we get there, I shall be near sixteen, and you will allow me to sit up a little later. – Yes, till half past ten. – Let it be eleven. Our conversation in bed lasts an hour, and your masters come early. – That is true, you will be obliged to go to bed at half after ten. – How! I obliged? – Yes, my dear, Papa, you will not refuse me what makes my chief happiness. – Consider it is unprecedented at Paris to go to bed at ten. I must give up all company. – You will be glad of the excuse; you do not love the world. – I regret it not when I give it up for you; but I like it, when I am in it. I am resolved to return into it to introduce you, and that will be soon. For example, when I am seventeen, there will be no reason against my sleeping in your room. – That I allow. – Well, Papa, you who are so kind will not refuse to abate me eighteen months, which are, in fact, but six; for we shall spend the rest in the country, and at the regiment I am so belong to. – Well, well, chatterer, go to sleep I will think of it.

You see, my dear Viscount, that it is not without reason I grant as a favour what I most wish. If Theodore was once to suspect his sleeping in the same room with me was, that I might be a spy on his actions, he would look upon my apartment as a prison, and me as on a tyrannical jailor. It is thus that the same precautions, taken inconsiderately or prudently produce useful or pernicious effects. I do not deceive myself; for I know that Theodore will one day find himself on a sudden under restraint from this engagement. I shall easily perceive this change in his mind by his indifference. I shall have foreseen this event, and of course be prepared with sure means of preserving my authority over him as strong as ever; you shall know them when this happens.

I was acquainted before with the quarrel between you and Madame de Gerville; and you ought to have received my letter, in which I owned myself not surprized at her treachery. Since I have lived in the world, I have never found a single instance of a person given to intrigues whole friendship might reasonably be depended on.

LETTER IX.

Madame d' Ostalis to the Baroness.

B E not alarmed, my dear aunt; Mons. d' Ostalis will never again leave me; the fancy which posessed him will not become a passion: I have followed your advice, and I have found all my happiness again. I told you in my letter from Versailles, that I had only suspicious; but I was soon out of doubt. It seems that his attachment to me, so solid and so lasting, had wearied every one of our acquaintance; for his change appeared to create universal joy. I saw that malignant pleasure shone through the testimonies of concern that many people gave me on this occasion; they wished to appear as if they pitied me; they feigned to be affected with my condition, but they had no other motive for their conduct than that of acquainting me with an event, at which they thought, perhaps, my self-love would be still more hurt than my heart; but, these envious and malicious people have been deceived in their intentions. I appeared not to understand their insinuations, and not to believe their positive assertions. Some laughed at my credulity; others thought I affected it in consideration of Mons. d' Ostalis. In general, this conduct has been much approved, and yet I was not without grief and inquietude; I saw Mons. d' Ostalis really in love with the most charming person who has appeared in the world these ten years; it is true, that I observed nothing in the Countess Anatolle, which could encourage the passion she has inspired; but she is only eighteen, very much incensed against her husband; she is naturally tender, and all her mother-in-law's society visibly countenance Mons. d' Ostalis. Madame de Blesac, equally deficient in understanding and penetration, and full of the most ridiculous vanity, thinks it impossible that a young person, who has the honour of being her daughter-in-law, can ever take a lover; and really believes Mons. d' Ostalis only goes to her house for the sake of being of her party at piquet. Delighted with his assiduity and complaisance, she is continually commending him; so that the Countess Anatolle hears eternally the praises of a man with whole sentiments she is doubtless acquainted, and a man too whose amiable qualities are sufficiently apparent without any body's taking pains to point them out. I reflected a long time, and at last determined not to alter my past conduct. I behaved to Mons. d' Ostalis with the same conformity, the same mildness, the same desire of pleasing and attracting him; only I go much seldomer to Madame de Blesac's, and cease intirely speaking of the Countess Anatolle. As her mother-in-law trusted her often with me before the journey to Spa, and as she came to breakfast with me two or three times a week, it was impossible to create wholly receiving her at my house; but I no longer seek those opportunities, and put them off as much as possible without appearing to do it purposely. When I am with her, I always treat her with the same friendship; which is very easy for me to do, as I have naturally a great liking to her. Mons. d' Ostalis well knew I saw through his heart: his embarrassment was redoubled: he saw I was determined not to complain or question him, he began to feel himself much in the wrong; his passion struggled with his repentance, and for an instant stifled his natural generosity. He thought, perhaps, I secretly prided myself on my moderation; he wished to lessen the merit of it, and seemed to think my mildness was occasioned by indifference. Then it was I testified my affection for him; this was not what he expected or wished; by making him still more cul-pable, I increased his anger. His temper could not fail being very much altered by the violent agitations of his mind; he became totally unlike himself; he saw my tears flow without being softened; he let me see he suspected me of false-hood and hypocrisy: I desired him to explain himself, which he refused. Oh! how severely I felt, in this dreadful situation, the misfortune of being separated from and deprived of you! I have friends on whom I can depend, but it is only in the bosom of my mother, my benefactress, that I can deposit such griefs; to what other person on earth can I be permitted to acknowledge the wanderings and faults of an object so dear to me! My sentiments are so well known on this sub-ject, that those who have the greatest friendship for me, Madame de Limours, Madame de S— , and the Chevalier de Herbain, have never dared say a single word to me on Mons. d' Ostalis' conduct; very certain, that on this point they could not obtain my confidence. Such was my situation, when I received your letter, which, at the same time, revived and gave me the advice I stood in need of; I apprehended, that it was equally dangerous to affect indifference, or to shew so much sensibility as to give myself up to pique and ill humour; I determined therefore to write a note to Mons. d' Ostalis, of which I have send you a copy:

'You shun me; you appear embarrassed when with me; and why? What reproaches do you fear from a person who owes you ten years of happiness? And who, during that time, has never ceased to be perfectly happy, till within these three months? I must have been very ungrateful, should I now think myself gen-erous: alas! I have neither the right nor the desire to complain with acrimony; I am a friend who would speak and open to you her heart ... do not refuse me this explanation; I promise not to question you; I only beg of you to hear me.' – This note, by dissipating a little of Mons. d' Ostalis's embarrassment, restored him part of his generosity; he returned me an answer full of tenderness, and yet without promising me the conversation I sollicited. The same evening we supped together at the Spanish Ambassador's; the Countess Anatolle was there, and I observed that Mons. d' Ostalis did not dare to feat himself by her side at table. I went away before twelve, and left him there; for, since his return from Spa, we never go together in the same carriage. Mons. de P— gave me his hand to the bottom of the stairs, and went out at the same time that I did; on turning into the street Traversiere, one of the hind wheels of my carriage broke, and it overturned. The shock was so violent, that both glasses were broke into a thousand pieces; and one of the splinters cut my forehead exceedingly. Mons. de P— , who had followed me till then, (for he lives near me) stopped at the same moment, got out hastily, and, with the help of his servants and mine, succeeded in taking me out of the coach. He offered me his, to take me home; but I refused it; and, as I was not many steps from Madame de S— , I walked there, and so got rid of Mons. de P— . Madame de S— was not returned, and, finding neither her horses nor carriage at home, I wrote to Mons. d' Ostalis, to beg he would send me his; and, not to alarm him, or make him think I wished him to come himself, I only told him I had left mine on account of a little fright; and I sent this note by one of Madame de S— 's servants, who had not seen me, and who knew nothing of the accident. In about a quarter of an hour I heard a carriage enter the court; and, in a moment, the door of the room I was in suddenly opened, and Mons. d' Ostalis appeared; I arose, but, scarce having strength to support myself, I fell again into the great chair. Figure to yourself, my dear aunt, the astonishment and the terror of Mons. d' Ostalis, on seeing me covered with blood, pale, dishevelled, and with a large wound in my forehead. He came towards me, and clasping me in his arms, with his face bathed in tears, asked me a hundred questions at a time, but did not listen to my answers: he rang all the bells, assembled all the family, and sent for a Surgeon and Physician; in the midst of all this confusion, Madame de S— returned with a Surgeon whom she had brought with her; one of her servants, having been to acquaint her with my accident, she went immediately to seek for the help I stood in need of. The Surgeon found me feverish, and said I must be bled, but not yet for some hours. Madame de S— intreated me to stay where I was; but I refused, and returned home about two o'clock. When Mons. d' Ostalis and I were seated in the coach, he all at once threw himself on his knees before me, and seizing one of my hands; ah, cried he, this explanation which you asked of me, why are you not in a situation still to demand it! ... What! interrupted I; when you love me with the same tenderness, when you have proved it to me in so affecting a manner, do you think you have not already restored me to happiness? ... But I am guilty, said he, in a low voice, if I have given you one moment's affliction. At least, do me the justice to believe, that I am sensible of my faults, and that I earnestly with to atone for them! ... He pronounced these words in a manner which affected me so much I could not answer him! ... I put my face to his, and embraced him; he took my hand, and kissed it with transport: you weep, cried he; these sweet and innocent tears pronounce my pardon, without which I could not live, and which afford me equal joy and gratitude; as he said these words, the coach stopped. Though I was very weak and much bruised, I would not complain for fear of affecting Mons. d' Ostalis: but he perceived how much I suffered, and, taking me in his arms, he carried me into my chamber. The next morning at six o'clock, I was bled; I had no return of my fever; my head was quite easy, and I had no other illness than a sprain, which occasioned my keeping my bed for four-and-twenty hours. The same evening I had a long conversation with Mons. d' Ostalis ... I know very well, said I to him, that love is not a lasting passion. I have never at any time in my life placed my felicity on so transient a sentiment: doubtless, it would be very pleasing to possess your affections intirely; but I only depended on your friendship and confidence. I had flattered myself I should always remain your true and faithful friend; and this was the happiness I feared to lose. Had you succeeded in seducing a young, innocent, and sensible woman, had she sacrificed to you her reputation and peace of mind, you would have wished to make her happy, her heart being naturally good. And what delicate heart can content it self with love? she would have been desirous of gaining your confidence and even your esteem. She would have said to you: 'You have ruined me; you have deprived me of that virtue which I loved, and which I lament; you have given to my friends, and to all who surround me, the dreadful right of despising me; and, if you will not be my friend, what is to become of me, when you cease to be my lover?' What could you have been able to answer, said I? You would have promised all she demanded. She is amiable; she has wit; she would soon have obtained those sentiments of friendship and confidence of which I am to jealous, and which my affection makes me worthy to possess intirely. Ah! cried Mons. d' Ostalis, be satisfied; you shall never see me attached to any one who can make you uneasy ... The sacrifice you ask from me is already made, and gives me no pain. Yes, I deceived myself in thinking I could prefer another object to you; I knew not my own heart ... Ah, when it is you who are beloved, inconstancy is nothing but an illusion!

You are sensible, my dear aunt, I may depend on the promises and the sincerity of Mons. d' Ostalis: therefore you will judge all my uneasiness is vanished. It is now eight days since we had this conversation. I did not write to you before, because I wished to tell you I was perfectly recovered. The wound in my forehead is almost well, and will leave no scar; in short, I am better than ever. I have not written to you since my long letter from Versailles, but in a concise manner, not being willing, at the distance we are from each other, to afflict you with an account of my uneasinesses, unless I could have been near to have consoled you. Now, that I am again restored to happiness, I can only enjoy it imperfectly, because you are ignorant of it; and yet this happiness is the work of your hands. I owe it to the education you gave me; to the husband you chose for me; to the advice you have given me. Oh, my dear and tender benefactress! every moment of my life, you are present to my remembrance. Every happiness I enjoy is derived from you; and this idea still increases my felicity ... My tears flow; you will trace them on the paper; and perhaps you will mix your own with them ... Adieu, my dear aunt! my heart is full! ... I can write no more ... Adieu; I shall expect your answer with the utmost impatience.

LETTER X.

Madame d' Ostalis to the Baroness.

Mons. d' Ostalis never behaved so charmingly to me before: he does not leave me; we go out together; we have no longer two carriages; in short, we are exactly on the same footing, as before we went to Spa, except that Mons. d' Ostalis shews me, if possible, more regard and affection. I forgot to tell you a little affair which passed the day after my accident, and which seemed to make some impression on him. Madame de S— and the Chevalier de Herbain were at our house. Madame de S— was saying, that Mons. de P—, who had assisted in raising up my carriage, and had offered me his own, was ill of a fever, and kept his bed. That is very natural said the Chevalier de Herbain; he is ill on account of the grief he felt on Madame d' Ostalis's situation, because he is in love with her. Ah, said Madame de S—, I am charmed to hear it; Madame d' Ostalis can no longer boast, that no one was ever in love with her a moment. Oh! cried I, maintain it, Mons. de P— does not think of me. But, said the Chevalier de Herbain, interrupting me, it is useless for you to deny it; for, it Mons. de P— loves you, it is not your fault; however, it is certain he does. He rose from his seat, and, smiling, drew Mons. d' Ostalis to the window, where they talked for a moment very low, and then went out together. In less than a quarter of an hour they returned, and both appeared to be much softened. The Chevalier de Herbain came to my bedside, and kissed my hand with an air of satisfaction, which made me think Mons. d' Ostalis had just informed him of what had passed between us, and I could not imagine what had been the cause of this explanation. When Mons. d' Ostalis and I were alone, he took a paper out of his pocket. The Chevalier de Herbain, said he, who was glad of an opportunity to give me a lesson, has shewn me this letter which he received this morning from Madame de Limours. He desired me to read it, and it was as follows: 'I have only seen Madame d' Ostalis for one minute this morning. I did intend dining with her, but I cannot go to, her till six in the evening. Do you know that Mons. de P— is ill? He told a person of my acquaintance, who has just left him, that the accident of yesterday was the cause of his illness; for that he really feared for the life of Madame d' Ostalis. – He did not, however, avow any particular attachment; but the person, who informed me of it, says, that he is in love. In love with Madame d' Ostalis, cried I; then he is very ridiculous! ... Oh! Madame d' Ostalis will now turn the heads of many people: she has lost her husband's affections, and it was only they that kept lovers at a distance. This expression struck me; make what use you please of it. What woman will now dare to flatter herself with preserving the tenderness of her husband.'

It appears to me, that what struck Madame de Limours so much had the same effect on Mons. d' Ostalis. At least, my dear aunt, the winter approaches, and gives me the prospect of seeing you again in four or five months, as you have promised me you will not prolong your stay in Italy. Mons. d' Aimeri and the Chevalier de Valmont expect you with great impatience. The Chevalier conducts himself to a miracle; you will find him perfectly formed; he talks rather more than he did, but with the same modesty which you admired so much; he is less bashful, but appears always reserved. Madame de Valcy thinks no more of him: her coquetry is addressed to another object, an acquaintance made at Spa, an Englishman, who stays here all the winter; a clumsy tall figure, very pale, and very insipid; yet he appears to gain general approbation, although his manners are rude and blunt; which I fancy would succeed very ill in our country-men. – In short, Madame de Valcy has learned English; and it is thought she has already said, *I love you*.[12] This is very possible, for she does not fix any great value on this expression. Her person is much altered. She is excessively thin: her face has pimples on it; and she is no longer pretty, though she is only one and twenty: Madame de S*** is nine-and-twenty, and is still as blooming and as beautiful as she was at eighteen. Such is the effect of innocence and a pure and tranquil mind! I am convinced, nothing preserves beauty so well as living a regular life. Adieu, my dear aunt; I hope now that every step you take will bring you nearer to us; and that your next letter will be dated from Florence.

LETTER XI.

The Baroness to the Viscountess.

WE set out to-morrow, my dear friend, for Florence. It is impossible for me to regret Italy, when I am returning to France; yet my departure from Rome will occasion some melancholy emotions. You know my attachments to the C— d—ts; I cannot divest myself of the idea that I shall never see him again. He enjoys here every mark of respect that high rank, superior talents, great experience, a thorough knowledge of business and mankind, with the most serupulous integrity, can acquire. He possesses equally those qualities which command our esteem, and the virtues which gain our affections. He has the art of uniting to the appearance of a person in office the natural and easy behaviour and the free conversation of a private person. He has neither state nor pedantry. (True dignity is derived from the soul, and owes nothing to affectation.) His face, his discourse, his air, indicates his character: by seeing him, you know what he is. He possesses that happy and rare union of prudence and openness, of nobility and good-nature.

I shall, besides, leave behind me at Rome the Count and Countess de Balmire, whom I shall always remember: Adelaide has a sincere regard for the Countess, and has been in tears these two days. Miss Bridget finds fault with a sensibility of which she has not the least conception; for she is most earnest to return to France; and, in spite of her concern, we pack up chearfully, and rejoice in the thoughts of being at B— in three months time. You, my dear friend, promised to be there to receive me, and spend with us two months; but you do not mention Madame de Valcy: should it be agreeable to you to bring her, I flatter myself you are assured that it would give me pleasure. I depend upon Mons. de Limours; I am sure of Madame d' Ostalis, and the Chevalier d' Herbain writes that he will not wait for leave to visit one after an absence of two years; so long separated from them, how delightful it will be to assemble all my dearest friends!

Well, I have finished another work upon Education – be quiet, it is the last. Sincerely it is not for pleasure that I spend my nights in writing eighteen or nineteen volumes on the same subject: a sprightly head and a female fancy are not easily fixed down to such an employment! but I absolutely wanted these compositions: there were none; I made them. It is necessary, that before I explain the plan of them, that I should acquaint you with the reflections that made me see their usefulness. I figured to myself my dear daughter married at nineteen, and gone out of my hands perfectly educated: I saw her possessed of excellent principles, sound judgment, a polished understanding, an upright heart, her character formed, and more experience than commonly falls to the share of others at five-and-twenty. I was convinced she would love virtue, and that she would have the command over herself. I feared neither bad examples, nor the power of the passions: yet I foresaw with apprehension, that she would often hear in the world dangerous opinions maintained in a subtle enticing manner, even by people without abilities, but abounding with all those destructive principles which they have learned by heart from those contemptible performances which particularly, for these last twenty years, have turned so many moderate heads. I saw Adelaide amazed, thinking such strong arguments unanswerable; compelled to admire reasons whose falsity her soul and conscience bore witness to, and which her understanding in vain sought to refute. Certain that nothing would tempt her to read the scandalous books which openly attack religion and morals, how could I hope that she might not wish to study some works unfortunately celebrated, which, containing the same bad principles, are the more to be dreaded, as they may be read without shame? I dared to believe, that the love of virtue was sufficiently instilled into Adelaide's heart to be always her guide, even without the assistance of reason: but it grieved me, that she might perhaps at times have melancholy doubts with regard to the most pleasing and comfortable truths. – How was I to prevent these dangers? Was she to read at fifteen the books I just mentioned, for me to discover to her the false though subtle reasons they contain? But such a refutation is of too great consequence, and would occupy one's thoughts too much to be possibly effected in reading fast with her; besides, the lectures would be very long, and of course take up much of our valuable time. – Upon reflection, I found I could solve this difficulty by binding myself to a troublesome business, which required patience, thought, and judgment. From all the books that appeared to me dangerous I made two extracts; the one of their bad principles, the other of the contradictions which in the same Author destroyed these principles: this done, I began a sort of epistolary romance. This is the plan: A young man of parts and good disposition, but with warm passions, leaves his Province, enters into the guards, and settles at Paris. He makes danger-ous connections, and reads, with rapture, books that shake his principles. He has left in his Province a sister seven or eight years older than himself, for whom he has a sincere affection. He gives her an exact and regular account of his adven-tures, his thoughts, and studies. His sister, in her answers, gives him advice, and attacks, in a plain and solid way, his opinions and errors. I have put into the young man's letters all my extracts of false and destructive principles: they are marked by asterisks; a note shews the volume and page of the work from which they are taken: in these notes I have recited the contradictions and false conclusions of the same author. The sisters invariably follow the brother's letters: his regular-ity makes the work appear formal and improbable, though I have endeavoured to make it interesting: however, it is not wrote for publication. There are forty letters and their answers. A fortnight ago I had the first letter from the brother, wrote fair into a copy-book; and, being alone with Adelaide, I said to her, You are now near fifteen, one should begin to form your mind: your extracts are well done: your last six months journal pleases me much: you must now learn to write correctly and elegantly, and more particularly to reason solidly. That this study may be easy to you, and even an amusement, I am about a novel, of which you shall compose half. – That will be delightful! – Every week I will give you a letter: you will consider it with care to answer it. To-day we begin. You are to imagine yourself a woman, married these ten years, and living in the country, and having a brother at Paris, a constant correspondent, who is led astray by hurtful exam-ples and wicked publications. – That is not Theodore! – No; we are to suppose that he had a bad education; and the misfortune to begin the world without an adviser: it will be your task to reclaim him. Is my advice to have any weight with him? – very great. – Well! I will bring him back to the right way. – Here is his first letter – Give it me, dear Mamma! – First hear me: This is the letter of a man whose mind is already spoiled, and whose heart begins to be faulty. I forewarn you that this, and all the other you will receive, contains only bad principles of false opinions. In reading it, remind yourself often that you have only to dispute every sentiment therein; carefully search for all the opposite arguments that are convincing ones: it will be your fault if you do not overturn his system. The dotted lines are extracted from various Authors, as the notes will shew; and other notes will explain how they most absurdly contradict themselves. – Mamma, can I contend with the Authors? Certainly, and even with success; for they reject the truth; you seek for it, and find it in your heart. – Mamma, I will read the letter, and answer it this afternoon. – No, reflect more seriously upon it; – I do not expect your answer for a week.

At that time she gave it me with my letter; and I explained to her the faults of her composition. Your arguments, said I, are not strong enough: there is a want of regularity and connection in your ideas: your style is not elegant, and often incorrect and obscure. I will now shew you how you should have done. I read to her twice over my second letter: she was delighted with it, and discovered that her's was good for nothing. I will in this manner give her all the young man's letters in their proper order, and, when she brings her answers, will produce those I had written. This will employ her for a year. When she is near seventeen, she will take it up again: and, then being more ready at her compositions, she will finish the forty answers in six months. Thus I shall at the same time form her style, her mind, and her reason: I shall guard her against those dangerous impressions which might have been made at a future period. I shall inable her to reason with good sense on all sorts of subjects; I shall make her an excellent Logician, a character seldom to be met with in our sex; at the same time I shall discover if she is a moderate, or an extraordinary genius; at all events, this method will give her solid understanding. Mons. d' Almane practises Theodore also in this work of mine. His first letter was like his sister's, but better; the advantage of age was apparent.

Adelaide's attention to her scholar daily increases. It is at the same time whimsical and interesting to see her always with her daughter at her elbow; checking her, sometimes scolding her with formal and cross looks, or caressing and playing with her, and at the same time affecting an air of condescension, which makes me laugh, and touches me. Poor little soul! how she will love the children![13] Her heart, already susceptible of such soft and pure feelings! may she enjoy happiness equal to what she occasioned in me.

She experiences already the pleasures of a good mother: the deeper impressions these make, the less insensible she is to her former amusements; she gives with the more joy half *her savings* to the poor, because she always selects those who have been mothers of families, and is tenderly anxious about those poor women who have daughters of five or six years old. The other day she was melted, even to tears, on meeting in the street a little beggar, who had a slight likeness of Hermine. Adelaide had her cloathed, and desired me to put her apprentice to a sempstress. My daughter appropriates the other half of her savings not to her own, but Hermine's fancies; and, instead of laying it out in gewgaws for herself, she buys play-things for her daughter.

Adieu! my dear friend, it is with sincere pleasure I shall see you again so soon, and that I shall find you more happy, on account of the improvement of Madame de Valcy's behaviour, and that the quarrel between Mons. de Limours and Madame de Gerville has restored him to you. Your happiness is essential to mine; and, whatever is my lot, I cannot praise my good fortune, when you are unhappy.

LETTER XII.

Monsieur d'Aimeri to the Baron.

YOU say very true, Monsieur, it is easier to give up an amusement which pleases us, than to use it with moderation. I have sometimes permitted my grandson to play at games at chance, provided it was done with prudence. He assured me, as he was not fond of play, that he should always have a command over himself in this respect; notwithstanding which, he has in one single night lost two thousand guineas! – Last Tuesday we were engaged to sup at the Ambassador's de ***, where was to be a large company. I had a violent headach, which prevented me from going; but, finding Charles wished very much to be there, and, I must own, thinking he was much more prudent than I have found him, I permitted him to go alone. The next morning, before I was up, I received the following note from him: 'I find myself obliged in honour to declare to you an inexcusable fault which I have been guilty of. I have concealed from you, that, for these eight days past, I have owed Monsieur de *** a hundred guineas, lost to him by thirty and forty at a time. The hopes of paying my debt to him made me play with him again last night. I did not win a single game. The excess of my bad luck put me quite out of patience; I should have gone on for ever. I will even confess to you, if Monsieur de *** had not left off playing, my extravagance would have had no bounds. In short, I lost two thousand guineas. – I throw myself at your feet, to intreat you will pay my debt! As to every thing else, I will receive, with equal respect and submission, any punishment you think proper to impose on me. But, if I dared to ask still one more favour, it would be, that you send me for five or six years to my regiment. – I should leave Paris and its pleasures with joy, if I thought my father would still condescend to follow me, to advise me, and to forgive me.'

When I had read this note, I sent for my grandson. He came pale and trembling to my bed-side, where he stood, without daring to speak or lift up his eyes. Charles, said I, with what uneasiness must your mind be penetrated! You are sensible of the small fortune which Monsieur de Valmont possesses, and that it is no more than fifteen thousand livres a year; mine is only twenty-five.[14] You might reasonably suppose, after all the expence I have been at for your education, that I am in debt: but you may be assured I am not; and, on the contrary, I have, by my frugality in the last twelve years, laid by the sum of four thousand Franks: this is half the sum you owe; the other half I will borrow from my banker; and to-morrow you shall have the two thousand guineas. Oh! Heavens! cried Charles, I have then madly spent in a few hours double the sum which you have been twelve years saving! – This sum was yours; I meant to increase it; and I intended it as a present to defray your wedding expences. – My wedding! – Ah, I shall never marry! – All my hopes of happiness are destroyed! – And this sum, which you are going to borrow, will take away all the pleasure of your life! – No, I have still eight or ten thousand livres worth of jewels which I will sell; and I will also give up my little cabinet of pictures which are worth six hundred guineas; so that ... Oh, my God! your pictures which you so much delight in! ... Oh! my dear father, how guilty do you make me appear! ... In reality you are so! As to me, it is only giving up these things; but you may lose your honour, and in consequence may cost me my life. Suppose Monsieur de *** had not left off play, or had gained a sum which it was impossible for me to pay! ... Ah, what a dreadful supposition! ... But, in short, I was out of my senses: and thus it always is, when we play at a game we are not thoroughly master of. We lose like dupes; and even when we win it is not in a lawful manner; for in general the winner has a great advantage over the loser, as he is more calm, and knows what he is about.[15] For example, do you think the two thousand guineas, which Mons. de *** will receive to-morrow, is money well gained? No, certainly; for, if you had been cool, you would not have lost it ... This thought alone is sufficient to make one dislike chance-games ... I could make many other remarks on them, but I will spare you the pain; as I see you are perfectly sensible of the extent of your crime, I forgive you, and will never more mention it ... Oh, Heavens! what excess of goodness! ... Yet, let me tell you, Charles, this indulgence ought to terrify you; since, if you should ever fall into such an error again, you would be utterly inexcusable – Ah, my father, do not fear it: I will give you my most sacred word of honour never more to play at games of chance ... I receive it, and I will depend on it; for you would be the most ungrateful and most despicable of men, if you fail in it. After this conversation, Charles expressed his gratitude in the most affecting manner, and I perceived the uneasiness he suffered, lest his loss at play should hurt his character, and injure him in the delightful scheme we have in view. I could only give him this consola-tion, that I thought Adelaide would scarcely marry for these two or three years; and that in that time he might have it in his power to prove himself wholly cured of a vice of which for some time this adventure would make him suspected. In short, I know very little of him, or this will be the last foolish action of the kind he will ever be guilty of. He has sense, honour, and delicacy; and knows how to make use of them: so that I am persuaded the lesson he has had will last him his life; and with greater certainty, as he has not in reality a passion for gaming. May you, my dear friend, after this account, be of my opinion; at least remember, that my grandson is only twenty years old; and that many years will pass before Madame d' Almane will seriously think of chusing a husband for the lovely Adelaide; do not, therefore, judge too hastily, and by that means deprive me of the hope which forms the chief happiness of my life.

LETTER XIII.

The Baron to Monsieur d' Aimeri.

Florence.

I AM, intirely, Sir, of your opinion, that the Chevalier de Valmont will not game any more. The best lesson that he could have received is not the having lost two thousand guineas; but the depriving you in one moment of the fruits of twelve years œconomy, practised for his sake, and the seeing you sell your jewels and pictures to pay for his folly. This ought to reclaim for ever a young man of feeling and generosity. Besides, I think, with you, that the passion for play is not innate in the Chevalier: had you not brought him up in a manner to preserve him from it, you would now attempt it in vain. A young man, educated in the modern style, without decency, principles, or restraint; from his cradle taught to think that riches alone can give him consequence; from having seen his parents contract debts to display their pomp, and be guilty of mean actions to procure money; such a young man at eighteen will be full of his most childish vanities. Be his fortune what it will, he must have trinkets, expensive cloaths, fine horses, magnificent carriages, a villa most elegantly furnished, and many other extravagancies; to support which, he will have recourse to the gaming-table. He little cares that his being a gamester may hurt his marrying, or his advancement. He seeks not a proper match; neither does he aim at places or honour. He is resolved not to marry at all, or for money; and, if he is ever ambitious, he turns courtier with a view of inriching himself. Unhappy father of such a son: You are the cause of his irregularities and thirst after riches. If you educated him yourself, the fault was in you: if you trusted him to another, you are yet more culpable. Was it worth while, for the sake of increasing his fortune, to make over to a stranger your most sacred and important duty? You should have made his happiness your object. He had better have been virtuous and moderate, than rich, vicious, and dissipated. What will lucrative posts, a government, and pensions avail, when your son dishonours and obliges you to sell your estate? Let us wave this disagreeable subject, and, to forget it intirely, let us reflect upon ourselves and our children: let us talk of Theodore and of the Chevalier de Valmont. Make yourself easy with regard to the future: you have instilled into your son religious principles, a taste for politeness and good manners, a contempt of pomp, and a laudable ambition of distinguishing himself by the united qualities of head and heart. Before he thought of my daughter, he proved himself incapable of being biassed by interested motives, by refusing a very advantageous match, because the lady was of an inferior birth. He will soon see Adelaide again. – Love will furnish what your care and example have begun. Such are my hopes; may they be realized to our mutual happiness!

Allow me, Sir, to recommend a matter of importance to you: to insist on the Chevalier's keeping an exact account of his expences: if he is not regular, he will get into debt, and to extricate himself may be tempted to game again. Under pretence of easing yourself from that trouble, require him to look into a part of your daily expences. For these last six months Theodore has done this for me: he examines and pays the weekly accounts of my Valet de Chambre. He buys my cloaths for me. Adieu, Sir, if the Chevalier's imprudence causes you the least inconvenience, I have *fifteen thousand francs* with Monsieur Girard, in *St. Nicaire's* street, much at your service; of which I advise him by this post. You never mention my new house to me; I hope, however, you have been to see it. The Viscount de Limours, who has undertaken the building of it in my absence, according to my plan, informs me that it is commodious and pleasant, and that the apartments for my children, my son-in-law, and my daughter-in-law, are very agreeable. I intreat you to carry the Chevalier de Valmont thither, and shew him the lodgings fixed on for my son-in-law. Once more adieu! Sir, please to direct for me at Turin.

LETTER XIV.

Baroness to Madame d' Ostalis.

Turin.

I SHALL leave this place the 25th, my dear daughter; and I hope, when you receive this letter, you will be ready to set out to meet me at B—. The Viscount-ess tells me Monsieur de Limours's affairs will detain him at Paris till near the end of May; therefore we shall be alone at B— for at least six weeks; for which, though I have a great friendship for the Viscountess, I shall not be sorry, as after so long an absence I have many questions to ask, and many things to tell you.

I much approve Monsieur d' Ostalis's desire of obtaining an embassy. He is prudent, sensible, and with ease speaks many languages: he has, besides, a noble, open, and agreeable person; and this last advantage, though not an essential one, is still useful to a courtier, and particularly so to an ambassador, who ought to attract, to win, and to conciliate; which it is not an easy matter to do, with a disagreeable and awkward person and behaviour.

I think, my dear daughter, you will be pleased with the present which Adelaide brings you: it is a charming port-folio of drawings, a pretty collection of Italian songs, and an assortment of impressions[16] of all the most beautiful antiques, which are found in the cabinets of the Curious in Italy, cast in sulphur. Adelaide has a similar collection, and she has amused herself with arrangeing them in a chronological order; by which means she has formed, in twelve drawers, a complete series of mythology, and of Greek and Roman history, which cost only twelve or fifteen guineas. It appears to me, that all young persons who draw should be presented with this collection, requiring them to class them as Adelaide has done. By this amusement they will acquire a pure, elegant, and correct taste for drawing, a just idea of the ancient manner, and will bring back to their memory mythology and ancient history.

No, my dear child; I am neither inchanted with the Italian operas nor their play-houses; which I imagined to be more beautiful than I found them. They are large, but their form wants elegance: with respect to the decorations, it appears to me, that we preserve the perspective better than they do. The Italians make great use of transparent scenes which are very dazzling, but form no representations of nature, and are only fit to correspond with fairy tales. I have seen a theatre large enough to contain a numerous company of soldiers mounted on real horses; but the poor animals marched with so much difficulty on the boards performed their parts so ill, and their riders conducted them so aukwardly, and at the same time appeared to be so apprehensive of falling; that the sight appeared to me much more ridiculous than surprising. I have heard many operas, the music of which appeared to be excellent; but the scenery was in general too much neglected and without any variety: the actors perform ill, without being absolutely absurd. Princesses are dressed like the Nobles of Genoa. They wear enormous hoops, which are very inconvenient to them. The lover, or his mistress, never fail, at the sound of the organ, even in the most passionate scenes, to turn their backs on each other, apparently, that they may not forget what they are about; and the audience encore the parts which best please them; which destroys all the illusion. I think we may be certain, that singing is carried to the highest degree of perfection in Italy. The women's voices all appear charming, because they are natural and easy, without appearing to come from the throat; which is the general fault of the French singers. The Italians, on the contrary, soften their voices in the high parts, and never raise them above the natural pitch, which makes them truly melodious. I have seen in Italy many pantomime dances, in the serious style, charmingly composed and executed. Among others, that of Orpheus,[17] which pleased me best of all: but the comic dances are so flat and indecent, that we should not even think them tolerable at a fair. As to their concerts, I assure you, they are not better executed than ours; and, upon the whole, we are more delicate, with regard to ear, than the Italians. Adieu, my dear child; when I see you, I will tell you, which of the Italian composers I like best; for a decision of so much importance ought not to be trusted to the post. Adieu, my child, in six weeks I shall embrace you; you will see Adelaide; I shall hear you say, *How she is grown! how pretty she is! how amiable she appears!* – In six weeks I shall be in France, at B— with you! – But, mean time, this vile Mount Cenis parts us, and I am at Turin, where I must stay an age, a whole month! – Oh, what happiness to find one's self in one's own country, after two years absence! This is the greatest pleasure which travelling procures us.

LETTER XV.

The same to the same.

I HAVE read with extreme pleasure, my dear child, the account you gave me of your daughters. There is but one thing which appears to want an explanation and to be examined into. You give your children money for their pocket expences, when they are only ten years old, and are too young to be capable of spending it properly. Duclos says,[18] 'All that the laws require, that morality recommends, and conscience dictates, is contained in this one proverb so well known, but so little explained: *do not do that to others which you would not have done to yourself.* The exact observation of this maxim leads to probity: *do to others what you would have done to yourself.* This is virtue. Her distinguished character and nature consists *in conquering yourself in favour of others.* It is by this generous effort that we make a sacrifice of our pleasures to those of other people.'[19]

We may inspire a child with probity, because it is founded upon a justice, which is to be found in all hearts; however narrow the understanding, the principles of it may always be conceived; but it will not make a child virtuous, because he is not made to attain to perfection, or even near it. If you would have a child of ten years old be learned, witty, understand Greek, talk on the beauties of Homer,[20] feel the charms and graces of Fontaine, and the sublimity of Corneille; that child will always be a fool and a pedant. In the same manner, if you expect him to be benevolent, prudent, a Saint, or a Hero, all the good actions you make him perform will appear to him painful. He will forget the end to be obtained and the object; and will only remember the sacrifice he has made, and he will find virtue too severe and too difficult for him ever to love it. Another inconvenience of this pernicious method is that of giving children false ideas, and confounding that which is their duty with perfection, probity, and virtue; so that they can never arrive at solid and immoveable principles; they will reproach themselves with crimes, when in fact they are doing innocent actions; will become superstitious and over-bearing; they will torment themselves with idle scruples, or, at least, which is more probable, they will reject such practices as they had thought indispensable; will abandon them all, and fall into the wildest extravagance.

Confine yourself then to the giving your girls exact honesty; form and establish their principles in this manner; but require nothing more from them than what Religion and the laws prescribe to them as their duty. He, who is sensibly penetrated with the truth of the Gospel, will doubtless be the most humane and perfect of men. And the divine goodness, in shewing us virtue in all its excellence, makes us admire and love it, and exhorts us to follow it; but does not command it, nor expect perfection from us; but earnestly requires us to have faith united to good morals and honesty. Even giving alms, this duty so sacred in all good minds, is in the Gospel laid down as advice; by exhortation, and not as a positive injunction. It is necessary, however, that children should have an idea of virtue, and that they should be early accustomed to admire it; shew them a noble and sacred image of it; let them see the model of it in your actions and conduct; prove to them, that it lives in the heart, and will render them happy; and be certain that they will love it in time. The desire of obtaining the character which you bear, the praises which are bestowed on you, will insensibly lead them to imitate you. Compassion will soon be awakened in their hearts; they will discover some of the pleasures attached to benevolence. A child, as sensible as Adelaide, might even experience these sentiments a long time before she is ten years old. Adelaide, when only six or seven, found an inexpressible pleasure in giving any thing to oblige, or to relieve the distress of an unfortunate person. Having no money, she would have given with great pleasure, if we had allowed her to do so, one of her frocks to a little girl whom she saw almost naked; and would give her play-things to her brother. But these actions were neither ordered, nor even advised: in that case she would have done them with reluctance. Besides, these gifts cannot be called sacrifices: Adelaide had no great merit in giving away an old frock, or a play-thing of which she was tired; for she never offered a new one. So that one may say she did as much as could be expected in her infancy; she was obliging, but not benevolent. At ten years old she began to be deeply affected by great examples of generosity. Yet I thought, if I had given her a certain allowance, she would have laid out all her money in trifles; so that, till she was near thirteen, she never had any; and, even now, I have never told her she must be charitable. But I have produced scenes of poverty and distress to her, which made her feel that she must be so; therefore her heart and her reason have made her benevolent. She asks my advice on these matters, and I strengthen this new-born virtue in her by my approbation and esteem.

Expect then with patience the time, when your daughters hearts and minds will be awakened to virtue; and that, in trying to hasten it, you will, instead of bringing it to perfection, spoil the Work of Nature. A gardener, with great trouble and art, may ripen fruit before its season, but this fruit will be worth nothing. – Adieu, my dear daughter. Thank Heaven, in six days we shall go from hence, and we are so rejoiced at it, that it appears as if we were out of our senses. Adieu! I shall write to you again on Saturday: embrace Seraphina and Diana for me.

LETTER XVI.

Count de Roseville to the Baron.

IN my last letter to my dear Baron, which he ought to have received at Naples, I acquainted him, that the marriage of Stolina with an opulent merchant was fixed upon; and that my young Prince, intirely cured of a passion, which had caused me so much uneasiness, was but slightly affected upon hearing the news. – But a total change has taken place; judge then, if I ought not to be seriously alarmed? The Count de Stralzi returned four months ago from a tour through the Provinces undertaken by order of the Prince; we compared his observations with those of the Baron de Sulback, and found the two travellers scarcely agreed in any one point – The Prince, having a real regard for the Baron, was inclined to give him the greater credit. – I agree with you, said I, in entertaining a better opinion of Mons. de Sulback's character and sense; but I may without further proof be deceived. It is possible, that with the best intentions he may have formed a wrong judgment. – The state of the Provinces you are to govern ought to be strictly investigated ... How then can I come at the truth of the accounts they have given me? Go and travel then yourself upon the spot. – I wish much to travel, for a Prince can only come at the truth by his own inspection ... Agreed. – Recollect, however, that such trouble is not to be taken for things of small importance. – A Prince cannot examine every thing himself – trifles are below his notice; they cramp his genius and take him off from the pursuit of more worthy objects. – I am of opinion that a Prince should have a perfect knowledge of his Ministers; if he has had no opportunity of proving their probity and abilities, he should at least chuse those of an unblemished and thoroughly established reputation. – Certainly, he ought to learn the general opinion; besides making his own particular inquiries, he should know (as Abbé Duquet advises) 'What their former conduct has been; what their pursuits; what their connections; what the management of their own estates; what authority they have kept up in their own families; what their prospects in the establishments of their children;

what delicacy they have shewn with regard to wealth ill acquired, in not partaking of it by alliances; with what regularity they have paid debts not contracted by themselves, but charged on their estates; with what equity they have finished those law-suits which were unavoidable?'[21] – How can one be informed of all these particulars, observed the Prince? – Employ different people, unknown to each other, and compare their accounts? – One can easily learn the truth of facts only. – It is sufficient to ask questions, and to believe neither the friends nor enemies of the party, nor those who aim at the same employments; then it is that a friend may be useful to the Prince who desires and seeks after truth. – You will deserve to be beloved for your own sake. – You will be loved. – I have the vanity to believe, nay, I am sure, that your friends will not be unworthy of advising a great Prince. – However, avoid an unbounded confidence; ask the counsels of friendship, but weigh them well and follow them after mature deliberation; recollect, that the most virtuous and enlightened of men are subject to error. – Finally, resolve upon nothing without advice and that well digested – and, though your friend be ever so meritorious, do not suffer yourself to be biassed by him alone, in the choice of those you employ. – He may be partial – for he is a man, and may be for a moment unjust.

Some time after this conversation the Chevalier de Murville acquainted me, that Mirandel, the merchant, and destined spouse of Stolina, had retracted his promise, without giving a reason for a conduct so extraordinary, considering the love he had shewn for her. – I commissioned the Chevalier to find her another husband. He told me he had in his thoughts a person who would certainly return to *** in two months. The next day but one, he wrote me word, that Mirandel was constantly walking near the lake C*** of Stolina's house, and that he thought the match might be brought on again. He was authorised to try ... Failed, and the scheme was given up. The sixth of last month the Prince saw the Count de Stralzi for a moment, and proposed his hunting with him. The Count excused himself, and left us with an air evidently embarrassed. Just as we were going out, the Prince was told, that an old Officer, by his appointment, waited his commands. Oh! say the Prince, he is come too late; the time I fixed is past; tell him I am going a hunting. The poor man, replied I, flattered himself, that you would to-day listen to a recital of his misfortunes; he will return home in despair. – It is his own fault; why did not he come to his time! He is not here to give his reasons; perhaps they are good ones. Well let him come in then, said the Prince a little peevishly. Immediately a venerable worn out old man, with a wan countenance, and his arm in a sling, made his appearance. Sir, says the Prince, did not Mons. de Sulback desire you from me to be here at ten o'clock? He did, answered the Officer in a faultering voice: and yet, says the Prince, it is almost twelve. These words, uttered in an imperious and angry tone, so intimidated the unhappy veteran now for the first time at the Levee, and in the presence of the son of his Sovereign, that he could not reply.

He looked down, and stammered out some innocent words. I perceived he was unable to proceed; and, willing to give him time to recover himself, I accosted him thus: Probably you live at a distance from the Palace? It was not that – I was detained – by a trifling accident. – What accident? asked the Prince, with more good-nature. An accident – which deserves not – only – I broke my arm this morning. Heavens! cried the Prince, this morning! And yet you are come! and remain standing, when you can scarcely support yourself upon your legs! This said, he instantly drew forward an elbow-chair, and, taking the old man's hand, desired him to be seated. What for me? said the Officer, can your Highness think me worth your attention? Rest yourself, replied the Prince, and, still holding his hand, made him sit down. Oh! Sir, what goodness of heart! What goodness of heart! The veteran's tears hindered his saying more. What! Are you surprized at finding in me some marks of humanity? Ah! Sir, this moment repays forty years misfortunes. – The Prince wiped his swoln eyes, and, after a short pause, said, you suffer too much to be able this day to explain your business; I am even hurt that you came. – Sir, I came to solicit for my son! – Give me your memorial, and rest assured of my active and most interested zeal. – The old man, unable to answer, presented it, and got up to go away: the Prince, perceiving that he walked with difficulty, supported him by the arm as far as the door, in spite of the faint efforts made by the Officer to disengage himself, who, equally confused and struck by the Prince's good-nature, received his support with tears of joy and frequent exclamations of surprize and gratitude. When he was gone, I asked the Prince, if he did not think the excuse a good one, for not coming to his time, and if he repented having delayed his hunting? O! my God! what would this unhappy man, who came in so much pain, have suffered, had I not heard him? Therefore never hesitate to sacrifice your pleasures to good works; or, to explain myself better, permit not any particular amusement to take such hold of you as to be relinquished with real concern. Your only passions should be virtue and glory. – How much do I repent my haughty treatment of the old man, which seemed so much to distress him! – In fact, you cruelly frightened a man who had for forty years served the State with valour, a man covered with honourable wounds, a man who had undauntedly faced dangers and the enemy: yet this brave and respectable veteran trembled before you, before a boy of sixteen! Tell one, Sir, do you pride yourself in being the cause of such emotions? ... Quite the reverse; I am humbled and repent my conduct. That man must have thought me unfeeling and imperious, because he was so easily disconcerted ... He supposed you were possessed of that brutal pride which marks the characters of tyrants: he thought a broken arm would not be allowed to be a sufficient excuse by you. He even ventured to mention it only as a trifling accident. He imagined, that you looked upon men in a lower class as beings of an inferior kind to yourself; convinced of the absurdity of such an opinion, yet he wanted your aid. – He trembled. – Many Princes are narrow-minded enough to be vain of inspiring such servile fear: they are ignorant, that contempt and hatred are its companions. Haughtiness, disdain, and caprice, joined with power, may make one formidable, and inslave those who can only revenge their humbled state by aversion. It is virtue alone that can implant respect, and obtain faithful services. Always reflect, Sir, upon your most shining title, your first dignity. Remember you are a man, and that you cannot lessen another without humbling yourself. The Prince was convinced of this truth. He immediately talked of the old man; and said, that, let the fate of his petition be what it may, he shall not have made a fruitless journey with his broken arm; for he shall receive, to-morrow, the first quarter of a pension for life. I will afterwards ask him, how he came to form so strange an opinion of me? For surely I have not deserved the character of being absurd? By no means said I. But this man never came to Court but to ask favours there of impertinent clerks in office, and of Ministers too often capricious: rejected, probably, by one and by the other. He concluded, that power of authority made men hard-hearted, unjust, and contemptuous: and the masters of these people would of course be less easy of access and more inhuman. – How hard it is that a Prince should lose the affections of part of his subjects by the caprice and rudeness of his Ministers? Happily, replied I, this evil has its remedy. We were here interrupted by their asking if the Prince meant to hunt? Late as it was, he seemed to wish it: I made no objection even to stay out till night. He took me at my word, for, at dusk, we were six leagues from *** : It was then time to go to our carriages. Just as we entered a small and very thick wood, the horse of one of the Prince's equerries ran away with and flung him; he was thrown under the beast; from which we released him, and perceived he was covered with blood and dangerously wounded, chiefly about the head. The Prince was the more affected, the young man being his favourite. A huntsman went for the carriages; but the wounded man could not suffer himself to be carried six leagues in his deplorable situation. He recollected the country-seat of the Count de Stralzi must be near, and he desired to be carried there. A huntsman knew it to be within a quarter of a league, and that it was but two leagues from the village of *** , where both a Physician and Surgeon might be met with. The Prince, with a laudable compassion, would himself conduct the wounded man to the house, and recommended him to the care of the Count's servants. We got there by six o'clock, the night very dark. Some of his people said the Count was at home. We were surprised at it; he had told us in the morning, that some business of consequence would detain him in *** all the day. The whole house was in an uproar: some servants seeking their master; others, confused by our questions, answered them ambiguously. Our numerous company filled all the apartments. We had settled our sick man in a commodious room, and left him to go to our carriage, without knowing whether the Count was from home, or had concealed himself; when, just as we were passing thro' a grand saloon, he made his appearance: he approached us with such an embarrassed air, such a gloomy countenance, and such extraordinary agitations, that the Prince and I, equally astonished, looked upon one another with some degree of terror. The Count muttered some unintelligible excuses: the Prince without hearing them fixed his eyes upon him, and then said with a smile, I will endeavour to take a proper time for my next visit. The Count blushed, and sought in vain to disguise his extreme perplexity. The Prince changed the discourse to his equerry's accident, and, recommending him to the Count's care, stept forward to go away: at that moment a shriek was heard: we started. – The Prince stopped short. The Count trembled and pushed forward with dismay to the door, which was hastily opened: an Angel, a celestial figure, the divine Stolina, flung herself at the Prince's feet, imploring thus his protection. You, Sir, who formerly rescued my family from misery and death, vouchsafe now to preserve what is most valuable to me! Defend my honour! Be assured of that, said the Prince: innocence and beauty will never be refused my assistance. He affectionately raised Stolina from the ground, and, holding her by the hand, as if fearing she would quit him, or be forced from him, looked with rage for the Count, but in vain, I had favoured his escape. I made a sign to be left alone with the Prince, and then asked him, Well, Sir, what do you mean to do? You surely guess; to conduct her where she wishes. He spoke this in a very unusual manner to me; I perceived he was influenced by a power superior to mine, and put on this air of independence, that I might not oppose his intentions. I was convinced he would not brook contradiction, and, at the same time, would make a bad use of indulgence. I took the resolution of appearing ignorant of his thoughts, and, with great good-humour, said it is worthy of you to conduct *Stolina* to a creditable place of safety: but first let us hear her story. The young woman blushed, and told us that the Count de Stralzi, returning one day from the Chevalier de Murville's garden, saw her walking with her mother in the fields; that he wrote her many letters, of which she only read the first, and sent the others back unopened; at length he had desisted from his unsuccessful pursuit.

This morning, continued she, I rose as usual at day-break: Scarcely out of bed when an old maid-servant told me, one of my neighbours, for whom I had a particular regard, had just sent, desiring me to come directly to her: I went out with the maid, for my mother put great trust in that wretch. We crost a large orchard, and entered an avenue of elms: at the end there stood a carriage, which surprised me, this being an unfrequented spot. I would have taken another path, had not the maid told me the carriage was the Prince's, who was walking on the banks of the lake. (At this period Stolina paused, blushing exceedingly: and there was a momentary interval of silence. Well, replied the Prince, with a faultering voice, you believed it was my carriage? – Yes, Sir, and I did not take another path. – O Stolina! had I but been there – I should have preserved you from the villainous attempt: Well, interrupted I, it was the Count de Stralzi? No, Sir, his vile emissaries: they seized and forced me into the carriage, with my base servant, who wrapped my head in a handkerchief, so that I could neither see nor be heard.

They brought me to this house, shut me up in a room, and, about an hour before the Prince's arrival, the Count came to me. Promises, protestations, and intreaties being ineffectual, he was about to use force, when a great noise of horses and carriages was heard; at the same time one knocked at the door to acquaint him of the Prince's being come: he, doubtless, perceived the joy this intelligence gave me: his rage increased, and, after much hesitation, he left me locked up in the room. He was scarcely gone, when I opened the window, and resolutely jumped out of it. I fell on the grass in a small garden; its gate being open, I got into the courtyard, and some of the Prince's huntsmen, whom I met there, conducted me to this apartment. The seducing Stolina here finished her recital. Heavens! exclaimed I, to what shocking lengths do our passions carry us! What happiness is yours, Sir, to have rescued innocence from the attempts of vice? But it is seven o'clock, let us lose no time; Stolina is doubtless impatient to return to the embraces of her father and mother. Hearing this, she with tears intreated the Prince to send her that night to her parents. I will carry you there myself, said he eagerly. I can easily conceive, interrupted I, that you are desirous of restoring, with your own hands, to those worthy people a daughter so deservedly dear to them; but this adventure will make a noise; it will be known that she was carried off: the public are too apt to misrepresent the most trifling events and actions. Should it be known that you yourself carried Stolina home, depend upon it that many will through folly or malice confound the protector with the ravisher. Let me advise you to send her home under the care of young Sulback. The unsuspecting air of confidence and good-humour I put on intirely took from the Prince all desire of opposing me, and he heard me with complacency. Nevertheless, he observed, that Alexis Stezin's house being but three leagues off, we should only be an hour longer in returning to — . I remarked, that this circumstance could not affect my argument, in which the Prince acquiesced. We put Stolina into a carriage with Sulback for her guard, and got home ourselves at half past nine at night. I told the Prince I would immediately give an account of this adventure to his father. I returned in half an hour. Well, said the Prince, what does my father think of Stralzi's behaviour? He knew it all, replied I; that unhappy young man, on his escape from his house, confessed it all to his uncle; who flung himself at your father's feet to implore his mercy: and what answer did he receive? That you, Sir, should determine his punishment. What I? Yes, Sir: because, you being the best acquainted with all the particulars, are more able to give an equitable judgment. You may easily imagine, continued I, that the Prince your father, has a mind on this occasion to make a trial of your discernment and justice; and that if you were to pronounce too severe a sentence. – Yet the Count de Stralzi deserves punishment – without doubt, but recollect that maxim which pleased you so much when you read it: 'There is a meanness in hatred of which a great soul is incapable. A Prince must sometimes punish, when absolutely necessary;

but it should then be done without harshness or malice, and without giving himself up to the pleasures of revenge. He has no other interest but those of the public, and admits into his breast no secret aversions to disturb his peace, and deprive him of his candour and benevolence?'[22] – Reflect on this, continued I: you are to give an answer in two days: at the expiration of that time, I think, said the Prince, Count de Stralzi's youth intitles him to some indulgence: he should not be lost, but amended. Let him only be banished from Court for one year: I will request of my father to have the goodness to pronounce himself this sentence upon him, and to add at the same time, that, in case of his sincere reformation, the remembrance of his fault shall not prevent his receiving any honours his birth intitles him to. Does there appear to you, added the Prince, colouring, any harshness, any spirit of revenge in this sentence? On the contrary, answered I, there is too much lenity and indulgence, but arising from such laudable motives that your father will most readily confirm it. I had the greater reason to commend the Prince's good-nature, he having the day after the adventure confessed himself to be desperately in love: an unmanageable passion at sixteen and an half! I was at a loss how to act, when I heard that Mirandel had renewed his addresses to Stolina. He acknowledged that the Count de Stralzi had taken him off from his pursuit, by placing the Prince's favours to Alexis Stezin's family in a suspicious light. The forcibly conveying her away opened Mirandel's eyes, and renewed his former affection. I would have availed myself of this, and hastened the marriage; but Stolina herself objected. She positively refused to her father's intreaties a pardon to a lover whom inclination and repentance had restored to her. I know not what to think of this refusal: when the Prince himself one morning cleared up all my suspicions: he brought me a letter opened; he was much disturbed; anger and indignation were visible in his countenance. I promised, said he, to conceal nothing from you: I have just received this letter; here it is, read it. I took it, it was too moving, and from Stolina: she conjures the Prince, as her protector, as her deliverer, her only support on earth; to defend her from the persecutions of a man, as violent as he was contemptible; who, after having refused and basely aspersed her, was resolved to wed her, though she had so fixed and just an aversion to him. Well, Sir, said I, after having read the letter, Stolina must be accused of sickleness, since she now refuses an offer, which, but a few months ago, she willingly accepted. Be that as it may, said the Prince, he shall never gain her by compulsion. Who will compel her? Perhaps her parents – Yes. Stolina would have you think so? – But she deceives you. She deceive me! – Would you believe her sooner than me? But what advantage can it be to her? She is not ignorant of your passion. This has intoxicated and made her despise her former lover. What absurdity! Can you believe? I tell you nothing new; her father speaks plainly, that she can only love her deliverer, her only support on earth. Ah! Sir, you have banished the Count de Stralzi for attempting to debauch an innocent girl; what punishment will you inflict on yourself? What? – You have corrupted this young woman by discovering a passion which misleads you. You have robbed her of her reason and of her virtue. She dares to write to you, unknown to her parents: in short, to have a preference of applying to you, she is guilty of an abominable falsehood. She scandalises her father; she represents him as a tyrant, that she may make an offering of herself to you, under the specious form of a victim. It is certainly your work, that a mind, once so pure, is now so full of deceit. But are you sure she will not be obliged to marry this man? You may be certain of that: by sending to Mirandel's house you will find he is set out this evening for France, his native country. Besides, Alexis Stezin has no induce- ment to thwart his daughter's inclinations: the portion which the Prince your father gives her insures her an honourable match. Struck with these words, the Prince, sighing, looked down. You are convinced, continued I, of the bad conse- quences of your misconduct. It is not enough to be conscious of our faults; we must amend them. What must I do, interrupted he, with anxiety and eagerness? Cure yourself of a passion that degrades you. Alas! I can lament it; but for a cure – Is it you who talks thus? The son of a great Prince, born to govern men, yet unable to conquer the weakest of all passions? Besides, is it possible you can be in love with a person you have seen only two or three times? That was enough to inspire love – from my childhood she always was in my thoughts – what expecta- tion can you form from this? Would you seduce and ruin her? That thought strikes me with horror – Endeavour then to get the better of your attachment! Impossible! – I will propose the means. We were to travel some months hence: let it be directly. The Prince considered a short time; then offering me his hand, I consent to it, said he, to prove myself, notwithstanding my folly, worthy of your esteem, will be my chief pleasure. I am delighted with you, but not surprised, exclaimed I. No passion contrary to your duty could ever disturb me; I was cer- tain you would get the better of it. You, continued I, should write to Stolina, promising her your protection, and that she should never be compelled to enter any state of life, that was disagreeable to her. The Prince, delighted with this permission, squeezed my hand, and sat about writing. His answering her imme- diately pleased me, for I was certain, in his present disposition, the letter would be as I wished it. He desired me to read it. It was as harmless as if I had composed it myself. The next day the departure of the Prince was announced publickly. We set off in two days for those provinces of which Monsieur de Sulback and the Count de Stralzi had made the tour, by order of the Prince. We mean to form a judgment ourselves of the facts contained in their journals. We shall travel incog. with few attendants. The Prince expects to return to – in three months; but we shall be much longer absent. The whole of my scheme shall be explained to you in my next letter. You see, my dear Baron, though I write but seldom, I make it up to you by the length of my letters. You and my sister are my only correspondents: to you alone, I conside these occurrences. To my sister. I only speak of the Chevalier de Murville; whom she loves the more, since I have informed her that he is dying of a consumption: in this I exaggerated a little, to make my court to the Viscountess: yet the poor man is really in a weak state, and I fear, in some danger. Adieu! my dear Baron. Direct my letters, under cover, to the Comte de Riller, who will forward them.

LETTER XVII.

Mons. de Aimeri to the Baron.

YOU have no idea, Sir, of the joy my grandson experienced, when I shewed him your letter, dated B— Castle. Adelaide is then in France! cried he; this emotion was much more lively, as the night before last we supped at the Intendant's, where we saw Mons. D— , who was just returned from Turin, and who talked of nothing but Madame Almane and the charming Adelaide. Charles asked him many questions, and was informed that Mademoiselle Almane was the handsomest person living; the most amiable, the most natural; that she possessed all the candour and simplicity of infancy, and all the graces of youth; that she sings in Italian, and plays on the harp like an Angel; that she draws in a superior style; that she educates a little orphan; that she is the best as well as the youngest and most charming of mothers. Mons. D— related a thousand marks of Adelaide's and Hermine's mutual tenderness. This singular adoption has interested even people who do not know you. Charles was melted almost to tears; he knows by heart all the little stories Mons. D— recounted; and he talks of nothing else to me. As an imagination of twenty years is easily inflamed, he is anxious to have the time of his duty over, in order to fly to Languedoc; but, not with standing his impatience, it is impossible that we can depart from hence till the 25th of July. Adieu, Sir! I hope, as you have now fewer occupations, you will write oftener to me; and think with great pleasure, that I shall receive no more letters fifteen days after they are dated.

LETTER XVIII.

The Baron to the Viscount.

THE Castle of B— is at present very gay, my dear Viscount. We are happy in celebrating the event which interests all France; and, although at two hundred leagues from Versailles, I have illuminated my four towers and my gate-way – my peasants eat, drink, and dance in my garden; and I have, as well as you, the pleasure of hearing, Long live the King! a sound which must be pleasing to every Frenchman, particularly at this distance from Court; for, in the midst of a remote province, such exclamations can proceed only from the heart; they here express real joy and gratitude – you will not see an account of my entertainment in the Gazette;[23] it is a citizen, and not a courtier, who gives it – The most virtuous sentiments, sentiments which at all times have produced the most shining actions, are now treated as prejudices; insensibility and licentiousness, under the specious names of reason and philosophy, break without scruple the most sacred ties, and glory in despising all decency. They speak of State affairs with a freedom, which even the presence of their children and domestics cannot restrain – For my part, occupied intirely by the education of mine, I have seldom time to go to Versailles – but I would have Theodore love his King, because he was born to serve him, and to receive his favours – I would have him love his country, because it is his duty to defend and to shed his blood for it. – In this, as in very thing else, I inforce my precepts by example; and I conduct myself so as to prove to Theodore, that I interest myself equally for the happiness and glory of France and of the Sovereign who governs us. – I never fail to shew my satisfaction at every event that happens for the good of my country, by giving a little feast within my own walls, which, while it amuses my children, makes them take a sensible part in the public felicity.*

I am concerned, my dear, Viscount, that you cannot come to see us these six weeks – for by that means I shall pass only a fortnight with you, as my son's entrance into the army will oblige me to leave you by the beginning of June; we shall then go to Strasbourg to remain till January, for I intend that Theodore shall begin a course of civil law, which will employ him the following summer.

I send you a letter for Porphiry, whom I have engaged to accompany you into Languedoc; I have a strong desire to see him again, and to hear him read a performance of which Madame d' Ostalis speaks highly. – Adieu, my dear Vis-

---

* This last idea is not my own, I willingly yield all the merit to its unknown Author. I read in the *Paris Journal*,[24] about two years ago, several clever letters, signed Bonnare Pere, (a fictitious name.) In one of those pretty letters, this was his picture of a good citizen – I was sufficiently struck with it to remember it at the end of the year, and to give the honour of it to the Baron d' Almane.

count. Let me know if I must absolutely relinquish all hope of seeing you before the 20th of May.

LETTER XIX.

The Baroness to the Viscountess.

COME then, my dear friend; we are preparing plays, entertainments, and charming *surprises* for you. – A small theatre, where you see the actors through gauze, in imitation of the magical pictures of Azor and Zemira:[25] pantomimes acted by our children, Diana, Seraphina, Adelaide, and Hermine; – others, where you will see Theodore, Mons. d' Almane and Dainville; an orchestra composed of two harps, Madame d' Ostalis and me. And then we have balls, and run races on foot, with shepherds and nymphs; and we have concerts *trios* and *quartets*. – In short, our rehearsals are over, and we wish for the happy time when we are to begin our representations. I have had on this occasion an opportunity of giving Adelaide a very important piece of advice. The day before yesterday we rehearsed one of our pieces before Monsieur and Madame de Valmont and some other persons: Seraphina played her part very boldly. Her mother scolded her, and disconcerted her so much, that, in the midst of a very comic scene; she burst into tears; and Madame d' Ostalis sent her away to her chamber. We all returned to the saloon. Adelaide, very much concerned at this accident, told Madame de Valmont, that it was not at all surprising that Seraphina did not act properly, and that she had been so much affected by her mother's anger; for that she was not at all well, having a very bad head-ach, and even a little fever. I heard what she said; and asked her aloud, if Seraphina had really told her she was ill? Yes, Mamma, answered Adelaide, but in a low voice, and blushing at the same time. I took no notice of it, but went out, and returned in half a quarter of an hour. – A moment after Madame d' Ostalis came in with great emotion. She told me softly she wanted to speak with me, and made a sign to Adelaide to follow us: we went into a little room, and Madame d' Ostalis said I am very angry. Seraphina has just told me a lye, and maintains it in the most positive manner. – What is it? – Why, indeed, my dear aunt, she denies positively that she told Adelaide she had the head-ach. – What, interrupted Adelaide, have you told her? – Yes, replied Madame d' Ostalis, my aunt told me you assured her Seraphina was ill; that she told you of it; and this is what she denies; but you may suppose I do not hesitate to believe you, and that I have treated her ... Oh! Heavens, cried Adelaide, the poor little girl was right. With a design to excuse her, I thought an innocent falsehood might be permitted, and instead of this I have occasioned her punishment! – Go, then, said I, to Madame d' Ostalis, give her her liberty, and to make her amends, forgive her intirely, and allow her to come to supper with us. As soon as we were alone, How, said I, to Adelaide, could you invent this story, not only to Madame de Valmont, but to me also! – It is true, Mamma: you know I hate lyes; but I thought, when no person was hurt by it, and that it might excuse one I loved, I might be allowed to make use of a falsehood. It is permitted to be used in these circumstances, when it serves to excuse a real fault, or to conceal secret either of our own, or one confided to us.[26] These are the only cases where falsehood may ever be permitted. The fault, which Seraphina was guilty of could neither give a bad opinion of her heart, or of her disposition: it was not a crime. Therefore neither your friendship for her nor your attachment to Madame d' Ostalis, obliged you to tell a lye on this occasion: and every time you do so, however harmless it may seem, unless there is an extreme necessity for it, or a great deal depends on it, you will always be to be blame, and at the same time act very imprudently; for in using yourself to tell this kind of lyes, you will lose the right of being credited, when you wish to defend your fiends. Every body knew, that Seraphina had no head-ach: another time, if you should wish to excuse any little faults you will be suspected of, even if you tell truth; and, if you was not so young and so well known here, people would be apt to believe you naturally given to falsehood, since you was guilty of it without any kind of necessity. We ought to do every thing to serve our friends, except exposing our reputation for them. Honour is too estimable for us ever to sacrifice it on any account. If you tell a lye, in order to do your friend a small service, they who discover it to be a falsehood, have a right to suppose you a lyar; therefore, you ought never to tell a lye. If you conceal the truth, or deny it, in a matter which concerns the happiness of your friend, it will not hurt your character; it has its excuse in the necessity of it: this therefore is allowable, and friendship renders it your duty. I see plainly, replied Adelaide, how seldom it is that the most innocent lye is not attended with inconveniencies. I wanted to serve Seraphina, and all the success I had was to occasion her anger, and take from myself the power of defending or excusing her for a long time! ... Remember, said I, never to depart from these principles; the contrary would lead you far astray. It is not enough to do a good action; it must also be united with justice and integrity ... Can it be possible to depart from integrity in doing a good action? ... Let us suppose that we have two neighbours, one of them poor, virtuous, and the father of a numerous family; the other rich and a bad man, who has acquired his fortune by thieving and cheating. Your poor neighbour tells you he is perishing with hunger; and, as you have no money, he leaves you in despair. A moment after the walls which separate you from your rich wicked neighbour, tumble down, and discover a large room, entirely filled with gold. You are sure, that the owner of this money does not know the amount of it, and that you could take some without his finding it out; and consequently without exposing your reputation. You recollect; you think you still hear the piercing cries of the good father of his family; you can save his life and those of his wife and children. A hundred guineas would make him happy; this money, gained by vice, would pass from wicked hands to those of virtue; the wicked man could not only spare it, but does not even perceive the loss of it; while on the other hand, this sum would snatch a whole family from the grave! ... Oh, Mamma! do not tempt me any farther ... I only ask you, in this situation what would you do? ... Ah, the unfortunate father of the family! ... You would steal then! you would be guilty of a crime which merits death! ... Oh, Heaven! I should rather die myself ... But would such an act of compassion be pardoned? ... Compassion, when opposed to honour and honesty, is only a weakness which ought to be conquered. I perceive it, and that, in effect, nothing can excuse a thief ... But at least, Mamma, you will allow this to be a very distressing situation ... Yes, for a person who blindly pursues the impulse of the moment, without considering justice or prudence: But for Adelaide, when she is eighteen years old, it will only be painful, not distressing. When you are of this age, you will know perfectly the impossibility of being virtuous, unless you constantly attend to its principles, and act from a regular and settled plan: *Never do what religion or the laws of your country forbid.* This is the sacred precept which must be the rule of all your actions; and no pretence, or situation, however extraordinary, can dispense with your observing it ... If there is a circumstance which may make you think stealing excusable, you might perhaps find another which might make murder appear lawful ... Murder! oh, no! ... Yes, murder, even parricide! ... History, you know, furnishes us with more than one instance of these dreadful actions, produced by motives which have produced the most virtuous actions, the love of one's country and the desire of serving it. Thus it is, that our most laudable pursuits, our most noble sentiments, even our virtues, may lead us astray, if we renounce our principles. So pity and humanity might inspire as with the desire of stealing ... A crime is always a crime, however useful it may be, or whatever good it may produce, and even if it insured the felicity of a whole nation. He, who commits so mean an action, dishonours himself, and becomes a villain. Ah, Mamma! I will never forget this precept, so easy to remember: *Never to do what religion and law forbid.* I will never tell an untruth again on a trifling account, since religion and conscience forbid lying. I will never dissemble the truth, but when prudence, discretion, and friendship make it absolutely necessary; and I will never steal, in order to be charitable. But, Mamma, one word more about lying; for you have just made me very scrupulous on the subject. There is not a day passes that we do not tell a thousand stories; for instance, when you order yourself to be denied! – It would be a folly to call that lying; every thing of that kind, which is done through politeness, is only a common compliment, which is the more innocent, as it deceives nobody.[27] – Yes, Mamma, when you do so, because you do not insist upon it: but I have seen people say the same thing, with so much apparent sincerity, that I should have been deceived by it, if I had not afterwards discovered that it was false. – This is indeed different, when one says such things, with earnestness and a tone of affection, it must then be called falsehood, not politeness. – Then, Mamma, to be polite, I think it is not necessary to say continually, *I am much afflicted.* – Not at all; though formerly the matter was carried still farther; for people said they were in *despair* on those occasions; which, at this time, makes them only *afflicted.* In short, the most simple expressions are always the best of this sort; and it is difficult to preserve an air of true politeness, if you use yourself to such expressions. – I remember you forbid me to say, *that is incredible, unheard of, – I am inraged* – and then, *this is ravishing charming* ... And many other such words and sentences, of which I have formed a list, that I may not make use of them when I come into company. I have not intirely forbid you to use them, only recommended you not to repeat them constantly, or when they are improper. Nothing can be more disagreeable than this way of talking, and the being so lavish of such strong epithets; it deprives you of the possibility of expressing either astonishment, affection, or joy, when you really feel these sentiments. Thus people use the most passionate expressions where enthusiasm is ridiculous, and appear cold when they wish to shew their tenderness ... Adelaide retired to her chamber after this conversation, in order to write down a part of the advice I had just given her. It is a custom she has used herself to for some time: she makes a kind of journal of all our conversations, and she writes an exact account of the principles and sentiments which strike her the most. I only require that she should submit this little Work to my censure, in order that I may see whether she thoroughly understands it, and may correct it, if by chance she should be mistaken. But what engages her time the most is the Novel in Letters, which I mentioned to you. She already sees with great pleasure, that the last letters are much superior to the first. She even enjoys her own improvement. She perceives new ideas open to her. Her understanding is clear and just, because she has learned nothing from conversation which is above her comprehension. She is very impatient for the time when she may read the best Authors in the three languages of French, English, and Italian;[28] but her confidence in me moderates her impatience; for she is certain, that I only defer giving her this pleasure, that she may be the better able to enjoy them; and we have agreed to defer this interesting study, till she has written all the answers to my letters, which will be nine or ten months hence. Adieu, my dear friend; come to us, and by the addition of your company render the Castle de B— the most delightful place in the world, and, at the same time, complete the felicity of your happy friend.

LETTER XX.

Madame de Valcy to Madame de Germeuil.

B— Castle.

YOU wish to hear a particular account of the life we pass here and of our amazing pleasures; so I will satisfy you: we have had many most splendid entertainments, moral Comedies without love; Pantomimes acted by children; dancing by the country-fellows and waiting-women; and parties on the water; we sup at nine, and are all in bed by eleven. Judge now, how little all this suits my inclination! But yet I am the only person who is not delighted with this rural life: my mother is in continual extacy: Madame d' Ostalis always appears charmed before her aunt, and commends every thing she likes: my father regrets neither the Opera nor Mademoiselle Hortensi;[29] the Chevalier de Herbain gives up small talk, and is as insipid as he is naturally satyrical and severe: even Porphiry writes only little Poems and Eclogues, in which he paints and celebrates the virtues of Madame d' Almane, the charms and accomplishments of Adelaide, and the innocent felicity which every one enjoys in this delightful place. As I am to give you an account of all the people that are here assembled, besides those I have already mentioned, we have the Chevalier de Valmont's father and mother; as to the first, he is an absolute rustic of the worst sort; always laughing, and calls his wife, his heart, and his puss, impertinent, proud, and never inclined to be silent, till Madame the Baroness d' Almane is disposed to speak. As for Madame de Valmont, though there is a most uncommon insipidity in her, yet she would be well enough and really has something almost noble in her manner, if she would not net so much, and did not constantly wear a tippet of moleskin, with tufted fringe. Now figure to yourself all these personages surrounding Madame d' Almane, and neither seeing nor hearing any thing but her; then add to the picture a parcel of children; Adelaide, Hermine, Theodore, Constantia, Seraphina, Diana, tiresome little wretches, who all follow Madame d' Almane and listen to her as to an oracle; then imagine this society assembled in a vast large Castle, the very furniture of which is enough to give you the vapours, for you see nothing but stern profiles of most melancholy figures, with enormous Roman noses. Now, pray bring all these circumstances before you, and then you will conceive what sort of countenance I must put on it this peaceful sanctuary *of virtue and happiness.*

You wish for a faithful description of Adelaide, that little miracle, that masterpiece of Nature and education; I will satisfy your curiosity, and be very particular; she is not tall for her age, but remarkably slender; has a little round face, with delicate features, and a very childish look; at first you are only struck with her eyes, which are really beautiful and singularly expressive; her whole countenance is naturally pleasant and sensible; she has an agreeable and clever smile; her complexion is pretty, though not remarkably fair; she has but little colour, but then she blushes every instant, and only in her cheeks; and her beauty improves when she either speaks or sings; she has a charming mouth and teeth, and very pretty hands; she is not so handsome as my sister, but yet she eclipses her, or, to express myself more properly, you forget to look at Constantia when Adelaide is present. – This little figure will soon be much talked of, and I am certain, when she appears in the world, we shall hear no more mention of the Countess Anatolle. With regard to her education, which is so much praised and cried up, I see nothing particularly in it; for it appears to me as if she owed nothing but to Nature: she is so obliging and good-humoured, that it is impossible to dislike, or indeed not to have a regard for her; as to any thing else, she is very bashful, speaks little, and that only in a common sort of manner, and appears more childish than people generally are at her age, for she plays with Diana, Seraphina, and her little Hermine, not the least out of complaisance, but for her own diversion; they say she has knowledge, but, though conversation often turns her on *History*, the *Arts*, and *Literature*, Adelaide listens with an attention which shews nothing but curiosity, for she never assumes the air of satisfaction, which every one has, who hears what he already knows; and she never joins in those conversations which must be owing to ignorance; for how is it possible to persuade one, that a person of only fourteen years of age can be sufficiently modest always to hold her tongue, when by conversing she could astonish the company, and gain herself admiration? She has a charming voice: I am no judge of her talent for musick and drawing; you know the little taste I have for the *Arts*. I perceive she can with equal readiness converse in English and in Italian, and has a number of pretty little accomplishments which she owes only to herself. It is she who puts in order the fruit for the table, and she can cut out the prettiest things in the world; she also does cyphers for rings on hair and landskips, and all those different things she learned in her idle hours. – Theodore, the other prodigy, is not so handsome as his sister, nor has he, like the Chevalier de Valmont, the interesting figure of a *Hero in Romance*. – However, he is tall and perfectly well made; he has a form equally active, easy, and noble, a good face, and an interesting countenance; but he is as bashful as his sister; and *not more knowing*,[30] I would lay a wager, though he is fifteen and a half ... Theodore is neither deficient in the graces, nor in politeness, though he knows not yet how to compliment a woman, or even look at one. – My mother understands much better how to educate her pupils; for (without talking or commending myself) Constantia is very forward for her age. She has already formed a passion, a violent affection, and with the person who I make no doubt will determine the future destiny of her life ... She absolutely loves Theodore to distraction; she has got to her *emotions*, – her *blushes* – and *reveries*. – In short, nothing can be more visible, or more ridiculous – at thirteen, I was only a coquette, but Constantia has an absolute passion. The difference which appears to exist in the educations is only in name; for coquetry and love generally make people run the same length; so what signifies the answer where the effects are alike! Adieu, my dear; during your circle, you was the object of my tenderest compassion; at present, you may return the compliment, for I do assure you I am as much out of my element here as you was with your country Squires.

LETTER XXI.

The Baroness to Madame d' Ostalis.

Castle de B—

DO not regret leaving the Castle so much, my dear child; you have quitted us, and it is no longer the same; we have lost the most agreeable part of our company. Since your departure, the weather has been so extremely hot, that it has been impossible, particularly for Parisian Ladies, to stir out of doors before eight o'clock in the evening. The Viscountess has established a reading party, where we all assemble, though not compelled to it; it lasts about three quarters of an hour; and it is Adelaide, who reads aloud *The Theatre de la Chausèe*.[31] As she has a very sweet tone of voice, acts well, and reads Poetry with great propriety,[32] she even attracts the attention of Madame de Valcy, who piques herself greatly on having a very particular affection for Adelaide; which proves to me, that it is impossible for those who are possessed of native innocence and mildness, not to please even the most envious or censorious persons in the world. In three weeks we shall be left in solitude; I shall remain here only one month after the Viscountess goes; so that I shall certainly be at Paris by the beginning of November. We expect every day Mons. d' Aimeri and the Chevalier de Valmont; the first has had a fit of the gout, which confined him a month to his bed, and retarded his departure from de *** ; but he is now recovered, and his last letter informs us of his speedy return. I own I am not sorry that the Viscountess will be gone before his arrival, because the interview between Adelaide and the Chevalier de Valmont will be very interesting; and I fear the penetration of the Viscountess, as well as the malignity of Madame de Valcy. Adelaide will be fifteen in less than two months ... I am very certain that the Chevalier will not see her without surprize and emotion; and witnesses at such a time would be very troublesome. Adieu, my dear child; I will write to you again, when Mons. d' Aimeri arrives; and will acquaint you with all the particulars which your friendship has a right to expect.

I have this day received two letters from Strasburg. Mons. d' Almane and Theodore are in perfect health; they tell me it appears as strange as it is afflicting, that they should rise in the morning and go to bed at night, without embracing me once throughout the whole day. You can tell whether I do not partake of the same sentiments ... Adieu, my dear child: How happy will the month of January make me, for then I shall be again united to all whom I love!

LETTER XXII.

The Baroness to the same.

From the Castle de B—

AT length, my dear child they are arrived; they came the day before yesterday, and the very day after the departure of the Viscountess, Madame de Valmont, Adelaide, Hermine and I were reading in my closet, when a messenger came to inform us he had left Mons. d' Aimeri and the Chevalier de Valmont, four leagues from B***: on hearing this Adelaide's cheeks became very red, but, as the least surprise has the same effect on her, her blushing did not appear at all particular. I lent my coach to Madame de Valmont, who set out to meet her father and her son; and Adelaide went to her own chamber to play on the harp; I followed her thither, but did not perceive she felt the smallest emotion. At seven o'clock I heard the sound of a carriage; I left Adelaide, and went to the great Vestibule, where I found Mons. d' Aimeri and the Chevalier de Valmont. I embraced them both, and we entered the saloon. Mons. d' Aimeri inquired after Adelaide; the Chevalier asked me many questions about Theodore, but seemed to be very absent, and kept his eyes fixed towards the door ... At eight o'clock the door opened very gently, and Adelaide appeared, leading Hermine by the hand. At this instant, I fixed my eyes on the Chevalier, and I saw he was affected by pain, joy, and friendship ... in short, all that I could wish. After the first compliments were paid, the Chevalier addressed himself to the little Hermine in Italian, which surprised us, as he was ignorant of the language, when he left us. He told us, with great politeness, he had learned this language, in order to converse with Mademoiselle Hermine, because he knew she could not speak French. Adelaide was perfectly sensible of this gallantry, and appeared much flattered, that the Chevalier already knew Hermine by character. The next day, Adelaide was dressed with her usual simplicity; her hair was tied with the same ribband which she wore the evening before; nothing was particular or new; but Hermine's dress was quite studied, and I saw that Adelaide wished the Chevalier to admire her and think her pretty: he, not venturing to praise her Mamma, repeated every minute, how pretty Hermine is! He took great notice of her, and played with her, but with a certain air of affection, and even respect, which was very pleasing. Adelaide was much flattered with this complaisance, though I am sure she did not know either the motive or the merit of it. Madame de Valmont returns home to-morrow with her father and son, but will come again to visit us, and they are to spend the two last days with us that we stay here. Adieu, my dear child. – The Chevalier de Valmont is truly amiable, and has a mildness and delicacy which are equal to every other good quality he possesses.

I beg of you, my dear child, to order fires to be made in all the rooms of our house. I know it has been built these eighteen months, and that the walls must be dry; but it is not on my account that I am fearful, and, if I was to live in it by myself, I should not take these precautions.

LETTER XXIII.

The Viscountess to the Baroness.

Paris.

I OUGHT to confess to you, my dear friend, that the day before yesterday I had a little return of youth – for on Monday I carried the Countess Anatolle to the masqued ball which was given by the Ambassador – It is a long time since I was at such an assembly, and in truth I do not think I shall ever go to another. – Oh what an insipid thing is a ball, when one is no longer a coquette! As I had no part to act and was only a spectator, I endeavoured in vain to discover one out of the many attractions such an assembly used to afford me; for now those things appeared ridiculous which had formerly charmed me. I soon discovered Madame de G— who still enters into the spirit of a ball to perfection; but so far was she now from diverting me, that she appeared in my eyes an insupportable prating woman; extravagant in cool blood, affectedly giddy; without gaiety, wicked without refinement, and for four whole hours uttering only idle impertinence or dull nonsense; and that with a squeaking strained voice, which certainly must disfigure and make the person the most amiable and entertaining, appear ridiculous and troublesome. – One of the things, which struck me most at this ball, was the ridiculous affectation of the men who were unmasked, almost all of them affecting indifference and fatigue, and answering the masques with the greatest disdain. They form in the gallery several parties, but only appear fixed in their situations, that they may spoil the ball, or from their laziness be able to steal off to bed. – For my part, I prefer those who go to make their intrigues known which were only suspected, and to let the world know the woman who was so well disguised, and who fancies her secret to be unknown to the universe. Others, still more amusing, had put on a mysterious air from mere foppery; and pass one part of the night with some suspicious characters, with whom they have no acquaintance, in order to make people suppose they are deeply engaged in an intrigue; how one's eyes change with years; I had been two hundred times at the Opera-ball, and had never seen all this before; the reason is, because it is impossible to be at the same time actor and spectator. This shews why we sometimes live twenty years in the world without knowing it. So long as we maintain those trifling inclinations which make us act any little *parts* in the world, we are blind to what passes in it. – As you will now soon return here, I must instruct you how affairs stand in the circle of our society. Mons. de Merange and Madame de Clemis are at last declared enemies, and, what makes it still more surprising, they were never either lovers or friends. This aversion proceeds intirely from rivalship of pretensions; it is seldom that a man and woman hate each other, only because they are envious; but when it does, happen, that sort of dislike is the most inveterate. Do you ask why? Perhaps because naturally men and women were formed to love each other as hatred they say, is the most violent between nearest relations.

You will find Madame de Lurey in affliction: she has lost her best friend and dearest *confidant* Monsieur de C— , who is just dead of a malignant fever. The women, as I before informed you, love each other with an extreme affection: however, for some time past, they have only intrusted their *real secrets* with the men; it appears much more natural to confess one's faults to a person of one's own sex; and I am certain, that women only chuse male confidants, in order to look out for successors to their gallants. It is without doubt a prudent precaution; for nothing is a greater proof of understanding than to have many resources quite ready in case of misfortunes.

You will meet at my house Madame de Fervaques, as chance has again revived our acquaintance; she was once under great obligations to me; but those were private, and not known to the world, so were soon forgotten by her. She very soon neglected me, and at last gave me up intirely, without any reason or quarrel. I lately did her a trifling piece of service, but which was well known and much talked of; and Madame de Fervaques made me the most grateful acknowledgments. She came to see me immediately, and loaded me with professions of friendship, which only served to convince me, she is as hypocritical as she is inconstant. – As you have only met her, you will not dislike my giving you her picture. Madame de Fervaques is a person without character, and has neither passions nor virtues; but all the great faults which vanity can give. She has a perfect knowledge of all the rules of common politeness, and is what is called highly fashionable; but she lays so great a stress on this science, that she is an absolute slave to it; and has no real esteem but for those who possess it; – she is most strictly polite, but her civility is never obliging, and often misplaced; for she is as polite even to the domestic part of her family as if she was in the drawing-room: polite to her most intimate friend; in short, polite every instant of her life. She had rather a hundred times have a serious quarrel with any person than be deficient in any form of civility: she is capable of forgetting an essential service, but she has never forgotten to return a visit. – After such a description, it is possible to conceive one may have a respect of civility for Madame de Fervaques; and that she deserves more than any other person for one to send and make all sorts of *obliging inquiries* after her health; to leave a ticket at her house, and go to see her when her doors are open; – but at the same time she is a person that one is not at all obliged to esteem.

But now, to finish my instructions, I must inform you of one thing that as yet I have omitted telling you, that absolutely you must alter your manner of speaking, as the French language has undergone a great change since your departure: we talk French as the lowest rustics do, leaving out half the letters, and, instead of *cette, votre, notre*, we call it *ete, vot, not*; to express one's self with propriety is now thought a vulgar kind of pedantry; so that a peasant talks much more in the style of the Court, than our scholars do;[33] and we have all carefully adopted this manner – We have also spoiled the pronunciation of many words, which in your time were spoken with propriety; we say *segret* for secret, *inmense* for immense; but I have made a collection of all these alterations, and you must absolutely learn the list by heart, before you receive company; otherwise you will have the appearance of rusticity or a finical exactness. However, you are at liberty to use pedantic expressions in your conversation, and to pay great attention to your phrases when you are speaking; and, if you happen to make a repetition, you may stop to find the synonymous word to that which you was so unfortunate as to use twice over: and lastly, you may aim at eloquence in familiar conversation. If you acquire all this, it will make you appear a very sensible woman; for, provided you only pronounce your words like your waiting-maid, you will never be accused of affectation; and, however stiff and studied you may be yourself, you will always be thought perfectly easy and natural.

Adieu, my dear friend; every one here anxiously waits your return; I am charged with a thousand kind messages, particularly from Madame de Irec, who is dying with impatience to converse with you on Education, as she thinks her talents superior in that particular, because she dresses her daughter, who is six years old, as a sailor, which you will find here a general fashion; but yet I do not imagine that Adelaide will adopt it for Hermine.

LETTER XXIV.

Mons. de Lagaraye to Porphyry.

I HAVE read your manuscript twice over, my dear Porphyry; and I know no work which so faithfully describes the manners of the world: you boldly satyrize its follies, absurdities, and vices; a more daring attempt than that of which fools are so vain; their attack upon Religion, upon Kings and government – in the midst of a general corruption, insolence and impiety never fail to meet with admirers; but you dare to expose vice; you dare, without reserve, to assert useful truths; and nothing that deserves it escapes your censure. – At the same time you pay a sincere deference to religion, you praise virtue without parade and from the bottom of your heart; and you prove, 'That there is no happiness without it.'[34] Believe me, the modern writings, which appear to be the boldest, are not half so much so as your's. Your motives are laudable, and you make the best and noblest use of your abilities. Nevertheless, not to deceive you, my dear Porphyry, if you expect much admiration and success, you will be disappointed; we must not look for praise from those we expose. – What courtier, in Fenelon's time, would praise Telemachus? – so, when you have finished a master-piece, the greatest part of the public will be against you: you will always meet with enemies in the atheists, the ambitious, coquets, and pedants; bad fathers, people without morals, and without principles; and the generality of the world. – Proceed, my son; work for glory, and not for applause. Do still better, seek only in your own breast for the reward of your labours; for will you be worthy to paint virtue, and to delineate its charms, if virtue alone will not content you? – If injustice should disgust you, if calumny should blacken your character, if malice should persecute you, reflect, that this work of yours may guard unexperienced youth and innocence from the detestable snares of vice, that it may bring back into the right way wandering and depraved characters, that, if your enemies should decry it, it may nevertheless be read with approbation and gratitude by good fathers and tender mothers of families.

LETTER XXV.

The Viscountess to the Baroness.

Paris.

My dear friend,

I AM at this instant in such an agitation, and so miserable, that I absolutely must write to you, though I am certain of meeting you to-morrow; but on your first arrival it will be impossible for me to see you alone; for which reason I shall send Renaud to – where he will wait for you; and, during your journey, you will read my letter, and my misfortunes will feel less severe, when I have intrusted you with them. It is now impossible for me to flatter myself, that Madame de Valcy will ever repent, for her heart is corrupted beyond all remedy: Corrupted! good Heavens! and can I pronounce that dreadful word, without expiring with grief! It is my daughter of whom I am speaking! my very soul is torn! but listen to this dreadful story, and then judge of my situation.

Madame de Valcy and Madame de Germeuil had a great quarrel the other day, and the latter had the cruelty to send me many of Madame de Valcy's letters, in which I am treated with great indignity; but I will copy that of the latest date; it was written three weeks ago, and is as follows:

'Once again I tell you, nothing shall prevent my buying that little place of St. Mandée, and in my own name; as that old woman will not allow of Duplessis; you propose a fine expedient, that the Marquis de – should purchase it, as for himself: but then, he will put in one of his servants, who will serve by way of keeper; and suppose I wish to go there without him, even without his knowledge ... you laugh, I am sure, or else are indignant, and talk of *sentiment* and *love*; I answer, *coldness* and *inconstancy*; in short, one should foresee every thing: I mean to dispose of my time according to my own fancy at this delightful house; so I again repeat, conclude the purchase in my name, and I will take precaution that it be not discovered; but, though it should be found out, what great harm is there! Are we forbid to love the *country*, solitude and agriculture? or to take delight in a charming garden? You pretend that my mother would fly out: Oh, do not suppose she is so morose; for be assured you do her injustice. Her female friend dictates a few severe expressions; but then her male one inspires her with much softer sentiments ... however, at the worst, if she is angry, we will flirt with the Chevalier d' Herbain, and then he will soon make our peace, for he'll think the affair trifling; and he will not let people be so *inconsistent* as to scold about it. Adieu! my dear little creature, and finish quickly with your old devotee; and, as a recompence, you may, as often as you please, go to muse and meditate in my hermitage.'

Now is it possible for any person to be more depraved or wicked! to avow, without the smallest necessity, that she loves not her gallant; and with indifference to declare she means to leave him: to accuse her mother falsely, merely from a wantonness of heart, and to renounce all principle and modesty, without even the excuse of passion or warm fancy; and in cool blood to dishonour herself! but her wickedness and vices distress more than anger me! and, when I reflect on the education she received, I accuse only myself for all her faults; and I have no right to be displeased or angry, and I ought to feel only remorse. For twelve years I thought of nothing but dissipation and trifling amusements, and, during that whole time, forgot that I was a mother, and intirely abandoned my daughter. Heaven this day punishes me for that criminal carelessness! I can no longer deceive myself; it is a vice proceeding from education, which has corrupted her soul; coquetry has been her ruin! Unfortunate girl! if she had been blessed with a mother such as you are, she would have been sensible and virtuous, esteemed and happy! She calumniates and hates me! Ah! I can only pity her; I ought to forgive her.

This dreadful misfortune I shall conceal at the bottom of my heart: I shall neither mention it to Monsieur de Limours, whom I am afraid to exasperate, nor to Madame de Valcy: but now it is all over with me; the happiness of my life is gone, and I look forwards to misfortunes, which I cannot even bear the idea of: she will, I am certain, finish her ruin by some exploit which will be publicly known. Oh, my dear friend, was I not sure of seeing you to-morrow, and of weeping over all my misfortunes in perfect freedom with you, I believe I should lose my senses. Oh, virtuous and affectionate mother! you will obtain for your miserable friend a pardon from Heaven for all her faults, and you will procure for me the preservation of the only comfort I can enjoy! my dear Constantia! Alas! I feel myself so culpable, that all that can still make me happy appears hardly possible! and every reflection lessens the hopes of my heart. Oh! come and restore to my distressed thoughts that fortitude which has now abandoned me: Come to me, for you are the only person who can afford me comfort!

LETTER XXVI.

Monsieur d' Aimeri to the Baron.

MADAME d' Almane set our yesterday for Paris, and we vainly seek her where she is no longer to be found. This morning the Chevalier proposed our going to the Castle de B—. We went thither on horse-back, and stopped on the bank of the river: here is was, said the Chevalier, that I saw Mademoiselle

Adelaide for the first time. My mother came to visit Mademoiselle d' Almane. They were walking on this grass; we were conducted to them; and in going thither we met about a hundred paces from them a lovely little girl who was diverting herself with running. I was struck with her figure. Her beautiful black hair concealed half her face, but allowed me to see a pair of the finest eyes in the world! – As Charles ended these words, we found ourselves at the gate of the Castle; he stopped, and, shewing me a large service-tree, he said, at the time I am speaking of, I climbed up this tree, and, fell from it: Adelaide desired a branch of the tree ... You was more eager than dexterous ... I fell on my head which received a large wound; but Adelaide wept at it; and, tearing off the handkerchief which covered her neck, bound it on my forehead! – In saying these words Charles had tears in his eyes, and fell into a deep reverie. We went into the garden, where he recollected many other circumstances. In this place he had found a bird's nest, which he had presented to Adelaide, and which she accepted with pleasure. There Theodore and Adelaide used every evening to amuse themselves with different sports. – In this arbour of honey-suckles, he had taken leave of Adelaide, when we went upon our travels to the North ... In short, every object brought something interesting to his remembrance. Charles recollected with tenderness these happy days of innocence: days in which the charming Adelaide expressed extreme pleasure in seeing him; and told him, when he went away, *If he would but return soon, she should love him very much.*

You may judge, Sir, by these particulars, whether the Chevalier is in love. He is absolutely almost out of his wits; and I am not surprised at it, for nothing can be comparable to Mademoiselle Adelaide. She has, in her person, manners, and deportment, inexpressible charms, which, the oftener you see, the more amiable she appears; and all these are united to knowledge surprising for her age; so great a genius, with modesty and innocence, which would disarm even envy itself. She is always gentle, kind, and obliging; and it is plain, that these qualities are really in her heart, without any disguise or affectation. Politeness is so natural to her, and she has so much the habit of behaving with the utmost propriety, that one would almost be tempted to believe, she was born perfect, and indebted for nothing to her education. She is so much at her ease, and has so little art, that one can scarce persuade one's self she was not intirely the work of Nature. Adieu, Monsieur, we intend going to Paris in three weeks. Pray let me know whether you do not mean to leave Strasburg before the end of December.

LETTER XXVII.

Count de Roseville to the Baron.

YOU will see, my dear Baron, by the Gazette, that we are still on our travels. You will with the less surprize receive a letter from this place. We have thoroughly investigated the facts contained in the Journals of the Baron de Sulback and of the Count de Stralzi, by which means we have proved the veracity of the former, and of course the falsehood of the latter. Three weeks after we left the Court, the young Prince received a letter from his father of which this is a copy:

'It is with inexpressible pleasure, my dear son, I learn the consequences your presence produces wherever you go. Deserve these marks of attachment by your sensibility of gratitude. Promise yourself to be the means of happiness to a people that love you, trusting you will one day be a blessing to them. Never receive coldly proofs of their affection. They not only claim their happiness from you but your love; theirs is given you at that price. Justice alone will intitle you to their respect; their allegiance must be your's, were you a tyrant:[35] a parental affection towards your subjects will exalt you to the rank of the greatest Monarchs; by the high esteem they hold you in they will immortalize your name. Their happiness will depend on you, your fame of true glory on them. By endearing yourself to my subjects, you will increase their regard for me; they will be convinced of my good intentions towards them by my care of your education. They will load me with blessings for rendering you worthy of the throne. Continue your journey six weeks longer in my provinces, and bring me back a descriptive and exact Journal. Should you find, in any remote province, merit and virtue languishing in obscurity, perhaps oppressed, bring it forth to light. – Whilst I am confined by the cares of Government to a deceitful Court, where the voice of my people and complaints of the unfortunate cannot reach me, you, my son, still at liberty, will perform the sacred duty of a faithful subject and tender friend; instruct yourself to enlighten me.

When you have examined all my provinces, I would wish you to acquire the very useful knowledge of the neighbouring States. Travel among them for seven or eight months; acquaint yourself with their strength and resources; examine attentively their public establishments and manufactures, &c. Proceed, my son, to inform yourself; bring your reason to maturity, and render yourself worthy to govern one day a nation ready to undertake any thing for its Sovereign and for glory.'

The Prince read the letter with a sigh, and with some chagrin at the positive order not to return to *** for ten months. He did not, however, complain; his respect for his father is not merely form; he feels for him that profound reverence and affectionate attachment which high esteem and gratitude inspire in great souls. We have now been four months in foreign countries; have frequented different companies in all the towns where we resided. The Prince is amiable, engaging, and polite; he is easy and graceful, and constantly keeps to the character of incognito as agreed upon. In all company he is the Count de Gemrid; by which means he is never under restraint. We hear opinions of the Court and State affairs. We hear them praised and blamed without reserve. The Prince often, when we are alone, testifies his surprize at the freedom used by the censorious; it is, said he, equally extraordinary and imprudent. – Doubtless it is very blameable, but not extraordinary; it is so every-where. Every-where? What in my father's dominions! – There are in all States factions and male-contents. A Prince should overlook what ill humour says against him. He abuses his right of punishing, if he does it out of revenge ... but if they should attack his honour ... A Sovereign's honour is determined by the general opinion of his subjects, not by the prating of silly people. Let us suppose you defame one of your courtiers, his character is blemished, and he can have no redress: at the same time, was he guilty of a like fault towards you, he would be in danger of ruining himself, and could not hurt you. Under these circumstances, justice teaches you forgiveness. Malevolence may offend, it can never hurt you, therefore despise it ... Should the Author of a libel that abuses a Prince without mercy escape with impunity? ... No, certainly. Bad men deserve punishment; I only alluded to common talkers. You will probably meet with people mean enough to tell you who those are who speak disrespectfully of you! Then, Sir, let your indignation fall on the informers! ... Am I not obliged to those who tell me what faults are found with me? ... That depends upon circumstances ... If friendship does it expresly to reform you, the accuser should be concealed. An honest man, a witness to errors, looks upon them as secrets intrusted to him. If they speak without reserve in my presence, it is because they trust to my discretion: I am the more honoured by the confidence arising from my character, rather than from friendship. A stranger, even an enemy, putting his trust in me, depends upon my honour; by betraying him, I disgrace myself. But should a supposed friend traduce me? ... If he did it in the height of passion and discontent, I would not tell you of it ... But if deliberately and with premeditated malice ... Yes, I would then acquaint you with it in his presence. Consider, Sir, there is always either rancour or cowardice in secret accusations; despise the tale-bearer who discovers to you the faults of others and wishes to have his name concealed. We depart to-morrow, for ***. The Prince leaves this place with regret, and with a character most satisfactory to me; from his travels he will reap real advantages, as he has no desire to display those already acquired. He speaks little, asks many questions, and listens with attention. He writes down every night all that has happened in the day worth remarking.

Do you remain, my dear Baron, at Strasburg? Or do you at Paris enjoy the pleasure or your friends and amiable family? Write to me about yourself, Madame d' Almane, your children and the Chevalier de Valmont, for whose interest I have an affectionate regard.

LETTER XXVIII.

The Baroness to Madame de Valmont.

Paris.

I ASSURE you, Madame, it was Adelaide's own desire to write to you the day after our arrival. Since she has given you a description of our new house, I shall only mention her apartment and her brother's, because she is acquainted with neither. I must explain this, as it will no doubt surprize you. Mons. d' Almane lodges on the ground-floor, and I up one pair of stairs; adjoining to my bed-chamber there is a pretty large closet in which Adelaide now sleeps; at the farthest end is a door fast locked. Adelaide asked me to what that door led; I answered, to some long galleries which I should hereafter have laid out in apart-ments for her, in case she married, and her husband was willing to live with us. These pretended galleries are in reality delightful apartments, consisting of six rooms, all fitted up. There is no gilding, and it is furnished with the greatest simplicity; but it will suit my daughter better, for her taste is good enough to prefer elegance and convenience to magnificence. I certainly shall not wait for her marrying to procure her the pleasure of being so agreeably lodged. She is above fifteen. Next year I intend opening the prohibited door and settling her in her new apartment. Theodore will likewise experience a similar surprize. Mons. d' Almane being desirous of retaining his son a year longer in his own room, and being unwilling that he should have a wish to occupy any other, is the reason of our secrecy.

Mons. d' Almane arrived at the end of last week; so here we are all reunited and perfectly happy. My children are not yet in the world; but, as we sup at half past nine, Theodore sups with us, but goes to bed before eleven, and his father retires with him. I remain with my company until near one. Adelaide sups in her own room with Miss Bridget and the little Hermine at eight; therefore she always gets up two or three hours before me. Although in that time Miss Bridget presides over her studies, I take care to direct them in such a manner that I may judge at my waking, how well she has employed her time. For example, I do not allow her to practise music; but I make her draw, write, and cast accounts. She is at present taking Extracts from history, in English and Italian, which will accustom her to write those languages, without being obliged to dedicate a particular hour to that study. She takes Extracts in French from the Plays and Letters which I have written. When I am up, I correct the faults in her style and language. Afterwards I make her sing, and play on the harp till noon, when, if the weather permits, she walks or reads. We all dine together at one; after dinner she embroiders, or works tapestry for half an hour. From three to five she is engaged with her two masters for singing and dancing. We then are shut up in my closet, and read an hour. At six the academy begins. She draws by the lamp and from nature. You see, Madame, from this relation, that Adelaide is engaged in a new study. She begins to paint miniatures: she will keep this Master till she is eighteen, and during that time she will spend two hours every day in drawing. Being accustomed by degrees to be always employed, and never to lose a moment, this continued application cannot fatigue her; the variety of her occupations will refresh her. Moreover, having surmounted all the first difficulties, study will in general appear much more agreeable than painful to her, and a habit of labour will make idleness insupportable. I procure her three times a week a recreation equally amusing and instructive. Directly after dinner I get into my carriage with my two children, and we visit the cabinets of pictures, gems, medals, or we see fine monuments or manufactories: if it is manufactories, we never fail, before we set out, to read in the Encyclopædia[36] an explanation of what we are going to see, by which means we perfectly comprehend all that is done; and we shall continue this kind of course till May. I obey you, Madame. I write of nothing but Adelaide: your goodness to her will make all my relations interesting to you; and you see how confidently I avail myself of means so delightful to myself, to amuse and please you.

LETTER XXIX.

The same to the same.

MADAME, Mons. d' Aimeri and the Chevalier de Valmont arrived yesterday in perfect health. My son's gratitude is boundless for the friendship the Chevalier testified on seeing him again. Before my departure for Italy, Theodore was too young to be considered and treated as a friend; he is now sensible of all the joys of friendship. The trifling difference in their ages is scarcely discernible at present, and will not be at all so in another year.

Yes, Madame, I have made an acquaintance with that charming Countess Anatolle whom the Viscountess extolled so highly. She is really extremely pretty and very amiable; but I grieve to see the dangerous connections she is allowed to form.[37] She begins to enjoy her liberty; she goes by herself, because she has just lain in. Mothers ought to be prudent; nevertheless at eighteen it is impossible to do without a guide, particularly with a neglected education. Farewell, Madam; I give no account of your commissions, since Adelaide undertook them. She employs herself with that activity you admire in her; and her ardour redoubles when you are the object.

LETTER XXX.

The Baroness to Madame d' Ostalis.

NO one truly ever possessed more delicacy and sincerity than he! ... His is now a real passion, but still more affecting, as he shuts it up carefully in the bottom of his heart. He hardly dares look on Adelaide; he even seems to shun every opportunity of conversing with her, and has never taken the liberty of praising her; all his encomiums are bestowed on the little Hermine; all his marks of affection on Theodore who loves him to distraction. The Chevalier dined here to-day. When they rose from table, my son was talking of him to Porphyry, and said, *I love him, as if he was my brother!* at that word *Brother*, Charles ran to Theodore, seized his hand with an expression of sensibility beyond description! Instantly the fear of having committed an indiscretion without doubt struck him (for, when we are truly in love, we think that every thing betrays it.) He was embarrassed, blushed, and cast down his eyes. Adelaide was embroidering by me. I looked on her, but could not see her face. She had just dropped her needle, which she sought very attentively, bending down her head on the frame ... She remained in this attitude long enough to make it appear a little suspicious ... She rose up very red. Was it confusion, or merely the effect of the blood in her face? I know not.

With regard to her affections, I am very sure she has no decided ones, and I am as certain reason will always regulate them. I think I have observed she speaks with more esteem of Madame de Valmont, since she has seen her son; and that she experiences a sort of pleasure in pronouncing the name of Valmont. She has taken the pretty collection of pebbles out of the box which the Chevalier gave her before we went into Italy.

These pebbles, forgotten during three years and an half, are now arranged in great order on pretty shelves of Acacia wood bought on purpose. These are all the indications I can collect at present. As to the rest, Adelaide is neither thoughtful nor distracted, she is as lively as ever. On those days in which the Chevalier is not admitted, that is to say, at least five days in the week, I cannot perceive the least alteration in her temper. In fine, I dare assure you, if she feels any preference, she is but slightly affected, and it does not disturb her tranquality.

The Marquis de Hernay, the young man we saw in Italy, is returned; the Chevalier met him here one evening. He knows that the Marquis is unmarried, that he is very rich and well spoken of; and I thought I remarked an uneasiness in the Chevalier on seeing Mons. d' Almane take so much notice of him.

The Countess Anatolle supped with me last night. Mons. de St. Phar, who is said to be in love with her, staid till near nine, in hopes of being asked to supper; but, as I have not yet adopted that fashionable method of drawing company to my house, I did not invite him. The Countess was rather melancholy all the evening; she complained of the vapours! after supper there was half an hour's gossip between her, Madame de Valcy, and Madame Clairford; then she went to bed. She cannot as yet be reproached with any thing essential; but she grows coquetish, and gives herself up to Madame de Valcy ... You will see the ill effects of all this. It is a pity, for she certainly has an excellent understanding and a charming disposition. Adieu, my dear child, send me intelligence of Madame de S— ; I already know that the inoculation has taken, and that she has not much fever. I hope you will return in three weeks; I cannot accustom myself to the thoughts of your being but a league from me, and not to see you for so long a time; but I highly approve of your not returning before the time prescribed. Many people make no scruple of deceiving the world in this respect, and bringing the small pox to Paris; this nevertheless is a very cruel thing, and equally inconsistent with justice and humanity.

LETTER XXXI.

The Baroness to Madame de Valmont.

April 25.

OUR departure for Holland is at last fixed; and Mons. d' Almane, my children, Dainville, and I set out in eight days. I need not tell you, Madame, that Hermine is to be of the party, as her mother and she are always inseparable. We shall certainly return in a month. The Chevalier de Valmont had a desire to see Holland and go with us; but instead of that he sets out to-morrow for his garrison. You know, without doubt, Madame, that Mons. d' Aimeri does not attend him; it is high time to trust him to himself, that he may shew the use he will make of intire liberty. He goes to a city where they play very high; he will be there without a *Mentor*, and surrounded by a croud of young men who will give him none but bad advice. He will have great merit in behaving well. He took leave of us to-day, and was really affected when he embraced Theodore. They promised to correspond, as they will not meet again till next Winter. Adieu, Madame; direct your first letter to me at the Hague. Since I am acquainted with your taste for flowers, you may depend on a little box of the best Hyacinth roots Haerlem will produce.

LETTER XXXII.

The Baroness to Madame d' Ostalis.

Amsterdam.

I AM this moment, my dear daughter, returned from Broëk, two leagues from this place.[38] One cannot describe this village without being suspected of exaggeration; yet all I can say of this delightful spot must fall infinitely short of reality. The inhabitants, though mere peasants, are very rich. The streets are paved in Mosaic work of different-coloured bricks, and as neat as could be in your own apartment. The houses are painted, and as clean as wainscots, the best looked after. All, even the tiles, are shining bright and appear new. Each house has a garden and a terrace, both inclosed only by low and open fences which conceal nothing. The terrace is usually before the house, the garden behind, and separates it from the next house. Both sides of the street are laid out in the same manner. The ornaments of the gardens are China vases, grottoes, flowers, trees, and parterres, some laid out artificially with glittering pieces of glass of different colours, others of shells, as carefully arranged as in a cabinet. Large fertile meadows full of cattle are behind the houses, as are the sheds of stables, so that the carriages and cattle never come to dirty the neat streets. The insides of the houses are equally astonishing as the outsides. The floors are checquered with black and yellow shining stones: the best rooms are furnished with wainscot of its natural colour, neither varnished nor painted, but carved very ornamentally. In the best room there is always a large cupboard with glass-doors, through which are shewn most beautiful china, and quantities of plate, to all appearance new from the goldsmith. The same order of neatness prevailed in all the houses we went into. By this uniformity, one would imagine, all the fortunes were equal: when we have seen one, we have seen all the houses at Broëk. They have all two doors, one of ceremony, only made use of at marriages and deaths. The new-married couple enter by it, and never go out of it but to their graves. The peasants of Broëk have also a room which is never made use of but on the wedding-day and ever afterwards held sacred: it is more ornamented than the rest, and the bed excessively adorned and covered with fine lace: on a table is placed a pretty basket containing the bride's wedding cloaths: they never go into it, but to clean, put it in order, and shew it to strangers.

The same uniformity is observable in their dress: that of the men very plain, the women's very expensive. They are clothed in beautiful Persians,[39] the finest of linnen, and many trinkets of gold and pearls. – A hood of white cambrick conceals their hair, fastened on each side by two gold pins set with pearls. I have seen even servant-maids drest in this style: their mistresses exceed them only in more valuable necklaces and rings, and the fineness of their linnen.

The manners of these people are irreproachable; the strictest harmony unites them. They have a most tender affection for their children. The little infants are so used to be caressed, that they court you for it. I could not help stopping when I saw any of them, and they ran of their own accord to kiss me. The inhabitants of Broëk are very unsociable. On the first sight of strangers, they shut themselves up, and refuse to open their doors: but they have a natural politeness, or, to speak more properly, a certain respect for women that makes them act very differently with regard to them: they no sooner see them, than they hastily assemble, follow, and conduct them, with their male companions, to shew them their house in the most easy and polite manner. Thus were we treated for three hours. Their wives never stir from Broëk. A young woman would find it difficult to marry at any distance from it. They know as much of London, or Constantinople, as of Amsterdam. Their happiness is placed at home. Broëk is to them the whole world, for which reason their customs and virtue remain the same. They always intermarry: many Nobles of the country have wished to espouse the young women of Broëk, for their riches; but no one has as yet succeeded. The inhabitants value themselves on their plainness and state of peasantry. They live frugally: to beautify their houses is one of their greatest pleasures: to be united and quiet is what they vgalue most. Beautiful as the human race is in all Holland, it is remarkably so here. The children are all charming, the men robust, and the women large, well made, and in general handsome. – Their complexions are almost supernatural. In short, this village presents a picture singular in its kind. Every thing charms the eyes and heart; no one disagreeable or unhappy object to spoil the piece. You not only meet no beggars, but every one seems to be in easy circumstances. There are no cripples, no infirm old people, no houses out of repair. Health, all things necessary to ease, every elegance of industry and neatness, simplicity, humanity, virtue and happiness; these are the inestimable advantages and charming prospects we there meet with, which, joined to the interesting singularity of their dress, houses, and customs, make it, altogether, the most extraordinary place within one hundred leagues of us.

I was yesterday at Sardam (where Peter the Great resided)[40] a larger and richer village than Broëk, with almost the same manners and customs, but not near so pretty, clean, or singular.

Here we finish our course of manufactures. We have seen those of paper, ropes, and cables, &c. At Haerlem we saw a foundery of types for printing and likewise diamond-cutting. Our children are delighted with Holland. The manner of travelling is very agreeable in a fine yacht, or rather a handsome saloon. We coast along beautiful shores. We can read, write, and practise on Musick, as conveniently as in a house.

Italy and Holland seem to me the most contrasted; in the former, Nature is majestic and diversified, presenting every-where to the view most grand effects, enormous rocks, high mountains, precipices, and cascades: in the latter, the country is flat; canals, verdure, and small plantations are every-where to be seen. In Italy, ancient monuments at every step remind us of the most glorious actions recorded in History. The modern Architecture is magnificent, noble, and calculated to strike the imagination, and will bear the most strict examination. The pictures, like every things else, are in the heroic and sublime style. In Holland, no monuments remain: every thing appears new: the effect of the whole together must be considered separately; each part loses its value, and appears mean and in bad taste; each particular object is trifling. Architecture and the Arts are there equally unknown. Every thing pleases, but in a low taste and without grandeur. The pictures are small but extraordinarily highly finished; the subjects generally very mean. In Italy, they paint Heroes and Demi-gods: Here, drunken sailors, greenstalls, and fishermen. The Italians are vain, artful, and idle: the Dutch honest, plain, and industrious, despising pomp and magnificence.

Adelaide has finished writing answers to the Letters of my Work: and, according to my promise, we are now reading those capital Authors we have so long wished to be acquainted with. The day we imbarked at Maerdike, I put into my daughter's hands Madame Sevigne's Letters and the English *Clarissa*. She read in the yacht these Works alternately, with a pleasure and attention which gave me great satisfaction. She is sufficiently founded to feel the beauties of Madame de Sevigne's style, and is deeply touched with the sublime of *Clarissa*. She was much struck with the black character of Lovelace, and shuddered at his arts of hypocrisy: This is what I wished. It is very important for young women early to distrust men in general. No book is better calculated for that wide purpose than *Clarissa*. Adieu! my child! To-morrow we go to Utrecht: in fifteen days I shall embrace you. Theodore has received already in Holland these letters from the Chevalier de Valmont: they are surprisingly affectionate! – Sure never was friendship so tenderly expressed!

LETTER XXXIII.

The Viscountess to the Baroness.

I HAVE news to tell you, my dear friend, that some time ago would have given me the greatest uneasiness, but to which at present I am indifferent. Madame de Valcy is taking a house of her own, and quits mine, as one would an inn. Her mother-in-law is just dead, and has left a very considerable fortune, which she had been in possession of these two years by the death of her brother.

This event makes Monsieur de Valcy immensely rich; and renders him worthy of all the affection of his wife: but I believe he will set no great value on these proofs of her regard: however, he is quiet, weak, and very limited in his ideas; for though he is not deceived, yet he suffers himself to be managed. He has a very grand establishment: neither Monsieur de Limours nor myself are the least consulted about their affairs; but we do not complain; for it is surely wrong to expose a daughter's faults to the world! Madame de Valcy is so overjoyed, she humbles me, and yet moves my compassion: when riches cause such emotions, how are they to be pitied who possess them! as they are rendered incapable of our experiencing the feelings which flow from a generous heart! Adieu, my dear friend; I expect your return with the greatest impatience, as I have a thousand things to say to you which cruelly afflict me, and which it is impossible for me to write.

LETTER XXXIV.

Mons. de Lagaraye to Porphyry.

A LITTLE adventure has just befallen me which seems made on purpose to interest a young philosopher, and give birth to new and useful ideas. You know that a neighbour of mine, Mons. de Valincourt, is bringing up an unfortunate nephew born deaf and dumb. You may have seen this youth at my house, whose name is Hipolytus, and who is very remarkable for a countenance full of expression: yet, as it is two years since you were at Lagaraye, you may probably recollect him but very imperfectly: it will therefore not be improper to describe him: Hipolytus is not handsome, but his countenance is so sprightly, with so sensible a smile, and so piercing a look, that it is impossible not to be struck with his figure. The rapid and perpetual motion of his eye renders his countenance as animated as it is ingenuous. By his eyes he hears, understands, and expresses himself. In them are painted an habitual and constant curiosity; it is easy to discover in them his thoughts, feelings, and every sentiment of his soul. It is now near two years since his uncle set out for Paris, and, as he proposed only to stay six weeks, did not take him with him. I undertook the care of him for that time; and Hipolytus, who was then but fourteen, came joyfully to Lagaraye. As he is naturally sensible and good, and his misfortune adding to the interest he inspires, he is beloved by all who know him. He has been brought up by a virtuous uncle, always indulged and treated with tenderness. He has never had any but excellent examples, and his heart is as gentle as it is pure and grateful. In a week after his uncle's departure, he fell suddenly ill of a malignant fever. He was in the utmost danger for twenty-nine days: I attended him with true affection, and watched by him several nights. He proved to me, that Gratitude needs not the aid of words to make herself understood. His eyes spoke in terms less deceitful and more moving than the most eloquent discourse. I had the happiness to restore him to health. He was perfectly recovered when I received a letter from Monsieur de Valincourt, informing me that important business would detain him at Paris, at least seven or eight months, intreating me to send Hipolytus, and to trust him to his steward who was just setting out. He did not leave me without shedding many tears. I begged his conducter to let me know how he did, as soon as he got to Paris. Monsieur de Valincourt wrote himself to thank and inform me, that his nephew was perfectly well; from that time I was eighteen months without hearing of them. Yesterday I received a letter by the post. I opened it, and saw a bad hand which I knew not; I looked for the name; judge of my surprise in seeing that of Hipolytus and de Valincourt! ... I then read with as much emotion as curiosity, a letter conceived in the following terms:

'Oh! what transports can equal mine! ... I am now assured that all my gratitude will be known to you! I can pay my thanks in your own language ... My father! oh do allow me to call you by that tender name, since you saved my life, since I feel for you the most affectionate sentiments of a son! ... My father, (how great is my happiness!) a man* as good and benevolent as yourself,[41] procures me the inexpressible pleasure of speaking to you; of laying open my whole heart to you; and of understanding you, if you desing to write to me! ... I had only detached ideas; now I think, I reflect, I enjoy in its full extent all the felicity, all the sweets connected with the state of man! ... What sublime truths has my new benefactor made known to me! Before I was instructed, I doubted of the existence of a supreme Being, Creator of Man and of the Universe; – but I was ignorant of his law: without my respectable, my dear instructor, I should never have read the Gospel! Oh, ought we to be surprised, that man is so good, so virtuous, when he finds in this divine book all the knowledge of his duties and every incentive to virtue! – I will acknowledge, that, at the bottom of my soul, my weak reason has been astonished and confounded by the excess of your benevolence. Humanity was truly dear to me, compassion lorded it in my heart; but I could not conceive the possibility of devoting one's self entirely to such melancholy and painful cares! Alas, I was acquainted only with the law of nature: I was not made to comprehend perfection. Now that I am enlightened by Religion, I

---

* The Abbé de L' Epic, whose elogium cannot be properly made, but by describing the actions of his life. He confeciates his fortune to the relief of the poor; his understanding and talents to the instruction of the deaf and dumb. He snatches these unfortunates from error and ignorance; he restores them to Religion, to the State, and to Society. He teaches them, by a method he has himself invented, Reading, Writing, and Arithmetic. He is the Author of a work (as estimable as it is ingenious and useful) intitled *Institution des Soards & Muets de Naissance*.

admire without surprise your sublime virtues, and those of the Sages to whom I am indebted for my new existence. I easily conceive, that man is a perfect Being, since Religion, the Laws, Honour, and Nature, all unite to prompt him to good! Can he even need the fear of punishment to keep him from evil? ... Is it not sufficient for him to know he will be hated if he is wicked? ... Wicked men! ... If it should be true, that there are any such existing, this doubt troubles and afflicts me! ... But, should there be any such, these mad monsters are surely too rare for me ever to fear meeting one; I may therefore flatter myself never to see any but good and sensible men ... During my abode here, I have had occasion to observe various ranks, and they have all been virtuous. At the school where I, together with a croud of children and young persons of my own age, are instructed, I have often seen strangers assist at our lessons; amongst others the presence of the Emperor,[42] proved to me by the marks of esteem and veneration he paid my master, that Kings can distinguish honour and reward merit and virtue.

Finally, every new object I behold, all the the knowledge I acquire, increases my affection for the human species. Oh, my father! when I can return to Britanny, will you sometimes permit me to assist in the sacred employment you impose on yourself? I cannot be happy but in dividing my life between my uncle and you.'

Well then, my dear Porphyry, do you not envy the fate of Hipolytus? He has never dwelt but in solitude and with worthy people: he has never heard mixed conversation; indiscretion, slander, and calumny are vices he has no idea of; he judges of men from the most deceitful appearances: he sees them smile, embrace, and treat each other with as much friendship as respect. He mistakes falsehood for affection, and politeness for sensibility. He imagines himself in a terrestrial paradise; he looks on all men as his friends and his brethren ... Sweet and charming illusion! which reading alone will soon destroy. Alas! what will become of him in running through the bloody pomps of history? With what grievous astonishment, with what profound indignation, will he not read the encomiums lavished on barbarous conquerors who have depopulated the world! Oh, Porphyry! to have a good opinion of mankind, must one then be born deaf and dumb![43]

LETTER XXXV.

The Baroness to Madame de Valmont.

Paris.

MONS. d' Almane set out yesterday with Theodore for Strasburg, and I, instead of remaining in my own house, have brought Adelaide this morning to a small apartment I have hired in the Convent of *** where we shall pass the

Summer and Autumn. I tell my daughter, that oeconomical reasons determine me. But the truth is, that, as she is to begin going into company next Winter, I wished her first entrance into the world to be preceded by six months of total retirement. I also am not sorry to have her see the pensioners; by knowing the manner of education in a Convent, she will set an higher value on her own.[44] As we were walking this afternoon in the garden, a number of young Ladies of Adelaide's age met us. At sight of us they burst out a laughing, and ran away as fast as possible to avoid us. Adelaide asked me the reason of this strange procedure. Why do they run away and laugh, says she? – Is it our figures which excite this fear and mirth. – But what is there in us either formidable or laughable? – Nothing in reality; therefore they only make a joke of us. – Make a joke of us! and why? – Malignity seizes on a ridiculous circumstance, and makes a joke of it; foolishness laughs without any cause ... Then all these young people are simpletons? – Perhaps their understandings were naturally good; but they have all the folly a bad education can bestow, viz. childishness, wildness, rudeness, and vulgarity ... What! and does no one reprehend them for these faults? – Abandoned by their mothers, they are given up to Governesses who are incapable of educating them properly, and who, moreover, leave them all day to themselves, without taking the pains to observe or attend them. – Oh, unfortunate children! It is not their fault, if they are ridiculous; we ought only to pity them! ... Had I been placed in a Convent, had I not had the tenderest of mothers, I should have had all these faults. – Doubtless, my dear Adelaide; and this kind indulgence you manifest is in reality no more than justice; preserve it carefully; should you love it, you would tarnish the lustre of all your virtues, and you will become ungrateful towards me; for you cannot pride yourself on the qualifications and talents you possess, without recollecting it is to me you owe them.

Be not afflicted, Madame, when you figure to yourself Adelaide's little countenance through a grate. We receive no visits, but from Madame d' Ostalis and Madame de Limours, and they are admitted into the Convent. So we shall never go into the parlour, unless it is to take a lesson in painting or dancing; and that is not through the grate, but in the outward parlour. We shall spend our time delightfully; books are our greatest enjoyment. We now read *Telemachus* in the morning, and Fontaine's Fables in the afternoon. Adelaide, transported, thanks me at every page, for having refused her these admirable Works, whilst she was too young to know their value; and she cannot conceive, what folly can make people allow children to read them. If I was not very careful, her fondness for reading would make her neglect her other avocations. In short, this appears to me so good a method, that I cannot think it possible but that it must be one day universally adopted.

LETTER XXXVI.

Baroness to Madame de Valmont.

MY poor Adelaide has gone through many vexations, with the causes of which, Madame, I am going to acquaint you. Among twelve or fifteen pensioners who are in this Convent, there is one called Mademoiselle de Celigny, who is about seventeen years old, and has a very agreeable person; in other respects, she is as ill educated as the rest, but has wit enough, when she chuses it, to conceal her faults, particularly to a girl of fifteen and a half. She took great notice of my daughter who, naturally sensible and grateful, was much pleased with her attentions. I saw plainly this connection would not suit Adelaide; but I wished it might serve her as a lesson, and I left it to her to find it out. In consequence of this design, I permitted Adelaide to ask her sometimes to breakfast, and sometimes to dine with us. As I never quitted Adelaide a moment, I found my making a third person with them was very distressing to this young Lady. One day, when we were going to take a walk, I pretended to be tired, and sat down again, telling Adelaide she might walk with Mademoiselle de Celigny for half an hour; on their return, I perceived that Adelaide looked much dissatisfied, and that she treated Mademoiselle de Celigny with great coldness. I suspected the cause of it, but I asked no questions, and we went to bed without any explanation. The next morning, when Adelaide was writing her copies, I went and made a visit to Sister Saint Helena, one of the Nuns who was a friend of mine, and who always had the news of the whole Convent before any body else ... I told her my curiosity to know what it was Mademoiselle de Celigny had said to my daughter: sister Helena (who already knew the disposition of Mademoiselle de Celigny, and had given me a caution in secret respecting her) told me, that this young Lady pretended Adelaide had complained of the slavery, in which I kept her, by always following her like her shadow. After this recital I returned to Adelaide, and told her what sister Helena had said. She heard me with that tranquillity which convinced me she did not think I believed a word of what I had been told. Is it possible, said she, that people can carry their falsehood and wickedness to such a height? ... Now, Mamma, I will tell you the truth ... Mademoiselle de Celigny, displeased with my coldness, imputes to me all that she said herself ... You tell me nothing new; I guessed by your manner yesterday what you have just now informed me of. I was also very certain the particulars of your conversation would be very unjustly repeated; and I only asked sister Helena about it, in order to let you see you was deceived in Mademoiselle Celigny. – What then, Mamma, you knew she was not good? – I saw she had no good principles; that she was a great talker and a gossip, and consequently thought she might not scruple telling lyes and being deceitful. – Oh, Mamma, why would you not condescend to enlighten me? – I only wished experience should undeceive you. – Oh, Mamma, you have set my heart at ease; it would have given me great pain to have told you, she gave me very bad advice, though I was determined to tell you of it, as I was never to see her again, even though you had not acquainted me with her having told stories of me ... Never to see her again! ... I shall not allow this ... How then, Mamma? ... You must avoid an open rupture, which will make a noise, and injure the character of both persons who disagree. It is easy by degrees to break off your acquaintance, which will prevent the publick from making a history of it to amuse themselves with. In short, you must remember it is more prudent to *disunite* than it is to *break*. – What, Mamma! shall we often see Mademoiselle de Celigny then? ... You need not send for her, but you must receive her with politeness; you are not obliged to tell her you love her, but you may behave to her as usual ... It is very hard, however, to associate with people you despise ... It is necessary to learn how to live with chattering, mischievous, indiscreet persons; because, when you meet with them, you should be able to guard against them; but, when you have found them, or connected yourself with them, it is necessary to submit patiently to them. – Oh, what imprudence have I been guilty of! I will never do so again: before I form an attachment, I will study the disposition of the person I am inclined to love ... You will do well also to study her character, and even that of her family and friends; for one may frequently judge of people by their connexions; which is a still stronger reason why we should fix upon those who are most esteemed.

After this conversation Adelaide has determined to see Mademoiselle de Celigny again, and to treat her in the manner which I have advised; but this obedience will cost her some pain. In continual fear of Mademoiselle, she will speak of nothing decisively but the *rain* or *fine weather*, fearing always on her side a bad interpretation; and, to prevent her from inventing new stories of her, she is cautious never to speak to her in a low voice and not to remain alone with her a moment. This restraint accustoms her to prudence and circumspection, and, at the same time, maintains the bitter repentance she has felt for forming an attachment so ill judged and so little considered.

Adieu, Madame; I received yesterday a letter from ***, in which I am told the Chevalier de Valmont is neither confused nor hurt by the jests which his young friends make on his wisdom; they even add, that those who least resemble him pardon him his opinions on account of his graces and artless behaviour. I very sincerely share with you, Madame, in the joy which his conduct and his success must give you.

LETTER XXXVII.

The Count de Roseville to the Baron.

AT last, my dear Baron, we are returned to ***. I have brought back my pupil in his nineteenth year, with his principles sufficiently strengthened to resist the alluring arts which love was preparing to practise upon him. Stolina, still unmarried, lived with her father upon the banks of the lake. She had found means to avoid and put off every proposed match, during our absence, under various pretences, and chiefly under that of a weak and worn out constitution. The day after our arrival, the Prince received the following note: 'I am dying – Alas! may I flatter myself with the hopes of seeing, before I expire, my benefactor and my protector! If this favour is refused me, my last moments will be as grievous as my life has been unhappy. STOLINA.'

The Prince, with tears in his eyes, brought me this note, without allowing me to speak he said; no objections of yours will prevent my going immediately to Alexis Stezin's house. – Do you think me, interrupted I, capable of dissuading you from an act of benevolence? O, my friend! said the Prince, warmly embracing me ... I desire only, replied I, that a Physician, in whom you put the greatest trust, may accompany us. He fixed upon Dr. Walter; we set off as soon as he came, and found Stolina in an elbow-chair, with all the outward appearance of a sick person, pale and languishing, but more bewitching and beautiful than ever. Her agitation of joy at the sight of the Prince was too evident. Her colour went and came, and she burst into tears. She attempted to rise from her chair, but fell back. The Prince, equally affected, seated himself, muttering some incoherent words. He then told her mother he had brought a Physician, and ordered him in. During this discourse, I earnestly examined Stolina's looks, and plainly perceived her displeasure at it. We left the Doctor with her, and withdrew to another apartment. He came to us in about five minutes, and positively declared, that, so far from Stolina's being dangerously ill, she could not possibly imagine herself to have the least complaint; and I am obliged in conscience to assert, continued the Doctor, that there is some design in this. The testimony of a man so honest and skilful, whom no one could have influenced, struck the Prince very forcibly. He traversed the room in great trouble. At last, says he, let us depart; nothing now detains me. He hurried away: I followed, highly pleased at his being able to tear himself away from the dangerous Stolina, without even taking leave. He was scarcely seated in his coach, before he blamed his cruelty. He figured to himself Stolina in tears: he favourably attributed their little artifice to her love for him; and, as if he had a mind to revenge on me the pleasure this victory over himself had given me, he openly avowed his weakness and distress. I took not the least notice. My composure provoked him: he would have much preferred a serious discourse. Any remonstrance from me, besides giving him pleasure at my uneasiness, would have produced a regular debate on a subject so interesting to him. The conversation now ceased of course. When I perceived the Prince was about to put himself seriously in a passion, I said to him, you will fail in your endeavour to discompose me, for I know, though you are subject to say disagreeable things through pique, yet honour and reason are always your guides in affairs of consequence; what therefore do your speeches signify, when I am secure of your actions? These words flattered the Prince much, being pronounced in a blunt manner, and as if truth alone had forced them from me. He grew calm; the desire of meriting my esteem restored him to himself. He offered me his hand, and, fetching a deep sigh, said, you know me better than I do myself ... Your trust in me gives me strength, and exalts me in my own esteem enough to make me flatter myself I am worthy of your's.

Soon after, at my desire, the Chevalier de Murville called on Stolina, and represented to her so forcibly the bad consequences of her behaviour, that she, after some wavering, consented to complete the happiness of the faithful Mirandel; they are married and settled in the province of *** one hundred leagues from Court. This distance frees me from a very serious anxiety. The Prince heard the news with resolution. He is pensive, but strives to divert his melancholy by a closer application than ever to his studies. Some time ago the Prince his father, who wishes him married this year, conversed on that subject with me. I approve his intention, but not the proposed Princess. She is very ugly and six years older. If it is necessary in such situations to be chiefly guided by political views, is every tender feeling to be given up? I think that present advantages alone are considered in the marriages of sovereign Princes. It is a misfortune that very little future benefit is to be expected from their union. Ambition easily breaks the most sacred ties. It is the moderation of the Prince, the strength of his dominions, the prudence of his government, and not great alliances, that preserve the blessings of peace. After these reflections, I mentioned a young Princess lovely in her person, excellently brought up, and who by the sweetness of her temper and by her accomplishments would insure the happiness of the Prince, and be an ornament of the Court. When this so suitable an union takes place, I shall only have this wish to assist at the nuptials of Theodore and Constantia. It is delightful, after twelve years absence from one's country, to return to it, to one's friends and family. I cannot quit *** without severe pangs, or, to speak more plainly, without a fixed resolution of returning. I shall leave behind me the object that for twelve years has intirely possessed my thoughts. You can best judge, my dear Baron, the grief such a separation must occasion to me.

Your's dated the 25th is just come to hand. I perceive by it my last has not yet reached you. Be at ease with regard to the Count d' Ostalis; every proper step has been taken! act with confidence on your side. What pleasure I shall have in renewing at *** my acquaintance with Mons. d' Ostalis? He alone will make me not regret the loss of our present Ambassador.

LETTER XXXVIII.

The Baroness to Madame de Valmont.

Y ES, Madame, the first of November was a joyful day for Adelaide and Theodore. We were still in the Convent, when at eight o'clock in the morning we were told, that Mons. d' Almane and Theodore were waiting for us in the parlour. Adelaide took Hermine by the hand, and we went down stairs with that eagerness which one feels to see two persons so dear to one after six months absence. We passed the grate, and flew into the outer parlour. Adelaide threw herself into the arms of her father, while I received Theodore in mine. Adelaide embraced him in her turn; after which we left the Convent, and got into our coach. On our arrival at home, we entered my apartment, where we found Madame d' Ostalis and Madame de Limours. Adelaide had no sooner set her foot in my chamber, than she perceived the china which used to ornament it, and the tea-table, were no longer there. On her making this remark, Madame d' Ostalis led her into my closet, and shewed her it was deprived of all the impressions, drawings, and miniatures with which the wainscot had been adorned the past Winter. Adelaide, astonished at this alteration, asked the reason, at which every body smiled, but made her no reply; at length Madame de Limours, coming to me, said, Adelaide is to give us a breakfast this morning, if you will permit her. She has some excellent tea, which is now waiting for us in her apartment. We all followed Madame de Limours, and entered Adelaide's chamber, where we found nothing new, only that her bed was not in the room. Adelaide surprized, asked me how it happened. When on a sudden the door, which had been condemned, opened and discovered a delightful apartment. Little Hermine flew thither, uttering a cry of joy. Adelaide threw herself on my neck, saying to me, Oh, Mamma! I am sensible of your goodness, but you send me farther from you; I was nearer to you in this room! ... As she finished these words, Madame de Limours took her hand, and led her into a beautiful bed-chamber. There my daughter, looking round her, saw part of the ornaments which used to be in my apartment, and easily guessed the rest were distributed in the other rooms. Madame d' Ostalis opened a commode, and took out a little box, in which Adelaide found the few diamonds and other jewels I was mistress of.[45] Very far from expressing any pleasure at this sight, Adelaide looked very gravely on all these riches. Ah, Mamma! said she to me, I cannot see with any pleasure that you have deprived yourself of these ornaments for me; do you think it is possible I can enjoy them? ... Make yourself easy, my dear child; amuse yourself with these toys which are made for persons of your age. Whenever I purchased any of them, or was pleased with them, it was because they were destined for you. Reward me then for my attention by appearing pleased with my present. Adelaide embraced me, and pressed me in her arms, without being able to answer me. Madame de Limours came and parted us, in order to shew Adelaide the rest of the apartments; after which we returned to her chamber to drink tea, and after breakfast we conducted Theodore to his apartment. He expected the *condemned door* would be opened for him also; but he had not this agreeable surprize; however, he was delighted with his new habitation. When Adelaide and I were left alone, she expressed her gratitude in the most affecting terms. You have given me, said she, at one and the same time, every thing that can indulge the fancy of a young person who has not had the happiness of being thought up by you. Your presents are far above my wishes; yet they are only precious to me, as they belonged to you ... You must then be sensible, my dear Adelaide, of the extreme pleasure I feel in giving you all these trinkets. Yes, certainly; but nevertheless it gives me pain to see your chimneys and shelves unfurnished, and that horrid little tea-table of English queen's ware,[46] which supplies the place of your fine china. Hear me my dear child, and you will cease to pity me. Is it not true that a dish of tea or coffee drinks as well out of a cup made of earthen ware as out of the finest *china?* Yes, only the pleasure of looking at it ... Supposing the sight of my china gave me pleasure, which it never did, it could only have been during the novelty of it. Besides, nothing is more inconvenient than to have one's chamber filled with vases, monkeys, and other pieces of china; and one would never place these ornaments in a room where nobody came; so that one has these things only for the pleasure of letting them be seen, that is, from motives of vanity to prove one's taste and one's riches. For my part, I have another kind of vanity, which is to prove that I only esteem these superfluities in order to give them to my daughter. I shall have much more pride, when those who visit me look with amazement on my shabby set of earthen cups and saucers, than when they praised the elegance of my tea-table. I have no need to assure you that this way of thinking contributes in no respect to make me do what I do to oblige you, though it may sometimes help to reward me for the sacrifices I have made on your account. I need only to consult my own heart in order to do things which will give you pleasure. – Mamma, you inspire mine with noble sentiments by your tenderness and your example. At present I cannot conceive how people can value themselves on such trifling things. It appears to me that nothing is wanting but good sense, and a proper degree of pride, to make us conduct ourselves as we ought. Is it possible that proud and rich people should value themselves on their fine houses, their sideboard of plate, and their jewels, when every step they take they may find people who not only equal but even surpass them in magnificence? If, on the contrary, they would distinguish themselves by their moderation and benevolence, they would meet with few competitors; and the praises they would then obain would really be gratifying ... You say very right, but, however wise such an observation may be, a bad heart will never make it. Mamma, I promise you I will always avoid this ridiculous ostentation ... To have a house convenient and neatly furnished and elegant by its plainness, with fashionable cloaths, which are nothing remarkable either in their form or for their magnificence, a box either at the opera or the play which one likes best, and to give good suppers, are all the advantage to be derived from riches. As to plate, jewels, and expensive furniture, they are merely for ostentation,[47] and wholly unfit for persons in private life, and very ridiculous and indecent in people who by their birth and situation are excused from making any kind of figure or appearance. Always remember then, that pomp shuts its eyes to the sufferings of human nature, and witholds from it the assistance which it ought to give; and that no one can admire it who has not a depraved heart and the most childish vanity.

At present, Madame, Adelaide enjoys almost all the privileges of a young married woman. She has a waiting-woman to herself; Miss Sally, whom I sent for from England, a young person well educated, about four-and-twenty, and who does not know a word of French. Adelaide has an allowance with which a married woman might be satisfied, and I only charge myself with paying her's and Hermine's masters. I have insisted, that Adelaide should not suffer her woman to keep her accounts; therefore, every night, Miss Sally gives her a little memorandum of the expences of the day, which Adelaide pays immediately, and then sets down the account in a book which is appropriated to this use. This book is brought to me every fortnight, that I may see whether my injunctions be regularly observed, and whether the expences be reasonable. Besides this, Adelaide has another book, in which she makes all her trades-people write their receipts. She is every morning employed in looking over the expences of my houshold and settling the account. These little matters do not take her up more than a quarter of an hour in a day, and by this means she learns the price of all the different articles used in house-keeping; and, being accustomed from her infancy to these things, it is no kind of flavery, and it does not even appear strange; her accounts only are more extensive: but, having been led to them by degrees, she finds them no more troublesome.

Adelaide begins now to go into company; at sixteen it is time she should appear. She sups with us, and comes into the saloon about half an hour before supper; and retires to her chamber, when we get up from table; for it is necessary she should go to bed and rise early, while she has masters, which will be for two years to come. I intend also, this next fortnight, to take her with me to pay visits.

But the greatest pleasure she can enjoy, at her time of life, is the continuing the new plan of reading, which we began in Holland, and to go often to the French Comedy, to see the best Plays of our Dramatic Authors. The day before yesterday she saw *Phædra* performed, which she had never read. It is impossible to describe the impression which this Piece made on her; an impression she will feel so often and for so long a time. Imagine, Madame, what delight it must afford a young, sensible, and well instructed person, to see, in the course of Winter, the best representations of *Cinna*, of the *Horaces*, of *Rodogune*, of *Athaliah*, of *Andromache*, *Zara*, the *Misanthrope*, *Tartuffe*, *les Femmes Savantes*, &c. &c. &c. and to be able to say, in the Spring, this pleasure is far from being exhausted, next Winter I shall see other Plays equally good and well represented.[48]

To give you an account, Madame, of all our employments, we have begun a course of Philosophy. There are about fifteen of us who attend the Lectures, which are twice a week, and will last two months. We shall attend for the same time Lectures on Chymistry; and we shall finish, by going through a course of Natural History; which will carry us to the month of May. We shall repeat them all again next Winter, as that is the only means of making them useful, for it is impossible to reap the smallest advantage from them, attending each only once. Adelaide and Theodore are neither of them strangers to Natural History; and they have acquired some knowledge of minerals, and shells, as well as of plants. They read in their infancy, and almost know by heart, the *Spectacle de la Nature*,[49] and a *Histoire des Insectes*[50] in two volumes, well written, and very interesting; and in four months they will read that immortal work, which even without a taste for Natural History one must read over and over again.[51]

Do not imagine, Madame, that my intention is to make Adelaide *learned*; you know my sentiments in that respect, which are not at all changed. I only mean to give her a little knowledge of these things, which may serve to amuse her sometimes, and prevent her from being tired at any time, should her faher, her brother, or her husband, chuse to talk on such subjects; at the same time it will preserve her from an infinite number of prejudices which are adopted by ignorance.

LETTER XXXIX.

The Baron to the Viscount.

Since you do not return from Ghent till next month, my dear Viscount, I must send you some account of our children. For some time I had observed a visible alteration in Theodore; he was become absent and thoughtful: at one time he fixed his eyes on the Countess Anatolle (who sups here often) at another he passionately admired the charming figure of the beautiful Constantia. I found it was necessary for me to speak to him. One day, after having dined with Madame de Limours, where for the first time he had heard Constantia, sing, I said to him, I perceive with pleasure the impression your cousin has made upon you. At these words Theodore blushed; surprise and joy was painted in his countenance. Yes, my son, added I, Constantia is perfectly well educated; charming in every respect; and my warmest wishes will be completed in having her for my daughter-in-law. I own, said Theodore, I have often suspected you had such intentions: but your silence to me on that head made me reject these thoughts. – You was too young to be acquainted with a project in embrio, and which even now has no certainty. Yet the ties of blood and friendship which bind you to Mons. de Limours. – Surely the match would be a very proper one; but above all you must, I desire it most earnestly – Do not doubt that in the least – The heart of Constantia must also not make the least objection: and it must be the merit that your conduct will acquire, that will induce her parents to prefer you to the many that will seek their alliance: she is now but fourteen, will certainly not be married till she is seventeen: if till that time you do not act up to the hopes formed of you, or if you appear to have formed another attachment, Monsieur de Limours will never give you his daughter. O, my father! answered Theodore, I shall be always with you; I shall reveal to you my most secret thoughts and shall follow blindly your advice: can I then fear going astray for a moment? – No, doubtless, if you persist in this resolution. – If I persist, O! have no doubts of that! Have you not taught me two essential truths, that virtue alone insures a happy life, and that a guide to my youth is absolutely necessary. If the best founded gratitude, and the most tender affection, did not attach me inviolably to you, reason and self-interest would make me seek your advice and prefer your's to all other company. It is enough to be acquainted with your wisdom and knowledge of the world for me to consult and obey you. Figure to yourself the absolute power which you, my benefactor, a father, as affectionate as instructive, and a friend as indulgent as agreeable, have over me ... Theodore uttered these words with that animated tone, that feeling and sincere air, which so much inhances the value of professions of friendship. – Delightful child! how all my labours are rewarded!

He has promised to keep secret from Constantia his hopes of being her's, and from every one else, except Madame d' Almane. I am sure he will keep his word. Since this conversation, he takes a warmer interest in Constania, and is much less struck by the charms of the Countess Anatolle. She is no longer visited by Monsieur de St. Phar. Some say there never was a sincere attachment between them: others, that he has sacrificed the Countess to Madame de R***. However it is, she has lost her character, and is the less spared on account of her superior beauty: they take her cruelly to pieces; and she is much to be pitied, if she has nothing to reproach herself with, except being a coquet.

LETTER XL.

The Baroness to Madame de Valmont.

THEY are in the right, Madame, to say, that a mother is very proud the first time her daughter has an offer of marriage. I have just experienced that satisfaction. The Marquis de Hernay, a young man whom I saw in Italy, is very desirous of marrying Adelaide; he hinted the subject to me near three weeks ago. I gave an indirect answer, and spoke of it to my daughter the same day: at the first mention of marriage, before I had named the Marquis de Hernay, she changed countenance! What! Mamma, cried she, do you already think of marrying me? Not immediately, answered I, since you have a good fortune and are well situated. Nothing can determine me to marry you till your education is quite completed. But I can from this time, if you consent to it, enter into conditional engagements. In short, he that makes proposals ... is the Marquis de Hernay ... a very proper person, whose fortune and family ... Oh! Mamma, interrupted Adelaide, smilling, was his family still more noble, and his fortune more considerable, it is impossible *that* man should be destined to call you mother. But Adelaide, you are very censorious ... I think he does me great honour ... but I confess, that he does not appear to me worthy of being your son ... nor your husband. Do you agree to that? ... Confess, Mamma, that you are of my opinion! ... Let us speak seriously: why have you so great a dislike to him? ... because, Mamma, you think him a coxcomb ... I never told you so ... but I observed it, and your opinion will always determine mine ... Well, if it should be true that he is a coxcomb, if he is worthy ... My dear Mamma shall find me a good husband and one who is not a coxcomb ... Take care, Adelaide, that you form no idle chimeras, nor carry your delicacy too far ... I cannot do that; for I assure you I never in my life considered the turn of mind I should desire in a husband. I know I should not have knowledge or experience enough to chuse properly; and that I should be just as foolish as ungrateful, if I did not trust my happiness intirely to you ... Then you will readily accept the husband that I shall seriously propose to you. Yes, Mamma; be assured of it, whoever he is. I deserve this confidence; but how important is the choice! if you knew, my child, how difficult it is to judge of men ... their manners are so different from our's, and then they know so well how to dissemble when they think proper ... How well Richardson has described this! that horrible Lovelace! what a hypocrite! what a monster! – it is true that they are only taken up in deceiving us, in feigning affections they do not feel, to seduce us, that they may boast of it afterwards ... It makes one tremble. But how can a woman be so foolish as to sacrifice to a man her happiness and reputation? – That is the abyss into which a disordered imagination leads us. We persuade ourselves that our love is unconquerable; we make no efforts to oppose it; we yield to it; and we are not undeceived, till our character is intirely lost. Rational people, though possessed of great sensibility, will never be violently in love; therefore you see how careful Richardson has been (who certainly knew the human heart) not to represent Clarissa in love; even at the time when she is deceived in Lovelace, she has only a small degree of preference for him, and never any love: yet she has a tender heart; but she has virtuous principles, a superior understanding, and great prudence; and consequently it is impossible she should be susceptible of an affection which cannot fill the heart till it has turned the head; and from which reason will always preserve a person of reflection who has a command over herself. After this conversation it is unnecessary to tell you that I have not accepted the Marquis de Hernay's offer: he desired a positive answer, and since that time he has intirely left off visiting here.

You are anxious to know, Madame, what impression going into company has made upon Adelaide; as she has all her senses about her, she is very much struck with the absurdities she perceives. I carried her the other day to Madame de B— 's, where there was a great deal of company, and we staid some time. She made many observations, which she communicated to me, when we were alone. Can any thing be, she asked me, more amiable than Madame de B—? no, certainly, replied I, and you will find very few persons to be compared to her. She possesses that true politeness that always pleases and never fatigues. She has the art so infinitely rare of speaking well, of expressing herself with elegance and purity, without its being possible to accuse her for one moment of pedantry. You may say of her conversation the same that they say of Madame de Sevigne's writing, that it is never far fetched, nor ever vulgar. She has so sweet a disposition, that we are more charmed than surprised at her most lively sallies, and reflection convinces us of her superiority. – With what warmth, Mamma, you make her elogium, and yet she is not one of your friends! ... Was she my enemy I should say, the same things of her; it is so pleasing to speak of her as she deserves ... Mamma, what is the name of that young Lady who was seated by Madame de B—, who had her handkerchief so trimmed and so many flowers shaking on her head? ... Madame de – How do you like her? – She is not at all pretty, and she has a disagreeable manner of turning her head to the right and left every moment ... and of making faces! ... what a group of them she drew round her! ... As soon as she went into another room, all the men who were there also came and surrounded her also. – I lay a wager it was on account of the faces she made; for it was very droll to see her near ... Yes; this is what is called coquetry; which men despise so much and which yet attracts their notice. – Mamma, did you remark when Madame de B— said so much in praise of Madame C—, with what coldness Madame de *** answered her! ... Yes, she was not able to dissemble her chagrin; for envy is a vice which no art can conceal ... You see the proof of it: since you, who are so young and so little experienced, have discovered in a moment, that Madame de *** was envious. – And how can one be so! how at least can one be insensible to the noble pleasure of doing justice to others.

You see, Madame, how ridiculous Adelaide finds coquetry and envy as disagreeable. If she had seen company at my house from the age of eight years, she would have been accustomed to all these things: she would not have remarked them, or at least she would not have been shocked by them; and in that case how should I have acted, in order to have preserved her from the same faults; instead of which, I have no occasion to tell her how hateful the vice is, her eyes are open, she sees and detects it.

Yes, Madame, the Chevalier de Valmont conducts himself always as well as your affection can wish: his connexions are not very much extended, because he has chosen his friends with propriety. He is particularly attached this Winter to the Marquis de *** that young man so distinguished by his virtues, by his genius, and brilliant qualities, and whose conduct has given every father of a family the satisfaction of being able to offer to his sons a model worthy to be imitated. The Chevalier de Valmont shews the most sincere attachment to Theodore; they have both the same principles and the same sentiment, and they are made to love each other throughout their lives.

LETTER XLI.

The Baroness to Madame d' Ostalis.

WELL, my dear child, does the affair succeed? Will Mons. d' Ostalis obtain his wishes, and be appointed to the Embassy? Send me a messenger to tell me the *Yes* ... and even the *No*; that *No* which will make you remain at home! ... In preference to every thing, I wish for the advancement of you husband and all that will contribute to his honour and the increase of his fortune ... But I am in the most difficult situation; for that which my heart wishes for my reason condemns! ... For me to wish to see you setting out for La ***! No, do not imagine it! ... Ah, my daughter! ... How often have I reproached myself during the two years I staid in Italy, at such a distance from you, and which I might have spent with you! ... But let us say no more of it; let us wait the event with resignation, and prepare ourselves to support it with courage.

I supped last night at Madame de Valcy's for the first time this Winter. The Viscountess made such a point of it that I could not deny her. There were near forty people of the best fashion. We have seen the time when Madame de Valcy was not well received in company, but, now that she has a hundred thousand livres a year, all the world flock to her with eagerness.[52] She is very much elated at it; she is ignorant that she has no better qualities, than her riches, to attract their notice, – People, who keep such excellent houses, are like Kings who never know what is said of them. A good supper as often makes people guilty of meanness and falsehood as ambition. Duclos has said very justly, 'Men never judge, but by appearances. Are they made dupes of? It is because those who deceive them are basely, as well as dexterously, perfidious.'[53] It is also true, that, unless one is blinded by an immoderate share of vanity, a very little experience may inform one, that, whenever one pleases, one may draw company to one's house, even without giving them suppers; it is not necessary for one even to be amiable; one has only to keep one's chamber and open one's doors. This is a useful lesson for young people in order to keep them from the absurd folly of setting a high value on their extensive connexions. This eagerness for drawing all Paris to one's house occasions a loss of time, which is not repaid by any real pleasure. In the midst of such a vortex, it is impossible to cultivate the mind or improve it, and to preserve an inclination for study or business. – My intention is certainly not to let my daughter live in solitude; and I shall have no objection to her being in places sometimes, where she may meet with fifty or sixty people, provided she does not receive so many at her own house, where I would have her entertain only her friends and those that are really amiable; and, in that case, she will never have forty persons to supper. Mons. and Madame de Valcy are minding themselves; their pride pays very dear for the boast of keeping one of the best houses in Paris. Adieu, my dear child; I do not press you to write to me; you can judge by my affection for you of the impatience with which I wait to hear from you.

LETTER XLII.

The Baroness to Madame de Valmont.

M ONS. d' Ostalis is named Ambassador to ***. He sets out in two months, and his wife attends him. Far from exacting such a sacrifice, he pressed Madame d' Ostalis to remain in France; but, doubtless, he was certain she would listen only to her duty! ... Yes, such is the duty of a wife! She must without hesitation quit her friends, her family, her mother, to follow her husband. Adelaide may one day be called upon perhaps to perform these same duties! ... This cruel thought deprives me of my only consolation ... Madame d' Ostalis rends my heart, when she says Adelaide remains to you. Alas! who can assure me she will always remain? What a melancholy Summer will this be to me! Mons. d' Almane and Theodore set out in six weeks; and I, a fortnight after, shall fix myself at S***, on that little estate we have six leagues from Paris; where I shall stay till the beginning of November. Adieu, Madame; – pity me ... You know better than any body how much I ought to suffer at this time.

LETTER XLIII.

The Baroness to Madame de Valmont.

Y ES, Madame, without doubt the interest of those who are dear to us is able to make us support with courage the most cruel disappointments. Have I not myself taken all the steps that could possibly be useful to Mons. d' Ostalis? If I could be sure that Adelaide would be happier two thousand leagues from me, do you think I should hesitate a moment to separate myself from her? I should not even then sacrifice all my felicity to her; in securing her's, I could not think myself unhappy.

I shall only receive my particular friends here; I have brought with me a Miniature Painter, the only Master Adelaide wants at present; for I can supply the place of all the others. Mons. Leblanc, Mons. d' Almane's Steward, will stay six months with us, and will give my daughter some general knowledge of those affairs in which a woman may find herself engaged. So it is recommended by the wisest and best of Instructors, 'It is right,' says Mons. de Fenelon, 'that young people should know something of the principal rules of the laws; for example, the difference there is between a *Will* and a *Deed of Gift*; what is the meaning of a *Contract*, an *Entail, a Division*, and *Coheirs*; the principal laws of the country where we live, and the customs which render these acts valid; what is meant by *Property*, by *Community*, by *real* and *personal Estates*. If they are married, their principal business will turn upon these things ... Girls of family and large fortunes ought to be instructed in the duties of their situation ... With regard to these estates, it is right to teach them what they may do, in order to avoid being cheated, and all those artifices so common in the country. Add to this the means by which they may establish little schools and hospitals for the sick and poor. In explaining the duties of landlords, do not forget their rights; tell them what are *Fiefs, Vassals, Homage, Rent, Impropriations*, the *right of Field Rent, Fines of Alienation, Indemnities, Mortmain, Acknowledgement, Court-rolls*, and such things, to be acquainted with which is necessary, since the management of estates intirely depends on all these matters.'[54] We have every morning a conversation of three quarter of an hour with Mons. Leblanc on this subject. In the afternoon, Adelaide writes down all she is able to retain in her memory. Mons. Leblanc corrects it the next day, and adds in the margin the words she has omitted. Adelaide will preserve these papers, in order to remember what they retain. It will be sufficient, if she only reads them once a quarter. I do not allow her to write at the time, because she would not listen with so much attention, if she was not obliged to take an account of the conversation four or five hours after; and I have not allowed her Master to write these papers, because the clearest explanation, and what we never forget, is that which we make ourselves.

Adelaide finds the country, where we now are, not half so agreeable as our situation in Languedoc. She is also surprised and much hurt by perceiving the wretched poverty of the peasants, who surround this little estate. What, said she to me! so many unfortunate people so near Paris; so near this multitude of rich persons! ... Can you be astonished at it, replied I, when this poverty exists even at   Paris itself? It is not in the regions of pomp and ostentation that you will find benevolence. Luxury supports the manufactures, gives bread to a number of workmen, that is, when it is moderate; but carried to excess it equally ruins the workmen, and those who employ them: the last never pay, and the first die of hunger, and every tradesman is made a bankrupt. In short, how is it, when you have fifty thousand livres a year, and spend eighty, that you can do any good actions? ... Mamma, I shall never contract any debts, and shall always have some money left of my allowance. I wish you would have the goodness to direct me how to employ a sum which I design for the poor ... And what is this sum? ... Five hundred livres a year certain,[55] and my brother will give the same: but we wish to devote this money to a certain object which is not to be changed.

I promise you I will think about it, answered I and even to second you in this project. Mamma, said Adelaide, could not we form a little association with some of our acquaintance? ... It is possible we may; but we must never make proposals of this kind, except to particular friends ... You do not then approve of those collections that are frequently made in company? ... Not at all; let us give as much as we can; it is all that religion and humanity require of us. We are not ordered to beg alms to give away. For my part, I had much rather dispose of some of my goods to support an unfortunate person who asks my charity, than to beg money of thirty people whom I do not know, and who give it with reluctance and an ill grace: for my part I never submit to this contribution but through politeness. – How can I be certain that the object of the charity is really worthy my compassion? I know nothing of the matter; I have my own poor whom I love; the money they ask me for belongs to them; the begging Lady would take it from them, and also take from me the merit and delightful pleasure of giving it. She alone will enjoy the little portion of gratitude that is due to me. If it was not unpolite, I should have a perfect right to say to her, deny yourself one or two superfluities, and you will complete the sum you now ask for, in a manner much more noble and more meritorious. It is very likely this discourse may make little impression; for I imagine it is much easier in general to be troublesome and indiscreet than charitable and benevolent ... Yet, Mamma, I have often heard you praise Madame — , for her benevolence, and she is a begging Lady ... If the benevolence of all the begging Ladies was as sincere and as universally known as hers, I should no longer condemn the custom; it would appear respectable, though, even then, I should still be determined not to adopt it. I repeat, let us return to our first principles, and we shall never deviate from them. Above all, it is necessary to be strictly just ... And it cannot be called justice to obtain money from those who give it with regret; and this reason alone would give me an aversion for collecting money in company.

The same day that we had this conversation, I told Madame de Limours and Madame de S*** who were here the scheme of Adelaide; and it is agreed that we should form an association with some more persons, in order to found a little establishment about two leagues from Paris; and that each member should preside over it in turn. We have not yet made our calculation; we have only determined at present on having a school for six very poor girls,[56] whom we shall chuse, with agreeable persons and healthy constitutions, and about ten years old. These six children we shall have taught to read, write, and cast accounts, and to work at their needle. We shall take a small house for them, and put at the head of it a good workwoman, and a man who will be the steward, and at the same time the schoolmaster. We shall also give them a cook and a maid-servant. We imagine this establishment will cost us possibly six thousand livres a year.[57] Our intentions are to keep the girls only seven years, the two last of which they are to work for their own profit; and they will be employed by the Ladies who establish the school and by their friends; so that, when they leave it at seventeen years old, they will have a small sum of money, understand reading, working, writing, and accounts: the Governesses of the society will have the liberty of letting the girls they present be taught other things, such as embroidery, making caps, and working tapestry, &c. These girls, having received an excellent education for their stations, will be easily settled in places either at Paris, or in the country; and the sooner, as they will have the protection of all the Governesses. On the day they quit the school, six other girls of the same age will take their places; and so on, as long as any of the Governesses live; who enter into new engagements every seven years. Adelaide is employed in forming the regulations of the school and the Christian and moral instructions for the girls: the Governesses are to be the judges of this work, and to correct it as they see occasion. You, Madame, who take so much pleasure in doing good, will easily imagine how much this scheme employs us; we talk of nothing else, and Adelaide has already drawn up a part of the instructions destined for the girls.

I punctually receive news of the Chevalier de Valmont from my son, who is very happy to find himself this year in the same garrison; and the praises of the Chevalier always take up a whole page of every letter I receive from Theodore.

LETTER XLIV.

The Baroness to Madame de Valmont.

From St.***

I HAVE made acquaintance, Madame, with a person you often met with at Narbonne in the Winter you spent there: it is Mons. the Count de Retel. He gave me the pleasure of talking of you, which was sufficient to make him agreeable. He has, besides great knowledge and understanding, a little roughness and singularity, but an excellent character and an air of freedom which pleases me much. He has a charming house about three quarters of a league from mine: he gives us the liberty of walking in his garden; which has been the means of bringing us acquainted. He has no great opinion of the knowledge or talents of women. He smiled when he saw the plan of my garden raised by Adelaide, as well as at the landscapes, flowers, and miniatures of her drawing. I suspect he may more than once have been deceived in this way, and that experience has made him incredulous. Rousseau says, 'At Paris the rich understand every thing; the poor only are ignorant. This capital is full of artists of rank, particularly females, who finish their works, as Monsieur Guiallaum invented his colours. I only know three fair exceptions to this rule among the men, though there may be more, but I know not one among the Ladies, and I doubt whether there is any.'[58]

For my part, I know two exceptions already, which are Madame d' Ostalis and Adelaide, and therefore I believe there may be more; though I have not seen any other female artists draw landscapes from Nature, or make good and correct likenesses in their portraits.[59] But at length Monsieur de Retel has seen Adelaide drawing in a garden: he has seen her paint from Nature; he has examined into her improvements, and is now convinced there is no treachery. This discovery has made him go from one extreme to another; for he is become one of Adelaide's greatest admirers. The other day we were playing by chance, at a game where every one is to make a verse in their turn. The prettiest hand-writing in the world discovered all those which were written by Adelaide. Monsieur de Retel, after praising the writing, examined the poetry with great attention. How, said he, there are not only no faults in the spelling, but not one line bad of the verification! ... So then, Mademoiselle, said he, with a tone rather ironical, you have learned to make verses, and doubtless we may flatter ourselves one day or other with seeing some of your productions. It is true, replied Adelaide, that Mamma, to make me better able to judge of the measure of verse, put me upon making some myself; but at the same time she taught me, that unless one possessed this talent in a very superior degree, it would render a woman ridiculous ... Well, Mademoiselle, interrupted Monsieur de Retel, why should you not hope to be able, some time, to equal any of the ladies who have distinguished themselves in this way? ... Because my vanity does not hinder me, said Adelaide, from perceiving that the verses I make are good for nothing. The paper I have in my hand, said Monsieur de Retel, proves that your modesty deceives you. This is only your gallantry, said I, in my turn; but Adelaide knows very well, that with much labour she could only produce very moderate verses. Besides, it is much better to write well in prose. The name of Madame Sevigny will be immortal: and Mademoiselle Barbier[60] is known to very few people, though she died only in 1742, and though she wrote several operas and tragedies, which were very well received at the time: But why is this? Because Mademoiselle Barbier's tragedies are very indifferent, and Madame de Sevigny's letters have every degree of perfection of which this kind of writing is susceptible. Thus it is, that there is more merit in writing a song that is perfect than a whole Epic poem, if it is ill done. Four verses only have raised the reputation of Monsieur St. Aulaire[61] for ever; and Chapelain[62] would have been long since forgotten, if some Authors had not taken the trouble to criticise him. Therefore, since Adelaide writes a very good letter, and makes bad verses, I advise her always to keep to prose: But suppose, said Madame de Limours, some time hence, born with so much wit as she has, and educated with so much care, she should distinguish herself, and become an Authoress, would you dissuade her from it? ... No; I would not; for, though I am not certain she would make an excellent work, yet I am very sure it would not be a bad one, when her understanding is perfectly formed ... But you say, that good works alone pass to posterity? ... Yes, works of mere entertainment and pleasure; but a work of mere morality, provided it is well written, may be excused for its want of genius and superior talents. An Author, who wishes only to shine, has no right to this indulgence; if he does not please, he is to blame and is good for nothing: but I can pardon great faults and an indifferent style in one who means to instruct and inlighten me. I could not without ingratitude judge him with severity: his book would merit esteem, were it void of all entertainment, and even tiresome; as long as it is useful, it will always be read. It is thus, that many works on science written without genius, and several books on morality which are but moderate performances, have descended to posterity, merely because they are useful. For these reasons I would always endeavour to prevent young people from the madness of turning Poets: there can be nothing really useful in that kind of writing which consequently requires a superiority of genius;[63] therefore, it is much wiser to prefer prose, in which one is sure of distinguishing one's self, it does but convey instruction and good sense; and may, with the addition of genius, be reckoned in the number of the best Writers, and equally valued for every great talent and the use made of them.

This conversation has put an end to Monsieur de Retel's fears, lest Adelaide should turn Poetess. Madame de Limours is persuaded it will conclude by his falling in love with Adelaide. This establishment would be far above any thing I could expect for my daughter, and yet it would give me no pleasure; Monsieur de Retel has a hundred thousand livres a year,[64] and is of a very good family; but he is seven and thirty years old, and has a person which cannot be agreeable to a young woman. If his being so very plain did not absolutely create an aversion to him, it would at least make it probable that his wife could never love him; and, though I am far from desiring that Adelaide should be violently in love with her husband, yet I should wish her to like him, and consequently would have nothing to be disagreeable in him. I am very sensible that in general this consideration has no weight, and that a man of family and fortune is seldom refused on account of his person, however disgusting it may be. But I confess I am of a different opinion; and, even if the happiness of my daughter were less dear to me, Religion would prevent me from sacrificing her to ambition, and from giving her a husband who might inspire her with aversion: and, even if it were her own choice, I should oppose it, unless she was five and twenty years old, as I should think it was owing to her simplicity, rather than her understanding.

LETTER XLV.

The Baron to the Viscount.

From Strasburg.

WE must, absolutely, my dear Baron, alter something in our plan; or, better to express myself, remedy the troubles Madame de Limours's rashness has caused. Theodore talks of Constantia with pleasure, but is too certain of having the happiness of belonging to you, to be warmly interested in that thought. He depends upon it; which is enough to take away his anxiety. All my endeavours to diminish his hopes will be in vain: the last farewells of Madame de Limours are too strongly in his thoughts ... Nevertheless the Countess Anotolle is arrived (for you know her husband's grandmother lives at Strasburg) she is every day the object of a new entertainment. She takes particular notice of Theodore, and they will meet this Winter at Paris. All this gives me uneasiness. The result of much reflection upon this subject is, that I think *you and I must fall out*; not publicly, for appearances must be kept up. Desormeaux's business will be a good pretence. Our interest clashed there, and I succeeded: do you take it in ill humour, and write me a formal letter: I will shew it to Theodore. On your side complain of me to the Viscountess: on our return to Paris, we shall find her uneasy and alarmed. This is all I ask of you; I will manage every thing else myself. Adieu, my dear friend! In expectation of this quarrel be assured that nothing can diminish my affection for you.

LETTER XLVI.

Baroness to Madame d' Ostalis.

St. ***

SINCE you have been at ***, my dear child, I have received two letters from the Count de Roseville; for it is true that I wished to hear news of you from more hands than one; he has very particularly answered all my questions about you and your children. He not only tells me that you are beautiful as the day, but that you have no appearance of sadness nor dejection, and that you was not in the least fatigued with your long voyage. In short, his account intirely agrees with your's, and this confirmation was very necessary to me. I do not doubt your sense; I rely upon your promises; but you know the most trifling and idle tears ought to be excused, when they proceed from real affection.

At length, my dear, the Count de Retel has justified Madame de Limours's prediction. This is the copy of a letter I received from him last night:

'You know, Madame, that to be able to talk on important affairs, it is necessary to have all our senses about us, to have a cool head and a heart free. I am now in that situation, but I have not a moment to lose, if I would profit by it. For near six months, since I had the pleasure of knowing you, I am become less incredulous. I did not believe the education of a young person could contribute to her establishment. It is true I have scarcely till now seen any instance of education which deserved to be looked upon as of importance; but at present I can conceive it very possible for our heads to be quite turned by a person who unites to the most striking talents a cultivated mind, an elegant figure, and an amiable temper. Such a person can equally seduce the most trifling, as well as the wiser men. She has but to shew herself, and she will attract all hearts; she will fix them by making herself known. Why, when we wish to marry, do we only ask for fortune? It is, because it would generally be in vain to demand a good education. We never ask for things which appear imaginary to us, and we often seek only for a rich wife, despairing to find one at the same time handsome, amiable, sensible, and ingenious. In short, Madame, I am thirty-seven, and Mademoiselle d' Almane (I may as well speak plain) is but seventeen. She is lovely in all respects, and I have nothing to offer in my own favour but the desire I should have of making her happy, and my attachment to you, Madame! ... I am not ignorant that you think her education will not be completed till she is eighteen and a half; and I too much admire your Work not to wish it brought to perfection. If you have other views, I have no right to demand your secret; but I have a right to expect from such a character as your's a frankness that will preserve me from the misfortune of entertaining vain hopes. I again repeat it to you, Madam, I am not yet in love; but, if your answer is not favourable to me, hasten to send it, and deprive me of all hopes.'

After having read this letter, I called Adelaide, and shewed it to her. What do you think, said I, of this new proposal? I could marry Mons. de Retel without reluctance, replied Adelaide. ... Without reluctance! that is not sufficient. – I do not think I can ever marry with pleasure, I am so happy in my present condition! ... Mons. de Retel is a man of honour, he has good sense; by asking for your hand, he proves that he loves you, since he has a hundred thousand livres a year, is of a good family, and has a title. Ambition and vanity will never determine your daughter's choice ... yet I should perhaps be more sensible of the value of a considerable fortune than most people of my age. You have taught me how much riches can add to our happiness, when we know how to make a proper use of them; but I confess I should feel a kind of repugnance in uniting myself to a man for whom I should be but a bad match; and more so, if like Mons. de Retel, he was intirely destitute of all external graces: for I should fear he would suspect that I had not so much consulted reason and esteem as interest and ambition. I understand you, said I smiling; you would be better pleased with Mons. de Retel, if his person was agreeable, and if he was some years younger. We may easily comprehend this delicacy. – Joking apart, replied Adelaide, if Mons. de Retel, such as he is, had only a fortune equal to mine, and that you assured me he really possessed all the good qualities he appears to have, I could determine to marry him without any trouble; and I am very sure I should be happy with him. My motive for chusing him could not then be suspected; – by preferring him to a young man, I should shew sense above my years, and I should deserve his affection and the esteem of the Public. – I approve this manner of thinking, my dear Adelaide; it is quite conformable to my own, and I will thank Mons. de Retel. – I am very glad of it, I confess, Mamma; yet I must again repeat to you that it is not his age which makes me dislike him. I know very well that a man is not old at seven and thirty; it even appears to me that I should be flattered by having a husband of experience and consideration. I have yet seen but little of the world; but I have already observed how unhappy young men make their wives; the Count Anatolle, for example, and many others ... I protest to you, Mamma, I should like better to marry an amiable man of thirty-seven than a young man of three and twenty. Scarce had Adelaide pronounced the words *three* and *twenty*, than she blushed most violently, as if she had named the Chevalier de Valmont. It was in effect the same thing; for he was in her thoughts. I was delighted that she gave me an opportunity of speaking about him to her. I was careful however not to increase her confusion by appearing to fix any particular meaning on the words that had just escaped her. Indeed, said I, laughing, there is a vast deal to blush at: because you think of the only young unmarried man you are acquainted with, could your fear from me an improper interpretation. – Ah! Mamma, replied Adelaide, embracing me with some remains of emotion, I never shall fear your reading to the bottom of my heart. – I am very certain of it; and be sure that all your sentiments are perfectly known to me ... Well, Mamma, I hope I have none that you can disapprove. Adelaide's appearance of uneasiness at saying these words, and the simplicity of the question itself made me smile. What then, replied I, are you not sure of it? ... but I believe you better than myself ... be composed then, for you are perfectly right ... I really thought so ... The Chevalier de Valmont is the son of a Lady you have loved from your infancy; he is your brother's friend; he has many agreeable qualities; he promises to be amiable; he ought to inspire you with more affection than any *other young man* of his age. But you have often heard that his aunt Mademoiselle d' Olcy has for a long time had views for his establishment; and, besides, you know very well that you may pretend to a much more advantageous match. You know still better that you are not at liberty to dispose of your heart; and that we are to direct its inclinations ... Be also very sure, Mamma, that I never thought for two minutes together of the person you mention. It is true I am more interested about him than about any other young man; but, though I have often seen him, he is too young for me ever to have been able to converse with him. I can neither judge of his sense nor his disposition. I know Mons. de Retel much better than I know him; so that, unless my head had been absolutely turned by foolish Romances, where we see so many examples of pretended unconquerable passions which spring up suddenly at first sight, how could I persuade myself that what I feel for him is a real sentiment of preference? My brother loves him tenderly; but he knows how improper it would be to converse with me about a young man of the Chevalier's age, and he never in his life mentioned his name to me. I never hear him spoken of; and I am absolutely ignorant what his disposition really is. I have only a good opinion of him, as my father permits his connexion with my brother; but I cannot know whether he has any particular attachment, or any essential faults in his disposition. In a word, I find his person agreeable; he appears to me honest, polite, reserved; is sufficient to inspire favour, and not to generate friendship. This is the way we always think, replied I, when our imaginations are not heated; in short, when we possess the sense, reason, and purity of heart of Clarissa, Miss Byron,[65] and Adelaide. I see with pleasure, that you have too much good sense to exaggerate to your own affections yourself, an illusion which has ruined so many young people. Nevertheless it is sufficient that you have discovered that preference at the bottom of your heart of which you have been speaking, that you may carefully avoid the object of it, and drive from your imagination all that can recall him to your remembrance. It is a duty which modesty and prudence equally impose upon you. It is right already to accustom yourself to discharge scrupulously this duty now indispensable, and which will become sacred when you are married. For example, your husband will certainly be a Gentleman, because I shall chuse him for you; but I shall be too intent upon essential qualities to be able to promise you that he shall have many graces; so that it is very possible that you may meet with many people more amiable. The smallest degree of preference will not then be allowed you; as soon as ever you feel it, it is necessary to oppose it and destroy it; an effort which will never be painful to you. It is very unusual that a person perfectly discreet should not be secure from these little surprizes, however slight and transient they may be. Duty, acquaintance, esteem, and gratitude form real attachments; so that the husband I shall give you will certainly become too dear to you, for you ever to value in others those graces which he may not be possessed of. You well know that the Chevalier de Valmont is not, strictly speaking, a suitable match for you; yet he is free, and you are not married; so that the kind of preference which he inspires you with does not amaze me; but if I should to-morrow tell you my choice was made, if I was to present to you the man who is to be your husband, I am certain that from that moment the Chevalier de Valmont would be banished from your memory. Oh!

yes, Mamma, cried Adelaide, do not doubt it. Very freely, I should no longer think of him, indeed I scarcely think about him now; and I am sensible how just and reasonable every thing is that you have said; and I promise you to intirely banish from my breast this little inclination: if it was still stronger, I could do it without trouble, I have so many employments that please me! Objects that are so dear to me! ... My little Hermine alone would be sufficient to divert me from an affection a thousand times more serious. – Ah I do not question it. – We are going back to Paris, and he is returning from Strasburg: how ought I to behave? ... I shall more rarely ask him to supper, and never but when we have much company. On those days I shall be careful to invite Mademoiselle de Limours; she never sits down to table; you will remain in the saloon with her, and, when we return, you will retire to bed. As for the rest, think no more of it, and never speak to me again about it; for all conversations hereafter are needless, since this has not left in me the smallest inquietude. At these words I embraced Adelaide, and changed the subject. You may judge by this account, if I ought not to be satisfied with the sense and discretion of Adelaide. She is nevertheless in the most dangerous situation in which a young person can possibly find herself. She has from her infancy been acquainted with an amiable young man, her brother's friend, and the son of a woman with whom I am intimately connected. She knows besides, that if by marrying the Chevalier de Valmont she should not form a splendid alliance, at least it could not be found fault with. In short, she has great sensibility, and yet she has no violent passion; this is in fact, because she has true feelings; because her heart is filled with the softest sentiments. The want of love does not disturb her, since she is satisfied. She does not spend her evenings in reading *Zaide*, the *Princess of Cleves*, the *Siege of Calais*,[66] *Cleveland*, &c. She read these Romances with me when she was thirteen. She may read them again now without danger; the first impression is made. She will see in similar works only the delirium of an inflamed imagination. She reads *Clarissa*, *Pamela*, and *Grandison*; she sees there how little power love has over the heart of a sensible woman. She will say to herself, these three Works are universally looked upon as the best of their kind; they have lost none of their reputation; they present a faithful picture of the human heart; for what merit can there be without truth? If Richardson's Heroines are not imaginary beings; if the angelic and sublime Clarissa, the virtuous Pamela, are not unnatural characters; if they are equally interesting and affecting; these novels are master-pieces, and we must despise all the others; we must necessarily believe, that it is to the errors of imagination, and not to sensibility of heart, that love owes its greatest power; and that a prudent, modest, and virtuous woman will be always secured from the violence of this passion, even when she might lawfully yield to it.

Good night, my dear child; the courier does not go till Monday; to-morrow Adelaide will bring me her dispatches for you, and I shall then add something in her letter.

LETTER XLVII.

Madame d' Ostalis to the Baroness.

I CAN now, my dear aunt, give you the accounts you desire of this country. Every thing you have been told concerning the young Prince, pupil of the Count de Roseville, is infinitely short of the praise he merits. It is impossible to be more polite, more amiable, or to behave with more dignity. He brings to my mind the definition of La Bruyere, who says, 'False grandeur is fierce and inaccessible; as it knows its weakness, it endeavours to hide itself, and will only appear when it means to deceive, and is not likely to be discovered to be what it really is, that is to say, really littleness. But true greatness is free, mild, familiar, and popular ... It loses nothing by being looked at; the more you know it, the more you admire it ... and one approaches it at the same time with freedom and with humility, &c. &c.'[67] The Prince has as much knowledge as politeness. He is equally unaffected, good-humoured and sensible. He has, without any attempts to shew it, all that variety of wit and delicacy which is improved by a good education. He does not speak to an old man with the same tone and air with which he talks to a young one: and, if he addresses himself to a Lady, it is with that gentle and softened voice which gives to the most common expressions the appearance of deference and respect. He speaks in a plain but correct manner; and every thing he says appears obliging, because he listens to the answers made him, and never interrupts you by his inattention. He has a very pleasing smile, which he does not lavish on every one alike; but has always an open and serene countenance, which expresses better than I ever saw goodness and benevolence. He protects and encourages arts, sciences, and letters; and he does it with great discernment. He has just founded two prizes of gold medals to be given annually by the Academy of ***; one for men of wit and learning who compose the best work in the course of the year: and the other for painters and sculptors. The first is under express conditions, that no one shall be intitled to it who does not bear a good character; or who has ever written any thing contrary to religion, government, or morality. From the choice made by the Academy there lies an appeal by the Prince; which makes it doubly honourable to obtain the medal, since it is at the same time the reward of virtue as well as of ingenuity, and is a certain proof of the protection and esteem of the Prince. The Academy of Painting give on the same conditions a gold medal alternately to the best sculptor or most distinguished painter, provided, as you may suppose, they do not disgrace their talents by one single indecent production. The Prince since his marriage has formed many charitable establishments; and, besides giving money to them, he has formed their administration in the best manner possible, and has himself selected the persons to conduct them. In short, he is beloved by all who see him: he is adored by his own people; he is the delight of a tender father, and the pride and happiness of his Governor who has been able to form such a Prince.

I saw last week, for the first time, the unfortunate Chevalier de Murville. I went to his house; for the bad state of his health will no longer permit him to come to ***. He learned from the Count de Roseville, that I knew Cecilia; he spoke of her to me. Time and reflexion, said he, have in some measure restored my tranquillity; but I must own the unexpected meeting with Monsieur d' Aimeri, the sight of Charles, ... the news of the death of Cecilia, and the particulars which attended it: all these events have been a mortal stroke to me! My life, if not intirely insupportable, is become a burthen to me, and I see the approaching end of it with joy. His eyes, while he spoke, were filled with tears. I pity him! he is sensible; he is patient; but I am far from admiring his sentiments. If he had not taken pleasure in nourishing his grief, he would not at this time have been sinking under it. With his understanding, and a less Romantic turn, his strength of mind would have been able to triumph over a passion to which he is now a victim. He regards his weakness as a virtue, and his grief as a duty, being ignorant that the first duty of man is to preserve his reason, which was given him to heal the deepest wounds of his heart, and to inable him to support with fortitude all the changes of fortune.

Adieu, my dear aunt, I may well recommend fortitude, when you are at Paris, and I am at ***, and when no body perceives the smallest alteration in my temper and disposition.

LETTER XLVIII.

The Baroness to Madame d' Ostalis.

From Paris.

W E were no sooner arrived this morning than Adelaide ran hastily into her chamber, and in about a quarter of an hour returned, bringing a large box which I recollected in a moment. Here, Mamma, said she, blushing, I am going to part with every thing that can call to my mind the *smallest remembrance* ... Therefore I bring you this little collection of pebbles and the pretty box of Acacia – That is filled with play-things belonging to Hermine. As I took the box from her, I thought I heard her utter a gentle sigh ... I shall lock up this collection carefully, as I received it only as a deposit, which I have no doubt one day or other I shall return to her again.

Madame de *** died yesterday; she could not support the loss of her daughter! If there is any misfortune, for which we are not to be consoled; if there is any grief which our reason will not help us to conquer; it is doubtless that which Madame de *** has sunk under. She has fallen a victim to the most innocent and most natural of all affections, and this Lady, whose grief has carried her to her grave, whose fortune was half given away in charity, and who was in every respect so estimable, appeared reserved to many people. She neither boasted of her tenderness for her daughter, nor the pleasures of benevolence: she never amused herself with talking of it, but she really performed it. She neither prided herself on being a good mother, nor for being charitable; but she was both the one and the other, and she did not suppose she merited praise for doing what she thought her duty. When her daughter died, there were no accounts of affecting scenes and tragedy-speeches; her grief was not painted with eloquence! ... At the time Madame de Blinville became a widow, we heard of nothing but the excess of her affliction; people repeated proofs of it, in the most interesting and pathetic terms. She would renounce all *amusements and company*, and would *consecrate the rest of her days to friendship and solitude* ... But see the difference; in the space of eight months Madame de *** no longer exists, and Madame de Blinville is just returned to the world more admired, more brilliant, and more artful than ever. It was not necessary to console herself so quickly, when she had made a resolution to afflict herself for ever. When, labouring under similar misfortunes, we are supported by reason, we submit, though we are not consoled; we bear our loss with fortitude, but we feel it. Time weakens the remembrance of it, but does not cure us intirely; insensibility alone makes us forget it. Real affliction is never totally effaced from the mind, even when you have conquered it. We never thoroughly recover our former state of mind. When we have lost the person the dearest to us in the world, if at the end of one, or even of ten years, we have the same disposition, the same appearance, and the same behaviour, which we had before our loss, we never truly loved.

Madame de Limours is in despair; she really believes Mons. de Limours and Mons. d' Almane have quarrelled on the affair of Desormeaux. The Marquis de Hernay, who wanted to marry, was very desirous of paying his addresses to Constantia, whom he often saw at Mons. de Limours's, where he was received with the greatest politeness. The Viscountess, as usual, saw every thing in the worst light, and was certain every thing was settled, which she dreaded. It was painful to me to see her grief, and not relieve her mind; but, if I had told her the truth, Constantia would have known it a quarter of an hour after: the whole house would have been told it in the course of the day, and Mons. d' Almane would never have forgiven me. The poor Viscountess afflicts herself with imaginary distresses, and her intimate friend dares not undeceive her; see to what evil indiscretion leads us! When she talks to me of her fears, I always tell her she alarms herself without reason, and that, for my part, I am perfectly easy about it. But she will not hear me, and nothing can convince her. On the other hand, little Constantia makes herself miserable. Having an idea from her infancy, that she was one day to be the wife of Theodore, she has conceived a passion for him, which at present makes her unhappy, and which is indeed too ardent ever to make her otherwise! And, if in reality the Viscount and Mons. d' Almane should quarrel, if he should chuse another husband for Constantia, what would become of her? ... She is only fifteen, and her heart is no longer her own. She is melancholy and indolent, and nothing seems to amuse or please her; even friendship seems to affect her very slightly. She loves Adelaide, not on her own account, but because she is Theodore's sister. In short, her imagination is fixed on one object, and her heart is affected by a passion which absorbs all her faculties. This is not, I confess, the daughter I should have wished; however, she has some excellent qualities. She is extremely sweet-tempered, and so diffident that she does not think herself handsome, she has some useful and agreeable talents, and does not want knowledge. But she is too bashful, and too indolent, to appear to the best advantage; and has not resolution enough to attach herself to her tender friends; but she will be liked in general, and will not create enemies. Adieu, my dear child; I have answered all your questions, which is more than you have done by mine. For instance, you have not told me any thing of the people with whom you live on an intimate footing. It is true, I am not acquainted with them; but what does that signify? If you like them, and they are your friends, I wish to know their names, their characters, and even their persons: I wish to figure to myself the persons who surround you. Adieu, my dear child; I sup this evening at Madame de Limours's, with Madame de S—, the Countess Anatolle, and the Chevalier de Herbain. You may guess whether we shall not speak of de la ***. Yet the Viscountess is rather angry with you for not admiring her Hero, the Chevalier de Murville; she says, you are *not worthy of being witness of the great example he has given.* Adieu, my dear, and lovely friend; tell me more of yourself, and of those you are with; or I will give you shorter accounts from hence.

LETTER XLIX.

The same to the same.

AT length Theodore is really in love with Constantia; his anxiety has betrayed his passion; and he loves the more ardently, as he perceives he is beloved again. I have made a discovery which I shall only impart to you. It is, that the Countess Anatolle has persuaded herself, that she has an affection for Theodore. Madame de Valcy never had a more lively attachment than at this time she has received for Mons. de Remicourt, who has no great merit, but, with a serious and discreet appearance has already ruined three or four women; consequently he is quite the *ton*; which of itself is a very good reason for Madame de Valcy to admire him. You will judge then of her uneasiness in seeing Mons. de Remicourt intirely taken up in admiring the Countess Anatolle. The only thing for her to do in this case is to persuade the Countess that she has a secret attachment to Theodore, which is easily done with a young woman of nineteen whole ideas are so lively. If the Countess thought Theodore loved her, she would give no encouragement to Mons. Remicourt; besides, Madame de Valcy hates her sister, whose sentiments she has found means to penetrate; so that, if Theodore would but attach himself seriously to the Countess Anatolle, Constantia would lose her lover whom she adored, and a husband who had been destined for her from her infancy; all which would give great pleasure to Madame de Valcy. This discovery I have made by spending two or three evenings with Madame de Valcy, the Countess Anatolle, and Mons. de Remicourt; and I hope, my dear, I shall be able to prevent her succeeding in her intended mischief.

Yes, my dear child; I am perfectly satisfied with the impression Adelaide has received of the world. The more she sees of it, the more she is confirmed in the principles I have given her. The world will help to spoil a bad understanding, but it will improve a just one; according to this maxim of Mons. Dumarsais, who says, 'That every thing which is received depends on the person's situation and disposition who receives it: thus it is, that the rays of the sun harden clay and soften wax.'[68] We are continually saying the world is very dangerous for young persons: it is our own fault: let us educate our daughters properly, and the world will afford them useful lessons.

Madame de Narton is returned from England; Adelaide saw her the other day at my house for the first time, and the next day she dined with her. She asked me several questions about Madame de Narton, and whether it was true, that she had ever been handsome? Yes, I told her; fifteen years ago she was a very beautiful woman. – She had then every requisite for pleasing? – No, far from it; she was not at all amiable ... She had a very bad education, and was extremely ignorant. Her disposition was as little attended to as her mind; she had a thousand faults, and was so ill-tempered, capricious, and ill-bred, nobody could live with her: but, having good sense at the bottom, she has at length perceived her own defects, and has by degrees corrected them. She is become mild, gentle, and obliging; and, conscious of her ignorance, she has read a great deal; in short, she *has educated herself.* – What a pity that her parents did not take that trouble; for, without reckoning what she must have suffered in reforming her own mind, she has not had the pleasure of appearing in the world with all the advantages which she might, and the most valuable are those which she last became possessed of: for, if she had had a good education, she would have been, at the same time, amiable, sensible, well instructed, young and beautiful. After this reflection Adelaide made many more on the happiness she enjoyed by having a tender and sensible mother. She amply rewarded me for my cares, not only by the success I have had, but by an affection and gratitude which seem to increase every day.

You know, my dear child, that Mons. de Resan is married to Mademoiselle de Sevanne; and, as he is a friend and relation of Mons. de Limours's, the Viscountess has made acquaintance with the Ladies of the Sevanne family. The bride's sister-in-law is the most tiresome creature in the world; she is still young and tolerably pretty; but, joined to the misfortune of not having common sense, she has the absurdity of supposing herself one of the greatest wits of the age; and is not only always talking, but it is always of herself. She is continually replying to every thing that is said, *Oh, yes, I am of this opinion; I did that, or I said this*; and this I is repeated without ceasing, and forms the chief part of her conversation. We were talking yesterday of the *Persian Letters*;[69] the Chevalier de Herbain mentioned this charming observation: 'Happy is the person, who has guard enough over his vanity never to praise himself; who is diffident of those who listen to him, and never off ends by opposing his own merits to the pride of others.'[70] Upon this, Madame de Sevanne extolled the beauty of the thought; and added, that people who were always speaking of themselves were insupportable: and yet the force of custom made her say at the same instant, *for my part, I never talk of myself* ... A general laugh ensued, and Madame de Sevanne asked very seriously, what we laughed at? She has many other *singularities; the least thing that happens surprises her; as wonderful to relate; she has the strangest antipathies which were born with her, and are unconquerable; she has fainted away with eating gooseberry-jelly into which one single rasberry had fallen.* Even her illnesses are very extraordinary; she has for there two years laboured under complaints which the most able Physicians have not been able to find out; and these complaints we are forced to listen to from day to day! ... In short, though she is in perfect health, you may every moment hear her complain of the head-ach, or of her nerves; or the weather is either too cold, or too hot, or too damp. Every thing of this kind, she says, affects her, and makes her suffer more than any body living. Adelaide hears her, and considers her with the greatest astonishment; and is convinced by her own observation, how absurd and tiresome it is to be always making of one's self.

Our little school is established: we have taken six little girls from the most miserable state of poverty. They are all pretty, which was what we wished; because there is more danger of such than if they were plain. Our head Manager was formerly a writing-master; he understands writing and accounts thoroughly, is perfectly honest, and is taken from great distress, as is also a semstress, whom we have appointed to teach the girls. I have deposited with Monsieur Browne, our Banker, the sum which you sent me for this purpose: we are in all fifteen Members, or Governors; Mons. and Madame de Limours, Constantia, Madame de S***, the Countess Anatolle, the Chevalier de Herbain, Porphyry, Mons. d' Aimeri, the Chevalier de Valmont, the Count de Retel, Mons. d' Almane, my children, and myself: we each give a sum according to our abilities. Some only give two hundred livres a year; nobody gives more than five hundred, except Mons. de Retel, who, being the richest and a single man, gives five-and-twenty louis d'ores; and is also at the first expence of furnishing the linen and other necessaries to equip the little girls, which will nearly amount to a hundred pistoles. The yearly expences at the outside will amount to six thousand livres, and this sum will provide for ten persons including the cook and maid servant: and, as all the girls are renewed every seven years without additional expence, the benefit produced by this establishment will not be confined merely to ten persons.

Adieu, my dear child; I have no news to tell you, unless it is, that Madame de Germeuil is separated from her husband, and absolutely banished from society; for the world, so mild in general, has for some years past never pardoned those who are separated. It is indeed necessary for all those who separate to have the strongest reasons for it, and to have a just right to the esteem and good opinion of the publick; otherwise the noise, which such an affair makes, deprives them of all consideration, let them be ever so much intitled to it.

LETTER L.

Madame de Valcy to the Countess Anatolle.

WHAT! in the middle of winter to leave Paris all at once, and to go and spend six weeks with an aunt of an husband one no longer loves! What, my dear, is the meaning of this whim? ... You wish to conceal your secrets from me, but, notwithstanding your want of confidence, I cannot forbear opening your eyes, and giving your that advice you are at present in want of – you *fly to cure yourself*! – the medicine is worse than the disease; it is therefore absurd. Besides, custom forms and strengthens friendship, but it destroys love; expect then nothing from absence; it makes one forget a friend, but it renders a lover more dear; because the imagination always represents him more amiable than he really is: so that, by continually feeling the person on whom you have placed your affection, you will in the end love him less: but this your romantic ideas will not suffer you to credit: if you pretend to triumph over your passion, you flatter yourself with a vain conceit; take my advice, reckon more on your virtue, and less on your reason ... Do not fear that the love, with which you are possessed, can conquer your principles; but do not hope that you can tear it from your heart. What, indeed, cannot one love passionately without disgracing one's self! I am not ignorant, that in general this sentiment is not believed to exist;* but it does exist, and you cannot doubt it, for it was certainly made for you: – Cease then to be your own tormentor by reproaching yourself for a sensibility less dangerous in you than in any other. – I know exactly what passes in your soul; for you think they are bound by the sacred engagement; this is an error: there has not been even a promise given,[71] and at this very moment they are forsaking the vain projects planned in former times. You must suppose I am well informed on this subject, and you may rely on the truth of what I have told you. I shall feel happy, if it is in my power to afford you any comfort, and be the means of restoring your tranquillity; for I am certain you are now in a cruel agitation, and my compassion for you is more than I can express: if your's was only a common affection, I would exhort you to get the better of it; but you have too much energy in your soul to love slightly; recall all your principles, and promise yourself never to deviate from them: conceal your affection from the object which inspires it; never let a positive confession escape from your mouth; and be sufficiently generous to demand only friendship in return for violent love: this now is the only advice which can be given you, and all that can be expected from a heart sensible, generous, and innocent as your's. – Adieu, my dear friend; write to me punctually, and be more sincere with a person who is equally interested for your happiness and your reputation.

---

* And very properly; but those who wish to corrupt a young person will begin by talking to them in this manner.

LETTER LI.

The Baron to the Viscount.

Versailles.

OUR affair, my dear Viscount, is settled; we set out for L— on the first of April. It is needless to recommend caution to you who know all my reasons for wishing to have this secret kept faithfully: I have told it to my son, on the following occasion: On Monday we supped at Madame de G— 's. The Countess Anatolle was there; we had not seen her since her return: she wished to play at trictrac;[72] and, finding no one to make up her party but a Lady who knew little of the game, she desired Theodore to make one, and took him into a closet joining the saloon where the table was; by this means I lost sight of him all the evening. At supper he appeared thoughtful; his eyes and those of the Countess often met. On leaving the table, we all went to the Villa of Mons. de G— situated in the approach to Versailles. There was a delightful sight; – and Theodore was placed close to the Countess: I was so situated as to observe them without being seen. My son spoke little, but heard and saw nothing but her. She seemed only to talk to him by stealth; being so near, she dared not look at him. She sat upright in her place, without turning her body; and yet she every moment cast her soft and languishing eyes towards him, and hastily turned them down to the ground! a glance well understood, and which speaks very plain! – The Countess, after a moment's thought, talked with a Lady that set next to her, and for a time seemed to forget Theodore, who in the mean while was admiring two very long braids of the finest hair in the world, and waiting with impatience for the end of her conversation.

After the sight, Theodore, handed the Countess to her carriage: we got into our's, and discoursed of our amusement and indifferent subjects, and never mentioned the name of the Countess till we went to bed. The next morning, as soon as I waked, my son came into my room. He dismissed my servants, and, seating himself with his back to the window, that the light might not shew his face, he took and squeezed one of my hands between his: he was much moved, and at a loss, and for some time unable to speak. I embraced him, and, smiling, said to him, Do you know that you would make me very uneasy, if I was not perfectly acquainted with you? I see that the heart of my Theodore wants to relieve itself, and that he wants to trust a secret to his friend. – But I cannot imagine this confidence can be distressing to you, or afflicting to me. – I thank God! I have nothing as yet of real consequence to reproach myself with; – but I am in a particular situation! ... Particular! ... not at all. You love a person worthy of the firmest attachment, and at the same time suffer yourself to be flattered and seduced by the coquetry of a woman as sickle as she is imprudent. Such a situation is not extraordinary ... How could you find it out? – The Countess Anatolle's conduct is well known to me ... I own, my father, that I did not believe her to be a coquette. – I conceive it to be flattering to think she has sensibility. If our self-love did not often produce similar deceptions, coquettes would never seduce us. Your want of experience renders your fault excusable: besides, the Countess Anatolle is one of those coquettes who mistake themselves: she is lively, and thinks she loves you ... How then is she mistaken? – Because she before thought she loved Monsieur, de St. Phar, and because you are too young to inspire a passion in a woman who has been four years in the world. Well, I am comforted: you have read my heart; but what must I do? ... Avoid the Countess; never place yourself near her, nor look at her: it will cost you but little to do this, as you have a command over yourself, and if you love Constantia ... If I love her! You know, Sir, there is no sacrifice I could not chearfully make for her sake: her idea alone possesses me: I think only of her: yet I mistrust myself; and I fear, I own, the Countess Anatolle. Her remembrance never troubles me; when she is near Constantia, I do not even see her; but, ... when you play at trictrac with her in a small closet, you find her very handsome and very bewitching; particularly when she tells you that she only took her journey of a fortnight (which ought by the bye to have been for six weeks) to snatch herself from the danger of seeing you. – Here Theodore blushed exceedingly, and had the greatest surprise marked on his countenance. You take me for a conjurer, added I, laughing; really I did not hear one word that passed at your tête à tête; but I have known by heart, for these five and twenty years, what she said to you yesterday ... Coquettes are not dangerous, when they are so easily discovered. I promise you, my father, to avoid the Countess Anatolle with the greatest care: yet politeness will often forbid my quitting her as much as I could wish. – Well, you must keep yourself out of her sight long enough for her to forget you: for example, a year. – A year and Constantia? – You shall leave Constantia without regret: I propose to you a way of making yourself more worthy of her. – War is broke out in – Let us go – You know that the Chevalier de Valmont and I had that intention last summer – I have been earnestly busied since upon that object; I have now hopes of being employed; should that be the case, I will take you and your friend with me. Theodore, transported with joy, flung his arms about my neck. In that moment he saw nothing but glory; he forgot all the sacrifices that were to be made to it! Yesterday I told him my petition was granted, and our departure fixed for the end of March. He has given me his word, that he will, keep this a secret from his mother. I know perfectly Madame d' Almane's good sense and resolution: I am sure she will approve of a scheme which she herself would have advised: but I can too well judge how much she will suffer at heart! I will not distress her unnecessarily: I will not therefore impart this to her, till a fortnight before we leave her. Adieu! my friend, I will return to Paris on Tuesday night for certain, and will immediately join you in your box at the Opera.

LETTER LII.

The Baroness to Madame d' Ostalis.

From Paris.

I HAVE just experienced a very great pleasure, my dear child. A Tragedy of Porphyry's has been performed this evening for the first time; and it has had, as it truly deserved, the most brilliant success. It did not require the advantages of being well acted, or the addition of beautiful scenes; it will bear reading, and will confirm the good opinion the first representation of it has given. Porphyry has learnt by this the advantages which an Author derives from bearing an excellent character. He is certain before-hand of having the good-will of the Public, and that there will be no cabal against him. He has only written valuable Works. He has never taken notice of the criticisms which have been made by the envious and severe, and he does not pride himself on his moderation. We generally atrribute great merit to people who have a number of enemies. The reason is, because we see so many persons boasting of being hated, and repeating frequently, with such emphasis, *my enemies*, which in fact means *my rivals*. Porphyry is privately much afflicted at having gained enemies; but, so far from being proud of them, he has not even made a single complaint against them, which has much softened them. Incapable of envy or resentment, he can forgive their injustice, and finds a noble pleasure in extolling his rivals. He has always been intimately connected with the most celebrated men of letters; he was at all times desirous of their friendship and advice, and took every possible opportunity to oblige them. He thinks with La Bruyere, who says, 'Come in; all my doors are open to you ... Come always without ceremony; you bring with you that which is more precious than silver or gold: if I can oblige you, tell me so. What is there I can do for you? If it is to quit my books, my studies, my works, even this line which I have begun? What a pleasing interruption for me to be useful to you! [73] &c.' ... With such an obliging disposition, can any one be more capable of gratitude? If you solicit a favour for him and succeed, he will be infinitely obliged; if you are not successful, he will not be less grateful. Thus it is impossible to reunite more good qualities, or to have a more distinguished place in society. Every one is ready to acknowledge his superiority, because he does not appear to expect it. In short, his gentleness, his modesty, and simplicity appear less surprising in him than in any other person.

Men of the world can only shew their wit by their conversation. It is not therefore astonishing that they should aim at doing that which makes them shine. But a man of letters, whose merit all the world knows, ought not to be susceptible of this trifling ambition. *He has given his proofs*; what then can it cost him to be humble and modest? If he is not superior to such littleness, he is not worthy the glory he has gained. Besides, by employing himself in company to make others appear to advantage, he will always appear most amiable himself. People are always insupportable, when they wish to rule; and never obtain the success they aspire to but by attention, mildness, and modesty, with a desire to please and to be beloved.

I saw, by this first representation of Porphyry's Tragedy, how few people judge from their own sentiments. I supped with fifty people this evening; Porphyry is universally esteemed, his Play had met with the most brilliant success; and yet they only praised it with the greatest precaution, endeavouring, before they said any thing, to sound the persons who were thought to have the most judgment, and to collect the general opinion; and restrained their admiration, contenting themselves with saying, *This play has given me great pleasure; there are many fine lines in it and beautiful scenes.* – For before the Public had given their sentiments. They had not the courage to say, It is an excellent Piece, a Work of great genius. In short, people rather chuse to appear too difficult than not to be nice enough in their judgment. These very persons, who are so reserved in giving their opinions and approbation with regard to men of genius, make themselves amends for their prudence and restraint by judging freely on the conduct of society, which they boldly decide upon, and are not afraid of being contradicted by the Public.

Adieu, my dear child; I perceive the approach of Spring with concern, since at that time, as Theodore is entered into the army, I must part from him for many months. He yesterday proved his sensibility on this occasion, which affected me extremely. I was alone with him and his sister: Theodore, said I to him, you are every day more and more dear to me; so that I perceive I shall part with you this year with more reluctance than I have ever done yet! ... At these words Theodore looked at me in a manner which penetrated my heart; he then rose up, and went to the chimney; he turned his back to us, but Adelaide, who saw his face in the glass, flew towards him, and threw herself on his neck, crying out, *My dear Theodore*! Oh Mamma, look at him ... I got up: Theodore, bathed in tears, threw himself into my arms. He could not speak; and his emotions were so extraordinary, and so lively, that they appeared downright affliction; which surprized as much as it affected me. Adieu, my dear child; the twentieth of next month we shall have been separated a whole twelvemonth; in another month Mons. d' Almane and Theodore will leave us! ... I am very melancholy! ... Ah, when shall I see you again! when shall we be re-united?

LETTER LIII.

Count de Roseville to the Baron.

IN a year at farthest, my dear Baron, I shall have the pleasure of returning to you and to my country. An event, which will complete my pupil's happiness, is now my only delay. The Princess's pregnancy is announced, and the Prince, in the hopes of a son, is already busied in the choice of a Governor. I have recommended to him a book little known, (intitled a Treatise on the Education of Princes destined to a Throne, by Mons. de Bassedow, translated from the German by Mons. de B***.[74]) This Work is well worthy of notice, and makes essential remarks on the choice of a Governor, among which are the following: 'The King named for Governor to the young Prince, Polyprates, a distinguished Nobleman. It was not high birth, nor military and political abilities, that determined this choice. For, said he, the most experienced politician, the sagest civilian, may not have the necessary qualifications for educating a young Prince. Therefore the young Agatacrator was intrusted to Polyprates, as he had assiduously attended to the bringing up of his own children who excelled in prudence and learning all their cotemporaries ... Three years before he placed them under the tutor he had appointed, he made him qualify himself for that employment by reading the most approved Works on the subject, by consulting those who had succeeded best in their Plans of Education, and by making trials with poor people's children, which would at the same time give him opportunities of practising acts of benevolence. Polyprates had also procured servants, from whose conversation no harm could arise to the children. The intended tutor was directed to appoint them to their places about other children, that they might know how to conduct themselves about his own ... Without such a Governor, said the King, and a most scrupulous choice of all the Prince's attendants, it is impossible his education can be perfect. Neither trouble nor expence should be spared to seek, even in foreign countries, proper persons, and to prepare them by a well regulated course of experience.'

This is not all, said I to the Prince; your son will be first under the care of the women; to fix upon a fit Governess is much more essential than is generally thought. She will give him the first impressions; and the Prince will owe her gratitude and affection; she should be of an excellent character and well accomplished. Consider farther, Sir, after all these precautions, you will but imperfectly fulfill your duty, if you do not yourself watch over your son's education. What more important affairs can employ you even on a Throne? Your most useful and glorious actions will have only a temporary effect, if your successor is not a great Prince. He will bring to perfection or destroy your Works. Without him you may be great; but without him you cannot hand down your good name to posterity. Watch then over him, over his Governor, and all who attend him. Study his character, learn his inclinations, his faults, and his virtues. Always bear in mind that Augustus, master of the whole world, found leisure to superintend the education of his grandson. – At this audience I gave the Prince a short list of people in my opinion worthy of being appointed Governors. You will find there, said I, four names; a great many without doubt. Happy the Prince who can reckon at his Court four men truly meritorious! Out of these you should chuse a Governor; but I would advise you to study and observe them carefully, and not to determine hastily; for all your prudence and reflection is necessary in an affair of so great consequence. The Prince examined the list, without surprise, at the three first names. The Public had already approved them. At the fourth name he exclaimed, what Mons. ***? Do not you know his birth intitles him not to this honour? ... It is true he is not of an illustrious or an ancient family, but he is received at Court. What signifies his having fewer titles than others, while his merit is superior? In every other post, which essentially requires great abilities, high birth is never regarded. Nothing but merit is sought for in a Prime Minister. It is not equally necessary in a Preceptor? Is his a less important charge? You wonder, Sir, to see the name of Mons. ***, how much more would you have been surprised in reading that of Mons. d' Elford? – What, a man who is not even admitted at Court? – The same: a man replete with virtue and genius. It was not his mean birth hindered my proposing him, for that circumstance would have been an additional advantage in his appointment. What a noble lesson for a young Prince to find in his own Governor an example of virtue rewarded? With how much greater respect will he hear him, as knowing his qualifications and superior abilities gained that office? – But can I, without offending common prejudices, avail myself of Mons. d' Elford's talents to assist the education of my son in a lower degree ... If he is not at the head, and with the title of Governor, he will have but very little influence. The places, Sir, of a lower degree, which you mention, though very honourable for those of Mons. d' Elford's situation in life, are seldom accepted by men of real genius. They can do good but by halves; even should the Governor adopt their plan, they would not reap the most pleasing reward of their labour, the credit of it, and the gratitude of their country. – Do you suppose that common prejudices can influence me, when my dearest interests are concerned? – No, to be sure. – Why then did you not propose Mons. d' Elford? Because he never lived in the Court, or in the great World; and it is absolutely necessary that a Preceptor should have a knowledge of both. – You do not think then that a Prince, brought up far from Court and in ignorance of his birth, will be the fitter to reign? ... The heir apparent cannot be so treated: This plan is merely chimerical; of course I have bestowed little reflection upon what benefits might result from it. – But is it not very easy, without concealing his birth, to bring up a Prince far from Court? – It has no advantage that can sufficiently repay his misfortune of being from under the eyes of his parents. It is his duty to regard them in the highest light; his happiness to possess their affections; and, to effect these good purposes, he should live always with them. I am much pleased with the idea of a house of education seven or eight leagues from the Court, for the young Prince to spend there two or three months every year. At such a distance he would frequently enjoy the company of his parents, and this retirement would be of equal advantage to his body and his mind. – I am so struck with this thought, that I will certainly have such a house built; I am of opinion, that the plan is not to be trusted solely to the architect. Instruction should not only be gained from the tapestries, carpets, and other furniture of the apartments; one should meet with it in the Court-yards and gardens. It should be without gildings, looking-glasses, and other useless decorations. It should present every-where objects calculated to inspire virtuous sentiments in youthful minds.*[75]

You will easily believe, my dear Baron, that I shall engage the Prince to reflect seriously on the plan of this house, before it is built; and to consult those who are capable of giving the best advice on this head.

Adieu, my dear Baron. I write also by this post to Madame d' Almane, so I do not mention Monsieur and Madame d' Ostalis: Madame d' Almane will shew you my letter: the accounts contained in it will give you the greater pleasure, for you are sensible that I never allow myself to exaggerate in the least, even to give you pleasure.

LETTER LIV.

The Baroness to Madame de Valmont.

Paris.

AH! Madame, you alone can conceive the condition I am in and the griefs which surround me! ... To you I may disclose that grief of which here I conceal the greatest part in my own breast; you will share it; you feel it yourself. Alas! at break of day to-morrow they depart! ... They wished to deceive and persuade us, that they did not set out before Monday or Tuesday. I pretended to believe

---

* For example, pictures of the most noble actions, and, in the gardens and courts, statues and busts of the most famous men; their histories should be written on the pedestals. Without any additional expence, a King might select from his own collections pictures, drawings, prints, and statues, which hand down to us great men and their actions. These should be always before the eyes of the Prince, his son.

them; but I knew the truth this morning ... What a supper this last! ... Mons. d' Aimeri and the Chevalier dined here: they did not leave me till five, and Monsieur d' Almane and Theodore returned with them at seven: this eagerness alone would have made me suspicious. We supped together; the manner Monsieur d' Almane had placed us at table had something very remarkable in it: I was seated between him and my son, Adelaide was on her father's right hand; he told the Chevalier to sit on the other side of her; and he, fearing he did not hear right, obliged Mons. d' Almane to repeat this invitation twice ... The conversation was very melancholy and ill supported. You are sensible how difficult it is to forbear weeping when we speak; Adelaide and I were silent ... When we rose from table, I felt I had so little command over myself, that I resolved to retire for a minute ... At eleven Monsieur d' Aimeri looked at his watch, and I saw him make a sign to Monsieur d' Almane; presently they all arose; my husband and son drew near, and in an hesitateing manner bid me good night; on embracing them, I could not refrain my tears. I felt my son's flow; my face was bathed with them – Adelaide, shocked and comprehending but too readily that these embraces were a farewell, came and threw herself between her father and brother – At length Monsieur d' Almane snatched himself from our arms, and took some steps towards the door. – Adelaide, pale and trembling, seeing him go, attempted to follow him; but, unable to support herself, would have fallen, had not the Chevalier flown towards her, caught her, and carried her to a chair ... Monsieur d' Almane returned, to assure his daughter that they should not leave us that night; then, observing that the Chevalier and Theodore could no longer hide their extreme sensibility, took an hand of each and went abruptly out of the room. Adelaide cast herself into my arms, and we gave a loose to our tears ... We were above two hours together without speaking; we could only weep ... Besides, inquietude and sorrow sometimes inspire such dismal ideas that it is impossible to communicate them ... We have not courage to utter them; we experience a kind of superstition in our fears for those we love, which hinders us from expressing our most distracting thoughts. In this case, such terrible words occur, that one cannot resolve to pronounce them. I remember Adelaide at four years of age had a blow on her head; she fell ill at the time, and had a fever; I sent for a physician; I talked of the blow she had received; I asked whether her fever did not proceed from it. It would have been possible for me to have said, Don't you think she has fractured her skull? That horrid word *fracture* was uppermost in my thoughts night and day, but my mouth could not give it utterance ... Such is my situation at this moment, it would exceed my resolution to communicate all my thoughts to the person in whom I place the greatest confidence! Ah! Madam, when I reflect (and at what minute do I not think of it) to what an height of happiness I am raised, I tremble at my own good fortune: is it possible that such perfect felicity can be permanent? ... It is now four o'clock in the morning, and they depart at six; I know not if I can resist the desire of seeing them again for a moment and embracing them! My poor Theodore, how deeply is he affected! what goodness and sensibility! how dearly do I love him! ... and the Chevalier de Valmont! ... believe me, Madame, he also is very dear to me ... But in eight or ten months we shall see them again. They will have made a glorious campaign ... The will distinguish themselves, I am very sure ... Oh! what joy, what transports, on reading the letter which announces their return! ... When we know they are landed! ... Alas! what mortal fears, what pain must we support, before we taste such delight! but then, can it be bought too dear? Adieu, Madame; Monsieur d' Aimeri will spend three weeks with us at St. —. Then he will come to you; so you will certainly have the pleasure of seeing him towards the end of April.

LETTER LV.

The Baroness to Madame d' Ostalis.

De St. ***.

I HAVE been two days here, my dear daughter; the two most unhappy and painful days of my life ... Although naturally I weep with great difficulty, for these last forty-eight hours the tears have been continually in my eyes and every moment ready to flow. In hopes of amusing myself on Monday evening, I took up my harp and played some lessons, chusing those I knew not, in order to force my attention; but, as I was playing, my eyes were so darkened by tears that I could not see the notes. It is possible to banish reflection, but not fly from sorrow: a frightful weight always remains at the bottom of the heart! ... Hitherto I can reap no true consolation but from Religion, by addressing myself to God in prayers, by placing all my hopes in him alone. It is with a firm faith I dare implore him, and he has already deigned to revive and strengthen me: in every event of my life may I render myself worthy to be either sustained, consoled, or guided by him! The Viscountess and Constantia are here; the dejection of the latter fully evinces her attachment for Theodore; Adelaide readily sees into her sentiments: she pities but cannot comprehend her. As I do not chuse to have my daughter the confidant of such passions, I take the greatest care to prevent her being alone with Constantia, and have strictly forbid her ever talking to her of Theodore. The Viscount, to calm his Lady's fears (which are as tormenting as Constantia's) a fortnight before Monsieur d' Almane's departure, positively refused the Marquis de Hernay, and assured her at the same time, that in his heart he always preferred Theodore to any other. The Viscountess intreated him to make a contract with Monsieur d' Almane; but she could not prevail, which causes her much fear and uneasiness.

Adelaide is much afflicted, but her strength of mind equals her sensibility. She is continually employed, and has lost none of her activity.

Porphyry came here with me, but leaves me tomorrow; he has received a letter with the melancholy account of Monsieur de Lagaraye's being dangerously ill; and he is going to nurse his benefactor. Adieu, my dear daughter. Ah! why I must I be deprived of the consolation of confiding to you the most cruel incidents of my life! ... I write indeed, but when will you read this letter? When shall I receive your answer? ... God bless you, my child! I will write again on Thursday and give you more particulars.

LETTER LVI.

The Viscountess to the Baroness.

Paris.

I HAVE a great deal of news to tell you, my dear friend. Madame de Blemur has revenged herself in a very striking manner on Madame de Serville. A thousand circumstances united to make the latter ardently wish for the place which you know she applied for, and thought herself sure of obtaining, when Madame de Blemur returned from the waters. This event intirely changed the face of things: for she planned so deep and well-formed an intrigue, that she absolutely contrived to make the affair come to nothing; and then wrote to Madame de Serville to glory in the exploit. All the world have copies of her note, which are in the following words: 'In former times you experienced, Madame, I knew how to serve my friends; it is then but justice that you should feel I also know how to revenge ingratitude and deceit; it was owing to me that your schemes failed. I have not indeed returned you all the evil which you did to me, but yet feel myself satisfied at having it in my power to convince you that I am not to be deceived and betrayed with impunity.' – This extraordinary manner of making a boast of one's anger, and glorying in revenge, has, however, met with its success, and is applauded by many people; for they find in this proceeding a generous sincerity, and repeat all the common expressions you already know, which are so dangerous as well as false; 'that people of the greatest sensibility know best how to shew dislike;' and 'that grateful hearts are always the most revengeful.' Such maxims are now become proverbs, not on account of their truth, but on account of their being an excuse for wickedness. A feeling and grateful heart will always act nobly and generously, and will think of hatred with horror, and of revenge with disdain. Those who avenge themselves shamefully give way to a furious passion, and sacrifice honour and humanity to the most terrible of feelings. To think of employing one's thoughts without ceasing, only to injure and to endeavour to make the object of one's dislike for ever unfortunate, to find pleasure in the traits of so black a picture, to carry into execution so horrid a design, does it not shew, at the bottom, a savage character absolutely void of all feelings either of tenderness or affection? Madame de Blemur's friends say, by way of excuse, that she did not give herself time to reflect on this action, and endeavour to persuade one it was not premediated: but Madame de Serville's scheme could not be defeated in four-and-twenty hours; and it has been sufficiently proved, that this was the effect of more than two months intrigue; besides, never does a sudden fit of anger make a really good heart guilty of a bad action. If we ever give way to passion, reason forsakes us, and for a time we are lost to ourselves; but then the instinct of a natural good disposition is left, and will serve as our guide. – Another event is, that Mons. de Somires has just gained his cause. It was expected he would have acted in the most generous manner to his relation, who has a numerous family, and almost reduced to beggary by this event; during the three years which this law-suit has lasted, you are not ignorant of all that Mons. de Somires and his friends said on the subject; well then, after all that violent display of heroic sentiments, Mons. de Somires keeps all his fortune! It has been proved he has the right, and he shews he has the inclination also. – But I cannot endure to find words and actions so very contrary; why say, *I am more generous than another*, in order to prove in the end, that one is only an impostor? But yet, on the whole, I do not think it a bad plan; undoubtedly it renders one contemptible in the opinion of sensible people; but then it is sure of gaining one the esteem and admiration of fools, who are always more guided by expressions than actions. If Madame d' Inselin was not for ever talking of her own *rank* and *greatness* of *soul*, and did not pronounce these two words with such strong emphases; and if she was not herself to tell of her dislike to every thing that was *mean*, would any one talk either of her rank or greatness of soul? For she dearly loves money, is very parsimonious, and has nothing the least obliging in her manner. She seeks, cultivates, and flatters, all persons who can be serviceable to her: and she has spent her whole life in begging and soliciting favours, but assures people that her sentiments are perfectly noble; and they give her credit for it. Every one says the world is bad; as for myself, the longer I live, the more I see that it is equally credulous and foolish: and indeed there needs no great wit or genius to impose on it; nothing is wanted but impudence and art.

My last news is that Madame de Gerville is seized with a religious zeal; her pretence for this alteration is the death of her brother, whom it is well known she never loved: but the motive has made the change very interesting, and she is now quite restored to favour; which costs her only the sacrifice of her box at the

Opera; for now even the outward forms of religion are not so strict as they were formerly, and neither rouge nor head-dress is discarded; it is only forsaking public amusements, and assuring one's friend that one is a devotee. Thus, since my return here, I absolutely hear little else than the praises of Madame de Gerville for her sensibility. – All principle apart, I cannot hate her; though she is certainly the person in the world who has done me the greatest injury; yet she causes no alteration in my disposition. Was I to see her in distress, I should feel the same compassion for her as I should for a person wholly indifferent to me. – Even in the midst of her prosperity, I wish her no harm; but will confess to you, that the sight of her happiness is not pleasant to me, as I really think her not deserving of it; for she is a person I cannot esteem, and I do not take aversions without feeling contempt; I never hate what I once valued: for, even if any rivals of mine were to obtain the prize I wished to gain, and succeeded without using either artifice or falsehood, I should own the generousity of their conduct, though they deprived me of the happiness of my life; and I should never hate them. It is with the greatest ease I can forbear exposing in public the faults of those who are not my friends, and can even defend them when they are falsely accused before me: but I must own it does hurt me to hear them praised and extolled for virtues which I know they do not posses. It is then with difficulty I keep within bounds; but my anger soon ceases, and reflection restores to me ease and indifference. – Adieu, my dear friend; on Thursday I mean to come and spend three days with you. – I endeavour to amuse myself and divert my little Constantia; but yet we are not in spirits, and when alone can talk only of you, Mons. d' Almane, and Theodore.

I have received only one letter from Porphyry during the three months that he has left us, and I fear there is no hope of Mons. de Lagaraye's recovery. What a loss will he be to humanity! and with what regret must that good man leave this world, when he reflects on the numbers of those unfortunate people who, by his death, will be deprived of their only benefactor! – How terrible must his last moments be! What a shocking scene for our poor friend! – If you have heard from him since the fifteenth, pray let me know.

LETTER LVII.

Porphyry to the Baroness.

De Lagaraye.

OH, Madame! I have lost my benefactor, my father, my guide! ... His death was worthy of his life. The melancholy account, which rends my heart, can alone relieve it and procure the only consolation it is susceptible of at this dreadful moment ... Oh! can I better honour his memory, than by relating with fidelity his actions and his discourse, which will raise him higher in your estimation?

I informed you, Madame, in my last letter, that I then had some hope, but two days after I lost it intirely. Last Monday, Mons. de Lagaraye would not permit me to sit up with him; I lay in an adjoining closet. About four o'clock in the morning I was called, and informed he was much worse. I found him in a swoon and in Madame de Lagaraye's arms; which lasted for a considerable time. When he came to himself, his pulse became pretty good, which was thought a favourable circumstance. At six he desired we would quit the room and leave the Priest and him together. We went into his anti-chamber, and, in about an hour, the folding doors opening, judge, Madame, our surprize, on seeing his servants carrying him in a great chair; he just stopped, and told us he was going to visit *his sick*. These words struck us all with the same idea, that they were meant as his last adieu, which drew tears from every one in the room ... Mons. de Lagaraye desired me to announce his visit in the infirmary, that his presence might not alarm the invalids; which proved a very necessary caution, for they were transported beyond expression, all concluding that Mons. de Lagaraye was out of danger. Many exclaimed, now is life desirable! ... Others offered up to Heaven their most fervent prayers, expressive of their gratitude and joy. All renewed their promises to God of accomplishing their different vows for the re-establishment of their benefactor's health. The moment Mons. de Lagaraye appeared in the hall, they all drew aside their curtains, and leaned almost out of their beds to see him come in. There was a confused murmur of sobs and tears; their misfortunes were forgotten, their sufferings suspended, gratitude alone employed and filled their hearts. Mons. de Lagaraye ordered himself to be carried round the hall, in order that they might imagine he was past all danger. At the same time he exhorted them to resignation, in case it should please God to take him; and, for their greater consolation, he ordered that part of his will to be read, in which he had directed, that they should remain in the infirmary till they were perfectly cured. At last he informed them, that, as he found himself weak, he should not visit them again for ten or twelve days: he then retired, loaded with benedictions and thanks. As I followed him, I remarked that he looked back at the door, and with a profound sigh lifted up his eyes to Heaven. As soon as he got to bed, finding himself faint, he took a few drops of æther, and made some pretence to send Mons. de Lagaraye out of the room, as well as all his attendants, except myself; and, begging Lemire, his surgeon, and St. André to withdraw, and then holding out his hand to me, moments, said he, are dear to us, and there are none to lose. Has Lemire told you the truth? How, interrupted I, with inexpressible grief, what do you mean! He replied, on my situation ... This struck me dumb, for till then I had flattered myself; but now my hopes were fled, for I saw it was all over, and that he was sensible of it ... I laid my head on his hand; and he, perceiving that I bathed it with my tears, remained for a short time silent; then resuming the discourse: Regret me, said he, you ought; but do not pity me; think on my life and the reward which I shall receive, and be not so selfish as to be inconsolable for my death ... No, cried I; you will not die; no, it is impossible. Cease, replied he, cease, my dear Porphyry, to flatter yourself. I have not twenty-four hours to live ... You! Great God! It was for that reason that I wished to see the sick; I owed them that consolation. You, my father ... At sixty-three, then your career will be finished ... Well then, what occasion have you for murmuring? If I had lived fifteen years longer, I should have been rewarded later ... But these unfortunate people to whom your life is so necessary! ... I put them again with confidence into his hands, who first inspired me with the resolution of consecrating my life to them ... You think, perhaps, I bitterly regret all the good I could have done, had I ten years longer to live; if I had only worked for glory, it is true, I should die in despair; these two years I have been thinking on new plans, and was just about carrying some great things into execution. A few years more, and I should have left establishments which would have survived me. But death comes and destroys all these hopes. What does it signify? God, who reads the very bottom of our hearts, will keep an account of my projects as well as of my actions. All my designs are over-turned; but I had formed them, which will intitle me to the reward; so that I die fully satisfied, and twenty years more could not have made my last moments more sweet and tranquil. O admirable triumph of Religion, cried I! O my father! How you make me love this sublime piety that can alone, by inspiring heroic actions, even raise a great soul above glory! Ah, what signifies the judgment of men and the vain reputation of a moment, when we are under the eye of the Supreme Judge, who penetrates the motives, who knows the desires, from whom virtuous intentions are never hid, and from whom we must expect immortal recompence, for the good we have done, and for that we are willing to do. At these words, Mons. de Lagaraye, looking at me with eyes which expressed the sweetest satisfaction; promise me then, said he, to preserve these religious sentiments in a world where so many look on irreligion as a proof of strength and superiority of understanding. Remember, my dear Porphyry, that Corneille, Racine, Fenelon, Boileau, Bossuet,[76] and Pascal, were as much distinguished by their eminent piety as by the superiority of their talents ... Your example is sufficient for me; I shall compare the life of the slanderers of Religion with your's; and I shall preserve to my latest breath the principles you have instilled into me. On pronouncing these words, I fell on my knees at his bedside; he clasped me in his arms, and was some time before he could speak; then, raising me up, and making me sit down by him, he charged me with a painful commission, that of acquainting Madame de Lagaraye with his situation; and at the same time ordering me to take all necessary precautions that his death might be concealed from the sick till after their recovery; which the precaution he took of telling them he should not see them, for twelve days, the better inabled me to do. He finished by recommending to me a young man of his school, to whom he had taken a particular liking, and for whom you will easily believe, Madame, I shall have the greatest friendship. After this cruel and affecting conversation, I went in search of Madame de Lagaraye: the sight of me but too well prepared her for the dreadful news which I was charged to communicate: she, trembling questioned me, and soon discovered the extent of her unhappiness. She clasped her hands together, and, lifting up her eyes to Heaven, filled with tears, she remained some minutes in that attitude, without uttering a single word; – but the sublime and affecting expression of her countenance sufficiently declared her thoughts and sentiments ... She offered the happiness of her life as a sacrifice to God! and yet there was nothing violent or frantic in her grief; it appeared strong, but a perfect resignation softened the bitterness of it; so that my commiserations were in part lost in admiration ... At last, Madame de Lagaraye, wipeing away her tears, arose, and, leaning on my arm, Let us go to him, said she; be not under the least apprehensions that the sight of him will add to my weakness: on the contrary, it will give me firmness; for is it possible to want resignation or courage in his presence? I conducted Madame de Lagaraye to the door of the apartment, and stayed in the next, where I found St. André and Blanch. The first was standing, leaning against the chimney; he did not weep, but grief and consternation were strongly painted in his pale and disfigured countenance. You are, Madame, already acquainted with his history, and with the natural violence of his passions; and how sincere and violent his enthusiasm is for Mons. de Lagaraye. I went up to him; he pressed my hand, and perceiving my tears to flow, You are young, said he, this is an event you had reason to expect; but for me, who am so much older than him, and a useless burden upon earth, to survive him! – As St. André pronounced these words, we heard a dreadful scream; it was Madame de Lagaraye: terrified and trembling, we ran towards the door, and, entering the room, what a sight presented itself to our view! We saw Monsieur de Lagaraye ready to breathe his last; the frightful paleness of death had already overspread his countenance: his unhappy wife, seated on his bed, supported him in her arms. The Priest, standing by the bed-side, held one of his hands ... On perceiving us, he made a sign for us to draw near him; then, turning his head towards us, with a look full of mildness and serenity, Porphyry, oh, my son! said he, remember thy promise; and you, my dear St. André, continued he, never leave my wife; but do you and your family continue with her in such retreat as she shall chuse; and may Friendship, but above all, Religion, be your comfort. In pronouncing these words his head fell on his breast, and his eyes closed: the surgeon drew near to feel his pulse, and made a sign that he still breathed: a moment after he said aloud, *His Pulse revives*. Alas! how easily is the human heart impressed with hope! These few words caused an universal transport; every one repeated them, and expected a miracle ... I approached, and, looking stedfastly at Monsieur de Lagaraye, I perceived the paleness dispersing, his colour returning, his eyes opening, and a supernatural expression made his venerable appearance more and more striking ... All at once he lifted up his hands to Heaven, and with the most fervent emotion he said, Oh, my God! thou callest me; I come! These were his last words ... Struck with surprise, and seized with emotion, which such a sight never perhaps before produced, we all fell on our knees. We looked on his death without fear, and we considered the melancholy object of our loss without terror; because we were sure that he was happy. It appeared not as if death had approached and struck him; but the Almighty had descended from Heaven to call and to receive him. After having torn Madame de Lagaraye from his apartments, I recollected his last injunctions concerning the sick; I ran to the Infirmary, but too late; the screams of the domestics, the tears, the groans of the nurses, had but too soon divulged the melancholy news which I was charged to conceal. I stayed only a minute, and withdrew, penetrated with compassion and horror ... I was doomed to be a witness to a still more pathetic and dreadful scene.

The day before yesterday, that I intended for the funeral, I went at the time appointed into the school-hall, where the coffin then lay: in crossing the court I perceived it was filled with many of the inhabitants of the village and all the manufacturers in tears: on entering the hall, I found near sixty children kneeling round the coffin; St. André, in a long black cloke, was, at the top of the room, motionless and plunged in the deepest meditation, with his eyes fixed on the coffin, which he seemed to contemplate in the most melancholy and unhappy manner. His three sons were placed behind him; we were waiting for the Priest, when all at once six men, with the most terrifying aspects, pale, livid, and imaciated, cloathed in white sheets which covered them from head to foot; who could scarce support themselves, and appeared like phantoms; like ghosts coming out of their tombs; prostrated themselves before the coffin with the most hideous groans ... These unfortunate people stole out of the Infirmary to render their last homage to their benefactor, in the absence of their nurses, who had left them in the general trouble and confusion ... Two of these unhappy people fainted, and fell near the coffin: I had them removed, and went with them myself to the Infirmary, where I gave them all the relief that they stood in need of; and returned to the hall just as the Priest arrived, and immediately we were in motion. As soon as we came near the court, we heard more distinctly the lamentable groans of the multitude, who waited to join the funeral pomp; but, the moment they saw the coffin, an universal silence ensued, and an awful respect stopped their lamentations and tears. In about half an hour the numerous retinue arrived at the church. Alas! in my infancy I saw Monsieur de Lagaraye lay the first stone of this sacred edifice! We now approached the awful tomb which was going to inclose the precious remains of the most virtuous and best of men. The grave was half open, and the coffin placed on it: my heart was now torn asunder, and I turned my trembling eyes from it. At this moment I heard a plaintive voice, and saw the unhappy St. André staggering on the edge of the grave; his sons tried, but in vain, to drag him from it; lost and wandering he struggled in their arms, crying out, Oh, my Master! Oh, my Friend! ... and at that instant fell into the grave, and expired on his benefactor's coffin; a noble and striking victim of gratitude and friendship.

I cannot give you an account, Madame, of the conclusion of this melancholy scene, as I was deprived of my senses. Upon my recovery I found myself in my own room; they bled me, and obliged me to keep my bed, being in a high fever. Yesterday, finding myself a little better, I arose, in order to pay my respects to Madame de Lagaraye who communicated to me all her plans: she proposes to reside at Anjou, where she was born, as soon as the sick are recovered. She will there establish a charitable hospital and a little school for girls; to which she will devote the thirty thousand livres a year which were left her. She takes with her the unhappy family of St. André: the latter was interred this morning; and they have justly immortalized his memory and his death by placing his body in the same grave with Mons. de Lagaraye.

The heirs of Mons. de Lagaraye are all here, and treat her with the greatest regard and respect, which indeed they cannot refuse to her virtues; but it is already known that they will not keep up any of Mons. de Lagaraye's establishments. As to me, Madame, I know not when I can enjoy the happiness of seeing you: I shall stay with Madame de Lagaraye as long as I can render myself useful to her; therefore, in all probability, I shall not return to Paris till the beginning of the Winter.

LETTER LVIII.

The Baroness to Madame d' Ostalis.

From St. ***

IT is determined, my dear child, that I shall stay here all the Winter; for what should I do at Paris in the situation in which I am. Could I go to public places, or even mix with company? Even supposing dissipation was not wholly disagreeable to me; yet prudence would oblige me to renounce any pleasures it might afford me. How can a woman venture to shew herself at an opera or a ball, when her husband or her son are exposed to all the dangers of war? Madame de Limours came frequently to see me:[77] but you know it must be a little Paris to please her, as she owns herself; therefore she never stays more than eight or ten days at a time with us.

The Count Anatolle died yesterday of a consumption, or rather of the excesses in which he has lived for these two years. He has left a rich and lovely widow, and, I think, not an inconsolable one. One thing pleasant enough is, that Constantia is jealous of the Countess Anatolle; for she has found out her attachment to Theodore. So she never mentions her name; and, if by chance she hears any body speak of him with admiration, she blushes and appears hurt. So young and already to feel such strong passions! ...

Mons. de Valcy has sold one of his finest estates ... We hear he is nearly ruined; – you would not know his wife; she is at this time as red-faced, as ugly, and old as she was young and pretty five years ago. She seems more sensible of this misfortune than she is of her husband's ruin. Adelaide grows every day more lovely; she is quite capable now of being my friend. – Her sense is equally as good as her temper. No conversation can be more agreeable to me than her's: our sentiments and opinions are exactly alike ... We often spend whole days *tête à tête*, and they pass away quicker than others. We know how to employ them. We are equally lively, with the same tastes, the same manner of thinking. Can we ever be tired of being together? Even if I did not love her so much, her freedom and extreme candour would make me always prefer her society to any other. She is not only incapable of falsehood, but exaggeration is also as much unknown to her as telling lyes. She is in every action of her life as sincere as is consistent with prudence and politeness. This charming quality gives inestimable value to whatever she does or says; we are sure that neither interest nor flattery will ever dictate the praises she bestows. Her attentions are obliging; the proofs of her friendship really affect the heart. We listen to her with earnestness, and are interested in what she says, because truth in its most pleasing form comes from her lips: her looks, her gaiety, her smiles are all natural and without art. Was she not handsome, had she not so much grace nor talents, yet she would please; she would engage your friendship; she would still possess that inexpressible charm which truth and candour bestow. We cannot have this precious virtue without possessing many others; we can never be perfectly sincere without being noble, equitable and generous. We do justice to our enemies; we acknowledge freely their good qualities: we reject praises which are not our due; and, in short, we can neither intrigue nor flatter; for to do either we must make use both of cunning and falsehood.

Adelaide is not yet eighteen years old, and has already corrected all the faults natural to her age and sex. Since the Veillée des quarante, she has never been tempted to make a joke of any one; particularly on account of those things which are so common and trifling as clothes and headdresses, &c. At the same time she takes a joke herself; even if it were severe, provided it did not affect her character, she would receive it with good-humour and sweetness. She despises that kind of malignity so much, that such a joke would neither confuse nor distress her. – She tells me all her observations, and confides to me her private opinions on the persons we see: but never, before a third person the least suspicious, will she permit herself to criticise the smallest matter. As she has an excellent understanding, she is absolutely exempt from that trifling curiosity which women in general are so justly reproached with, and which is only occasioned by idleness and envy. Adelaide thinks such trifles of no importance, and wonders how people can disturb themselves for such things or wish to know a secret which cannot interest them. When she lives in the world, she will be the last to hear the scandalous reports which are circulated of quarrels, agreements, &c. &c. She will be witness to many treacheries, without taking any part in them; and often, without attending to them. People ridicule her on this account, and will be always asking her, *from whence she comes that she knows nothing*? It is true, she will be ignorant of them; but she will know how to find out the characters and dispositions of the persons with whom she associates. Wickedness, indolence, and gossiping often betray the little intrigues of society; but sense and prudence only can give penetration. Adelaide will seldom be deceived by false friends, (for what good heart is not sometimes made a dupe;) but she will not bestow her confidence, unless to those who deserve it; which is an essential matter: for, if you cannot prevent being treated with ingratitude, prudence at least will keep you from being betrayed. Adelaide never forgot our little retreat in the Convent de *** and Mademoiselle de Celigny. She will never more judge of people by their appearance nor expressions: she is cured of this infatuation. No one ever carried this weakness so far as Madame de Limours did; when she was young, to be amiable in her eyes, it was sufficient to have a long face, light hair, and an aquiline nose. On the other hand, all the Brunetts, who were handsome, she called lovely, striking, and witty; and those who were plain were cross and good for nothing. However, as it is very possible to have black eyes and a mild disposition, or a pale complexion with a peevish temper, the Viscountess frequently found herself deceived in her opinions; an error which experience alone could discover. Madame de Berniere, a fair and interesting figure, became her intimate friend in the space of eight days; and they intirely broke with each other in three months, after having had a dozen quarrels in the time. To this friendship Madame de Semire succeeded, a Brunette full of wit and vivacity. But the Viscountess soon put an end to this attachment, inraged at the insupportable folly and impertinence of a person she had thought so droll and so clever. I could tell you twenty stories of her on similar occasions ... We saw her for six months inseparable from a woman whom she called *my love, my dear*, and *my child*; and the very next Winter they were quite strangers. This conduct did much harm to her character, and her castoff friends aspersed her without mercy, and betrayed all the little secrets she had consided to them during their intimacy. The extreme youth of the Viscountess, and the bad education she had received, could only plead her excuse; and she had too much sense not to endeavour to correct her error, when she grew older.

No, my dear child, Adelaide's affection for Hermine is not at all lessened. On the contrary, she is every day fonder of her. Hermine is now ten years old, and is really as pleasing in her temper as in her person. She has all the sincerity of her little Mamma; a virtue which she intirely owes to her, as she had naturally a disposition to falsehood. The poor little girl has been under great trouble to-day, she had a little white cat which she took great delight in. This morning the unfortunate Azolin fell out of a window into a paved court, and two hours after died on his mistress's lap. At this shocking sight, Hermine turned pale as death, and then burst into tears, throwing herself into Adelaide's arms, who did not receive her without emotion! ... This scene made me recollect a picture of de Greuze, which represents a little girl weeping for her Canary bird[78] ... The tears of Hermine on this accident, gave me I know not what kind of pleasing sensation ... These infantine troubles are agreeable to contemplate, because they prove the innocence and felicity of that age. These pure tears, which fall for the loss of a cat, convince us that the heart has never experienced any real grief. Happy age! ... Adelaide has this evening given Hermine a squirrel. Should any similar accident happen to it in two or three years, may it be wept for as sincerely as Azolin! Adelaide and I have waited till near mid-night merely to talk of Hermine. Adelaide, like a true mother, pleases herself with building Castles for her. She looks forward to the time when Hermine will be twenty years old; she wishes she was so now. But in that case, said I to her, you would be eight-and-twenty, and no longer in the prime of youth? ... But Hermine would be in all the charms of her's! ... This is a sentiment which not only consoles a good mother for the loss of her charms, but makes her even desirous of growing older, that she may see the happy days destined for her children. She cannot be under any concern on the decrease of her own beauty, when she sees her daughter's every day improve. Time only takes graces from the mother to add them to her child.

Adieu, my dear child; on Tuesday I shall send to your Banker's a little picture painted by Adelaide, which represents her giving a lesson to Hermine. I hope the painting will please you as well as the resemblances.

LETTER LIX.

Baroness to Madame de Valmont.

From St. ***.

HOW happy we are, Madame! ... How great will your felicity be, what joy will you feel! Ah, who is more sensible of it than myself? ... Our children are equally distinguished; they are well! ... We shall see them in three months ... I send you all the particulars, and not only the letter Mons. d' Almane has written to you, but that which I have received from him, as I imagine it will give you still more pleasure, and I have nothing I wish to conceal from you! ... When this precious packet was brought me by the Chevalier de Herbain, I was with Madame de Limours, Constantia, and my daughter. I trembled so much I could scarce open my letter or speak ... At length I found it was from Mons. d' Almane ... I opened it; and judge what I felt on reading these words: 'Glory and happiness, my dearest friend!' ... I could not utter a word, – I threw myself on my knees ... My dear Adelaide came and flung her arms about my neck; all my friends surrounded me; their joy added to my felicity ... Why were you not here, Madame? How delightful would it have been for me to embrace you at that moment! What would I not have given, had you been here, that we might have read our letters together! ... Poor little Constantia was much affected, and the name of Theodore escaped her lips! ... and she shed a torrent of tears! ... Nevertheless, when I read an account of the action, I observed that Adelaide's transport and emotions infinitely exceeded her cousin's. Great souls alone are capable of feeling sentiments of this kind! ... After Constantia had heard that Theodore had received no wounds, the rest of the account appeared to have very little effect on her.

Adieu, Madam; remember me, I intreat you, to Monsieurs d' Aimeri and Valmont. Ah! that you were but all here! ... Adelaide has written you a very good letter, which she has just shewn me; yet she has not expressed half the part she takes in your joy ...

LETTER LX.

The Viscountess to the Baroness.

LAST night I took Constantia for the first time to one of the dressed balls; we staid to the very fast, and guess what time it was before we were in bed; absolutely half past three in the morning. – The Assembly was magnificent; an immense croud and all the prettiest women in Paris were there; but they only appeared to shew their fine clothes; for they came at two, and went away again at three; that is, as soon as they had been viewed by the whole Assembly, and when their rouge began to run, and their hair to get out of order: they gaped, complained of heat, and retired. Oh! in our time, people had more real spirit; I cannot conceive any thing more absolutely dull or inanimate than the flirtations now a-days; for they really consist in nothing more than grimaces and inquiries about dress. – I supped the other night with one of these fashionable flirts; it was Madame de Blemur; she is ugly, but thinks herself clever and agreeable; she has a flow of words, with a constant giggle which she styles wit; she has a positive manner, and her conversation is as insipid as it is common; and, when she particularly wishes to shew herself off, one may discover it in a moment, for she tosses herself about the room, never sits still, walks with a careless air, and even jumps to admire herself in the looking-glass; and finds a thousand occasions to shew a pretty foot, and she laughs quite loud. – These now are all the artifices of a fashionable Coquette: they appear to me perfectly innocent, because it is impossible that they can ever injure any one. – Constantia was with me the evening I met her, and all the company were full of her praises; indeed I never saw her look so well. Madame de Blemur had not sense sufficient to know she ought to disguise her envy; she could not perceive that Constantia was pretty; at first she used all her arts to endeavour to eclipse her, and tried all those graces which I have described; but, when she perceived all her arts were in vain, and that the eyes of the company were still fixed on Constantia, she was absolutely so disconcerted, that she took no further pains to conceal her envy or ill-humour. How much does a foolish and ridiculous envy disgrace and humble one! ... I remember when I was young, there was nothing I so much dreaded as the fear of being thought to possess a jealous disposition; and I not only agreed in the praises of all the pretty women, but really found pleasure in talking of their beauty, in hopes of persuading those who heard me, that I was absolutely exempt from this contemptible vice. But to return to Madame de Blemur: what completed my aversion to her was, that, when the conversation turned that evening on Madame de – , she, in my opinion, abused her in a most shameful manner, and wanted to turn into ridicule her love for her husband; she gave us several proofs, which, however, had a very different effect from what she expected, as all the company admired the character, sense, and behaviour of Madame – . Madame de Blemur agreed that she was a person quite *perfect* – but pronounced that last word in a most satyrical manner, and then added, that Madame de – tired one to death in conversation, and that she was romantic to the greatest excess: I had a great inclination to answer, they cannot be very tiresome who possess a good understanding, great sweetness of disposition, and much information, and I had rather be styled romantic than ill-tempered: for I am certain, that, if Madame de – was to shew that affection to a lover, which she shews to her husband, Madame de Blemur would then think her engaging, and would be always praising her for her sensibility. People, void of principle, have always an aversion to those who are amiable, and wish to make even virtue itself appear ridiculous! a difficult task! and which can only serve to discover their own faults and depravity of heart.

I yesterday made a hundred visits with Constantia, and carried her among the number to Madame de — . She returned delighted with a Mademoiselle de — ; in truth it is impossible for any person to have been better educated, or to be more amiable. She is neither shy nor confused in any company, and yet has all that modesty which is so desirable at her age, and that deference, and even respect for married women, which is always engaging in so young a person. Her manner of expressing herself is always gentle, unaffected, and obliging; and her figure is as pleasing as it is ingenuous; and I know, that she possesses as much knowledge as she has wit and grace. – But how is it possible for a mother such as her's not to make her children absolutely delightful? Adieu, my dear friend; I shall come and see you either on Thursday or Friday. There is no allusion either to you or me in those shameful verses which you have heard of: and that is all I know about them, as I absolutely refused to see them. At all times one meets with people (otherwise amiable) who are curious to see such abominable productions, will learn them by heart, and repeat them in all companies; but surely to read and repeat such horrid stuff is making one's self a partaker with the wicked Author of the calumny! I can hardly conceive how any persons of real principle can suffer themselves to read a libel; still less that any one can so much despise all decency as to talk of them and quote passages from them in company.

LETTER LXI.

The Baroness to Madame d' Ostalis.

St. ***

I HAVE been very uneasy these two days past, my dear child. Miss Bridget has been dangerously ill with a sore throat. The day before yesterday she was blooded for the third time; and at night Adelaide came into my room with tears in her eyes, telling me that Miss Bridget was worse. I beg, Mamma, added Adelaide, you will permit me to sit up with her to-night, for it is of great consequence that she should take the medicine which the Physician has just ordered her every hour; and it is impossible to trust to the care of a nurse or a chamber-maid. Very well, interrupted I, I consent to your sitting up to night: to-morrow I shall watch in my turn. Adelaide went out of the room, and I remained alone with Madame de Limours. What, said she to me, do you permit Adelaide to sit up a whole night! ... At her age all young people go to balls at night; so ... but Miss Bridget has a fever ... Miss Bridget's disorder is not catching; besides, to save my daughter a little fatigue, and even a slight fever, I would not prevent her discharging a duty ... Yet what could she do more for you? I do not know; and I flatter myself she herself does not; but, the more gratitude and attachment I see in her to her Governess, the more I shall depend on her tenderness to me. According to this manner of thinking, I have reason to be satisfied; for Miss Bridget has received from Adelaide the most tender marks of affection. She would not suffer her to pass the whole night with her. – Adelaide, to satisfy her, pretended to leave her at three o'clock; but concealed herself behind her bed, that she might watch the attention of the nurse. She did not dose for a moment; she put out the medicine every hour, and gave it to the nurse, whom she was obliged to wake several times. When the Physician arrived at nine in the morning, Adelaide was still in Miss Bridget's chamber, and gave the most exact account of the night. The Physician assuring her then, that Miss Bridget was absolutely out of danger, she burst into tears, and her joy so greatly overcame her fatigue, that she would not consent to lie down, but passed the whole day in her chamber. She was tired at night, but her spirits were not exhausted, as her resolution had kept them up. She slept twelve hours last night, is extremely well to-day, and Miss Bridget is perfectly recovered.

There has been a little dialogue to-night between Adelaide and Constantia, and account of which I am sure will give you pleasure. The Viscountess was a little out of humour this morning, and after dinner found fault with Constantia rather unjustly. – I went into my own room as usual at five o'clock; Adelaide went to her studies in an adjoining room, and left her door open, so that I could hear her sing, speak, and play, as well as if we had been together. You know that no noise prevents me from writing, and that I composed all my Works by the sound of the harp and harpsichord; and interrupting myself every minute to say, *that is wrong, you play out of time*, &c. I seated myself at my desk, and my daughter took up her harp. In about half an hour after I was informed that Mademoiselle de P— was coming; that her coach was in the avenue. I told Adelaide, that I was obliged to go down and stay in the saloon till supper. Coming out of my chamber, I met Constantia, and told her the same; but a moment after I found it was a mistake, and that Mademoiselle de P— was not come. So I went up stairs again, and, as there was a carpet in my room, I went in without making the least noise. I had left a candle upon my desk, seated myself in my great chair, and took up my pen; and, hearing Adelaide and Constantia talking, I thought it would be amusing to write their conversation, which forms the following dialogue:

Constantia. ... One quarter of an hour only?

Adelaide. Ah, my dear! I would converse with you with all my heart, if Mamma knew it; but she thinks I am busy at this time, and the thought of that would give me pain; it looks as if I deceived her ...

Constantia. At your age my aunt does not require you to study without some relaxation ...

Adelaide. She knows how much I love to be employed. I should have ill profited by her cares and her example, if putting aside my work would be any pleasure to me; but I repeat it to you, that the reason I had rather talk to you another time is, because I told my Mamma, when she went down stairs, that I should work hard.

Constantia. Well then, I must go ... but it is very cruel however ...

Adelaide. Constantia? ...

Constantia. What? ...

Adelaide. If you are angry, stay then ...

Constantia. You certainly do not love me ...

Adelaide. Do you think so? ...

Constantia. But ...

Adelaide. Come, let us talk then ...

Constantia. If you knew how unhappy I am to-day! ...

Adelaide. How so? ...

Constantia. You saw in what a manner Mamma treated me this afternoon ... We may speak before Hermine, she will not tell what we say.

Hermine. Oh! I read so attentively, I shall not even hear it.

Constantia. When Mamma returned to her chamber, I followed her. I wished to speak to her; but she received me with such severity, notwithstanding I was not in fault, as you was witness to.

Adelaide. Not in fault, my dear Constantia! do you consider what you say? ... You accuse your mother of injustice.

Constantia. I have not complained to any body else, but may I not to you?

Adelaide. No, for, if such an idea should enter into your imagination, you ought to reject it, and think you have deceived yourself. Would you tell my aunt you was not in fault? No, surely, on the contrary, you appeared to think she was in the right; the complaints which you have since made takes from you all the merit of the mildness you shewed her, and looked like hypocrisy. Besides, supposing it true that my aunt was for a moment out of humour, who will excuse it, and seek to conceal her little foibles, if you do not? This is the only proof of gratitude you can shew her. Have you a right to expect that she is perfect? Pardon my freedom, my dear Cousin; it gives me great pain to afflict you, but I love you too much to conceal the truth.

Constantia (weeping.) Yet I flatter myself you do not doubt my affection for my Mamma.

Adelaide. It is because I know the extreme goodness of your heart, that I speak to you with so much sincerity.

Constantia (still weeping.) I know you are in the right.

Adelaide. Amiable candour! embrace me, my charming friend.

Constantia. My dear Cousin, I wish I could resemble you!

Adelaide. You have nothing to wish for; you have every good quality; but, as I am older than you, it is not surprising that I should have a little more reflection.

Constantia. I am in despair; you have just made me sensible that my fault is inexcusable ...

Adelaide. Well, my dear Constantia, repair it; it is in your power.

Constantia. How?

At this part of the conversation I got up softly, and went to find the Viscountess. I did not tell her the whole of what I had just heard; but informed her that Constantia was in despair for having displeased her; and desired her to conceal my having heard the conversation. While we were talking, the door opened, and Constantia came in with her eyes much inflamed. Perceiving me, she was a little confused; I told her that Mademoiselle de P— was not come; and I suffered her to believe I had been all this time with the Viscountess. After a moment's reflection Constantia approached her mother in tears; the Viscountess embraced her; and Constantia, throwing herself upon her knees, frankly owned she had been complaining of her, and that Adelaide had made her sensible how much she was in fault. At these words the Viscountess, much softened, raised her up and praised her for her sincerity. Alas, Mamma! said Constantia, I have not had the merit of doing it of my own accord: it is Adelaide who advised me to make this confession! At this last proof of her sincerity the Viscountess and I both embraced her, and found it impossible to refrain from tears; for who could avoid being affected by such proofs of ingenuous frankness? I praised this action with enthusiasm, for indeed it was charming; but the Viscountess insisted that I should not have been so much affected by it, if it had not made Adelaide appear so amiable. Apropos of this little incident, the Viscountess is very desirous I should acknowledge what are Adelaide's secret faults. I must own, says she, I do not know myself that she has any; but I should think she must have one at least, however trifling it may be ... That would be my fault, since we are convinced that there are no imperfections, nor even vices, that education cannot destroy ... Then you really do not know one single fault she has ... But first we must understand each other; explain to me what is the having a fault? ... It is an inclination, more or less dangerous, which constantly governs us ... Which constantly governs us? What a terrible definition! ... I believe it just ... And I also, which is the reason that I have always thought it impossible to be perfectly happy, if we have a single defect. – And you think that education is able to extirpate them all? – If it corrects one, why can it not correct more? ... Oh, because it is not possible for us to be perfect. – Perfect! no, certainly; but consider it is a very different thing to commit a fault, and to have a fault. I protest to you that Adelaide has not one single defect; that is to say, one bad custom that has taken root, or rather, as you say, no dangerous inclination which constantly predominates; yet she is not perfect, since no mortal can be so. She is very gentle; yet it is possible certain circumstances may make her shew a little impatience and even anger; she may be deceived; she may be unjust for a moment, or out of humour. But, since she has no habitual faults, her errors will appear very rarely, and be very trifling, and can never hurt her reputation, or make her unhappy. – Then you think, if I had been better educated, I should have had a milder disposition ... I have no doubt of it ... In that case, replied the Viscountess, it is an excellent thing to be well instructed. – Adieu, my dear child; you often ask me for particulars and whole conversations. I hope you will be contented with this letter; but I should not be satisfied myself with it, if I had not written at the same time these long pages to Seraphina, merely to talk about you. – Embrace her for me, as well as her sister, to whom I shall write on Thursday.

I have opened my letter again to tell you news, of which Mademoiselle de P— had undertaken to acquaint the Viscountess. Mons. de Valcy has just quitted the army, and is totally ruined; of all his great fortune he has nothing remaining but an annuity of fifty thousand livres![79] Mademoiselle de Valcy has consumed all her fortune, for her debts far exceed the portion she received. Her husband went away last night; it is said he means to travel for two or three years. Madame de Valcy remains here without assistance, without advice, without resource, abandoned by all her friends, and even by Mons. de Remicourt. She is very ill and keeps her bed; at this moment the Viscountess sees only her misfortunes; she forgets the causes of them, and has just left us to fly to her assistance.

LETTER LXII.

The Baron to Mons. d' Aimeri.

I SHALL most certainly, Sir, be at Paris the beginning of April. I bring back our two children still more deserving of our affection, and of the happiness that awaits them. Could they have acted otherwise? They are Frenchmen! They have shewn as much knowledge and alertness as courage. In giving them due praise, we cannot say they have distinguished themselves; for, amongst such a number of young Frenchmen as are here, no one can distinguish himself by courage only.

I hope, Sir, to find you at Paris as well as Mons. and Madame de Valmont. I keep in reserve for our amiable Charles all the pleasure of surprising him. I think he entertains great hopes; he sees I love him as a son; but I please myself sometimes with perplexing him, at least I keep him in suspence.

Yes, we are about to form that union so much wished for, that union, the object of both our vows! Drive away then from you those dark thoughts which possess you. Forget, if possible, those melancholy reflections which have imbittered your life. Dare to think yourself worthy of happiness; you have acquired that right. Adieu! Sir; I beseech you to engage Mons. and Madame de Valmont to keep the secret, till Madame d' Almane has communicated it to the Viscount and Viscountess de Limours.

LETTER LXIII.

The Baroness to Madame d' Ostalis.

IMAGINE my happiness, my dear child; they are coming! ... We shall see them in two days! ... To-morrow we set out, and are in hopes we shall meet them thirty or forty leagues from Paris ... Oh, what could add to my felicity, if you were but here? You cannot conceive all that passes in my heart; no, though you know it so well, you cannot guess at it! ... I only returned from St. *** this morning. The Courier sent by Monsieur d' Almane came through Paris, and told me Madame de Valmont was just arrived and waited for me at my house. This intelligence I concealed from my daughter. I sent for horses, and we set out immediately. Adelaide had no suspicion of the event which was to fix her fortune ... When we alighted from the coach, we saw Madame de Valmont on the steps; Adelaide flew to embrace her and express her joy. As to myself, I was so much moved and softened to find myself in Madame de Valmont's arms, that I cannot describe to you what I felt ... We all three wept, without being able to say a word. However, as soon as we entered my apartment, I took Adelaide by the hand, and said to her, embrace Madame de Valmont again; embrace her, my dear Adelaide with the tenderness of a daughter, for soon you will become her's ... At these words Adelaide blushed and trembled; a flood of tears bathed her cheeks. For the first moment she saw only her mother ... She was struck with the ideas of fear and grief, considering that I was to be no longer arbitress of her fate ... We each took her in our arms. Adelaide leaned on my neck; she could only answer by sobs and sighs; she was indifferent to the caresses of Madame de Valmont. It appeared she wanted to let me see she could love no-body but me ... At length Madame de Valmont left us; and, when we were alone, she opened her heart to me without disguise: she confessed that she preferred this match to any other; and the more so, as she was sure the Chevalier de Valmont would never separate her from me. But she added, that she thought the Chevalier was too young, and she wished he was a few years older. I satisfied her on this matter by saying I perfectly knew his disposition, and that, when one has received a good education, twenty-four is old enough to avoid being corrupted. Monsieur and Madame de Valmont and Mons. d' Aimeri supped with us this evening; Adelaide, though for the whole time rather serious, behaved charmingly. I have had to-day a very high quarrel with the Viscountess. It was necessary to tell her, that Adelaide would be married in six weeks. This news, which was not confided to her, could not fail of exciting her anger. She told me, I put no confidence in her. I was obliged to reproach her with indiscretion. – Friendship, said I to her, does not require me to expose the peace and happiness of my daughter, in trusting you with a secret which I knew you could not keep. Did you not give me your promise, to conceal from Constantia your design of marrying her to Theodore? Did you keep it? ... At these words the Viscountess, having nothing to answer, rose up in a furious passion, which actually terrified me – I would have stopped her; but she went away instantly, declaring she would never see me again, as long as she lived. About an hour after I went to her house, where I found her alone with her daughter, who was in a dreadful situation, for she thought we had intirely broke with each other: and her mother at that moment, being governed by her passion and resentment, was more irritated than affected by her sorrow and tears. As soon as I appeared, she sent her away, and, coming up to me with determined rage, asked me *what I wanted*? I was so much affected with seeing her in such a situation, that I trembled as if I had been the guilty person. I am come, said I, to endeavour to restore the tranquillity which you have not only lost yourself, but have deprived me of. It is very true, that I have concealed from you the most important secret of my life. It is not my fault; – it is your's ... I could not depend on your discretion; but I never doubted your justice or your friendship ... As I finished these words, the Viscountess, bathed in tears, threw herself into my arms with that charming frankness, which accompanies all her actions ... I received this embrace as a pardon; it restored me to happiness, which I could not enjoy without her friendship. Our hearts were made for each other; – how then does it happen they are formed so unlike?

The Countess Anatolle, prettier than ever, came to see me this afternoon. She talked to me for an hour of Mons. d' Almane's return, and asked me a thousand questions about Theodore. Poor Madame de Valcy is dying of a consumption, and can scarcely live three months. Adieu, my dear child; it is two o'clock in the morning, and I must rise tomorrow before seven. Adieu; though the post does not go till Tuesday, I shall write every day: you may depend on a particular and exact Journal, since I have no other means of informing you of my sentiments and ideas.

LETTER LXIV.

The Baroness to Madame d' Ostalis.

Tuesday.

O! my daughter, they are here! ... I have seen and embraced them! ... They are here; and neither grief nor joy has been fatal. Scarce was I out of bed this morning, when I heard a carriage in the Court: thinking it mine, I finished dressing, when my door suddenly flew open, and I saw Mons. d' Almane and Theodore ... At the same instant, Adelaide, amazed, ran in and threw herself into her father's arms. What a scene! ... what happiness! after a year's absence, after having felt so many fears and anxieties! you, my daughter, who know my heart; you alone are capable of judging of the extent of my felicity! ... The meeting of Adelaide and the Chevalier de Valmont was at noon! He is so affected, so transported with his good fortune, that he is deprived of speech. He can only gaze on Adelaide, embrace his mother, and kiss my hands. Adelaide blushes more than usual, and redoubles her tenderness to me. Her eyes frequently are filled with tears, when she looks at me; but she does not avoid the Chevalier, nor even omit any opportunity of shewing her attention to him, or saying an obliging thing. Theodore takes a lively share in his friend's happiness; to-morrow evening he will be acquainted with his own; for Mons. d' Almane has sent an express to the Viscount who has been absent a week, and they only wait for his return to declare the marriage of Constantia and Theodore. You cannot form an idea of the affectionate joy of Mons. d' Aimeri, yet the indelible remembrance of the hapless Cecilia troubles him in the midst of his transports! Have I deserved so much happiness! said he to me this evening, I always dread losing it ... He pronounced these words in a voice that penetrated me: one single subject of remorse suffices to taint the purest felicity ... To enjoy true happiness, one must have merited it. God bless you, my dear child! I will continue this letter to-morrow, as it cannot go till Thursday.

Wednesday Night.

I HAVE this moment received your letter, in which you acquaint me of the Chevalier de Murville's death. I would not have Mons. d' Aimeri hear it, till the weddings are over: for in his present frame of mind I am sure he would be extremely affected. I have mentioned it to no one but Madame de Valmont, who agrees with me in the necessity of concealing it at present from her father; and we have taken all proper precautions, in case any parcel should arrive from ***, that this melancholy restitution may not be delivered to her in his presence.

The Viscountess is all in raptures; the Viscount is arrived, and it is agreed, that Constantia, Theodore, Adelaide, and Charles are to be married the same day. What a day for me! ... We are in hourly expectation of the Court de Roseville; his last letter was dated from ***. The return of so beloved and deserving a brother will complete Madame de Limours's bliss ... Mine, alas! will not be perfect, you will not be present! ... And what a space divides us! ... You will not read for a month all these particulars you so impatiently expect! ...

The Countess Anatolle came to see me to-day; I acquainted her with my son's marriage. She blushed, turned pale, and cast down her eyes. I took no notice of her concern, and changed the discourse. In a few minutes she told me she should leave Paris to-morrow for two months, and presently after went away. I own myself deeply interested for her. What mother does not in her heart pardon a weakness, of which her son is the cause.

I am writing to you, my dear daughter, surrounded by taylors, mantua-makers, milliners; no less than ten persons are in my room, and my bureau is covered with rich stuffs, flowers, gauzes, and lace. Adelaide will chuse nothing, and depends on my taste. This is trusting to me a business which I shall be very attentive to; it is the adorning and beautifying of Adelaide. No Coquette can be more taken up with ornamenting her own person than I am with studying what will best suit her's. During this time she attends to her books, her learning, and her musick, just as usual. Hermine did not know till to-day, that her Mamma was going to be married. She shewed the greatest astonishment; and, looking at Adelaide with tears in her eyes, said, Mamma, shall I still be your child? ... These words made Adelaide weep also; and, taking Hermine in her arms, she assured her, with a thousand embraces, that she should always love her dearly. This restored the little one's spirits; and she told me, she was very glad I had chosen the Chevalier de Valmont, because he was almost as amiable as her little Mamma.

What they informed you concerning Madame de Gerville was then true, but is now no longer so. She has given up devotion, and with it the character she had attained; and all for the sake of a young man just coming into the world, and whom she has undertaken to fashion and introduce. She only needed this kind of error, so scandalous in a woman of her age, to render her as ridiculous as she is despicable.

Madame de Valcy continues in the same state: it is said to be disappointment alone which kills her. The Viscountess's behaviour to her ought to augment her remorse, if she is really capable of any emotions of gratitude and repentance.

Thursday.

T HE Count de Roseville comes to-night; so we shall certainly sign the articles next Monday ... Oh what a day! ... I am really not myself ... I am continually moved, ever ready to shed tears. I neither sleep nor eat; I cannot speak; my looks are wild and stupid; I have but one thought, – but one idea.

I forgot to mention Madame d' Olcy; she behaves perfectly well on this occasion. Her vanity is flattered by her nephew's nuptials; she is at present the tenderest and best of sisters. She insisted on Madame de Valmont's lodging with her; she never leaves her, and she is always here; which inrages the Viscountess, who cannot abide her. Adieu, my dear daughter; were you but here, what happiness could equal mine!

LETTER LXV.

The Count de Roseville to the Prince.

AH! Sir, what an expression has escaped you! You praise, it is true, the moderation of the Prince your father; that virtuous principle which leads him to prefer peace to almost certain conquests: you add, however, 'that a war, though unjust, would have given you an opportunity of signalising yourself.' Is this your reason for discontent? – The much esteemed Author of the Institutions of a Prince, Abbe Duguet,[80] exclaims, 'Unhappy is the Prince who engages in an unjust war; he is the murderer of all the victims to his ambition or his other passions: he plunges the poniard into the heart of his subjects, and is the executioner of all those who perish in the enemy's army. All the carnage on both sides will be set to his account: the blood of both parties, that is shed, will be required of him. He will be found, in the sight of God, guilty of all the horrid consequences of war, of all the conflagrations and rapine committed both by his own troops and by those of the enemy: of the ravages and devastations, which the most active and humane Generals cannot prevent. All this dreadful heap of crimes and of wickedness will fall on his head,'[81] &c.

What a frightful and terrible picture of the shocking mischiefs ambition produces! – Does it not deeply affect you, Sir? To acquire merely fame, you need not be uniformly virtuous: even then, however, courage and ambition will fail you, unless attended by good fortune: it is only in prosperity that injustice can dazzle for a moment the eyes of the vulgar. Brilliant successes alone gain a vein of temporary triumph. Should Fortune abandon you, hatred, contempt and infamy follow of course. But a reputation founded on true glory is not subject to chance nor the caprices of Fortune. Be just, be merciful, and you will appear as great in adversity as in the most established state of happiness.

Your Highness will allow me to make some remarks on this question: 'Whether a Prince should suffer himself to read anonymous satyrical Works against himself, or his Ministers, his people in office, and those nearest his person?' Your Highness seems willing to think, that such writings may discover to a Prince his own faults and the true character and conduct of those about him. I agree with you, Sir, that useful truths may sometimes be extracted from such contemptible productions: those, however, which concern yourself, would disgust without improving you: for blame, dictated by malice, vexes, without amending us. If by chance, in a work of this sort, amongst the various accusations of your Ministers and people in office, there should be one found in justice, how are you to sift it out of the confused heap of impositions and calumnies? Is a Prince to seek truth in a libel? Is he to expect it from a coward or a villain?

Will you Sir, who detest and will not listen to a slanderer, read a libel without seruple? Will you not give up a blameable curiosity to the gratitude you owe to your Minister, or your people in place, who serve you with zeal and attachment? What! whilst they are dedicating their time to you, and labouring for your glory, and whilst your approbation is in their opinion the sweetest reward, will you in private read an infamous writing in which hatred and calumny seek to blacken and dishonour them? Ah! shudder, Sir! If you are not ashamed of being ungrateful, fear at least becoming unjust! If it should be in the power of imposture to deceive, lead astray, and deliver you up to fatal prejudices, ought you to expose yourself to this frightful danger? No man, scrupulously honest, will ever read a libel: a Sovereign should, if possible, be more delicate in this respect, and should look upon the man, who dares to quote a part of such a work, as a slanderer. I have heard of a great Prince, who, willing to give means to his subjects of informing him of the truth, placed in one of his closets a box which had an opening into the street, into which any one might throw a paper, and the Prince alone kept the key. This institution might be of great use, if the Prince should declare, that he would burn, without reading, all anonymous papers. If you, Sir, should ever be tempted to hold this kind of correspondence with an infinite number of people who have no other way of approaching, and writing to you let me advise you to insist particularly on the name and direction of each, and to impose it to yourself, as a fixed rule, to read none, till you are sure that the names and directions are not fictitious. Finally, Sir, without having recourse to this method, you may always discover the truth, if you encourage it, and have faithful friends. I learn with pleasure, that the Baron de Sulback becomes daily a great favourite with you. You are sensible of his integrity and knowledge. Consult him always. But I must repeat, Sir, that in affairs of real consequence, you should take the advice of more than one, and follow none rashly. I cannot but observe, notwithstanding my great partiality for the Baron de Sulback, that he is yet much too young to be your only confidant. He is well informed, rational, and virtuous; but he is only four and twenty: at that age, and at Court, one may easily degenerate and become corrupt. It will be soon perceived, should his principles be changed: he will grow more supple, more obsequious, and have less sincerity. The fear of your displeasure, of making himself enemies, or even more trifling considerations, will prevent him from telling you freely the truth. You will see him insensibly lose his disinterestedness and his moderation. He will value your favour more than your esteem. He will endeavour to form a party in his interest: he will be busied solely in making his own fortune, in removing his enemies from about your person, and in supplying their places with his own creatures. He will fear all persons of a truly distinguished merit, and will do his utmost to prejudice you against them. Attend to him strictly, and you will easily discover these arts; and, should there be such, you surely will not suffer yourself to be a dupe to him.

I will not repeat to your Highness, how happy your bounties and your remembrance make me. You know my heart: and that your success, your honour and friendship, constitute the chief comforts of my life. I must intreat you not to forget your promise to me of reading frequently Telemachus and the Thoughts of Marcus Aurelius.[82]

LETTER LXVI.

The Baroness to Madame d' Ostalis.

O, MY daughter, what an event! ... This unfortunate Mons. d' Aimeri ... Yet I believe his disease is not mortal: the Physicians give hopes; but he has such fatal forebodings, he sustained so cruel a shock! ... Yesterday, Monday, the day fixed for signing the articles, we all assembled at the Viscountess's: Monsieur d' Aimeri had a slight attack of the gout on Sunday. We had not finished our business above a quarter of an hour, when a servant whispered Madame de Valmont, that a person desired to speak to her on an affair of great importance. She turned pale, and desired the man might be conducted into the Viscountess's closet. She then rose, and communicated her suspicions to me. I recommended shutting herself up in the closet, and she went out directly. Monsieur d' Aimeri, having observed her trouble and agitation, was questioning me anxiously, when all at once we were alarmed by the sound of an unknown voice, crying aloud, Help, help. I attempted in vain to detain Monsieur d' Aimeri; he burst from me; the Viscountess, Mons. de Valmont, and myself followed him; we met a man in deep mourning, who told us, that Madame de Valmont had fallen down in dreadful convulsions ... Monsieur d' Aimeri quickened his pace; we entered the closet; I got before him, saying, For Heaven's sake go; in the name of Friendship, I intreat you to absent yourself for a moment ... I would have forced him, but he pushed me away, and advancing, saw Madame de Valmont in a fit by a table, on which stood a box half open ... He flew towards his daughter, caught her in his arms; he raised her up. At that moment a parcel slipped from under her gown to the ground ... He made a false step, he staggered, recovered himself as he was falling; cast his eyes on the floor ... Heavens! what an object struck him! the wretched man trod under his feet the hair of the unfortunate Cecilia. ... He could not avoid knowing this dear and sacred relic ... Madame de Valmont's situation, the box, the stranger, all confirmed it ... He shuddered, turned pale, and trembled; he seemed to receive a mortal wound! ... I drew near, and hid from his eyes the melancholy object which had just renewed all his remorse. Mons. d' Almane advanced at the same time, took him in his arms, and carried him into the next room. They were scarcely gone, before madame de Valmont recovered her senses. There were then in the closet only the Viscountess, Mons. de Valmont, the stranger, and myself. What I have been relating, all past within three minutes. I had the precaution, on leaving the saloon, to forbid our children following us, and they remained with Madame d' Olcy, the Ladies de S***, and all the company whom we had invited on this occasion. In the mean time Madame de Valmont sighed, revived, and some tears dropped from her half closed eyes! ... O, my sister! exclaimed she. Pronouncing these words, she raised herself gently; opened her eyes; saw the stranger; started; recovered her recollection; turning, she perceived me, and extended her arms towards me with transport: Oh! cried she, do you know? ... My son! ... the Chevalier de Murville? Yes, Madame, interrupted the stranger, addressing himself to me, I was commissioned to present that box to this Lady, and to request her to open it immediately, as it contains Monsieur Murville's will, by which he appoints the Chevalier de Valmont heir to all his fortune; that is to say, to seventy thousand French livres a year.[83] As the stranger concluded his speech, Madame de Valmont and the Viscountess embraced me, with the most affecting expressions which the tenderest friendship could inspire. Mons. de Valmont, who had hitherto appeared a more surprised than concerned spectator of what had passed, now took a true share in our joy. He wanted to run into the saloon, and to inform his son and all the company of this good news: but we convinced him, that it was necessary first to acquaint Mons. d' Aimeri. The Gentleman in mourning (whose name is Arnal, an old friend of the Chevalier de Murville) told us, that the will was in the hands of Monsieur *** a lawyer; and, after giving us all necessary information, he took his leave with a promise of seeing us again at seven the next morning. – We told Madame de Valmont the situation of Mons. d' Aimeri: she went directly to him with the copy of the will. He shewed much sensibility on the occasion, but persevered in his deep and heavy sorrow. The Chevalier received this news in a manner the most delightful to Adelaide and to me, testifying all the delicacy of the tenderest and most passionate lover. He is truly inamoured, and for life. Theodore is violently in love with Constantia; but the Chevalier's passion is as fervent and far more profound. Mons. d' Aimeri did not sit down to supper and went to-bed at ten o'clock. He encouraged us in regard to his health, and complained only of a little lassitude, Adelaide came into my room this morning, before I was up, in a visible agitation: she sat down on my bed-side, and I looked on her with an air of anxiety. What ails you, my child, said I, you seem to me to have been weeping? ... Mamma, I have a confession to make to you, which hurts me a little ... Hurts you! ... O how you surprize me! ... Condescend to hear me. Yesterday in my first agitation I wrote a letter before I went to-bed, which I intended sending this morning unknown to you, lest you should disapprove it; although my tenderness for you was my only motive for writing it: but I have recollected, that we must not swerve from our duty, even to do a good action ... I owe you an unlimited confidence; no motive can justify my concealing any important step from you: therefore I come to acknowledge that I have written to the Chevalier de Valmont ... and here, Mamma, is my letter. I embraced Adelaide, and, taking the letter she offered, I read the following words: 'My heart is rent by a cruel uneasiness which I cannot help imparting to you, since one word from you will dispel it intirely. Mons. de Murville's will makes a change in your situation, which alarms me. An inheritor of so large an estate, do you not form new schemes ... Will You be always satisfied with this plain and contracted apartment? ... which was even yesterday so charming in your eyes! ... Remember, Sir, that my mother, when she made choice of you, had a right to expect never to be parted from her daughter; with regard to me she deigned to consult, do you not think that so pleasing an expectation contributed to my ready compliance? ... You owe the preference, with which you have inspired me, to the regard my parents have for you, and to the attachment which I believe you have for them; in short, to my persuasion that you would be perfectly happy in the midst of my family. Alas, is it possible you should be capable of sacrificing such solid and gentle happiness for the vain desire of possessing a fine house and of displaying your magnificence? Can the most frivolous vanity make you forget the sacred rights of friendship and grati-tude? Yes, gratitude; you own it to my mother who loves you. She and my father adopted you in their hearts, even before your conduct justified their choice; and could you have the inhumanity to rob them of their daughter? Could you despise this habitation which has been destined for you these eight years; this habita-tion, which my mother planned herself, and which she pleased herself in decorating with so much care and delight? Could it be true, that you harbour so cruel an intent? Do not conceal it from me, it is not yet too late! ... It is still my duty to prefer my mother to you; and I declare that I do not hesitate. Thinking otherwise should I be worthy of the sentiments you profess for me? What could you expect from my heart, could I now be so ungrateful as to waver between my mother and you? What should I be at present but for the sacrifices she made for me, and for the attention and care which she has bestowed on me? What would become of me, was I deprived of her example and advice? ... I am indebted to her for all that can insure the happiness of my life. I owe to her a grateful heart, a love for virtue, those talents which please you, and the sentiments with which I have inspired you. O, if you really love me, how very dear should she be to you! ... Promise me you will never part us ... Since my mother has chosen you, you must be virtuous and benevolent ... To what worthy and satisfactory purposes may you not dedicate these unexpected riches which Heaven has granted you! O, consult only your own heart and understanding, and you will use them as I wish. Once more I repeat to you, Sir, that a single word will re-assure me; a promise

will annihilate all my fears, and dispel all my uneasiness.'
                              ADELAIDE.

You will easily conceive, my dear, how sensibly I have been affected by this
letter. Adelaide, seeing my tears flow, threw herself into my arms. O my child,
said I, how happy have you made me! ... not only by giving me so affecting a
proof of your tenderness, but by convincing me how very dear your principles are
to you, since you did not think you could send such a letter without my consent.
Persevere always in this manner of thinking, and never forget that a woman may
have good qualities, but never can be virtuous unless her principles are unshaken.
– But never will you permit me to send this letter? ... Recollect, my dear, that
(in the general opinion) you require from the Chevalier de Valmont a very great
self-denial. To content himself with an apartment at his father-in-law's; to promise to reside there always; to have no house; no kitchen of his own; not to have
it in his power to give a supper; is too much to ask of the owner of an estate of
100,000 livres a year ... He will be so much the richer, and may indulge far more
rational tastes. So far from your society's being new to him, he has no connexions
nor friends but your's ... Nevertheless no other young man of his age, with such a
fortune, would consent to what you demand; therefore you ought not to expect
it ... If he has only a common way of thinking, I shall not regret him ... You are
then resolved not to marry him, unless he promises what you require? ... Yes,
Mamma, if you will condescend to allow me to decide ... But, if Mons. de Retel
had had a more pleasing person, you would have married him, and yet he would
not have lived with me ... You, Mamma, have taught me, that our pleasures must
yield to reason and justice. Mons. de Retel had no obligations to you; I could not
expect a favour from him which I have a right to demand of the Chevalier ... The
latter is certainly incapable of deceiving you, and should he refuse! ... He will not
deserve me, should he only hesitate ... Have you considered the ill effects of such
a rupture, after the articles are signed, and even after an engagement still more
binding, the preference you have avowed? ... I feel all the force of that engagement; and that it binds me never to marry any other; but, if he obliges me to
give him up, I shall be wholly your's; my life will be devoted to you ... O do not
doubt it; I desire no better lot! ... Adelaide could not refrain from tears, as she
uttered these words. I strove again to persuade and divert her from her design;
but she interrpted me, and besought me so earnestly to permit her to send the
letter, that I could not resist her intreaties. – It was not without some inquietude
that she waited for the answer. At length 10 o'clock struck, and they brought
her a letter, which she received with a trembling hand ... She gave it to me, and I
opened a note which contained the following words: 'Who! me! I separate you
from so beloved a mother and so worthy of your affection! O Madame, since she
condescended to chuse me, ought not you to esteem me at least! ... You, who are

unacquainted with love, cannot conceive the extent of its dominion! ... But who is more sensible of the sacred rights of gratitude and of friendship? ... It is at the feet of Madame d' Almane. (Alas! I have not as yet a right to prostrate myself at your's.) It is at the feet of the best of mothers that I will renew an oath so dear to my heart and which I hope, will restore my happiness, which your unjust suspicions have disturbed, by dispelling all your fears.'

Adelaide did not conceal from me the joy this note gave her. We went down together to Mons. d' Almane, and shewed him the Chevalier's answer. At this first moment Adelaide shewed a sensibility which she had never before discovered; and Theodore left us abruptly in the midst of our conversation, saying he would go seek his friend, and assure him that Adelaide was no longer unjust. Adelaide ran after her brother to prevent his going out; but I believe she did not employ all her strength to stop him. Theodore returned in an hour, and told us that Mons. d' Aimeri suffered prodigiously with the gout, and that he had also a fever. Mons. d' Almane and I went directly to see him. His Physician and Surgeon did not seem to think him in a very dangerous way; but he is so violently affected with what happened yesterday; he is so struck with the idea that Heaven denies him the consolation of seeing his grandson married before his death; that he believes his illness mortal. He confessed and received all the Sacraments at noon. The Chevalier de Valmont is absolutely in despair. He is tenderly attached to his grandfather; and it will delay (supposing the belt) his marriage and Theodore's at least three weeks; – my son, you may believe, shares his sorrow. Mons. d' Almane and Theodore have been all the evening with Mons. d' Aimeri. Adelaide and I supped alone; the pleasure of talking together kept us up till midnight. I can, said she, at present have no doubt of the sincerity of the Chevalier's affection; but will these sentiments last for ever? – You are not speaking of love I suppose, you know that is a passion which can never last – His love will be over perhaps in a year; it certainly will not continue three. But, if you behave well, he will never feel a passion for any other, and you will be the object of his tenderest affection. If you know how to inspire this unalterable attachment, you will enjoy all the felicity this world can afford. You will obtain the only influence you ought to desire, the influence which we acquire by our conduct and virtue; you will never feel that you have a master; the sacred title of mother will not be a vain one to you; you will be consulted in the establishment of your children; you will preside over their education, and you alone will marry your daughters; you will become the friend and confidant of your husband; you will preserve him from the errors of youth; you will strengthen his principles, and increase his love for virtue; you will have part in all the respect he merits; for you can only share his glory and his success by obtaining his affection and making him happy. You will be ranked highly in the most distinguished societies; in short, your talents, your understanding and beauty, will add to the lustre of the example of your virtue, and render it more alluring. But virtue alone will not suffice for the attainment of such felicity; reason and prudence must direct and regulate all your actions, and you must form to yourself a fixed plan of conduct. For example, you should from this minute consider of a manner of behaviour to your husband from the first. Shew him only those sentiments which will always last. If you should be too fond at first, you will hereafter appear cool. By shewing much love, you will increase for a time that which you inspire. For some months you will be more ardently beloved; but it will be in a less solid and durable manner. Love is not a sentiment made for you, yet your heart is so tender, that you should perpetually strive to moderate your extreme sensibility; and if it should be sometimes too lively, know at least how to dissemble the excess of it. To pretend to sentiments which we do not feel is falsehood; not to disclose all we feel is prudence. Express only confidence and friendship; but be sure never to exact the cares and attentions of a lover; receive them with politeness and pleasure, but at the same time never expect them; and appear more affected by a mark of esteem, than by a proof of love. Finally, convince your husband that his presence is at all times most agreeable to you. The surest and only means of keeping him near you is to receive him always with equal pleasure. This is a duty, replied Adelaide, I shall certainly find no difficulty in fulfilling. Besides, the care of my own reputation would of itself be a sufficient inducement. Calumny can never fix her invenomed tooth in a woman who, so far from flying or avoiding her husband, wishes to have him a witness to all her actions, and the presence of the least amiable husband cannot be a restriction, provided she is totally exempt from coquetry. You are in the right, answered I, but few people have elevation and sense enough to think as you do. A young woman, who has never thought in her life, desires only two things in marrying: to attract attention and to go by herself, that is, without her husband or mother-in-law; and the former is generally reckoned the most offensive and tiresome of *Chaperons*. If by chance a husband takes it into his head to be fond of his wife, and chuses to sup frequently with her; she never fails complaining in secret of such tyranny. The bosom of friendship receives her groans; the friends declaim against the insupportable man, who is presently described as a jealous tyrant and a monster. All the young men speak of him with derision, and turn him into ridicule. Every one is in league against him; they all wish to be able to banish him from society; and the whole world deplores the hapless lot of his victim. It is true, that this woman, so interesting in the eyes of such a number of simpletons, loses at once her peace of mind, her happiness, her reputation, and the esteem of all sensible persons. – Nevertheless, Mamma, returned Adelaide, the jealousy of their husbands is a real torment to many virtuous women. – True, my dear; neither do I speak but in general; I always admit exceptions in every thing; but in this particular, which allows of none, namely, that a virtuous woman should never betray any suspicion of the jealousy of her husband; and, if she avoids every temptation that could give it birth, if she conceals it carefully, she will certainly cure him, without the world perceiving it. – But how is a man to avoid the imputation of jealousy, if the young men accuse him of it, merely because he is always seen with his wife? ... That is what never happens; let a beloved husband be ever so attentive, he will not be accused of jealousy. You know the Baron de T*** and Mons. D***; they and their wives are inseparable. Has it ever been said, that they are jealous? Yet the Baroness and Madame D*** are amiable, young, and handsome; but they are as much distinguished for their conduct as for accomplishments; and they do not think a husband's presence can be any trouble or constraint ... In this part of our conversation I heard the clock strike 12, and I sent Adelaide to bed, with a promise to renew the discourse to-morrow. Adieu, my dear daughter; it is three in the morning; but I would not go to bed till I had written all these particulars, since the Courier sets out to-morrow. I know the share you take in my conversations with Adelaide; and, as a mother and a friend, I assure you I relate them faithfully, and I believe without changing a word. You know the tenaciousness of my memory; so you may believe in truth, that it is as if you were by and listened; for you know exactly all we say. Finally, the sole idea that Diana and Seraphina will one day read all these letters would give me all that minute exactness which you so earnestly recommend. Farewell, my dear child! I shall continue my journal to-morrow, and go on with it until Mons. d' Aimeri's recovery.

The Count de Roseville has engaged to send your stuffs by a safe and speedy conveyance. He breakfasts with me almost every day, not only to see me, but to talk of you for hours together. Judge how agreeable his company is to me! Besides, he is truly interesting, by his wit, his way of thinking, and that extreme simplicity which is his characteristic. No man surely can have more knowledge and merit and be less assuming. Our friend Bruyere very justly observes, 'It is profound ignorance which inspires one with a dogmatical manner. He who knows scarcely any thing thinks to teach others what he himself has but just learned. He who knows a great deal thinks it hardly possible for any one to be ignorant of what he says, and therefore speaks with more simplicity.'[84]

LETTER LXVII.

The Baroness to Madame d' Ostalis.

Wednesday.

MONS. d' Aimeri is still nearly in the same state, yet they say he has less fever; but I find him more dejected, more depressed, than he was yesterday. He has been shut up for an hour to-night with two notaries: in short, he takes all the precautions of a man who thinks himself at the last extremity. At the same time I observed a change in him today which struck me; it appeared to me, as if he wished to flatter himself, or rather to deceive us, in regard to his health. He told me to-day, for example, that he had slept pretty well last night, which is not true. He added, that he was in less pain than yesterday; he no longer talks of his fatal presages; his heart appears quite hardened and he shews an insensibility which even extends to his grandson. I believe that his remorse, and his apprehensions, naturally violent at this time, give him up to the most cruel terrors; to such dreadful ideas that he can only think of himself. Nothing makes us so selfish as being in imminent danger; and how dreadful is that which looks him in the face! ... His tortured soul seems excluded from all hopes; he is inaccessible to the soft sentiments of friendship and to all kind of consolation. I spent three hours with him: I observed also, that he could not without extreme pain hear the Chevalier de Murville's will mentioned; but unfortunately Mons. de Valmont has not yet exhausted that subject of conversation, and it is absolutely impossible to make him understand, that it displeases Mons. d' Aimeri. He answers, that certainly his father-in-law must be delighted at Charles's having an estate of an hundred thousand livres a year; and of course he talks of nothing else; and still keeps praising *this good Chevalier de Murville, whom he knew formerly only a poor Gentleman of Picardy, but whole person deserved to have made his fortune; for he was as handsome as an Angel.* You know Mons. de Valmont; therefore can both hear him and see him. If, in the midst of this prating, any one makes a sign to him in order to silence him, he never fails asking aloud what they mean. He afflicts all Mons. d' Aimeri's nurses, except the Viscontess, whose attention is sure to be fixed by talking of the Chevalier de Murville; and I have even surprised her several times questioning Mons. de Valmont softly on this subject, in order to know what kind of man the Chevalier de Murville was in his youth.

Theodore conducts himself in a most delightful manner: instead of dining and supping at home with the Viscountess and Constantia, he stays with his friend, and never quits him but for one half hour in the day to come and see us just before dinner. He certainly cannot make a greater sacrifice to friendship. The Chevalier de Valmont is still more unhappy; for, since the day before yesterday, he has never seen Adelaide, who receives from him every day a most beautiful nosegay and a charming basket of flowers for Hermine.

To-night before supper, according to my promise, Adelaide and I resumed the conversation of yesterday. She questioned me very particularly on the Chevalier de Valmont's disposition. I am certain, answered I, that he has all the essential virtues, and that he has excellent principles; yet I will not assure you, that he is without faults. He is naturally inclined to melancholy, and it is very possible he may sometimes be out of humour. He will certainly love you passionately the first year of your marriage. Take advantage of this temporary, though boundless, empire, which love will give you over him, to acquire the right of speaking freely to him of his faults; which should always be with a tone of interest and tender affection. At the same time ask advice of him; and, if you wish him to receive your counsels, appear desirous of his. What an interest have you in correcting all his defects, and in forming his temper and mind as much as possible! Reflect, that his virtues will be your happiness; that your fortune, the establishment of your children, your consequence, your glory, will depend upon his conduct; in short, that if you render him better, he will become more dear to you, and you will attach him to you by the most lasting affections, esteem and gratitude. Engage him to cultivate his mind; to be always employed; and, above all, to make a good use of his fortune. Convince him, that every action of benevolence will make him dearer to you. What lover will not be desirous of distinguishing himself, and of acquiring glory, when his virtues give pride to the object beloved? But it is a virtuous woman alone that can inspire this noble enthusiasm. If you are not yourself truly estimable in all particulars, your husband will set no great value on your esteem. To deserve all his regard, be exactly that you are now; and, above all, preserve that sincere piety which distinguishes you: it will secure your happiness, it will defend you from all the strokes of calumny, and it will certainly preserve your husband from injurious suspicions of jealousy. So it is necessary, from the first year of your marriage, that your husband should be acquainted with your principles and your virtues; it is necessary for you to employ yourself in studying his disposition, and to accustom him to gently hear you tell him the truth ... It is very essential also, that I endeavour to gain his confidence ... You have a very easy method of doing that; give him your's, and he will not refuse you his. When we are well disposed, we have at the bottom of our hearts a natural equity, which, without the assistance of reflection, will make us feel and partake all the reasonable sentiments we inspire. If you would be loved, avoid artifice; it subdues sometimes, but never attaches. – Love in good earnest, and you will be beloved. One attracts, one obtains confidence, in the same manner as friendship. If you have discovered to me your prudence and discretion, and if you are desirous of reading my heart, trust me with your most important secrets, and mine will escape me. Besides, my dear Adelaide, the knowledge you have gives you a right to your husband's confidence in all things. Though he should have the most perfect esteem for you, if you did not understand business, he could not converse with you about it. But Mons. Leblanc's instructions[85] have made you capable of discoursing sensibly on all kinds of affairs. To preserve the confidence he will grant you, never boast of it; if he should think you wanted to persuade people that he consulted you in every thing, he would not easily pardon this trifling vanity, as his pride would be hurt; and, even exclusively of this reason, if he knew that you imagined he concealed nothing from you, prudence alone would set bounds to his confidence. – I once knew the friend of a Minister of State, whose vanity of this kind rendered him very ridiculous. He was every moment telling people how great a confidence was reposed in him; and it was impossible for him to talk in that manner without his being guilty of many indiscretions; therefore such a person is the most dangerous confidant a Courtier could rely upon. A little political secret might easily have escaped him without his perceiving it; and a mysterious and cunning look, or even an affectation of silence, would be sufficient to make a discovery. I remember, once my father-in-law solicited a favour of great importance; the Minister's friend came to acquaint him privately, that his request was granted. This attention did not arise from friendship, but was merely an indiscretion occasioned by vanity. – He only wanted to shew, that he was the first who knew it; and that he had heard it, even before the person most interested in it. This was a conduct well calculated to expose the Minister, who had so injudiciously placed his confidence. As to you, never think of gaining any one's confidence, except your husband's. – All the world will imagine you possess it; and this opinion will neither hurt his consequence nor his fortune; which far from being established by your indiscretion, will be founded on your merits and your virtue.

I have still one thing more to advise you about, my dear Adelaide. You have an unalterable sweetness and gentleness of disposition; but yet you must not flatter yourself, that you will have no disputes with your husband. In all the little arguments you may have together, I recommend you always to wear an air and tone of respect; and at the same time never to suffer from him any expression that can wound your delicacy, without appearing much concerned at it. In short, in all situations, the more regard you shew him, the more he will shew for you.

After this conversation, I went and fetched your letters, and read to Adelaide that, which you wrote me some years ago on the subject of the attachment Mons. d' Ostalis had conceived for the Countess Anatolle.[86] During my reading it, Adelaide was in an agitation, at the same time affecting and comical. Her anger against Mons. d' Ostalis at least equalled her admiration of you; and I am not yet certain, whether she has not still a little rancour at the bottom of her heart against Mons. d' Ostalis. But she was much struck with the prudence of your conduct; and she said with a deep sigh, I promise you, Mamma, to follow so good an example, if ever I should be in a similar situation.

Thursday Evening.

MONS. d' Aimeri is much worse. I am just returned from him, overwhelmed with grief, tenderness, and compassion. About six in the evening, he became confused in his head; and insensibly grew delirious to the most frightful degree. Every moment he called out, Cecilia; this name, from his lips, made me tremble!

... At other times, he cried with a voice half choaked, and in the most piercing accents, take away that hair, take it away from me ... He thought he saw it on his bed; he shook the bed-cloaths with all his strength; and turned his head away with grief and terror painted most forcibly in his eyes ... At seven o'clock, he grew calmer; he recovered his senses, and demanded a Confessor; and we all left the chamber. In about half an hour he sent for me; I found him so moved, so softened, that he could not speak. I seated myself near his bed, and, after a moment's silence, he wiped his eyes, and said, I am going to tell you a thing which gives me great consolation ... You know, Madam, that Mons. *** the Notary, has in his hands twenty thousand crowns, which belong to my grandson. The first day of my illness Charles took ten thousand livres upon this sum, with which he has delivered thirty prisoners, detained at Fort l'Eveque,[87] till they had paid the expences of their nurses. He has not only carefully avoided boasting of this action, but he has taken great precaution not to let it be known, that he was the author of it. However chance discovered it this day to the Abbè Moreau, who has just informed me of it. This is not all, said Mons. d' Aimeri; he has employed my steward to purchase a piece of ground, which joins to our little Charity School. He means to build a house, which may hold ten girls; and he charges himself with the whole expence of this second school, which will be established on the plan of the other. How happy ought you to think yourself, interrupted I! the Chevalier de Valmont is your own work; he is indebted to you for all his virtues, as he owes his education wholly to you! ... At these words, Mons. d' Aimeri raised his eyes to Heaven, fetching a deep sigh. – Do me the favour, Madame, said he, to fetch Mons. d' Almane, Monsieur and Madame de Valmont, and my grandson, and return with them. I went out immediately. When I came into the saloon, every body surrounded me to enquire after Mons. d' Aimeri. – I was so much affected, I could not speak; and the besides, at that moment I saw nobody but the Chevalier de Valmont; I ran to him, and embraced him with the affection of a real mother ... I afterwards acquitted myself of my commission, and we returned to Mons. d' Aimeri. As soon as he saw his grandson, he held out his arms with the most affecting tenderness. The Chevalier flew to him, and Mons. d' Aimeri pressed him to his bosom. Oh, Charles, said he, you have established peace and tranquillity in my soul ... Yes, Heaven will pardon me on account of your virtues? ... Think, my dear child, that every good action of your life will be an expiation of my crimes ... The Chevalier could only answer by sobs and tears; – and Mons d' Aimeri was so much affected, that finding his strength failed him, he made a sign for us to lead his grandson into the next room. – Before I left him, I asked the Physician's opinion, who did not seem to be intirely without hope. You may easily imagine, how much Adelaide has been delighted by these particulars ... The school for girls has above all given her infinite pleasure. She flatters herself, that love has had a great share in inducing the Chevalier to perform this noble action; and this is a motive, which does not lessen the merit of it in her eyes. Adieu, my dear child; as the post goes to-morrow, I must finish this letter; but be assured the journal shall be exactly continued till the wedding-day.

LETTER LXVIII.

The same to the same.

Friday.

THIS unfortunate Mons. d' Aimeri! ... Alas! his forebodings were but too just! Heaven has not permitted him the happiness of conducting his grandson to the altar. He retained his senses to the last; and died this morning at six, after having insisted on Mons. de Valmont and Mons. d' Almane giving their words of honour, that the weddings should be celebrated the 18th: that is to say, in four days. The Chevalier is in a pitiable condition. He was here this evening for the first time, since the articles were signed. His interview with Adelaide was truly affecting: he enjoyed the purest of all consolation; that of seeing the object of his love a sharer in his sorrow. He has seen Adelaide weep, and her tears fell for him.

In conformity to the last request of Mons. d' Aimeri, the weddings are fixed for next Tuesday at nine in the morning; there is to be no parade; and we go from the Church to Saint *** on Tuesday the 18th of April; what a day for me! what an epoch in my life!

Saturday, 15.

THE Viscountess has discovered a secret concerning Theodore, of which I was intirely ignorant. The day after his arrival, the Countess Anatolle sent him a letter, which contained a full acknowledgment of her sentiments, and an offer of her hand. She added, that his success and behaviour during the campaign had completed the discovery of a passion to her, which she had long endeavoured to suppress, &c. A person must have a weak head, and very little greatness of soul, to make such advances to a man of ninteen and a half. It is true, she had not thought of the possibility of a resusal; our engagements with Mons. de Limours were unknown to her, she has a vast fortune, is only twenty-one, and perfectly beautiful. Not doubting her success, she trusted the secret to a friend, who told it to another, and from friend to friend it reached the Viscountess; who related all these particulars to me this morning. Mons. d' Almane tells me, that Theod-ore had no certainty of marrying Constantia, when he received the Countess's letter. Yet, as you will easily believe, he did not hesitate, but sent immediately an answer full of respect and acknowledgments, but declared that his heart was engaged. The Viscountess, in order to raise Theodore in Constantia's eyes, told her all this History, which I highly disapproved. – She is naturally inclined to jealousy. She must meet the Countess Anatolle frequently at her relations, and in publick company, and she will never see her undisturbed. I received a letter from Porphyry yesterday, which announces his long expected return. He has spent near a year with Madame de Lagaraye. This conduct adds greatly to the esteem and friendship I already felt for him. He informs me, that the sole reason of his coming is to enjoy for a moment the fight of my happiness; and that he shall then return to Anjou, to the widow of his benefactor, whose affairs are not absolutely settled. Good night my dear. Still two days to Tuesday.

Sunday, 16.

WHAT a delightful morning has this been to me! Although I did not go to bed till two, I was up again at seven; for how is it possible to sleep an instant, when the most interesting day of my life is so near! ... I have been breakfasting with Mons. d' Almane and my children. Adelaide was seated between us, and Theodore kneeled on a stool before us. He talked to us with as much affection as animation, of the excess of his happiness, and of his gratitude to us. You unite me to her I love, said he; every wish of my heart will after to-morrow be gratified. Constantia will have pledged her faith to me; I shall call my beloved friend by the dear name of *Brother.* Within three days Constantia and Charles will be your children; they will be there! ... We shall never breakfast without them ... Adelaide and Constantia will be placed between my parents; Charles and I shall be at their feet. During this discourse, Adelaide, reclining gently on my shoulder, with her eyes full of tears, looked tenderly on her brother, and from time to time pressed one of my hands, which she held in her's ... Theodore left us at nine to go to Madame de Valmont; and Adelaide retired to write some letters: – only Mons. d' Almane and I remained; and the pleasure of talking of our children kept us together till dinner. We not only were transported with our present prosperity, but we enjoyed all the felicity which we discovered in future days. I see you returned to Paris; and your children and mine educated in the same principles, forming but one family, too numerous, too united not to constitute a society in themselves. Their virtues, their affection, and their behaviour making the happiness of our lives! Such delighful hopes cannot be chimerical: we have a right to expect what we have deserved to see realised. You have no idea of the joy which fills this house; Adelaide and Theodore are adored, and they now receive the most affecting testimonies of affection from all the servants. But there are two persons who partake almost all the sentiments which I feel, Dainville and

Miss Bridget. He has already made ten allegorical pictures upon the marriages of Theodore and Adelaide. Besides he shews his satisfaction by an excess of gaiety, which makes him appear mad. As for Miss Bridget, she is much more deeply affected: she says, she is charmed; in effect she can neither speak nor weep. She was never very explicit; but now, she cannot even return the compliments made her on Adelaide's nuptials; she can only bow her head, and repeat, that she is charmed. Theodore presented Dainville this morning with an annuity of 1500 livres, and Adelaide did the like for her dear Miss Bridget. For the rest, these two persons, who have been of such great use to me in the education of my children, will end their lives with me; they will remain in the same rooms which they now occupy; and they both look forward to the time, when they can devote their talents to the education of my grand-children. My grand-children! ... In a year most probably I shall be a grandmother! Oh how I shall doat on the children of Adelaide, and on Theodore's! How extremely dear will the daughter of Adelaide be to me! To me who can never hear her call Hermine *my child* without emotion.

The Chevalier de Herbain to the same.

Monday, 17.

I AM commissioned, Madame, to continue the journal; and I must send it to the Count de Roseville before nine o'clock this evening. Madame d' Almane, surrounded by fifteen people, who will not leave her till midnight, will not be able to write till after supper; therefore, I hope you will excuse my being the relator this day: but without partiality you will lose nothing; for, in reality, I am the only person in the house who is at leisure to write, joy and happiness have turned all their heads. The business of the day is the acceptance of the *wedding-basket* sent by the Chevalier de Valmont. First of all you must know, if you have not already some idea of it, that Mademoiselle d' Almane has declared she will neither accept of diamonds nor trinkets; in fact, the gifts of Madame d' Almane and the presents from uncles and aunts would have been sufficient to gratify the wishes of a much less sensible and moderate young person, than our charming Adelaide. At five o'clock the arrival of the basket was announced, which made us eager to have a peep at it. Madame d' Olcy, with whom I am a favourite, whispered me, that she had not been consulted, and she was sure, it would be in a frightful taste. She went into Mademoiselle d' Almane's closet, where we saw the basket, and it really was rather a mean-looking one. Madame d' Olcy put on a scornful look; I winked at her, and opened the basket; being a nice observer, she presently judged the contents (millenary) were not worth 4000 livres. Judge, Madame, of her indignation: while she was attacking her sister and nephew with the most ill-natured pleasantry, Madame de Limours finished emptying the basket, and discovered a very pretty pocketbook at the bottom, on which was written Hermine's name. Little Hermine came running to us quite delighted: Madame de Limours gave the pocketbook to Mademoiselle d' Almane, who opening it, found written on a piece of paper, with something inclosed therein, *A wedding gift from Madame de Valmont to her daughter.* Adelaide blushed and looked at her mother, who, on opening the paper, found it inclosed a settlement of 4000 livres a year on Hermine during her life. Madame d' Almane, and Madame de Limours embraced the Chevalier de Valmont. Madame d' Olcy in a cold constrained manner exclaimed, *that is delightful*! and Mademoiselle d' Almane with a most inchanting grace took Hermine by the hand, and said, you may accept of this present, my dear girl, for to-morrow he will be your father. Then leading Hermine to him, told her to embrace him, and he returned it with the greatest transports, holding her for some time in his arms. All this while Theodore, from whom no secrets are hid, being impatient that all the treasures of the basket should be discovered, listed up a kind of pocket which contained a bit of pasteboard. – Here is a plan, said he, for a charity-school for ten young girls; it is you, sister, who are to be the foundress, and for whom this is intended, as what was supposed would be the most agreeable to you. Here Madame d' Olcy cried out again, *delightful, delightful*! Because she is all politeness; but I am very sure she thought that a basket made by Miss Bertin, would have been much more desirable than this. You will allow, Madam, that such wedding-gifts as these are still more honourable to those that receive, than to those that give them. For my part, what I almost as much admired, was, that out of sixty persons, who have been here to pay their compliments to Madame d' Almane for the last two hours, there is not one knows the contents of the basket. It is true, Madame de Limours went home, or she alone would have made it public; for Monsieur and Madame d' Almane never speak of what passes in the family to those whom it does not concern. Besides, in this house, great, delicate, and virtuous actions are not remarked; they give satisfaction and pleasure, but never that extreme surprise which makes them esteemed miraculous, and worthy of being the common talk of the week: as a proof, after having examined the basket, we left the closet; and though there was none but the family, Madame d' Almane changed the conversation, and no more was said of the basket. There is in this simplicity of acting something so sublime, that it demands from the bottom of the soul the utmost of our admiration.

Porpyhry is just arrived in time to compose the nuptial songs. I am writing, Madam, in a closet adjoining the saloon, and am interrupted every minute by one or other with some message for you: among others, there is Porphyry, who complains of your silence; and Madame de Puisigny, the widow of a relation of Madame de Valmont, who spent some time with you in Champagne, at your mother-in-law's. This Madame de Puisigny is one of the most agreeable persons I ever met with: she is lively and easy, without being capricious: she argues without severity, and contradicts without displeasing; she has read and seen a great deal, and her conversation is as instructive as it is entertaining: in short, the goodness of her heart keeps pace with her wit and agreeable manner, and must be productive of the most lasting and solid friendship. It gives me pain that you were only eighteen years old when you last met her, as I am afraid you will not recollect her, particularly as her age would make you feel so much respect for her, that you could not form an exact estimate of her worth. Adieu, Madame; accept with your usual goodness, my professions of that real attachment for you, which I have vowed for life. The only person in the world, who can possibly love you better, insists upon my pen, and I cannot refuse it.

Oh! my daughter! my dear daughter! to-morrow is the day! it must be within twelve hours! ... Consider the agitation and confusion I am in! ... I can write no more; my hand trembles so, and my heart is so full! Adieu, my child! ... I am happy ... and I love you *beyond expression.*

LETTER LXIX.

The Baroness to Madame d' Ostalis.

Saint ***.

Tuesday April 18.

SHE is married! ... O God, grant that it may be for her happiness! ... that hope alone directed me. Neither interest nor ambition determined my choice: I may therefore be allowed to expect from this union all the joy of my life.

You will credit me, that I never closed my eyes this night: No sooner did I behold the first dawn of day, than I rung. I rose hastily, and was going down to Mons. d' Almane, when my daughter came into my room: she threw herself into my arms; afterwards she fell at my feet, bathed in tears, and eagerly embracing my knees ... Oh, Mamma! exclaimed she, you are going to give me a new master; but in delegating to him those sacred rites which you have over your daughter, promise me at least to preserve and exert them yourself in their full extent. On my part I vow you the same submissive obedience I have ever paid you. The first and dearest wish of my heart is, to take you for my model, to copy you, if it be possible; to observe all your advice, to devote my love to you. I am sensible, that all your happiness depends on my conduct. Ah! I will justify your expectations! ... Did I not respect my duties, I would fulfill them, to insure your felicity; I would fulfil them for your sake, who was to me in the place of a Governess and an instructress; who was my dear benefactress, my tender mother! ... At these words she raised her arms towards me; and looked at me with those melting eyes, which so justly describe the tenderness and purity of her soul! ... I raised her up, and embraced her a thousand times. I could not speak, but she saw into my heart

In about half an hour Mons. d' Almane and Theodore came to seek us. My son, already dressed, hastened us to our toilets. Mine did not take long. I would myself dress Adelaide. What a pleasure I felt in decorating her; in placing in her head that little sprig of orange flowers!* in putting on her nuptial robe! ... Adelaide, who is commonly only pretty, was beautiful to day. A soft melancholy was spread over her features, and added to the beauty and nobleness of her figure, made her modesty more affecting.

I shall not pretend to describe what I felt in conducting her to church, in seeing her at the altar! ... You will one day marry a daughter, and you will then know all, that passed in my heart ... As soon as the ceremony was over, we all set out for Saint *** ; where I shall remain all the Summer and Autumn; my son-in-law, or rather my second son, and Theodore, will stay till the time of the Summer campaign; that is to say till the month of June. The poor Viscountess is obliged to leave us to-morrow, in order to return to her attendance on Madame de Valcy, who cannot live a week longer. It is settled, that Theodore and Constantia shall only reside four years with Monsieur d' Almane; and then they are to take possession of an apartment, which is allotted them in the house which the Viscountess is building.[88] It is but just, that he should enjoy the company of the only child that is left him, and for whom he has for these last two years conceived the most tender affection. In four years Theodore will be twenty-four; he may then quit the paternal dwelling without danger: besides, the Viscountess's house will be so near this, that this separation cannot be felt.

I am now, my dear child, going to give you a description of the wedding present I made my children. I took Adelaide and Theodore into my closet; and fetching from my bureau two copies of a Work in three thick volumes: This, said I, my children, is all I have left to give you. It is written for you; and entitled, LETTERS ON EDUCATION[89] ... You will find in them a faithful picture of the manners and fashions of the world. In this sketch of human life, I wished to point out to you the road which leads to happiness; to mark the rocks you should avoid, the crosses and errors from which you should preserve yourselves. This undertaking required courage! ... I knew it; nor was I ignorant of the numberless dangers to which we expose ourselves by attacking without reserve vice and folly! ... But neither fear, nor any other consideration could stop me when I was writing for you. I had no difficulty, or even any merit in speaking the truth:

---

* A confecrated nosegay, always worn by Brides.

my wish was to inlighten you. It was labouring for your happiness and my own. I am still young enough to flatter myself with the hopes of superintending the education of your children: but if death should rob you of your mother, you will find in these books all the advice she could have given you. This book is adapted to youth, not to childhood: it reveals all the secrets of education. If you adopt my method, do not give it your children before their wedding-day. In fine, you alone can judge, and prove to others, if my system really deserves to be preferred. If you never swerve from your duties, if you preserve your principles untainted, if you are always virtuous and benevolent; if your knowledge and your talents daily procure you new pleasures; in short, if you find an inexhaustible spring of happiness in the constant pursuit of benevolence, and the practice of every virtue ... then my plan is a good one; my system is not chimerical; and my work is no romance. O, my dear children! I do not doubt but you will prove the utility of this work; – when your characters and your hearts are known, the method I have followed will be applauded.

FINIS.

Course of Reading pursued by *ADELAIDE, from the Age of six Years, to Twenty-two.*[1]

ADELAIDE could read perfectly well at *six* years old; but then she only read by way of lesson, and did not understand what it was about. And though by that time she knew the History of the Bible, she learned it solely, by means of the Magic Lanthern.[2] She had also some notion of Geography, which she learned by means of Perspective Glasses; and she had seen Pekin, Canton, Moscow, Kola,[3] &c. a thousand times. She not only knew the Capitals, but the principal rivers, and other things worth notice; which she learnt in the same manner, by amusing herself with Madame d' Almane and Miss Bridget, in looking through the Perspective Glass. She spoke French and English equally well. Such were Adelaide's improvements, when she arrived in Languedoc. Although she appeared to have both penetration and sense at that age, yet Madame d' Almane did not think it would be any advantage to her to read those little Tales, which are composed for children in their infancy. She thought it better to give her six months preparation for reading them, by teaching her to read little true stories still better adapted to her capacity, but which were not worthy the notice of the publick. Madame d' Almane had five of six sets of these little works printed; but took care to conceal her being the author. When she arrived in Languedoc, she waited for a proper opportunity to produce them; for she would not give them to her daughter, but at the time when they might be useful. Adelaide was very impatient to read to herself; and her eagerness was encreased by deferring to satisfy it; – however, one day, that she had been contradicting her brother, there came a pedlar to the Castle with books, one of which she was permitted to choose; she did not fail to take the only one which was bound; indeed it was in Red Morocco, with a gilt edge; when she had purchased it, she found it was called, *The History of Cephisa*, a charming little girl, very mild and obedient, who never contradicted her brother in her life. She read this history with great delight; and that very evening Adelaide asked her brother's pardon, and assured him she would never more behave ill to him. A week after came another pedlar, and brought another book, which was a new lesson*. In short, in six months Adelaide had read, and got by heart, all the little neatly bound books, in which were Madame d' Almane's histories.[4]

---

* Madame d' Almane made use of, more than once, this indirect method of giving instruction. When Adelaide left Languedoc to return to Paris, she was ten years old, and during that Winter

At seven years old she had read The Bible, *The Conversation of Emilius,*[5] and *Les Hochets Moraux,* by Mons. Monget;[6]which are pleasing Tales in verse, dedicated to Mademoiselles d' Orleans and de Chartres; these Adelaide got by heart*. At seven years and half she read *Plays and Dialogues for Children,* written by Madame de la Fite,[7] a work in two volumes, equally valuable and interesting, as well for the use it is of to children, as by the wit and graces with which it abounds. At eight years old she read the seven volumes *des Annales de la Vertu;*[8] *La Géographie comparée,* by Mons. Mentelle,[9] and a *Treatise on Heraldry.*[10] By this time Adelaide began to write a large hand pretty well, and instead of giving her one single sentence for a copy, she had a different page every day. The first she began with, was *le Catechisme Historique,*[11] which lasted her six months; and the next six months, she wrote *l' Abregé de la Géographie,* by Mons. le Ragois.[12]

At nine years old she wrote *l' Abregé de l' Histoire Poétique,* and *l' Instruction sur les Métamorphoses d' Ovide,* also by Ragois;[13] which lasted her till she was ten, when she read, and acted, five Comedies of the *Theatre d' Education; Agar dans le Désert; les Flacons; la Colombe; l' Enfant Gate* and *l' Aveugle de Spa.*[14] To these were added *Eléments de Poésie Françoise,*[15] three Volumes in Twelves, and *Robinson Crusoe.*[16] By this time her lessons for writing, were an Abridgement of *The Beauties of History,*[17] as she then began to write English, which before she could only speak. When she had written her English copy, we made her read it in order to pronounce it properly; and this taught her to read English; so that one lesson contained three, Writing, History, and the English Language.

At *eleven* years old she wrote over again all those books, which we have just mentioned; and she knew by heart the *Annales de la Vertu* so much the better, for having seen in the tapestries and magic lantherns the most remarkable incidents in History. She also read at this age, Rollin's *Ancient History,*[18] *The Imitation of Jesus Christ,*[19] *The Father's Instructions to his Children;*[20] and *le Theatre de Campistron.*[21]

At *twelve* years old she received the Sacrament; she read *les Quatre fins de l'Homme,* by Monsieur Nicole;[22] an excellent book, which, read in early youth, makes an impression not to be effaced. Echard's *Roman History;*[23] *le Theatre* de la Grange-Chancel;[24] and Macaulay's *History of England.*[25]

At *thirteen* she read the *Princess of Cleves,*[26] *Zaide,*[27] *Cleveland,*[28] the *Deane of Coleraine,*[29] *Anecdotes of the Court of Philip Augustus,*[30] the rest of the *Theatre d' Education;* a book on Mythology, by Madame d' Almane,[31] and the *Travels*

she used every morning at breakfast to read aloud the Paris Gazette. During this Winter, she read near sixty false sheets, which her mother had caused to be printed expressly for her, and substituted instead of the real news-papers; Adelaide and Theodore read all these with inexpressible delight. They contained pleasing histories; proofs of great courage; benevolence; filial affection, &c. &c. and many other similar lessons, which were thought necessary for the particular occasion.

*   *Les Hochets Moraux* are to be had at Lambert's and Baudüin's rue de la Harpe. [This is a note from the translator] *of Cyrus*:[32] and in the course of this year she wrote for her copies, a Collection of Poems taken from different authors; such as Bertaut, Godeau, Pavillon, Desmahis,[33] *&c*. *At fourteen* she read Tremblay's *Instructions from a Father to his Children*;[34] a good book, which contains a course of instruction well written upon all subjects; *The History of France*, by Velly,[35] &c.; *le Theatre* de Boissy;[36] *le Theatre* de Marivaux,[37] *le Spectacle de la Nature*, by Mons. Pluche;[38] *Histoire des Insectes*, in two vols.[39] and Lady M. W. Montague's *Letters*.[40] Adelaide began at this time to read Italian, which she already spoke very well, and set out with the translation of the *Peruvian Letters*,[41] and *les Comedies de Goldoni*.[42] She continued writing the Poems before mentioned, and began to answer the Letters written by Madame d' Almane, as mentioned in the third volume, and also took Extracts of what she read.

At fifteen she read *les Synonymes* de l' Abbé Girard,[43] *la Maniere de bien penser dans les ouvrages d' esprit*, one vol.[44] *Reflexions critiques sur la poesie & sur la peinture*, by the Abbé Dubos;[45] *Histoire de Pierre le Grand*;[46] Voltaire's *Universal History*;[47] *Theatre* de Destouches;[48] *Theatre* de la Chausee;[49] *D. Quichotte*;[50] *la Poétique* de Marmontel;[51] Hume's *History of England*,[52] and the Works of Metastatio in their original languages;[53] and this year she only wrote her Copies with a Master twice a week; she finished the Answers to Madame d' Almane's Letters; and made Extracts from the English and Italian Histories. At sixteen she read Virgil's *Æneid* and his *Georgics*,[54] translated by Mons. l' Abbe de l' Isle; Madame Sevigny's *Letters*;[55] Fontaine's *Fables*;[56] Translation of the Greek Theatre;[57] *Theatre* de Crebillon,[58] and some detached Pieces, as *Manlius*, de la Fosse; *Ariane*, and the *Comte d' Essex*, de Thomas Corneille;[59] *la Metromanie*; *Ines de Castro*;[60] the Translations of Plautus and Terence;[61] *Clarissa*,[62] and Thomson's Works in English;[63] and Pasto Fido, in Italian.[64] – This year Adelaide left off writing Copies, and only wrote Extracts, and made Verses. She also began again to compose Answers to the Letters Madame d' Almane had written; and in six months she had written forty Answers. At *seventeen* she read Voltaire's *Age of Lewis Fourteenth*, and his History of *Charles the Twelfth*;[65] the Poems of Madame Des Houlieres;[66] the Works of Gresset;[67] *Theatre* du Grand Corneille;[68] *Theatre* de Racine;[69] *Theatre* de Voltaire;[70] les Sermons de Bourdaloue;[71] and *Sir Charles Grandison* and *Pamela* in English;[72] with Ariosto in Italian.[73] She made Extracts from History, and from Corneille; she read Voltaire's Edition of the latter, in order to judge of it herself. When she had made her Remarks, Madame *d' Almane* corrected her opinions, by shewing her *Voltaire's*; at the same time observing, that his were not all equally just.* Between *eighteen* and *nineteen*

---

* Among others, the criticism on that beautiful imprecation of Camilla, in the Horaces; – and in that line in Rodugune is admirable, because it comes from Cleopatra; whose desperate character and motives of action it points out so well: after having heard her say these words: *Fall upon me Heaven, &c. &c.* we are not surprised to see her poison herself with a view of being revenged. Take she read *Theatre* de Moliere;[74] Boileau's Works;[75] Regnard; Dufreni;[76] the Poems of J. B. Rousseau*;[77] *Sermons* de Massillon;[78] with the Spectators in English,[79] and Petrarch in Italian.[80] After the marriage of Adelaide, Madame d' Almane engaged her to continue her reading as usual, which she did at her toilet; and as she received no company at her house for two years after she was married, she had time to pursue her studies from eighteen and a half to twenty years and a half. She read during that time *Letters on Education*;[81] *Emilius* and *Odyssey;*[82] Buffon's *Natural History*;[83] *Telemachus*,[84] *Flechier, Bossuet, Mascaron*;[85] *les Caracteres* de la Bruyere;[86] Rochefoucauld's *Maxims*;[87] and in English Pope's Works,[88] and Locke,[89] including the *Iliad* of Pope so elegantly translated;[90] with the History of Italy by Guiciardini,[91] and the Works of Dante, in Italian.[92]

From the age of *twenty and a half to twenty-two*, she read the *Pensées* de Pascal;[93] *Gil Blas*;[94] *Memoirs of the History of France*;[95] Hamilton's Works;[96] *Treatise on Wisdom*, by Charron;[97] *Persian Letters*; and *l'Esprit des Loix*;[98] in English, Milton and Shakespeare, and in Italian, *La Jerusalem déliverée.*[99]

At *twenty-two* Madame d' Almane gave her notice of all the New Works which were worth reading; and advised her to read over again the books she had been accustomed to from sixteen to twenty-two; which would last her, with some additional books which it was necessary she should be acquainted with, such as Fontenelle's *Plurality of Worlds, ses Discours Academiques*,[100] and some others, till she was seven or eight-and-twenty. This Plan of Study seems to be carried to a great length; yet it does not take in many works of which there are Extracts to be met with in the seven volumes of *Annales des Vertu*; such as the Histories of Scotland, Ireland, Germany, Poland, Turkey, Arabia, and Russia. It is remarkable that this plan of reading, at the beginning, only required half an hour each day; and only three quarters of an hour from the age of thirteen to twenty two, even supposing they did not read fast. There are only two or three of the Works which are voluminous; and there is not a year where one has more than fifty volumes to read. It must be observed that Plays are read in much less time than other books, because the names of the persons take up a great part of the room.

The studies of Theodore were much more extensive. Many Latin Books, of which Adelaide never read even the translations, as well as many books on

---

away this single speech of the Play, and the plot, which is the most beautiful of any on the Theatre, would appear no longer probable. The Author of *Zara* ought to feel, better than any one, the superior merit of the above excellent line. – Osmyn says, *I am not jeolaus: Have I ever been so!* – This beautiful piece of oratory, prepares us for every thing: it gives us the character of Osmyn; it shews us the unravelling of the plot. Take away this one line from the Play, and the murder of Zara would only inspire one with horror and amazement, and the catastrophe would appear no longer probable.

  *   The great merit of Rousseau's Poems depend less on his thoughts than on his harmony. It is necessary to have read a great deal of Poetry in order to taste the beauties of his; and for this reason Madame d' Almane did not hurry herself to give them to her daughter.

Laws and Political Subjects, were comprized in his reading. Yet there was not more time employed on that account. Theodore, from the age of sixteen to twenty-two, read every day about two hours and a half. He learned no music nor singing; he did not draw so long at a time as his sister. When the weather was not fit for walking, Adelaide amused herself with Embroidery, or other little works of that kind, and Theodore read, played at billiards, &c. So that Theodore had read infinitely more than Adelaide; yet she met with very few women who had so much knowledge as herself, or whose ideas were more clear and just; for she had learned and digested every thing she had read.

A Mother, who wishes to adopt this method of studying for her daughter, and who at the same time does not intend her to learn English or Italian, will have very little to alter. It will only be necessary to substitute translations from the principal Works in those languages. Therefore it will only be dispensing with seven books, which are not absolutely necessary to be read, and which Adelaide had learned by her Copies from ten years old to thirteen. These books are the *Beauties of History*; *Father's Instructions*; Macaulay's *History*; the *Travels of Cyrus*; Lady M. W. Montague's *Letters*; *The Peruvian Letters*; and Goldoni's Comedies. Instead of these, you may take *Models Militaires*, in two volumes,[101] *Histoire generale des Voyages*, abridged by Mons. de la Harpe,[102] twenty-one vols.; the Translation of the Fables of Phádrus;[103] and *Advice from a Mother to her Daughter, and to her Son*, by Madame de Lambert.[104] One may add more French Books, if one does not teach them English, because one can read much faster in one's own language, unless one is quite perfect in others, and then it makes little or no difference. But when Adelaide read English and Italian, they were not so easy to her as her own tongue; and therefore I have substituted for the foreign Works, more voluminous Works in French.

INDEX of LETTERS relative to the Education of PRINCES.

FIRST VOLUME.

LETTER XXIV. *The Count de Roseville to the Baron d' Almane.*   61
LETTER XXXVI. *Ditto.*   101
LETTER XLVII. *Ditto.*   125

SECOND VOLUME.

LETTER I.   169
LETTER IX.   206
LETTER XXV.   235
LETTER XXXVII.   258
LETTER XLVI.   312

THIRD VOLUME.

LETTER XVI.   352
LETTER XXVI.   375
LETTER XXXVII.   392
LETTER XLVII. *From Madame d' Ostalis.*   414
LETTER LIII. *From Count de Roseville.*   426
LETTER LXV.*   453

---

*   The Author has not entered into particulars relative to the Education of a Prince, because she has written a Comedy on the subject, called *Vatheck, or the Governor of a Prince*, in her Theatre of Education; and therefore would not repeat herself in this Work.

ENDNOTES

Volume I

1. *twenty leagues from Paris*: The second English edition includes a note by the translators which reads 'It is scarce necessary to observe that a French league is near three English miles'. See *Adelaide and Theodore; or Letters on Education: Containing all the Principles Relative to Three Different Plans of Education; to that of Princes, and to those of Young Persons of both Sexes. Translated from the French of Madame la Comtesse de Genlis. The Second Edition, Carefully Corrected and Amended*, 3 vols (London: C. Bathurst and T Cadell, 1784), vol. 1, p. 3.

2. *When I arrive at B—*: The disguise of the name of the estate that the Baron d'Almane is retreating to recalls Belle Chasse, where Genlis educated the Orléans children (see Introduction, p. xi).

3. *'Most people chuse Governors ... education of one'*: The quotation is from Book I of Rousseau's *Émile*, which reads 'One would wish that the governor had already educated someone. That is too much to wish for; the same man can only give one education'. See Jean Jacques Rousseau, *Émile: Or, On Education*, trans. by Allan Bloom (London: Penguin, 1991) p. 51. The Swiss Jean-Jacques Rousseau (1712–78) first published *Émile* in 1762. It has influenced debates on education since publication.

4. *I had already finished some Works on Education*: Throughout Genlis's works, she refers to her own writing, and in the early stages of her career in particular everything was destined for pedagogical purposes. The Baroness d'Almane here could be referring to the earlier *Theatre of Education* (1779–80) or indeed Genlis's *Confessions d'une mère de vingt ans* (*Confessions of a Twenty-year-old Mother*), a work she wrote during her first pregnancy when she was nineteen and which was never published.

5. *sending to England for a person to teach Adelaide the language of that country*: The practice of having native language speakers instructing children in foreign languages is an innovative one that Genlis adopted in the education of the Orléans children, notoriously in the adoption of two young English girls, Pamela and Hermine (see Introduction, p. xvi).

6. *Miss Bridget ... and Dainville both eat with us*: The democratic practice of dining with employees and domestics shocked British observers during Genlis's 1791–2 stay in England. Frances Burney reports a conversation about Genlis's household in Bury in her journal:

> They keep a botanist, a chemist, and a natural historian always with them. They are supposed to have been common servants of the Duke of Orléans in former days, as they always walk behind the ladies when abroad; but, to make amends in the new equalising style, they all

dine together at home. (Charlotte Frances Barrett (ed.), *The Diary and Letters of Madame d'Arblay (1778–1840)*, 4 vols (London: S. Sonnenschein & Co., 1893), vol. 3, p. 408)

7. *education of men and women ... differs in almost every other respect*: The Baroness can be seen to protest her case too strongly here, since the education of Adelaide does not differ dramatically from that of Theodore.

8. *in order to captivate those upon whom they depend*: Genlis is referring here to Sophie's education in Book V of *Émile*, where Rousseau argues that 'guile is a natural talent with the fair sex' and that a woman 'must have the art to make us want to do everything which her sex cannot do by itself and which is necessary or agreeable to it'. See Rousseau, *Émile*, pp. 370, 387.

9. *it will never procure her the esteem and attachment of a sensible man*: The comments on Rousseau here can usefully be compared to Mary Wollstonecraft's comments in *A Vindication of the Rights of Woman*:

    > The man who can be contented to live with a pretty, useful companion, without a mind, has lost in voluptuous gratifications a taste for more refined enjoyments; he has never felt the calm satisfaction that refreshes the parched heart like the silent dew of heaven – of being beloved by one who could understand him. (Mary Wollstonecraft, *A Vindication of the Rights of Woman*, ed. Miriam Brody (London: Penguin, 1992) p. 191)

10. *'walking in the fields or road'*: The full quotation, from Montaigne's 'Of the Education of Children', reads:

    > But, as the steps we take walking back and forth in a gallery, though there be three times as many, do not tire us like those we take on a set journey, so our lesson, occurring as if by chance, not bound to any time or place, and even mingling with all our actions, will slip by without being felt. (Michel de Montaigne, *The Complete Works: Essays, Travel Journal, Letters*, trans. Donald Frame (London: Everyman, 2003), p. 148)

    In the French version of the text, Genlis includes a lengthy note to this passage, which is translated for the 1784 edition:

    > It may be generally observed that knowledge of children, depending much upon the senses, it is necessary to adopt our instructions to the senses as much as possible, and infuse them, not by the hearing, but by the sight; this being the sense by which the strongest impressions and the most clear and distinct ideas are received. *Education of a Prince by Chanteresne*, 2nd part. We shall speak of this work more particularly elsewhere. (*Adelaide and Theodore ... The Second Edition*, vol. 1, pp. 34–5)

    'Education of a Prince by Chanteresne' refers to Pierre Nicole's (1625–95) *De l'éducation d'un prince, divisée en trois parties dont la dernière contient divers traitez utiles à tout le monde* (1670); see note 72 to Volume I, below.

11. *Ovid's* Metamorphoses: The Roman poet's *Metamorphoses* was, as Garth Tissol points out, 'well served' by eighteenth-century English translation: two collaborative translations appeared in 1717, edited by Sir Samuel Garth and George Sewell, and prose translations also appeared in the mid 1800s. See Stuart Gillespie and David Hopkins (eds), *The Oxford History of Literary Translation in English: Vol. 3 1660–1790* (Oxford: Oxford University Press, 2005), pp. 204–18.

12. *the Seven Kings of Rome*: Romulus (753–717 BC), Numa Pompilius (717–673 BC), Tullus Hostilius (672–641 BC), Ancus Marcius (639–616 BC), Tarquinius Priscus (616–579 BC), Servius Tullius (579–534 BC) and Tarquinius Superbus (534–510 BC).

13. *Constantine*: Roman emperor, Flavius Valerius Aurelius Constantinus, or Constantine I (*c.* 274–337) converted to Christianity and made it the religion of the state.

14. *the most celebrated Roman Ladies*: the events of the legendary Lucretia's life have been commemorated in literature by Livy and Shakespeare and others. She was raped by Sextus Tarquinius, and subsequently committed suicide. Aelia Flavia Flacilla (d. AD 385), first wife of Emperor Theodosis I, commemorated in literature by Madeleine de Scudéry's *Clélie, histoire romaine* (1654–60) a book Genlis frequently read in her youth. Cornelia, Cornelia Scipionis Africana, (190–100 BC) was worshipped as a symbol of virtue. Portia, Porcia Catonis (70–42 BC), wife of Brutus, committed suicide by swallowing burning coals. All these heroines of classical and modern literature were well-known to Genlis through her early reading.

15. *neither does it cost so much, and it will last for ever*: Genlis's original note to the French text is translated for the 1784 English edition: 'This tapestry, as we have described it, well drawn, mostly after the ancient medals, cost only 900 livres – 37 guineas and a half'. The translators have added the English equivalent to the French 'neuf cents francs'. See *Adelaide and Theodore ... The Second Edition*, vol. 1, p. 36.

16. *little coloured prints ... taken from the History of France*: Genlis's original note to the French text is translated for the 1784 English edition: 'These coloured prints may be made for about 16s. a piece, framed and glazed, if you would have them well executed; and for less, if you are not very nice about them'. The translators have converted the French price, 'dix-huit francs'. See *Adelaide and Theodore ...The Second Edition*, vol. 1, p. 36.

17. *Henry the Fourth ... with Sully at his side*: Henri IV (1553–1610), acceded to French throne after the assassination of Henri III in 1589. He converted to Catholicism to enable his accession, but introduced the Edict of Nantes that granted freedom of Protestant worship in 1598, and was therefore feted by Enlightenment figures such as Voltaire as a symbol of tolerance. Maximilien de Béthune, duc de Sully (1559–1641) was his most important minister, himself a protestant, who introduced the financial and agrarian reforms that help to repair the damage of the Wars of Religion.

18. True happiness ... an enemy to pomp: The French text includes Genlis's translation of this quotation as a footnote: 'Le vrai bonheur ne se trouve que dans la solitude, il fuit la pompe et le bruit'. The 1784 English edition's note includes only the reference: 'See the Spectator, Vol. I' (*Adelaide and Theodore ...The Second Edition*, vol. 1, p. 38). For the original quotation see D. F. Bond (ed.), *The Spectator*, 5 vols (Oxford: Clarendon Press, 1965), vol. 1, p. 67. The sentiments are repeated in volume 5, when the story of the happiest man is told: 'he was found to be an obscure Countryman, who employed all his Time in cultivating a Garden, and a few Acres of Land about his House'. See Bond (ed.), *The Spectator*, vol. 5, p. 86.

19. *Countess de Valmont ... has only one son*: This first mention of this character (Charles de Valmont, who will become the romantic hero and husband of Adelaide) calls to mind Laclos's character Valmont from his highly successful *Dangerous Liaisons*, also published in 1782, although contemporary readers would not have seen this connection. See note 37 to Volume III, below.

20. *There was a serious party at Reversis*: Here the translator mistranslates the original French, which refers to a card game, reversi, as the subsequent sentences make apparent.

21. *what do you think of Rousseau's method?*: The Viscountess de Limours is referring to Rousseau's writings on how to improve physical strength and health of children, which are spread throughout *Émile*, but can be found in particular in the opening pages of

Book II, when Rousseau recommends outdoors activity and non-restrictive clothing. See Rousseau, *Émile*, pp. 77–85.

22. *Rousseau ... with words that have in general no sense in them*: These ideas are discussed in Book II of *Émile*: 'If children understood reason, they would not need to be raised. But by speaking to them from an early age a language which they do not understand, one accustoms them to show off with words, to control all that is said to them, to believe themselves as wise as their masters'. See Rousseau, *Émile*, p. 89.

23. *Fontaine's Fables*: Jean de la Fontaine (1621–95), known for his *Fables*, which are still commonly learnt by rote by French children. Rousseau observes in *Émile* that 'all children are made to learn the fables of La Fontaine; and there is not a single one who understands them' (Rousseau, *Émile*, p. 113). Peter France points out that there are few eighteenth-century English translations of la Fontaine's work, and that 'imitation was more common than actual translation'. See Gillespie and Hopkins (eds), *The Oxford History of Literary Translation in English: Vol. 3 1660–1790*, pp. 310–12.

24. *Telemachus*: *Télémaque* (*c.* 1695) by François de Salignac de la Mothe-Fénelon (1651–1715) was written for the Duke of Bourgogne, Fénelon's royal pupil. It is a continuation of Book IV of the *Odyssey*, and was an important text in the Enlightenment period, in large part because of an episode where an ideal city-state, Salente, is described which was seen as a criticism of Louis XIV's governance. A prescribed text for students of French for two centuries, it was the text that was most often reprinted in the eighteenth century. See Peter France (ed.) *The New Oxford Companion to Literature in French* (Oxford: Clarendon Press, 1995), p. 794. It is referred to frequently in *Adelaide and Theodore*, particularly in reference to the education of the Prince, although Adelaide and Theodore also read it.

25. *Madame de Sevigny's Letters*: Marie de Rabutin-Chantal, marquise de Sévigné (1626–96) is the author of a voluminous correspondence (over 1,000 letters have been recovered), part of which was translated anonymously in 1727 and 1757–65. She was frequently admired by Genlis for her perfect model of the epistolary style. See, for example, the introduction to Genlis's *De l'influence des femmes sur la literature française comme protectrices des Lettres ou comme auteurs. Précis de l'histoire des femmes françaises les plus célèbres* (Paris: Maradan, 1811). No translation of this work (*On the Influence of Women on French Literature as Literary Patrons or as Authors*) exists, although it was known and reviewed in Britain.

26. *the Works of Corneille*: Pierre Corneille (1606–84), the author of thirty-two plays, the most celebrated of which are the tragedies *Le Cid* (1637) and *Cinna* (1640/1). Several were translated into English in the mid- and late seventeenth century, including *La Mort de Pompée*, translated by Katharine Philips as *Pompey* and staged in Dublin in 1663. Paulina Kewes points out that only three translations of Corneille's plays were printed post-1700. See Gillespie and Hopkins (eds), *The Oxford History of Literary Translation in English: Vol. 3 1660–1790*, pp. 319–21.

27. *Racine*: Jean Racine (1639–99), an important tragedian, author of plays such as *Andromaque* (1667) and *Phèdre* (1677). As Paulina Kewes notes, the anonymous translation of *Andromaque* did not find favour with the London audience who saw it in 1674, and throughout the eighteenth century, it was Molière (Jean-Baptiste Poquelin, 1622–73) rather than either Corneille or Racine, that was viewed as the French Shakespeare in eighteenth-century Britain. See Gillespie and Hopkins (eds), *The Oxford History of Literary Translation in English: Vol. 3 1660–1790*, pp. 321–2.

28. *Crebillon*: One of two Crébillons, Prosper Jolyot de Crébillon (1674–1762), playwright, or Claude-Prosper Jolyot de Crébillon (1707–77), novelist, could be meant here. It is likely, however, that Genlis intends her reader only to think of the older Crébillon, since the licentious nature of the younger Crébillon's libertine novels (one of which was partly translated from Eliza Haywood's *The Fortunate Foundlings* (1744)) would never have been suggested in the context of Adelaide's reading, even at an older age than she is represented in this letter.

29. *Voltaire*: François-Marie Arouet (1694–1778), philosopher and major Enlightenment figure, author of works of history such as *Le Siècle de Louis XIV* (*The Century of Louis XIV*) (1751) and tales such as *Candide ou l'Optimisme* (*Candide or Optimism*) (1759). Voltaire held a similar attraction/repulsion for Genlis as Rousseau. She was repelled by what she saw as his lack of religion, and published an edited version of his Louis XIV in 1820: *Le Siècle de Louis XIV* (Paris: Maradan, 1820).

30. *those plays ... which are recommended by Rousseau to preserve them from the fears ... of being in the dark*: The French is 'des jeux de nuits recommandés par Rousseau'. The 'night games' Rousseau recommends to prevent children from being afraid of the dark are described in Book II of *Émile*:

> for these games to succeed, I cannot recommend enough that there be gaiety in them. Nothing is so sad as darkness. Do not go and close your child up in a dungeon. Let him be laughing as he enters the dark; let laughter overtake him again before he leaves it. ... nothing is more reassuring to someone frightened of shadows in the night than to hear company, assembled in a neighbouring room, laughing and chatting calmly. (Rousseau, *Émile*, pp. 134–8).

31. *The word study is never mentioned*: The French is less emphatic, and we read that 'the word study is *almost* never mentioned' (my emphasis).

32. *practicing music in two hands ... the best way*: Genlis was an accomplished harpist, and published a new method for learning to play the harp in 1802, which involved practicing both hands separately: *Nouvelle méthode pour apprendre à jouer de l'harpe* (Paris: Mme Duhan, 1802).

33. *keep him from such a master, as would ... teach him to draw from designs*: In Book II of *Émile*, Rousseau states of his pupil that he will 'carefully avoid giving him a drawing master who would give him only imitations to imitate and would make him draw only from drawings. I want him to have no other master than nature and no other model than objects'. See Rousseau, *Émile*, p. 144.

34. *theorbo*: a popular late sixteenth- and seventeenth-century instrument similar to a lute, widely used in France in the first part of the eighteenth century.

35. *knotting*: the French 'parfiler' is perhaps best translated as 'untwisting'. Genlis explains the curious custom of 'fringe untwisting' in her *Memoirs*:

> The remarks on society in *Adèle et Théodore* raised me also many enemies, because they were true, piquant, and without exaggeration. All the fringe untwisters were furious against me: this fashion was so prevalent then, that I must explain the practice. The ladies were in the habit of asking all the gentlemen of their acquaintance for their old gold epaulettes, their gold lace sword-knots, or the laces on their coats, &c. which were thus taken from their servants, and which the ladies then untwisted – that is to say – they separated the gold from the silk, to sell the former afterwards for their own profit [...] In general an able untwister might gain at this singular trade one hundred louis a year! (*Memoirs of the Countess of Genlis, Illustrative of the Eighteenth and Nineteenth centuries. Written by Herself*, 8 vols (London: Henry Colburn, 1825), vol. 3, pp. 141–3)

36. *Rousseau ... exactly follows the system of Mr Locke ... he copies him literally*: John Locke (1632–1704) published his *Some Thoughts Concerning Education* in 1693, and an expanded version was published in 1695. The first book of the treaty is devoted entirely to the health of the child, with such advice as *'feet to be washed* every day in cold water, and to have his *shoes* so thin that they might leak and *let in water* whenever he comes near it'. See John Locke, *Some Thoughts Concerning Education and Of the Conduct of the Understanding*, ed. Ruth W. Grant and Nathan Tarcov (Indianapolis: Hackett, 1996), p. 12. Clara Reeve quoted from Genlis's passage at length in her *Plans of Education*:

> Locke's system of Education was admired by all wise and virtuous parents: it was admired but not followed. Madame de Genlis has accounted for this with her usual penetration and sagacity: 'Locke's work was translated into all languages. It was in everybody's hands when Rousseau's *Emilius* appeared; - but had not brought about any change in the systems adopted. Wisdom has less influence than enthusiasm, because it is always simple in its expressions, and scarce ever assumes an imposing or authoritative tone. The English philosopher only seemed to give his advice; Rousseau repeated the same things, but he did not advise; he commanded, and was obeyed.' She likewise observes that Rousseau follows the system of Mr. Locke in almost every respect; he copies him literally, but without quoting him, or acknowledging his obligations to him. It is thus that many other French writers have imitated our best authors on most subjects. (Clara Reeve, *Plans of Education; with Remarks on the Systems of Other Writers. In a Series of Letters between Mrs Darnford and her Friends* (London: T. Hookham and J. Carpenter, 1792), pp. 39–40)

37. *Fairy Tales, till they are thirteen?*: The French text refers to reading of an older age, fifteen. Genlis takes a dim view of fairy tales, as the next letter from the Baroness will show. In the *Tales of the Castle* (1782; trans. 1785), Genlis included a tale 'Alphonse et Dalinde' in which all that appears to be magical has a rational explanation.

38. *Madame d'Aulnoy's Fables*: Marie-Catherine Le Jumel de Barneville, comtesse d'Aulnoy (c. 1650–1705) wrote both fiction and history, and is now largely known for her *Les Contes des fées* (*Fairy Tales*) (1697) and *Les Contes nouveaux* (*New Tales*) (1698).

39. *Locke ... not a single work ... proper for infancy ... in the French language*: The Baroness is distorting Locke's comments on suitable reading material for children, which can be found in the section entitled 'Reading' in *Some Thoughts on Education*, where he recommends Aesop's *Fables* and goes on to say:

> What other *books* there are in English of the kind of those mentioned above, fit *to engage* the liking of children and tempt them *to read*, I do not know but am apt to think that [because of] children being generally delivered over to the methods of schools, where the fear of the rod is to enforce and not any pleasure of the employment to invite them to learn, this sort of useful books amongst the number of silly ones that are of all sorts have yet had the fate to be neglected. (Locke, *Some Thoughts Concerning Education*, pp. 116–18)

The Baroness is making a general point about the dearth of material suitable for children, which is not entirely accurate. Tales for children did exist in the French language prior to the publication of *Adelaide and Theodore*, although it would be another year before the most popular late eighteenth-century work for children, Arnaud Berquin's *L'Ami des Enfants* (*The Children's Friend*) was serialized in 1782–3. Madame leprince de Beaumont, for example, published her *Le Magasin des enfants, ou Dialogues d'une sage gouvernante et plusieurs de ses élèves* (*Dialogues between a Wise Governess and Several of her Pupils*) in 1756, and this work, which included the fairy-tale *La Belle et la Bête* (*Beauty and the Beast*) saw many editions throughout the remainder of the century.

With the Baroness and Genlis's mistrust of fairy tales, it is perhaps not surprising that none are thought to be suitable.

40. *We call it the 'Castle Evening'*: Here, as in other places in the novel, Genlis attributes authorship of one of her own texts to the Baroness. *Les Veillées du château* (1782) would be better translated as *Evenings at the Castle*: it appeared in English in 1785 as *Tales of the Castle*, translated by Thomas Holcroft.

41. *I shall then give her the 'Conversations of Emily'*: *Les Conversations d'Emilie* by Louise-Florence d'Esclavelles, Madame d'Épinay (1726–83) was first published in 1775. The second volume (1782) won a prize from the French Academy that had been founded by M. de Monthyon to reward the most useful and best written prose work in 1782, at the expense of *Adèle et Théodore* and *Les Veillées du château*. Genlis wrote of this work in her *Memoirs*:

> I thought it, as it really is, full of errors in the diction, and of vicious and vulgar modes of expression – and besides the ideas in it are all common-place [...] *the prize for the new work published in the course of the year, and esteemed the best written and the most useful* was decreed to the second volume of the *Conversations d'Emilie*! This work, even if it had been faultless, did not qualify its author to stand for the prize, as it was not a *new work*, but only the continuation of a former one. (*Memoirs of the Countess of Genlis*, vol. 3, p. 154)

The English translation of *Les Conversations d'Emilie* (*The Conversations of Emily; Translated from the French of Madame la Comtesse d'Epigny* [*sic*] (London: John Marshall and Co, 1787)) did not appear until after the publication of *Adelaide and Theodore*.

42. *Miss Bridget added more particulars ... to the praise of Adelaide's sensibility*: This tale of childhood charity and sensibility is similar to several accounts of the Clémire children's philanthropy in Genlis's *Tales of the Castle*. In one notable episode, Madame de Clémire and her son Caesar come across two frozen brothers, the elder of whom has taken off his jacket to warm the younger. Madame de Clémire comments 'O! my child, how sublime is pity, since it can inspire virtue like this', and this inspires Caesar in turn to offer acts of charity to the family. See the eighth edition of *Tales of the Castle*, 5 vols (London: G. G. J. and J. Robinson, 1806), vol. 1, pp. 112–13.

43. *Here begins our dialogue word for word*: This passage was particularly admired in the British Reviews. The *Gentleman's Magazine* wrote 'That incomparable incident, early in the book, where Adelaide is debating about the liberty of her bird, her mother writing in the room, is a dialogue that must for ever stamp the fame and powers of its author, had nothing else been written by her.' See *Gentleman's Magazine*, 53 (1783), pp. 860–2.

44. *Lacedæmonians*: Spartans, inhabited the Greek island of Lacedaemon, or Sparta, and were noted for their self-discipline as well as for the harshness of their regime with its emphasis on physical fitness.

45. *a pretty little box made for sweetmeats ... the strictest fidelity*: This episode is cited in Edgeworth's *Practical Education* (1798):

> Madame de Genlis, in her *Adèle and Théodore*, gives Théodore, when he is about seven years old, a box of sugar plums to take care of, to teach him to command his passions. Theodore produces the untouched treasure to his mother from time to time, with great self-complacency. We think this a good practical lesson. (*The Novels and Selected Works of Maria Edgeworth*, 12 vols (London: Pickering and Chatto, 2003), vol. 11, ed. Susan Manly, p. 131)

Such is the dominance of the Baroness's presence as educator, that Edgeworth does not remember that this lesson is actually taught by the Baron, Theodore's father.

46. *Milton, Tasso, and Ariosto ... Fenelon, Montequieu, Addison &c*: The claim that modern European classics rival the Latin and Greek poets is repeated throughout Genlis's works. Of particular note in this passage is the inclusion of authors from Britain, Ireland and Germany. The passage mentions only very few writers who are not mentioned elsewhere, including Jonathan Swift (1667–1745) and James Thomson (1700–48), whose *The Seasons* (1730) was much admired in France.

47. *The modern Authors Klopstock, Haller, Gesner, Gellert*: Friedrich Gottlieb Klopstock (1728–1803), the most celebrated German poet at the time of publication of *Adelaide and Theodore*. Albrecht von Haller (1708–77), Swiss botanist, anatomist, poet, and all-round Enlightenment figure. Salomon Gessner (1730–88), painter and poet. Christian Fürchtegott Gellert (1715–69), poet and author of fables which took La Fontaine as the model. The Baron's opinion that there was nothing of much note in German literature was not an unusual one to hold in France at the time. Genlis's rival Germaine de Staël's *De l'Allemagne* was not published until 1807.

48. *the education of the last Czar*: Peter III of Russia (1728–62), Emperor of Russia for only six months before the coup-d'état lead by his wife, Catherine II (1729–96). She became known as Catherine the Great from 1762 when she became reigning Empress, and was the Empress at the time of publication of *Adelaide and Theodore*, making Peter III 'the last Czar'. With this reference to Peter III as a flawed ruler with military pretensions (he sided with Prussia and withdrew from the Seven Years War), the Baron blames nature and nurture for his flaws.

49. *that glorious king of Sweden*: Charles XII (1682–1718) was King of Sweden from 1692 until his death. He was a celebrated military campaigner, but, as the Baron suggests here, was single minded to the point of foolishness: the end of his reign signaled the end of the Swedish Empire.

50. *'the Tutor may judge of his pace'*: the relevant section of Michel de Montaigne's essay 'On the Education of Children' reads:

> I don't want him to think and talk alone, I want him to listen to his pupil speaking in his turn. Socrates, and later Arcesilaus, first has their disciples speak, and then they spoke to them. *The authority of those who teach is often an obstacle to those who want to learn* [Cicero]. It is good that he should have his pupil trot before him, to judge the child's pace and how much he must stoop to match his strength. (Montaigne, *The Complete Works*, p. 134)

51. *a man born naturally good ... will always remain so'*: This 'quotation' from Rousseau is not a quotation in the original French, but rather a summary of Rousseau's ideas in *The Social Contract* (1762).

52. *'tear each other to pieces'*: Michel de Montaigne's essay 'Of Cruelty' reads, 'Nature herself, I fear, attaches to man some instinct for inhumanity. No one takes his sport in seeing animals play with and caress one another, and no one fails to take it in seeing them tear apart and dismember one another'. See Montaigne, *The Complete Works*, p. 383.

53. *'never pity children when they fall down or hurt themselves'*: This paraphrase of Rousseau's comments can be found in the beginning of Book II of *Émile*, when the tutor tells his reader:

> Whatever injury a child may do to himself, it is very rare that he cries when he is alone, unless he hopes to be heard. If he falls, if he bumps his head, if his nose bleeds, if he cuts his fingers, instead of fussing around him as though I were alarmed, I will remain calm, at least for a short time. The harm is done; it is a necessity that he endure it; all my fussing would only serve to frighten him more and increase his sensitivity. (Rousseau, *Émile*, p. 77)

Locke voices a similar opinion in his *Some Thoughts Concerning Education*:

> Many children are apt to *cry* upon any little pain they suffer, and the least harm that befalls them puts them into *complaints* and *bawling* [...] Help and ease them the best you can, but by no means bemoan them. This softens their minds and makes them yield to the little harms that happen to them' (Locke, *Some Thoughts Concerning Education*, p. 84).

54. *'how then can she be a good nurse?'*: In Book I of *Émile*, Rousseau writes 'There is no substitute for maternal solicitude. She who nurses another's child in place of her own is a bad mother. How will she be a good nurse?' See Rousseau, *Émile*, p. 45. Genlis's comments on breast-feeding in this letter are more sensitive to the demands on the mother herself.

55. *'the cares of an interested and mercenary woman'*: This is paraphrasing Rousseau's words which appear earlier in Book I of *Émile* than those quoted above: 'Since mothers, despising their first duty, have no longer wanted to feed their children, it has been necessary to confide them to mercenary women who, thus finding themselves mothers of alien children on whose behalf nature tells them nothing, have sought only to save themselves effort'. See Rousseau, *Émile*, p. 44.

56. *nor shall I hear Gluck and Piccini*: The Baroness d'Almane is referring here to a notorious public debate which placed the German opera composer Christop Willibald (von) Gluck (1714–87) in opposition to the Italian composer Niccolò Piccinni (1728–1800), known as 'la querelle des bouffons'. Genlis herself, like Rousseau (but unlike her character the Baroness who claims to admire both composers) tended to side with Gluck. The 1784 English edition includes the following note by the translators: 'Two celebrated performers then at Paris'. See *Adelaide and Theodore ... The Second Edition*, vol. 1, p. 98.

57. *a sister, who is a nun*: The story of Madame de Valmont's sister Cecilia, the beautiful nun, was included in the *Universal Magazine*'s translation of extracts from *Adelaide and Theodore*, and this translation was reprinted in *Tell-Tale*, 3 (1804) and *Gleaner*, 2 (1806), pp. 162–182. See Robert Mayo, *The English Novel in the Magazines* (Evanston, IL: Northwestern University Press, 1962) pp. 513–14.

58. *at Province*: The French reads 'en province', an expression which simply means outside Paris.

59. *her long and beautiful hair ... had been placed*: The original French includes a note by Genlis which is translated in the 1784 edition: 'It is customary to cut off a novices hair just before she pronounces her vows'. See *Adelaide and Theodore ... The Second Edition*, vol. 1, p. 105.

60. *continually reminded of the misfortune under which she groans*: A note by the translators in the 1784 edition reads: 'Though a woman of family, and as such visiting and receiving persons belonging to the Court; yet as wife of a Financier, she cannot appear there herself'. See *Adelaide and Theodore ... The Second Edition*, vol. 1, p. 111.

61. *concealed perhaps at La Trappe*: A note by the translators in the second edition reads: 'A most rigid order of Monks'. See *Adelaide and Theodore ... The Second Edition*, vol. 1, p. 112.

62. *Mons. de Fénelon*: François de Salignac de la Mothe-Fénelon (1651–1715); his *Traité de l'éducation des filles* was published in 1687. Genlis's note, translated in the 1784 edition, reads:

> Rousseau has taken a multitude of ideas from the work of Mons. de Fénelon, entitled *The Education of Daughters*, and among others this – 'The early age,' says Mons. de Fénelon, 'in which we give them up to women, often indiscreet, and sometimes dissolute, is nevertheless that in which the most profound impressions are made, and which have, consequently, a

great influence upon the rest of their lives. Before children can well speak they may be prepared for instruction, &c. Chap. 3. Children ought not to be put too forward; I even think that we ought to make use of indirect instructions, which may serve to raise their attention by examples, and which are not tiresome, like lessons and remonstrances'. With regard to the natural defects of women, the manner of curing them, the accomplishments which are proper for them, and the qualities which ought to form their character, Rousseau has scarce done more than repeat what Mons. de Fénelon has said on the subject. (*Adelaide and Theodore … The Second Edition*, vol. 1, pp. 116–17)

The quotation attributed to Fénelon is a truncated version of 'The First Foundations of a Right Education', the third chapter of his book *Instructions for the Education of Daughters, by M. Fénelon Archbishop of Cambray, Translated from the French and Revised by George Hickes, D.D.* (Glasgow: R.&A. Foulis, 1750), pp. 9–18.

63. *every thing that is truly useful in his book*: Genlis's note to this, translated in the 1784 edition, reads: 'Even the idea of making his pupil learn a trade is not his own: a law of the Alcoran prescribes it, and Locke advises to teach boys to learn gardening, and carpenter's work'. See *Adelaide and Theodore … The Second Edition*, vol. 1, p. 117.

64. *'the desire of making our scholars appear brilliant'*: Genlis's note to this point, translated in the 1784 English edition, reads:

> Even this idea is not new, no more than that of endeavouring to form the heart and the morals, rather than striving to load the memory with an infinite number of things, for the most part useless. Montaigne has said 'The end we aim at in our instructions is, not to make men prudent and good, but learned. We know what virtue is, but we do not love it.' The author of the *Education of a Prince*, by Chanteresne, after having drawn the portrait of a good preceptor, adds – 'The man of whom we are speaking has no set hour for his lesson; or rather, he gives his scholar a lesson every hour; for he instructs him often, as much in his amusements, visits, and conversation, as when he makes him read books; because his principal aim being to form his judgment, the divers objects which present themselves, are often more adapted to that purpose, than studied discourses. As this manner of instruction is imperceptible, the profit drawn from it, is in some sort so too; and this is what deceives persons of little observation; who imagine that a child thus instructed, is not more advanced than another, because, perhaps, he cannot make a better translation from the Latin, or because he cannot better repeat a lesson of Virgil,' &c. All these ideas are to be found in Rousseau's *Emilius*. (*Adelaide and Theodore … The Second Edition*, vol. 1, p. 117)

The quotation from Montaigne is from his essay 'Of Presumption', and the full passage reads:

> I gladly return to the subject of the ineptitude of our education. Its goal has been to make us not good or wise, but learned; it has attained this goal. It has not taught us to follow and embrace virtue and wisdom, but it has imprinted in us their derivation and etymology. We know how to decline virtue, if we cannot love it. (Montaigne, *The Complete Works*, p. 608)

For 'the *Education of a Prince*, by Chanteresne', see note 10 to Volume I, above, and note 72 to Volume I, below. The quotation is from points XVI–XVII of the first part, pp. 10–11.

65. *he offers almost in every page opposite inferences*: Genlis's note, translated in the 1784 English edition, reads:

> The Creed of the *Savoyard Vicar*, for instance, who after having declared his opinions, allows it may be dangerous to spread them, and that one ought to respect the faith of others, &c. This is known to have been the creed of Rousseau himself, who, after particularizing the

inconveniences that may result from the imprudence of making it public, prints it – Is it possible to be more inconsistent!' (*Adelaide and Theodore ... The Second Edition*, vol. 1, p. 118).

66. *'he would no longer have wished to be a Prince'*: The Count de Roseville is quoting Rousseau's remarks in Book I of *Émile*:

> Someone of whom I know only the rank had the proposal to raise his son conveyed to me. He doubtless did me a great deal of honour; but far from complaining about my refusal, he ought to congratulate himself on my discretion. If I had accepted his offer and my method were mistaken, the education would have been a failure. If I had succeeded, it would have been far worse. His son would have repudiated his title; he would no longer have wished to be a prince. (Rousseau, *Émile*, p. 50)

Rousseau differentiates between the education of the sexes, but he does not believe that the education should fit the future station of children. The Count de Roseville, and Genlis herself do not agree, as can be seen in such works as Genlis's *Discours sur l'Éducation de M. le Dauphin et sur l'adoption* (1790).

67. *Moncrief ... 'Essays on the Necessity and Means of Pleasing'*: The translator has anglicized the spelling of the author who is F. A. Paradis de Moncrif (1687–1770), author of a famous *Histoire des chats* (1727). His *Essai sur la nécessité et les moyens de plaire* was published in Paris in 1738. I can find no evidence of an English translation of this work.

68. *'to make ourselves beloved by them'*: Genlis's note, translated in the 1784 edition, reads:

> This is not a good answer, it sets too great a value on money; besides, the expression – *to do good to our fellow creatures*, is too vague; and conveys the idea that every body loves money. It is impossible to explain that question in one answer alone; a long discourse would scarce suffice. (*Adelaide and Theodore ... The Second Edition*, vol. 1, pp. 119–20)

The original quotation can be found in F. A. Paradis de Moncrif, *Essai sur la nécessité et les moyens de plaire* (Paris: Payot et Rivage, 2002), pp. 86–7.

69. *'we should speak to them of respect, deference, gratitude, friendship, &c.'*: Genlis's note, translated in the 1784 English edition, reads: 'Even though the child were destined to be master of the world; for the greater his rank the more important it is to accustom him to respect men truly distinguished by their virtue'. See *Adelaide and Theodore ... The Second Edition*, vol. 1, p. 120. The original quotation can be found in Moncrif, *Essai sur la nécessité et les moyens de plaire*, pp. 96–7: Genlis's rendering is a paraphrase.

70. *being a stranger*: the French 'étranger' is best translated as foreigner in this context.

71. *I shall say nothing of* Bellisarius: Jean-François Marmontel (1723–99) published his account of the life of the Roman general Belisarius *Bélisaire* in 1767. At least thirty English editions of this work had been printed by 1800. Genlis was to publish her own version of Belisarius's story in 1808; an English translation quickly followed, *Belisarius* (London: Henry Colburn, 1808).

72. *Chanteresne*: Genlis's note, translated in the 1784 edition, reads: 'Chanteresne is generally supposed to be a feigned name; some attribute the work to Pascal; but the most common opinion is that Nicole is the Author of it.' See *Adelaide and Theodore ... The Second Edition*, vol. 1, p. 123, and note 10 to Volume I, above.

73. *Abbe Duguet*: Jacques Joseph Duguet (1649–1733). The work in question here is his 1739 *Institution d'un prince, ou traité des qualities, des vertus et des devoirs d'un souverain*, 4 vols (London: J. Nourse, 1750). The place of publication is likely to have been faked to escape the censor, and it has been suggested that the work may have been published in

the Netherlands. Genlis's note, translated in the 1784 English edition, reads: 'The Abbé Duguet wrote his book for the use of the eldest son of the Duke of Savoy'. See *Adelaide and Theodore ... The Second Edition*, vol. 1, p. 123.

74. *because it is tedious*: Genlis includes a note to this in the original French which the translator does not give in the 1784 English edition. In the note Genlis laments Duguet's comments on poetry, in which he compares kings and heroes to pagan gods, and says that the depiction of them on stage and through music encourages idolatry. See *Adèle et Théodore ou Lettres sur l'éducation contenant tous les principes relatifs aux trois différents plans d'éducation des Princes et des jeunes personnes de l'un et l'autre sexe*, ed. Isabelle Brouard-Arends (Rennes: Presses universitaires de Rennes, 2006), p. 133.

75. *'Prudence ... for fear of being seen, she sees almost nothing'*: Duguet, *Institution d'un prince*, vol. 1, p. 231 (chapter XX, article III, paragraph VI). No English translation of this work appears to have been published, and I therefore give the reference to the French text, which opens 'La Prudence, quand elle est parfaite'.

76. *flattery ... 'compound with it'*: Duguet, *Institution d'un prince*, vol. 1, pp. 90–1 (chapter X, article II, paragraph XIII and XIV). The French text opens 'Ainsi, l'unique moyen de s'en défendre'.

77. *an excellent saying of an ancient Philosopher*: Seneca, *Letters to Lucilius*, XLVII.1.

78. *'Children should always be commended ... when they confess a fault, be it what it will'*: The English text quotes here where the French merely paraphrases. In Locke's system, lying is the worst crime that can be committed by a child:

> It should be always (when occasionally it comes to be mentioned) spoken of before him with the utmost detestation, as a quality so wholly inconsistent with the name and character of a gentleman that nobody of any credit can bear the imputation of a lie [...] The first time he is found in a *lie*, it should rather be wondered at as a monstrous thing in him than reproved as an ordinary fault.

Locke goes on to write of children's faults:

> If therefore when a child is questioned for anything his first answer be an *excuse*, warn him soberly to tell the truth; and then if he persists to shuffle it off with a *falsehood*, he must be chastised. But if he directly confess, you must commend his ingenuousness and pardon the fault. (Locke, *Some Thoughts Concerning Education*, pp. 101–2).

79. 'Dramas for the use of children and young persons': Once again, Genlis attributes one of her own publications, the *Théâtre à l'usage des jeunes personnes* (1779–80) or *Theatre of Education* (1781), to the Baroness.

80. Flaggons ... *the* Dove ... *the* Traveller ... The Ball for Children: All the plays mentioned in this paragraph form part of Genlis's *Theatre of Education*. The first two mentioned, 'The Flaggons' and 'The Dove' contain only female characters. They were particularly admired in Britain: the *London Magazine* in a review of Genlis's plays wrote approvingly that 'all love intrigues, low humour, and loose conversation, is secluded'. See *London Magazine* (December 1780), pp. 569–70.

81. *prefer such pieces to French Comedies*: A note added by the translators in the 1784 English edition reads: 'He [*sic*] means that he does not prefer these indecent pieces to those acted at the Theatre called *La Comedie Française*, which is always decent, and indeed the French stage is much more chaste than ours. Note of the Translators'. See *Adelaide and Theodore ... The Second Edition*, vol. 1, p. 149.

82. *Lord Chesterfield, in* Letters to his Son: Philip Dormer Stanhope, Earl of Chesterfield (1694–1773); his *Letters to his Son* were not published until 1774, after his death.

83. *'Women ... a man of sense ... neither consults them about, nor trusts them with serious mat-*
     ters': The translation of Chesterfield's remarks in the French text appears to be Genlis's
     own. She includes Chesterfield's original in a note, the text of which is worth quoting
     since it is slightly different to the text provided by the English translator:

> Women are only children of a larger growth; they have an entertaining tattle, sometimes
> wit; but for solid, reasoning good sense, I have never in my life knew one that had it, or
> who reasoned or acted consequentially for twenty and four hours together... A man of
> sense only triffles with them plays with them humours and flatters them as he does with a
> sprightly forward child: but he neither consults them about nor trust [*sic*] them with serious
> matters' (*Adèle et Théodore*, ed. Brouard-Arends, p. 150).

     Chesterfield's comments can be found in his letter CLXI, dated London 5 September
     1748. See *Letters Written by the Late Right Honourable Philip Dormer Stanhope, Earl of
     Chesterfield, to his Son Philip Stanhope, esq. together with Several Other Pieces on Various
     Subjects*, 9th edn, 4 vols (London: P. Dodsley, 1787), vol. 2, pp. 81–2.

84. *'true politeness ... can only be acquired by keeping good company'*: Genlis's note, inserted
     into the main body of the text by the translators in the 1784 English edition, reads 'Vol.
     II'. See *Adelaide and Theodore ... The Second Edition*, vol. 1, p. 151. Chesterfield's original
     letter is CXIV, dated London May 24 1750. See *Letters Written by the Late Right Hon-
     ourable Philip Dormer Stanhope*, vol. 3, p. 98.

85. *'not believing what we do not understand'*: Montaigne, essay 27: 'It is folly to measure the
     true and false by our own capacity'. The translators render this phrase almost incompre-
     hensible. It should read, 'It is a dangerous and fateful presumption, besides the absurd
     temerity that it implies, to disdain what we do not comprehend'. See Montaigne, *The
     Complete Works*, p. 163.

86. *their little country retirements*: The French text reads 'leurs petites maisons', which is an
     allusion that the English translator presumably did not pick up, in light of the translation
     'country retirements'. In fact, the term has faintly scandalous undertones, since a 'petite
     maison' was a secondary residence at which one could be 'at home' to callers one could
     not receive in the main household.

87. *my old friend Madame de Surville*: this character was seen at the time of the original
     publication as a pen-portrait of Genlis's aunt, Madame de Montesson, wife of the Duke
     of Orléans. As a satire of a pedant, the portrait was not a flattering one. The relationship
     between aunt and niece was never an easy one, as Genlis makes clear in the Preface to her
     Memoirs: 'In proving from facts that Madame de Montesson was never my *benefactress*,
     and that she has never in her life done me a single service, I have always spoken of her
     without animosity; I have never attacked her character or reputation'. See *Memoirs of the
     Countess de Genlis*, vol. 1, p. vi.

88. *to play at* Biribi: French game of chance, in which players place bets on a board with
     numbers marked one to seventy.

89. *Tantalus*: In Greek mythology, Tantalus, son of Zeus, was punished for cannibalism and
     human sacrifice by being condemned to stand beneath a fruit tree in a pool of water, and
     yet never be able to eat or drink.

90. *Moliere ridiculed the learned women of his age*: *Les Précieuses Ridicules* was first performed
     on the French stage in 1659. It is a satire of the novels of Madeleine de Scudéry, and
     female preciosity more generally.

91. *playing at Pharo*: or Faro, an extremely popular card game in both France and England in
     the eighteenth century.

92. *Reville ... d'Auberville*: Pierre-Louis Dubus (1721–99) actor at the Comédie Française, and Jean Bercher (1742–1806) dancer and later choreographer. The translator uses the original French spelling of Dauberville, d'Auberville, and misspells Préville as Reville. This suggests that the point being made in this passage, that the majority of the 'Ladies of our time' have undiscriminating tastes (Jeannot and the petit-diable symbolize the popular theatre) and are amused by everything, would only have been understood by English readers in a general sense, since they would not have picked up on the direct references in the text.

93. *Madame de Sevigny*: see note 25 to Volume I, above.

94. *des Houlieres*: Antoinette Du Ligier de La Garde, Des Houlières (1638–94) was a highly regarded French lyric poet, known for her pastoral poetry, who received the first ever prize for poetry awarded by the Académie Française in 1671.

95. *Grafignys*: Françoise d'Issembourg d'Happoncourt, Madame de Graffigny (sometimes still seen as 'Grafigny', as in the text here) (1695–1758) was the best-selling French author of *Lettres d'une Péruvienne* (1747). This work, the fictional letters of a Peruvian Princess in France, was a European success, and saw fifteen English editions between 1748 and 1787. Jennifer Birkett sees it as a case-study of the popularity of French romance in the latter half of the eighteenth century: 'The first translated editions appeared in 1748, to be followed by revised editions with sequel in 1749; new translations, editions, and reprints followed in 1753, 1759, 1762, and up to the end of the century. Roberts's lively version (1774), fairly accurate for the most part, took the liberty of adding a sentimental sequel of her own invention.' See Gillespie and Hopkins (eds), *The Oxford History of Literary Translation in English*, p. 345.

96. Tartuffe: comedy by Molière, subtitled 'The Imposter' and first performed in 1664.

97. Misanthrope: Molière's comedy *Le Misanthrope* was first performed in 1666, and is considered to be the playwright's best work.

98. *Louis le Grand*: Louis the Great or the Sun King, King Louis XIV of France (1638–1715). He reigned for the second half of the seventeenth, and into the eighteenth century, acceding to the throne shortly before his fifth birthday.

99. *Poems of Madame de Houlieres*: see note 94 to Volume I, above.

100. *Greuse's ... Danaë*: Jean Baptise Greuse (1725–1805), French painter, exhibited his Danaé (in Greek mythology the mother of Perseus, impregnated by Zeus in the form of a sunbeam) in 1781, stressing the contemporary setting of Genlis's novel.

101. Rodugune: *Rodogune*, a tragedy by Pierre Corneille which was first performed in 1645.

102. Les Battus payent l'amende ... Le Café des Halles: the first was a play by Louis-Francois Archambault, known as Dorvigny (1742–1812), performed at the 'Théatre de variétés amusantes' in June 1779; the second, by Charles Jacob Guillemain (1750–1799), was performed at the same theatre in 1780. See *Adèle et Théodore*, ed. Brouard-Arends, p. 646.

103. *The contents of a certain utensil*: The English translator here only obliquely refers to the vulgarity of the French play that is explicit in the original text. The 'certain utensil' is in fact a 'pot de chambre' (chamber pot), the contents of which fall on the unfortunate Jeannot.

104. *gardens formed after the English fashion ... within the walls of Paris*: Genlis here avoids the fashionable anglomania of her compatriots, in particular the Duke de Chartres himself, who created a 'jardin à l'anglaise' for his house in Monceau in 1773, formerly the outskirts of Paris, now forming part of the Parc Monceau in the seventeenth arrondissement of Paris itself. See also note 117 to Volume I, below.

105. *Emperor Vespasian*: (9–79 AD) ruled Rome from 69–79 AD and was founder of the influential Flavian dynasty.

106. *Madame de Lambert, in her* Advice from a Mother to her Son ... *it is offence*: Anne-Thérèse de Marguenat de Courcelles, marquise de Lambert (1647–1733). In the original French text, Genlis identifies the quotation in a footnote which reads '*Avis d'une mère à son fils*, de Madame de Lambert'. Both the first and the second editions of the English translation include Lambert's name in the main body of the text. Lambert's *Avis d'une mère à son fils* was written around 1700 and published in 1726; her *Avis d'une mère à sa fille* was published in 1726. An English translation 'by a Gentleman' of both works was published as *Advice from a Mother to her Son and Daughter* (London: Thomas Worrall, 1729). The passage in the text is a paraphrase of the following lines:

> Those persons, who find Occasion to backbite, and love Raillery, bear a secret Malignity in their Hearts. Between the softest *Raillery* and *Offence*, there is but one Step to make: the false Friend, abusing the Right of Pleasantry, often wounds you; but the Person attack'd, is the only Judge of your Intentions: the Moment the Jest carries a Sting, it's no more *Raillery*, but *Offence*. (Lambert, *Advice from a Mother to her Son and Daughter*, p. 37)

107. *Carcassone*: a fortified city, clearly the nearest large city to the family, although the time taken for the physician to arrive emphasizes their rural location.

108. *enquiries into the truth of this affair*: Genlis's note to the original French text is translated in the 1784 English edition:

> One ought to consider, says the Author of the *Education of a Prince*, that it is almost only in the time of youth that Truth presents herself to Princes with any liberty; she avoids them all the rest of their lives. All who surround them concur to deceive them; because it is their interest to please them, and they know that telling them the truth is not the way to do it: so that their life is commonly no more than a dream, in which they see nothing but false objects, and deceitful visions. The person, therefore, who is charged with the education of a Prince, should often recollect that the child, committed to his care, is very soon to plunge into a kind of night, in which Truth will abandon him, and to impress upon his mind whatever is most necessary for him to know, that he may be able to conduct himself, in that obscurity, to which his rank, in some sort, necessarily exposes him. The *Education of a Prince*, by Chanteresne. (*Adelaide and Theodore* ... *The Second Edition*, vol. 1, p. 195)

For the original reference, see Nicole, *De l'éducation d'un prince*, pp. 22–3.

109. *the most tender humanity towards his people*: Genlis's note to the original French text is translated in the 1784 English edition:

> When a Prince loves his people, says the Abbé Duguet, scarce any thing need be said to him concerning his other duties. Love has no need of precepts. Love is the consummation of everything. It may be allowed to do what it will, since it can do nothing but good. (*Adelaide and Theodore* ... *The Second Edition*, vol. 1, p. 196)

110. '*those who ought to be treated with distinction*': Duguet, *Institution d'un prince*, vol. 1 p. 241 (chapter XXI, paragraph VII, VIII and IX). The French passage begins 'peu de personnes connoissent'.

111. '*listened to in his councils with admiration, &c.*': Duguet, *Institution d'un prince*, vol. 1, p. 267 (chapter XXII, paragraph I). The French passage begins 'Ce seroit un grand avantage'.

112. *the* Princess of Cleves: *La Princesse de Clèves* (1678) is a work of prose fiction set in the sixteenth-century court of Henri II, written by Marie-Madeleine Pioche de La Vergne (1634–93). It is sometimes considered the first European novel.

113. Clarissa, *which is the best,* Grandison *and* Pamela: *Clarissa, or the History of a Young Lady*
(1748), *The History of Sir Charles Grandison* (1753) and *Pamela, or Virtue Rewarded*
(1740) all by Samuel Richardson (1689–1761). All these novels were greatly admired and
emulated in France, inviting many translations and imitations including Abbé Prévost's
translation of *Clarissa* which appeared as *Lettres Anglaises* in 1751, critical responses
such as Denis Diderot's *Éloge de Richardson* (1762) and even the most influential eighteenth-century French novel, Rousseau's *Julie ou la Nouvelle Héloïse* (1761). Genlis gives
an interesting account of a meeting with Richardson's son-in-law, Mr Bridget in 1785
in her *Memoirs*:

> I had the pleasure of sitting in Mr Bridget's garden on the bench on which Richardson
> used to sit, the right arm of the seat opened and held an inkstand; here he used to com-
> pose and write a great part of the morning. Mr. Bridget became so much attached to me,
> that he offered to give me a manuscript copy of the novel of Pamela, with corrections in
> the margin in the handwriting of Richardson himself, on condition of my giving him my
> word of honour that I would myself translate it literally. As it would have been impos-
> sible for me to have translated it without making many alterations, I declined entering
> into such an engagement, but I offered to have it translated under my own eyes, and with
> all possible care; this he refused. Richardson is not interred at Westminster: the English
> do not esteem this author so highly as we do, because he is not in the rank of their best
> writers, and because he has attempted to describe the great world, with which he was not
> acquainted; but he has so admirably described the human heart, and human passions,
> and virtues; he has laid open so skilfully the heart of a virtuous, ingenuous, and feeling
> woman, that he will always deserve to be placed in the first class of moralists. (*Memoirs of
> the Countess of Genlis*, vol. 3, pp. 303–4)

114. *which is called* Annals of Virtue: Once again, the Baroness is given the authorship of
one of Genlis's works. *Annals de la vertu ou cours d'histoire à l'usage des jeunes personnes par l'auteur du théatre d'éducation* (Paris: M. Lambert et F. J. Baudoin, 1781) was
partly translated by Elizabeth Mary James and published as *A Selection from the Annals
of Virtue containing the most important and interesting anecdotes from the histories of
Spain, Portugal, China, Japan and America: with some account of the manners, customs,
arts and sciences of France* (Bath, 1794).

115. *reading the life of Alexander the Great*: the infamous Greek king (356–323 BC), known
for his military supremacy and empire building is shown here to have a negative effect
on young princes.

116. *the mind of Charles the Twelfth, when a child*: Genlis may have read this in Voltaire,
who in his *Histoire de Charles XII* (1731) notes that even as a very young child, Charles
modelled himself on Alexander the Great. See *Histoire de Charles XII* in *The Complete
Works of Voltaire*, 85 vols (Oxford: Voltaire Foundation, 1970–) vol. 4, p. 167.

117. *he has the* Anglo-manie *to a great degree*: by making anglomania one of the faults of
the 'mere nothing' Mons. de Valcy, Genlis once again shows contemporary French
anglomania in a negative light. See also note 104 to Volume I, above.

118. *Bois de Boulogne*: vast park now in the western suburbs of Paris. In the late eighteenth
century, it was an area used by the royal family to construct retreats away from the
court at Versailles.

119. *efforts will be made to injure you with the Princess*: Genlis's *Memoirs* are expansive
on the subject of her position as lady-in-waiting to the Duchess of Chartres and the
indignities she suffered in this post (whilst neglecting to mention, as discussed in the
introduction, the relationship between Genlis and the Duke). Maria Edgeworth gives

another side of the story in an account of the Dowager Duchess from a letter written in July 1820:

> Today we are going to dine again at Neuilly with the other Duchess of Orléans, daughter-in-law of the good old Duchess, who by-the-bye spoke of Mme de Genlis is a true Christian spirit of forgiveness, but in a whisper, and with a shake of her head, allowed 'qu'elle m'avait cause bien des chagrins [she caused me a considerable amount of heartache]. (Christina Colvin (ed.), *Maria Edgeworth in France and Switzerland* (Oxford: Clarendon Press, 1979) p. 187)

120. *'where you sacrifice the present to an uncertain future'*: The passage is from the beginning of Book II of *Émile* and reads:

> What, then, must be thought of that barbarous education which sacrifices the present to an uncertain future, which burdens a child with chains of every sort and begins by making him miserable in order to prepare him from afar for I know not what pretended happiness which it is to be believed he will never enjoy? (Rousseau, *Émile*, p. 79)

121. *'let Emilius run about ... without shoes or stockings ... I would imitate him'*: The passage is taken from Book II of *Émile*:

> Let us always arm man against unexpected accidents. In the morning let Emile run barefoot in all seasons, in his room, on the stairs, in the garden. Far from reproaching him, I shall imitate him. I shall take care only that glass be removed. (Rousseau, *Émile*, p. 139)

122. *wakes him abruptly, to make him get up in the middle of the night*: These experiments in education, intended to harden Emile physically and accustom him to the dark, are related in Book II of *Émile*.

123. *'he will rely on you to preserve him from them'*: This quotation is an abridged version of the second maxim, presented in Book IV of *Émile*:

> Teach him to count on neither birth nor health nor riches. Show him all the vicissitudes of fortune. Seek out for him examples, always too frequent, of people who, from a station higher than his, have fallen beneath these unhappy men. [...] Let him see, let him feel the human calamities. Unsettle and frighten his imagination with the perils by which every man is constantly surrounded. Let him see around him all these abysses, and, hearing you describe them, hold on to you for fear of falling into them. (Rousseau, *Émile*, p. 224)

124. *every passion ... takes away your judgement and makes you blind*: British critics objected strongly to the passages in which the Baroness makes Miss Bridget play a part in the deceptions used to instruct Adelaide.

125. *I neither go to Balls nor Operas*: A note by the translators in the 1784 English edition reads: 'They are masked balls'. See *Adelaide and Theodore ... The Second Edition*, vol. 1, p. 258.

126. *two young women so very intimate ... concerned together in some imprudent affair*: This account of female friendships brings to mind the 'imprudent affairs' of Marie-Antoinette, whose close relationships with female courtiers, notably Marie-Thérèse-Louise de Savoie-Carignan, princesse de Lamballe (1749–1792) and Yolande-Martine-Gabrielle de Polastron, duchesse de Polignac (1749–1793) were seen as damaging to affairs of state, and were the topic of much debate in the 1780s. Accusations of lesbianism with Polignac in particular inspired several pornographic pamphlets. See Chantal Thomas 'The Heroine of the Crime: Marie-Antoinette in Pamphlets' and Lynn Hunt 'The Many Bodies of Marie-Antoinette: Political Pornography and the Problem of the Feminine in

the French Revolution', both in Dena Goodman (ed.), *Marie-Antoinette: Writings on the Body of a Queen* (New York: Routledge, 2003), pp. 99–116, 117–138.

127. *the most beautiful persons*: In the original French text, this is not marked in quotation marks.

128. *a statue representing Fidelity*: The translators include a note in the 1784 English edition which reads: 'Perhaps Constancy is a better word'. See *Adelaide and Theodore ... The Second Edition*, vol. 1, p. 279.

129. *drinks no tea nor coffee with cream ... will preserve her charming state of health, her beauty, and her complexion*: Genlis's correspondence shows her preoccupation with a strict and unvaried diet that included no rich food: in her letters to her adopted son, Casimir Baecker, she warns of the dangers of excessive alcohol and dairy products, and stresses the benefits of gruel and vegetable stock. In a letter dated 26 May 1811, she attributes her own longevity to these measures, writing 'Ma santé est parfaite parce que mon régime est réglé, invariable' (My health is excellent because my diet is regimented, unchanging). See *Lettres Inédites de Mme de Genlis a son fils adoptif Casimir Baecker (1802–1830) Publiés avec une introduction et des notes d'après des documents nouveaux par Henry Lapauze* (Paris: Librairie Plon, 1902), p. 127.

130. *If you should hear of this affair, deny the truth of it*: A note by the translators in the 1784 English edition reads: 'How does this agree with the strict adherence to the truth, which she recommends so much in her daughter? Note of the Translators.' See *Adelaide and Theodore ... The Second Edition*, vol. 1, p. 293.

131. Quinze: a card game popular in France in the late eighteenth and early nineteenth centuries.

132. Cleveland: *Le Philosophe anglais ou Histoire de monsieur Cleveland* (1731–9) by the Abbé Prévost was his most popular novel in the eighteenth century, rather than *Histoire du chevalier des Grieux et de Manon Lescaut* (1731), Prévost's most popular work today. The English translation of *Cleveland, The Life of Mr. Cleveland, Natural Son of Oliver Cromwell* was published in the same year as the original French, 1731.

133. Zaide: or *Zayde*, the comtesse de Lafayette's (1634–93) second novel, first published in 1670. Set in Moorish Spain, it is the tale of lovers who, since they are from different cultural backgrounds, cannot communicate directly, although the ending resolves these difficulties with conversion and marriage.

134. *Comedy of the* Dove: Genlis's note, included in the second edition of the translation, reads: 'A Comedy in the *Theatre of Education*, by the Author of these Letters'. See *Adelaide and Theodore ... The Second Edition*, vol. 1, p. 298 and note 80 to Volume I, above.

135. *provided it is not too much. I leave it to your own judgment, and I shall not even look at you*: the second edition modifies the text to 'Provided it is not too much; and I leave that to your own discretion'. A note by the translators signals their cut to the original French text:

> *Et je vous assure que je n'y regarderai pas – and I will not even look at you.* The Author here again forgets her own principles, and gives her daughter a lesson of untruth. We have therefore omitted this sentence: and indeed it seems unnecessary; for as the child is left to her own discretion, he may infer that she shall not be watched. Note of the Translators. (*Adelaide and Theodore ... The Second Edition*, vol. 1, p. 301)

136. *Madame de Lambert*: Genlis's note, translated in the second edition, reads: 'Advice of a Mother to her Daughter', thus identifying the source text.

137. *'which do not often govern mankind'*: See Lambert, *Advice from a Mother to her Son and Daughter*, p. 104. The passage in this translation reads:

> While you are young, form your Reputation, augment your Credit, and settle your Affairs in a good Posture: hereafter, you'll find a greater Difficulty to effect it. *Charles V.* said, *That Fortune lov'd young People.* In Youth, everything assists you; everything is offer'd to your Acceptance. Young Persons rule, without knowing they do so: in an Age more advanc'd, every thing forsakes them: that seducing Charm is fled, and all that then remains, is Truth and Reason, which seldom influence the World.

138. *Mons. and Madame de Lagaraye. This is their history*: Genlis's note, translated in the 1784 English edition, reads: 'This story is a certain fact. The Author has the particulars from a person who had the good fortune to know, personally, Mons. and Madame de Lagaraye, who died about the year 1752'. See *Adelaide and Theodore ... The Second Edition*, vol. 1, p. 308.

139. *the sudden and extraordinary death of their only daughter*: Genlis's note, translated in the 1784 English edition, reads: 'All these circumstances are true, except that the person, who thus died suddenly, was the relation only, not the daughter of Mons. de Lagaraye, who never had any children'. See *Adelaide and Theodore ... The Second Edition*, vol. 1, p. 309.

140. *They went through several courses of Chymistry*: Genlis's note, translated in the 1784 English edition, reads: 'Mons. de Lagaraye has even published some valuable Works on Chimistry, and made many useful discoveries. It was he who discovered the properties, and gave his name to the *Salts of Lagaraye*; improperly indeed called Salts; for it is only a dry extract of the Peruvian Bark.' See *Adelaide and Theodore ... The Second Edition*, vol.1, p. 309.

Volume II

1. *'there are certain engaging qualities'*: Duguet, *Institution d'un prince*, vol. 1, p. 67 (chapter VIII, paragraph VI). The French text opens, 'Les Princes ont ordinarement un goût fort exquis'.

2.. *everything breathes an air of gaiety, plenty and content*: The rural idyll described here is reminiscent of village life in the *ancien régime* and customs celebrated in Genlis's play 'La Rosière de Salency', which dramatizes the custom of crowning the purest maiden in the village the queen of virtue. The play was one of the most popular of Genlis's *Theatre of Education*: Maria Edgeworth writes in 1803 that 'we were eager to see [Genlis] after having seen her beautiful Rosière de Salency'. See Colvin (ed.), *Maria Edgeworth in France and Switzerland*, p. 96. Sara Maza's important article 'The Rose-Girl of Salency: Representations of Virtue in Prerevolutionary France', *Eighteenth-Century Studies*, 22:3 (Spring 1989), *Special Issue: The French Revolution in Culture*, pp. 395–412, places the festival and Genlis's play in cultural context.

3. The Life of St. André: This insert tale was included in *The Beauties of Genlis; Being a Collection of the most Beautiful Tales and other Striking Extracts from Adela and Theodore; the Tales of the Castle; the Theatre of Education and Sacred Dramas* (Perth: R. Morrison and Sons, 1787). In the magazines, it appeared in rival translations in both the *Universal* and the *Lady's* (see Introduction, pp. xvii–xix) and the *Universal* translation was reprinted as 'The Affecting History of St. Andre' in the *Weekly Miscellany* (Glasgow), 4:95–9 (13 April–11 May 1791) and in the *Gleaner*, 2 (1806), pp. 131–42. See Mayo, *The English Novel in the Magazines*, p. 449.

4. *Launceston*: The French original reads 'Lanceston'; the English translator has corrected the spelling of the Cornish town.

5. *a charming figure ... leading a little girl seven years old*: Genlis's note to this passage is not translated in either the first or second English editions. It reads: 'We have merely animated Greuse's [*sic*] excellent painting *La Dame de Charité* in this scene. We only offer, it is true, a feeble sketch; but the original is so beautiful, that the most imperfect imitation will always be interesting' (my translation). *La Dame de Charité* was completed in 1775, when Greuze was at the height of his career.

6. *The enchanted gardens of Armida*: refers to a garden belonging to a character in the sixteenth-century Italian poet Torquato Tasso's *La Gerusalemme liberata* (*Jerusalem Delivered*, 1580). The sorceress Arminda's garden would have been known to eighteenth-century readers through its incarnation in opera, including Handel's *Rinaldo* (1711) and Gluck's *Armide* (1777).

7. *an annual prize to good fathers and good mothers*: Genlis's original French note is not translated in either the first or second English editions. It reads: 'We have taken the idea of such a useful and respectable festival from the good people of Canon' (my translation).

8. *those agonising prayers sounded in his ears*: In the second edition of the French text, Genlis gets rid of this note which lives on in all the English editions. In her preface to the second French edition, Genlis explains that critics were shocked at her condemnation of the prayers for the dying being recited aloud by the bedside of the sick, and so she decided to suppress the note. See *Adèle et Théodore*, ed. Brouard-Arends, p. 288 for Genlis's original French text.

9. *successor to an Alexander*: Alexander the Great is meant here. See notes 115 and 116 to Volume I, above.

10. *those in their situation in particular*: Genlis was determined that the 'lower classes' should have literature written for their use. The fourth volume of the *Theatre of Education* contained plays 'solely for the education of the children of Shopkeepers and Mechanics; but people even of a lower rank, may find useful instruction in it: the lady's maid, young milliners, mantua-makers, and shop-women will here see a particular detail of their duties', see *Theatre of Education, Translated from the French of the Countess of Genlis*, 4 vols (London: T. Cadell and P. Elmsly, 1781), vol. 4, p. ii. The first play in the volume was 'The Queen of the Rose of Salency' (see note 2 to Volume I, above). Others used a book shop and a clothes-seller as their settings. Marie-Emmanuelle Plagnol-Diéval's study *Madame de Genlis et le theatre d'éducation au XVIII siècle* (Oxford: Voltaire Foundation, 1997) provides a full account of these plays.

11. *Mons. Bezout*: Étienne Bézout (1730–83) was a French mathematician. At least one English translation of his writings was published (*Elements of Arithmetic, Translated and Adapted to the use of American Schools* (Hallowell, ME: Glazier and Co, 1824)), but this post-dates *Adelaide and Theodore*.

12. *Cours de Latinite de Vaniere*: Ignace Vanière (d. 1768), *Cours de latinité* (Paris: 1759). I can find no evidence of an English translation of this work.

13. *Virgil ... Eneid*: The Roman poet Virgil's *Aeneid*, written between 29 and 19 BC.

14. *temples of Seraphis*: The temple of Serapis, or Macellum, named for the Egyptian God who was also worshipped in ancient Greece and Rome, is the emblem of the Italian town Pozzuoli. Genlis's note, not translated in the first or second English editions, reads: 'In the vicinity of Naples' (my translation). All the replicas in the Chevalier de Murville's

garden represent what would have been the best examples of classical antiquity to late eighteenth-century readers.

15. *Minerva Medica*: Genlis's note, not translated in the first or second English editions, reads: 'near Rome' (my translation). This temple to the Goddess Minerva had a large dome in the eighteenth century; it collapsed in 1828.

16. *Trojan's pillar*: Trojan's column in Rome is an elaborately carved pillar depicting the Trojan wars, topped with a statue of St Peter.

17. *Apollo of Belvedere*: a Greek or Roman marble copy of a bronze, the original of which is said to have been by 4th century BC Greek sculptor Leochares.

18. *Venus of Medicis*: The Venus de Medici, a life-size marble sculpture of Venus or Aphrodite was a high point of the Grand Tour, and greatly admired by the French: between 1803 and until Napoleon's defeat in 1815, it was housed in Paris.

19. *the grotto of Pausilipo*: The reputed site of Virgil's tomb. Genlis's note, not translated in the first or second English editions, reads: near Naples. The English rendering of the French 'grotte de Pausilipe' as 'grotto of Pausilipo' is confusing here, since 'grotte' would have been best translated not as 'grotto', but as Posilippo Cave or even *grotta vecchia*.

20. *Chevalier de Murville*: A note by the translators to this passage in the second English edition reads: 'In the original, he is sometimes called Monsieur, and sometimes the Chevalier, and this is agreeable to the French manner, who notwithstanding his title call a man Monsieur, as the Baron d'Almane Monsieur d'Almane'. See *Adelaide and Theodore ... The Second Edition*, vol. 2, p. 77.

21. *the Widow's Bridge*: Genlis's note, not translated in the first or second English editions, quotes from a publication which appeared in Geneva in 1780, *Essais sur l'Espagne, voyage fait en 1777 et 1778, où l'on traite des mœurs, du caractère, des monuments, du commerce, du theatre et des tribunaux particuliers à ce royaume*, by M. Peyron, from which she takes the tale of the widow and her drowned son.

22. *maxim of Mons. de Rochefoucauld*: In the French text, the reference to François, duc de La Rochefoucauld (1613–80) is in a footnote. La Rochefoucauld's maxims were popular with translators, with five different versions between 1670 and 1749. See Gillespie and Hopkins (eds), *The Oxford History of Literary Translation in English*, pp. 365–6.

23. *'something not displeasing to ourselves'*: See *The Maxims of the Duc de Rochefoucauld*, translated by Constantine Fitzgibbon (London: Allan Wingate, 1957), p. 151: 'we always discover, in the misfortunes of our dearest friends, something not altogether displeasing'. This maxim (no. 576) was printed in the 1665 Paris edition, but suppressed from subsequent editions during the author's lifetime.

24. *Broek, in Holland*: The reference to Broek being in Holland is in a footnote in the original French text, and not translated in the first or second English editions. Broek is one of the first stops in Holland that the Almane family make: see letter XXXII in Volume III (pp. 383–5).

25. *this is the reason learned men are so often reproached with an arrogant and supercilious manner*: The 1784 English edition translates Genlis's original footnote as follows: 'It is easy to perceive that the Viscountess, however inconsiderate she may be, speaks here only in general terms, and that she is by no means so destitute of good sense as not to admit of some exceptions'. See *Adelaide and Theodore ... The Second Edition*, vol. 2, p. 84.

26. *Pierre Corneille*: see note 26 to Volume I.

27. Education of Daughters *by M. de Fénelon*: the quotation is taken from 'Housewifery and Neatness', the twelfth chapter of Fénelon's *Instructions for the Education of Daughters*, p. 151.

28. *the age of Lewis XIV*: Louis XIV (1638–1715) reigned from 1643 until his death.
29. *Rollin's* Ancient History: Charles Rollin (1661–1741), author of *Histoire ancien* (1730–38). His influential *De la Manière d'enseigner les belles lettres* (1726–28) was translated and published in 1734 as *The Method of Teaching and Studying the Belles Letters*.
30. The *Age of Lewis XIV*: Voltaire's *Le Siècle de Louis XIV* (1751). See note 29 to Volume I, above.
31. *Campistron*: Jean-Galbert de Campistron (1656–1723), playwright and tragedian. A Dutch translation of his *Andronicus* was published in 1741: I can find no evidence of English translations.
32. *Langrange, Chancel*: The English translator has here separated the names of one playwright, François-Joseph de Chancel, sieur de La Grange (1677–1758), also known for *Les Philippiques*, five odes which were composed around 1717–18, and which were highly critical of the Duke of Orléans and the corruption of the Regency.
33. *Lachaussee*: Pierre-Claude Nivelle de La Chaussée (1692–1754) is now remembered as the inventor of the 'comédie larmoyante', plays written for their sentimental appeal, largely in the 1740s. Two of his plays, *L'École des mères* (1744) (*The School for Mothers*) and *La Gouvernante* (1747) (*The Governess*) may have had particular appeal.
34. *Destouches*: the pseudonym of Philippe Néricault (1680–1754), comic playwright. The six-volume anthology *The Comic Theatre, being a Free Translation of all the best French Comedies* (1762) by Samuel Foote and other contributors provided translations of works by Detouches and Molière among others.
35. *Marivaux*: Pierre Carlet de Chamblain de Marivaux (1688–1763) was a playwright, novelist and essayist. His plays were performed in French in London by visiting French troupes, and some were also translated, but it was his *La Vie de Marianne* (1731–42) that became a European best-seller. Often seen as the model for Richardson's *Pamela*, it was translated several times in the mid-eighteenth century, including an extremely popular 1743 translation by Mary Collyer entitled *The Virtuous Orphan*.
36. *Les Poesies de Fontenelle*: Bernard le Bovier de Fontenelle (1657–1757) wrote varied and diverse works including pastoral poetry, a history of the French theatre and scientific treaties. His *Entretiens sur la pluralité des mondes* (1686) in which the new world system is explained through conversations between a philosopher and a society lady, and saw three different English translations by 1688, including a translation by Aphra Behn *A Discovery of New Worlds*, which contains her 'Preface, by way of Essay on Translated Prose'.
37. *de Pavillon*: Etienne Pavillon (1632–1705), poet and member of the French Academy in 1691.
38. *Desmahis*: Joseph-François-Edouard de Corsembleu (1722–61), poet and dramatist.
39. Andronicus: Campistron's 1741 play: see note 31 to Volume II, above.
40. Cinna: one of Corneille's greatest plays, see note 26 to Volume I, above.
41. Les Horaces: *Horace*, a tragedy by Corneille published in 1641 and dedicated to Richelieu. William Whitehead's *The Roman Father* was adapted freely from *Horace* in 1750, and was 'one of the last theatrical adaptations of Corneille' in England. See Gillespie and Hopkins (eds), *The Oxford History of Literary Translation in English*, p. 321.
42. *in our day would have dishonoured and made a young woman the town talk*: It is useful to compare here the comments on the Genlis/Orléans household at Bury in Frances Burney's 1792 diary entry: 'They have been to a Bury ball, and danced all night; Mlle d'Orléans, with anybody, known or unknown to Madame Brulard [i.e. Genlis, who was

known as citoyenne Brulard during the 1790s]'. See Charlotte Frances Barrett (ed.), *The Diary and Letters of Madame d'Arblay*, vol. 3, p. 408.

43. *'cruelty, tyranny and treason'*: Montaigne's essay 23, 'Of Custom, and Not Easily Changing an Accepted Law' reads:

> There are fathers stupid enough to take it as a good omen of a martial soul when they see a son unjustly striking a peasant or a lackey who is not defending himself, and as a charming prank when they see him trick his playmate by a bit of malicious dishonesty and deceit. Nevertheless these are the true seeds and roots of cruelty, tyranny, and treason. (Montaigne, *The Complete Works*, p. 94)

44. *'make them return his blows with interest'*: This quotation from Rousseau is in a note in the original French text, as in *Émile* itself where it can be found as a footnote to a point being made in the main body of the text that a child does not attack people, but things:

> One ought never to permit a child to play with grownups as with his inferiors or even as with his equals. If he seriously dares to strike someone, be it his lackey, be it the hangman, arrange that his blows be always returned with interest and in such a way as to destroy the desire to revert to the practice. I have seen imprudent governesses animate the unruliness of a child, incite him to strike, let themselves be struck, and laugh at his feeble blows, without thinking that in the intention of the little enraged one these blows were so many murders and that he who wants to strike when young will want to kill when grown. (Rousseau, *Émile*, pp. 97–8)

45. *Madame de R— was perfectly satisfied with the conclusion of the adventure*: Genlis reveals that this is a true story in her *Memoirs*:

> The incident of the gown from which the fringes were pulled off, which is related in *Adèle et Théodore*, is true: I witnessed the adventure at Rainci; M. de Chartes was the person who played this gay frolic: it is the only personality I have ever allowed myself in my writings, but the fact was witnessed by fifty persons besides myself. (*Memoirs of the Countess of Genlis*, vol. 3, p. 143)

See also note 35 to Volume I, above.

46. *Variétés Amusantes* ... Le Fou raisonable: Isabelle Brouard-Arends points out that the Variétés Amusantes, also known as the Théâtre des Variétés was one of the most popular Parisian theatres of the period, so popular that the daily programme was published by the *Journal de Paris*. The plays mentioned in this passage (*Jérôme Pointu* by A. L. B. Robineau, known as Beaunoir, *Eustache Pointu chez lui ou Qui a bu boira*, also by Robineau and *L'Anglais ou le fou raisonnable* by Joseph Patrat) were all performed at the theatre in July 1781. Brouard-Arends argues that because this kind of play was rarely performed more than once, and therefore faded rapidly from the collective memory, Genlis needed to choose up-to-date examples for her satire to be effective (see *Adèle et Théodore*, ed. Brouard-Arends, p. 651, notes 28 and 29). English readers were unlikely to pick up the references, but the fact that the plays were not known would have been enough to get the point across: these were not high culture performances. In the 1784 edition of the translation, the translators clearly thought some explanation was needed for English speaking readers, and included the following note for the theatre '*Variétés Amusantes*, a theatre in the nature of Sadler's Wells' and for the plays, 'little farces acted there'. See *Adelaide and Theodore* ... *The Second Edition*, vol. 2, p. 116.

47. Phædra *or* Cinna: Racine's *Phèdre* and Corneille's *Cinna*: see notes 26 and 27 to Volume I, above.

48. *all Dancourt's, for example*: This is not the better-known French playwright Florent Carton Dancourt (1661–1725) but rather L.R. Dancourt (1725–1801), French actor and author of many plays in the popular and burlesque style.

49. traine-ballet: undoubtedly left in the original French by the English translator because they did not know the game (unlike 'colin-maillard' / 'blind man's bluff'). It seems to have been a game similar to the modern children's game known as 'I sent a letter to my love' or 'drop-handkerchief', where participants take turns to drop a handkerchief behind the back of one person sitting in a circle, who then has to get up. The two players race to get back to the original space, and the loser takes his or her turn to drop the handkerchief.

50. *I could name more than one mother who could educate her son as well, and perhaps better than the best father*: Here the Baron departs from Rousseau, who states in Book I of *Émile* that 'As the true nurse is the mother, the true preceptor is the father'. See Rousseau, *Émile* p. 48.

51. *'they corrupt both court and state, where they command'*: Duguet, *Institution d'un prince*, vol. 2, p. 182 (chapter X).

52. *'those she leaves us the more desirable'*: Montaigne's essay 26, 'Of the Education of Children' reads 'She is the nursing mother of human pleasures. By making them just, she makes them sure and pure. By moderating them, she keeps them in breath and appetite. By withdrawing the ones she refuses, she makes us keener for the ones she allows us.' See Montaigne, *The Complete Works*, p. 145.

53. *Oh that I had but such an overplus! I would send it to the poor woman*: This is reminiscent of several of the passages in the *Tales of the Castle*, in which the Clémire children rejoice at the prospect of charitable giving:

    > We must find out some poor old woman, very good; and if we could find a poor blind old woman, how happy we should be! Yes! We would send for a surgeon from Autun to perform the operation for the cataract – O! that we would – but we must take care, though, that our playthings and diversions do not cost much money, you know; for mamma is not able to give us money for such things, and for cataracts too – No, we cannot have everything. (*Tales of the Castle*, vol. 1, pp. 62–3)

54. *Moreover, the fashionable amusements here are walking, fishing, reading, and playing at Loto*: The translators included a footnote to the 1784 edition which reads: 'Loto, a sort of lottery, a game much played at in France; the cards are of a particular kind, having numbers on them'. See *Adelaide and Theodore ... The Second Edition*, vol. 2, p. 151.

55. *A set of periodical writers have amused and diverted themselves in burlesquing you*: Genlis was to expand on this critique of contemporary literary reviewing practices in her 1802 tale 'Le Journaliste' (translated as 'The Reviewer').

56. *there are few critics now-a-days who can write like V—*: Genlis is perhaps here thinking of Élie Catherine Fréron (1718–76), editor of the journal the *Année littéraire* who attacked the *Encyclopedistes*, and who was himself the object of several notorious satires by Voltaire. Genlis admired Fréron greatly.

57. *La Corniche*: the name of the sea-road round this part of Italy. The whole account of the Italian trip is remarkably similar to Genlis's account of her 1776 trip to Italy with the Duchess of Chartres, a detailed description of which can be found in *Memoirs of the Countess of Genlis*, vol. 3, pp. 4–49.

58. *the old castle of Montalban, taken by the French in 1744*: in the Battle of Villafranca, April 1744, part of the War of the Austrian succession. In fact, the French troops were fighting alongside Spanish troops who assisted in the taking of the castle.

59. *tower of Eze*: Eze, a medieval village situated high above Nice itself: there are panoramic views of the riviera from the ruined tower.

60. The History of the Dutchess of C—, written by herself: This tale was extremely popular in Britain, appearing in *The Beauties of Genlis* (1787) and as a separate novella publication into the nineteenth century. Chawton House Library has two different editions of the text, besides that included in this volume. The first, published without either the original author or the translator's name: *The Affecting History Of The Duchess of C***, Who Was Confined Nine Years In A Horrid Dungeon, Under Ground, Where Light Never Entered ... But Fortunately she was at last discovered, and released from the Dungeon, By Her Parents* (London: Printed and Sold by S. Bailey, 35 Threadneedle Street [1805?]) and the second attributed to Genlis *The History of the Dutchess of C— from Adela and Theodore* (Baltimore, Maryland: Printed for the Bookseller, 1819). It appeared in both the *Universal* and the *Lady's* magazines. The *Universal* translation was reprinted in the *New Magazine of Choice Pieces*, 2:17 (1810). In the *Lady's* there were two rival translations, since 'Female Fortitude, or the History of the Duchess of C—, written by Herself' was serialized between January and July 1786. Robert Mayo points out that '"Adela and Theodore" was being serialized in the *Lady's* (1785–9), when "Female Fortitude" began its seven-month's run, but the interpolated history of the novel was still several years in the future. Since "Female Fortitude" is an unacknowledged translation of Mme. de Genlis's story, the editor of the *Lady's* was probably unaware of the duplication'. See Mayo, *The English Novel in the Magazines*, p. 493.

61. *The author ... saw at Rome the Dutchess of C— and every day dined with the father of that interesting person*: Genlis gives an account of meeting the Duchess of C— in the third volume of her *Memoirs*:

> The Prince of Palestrina, was father of the Duchess of Cerifalco, who passed nine years in a subterranean cave – an astonishing history, which I have related in *Adèle et Théodore*. [...] I went and placed myself near her, in order to have a good opportunity of seeing her. Though she was but forty-six years old, she looked sixty-six. She had no longer any vestiges of beauty; her appearance struck me, and I drew her portrait afterwards from nature; her head and eyes were inclined towards the ground, and from time to time she had attacks of shuddering. The prince told me the whole story, of which I have put many details into my episode. (*Memoirs of the Countess of Genlis*, vol. 3, p. 35)

62. *at an assembly*: In the French original, Genlis uses the Italian word 'conversation', and explains in a footnote that, 'on nomme ainsi en Italie une *assemblée*' (this is what 'assemblies' are called in Italy). The English translator ignores this nuance in the first and second editions.

63. *The wheel, or turning box ... without seeing or being seen*: This is a note written by the English translator, not included in the original text. Presumably customs and practices in nunneries were thought to require some explanation for English readers.

64. *The unhappy Dutchess de C— ... she indispensibly wanted them*: This is Genlis's note.

65. *Cicisbeo's*: the male attendant of a married woman, often suspect of being her lover, although the position was said to be platonic. The practice seems to have been the topic of much interest in eighteenth-century Britain as well as France, and was frequently commented on in travel literature and journals written in Italy in the period.

66. *Cicisbeo*: The French use of the Italian 'Cicisbea' makes it clear that it is the mistress who is being referred to here. The 1784 edition corrects the error. See *Adelaide and Theodore ... The Second Edition*, vol. 2, p. 157.

67. *Veilla delle quarante*: literally, the ball of the forty women.

68. *magnificent entertainments*: The translator includes the original French for this phrase and other translations on this page, a rare intervention on her part in the 1783 edition.

69. *The Duke de C— is like Bluebeard*: There are certainly resemblances with the tale of Bluebeard in the tale of the Duchess of C—. Genlis, having taken care to insist that the story was true, now establishes a critical distance from it by having the Chevalier d'Herbain compare it to Charles Perrault's fairytale.

70. 'they always talk of themselves': 'The reason why a lover and his mistress are never bored in one another's company is that the talk is constantly of themselves'. See *The Maxims of the Duc de Rochefoucauld*, p. 93 (no. 312).

71. *the only mountain I shall make her climb, shall be that of* Bons-hommes: The Vicountess is here stressing her intention not to leave France: the Bonshommes mountain path is the Pyrenees, and therefore near the Languedoc estate of the Almane family.

72. *in the cavern of the Dutchess*: The French is explicit that the Duchess mentioned here is the Duchess of C—.

73. another new work ... *upon Mythology; or Poetic History*: The Baroness is here credited with the authorship of a work that Genlis did not publish until almost thirty years after this mention. The impressively titled two-volume work *Arabesques mythologiques ou les Attributs de toutes les divinités de la fable en 54 planches gravées d'après les desseins coloriés de Mme de Genlis* (Paris: Charles Barrois, 1810) showcased Genlis's talents as an illustrator. There was no English translation.

74. *she is breeding*: The French is more explicit, telling the reader that Madame de Valcé is four months pregnant.

75. *Ninette a la Cour*: Charles-Simon Favart (1710–92) wrote many successful comic operas, including *Bastien et Bastienne* (1753) and *Les Trois Sultanes* (1761), set to music by Mozart and Haydn respectively. *Ninette à la cour* was written in 1753.

76. *A cloak lined with fur*: This is the translator's note.

77. *the isle of Calypso, and the growing passion of young Telemachus for Eucharis?*: In Fénelon's writing of Telemachus's tale, the son of Odysseus (Ulysses) falls passionately in love with a young nymph, Eucharis, on Calypso's island. In conversation with Mentor (the goddess Athena, or Minerva, in male disguise) Telemachus agrees that it is his duty to leave Eucharis and search for his missing father. The message to the young prince (that duty is more important than passion) is clear.

78. *date always from Auteuil and from Pantin*: Auteuil, now part of the chic sixteenth arrondissement of Paris in the west, and Pantin, a suburb of Paris in the north-east of the city, were both independent villages in the late eighteenth century.

79. *we ought to have made children our study ... and consequently ought to have educated more than one*: This is a second refutation of Rousseau's comments in Book I of *Émile*: see note 3 to Volume I, above.

80. *I have a letter of yours by me, of an old date, on this subject*: This refers to Letter VI in Volume I, pp. 9–11 above.

Volume III

1. The Baroness to the Viscountess: The French text reminds us that this letter is sent from Rome.

2. *it was a beautiful little girl, of six years and a half*: The tale of Hermine's adoption mirrors the adoption of Pamela (later to become Pamela Fitzgerald, wife of the United Irishmen leader) and Hermine into the Orléans family (see Introduction, p. xvi). It was a feature

that reviews of the novel did not fail to remark on: the *Journal Encyclopédique* claimed 'La jeune Hermine, petite orpheline, confiée aux soins d'Adèle, nous a paru un trait des plus heureux, des plus piquans & des plus ingénieux de cet ouvrage' (Young Hermine, an orphan who is given up to Adèle's care, struck us as the happiest, most touching and ingenious feature of this work): see *Journal Encyclopedique*'s review of *Adèle et Théodore* (April 1782), pp. 191–211; p. 208. Throughout her long life, Genlis was preoccupied with what she considered to be the duty of people of means to adopt unwanted children: she recommended that the Ladies of Llangollen do just that when she visited them in 1785. She gave the following account in her *Memoirs*:

> The two friends of Llangollen had one means of securing to themselves a happy old age; it was to educate and to adopt children, and thus to form themselves a family, which might have cheered their solitude, and one day have comforted their old age. I know not whether they have followed my counsel. (*Memoirs of the Countess of Genlis*, vol. 3, pp. 299–300)

3.   *and the Veillée des quarante – and the* Bambolina Francese: Adelaide is referring here to the episode at the Italian assembly (the Veilla delle quarante) recounted in letter XXXIX of Volume II, pp. 297–300, above.

4.   *think themselves well on half a crown a day*: Genlis's note to this passage is translated in the 1784 edition:

> In all Greek houses, you find at the door of the apartment a man dressed in black; with a long white cravat, who is a kind of Swiss servant, and at Rome is called a *Decan*. The Cardinals and Nobility have also a person to do the honours of their houses, whom they call a Gentleman, and who commonly is so. The Cardinal Mazarine was such a Gentleman at Rome. (*Adelaide and Theodore ... The Second Edition*, vol. 2, p. 9)

Presumably the translators mean Italian houses, rather than Greek houses; the original French simply reads 'Dans toutes les grandes maisons', without specifying where, but since this letter is describing Italian customs, it must be assumed that there has been an error.

5.   *set out on Monday for Spa*: Genlis knew the Belgian town of Spa well, spending two separate periods of convalescence there, in 1775 and in 1776. One of the plays in her *Theatre of Education* was entitled 'The Blind Woman of Spa', and was particularly admired in Britain as the following extract shows: 'it affords an opportunity of doing justice to our national character, and particularly to that of Lady Spenser, whose charity and benevolence supplied the principal materials for the Countess de Genlis'. *London Magazine* (March 1781), p. 141.

6.   *Plombieres*: A Belgian spa resort, like Spa (see note 5 to Volume III), less fashionable in the late eighteenth century as the Viscountess's comments suggest.

7.   *'they have no occasion to resist them'*: The quotations are from Book V of *Émile*, the book that discusses the education of Sophie, the female counterpart to Emile ('Why do you say that modesty makes women false? Are those who lose it most completely truer than the others? Far from it. They are a thousand times more false. One gets to that point of depravity only by dint of vices all of which one keeps and which reign only under the cover of intrigues and lies') and the note to this point which reads:

> I know that women who have openly taken a position on a certain question claim that they make the most of this frankness, and swear that, with only this exception, there is nothing estimable which is not to be found in them. But I do know that they never persuaded anyone but a fool of that. With the greatest curb on their sex removed, what remains to restrain them, and what part of honour will they take seriously when they have renounced

that which belongs to them? Once having put their passions at ease, they no longer have any interest in resisting. (Rousseau, *Émile*, pp. 385–6).

8. *the Italian*: The English translation here is somewhat misleading: it should read 'the Italian language' or simply 'Italian', since Miss Bridget's disdain is for the language, rather than Hermine herself.
9. *he extols English liberty*: English liberty was celebrated in France throughout the eighteenth century in works such as Voltaire's *Lettres Philosophiques*, first published in London as *Letters Concerning the English Nation* (1773). Here Genlis reduces admiration of the English and disgust at the Spanish to a series of clichés that mock benefits of the Grand Tour.
10. Paradise Lost *was the finest poem in any living language*: John Milton's *Paradise Lost* (1667) saw many French translations (in both verse and prose) in the long eighteenth century, as well as several eighteenth-century editions of a translation of Joseph Addison's remarks on the poem.
11. *we walk on the mountain of* Annette and Lubin: Annette and Lubin were orphan cousins, who lived a pastoral idyll in the mountains near Spa, and who inspired several tales, including one by Marmontel, published in his 1761 *Contes Moraux*.
12. *I love you*: The words are in English in the original French text.
13. *how she will love the children*: The French, 'ses enfants' should be translated as 'her children': The Baroness is looking forward to Adelaide becoming a mother herself.
14. *it is no more than fifteen thousand livres a year; mine is only twenty-five*: A note by the translators in the 1784 edition reads: 'Fifteen thousand livres is 625 Guineas, and 25,000 livres is about 1041'. See *Adelaide and Theodore ... The Second Edition*, vol. 3, p. 48.
15. *as he is more calm, and knows what he is about*: The 1784 edition of the translation includes Genlis's footnote, with an interesting modification. Genlis's note reads:

> Reflexion utile, surtout pour les jeunes princes. Il est généralement reconnu que, dans une société de joueurs, le plus riche a sur les autres un avantage énorme à la longue, parce qu'il conserve mieux son sang-froid, et qu'en risquant plus d'argent il ne risque pas de se mettre à l'aumône. Un prince peut ruiner un particulier dans une séance, il peut l'obliger à vendre, pour le payer la seule terre qu'il possède; et ce particulier, avec *le plus grand bonheur*, ne peut ruiner le prince. (*Adèle et Théodore*, ed. Brouard-Arends, p. 470)

The English translation is as follows:

> A useful reflection, particularly for young Persons. It is commonly known in a company of Gamesters, that the richest man has the greatest advantage, because he keeps his temper better, for although he risks a large sum it will not distress him. A great Man may ruin a private Gentleman at one sitting, he may oblige him to sell his whole estate to pay his debt; but this private Gentleman, with the greatest good luck, cannot ruin the great Man. (*Adelaide and Theodore ... The Second Edition*, vol. 3, pp. 49–50)

As can be seen, an attempt is made to make the reflection more general by translating 'prince' with both 'young Persons' and 'great Man'.

16. *an assortment of impressions*: Genlis's note to this passage is not included in the first or second English editions. It explains that these are rubbings of ancient stones.
17. *Among others, that of Orpheus*: The story of Orpheus and Euridyce has inspired western classical music for generations: Gluck's *Orfeo ed Euridice* was composed in 1762. Isabelle Brouard-Arends writes that the only Italian ballet on the subject is Heinrich Schütz's work *Orfeo et Euridice*, written in 1638, but in her *Memoirs*, Genlis identifies the performance, which took place at Forli: 'there was delightfully performed a very fine

ballet pantomime by Novère. The subject was Orpheus and Eurydice'. See *Memoirs of the Countess of Genlis*, vol. 3, p. 48.

18. *Duclos says*: Genlis's note, not translated in either the first and second English editions, identifies Duclos's *Considerations sur les mœurs de ce siècle* (1751).

19. '*a sacrifice of our pleasures to those of other people*': See Duclos, *Considerations sur les mœurs de ce siècle* (Paris: Champion, 2000), p. 129.

20. *the beauties of Homer*: The French text refers to the *Illiad*, rather than the author of the work.

21. '*those law-suits which were unavoidable*': Duguet, *Institution d'un prince*, vol. 2, p. 151 (chapter XX, article III). The 1784 edition of the English translation identifies the source of the maxim by including Genlis's original note: '*L'Institution d'un Prince par l' Abbé Duguet*'. See *Adelaide and Theodore ... The Second Edition*, vol. 3, p. 71.

22. '*There is a meanness ... candour and benevolence?*': Genlis's original note identifies the source, '*L'Institution d'un Prince de l' Abbé Duguet*', but neither the 1783 nor the 1784 English translations repeat the reference. For the original text, see Duguet, *Institution d'un prince*, vol. 1, p. 98 (chapter XI, article II).

23. *you will not see an account of my entertainment in the Gazette*: The *Gazette de France*, so called since 1762, although it was founded as *La Gazette* in 1631, continued until 1915. At the time of publication of *Adelaide and Theodore*, this was the official weekly magazine in France: its objective was to report on Court and Foreign Affairs. By stressing that his celebrations will not be reported in the publication, the Baron emphasizes that they are genuine, rather than designed to be talked about.

24. *I read in the* Paris Journal: The *Journal de Paris* was founded in 1777, and continued until 1811.

25. *Azor and Zemira*: one of the plays in Genlis's *Theatre of Education*, a reworking of the Beauty and the Beast story that Le Prince de Beaumont made famous in her *Magasin des Enfants*. See note 39 to Volume I, above.

26. *a falsehood ... is permitted to be used in these circumstances, when it serves to excuse a real fault, or to conceal a secret either of our own, or one confided to us*: Genlis modified the text of this letter for the second French edition, making her condemnation of the lie Adelaide has told more emphatic by including lines such as 'votre mensonge était donc absolument inexcusable' (your lie was therefore completely inexcusable). For details of the changes in the French text, see *Adèle et Théodore*, ed. Brouard-Arends, pp. 492, 655, note 22. The translators have clearly used the text of the first edition, and there is therefore no difference between the 1783 and 1784 texts. They were, however, preoccupied with the question of 'acceptable' lies, as their note to the 1784 edition, below, makes clear.

27. *only a common compliment, which is the more innocent, as it deceives nobody*: The 1784 edition includes the following note by the translators:

> Language is a matter of agreement; and words convey only such a meaning as is agreed upon by common consent, or common usage; if therefore, when I say *I am not at home*, I am understood to mean only that I am busy, and do not wish to see company – I do not tell a lye. Note of the Translator. (*Adelaide and Theodore ... The Second Edition*, vol. 3, p. 84)

28. *three languages of French, English, and Italian*: Genlis's French text reads 'je lui permettrai de lire les chefs-d'œuvres des trois langues qu'elle sait', and includes those three languages in a footnote (see *Adèle et Théodore*, ed. Brouard-Arends, p. 497). Both the first and second English editions choose to include the three languages, French, English and Italian, in the main body of the text.

29. *Mademoiselle Hortensi*: I have been unable to trace this character (Hortense in original French) to a real singer at the Paris Opera. However, her unmarried status and the use of a first name, rather than a surname, reminds us that in late eighteenth-century France, as in late eighteenth-century Britain, the status of the Opera singer and the society courtesan was often confused. The suggestion is that the Viscount de Limours misses the Opera for the Opera girls, rather than for the music.

30. not more knowing: The French original, also in italics, is *pas plus instruite*, which would be better translated as 'not more knowledgeable' or even 'not better educated'.

31. The Theatre de la Chausèe: A second mention of the playwright Pierre-Claude Nivelle de La Chaussée. See note 33 to Volume II, above.

32. *reads Poetry with great propriety*: Genlis's original lengthy note to this passage is included in the second English edition:

> Teaching children to declaim is giving them a talent without which pronunciation is always imperfect. When a person understands declamation, he prefers verse to prose, is fond of Tragedy, and prefers seeing *Cinna* or *Athalia* represented to a Comedy in prose. This talent, so pleasing in a young person, is also useful to a man, and even to a soldier. There are many employments and offices where it is necessary to harangue, and speak in public; which would be done with an ill grace without some idea of the art of Declamation. It is absolutely necessary to be learnt by Magistrates, and by those destined to the church. Some respectable men, through pious motives, would banish theatrical declamation from their course of education: but it is hazarding the loss of an art which gives great energy to the voice of innocence, and to the word of God. *Cours d'éducation, par M. Verdier en un Vol.* It is true that nothing is more ridiculous than bad declamation; therefore it must be formed from the instructions of the best Masters, or else wholly avoided. (*Adelaide and Theodore ... The Second Edition*, vol. 3, p. 91)

33. *a peasant talks much more in the style of the Court, than our scholars do*: The degradation in spoken and written French was something that preoccupied Genlis after her return to France from Germany at the beginning of the nineteenth century, when she lamented the modern ways. Her *De l'Esprit des etiquettes et des usages anciens comparés aux anciens* (Paris: P. Mongié aîné, 1818) contains comments on the linguistic changes; no English translation exists.

34. *you pay a sincere deference to religion ... and you prove 'that there is no happiness without it'*: Genlis was to publish *La Religion considérée comme l'unique base de bonheur et de la veritable philosophie* (Paris: Imprimerie polytype, 1787), translated as *Religion considered as the only basis of happiness and true philosophy* (London: T. Payne and Son, 1787), a work which originated from the notes she had made to prepare Louis-Philippe for his first Holy Communion. In it, she attacks the eighteenth-century *philosophes* such as Rousseau and Voltaire, and includes lengthy quotations from works such as Pascal's *Pensées* to support her argument.

35. *Justice alone will entitle you to their respect; their allegiance must be your's, were you a tyrant*: A note by the translators in the 1784 English edition reads as follows: 'This sentiment may suit the latitude of Paris. Note of the Translators'. See *Adelaide and Theodore ... The Second Edition*, vol. 3, p. 107.

36. *we never fail, before we set out, to read in the Encyclopædia*: Diderot and D'Alembert's 1750–2 venture *L'Encyclopédie, ou Dictionnaire raisonné des sciences, des arts et des métiers*, one of the most important and ambitious projects of the French Enlightenment. Genlis used some of the plates included in the volumes to get scaled models of different

manufactories made for the use of the Orléans children: these 'maquettes' can be seen today in the Musée des Arts et Métiers in central Paris.

37. *I grieve to see the dangerous connections she is allowed to form*: The English translation misses an important allusion here. The original French reads: 'je vois avec peine qu'on lui laisse former des liaisons bien dangereuses' (I see with sadness that she has been allowed to form very dangerous liaisons). This naturally reminds a contemporary reader of the most famous French work first published in 1782, Laclos's *Les Liaisons Dangereuses*, but it was very much a theme in the air at the time: Genlis's own mother, Madame de Saint-Aubin wrote a work entitled *Danger des liaisons* in 1762, and Genlis herself published a play on the theme entitled *Les dangers du monde*.

38. *returned from Broëk, two leagues from this place*: The first phrase of the French text reads as follows: 'Je reviens de Broëk dans l'instant, ma chère fille', with a note to the passage which reads 'Qui se pronounce *Brouk*. Ce village est à deux lieux d'Amsterdam'. See *Adèle et Théodore*, ed. Brouard-Arends, p. 517. Both the first and second editions of the English translation give the distance between the two places in the main body of the text, and neither gives a guide to pronunciation.

39. *clothed in beautiful Persians*: 'Perse', the fabric in question here, is a luxurious printed cloth.

40. *I was yesterday at Sardam (where Peter the Great resided)*: Genlis's original French reads: 'J'allai hier à Sardam, autre village plus étendu, plus riche encore que Broëk' and her footnote tells us 'Village immortalisé par le séjour que Pierre le grand y a fait'. See *Adèle et Théodore*, ed. Brouard-Arends, p. 519. Both the first and second editions of the English translation incorporate the information about Peter the Great's stay in Sardam into the main body of the text, and the second edition includes the following footnote: 'Broëk is two leagues from Amsterdam'. See *Adelaide and Theodore … The Second Edition*, vol. 3, p. 121. Peter the Great (1672–1725) visited Holland in 1697 as part of his tour in Western Europe (he also visited Vienna and England) to learn new techniques, and in particular to study ship-building.

41. *a man as good and benevolent as yourself*: Abbé Charles-Michel l'Epée (1712–89), philanthropic educator and author of *L'institution gratuite des sourds et muets* (The Free Institution for the Deaf and Dumb) (Paris, 1774), as Genlis's note indicates. It was translated as *The Method of Educating the Deaf and Dumb; confirmed by long experience* (London, 1801).

42. *the presence of the Emperor*: Genlis's original text refers to 'un grand souverain' and includes 'l'empereur' in a footnote. See *Adèle et Théodore*, ed. Brouard-Arends, p. 524. The Emperor in question here is Joseph II of Austria, Marie-Antoinette's brother, who visited the Abbé l'Epée's institution during his 1776–7 visit to France.

43. *must one then be born deaf and dumb*: The 1784 English edition includes Genlis's lengthy note, giving the source of the story in this letter, which is Edward Moore's *The World* (London: Dodsley, 1772):

> The Author takes his idea, on the subject of this letter, from an English book entitled, The World, Vol. Ist in which is the following Story: 'At the village of Aronche, in the province of Estremadura, (says an old Spanish author) lived Gonzales de Castro, who from the age of twelve to fifty-two was deaf, dumb, and blind; his cheerful submission to so deplorable a misfortune, and the misfortune itself, so endeared him to the village, that to worship the Holy Virgin, and to love and serve Gonzales, were considered as duties of the same importance, and to neglect the latter was to offend the former. It happened one day, as he was sitting at his door, and offering up his mental prayers to St Iago, that he found himself, on a

sudden, restored to all the privileges he had lost. The news ran quickly round the village, and old and young, rich and poor, the busy and the idle, thronged round him with congratulations. But as if the blessings of this life were only given us for afflictions, he began in a few weeks to lose the relish of his enjoyments, and to repine at the possession of those faculties, which served only to discover to him the follies and disorders of his neighbours, and to teach him that the intent of speech was too often to deceive. Though the inhabitants of Aronche were as honest as other villagers, yet Gonzales, who had formed his ideas of men and things from their natures and uses, grew offended at their manners. He saw the avarice of age, the prodigality of youth, the quarrels of brothers, the treachery of friends, the frauds of lovers, the insolence of the rich, the knavery of the poor, and the depravity of all. These, as he saw and heard, he spoke of with complaint, and endeavoured, by the gentlest admonitions, to excite men to goodness. From this place the Story is torn out, to the last paragraph, which says that he lived to a comfortable old age, despised and hated by his neighbours for pretending to be wiser and better than themselves, and that he breathed out his soul in these memorable words, that he who would enjoy many friends, and live happy in the world, should be deaf, dumb, and blind to the follies and vices of it. (*Adelaide and Theodore ... The Second Edition*, vol. 3, pp. 128–9)

Genlis's original text includes a literal translation of the passage into French directly after the English quotation; see *Adèle et Théodore*, ed. Brouard-Arends, pp. 524–5. Brouard-Arends points out that the translation is Genlis's own, rather than the published French translation, and was undoubtedly included to demonstrate Genlis's expertise in the English language.

44. *knowing the manner of education in a Convent, she will set an higher value on her own*: Genlis was to publish a work on convent education in the decade after publication of *Adèle et Théodore*, when national education was very much a topic for debate: her *Discours sur la suppression des couvens de religieuses et l'éducation publique des femmes* (Paris, 1791). In this work Genlis argues that although convent education is flawed in both method and in subject matter, it would be better to reform them than destroy France's only system of female education. See Lester Gilbert Krakeur, 'A Forgotten Participant in the Attack on the Convent: Madame de Genlis', *Modern Language Notes*, 52:2 (1937), pp. 89–95.

45. *the few diamonds and other jewels I was mistress of*: Genlis's note to this episode is translated in the 1784 English edition:

If, according to this thought of Madame d' Almane, it might perhaps be said, it is very easy in a romance to give such examples, I shall answer, that in the whole progress of this Work I have introduced nothing which has not been really done, and that I knew a Mother, still younger than Madame d' Almane, who made to her two daughters the little sacrifices just mentioned, if the pleasure of giving your children these trifles can be called sacrifices. The Philosopher Charon, who was a disciple of Montaigne, says: Parents ought to receive their children into their society, and participation of their fortunes, as soon as they are fit for it, and converse with them on their situation and domestic affairs, and also communicate to them their intentions, opinions, and ideas, and contribute to their innocent amusements all in their power, at the same time preserving their rank and authority over them. *De la sagesse*, Liv. 3. Chap. 14. As we have mentioned Charon, I cannot but observe that Rousseau has taken a great many of his sentiments from this Author, particularly what he says against those mothers who do not nurse their own children. (*Adelaide and Theodore ... The Second Edition*, vol. 3, p. 140)

The mother 'still younger than Madame d' Almane' was Genlis, who gives the following account of her actions on the marriage of her eldest daughter in her *Memoirs*:

> I gave my daughter, on her marriage, a quantity of splendid dresses in pieces, which I had been collecting for the last ten years with this intention; besides, I had a great collection of china, gilt and plate, which I divided equally between my two daughters, without reserving a single cup to myself. I immediately put Pulchérie [her second daughter] in possession of her share, which I caused to be carried into her room. I bought myself a collection of earthern ware, and while I remained at Belle Chasse, I never deviated from that simplicity, which I have ascribed to Madame d' Almane in *Adèle et Théodore*. (*Memoirs of the Countess of Genlis*, vol. 3, p. 107)

46. *little tea-table of English queen's ware*: The translator here inserts a reference to Wedgwood's cream-coloured earthenware, known as Queen's ware after Queen Charlotte (1744–1818) became Wedgwood's patron in the mid 1760s, and still popular in the 1780s. The French 'terre de pipe' only refers to earthenware. The 1784 edition of the translation refers only to a 'little tea-table of English ware'. See *Adelaide and Theodore ... The Second Edition*, vol. 3, p. 141.

47. *plate, jewels, and expensive furniture, they are merely for ostentation*: Genlis's original footnote is translated in the second English edition and reads:

> We live not, says Charon, for ourselves, but for others: we care not so much about what we really and truly are in ourselves, as what we are in the estimation of the public: so that we stint ourselves, we abridge ourselves of the conveniences of life, and torment ourselves to make a shew in the opinion of the world. This is true not only with regard to external things, and those which relate to the body and to the use and expenditure of our fortunes; but also with regard to the endowments of the mind; which we look upon as useless unless they are displayed to view for the approbation and entertainment of others. Lastly, the summit and perfection of human vanity, shews itself in seeking, delighting and placing its whole felicity in things which are frivolous and vain; and which are by no means necessary to the comforts and conveniences of life; whilst it is not solicitous, as it ought to be, about those which are real and essential. God has in himself whatever is truly and essentially good, evil exists in him, in *idea* only: man, on the contrary, possesses his good things in idea, and his evil things in reality. Brutes do not feed and satisfy themselves with opinions and fancies; but with what is present, palpable, and real. Vanity is the lot of man alone: he runs, he bustles, he bestirs himself, he flies, he pursues, he catches a shadow; he courts the wind, and a mere straw is the reward of a whole life of toil. (*Adelaide and Theodore ... The Second Edition*, vol. 3, p. 143).

48. *other Plays equally good and well represented*: All the plays mentioned in this section are discussed in Letter XIV, Volume II (see pp. 215–17).

49. Spectacle de la nature : Abbé Noël Antoine Pluche's work *Le Spectacle de la nature, entretiens sur les particularités de l'histoire naturelles* was published between 1732–51, and was immediately translated into English, appearing as *Nature Delineated: Being Philosophical Conversations. Wherein the Wonderful Works of Providence in the Animal, Vegetable and Mineral Creation are Laid Open* (London: James Hodges, 1740).

50. Histoire des Insectes: I have been unable to trace an exact reference to a History of Insects: many eighteenth-century works with similar titles could apply.

51. *that immortal work, which even without a taste for Natural History one must read over and over again*: The Baroness is referring to George-Louis Leclerc, comte de Buffon (1707–88) and his *Histoire naturelle générale et particulière* (1749–1804). There were several editions of English translations, including abridgments and English-language works that 'borrowed' the French author's work without acknowledgement. Buffon was perhaps the French *philosophe* who work was most widely read in late eighteenth-century Britain (see Gillespie and Hopkins (eds), *The Oxford History of Literary Translation in English*, pp. 85, 362). A translators' note to the 1784 edition reads: 'Meaning, we suppose, Mons.

Buffon's *Natural History*. If this Author continues publishing much longer, a short life will not be equal to the task. Note of the Translators.' See *Adelaide and Theodore ... The Second Edition*, vol. 3, p. 146.

52. *now that she has a hundred thousand livres a year, all the world flock to her with eagerness*: A translators' note to the 1784 English edition reads: '4166 Louis d'ors, or Guineas'. See *Adelaide and Theodore ... The Second Edition*, vol. 3, p. 154.

53. *'dexterously, perfidious'*: Genlis's note to the original French text gives the reference to the Duclos text, *Considérations sur les mœurs*, and the 1784 edition of the English translation reproduces the reference. See *Adelaide and Theodore ... The Second Edition*, vol. 3, p. 155.

54. *'the management of estates entirely depends on all these matters'* : The quotation is a truncated version of Fénelon's writings in Chapter XIII, 'Other Duties and Accomplishments', from *Instructions for the Education of Daughters*, pp. 155, 161. The second edition of the English translation translates Genlis's original reference in a footnote: '*Education des Filles* par M. de Fénelon. The great advantages women derive from this kind of knowledge, is much better explained in an excellent English Work, entitled *The Governess and Lady's Library*, which deserves to be read with attention by all mothers of families, and young women'. See *Adelaide and Theodore ... The Second Edition*, vol. 3, p. 158.

55. *Five hundred livres a year certain*: A note by the translators reads 'About 21 Guineas'. See *Adelaide and Theodore ... The Second Edition*, vol. 3, p. 159.

56. *we have only determined ... on having a school for six very poor girls*: Genlis was interested in the education of all social classes. In her *Discours sur l'Education publique du peuple* (Paris, 1791) she mentions the only school she knows of in Europe that educates the children of the working classes, tells her reader it is near Abergavenny and that it was founded by a woman. She seems to be referring to Hannah More's Mendip Schools. Later, Genlis published a work *Projet d'une école rurale pour l'éducation des filles* (Paris, 1801). Neither of these works was translated into English.

57. *We imagine this establishment will cost us possibly six thousand livres a year*: A note by the translators reads 'Two hundred and fifty Guineas'. See *Adelaide and Theodore ... The Second Edition*, vol. 3, p. 161.

58. *'I doubt whether there is any'*: In the original French text, Genlis gives the reference to the quotation as *Emile*, Book II. The quotation actually comes from Book III:

> Good mother, protect yourself about all against the lies which are prepared for you. If your son knows many things, distrust everything he knows. If he has the misfortune of being raised in Paris and of being rich, he is lost. So long as there are skilful artists there, he will have all their talents; but far away from them, he will no longer have any. In Paris, the rich man knows everything; the only ignoramus is the poor man. This capital is full of amateurs, especially among the ladies, who produce their work as M. Guillaume contrived his colours. I know of three honourable exceptions to this among men; there may be more. But I know of none among women, and I doubt that there are any. (Rousseau, *Émile*, p. 202)

59. *I have not seen any other female artists ... make good and correct likenesses in their portraits*: Genlis is much more supportive of female artists in her later *Tales of the Castle*, where she provides a striking 'defense' of the artists Elisabeth Louise Vigée Le Brun (1755–1842) and Angelica Kaufmann (1741–1807). She concludes the discussion with a paragraph that explains that any deficiencies in the style of female artists are owing to deficiencies in their education:

> If a painter intend [*sic*] to instruct his daughter in his art, he never conceives the project of making her a painter of history, but will continually repeat, she should attempt only to paint portraits, miniatures, or flower-pieces. Thus is she discouraged, and thus is the fire of fancy stifled: she paints roses; she was born, perhaps, to paint heroes. (*Tales of the Castle*, vol. 4, pp. 57–61).

60. *Mademoiselle Barbier*: Marie-Anne Barbier (1664–1742/5?) author of several tragedies performed in the first half of the eighteenth century, but, as the Baroness points out, largely neglected in the latter half of the century. Despite the short shrift Genlis gives Barbier here, the playwright is one of the women feted in Genlis's *De l'influence des femmes sur la littérature francaise* (1811).

61. *Monsieur St. Aulaire*: Genlis's note in the French text refers her reader to Saint-Aulaire's verse written for the Duchess of Maine. The poet (1745–?) was only known for this verse at the end of the eighteenth century.

62. *Chapelain*: Jean Chapelain (1595–1674) was a French critic and theorist. His epic *La Pucelle* (1656) was criticized by his contemporary Nicolas Boileau-Despréaux (1636–1711), now known as Boileau. Boileau's influence on literary taste in France in the eighteenth century meant that Chapelain was on the losing side of the battle, as the Baroness is clearly aware.

63. *requires a superiority of genius*: Genlis's original note is translated in the 1784 edition of the English translation:

> I know that Molière's Comedies have reformed many follies, and that Corneille's Tragedies are formed to elevate the soul; but in all Dramatic Works, not excepting those of this great man, (Corneille) the moral is only an accessory, not the principal aim. The real intention of the Author is to please and to move the passions; all that is expected of him is, that the catastrophe be instructive. He may be as loose as he pleases during four acts and an half, provided the last scene be moral. Mons. de la Motte, speaking of theatrical representations, adds: 'The instructive part is of short duration; but the seductive lasts a long time; the remedy is feeble, and comes too late.' *Œuvres d'Houdar de la Motte*, 5th vol. (*Adelaide and Theodore ... The Second Edition*, vol. 3, p. 166)

64. *Monsieur de Retel has a hundred thousand livres a year*: In the 1784 edition of the English translation, the translators include a note which reads 'Above 4000 l.' See *Adelaide and Theodore ... The Second Edition*, vol. 3, p. 166.

65. *Miss Byron*: Harriet Byron (Biron in the French original), heroine of Richardson's *The History of Sir Charles Grandison* (1753).

66. *the* Siege of Calais: Claudine-Alexandrine Guérin, marquise de Tencin (1681–1749) published her historical novel *Le Siège de Calais* in 1739. It was translated into English the following year as *The Siege of Calais by Edward of England: An Historical Novel. Translated from the French original* (London: T. Woodward, 1740).

67. *'with freedom and with humility'*: 'Of Personal Merit', in la Bruyère, *Characters: or the Manners of the Age with the Moral Characters of Theophrastus. Translated from the Greek. To which is prefixed an account of his life and Writings* (Dublin: J. Chambers, 1776), p. 33.

68. *'the rays of the sun harden clay and soften wax'*: Genlis's original note refers readers to '*Logique de M. Dumarsais*'. Neither of the English editions reproduce the reference. The quotation can be found in *Œuvres de Du Marsais*, 7 vols (Paris: Imprimerie Pougain, 1797), vol. 4, p. 311.

69. *We were talking yesterday of the* Persian Letters: Montesquieu's *Lettres persanes* (1721), a tale of two Persians, Usbek and Rica, and their stay in France. It was translated by John

Ozell in 1722, and by Thomas Flloyd in 1762. Genlis's note in the original French text refers her reader to p. 142, and the 1784 edition of the English translation does likewise. See *Adelaide and Theodore ... The Second Edition*, vol. 3, p. 186.

70. *'his own merits to the pride of others'*: see *Lettres persanes* (Paris: Garnier Flammarion, 1995) p. 162.

71. *a promise given*: The French text, 'parole donnée' is in capitals in the original text.

72. *trictrac*: an extremely popular game in pre-revolutionary France and is played by two players play on a board which resembles a backgammon table.

73. *'for me to be useful to you'*: 'Of the Goods of Fortune', in la Bruyère, *Characters: or the Manners of the Age*, p. 82.

74. *translated from the German by Mons. de B****: Genlis's note reads 'Qui a pour titre: *Education des princes destines au trône*, par M. Bassedow, trad. de l'allemand, par M. de B***', and both English editions include the note in the main body of the text. Isabelle Brouard-Arends identifies the work as *Éducation des jeunes princes destines au trône*, translated from the German by M. Bourgoing (Yverdon: Imprimerie de la société Littéraire, 1777). I have been unable to consult this work, and there seems not to have been an English translation.

75. *objects calculated to inspire virtuous sentiments in youthful minds*: This description naturally reminds the reader of the Belle Chasse estate where the Orléans children were educated by Genlis.

76. *Bossuet*: The only author in this list who has not already been referenced in the notes is Jacques-Béninge Bossuet (1627–1704), a leading intellectual in Louis XIV's court, appointed as tutor to the Dauphin in 1670.

77. *Madame de Limours came frequently to see me*: The tense error is confusing here: the phase should read (as the original French text) 'Madame de Limours comes frequently to see me'.

78. *a pictures of de Greuze, which represents a little girl weeping for her Canary bird*: Greuse's *La Jeune Fille que pleure son oiseau mort* (A Girl with a dead Canary) was exhibited at the 1765 salon, and was much admired by Diderot for its depiction of contemporary sensibility.

79. *an annuity of fifty thousand livres*: the translators insert a note in the 1784 English edition which reads '2083 Louis d'ors – or Guineas' See *Adelaide and Theodore ... The Second Edition*, vol. 3, p. 238.

80. *Abbe Duguet*: Genlis puts the name of the author in a note.

81. *'crimes and wickedness will fall on his head'*: Duguet, *Institution d'un prince*, vol. 2, pp. 391–2 (chapter XXII).

82. *the Thoughts of Marcus Aurelius*: Marcus Aurelius's *Meditations*, in which the Emperor's Stoic philosophy is explored in Greek was written on campaign between 170–180 AD. Tom Winnifrith points out that he is of interest to all ages, and that the eighteenth century saw two new translations (in 1701 and 1747), but also states that he 'was too elevated for the general reader'. See Gillespie and Hopkins (eds), *The Oxford History of Literary Translation in English*, p. 255.

83. *to seventy thousand French livres a year*: the translator inserts a note in the 1784 English edition which reads 'Three thousand three hundred and seventy-five Guineas.' See *Adelaide and Theodore ... The Second Edition*, vol. 3, p. 253.

84. *Bruyère ... speaks with more simplicity'*: 'Of Society and Conversation', in la Bruyère, *Characters: or the Manners of the Age*, p. 78.

85. *Mons. Leblanc's instructions*: The 1784 edition of the English translation includes Genlis's reference: 'See letter XLIII of this Volume'. See *Adelaide and Theodore ... The Second Edition*, vol. 3, p. 267.

86. *the attachment Mons. d' Ostalis had conceived for the Countess Anatolle*: Although Genlis's original French text includes a reference to this letter in a footnote, neither English edition of the translation does so. The letter in question is Letter IX of Volume III (pp. 336–9, above).

87. *thirty prisoners, detained at Fort l'Eveque*: this Paris prison housed the Marquis de Sade for non-payment of debts in 1771: it was demolished in 1780.

88. *the house which the Viscountess is building*: The French text refers to the Viscount, rather than the Viscountess, building the house, which makes the pronoun in the next sentences correct.

89. *it is written for you and entitled LETTERS ON EDUCATION*: The presentation of the book within the book is striking, and was used by Mary Wollstonecraft in her 1788 *Original Stories* when the female educator Mrs Mason presents her young charges with a book at the end of the text.

Course of Reading Pursued by Adelaide

1. from the Age of six Years, to Twenty-two: Adelaide's course of reading is remarkable for its breadth and scope, for the attention paid to foreign works, and for the insistence that the reading of the female and male child should not be dramatically different. Although nearly all of the works mentioned in this reading list have been referred to in the main body of the novel, and have therefore already been referenced in endnotes, I have included new references here for the reader's convenience.

2. *means of the Magic Lanthern*: A note by Genlis in the French text refers her readers to Vol. I, p. 86: this is Letter IX of Volume I, pp. 16–20, above.

3. *Kola*: the Kola peninsula is in the far north of Russia.

4. *Madame d' Almane's histories*: A note by Genlis in the original French text refers her reader to Vol. I, p. 94: this is Letter XIV of Volume I, pp. 32–4, above.

5. The Conversation of Emilius: not Rousseau's *Emilius*, but rather *Les Conversations d'Emilie* (1775) by Louise-Florence d'Esclavelles, Madame d'Épinay (1726–83).

6. Les Hochets Moraux, *by Mons. Monget*: This work (*The Moral Toys*) was dedicated to the Orléans twins, Mademoiselle d'Orléans et Mademoiselle de Chartres, and published with Genlis's own (Paris: Chez Lambert & Baudouin, 1781). An 1806 French edition printed in London seems to have been published to teach British children to read French. See *Les hochets moraux, ou contes pour la premire enfance. Ouvrage orné de seize grauvres. Par M. Monget* (London: Didier and Tebbitt, 1806). I have been unable to trace biographical information about this author.

7. Plays and Dialogues for Children, *written by Madame de la Fite*: Marie-Elisabeth Bouée de Lafite (?1750–94), *Entretiens, drames et contes moraux* (1778).

8. Annales de la Vertu: Genlis's own publication, *Annales de la vertu ou cours d'histoire à l'usage des jeunes personnes par l'auteur du théatre d'éducation* (Paris: M. Lambert et F.J. Baudoin, 1781).

9. La Géographie comparée, *by Mons. Mentelle*: Jacques Mentel, *La Géographie ou analyse de la géographie ancienne et moderne des peoples de tout âge* (Paris, 1776).

10. *a Treatise on Heraldry*: possibly Anselme de Sainte-Marie (1625–94), *Le palais de l'honneur [Texte imprimé], ou les Genealogies historiques des illustres maisons de France, et de*

plusieurs nobles familles de l'Europe, ensemble un Traité particulier pour apprendre parfaitement la science du blazon (Paris: Etienne Loyson, 1663).

11. le Catechisme Historique: Claude Fleury (1640–1723), *Catéchisme historique contenant en abrégé l'histoire sainte et la doctrine chrétienne* (Paris: P. Aubouin, 1690)

12. l' Abregé de la Géographie, *by Mons. le Ragois*: Claude le Ragois (d. 1683), *Instruction sur l'histoire de France et romaine, par M. Le Ragois,... On y a ajouté un Abrégé des Métamorphoses d'Ovide, de l'histoire poétique, de la géographie, et une chronique de nos rois, en vers, le tout en faveur de la jeunesse* (Paris: J. Barbou, 1778)

13. l' Abregé de l' Histoire Poétique, *and* l' Instruction sur les Métamorphoses d' Ovide, *also by Ragois*: see note 12 to Course of Reading, above.

14. *five Comedies of the* Theatre d' Education; Agar dans le Désert; les Flacons; la Colombe; l' Enfant Gate *and* l' Aveugle de Spa: See Genlis's *Théâtre à l'usage des jeunes personnes* (1779–80) or *Theatre of Education* (1781).

15. Eléments de Poésie Françoise: probably *Eléments de Poésie françoise, par Joannet* (Paris: Desaint et Saillant, 1752).

16. Robinson Crusoe: Daniel Defoe (1660–1731), *The Life and Strange Surprising Adventures of Robinson Crusoe, of York, Mariner. Written by himself* (1719).

17. The Beauties of History: L. M. Strech, *The Beauties of History, or Picture of Virtue and Vice, Drawn from Real Life* (London: printed for the author, 1770).

18. *Rollin's* Ancient History: Charles Rollin (1661–1741), *Histoire ancien* (1730–8).

19. The Imitation of Jesus Christ: *Imitation of Christ* (or *De imitatione Christi*), by Thomas à Kempis (1380–1471), first published in Latin around 1418. There were many French and English translations in the eighteenth century.

20. The Father's Instructions to his Children: Thomas Percival, *A Father's Instructions to his children, consisting of tables, fables and reflections, designed to promote the love of virtue etc* (Dublin: Caleb Jenkin; Beatty and Jackson, 1777).

21. le Theatre *de Campistron*: : Jean-Galbert de Campistron (1656–1723), playwright and tragedian.

22. Quatre fins de l'Homme, *by Monsieur Nicole*: Pierre Nicole (1625–95), *Essais de morale* (Paris: G. Desprez, 1678).

23. *Echard's* Roman History: Laurent Echard, *Histoire Romaine* (Paris: J. Guérin, 1734).

24. le Theatre *de la Grange-Chancel*: François-Joseph de Chancel, sieur de La Grange (1677–1758).

25. Macaulay's History of England: Catherine Macaulay (1731–91), *History of England from the Accession of James I to that of the Brunswick Line* (1763–83).

26. Princess of Cleves: Marie-Madeleine Pioche de La Vergne, comtesse de Lafayette (1634–93), *La Princesse de Clèves* (1678).

27. Zaide: or *Zayde*, Lafayette's second novel (1670).

28. Cleveland: Abbé Prévost, *Le Philosophe anglais ou Histoire de monsieur Cleveland* (1731–9).

29. the Deane of Coleraine: Abbé Prévost, *Le Doyen de Killerine* (1735–40), translated and published as *The Dean of Coleraine* in 1742.

30. Anecdotes of the Court of Philip Augustus: Marguerite de Lussan (1682–1758), *Anecdotes de la cour de Philippe-Auguste* (1722–38).

31. *a book on Mythology, by Madame d' Almane*: Genlis's *Arabesques mythologiques ou les Attributs de toutes les divinités de la fable en 54 planches gravées d'après les desseins coloriés de Mme de Genlis* (Paris: Charles Barrois, 1810).

32. the Travels of Cyrus: Andrew Michael Ramsay, *The Travels of Cyrus ... To which is Annex'd, a Discourse upon the Theology and Mythology of the Ancients* (London: T. Woodward, J. Peele, 1727)

33. *Bertaut, Godeau, Pavillon, Desmahis*: Poets Jean Bertaut (1552–1611), Antoine Godeau (1605–72), Etienne Pavillon (1632–1705), Joseph-François-Edouard de Corsembleu (Desmahis) (1722–61).

34. *Tremblay's* Instructions from a Father to his Children: Abraham Trembley, *Instructions d'un père à ses enfans sur la nature et sur la religion* (Genève: J. S. Cailler, 1775).

35. The History of France, *by Velly*: Paul-François Velly (1690–1759), *Histoire de France, depuis l'établissement de la monarchie jusqu'au règne de Louis XIV* (Paris: Desaint et Saillant, 1761).

36. Theatre *de Boissy*: Louis de Boissy (1694–1758), playwright.

37. le Theatre *de Marivaux*: Pierre Carlet de Chamblain de Marivaux (1688–1763).

38. le Spectacle de la Nature, *by Mons. Pluche*: Abbé Noël Antoine Pluche, *Le Spectacle de la nature, entretiens sur les particularités de l'histoire naturelles* (1732–51).

39. Histoire des Insectes, *in two vols*: unidentified.

40. Lady M. W. Montague's Letters: Lady Mary Wortley Montagu (1689–1762). The letters are presumably her *Turkish Embassy Letters*, written in 1716. These letters were popular in France, mentioned by writers such as Voltaire in his *Lettres Philosophiques* (1734) and *Letters concerning the English Nation* (1733).

41. Peruvian Letters: Françoise d'Issembourg d'Happoncourt, Madame de Graffigny (1695–1758), *Lettres d'une Péruvienne* (1747)

42. les Comedies de Goldoni: Carlo Osvaldo Goldoni (1707–93), Italian playwright.

43. les Synonymes *de l'Abbé Girard*: Gabriel Girard (1677–1748), *Synonymes français, leurs significations et le choix qu'il faut en faire pour parler avec justesse* (Paris: 1736).

44. la Maniere de bien penser dans les ouvrages d'esprit : Dominique Bouhours (1628–1702), *La Manière de bien penser dans les ouvrages d'esprit* (Paris: F. Delaulne, 1705).

45. Reflexions critiques sur la poesie & sur la peinture, *by the Abbé Dubos*: Jean-Baptiste Dubos (1670–1742), *Réflexions critiques sur la poesie et la peinture* (Paris, 1719).

46. Histoire de Pierre le Grand: Voltaire's history of Peter the Great (1759–63).

47. *Voltaire's* Universal History: Voltaire, *Essai sur les moeurs et l'esprit des nations* (1756), known as *Histoire Universelle* in France.

48. Theatre *de Destouches*: pseudonym of Philippe Néricault (1680–1754).

49. Theatre *de la Chausee*: Pierre-Claude Nivelle de La Chaussée (1692–1754).

50. D. Quichotte: Miguel de Cervantes (1547–1616), *Don Quijote de la Mancha* or *Don Quixote* (1605 and 1615).

51. la Poétique *de Marmontel*: Jean-François Marmontel (1723–99) wrote articles on aesthetics for the *Encyclopédie*, one of which was reworked as *Poétique française* in 1763.

52. *Hume's* History of England: David Hume (1711–76), his magisterial *History of England* was published between 1754 and 1762.

53. *Works of Metastasio in their original languages*: Pseudonym of Italian poet Pietro Antonio Domenico Trapassi (1698–1782) who was extremely popular with French audiences.

54. *Virgil's* Æneid *and his* Georgics: Virgil's *Aeneid*, written between 29 and 19 BC, and *Georgics*, written 29 BC.

55. *Madame Sevigny's* Letters: Marie de Rabutin-Chantal, Marquise de Sévigné (1626–96), author of a volumious correspondence to her daughter.

56. *Fontaine's* Fables: Jean de La Fontaine (1621–95), *Fables choisies, mises en vers* (1668).

57. *Translation of the Greek Theatre*: Many translations could apply here: the point is that Adelaide reads neither Latin nor Greek.

58. Theatre *de Crebillon*: presumably Prosper Jolyot de Crébillon (1674–1762), playwright. See note 28 to Volume I, above.

59. Manlius, *de la Fosse*; Ariane, *and the* Comte d' Essex, *de Thomas Corneille* : Antoine de la Fosse (*c.* 1653–1708), *Manlius Capitolinus* (1698), Thomas Corneille (1625–1709), *Ariane* (1672) and *Le Comte d'Essex* (1678).

60. la Metromanie; Ines de Castro: Alexis Piron (1689–1773), *La Métromanie*, five-act play first performed in 1738, and re-edited throughout the eighteenth century. Antoine Houdar de La Motte (1672–1731), *Inès de Castro*, a tragedy first performed in 1723. Genlis was to publish a historical novel entitled *Inès de Castro* in 1817.

61. *the Translations of Plautus and Terence*: comic Roman playwrights Maccius Plautus (*c.* 254–184 BC) and Publius Terentius (*c.* 190–158 BC) were popular in vernacular translations throughout the eighteenth century.

62. Clarissa: Samuel Richardson (1689–1761), *Clarissa, or the History of a Young Lady* (1748).

63. *Thomson's Works in English*: James Thomson (1700–48).

64. *Pasto Fido, in Italian*: Giovanni Battista Guarini (1538–1612). The celebrated play *Il Pastor Fido* (The Faithful Shepherd) was written in 1590, and was popular in translation throughout Europe in the seventeenth and eighteenth centuries.

65. *Voltaire's Age of Lewis Fourteenth, and his History of Charles the Twelfth*: *Le Siècle de Louis XIV* (1751) and *Histoire de Charles XII* (1731).

66. *the Poems of Madame Des Houlieres*: Antoinette Du Ligier de La Garde, Des Houlières (1638–94).

67. *the Works of Gresset*: Jean-Baptiste-Louis Gresset (1709–77), poet and dramatist.

68. Theatre du *Grand Corneille*: Pierre Corneille (1606–84), playwright.

69. Theatre *de Racine*: Jean Racine (1639–99), tragedian.

70. Theatre *de Voltaire*: Voltaire's plays include *Oedipe* (1718).

71. *les Sermons de Bourdaloue*: Louis Bourdaloue (1632–1704), Jesuit preacher, extremely fashionable in his day, and much in demand as a confessor.

72. Sir Charles Grandison *and* Pamela *in English*: Samuel Richardson (1689–1761) *The History of Sir Charles Grandison* (1753) and *Pamela, or Virtue Rewarded* (1740)

73. *Ariosto in Italian*: Ludovico Aristo (1474–1533), Italian poet and author of epic *Orlando Furioso* (1516).

74. Theatre *de Moliere*: Molière, pseudonym of Jean-Baptiste Poquelin (1622–73), generally recognized to be France's greatest comic playwright.

75. *Boileau's Works*: Poet and critic Nicolas Boileau-Despréaux (1636–1711), known to his contemporaries as Despréaux, but referred to as Boileau in the late eighteenth century.

76. *Regnard; Dufreni*: Jean-François Regnard (1655–1709), French comic playwright, Charles Rivière Dufresny (1648–1724), playwright who collaborated with Regnard in the 1690s.

77. *Poems of J. B. Rousseau*: Jean-Baptiste Rousseau (1671–1741), known as 'le grand Rousseau', lyric poet who also wrote paraphrases of the Psalms.

78. Sermons *de Massillon*: Jean-Baptiste Massillon (1663–1742), popular Versailles preacher who officiated at Louis XIV's funeral oration.

79. *the Spectators in English*: Genlis was a great admirer of the *Spectator*, the periodical founded and jointly conducted by Richard Steele and Joseph Addison, which appeared daily from March 1711 to December 1712. See note 18 to Volume I, above.

80. *Petrarch in Italian*: Francesco Petrarca (1304–74), humanist scholar and major poet of the Italian Renaissance.
81. Letters on Education: The version of Genlis's own *Adelaide and Theodore* that is presented to Adelaide on her wedding day in the final letter of the novel. Many of the works Adelaide reads after her marriage have a focus on education, as subsequent notes will show, presumably to further prepare her for becoming a mother.
82. Emilius *and* Odyssey: Rousseau's *Émile* and Homer's *Odyssey*. This reference is unusual in that Genlis does not specify her preferred translation for the *Odyssey*.
83. *Buffon's* Natural History: George-Louis Leclerc, comte de Buffon (1707–88), *Histoire naturelle générale et particulière* (1749–1804).
84. Telemachus: François de Salignac de la Mothe-Fénelon (1651–1715), *Télémaque* (*c.* 1695).
85. Flechier, Bossuet, Mascaron: Valentin-Esprit Fléchier (1663–1742), poet, Jacques-Bénigne Bossuet (1627–1704), orator, educationalist and political thinker, Jules Mascaron (1634–1703), like Massillon, a preacher under Louis XIV.
86. les Caracteres *de la Bruyere*: Jean de La Bruyère (1645–96), *moraliste* and author of *Les Caractères* (1688–1694)
87. *Rochefoucauld's* Maxims: François, duc de La Rochefoucauld (1613–80), *moraliste* and author of *Réflexions ou Sentences et maximes morales*, published in several versions between 1665 and 1678.
88. *Pope's Works*: Alexander Pope (1688–1744), poet and satirist.
89. *Locke*: John Locke (1632–1704), philosopher. Genlis puts his complete works on Adelaide's reading list. It is his *Some Thoughts Concerning Education* (1693) that is quoted at length in the main body of the novel.
90. *the* Iliad *of Pope so elegantly translated*: see note 88 to Course of Reading, above. Pope's translation of Homer's *Illiad* into heroic couplets was published between 1715 and 1720.
91. *the History of Italy by Guiciardini*: Francesco Guicciardini (1483–1540). His *Storia d'Italia* gave a comprehensive picture of the country in the period 1494 and 1532. Genlis was probably aware of the French translation *Histoire des guerres d'Italie*, translated by J. Fabre (London: 1738), but seems to want Adelaide to read the work in the original language.
92. *Works of Dante, in Italian*: Dante Alighieri (1265–1321), author of *The Divine Comedy*, written between 1308 and 1321, one of the greatest works of the Middle Ages.
93. Pensées *de Pascal*: Blaise Pascal (1623–62), mathematician, scientist and advocate of Christian ideas, his *Pensées* were published posthumously in 1670.
94. Gil Blas: Alain-René Lesage (1668–1747). *Histoire de Gil Blas de Santillane* was published in three installments between 1715 and 1735.
95. Memoirs of the History of France: the English translation omits 'quelques', which indicates that this is not one work of memoirs, but rather several.
96. *Hamilton's Works*: Anthony (or Antoine) Hamilton (1626–1740), of Scottish and Irish extraction, was raised in France after Charles I's execution. His most famous works, in French, were his memoirs of his brother-in-law *Mémoires du comte de Grammont* (1715).
97. Treatise on Wisdom*, by Charron*: Pierre Charron (1541–1603), moral philosopher and author of *De la sagesse* (1601), which relies heavily on the writings of Michel de Montaigne (1533–92).

98. Persian Letters; *and* l'Esprit des Loix: Charles de Secondat, baron de Montequieu (1689–1755), champion of the Enlightenment and author of the *Lettres persanes* (1721) and *De l'esprit des lois* (1748).

99. *in Italian,* La Jerusalem déliverée: Torquato Tasso's *La Gerusalemme liberata* (*Jerusalem Delivered*, 1580). The French text refers to Adelaide rereading this work age twenty, since she already read it at sixteen. The English translation omits the first reading. See note 6 to Volume II, above.

100. *Fontenelle's* Plurality of Worlds, ses Discours Academiques: Bernard le Bovier de Fontenelle (1657–1757), *Entretiens sur la pluralité des mondes* (1686) and *Histoire de l'Academie des Sciences* (1702). See also note 36 to Volume II, above.

101. Models Militaires, *in two volumes*: Possibly the anonymously published *Modèles de l'Héroisme et de vertus militaires ou histoire abrégée des plus célèbres guerriers anciens et modernes* (Paris: Nyon, 1780).

102. Histoire generale des Voyages, *abridged by Mons. de la Harpe*: Jean-François de la Harpe (1739–1803), his *Abrégé de l'histoire générale des voyages* (Paris, 1780) was an abridgement of a work by Antoine-François, abbé Prévost (1697–1763), the fifteen-volume *Histoire générale des voyages* (1746–59). Genlis perhaps includes the work to pay hommage to La Harpe, who was a close friend in 1781 and early 1782, although they were later to have a very public falling-out.

103. *Translation of the Fables of Phædrus*: Phaedrus (fl. 15 BC–AD 50) was widely translated in both prose and verse, in French and English, in the eighteenth century. For further information see Karina Williamson's article in Gillespie and Hopkins (eds), *The Oxford History of Literary Translation in English*, pp. 291–7.

104. *Advice from a Mother to her Daughter, and to her Son, by Madame de Lambert*: Anne-Thérèse de Marguenat de Courcelles, marquise de Lambert (1647–1733), *Avis d'une mère à son fils* (1726) and *Avis d'une mère à sa fille* (1726). See also note 106 to Volume I.

For Product Safety Concerns and Information please contact our EU
representative GPSR@taylorandfrancis.com
Taylor & Francis Verlag GmbH, Kaufingerstraße 24, 80331 München, Germany

www.ingramcontent.com/pod-product-compliance
Lightning Source LLC
Chambersburg PA
CBHW070925100726
47908CB00001B/100

* 9 7 8 1 1 3 8 2 3 5 9 4 6 *